THE RED TRIANGLE

THE RED TRIANGLE

A Novel

by

Tapan Gupta

KALPAZ

The Red Triangle

ISBN: 978-81-7835-897-0

Published in 2011 in India by
Kalpaz Publications
C-30 Satyawati Nagar Delhi-110052
E-mail: kalpaz@hotmail.com
Phone: 9212729499

Leser Type Setting by: Square Vision, Delhi

Printed at : Chawla Offset Press, Delhi

To Jatin,
My elder brother, my mentor
who inspired me to write this book.

To Whom it may concern

Donkey.... donky
old and grey
open your mouth
and make a bray

Contents

A Vision

Nidhi Apartments
New Greater Noida
1st January 2031
Wednesday 4.30 pm

Hi, I am Tapan and this is the first evening of the 'New Year'. I woke up just half an hour before. And this is because I couldn't sleep last night reading e-mails and attending congratulating phone calls of friends and relatives, and responding all of them the same as well.

The New Year eve yesterday was foggy and chilly outside, while I had my dinner with my family of 4 -1 = 3 (My son is away for his graduation) in a restaurant peacefully. I usually avoid any club party, friends and those boring boozy New Year Hungamas on this special day. Now I am feeling relaxed and contented enough to start this first page of my diary.

The very place where I am sitting at the moment is the balcony of my flat on the fifth floor of this building. This is my favourite relaxing point on off days and it overlooks the New Greater Noida highway. Aha... it is so big and beautiful to watch! It seems to be an enlarged facsimile of Nariman point Bombay.

By the way, at the mention of Bombay I must be

thankful to our Central Government for having retained its ages old heritage name once again. It sounds so promising and dreamy. It was almost 17 years back when keeping in view of the growing public demand, an online opinion-poll was conducted nationwide and 92 percent of the country folks including Maharashtrians voted in favour of the old name and against Mumbai. Not only this alone, some other favourite oldies like Calcutta, Madras and Simla also came back later on, indicating how the people still loved their country's ancient values.

I have taken a short break here to finish my remaining chai. And while doing so, do cast my eyes again at the shimmering elegance of 'N.G.N. Highway' in a longing manner. However, I can see only a small part of it from here, yet it is stunning to the eyes. On both of my sides, the dark grey metallic eight-lane wide road is stretching straight even beyond the limit of my vision. It is flanked by an array of tall and lanky looking multistoreyed skyscrapers standing solemnly.

Most of these are full of illuminated dots, as the evening has become dusky now. A number of neon-signs have also begun to emit the colourful and intermittent glows in the gathering haze. And a battery of cars and other vehicles cascading through the smooth roads seem to provide a lifegiving energy to the whole highway.

But the real pride of the N.G.N. is the world's tallest manmade structure on earth and that is visible from here less than an aerial mile away to the left of me. It is standing so stately upright that it has literally dwarfed all the buildings around. Its name is written on the façade in the bold letters in Hindi and English alternately. But in Hindi first, as per the unified law of the nation. Although it is obscured a bit from this distance, yet it reads.

Vyom Bhavan Towers (Hindi)
Vyom Bhavan Towers (English)

Well, I must conclude the subject now as it is going lengthy and return herefrom to myself. As far as my personal life is concerned, my past had been remarkably eventful, future... I don't know about, and the very present is here that I am happy with and am enjoying as well. I am fortunate that sometimes my family also gives me the company here and we sit for hours, discussing all those important family matters.

Tina, my wife is usually over busy with her beauty business and my only daughter Anushka helps her as an apprentice. She is doing bachelor course of cosmetic surgery. My only son Harshvardhan moved to the hostel to get his degree in Space Engineering last year. So at home Anushka is like my close friend. She takes proper care of my diet and health. We talk a lot together and here I would like to insist that especially the girls are so caring about their Dads.

It was only she, who gifted me this diary a couple of days before with strict instructions to start it right from the New Year positively. And so have I done as per her wish. She knew that I was fond of writing diaries way back in the times of my college days and continued even up to a few years after marriage. But then the seasons flew away and I completely yielded myself to my business and faster changing life patterns and thus gave it up as a result.

However, I do admit now that at this point of my life, after having celebrated my 21st marriage anniversary recently, I am becoming more and more obsessed by my past and my pen now runs easier every passing moment and the mind slowly tingles with all those recollections of honey memories. Every moment of which gives me a bit of sadness to think about.

I remember my college, my friends... and the jackpot of adulthood, when I entered the degree college for the first time in my life. And after entering the college, I began to assume that I were above par the other new entrants. And that I could do anything in the world I wished to. I even started fancying that I were the real prince charming at the campus and the girls looked so pretty to me like colourful butterflies. I must confess to myself that I always yearned to touch one or the other to feel the feminine stuff for the first time. What a Cinderella of sweet young age!

Many mixed up and vague images are emerging in mind at the same time as if being superimposed on each other. My favourite bunch of half dozen select friends including me, who were all co-accessories in a unique melodrama that had taken place in strange circumstances. Our mutual bonding, affections, quarrels, secrets and stupidities that we always reciprocated with each other. And also those frustrated arguments over the contemporary Indian Politics.

I remember how intensely every one of us desired to bring about the revolutionary changes in the system. And above all, that magical tryst with the Angel friends still stands out in my memory afresh. Many thanks to God... for their satisfied souls are not only resting in absolute peace now,but have reincarnated as well. More important thing is that the very seed they had sown in this holy soil has now ultimately grown into a tree, big enough to bear the fruits.

Yet the very feeling makes me dejected at times that I may never be able to meet them ever again physically. Sometimes certain questions do bounce in and out of my mind to put me in a state of contingency and I do start asking myself and wondering also as well, whether they are today aware or not about some startling facts that...

- *India is the most developed country in the world today?*
- *Delayed justice and terrorism are now the things of past?*
- *We have the vast territories on Mars and Moon?*
- *Cast-creed and minority-majority factors exist here no more?*
- *The new constitution is working absolutely wonders?*
- *And India is the Golden Sparrow once again?*

There is a long similar questionnaire but the answer to all is only one and that is 'Yes'! For the Red Triangle had foreseen the materialization of the same long before.

Now, what is this Red Triangle? And who were our divine friends? This query might be as complex to any one as the first appearance in Mock-CAT for a prospective MBA aspirant. But for the first time I will reveal all the extraordinary secrets in this Timebook step by step for my own satisfaction. I shall also keep the contents away from the prying eyes of the others, as I fear nobody will ever believe me. I know that I do own nothing in material to establish the credence of the successive events that took place way back in 2008-10, and the same may be dismissed as being merely concocted.

Although I have a strong desire to jot down everything all at once, but it is a long and wonderful tale and will take ample time to be accomplished. Let me begin to climb the ladder from the very first rung as a rule, as I am confused at the moment to guess how and where to start from. I may also miss the exact dates and falter in the chronological repetition of events at some places.

But fortunately, I still have a couple of randomly written old diaries, being tucked away in some dusty corners of my book shelf. They do contain the needful statistic details, stray incidents and other related references that I will necessarily require to proceed. So going through them beforehand shall be helpful. Hence, I will have to take a long break here till the coming Sunday to resume the writing with more energy, knowledge and authenticity.

Well... it is now getting dark fast and I didn't get a chance even to have a glance at the newspaper that is still lying folded up on the table in front of me. So picking it up, I do whisk through the headlines on the front page. Here are some of the headlines...

- *Parliament sanctions Rupees 2 trillion monetary aid to USA.*
- *Visa ban for Chinese and Americans for next six months.*
- *Euro gains 7 paisa at 2.05 per rupee.*

Crap! All the so common and boring news. Nothing new and noteworthy. I flip through the pages rapidly and another report catches my eyes.

Tourist booking to MARS full, up to June, 2031.

Go to hell!... I prattle in anxiety. Every body is rushing to mars to contaminate it, as they have already done to the moon. Bookings for the Hell must also be started as soon as possible. The curious fools may also make a beeline for that extraordinary journey.

And finally here is something that's quite cool to the eyes. The last waxy page of the paper displays the lifesize Luxury model of a car. This is Maruti, the most trusted car company all over the world with 100 percent Indian stake. An ultramodern, bonny and evenly latest model of a glamorous human female poses in front of it in style with her one hand resting at the bonnet. The name of the latest model (Automobile) instantly looks appealing to me. Written below the bold name is a line of most assuring words. It reads...

MARUTI 'TITANICA'
Be sure, it will never sink you!

I read it again and a spontaneous appreciation comes to my lips.

Fantastic!

The functioning features of the same do entice me and I can't resist myself to read. But as I go through it, my palmtop starts beeping.

Parivartan

'Good Evening Tapan... it is 5:30 pm, and you have to move. Say 'Yes' if you want the hot water ready at bath.' My P-top squeaked in enquiry and responding instantly in the suggested manner, I jumped up to get ready.

It took me half an hour to brush, shave, have a refreshing hot bath and get dressed. I had promised Anushka to reach our beautysalon Parivartan by 6:00 pm and it was to take me another 20 minutes to reach there, although it is not far away. So coming out of the flat, I headed for the stairs as I usually avoid the lift to take some body exercise. In the mean time, I prefer to instruct my car by my p-top to come out by itself from the underground parking l ot of the building to near the main exit so as to save at least 10 minutes of delay.

By the time I reached there I found the car waiting as calculated; with the parking lights on. I slid the small I.S. panel (Identity Sensor) open near the handle of the car door, and gave my thumb impression on the equallysized screen to request the automobile to unlock and let myself in. It did rightly so gently. My faithful car recognizes only four people in the world and that is my very family.

At Parivartan, which is a bigsized salon, I found my wife at her office. The salon's interior is tastefully decorated by the intellectual placements of art objects and greenery as well, at the selected places by Tina. However, I was welcomed by her with an involuntary smile.

'Thank God... you have woken up finally! Had a good sleep?' She exclaimed as she saw me.

'Yes

'Ate something?

'Some cheese-bread and chai

'Anushka had been waiting for you. She just got busy with a client... but will be coming soon. My God... this girl is always so crazy about shopping.'

'Shopping and gossiping are the two things she is crazy about. However, how is she doing?'

'She is excellent! But hello... you are appearing younger and smarter day by day. What is the matter?' She suddenly changed the subject and flirted in a manner the newlyweds do.

'Me?' I examined myself with surprise.

'It is obviously you...' And she laughed exuberantly.

'Have just taken the bath and this may be the reason'... I answered like a fool.

'Ooff... you are so boring. Leave it...' She became frustrated and it was then that I grasped at the special feminine gesture and tried to make amends with the same flattery.

'Darling... you are looking so romantic today. What is the matter?'

'Why... is the romancing your own monopoly?'

'I didn't mean that, and I love whenever you do it. But women generally give up that funky toying and sex-vex earlier than the men do, and keep rejoicing themselves in their Naani or Daadi status for the rest of their lives, whereas you know... man and horse are the two exceptions in the world who never grow old!'

'Hmm... that's why you kept me awake for the whole of last night? I must buck you up for the feat. Shabaash... my green old man!'

I was made to laugh the way she nodded and I said 'Tina... I love this vitality of your speech. And thanks for those younger and smarter type compliments for me. The real credit goes to your daughter who has reduced at least 10 years of my age by giving me this magical facelift... or 'Parivartan' (Change).' I ended and groped at my face in appreciation with my right hand.

'We must thank God instead for the finesse she has in her fingers... touch wood.' Tina heaved a motherly sigh and added, 'Operates botox with perfect expertise and has done real magic with you specially. And why not? She was operating her Dad after all!'

'May God bless her!' I closed my eyes for a moment in earnest prayer to the almighty, as the fearing parents always do.

Just then Anushka entered the office. The receptionist had informed her of my arrival most probably. And immediately she came to the point even from near the door.

'Hi Dad! Ready to move?'

'Always ready at your service my juke box.' I molested her as I always did and she rolled her eyes in anger.

'Again Dad... you will never mend your ways. Ok... get up now and come.' She however, subsided soon and motioned to turn when Tina stopped us.

'Wait a minute. Today is the beginning of the New Year, so first of all go straight to the Mandir and get the blessings of Sri Sai Baba and Swami Ji... right?' She advised

'Right.' I repeated in a manner similar to that of a teacher student classroom interaction scene.

'And Anushka...' She called again, 'Don't forget to buy lattice and... and some fruits and vegetables too as you like...'

'Okay mom. Bye...' Anushka replied and exited from the office and I followed like a faithful assistant while joining her in the process of coming out of the salon.'

'What do you do with the lattice exactly? Sounds like latex... the foul feeling rubber material?' I enquired curiously.

'It's nothing like that. Just a type of cosmetic chemical and is applied to the feminine eyelashes to make them thicker and longer.' She replied.

'Longer... how much longer?' I amused.

'How much longer? You are so funny Dad...' She suddenly began to laugh and we both threaded our way through the streets towards the Shirdi Mandir, talking like that. The idle mind drifted other way in the meantime and I felt a strange feeling of relief within me.

My life is going smooth and business is well established also. Tina has already become the noted personality in her profession. Anushka... my girl is learning faster as her mother's assistant. And my only son Harshvardhan, a studious boy, who was so inspired and resolute after our eight day's long Visit to Moon last May, that he decided to do engineering in the space science and is going on well with it.

Incidentally, he was first to wish us New Year, while both Tina and me sat awake cozily in the Rezaai (quilt) yester night. We just chatted and waited for calls and e-mails to flow in. And yes... among the numerous usual e-mails, I got an unusual and unexpected e-mail at the same time that sent shocks of surprise and confusion within me. I have read it again and again since, but have not understood the meaning of the same so far.

Samadhaan

Shri Sai Baba *Shirdi Mandir*
Shirdi *Muslim Ibaadatgah*
Mandir *(Mosque*

I was so engrossed in my thoughts that I suddenly found myself in front of our wellknown destination, where the abovementioned scripture adorned the pillars of the sacred place on both the sides... one on each in Hindi. As we entered the arched main entrance of the shrine, I was accosted by one of my old acquaintances, who was coming out from inside and was accompanied by a young man.

'Jai Hind Gupta ji... how are you?'

'Arey Sadiq Bhai what a chance meeting!' And we were locked in a friendly embrace together. 'Tell me how the life is going on... and is he your son, Nazir?'

The introductions and Jai-hinds were exchanged turn by turn between all four of us formally. I must explain here that Jai-hind is the unified and accepted form of addressing each other nationwide now. Our modern text books teach us that the religion of every citizen of the United India is only one, and that is Indianness, faiths may however, be different, and they are insignificant.

'After the graduation, I took the poll tests successfully to become an MLA from my constituency...' Nazir told about himself during the course of conversation, 'I was again fortunate to make the final place for the parliament through the online talent show when the viewers voted in my favour and allowed me to serve the country for the two year regular tenure.'

'My wishes and blessings are with you Mr. M.P... sir. You are now an exclusive part of the Government and your father must be a proud man...' I encouraged but he protested politely.

'Uncle... we are no more the elite class of politicians of a few decades back. MPs and MLAs today are the disciplined public servants who attend the houses five days a week like office to work collectively and have no superfluous status anymore. We belong to no party or banner. Thanks to the legislative policies that we are provided the Government. jobs at the end of our respective terms.'

'Gupta ji... the parliaments and assemblies today are no more the dens for criminals and corrupt to take shelter in, nor are they the rings of circus to just somersault and get the luxury lives in the bargain like they did in the old times. The scene has changed now...' His father also gave his opinion with a smile.

'Yes Sadiq Bhai, the advent of new governing system came like sunrise and this new class is doing a good job. Now, you are a lawmaker yourself Nazir... how do you enjoy the work at the house?' I asked him.

'Well, the Parliament is doing its solemn duty...' He began to explain, 'You know this is not the legislator's duty to bring the area or people's problems to the houses anymore. The problems do come more freely now from different parts of this vast country online and also through the specially designed offices 'Samadhaan', scattered over every town and city for the purpose.'

'All the received issues are being acknowledged, scanned and then resolved within the same week as compulsory. Our work is to stamp the legal 'Yes' or 'No' to the suggestions and proposals brought to us by the specially formed IAS panels for the job. You know, the system is so transparent that it has no place for bribery or commissions.

In the mean time, evening Aarti had finished inside the sanctum-sanctorum, and the devotees had started to come out to disperse. However, in the verandah around the courtyard, a few of others having Muslim faith, were still offering their Maghrib-Namaaz (Evening time prayer) and some prepared to leave who had finished. The head priest whom I called Swami Ji ambled about leisurely among them, chatting and supervising the Bandobast. He was also offering them chai in paper cups as it was extreme cold in the atmosphere. An attendant helped him in the job.

Taking leave from my friend and his son, we both entered the holy interior. We offered our prayers at the altar, sought the blessings of the almighty and received Prasada from the Asst priest, who had performed the routine rituals. We finished in a reposed manner, as the presence at a sacred place cools the conscience deeply. Finally, we moved from there and joined Swami Ji outside.

He was winding up his job ordering the Attendant who quite heedlessly busied himself collecting the blankets used as prayer clothes by the Namaazis. The Gandhi-Topis (caps), provided by the temple administration to those who were bareheaded at the time of prayer were also scattered around. There were a few piles of small blankets and caps in a corner of the verandah. It was a 2.5 feet high and 6 feet wide platform, interspersed by dozens of round pillars for support. It bordered the paved courtyard in the middle, well over the size of a badminton court, and a big Peepal tree stood in the middle of it.

However, I wanted to slip away silently to outside at first, as we were already getting late and a possible meeting with priest was sure to consume at least 15 minutes more. But I hesitated to do so, for he had seen us come in and any such action would be against the manners of courtesy. Furthermore, he was fond of me and always liked to have a chat.

He sprawled his large body on a blanket laid out on the platform and rested himself against a column. He intimately ordered us to sit nearby, after our initial formalities of bowings and blessings were over.

'Just wanted to see you Swami Ji. We are in a hurry today...' I tried to make excuse but he insisted.

'Why making so much haste, son? Come... relax! I wouldn't let you go without Chai.' It is shivering nip in the air and the new cook at Mandir kitchen produces a good brew. With this he motioned for attendant to go for that and I was speechless.

'Tina was here in the morning as she usually does, but Anushka baby seldom accompanies her...' aiming at her, he asked complainingly. 'Do you still fear this terrorist Baba?' And then, he began to itch his favorite long white beard.'

His jesting question made me laugh while Anu looked baffled.

'Terrorist Baba? What is this Dad?' She asked.

'It's quite amusing past and will tell you about on the way back...' I said still laughing and then turning to the priest

I proceeded in the conversation at random.

'So looking after the arrangements yourself today?'

'The devotees of both the faiths have increased for the time being...' He told. 'You are already aware that a lot of people from Kashmir, Gandhar, West Punjab and East Bengal (Former Pakistan and Bangaladesh respectively) who have the Muslim faith are working in the NCR. They live around here and do require the convenience of offering the prayers...

Fortunately, for us, there is no more a social gap between Mandir and Masjid now. The only difference is that the Muslims stay outside, and the Hindus go inside to the icon. Thanks to God for both the sections of the society have accepted the nation's "uniform civil code" whole heartedly and are enjoying together the bread-and-butter relations ever since. It is something like that'...

He gave a thoughtful pause here and remained silent for few moments to find the appropriate words and then asked me unexpectedly.

'Have you ever seen a rainbow after the rains?'

'Yes...' I replied.

'Just like that! So many diverse colours of humanity, being united to make a rainbow of integrity. And these are the photogenic moments for my old and dimmed eyes. Ah...' He discharged a lot of relieving fog from his mouth as if he had taken a puff at the hookah! He then closed his eyes in contentment.

Chai had come in the mean time and been distributed to us. I took a sip and commented like a saint.

'God is undoubtedly one and exists everywhere. Sri Sai Baba had also expressed the same himself. We can't confine the Supreme being to a particular place of worship... and this truth has dawned upon the people at last, I think.'

'Very truly so my son. The nights in winter are cool, dark and lengthy, yet the sun ultimately comes out to give light and warmth. The fall of party clan and the opportunist rulers was the rise of new India similarly. The only tragedy in our case was that the same darkness lasted for 62 long years, before the dawn came in 2010. But my son...' He suddenly stopped here to appear intrigued, much to the credit of the shadow of a column that fell on his face and eyes obliquely and almost concealed that part of his face from the rest. He nearly whispered while looking into my eyes.

'One thing I still wonder to this date... as to how that miracle happened all of a sudden? Don't you think it was quite an unbelievable change?'

'Yes Indeed. I smiled in a queer manner.'

'Although nobody knows exactly... He said again, 'but people used to argue at Paan shops and street nukkads (Corners) that the dramatic transformation was driven by some invisible and other worldly force. Can it really be possible on earth?' He asked again with the same mystique.

'This is your own department Swami Ji. You are so close to God every time, so why don't you ask him rather directly?' I suggested plainly and he got embarrassed with that. He straightened his back up to look sagacious.

'Yes, yes... it is certainly possible in everyway. The old scriptures clearly preach us that whenever there is increase of Adharma and decrease of Dharma, God Himself physically incarnates on earth. And has been doing so since the time immemorial.'

'Then this may also be the similar case... I somehow tried

to conclude and fidgeted to get up, but his next question again fixed me at my place.'

'Do you still remember the day when the then president addressed the nation all of a sudden and the people were totally out of their wits? And when he declared the dissolution of the Parliament and state assemblies all over the country with immediate effect? It was like a tremor of a very high magnitude and yet every thing was so cool and calm that people just waited, watched and calculated'

'Yes, it was a unique tremor, that was quite benevolent for the country, but brought devastation to the entire crop of leaders, their parties and their sycophants, whose shops were shut down so shockingly for ever.' I gave my opinion.

'And unfortunately, my (late) father was also one of them, who could not sustain that shock and took to the bed...' He said.

'I know he was an M.L.A at that time...' I acknowledged and again became restless. I looked for Anu who in the meantime, was just ambling about in the far corner of the verandah to kill time. But here, the dogged Swami Ji was quite determined to have all his say today. So being apparently ignorant of my uneasiness, he crooned further without a break. However, his tone became a bit emotional this time.

'He died within two months of the historical day. He feasted on Brahman votes for 20 years on successive terms to exercise the same damned democracy of caste politics. Brahmins did get nothing in bargain but he amassed considerable wealth and influence. He was a brash and bullied officials and the administration to get his works done...'

He paused for a moment and heaved a sigh before continuing, 'But you know, ill-got ill-spent is rule of the nature. Everything has since gone and nothing left now. He lived like a king... and both me and my brother like princes. I can't forget those days when our security men used to massage our bodies, iron clothes, polish shoes and did all other household chores like slaves'

He had not yet finished, when all of a sudden, Anushka let out a loud and frightened shriek from that corner of the verandah. It was comparatively dark there owing to the low hanging Peepal leaves, which prevented sufficient light down in that area. I instantly bolted from my seat and reached there in no time.

I found her trembling and shrunk in panic, with her hands reaching out to hold her face as girls naturally do in the similar situations. Although she was in much control of herself now, yet I promptly held her in my fondling arms like a good dad and enquired.

'What is wrong my son?'

There... she pointed to the corner, 'Someone is lurking behind those blankets'

I turned to see but could make out nothing there except a small pile of unused and folded blankets placed neatly. When I strained my eyes to make them accustomed to darkness, I saw the bust of a man behind. The figure was quite motionless and apparently rested against the wall.

'Who is there?' I threatened

There was no answer

By this time Swami Ji had also followed me hurriedly there. He drew near the platform and craned his neck forward to have a closer look for some time. Then, he climbed the platform in a single effort despite his old age and fearlessly approached the looming silhouette.

It was there that he heard a low wailing which reached a crescendo as he squatted beside the stranger. The Attendant also came running with a torch and joined his master, who took the torch and threw a beam of bright light on the figure.

He was a middleaged bearded man of about 35. His graying hair were dishevelled and dirty as if he had not taken bath for weeks. He wore jeans, dirty offwhite shirt and a rugged jacket. He sat still against the wall, with his legs outstretched and eyes closed. He drew deep, short and irregular breaths as an asthmatic patient usually does.

Watching him closely, the attendant whispered something in his master's ears and they both again began to examine him.

The trickles of his tears, both dry and wet shining under the torch light indicated that he had been crying. His drawn face was so pale and dead as if his corpse were exhumed from his grave a short while ago.

'Who are you brother? Swami Ji asked in a soft voice in the end and waited.

But he didn't move. His posture remained quite unchanged. Yet the suffocated hiccups convulsed him every now and then. This time the former placed his hand on his shoulder sympathetically and gave a slight jerk, while asking again.

'Who are you brother... and why are you crying like this?'

This time, he opened his eyes and looked at the questioner and as he did so, his red eyes turned hostile. A tinge of hatred contorted his face. He flapped the former's friendly hand away from his shoulder with disgust and glared at him.

'Don't touch me... you the son of a swine!'

An ominous hush fell upon everybody. This was quite unexpected gesture that might have irritated even the coolest of saints. Even I felt anger arousing inside me at the rude behaviour of the stranger. Anushka had now recovered from her initial shock and watched him in a mixed expression of fear, astonishment and rejection. However Swamiji kept his cool in wonderful resistance, and didn't react at once. Instead he directed the servant rightly to fetch a glass of hot water and a towel, and having done this he said again:

'I don't know who you are. I have not seen you ever before, but my assistant told me that you have been coming here since last week to offer Namaaz at least twice daily and do spend a lot of time in the same corner. Please tell me what is your name and the real purpose of coming here. Don't fear... let me assure that you will be treated as a friend here'

'I don't fear anyone except Khuda. And I have no fear also in letting you know that I wanted to kill you! 'The man blurted out.

'Kill me?' The old priest opened his bearded mouth in awe.

'Yes... but you are fortunate enough to have survived the blade.' With this, he produced a dagger from inside of his jacket to show. And, as he did so, a sudden spasm of cough shook him. Soon he went out of his breath, dropping the dagger on his thigh while trying to control himself and everyone watched him in a silent but precarious manner.

It took him a long time before he returned to normal. He then slowly accepted hot water, towel and then chai without any protest. Maybe it was that obstinate hospitality of his enemy that had softened him to some extent. The dagger had been removed from there in the mean time. Swamiji waited gravely until he finished his chai, and then asked him again softly.

'Now tell me, why you wanted to kill me? Have I done any harm to you? Have I knowingly or unknowingly sinned against you? Please relax! And tell me everything in detail, as I don't remember anything of the nature...'

'Your only sin is that you are the son of a monster who killed my father...' He moaned.

'But my father is no more! He is long dead and it is more than two decades now.' Swamiji exclaimed in astonishment.

'Father never dies... he continues in his son' The intruder growled in return. 'Your father has already gone to his deserved place in dojakh (hell), but you still represent him on this earth as his survivor. I have nursed the revenge in my heart for not less than 22 years. I can never forget that fateful evening when my father was brutally tortured to death by the accused and my mother watched helplessly, while clinging her 11 year old son to herself in panic... and that was me.'

His voice had turned husky due to the emerging emotions. With deepest grief, he lifted his hands in prayer and earnestly implored a curse while looking up at the heavens.

'O... 'Khuda', may he never rest in peace, for he has ruined us... Ameen!'

With these words, he began to wail again and then wept bitterly. His overall mental condition was weak and topsy-turvy. He clearly appeared broken, both physically and psychologically. And after some time, he went on to relate the narration of his tragic childhood with intermittent fits of cough. The different expressions came on to his face like sun and shadow.

Both Anushka and me had taken our seats on the platform, with the blankets underneath and listened to him intently. I was in no hurry now and so was Anu. She just sat silently on the corner of verandah, with her back resting against the pillar and one leg dangling down. The subtle shades of her countenance could be seen transforming slowly from sheer abhorrence to sympathy as he went on. On the other hand, Swamiji's face sank in shame over the misdeeds of his late father. He had begun to remember all as he was young at that time.

The incident had taken place way back in 2008 and root of the concerned man's current destruction was the political system prevailing at that time. It was based mainly on a single or two parties who enjoyed the power of states and center either alone or alternately between them. It was a whopping multibillion business at the time.

These parties were like the family trusts consisting of mainly corrupt, old and inefficient people with the life memberships. A mandate was forced out of citizens in the name of democracy by them and they plundered the country for 62 years in many ways.

Umakant Misra the father of Ramakant Misra alias Swamiji was an M.L.A. of the same cult in U.P. state. Unfortunately, Ashraf Wahaab, the father of Abdul Wahaab, who sat in front of us at the moment was posted as XEN (Executive Engineer) in the same district. Mishra unsuccessfully tried to tap him on many occasions, and began to nurse a grudge against him as a result.

As the bad luck would have it, birthday of a big state leader fell at the same time, and considering it the appropriate moment, the M.L.A. demanded huge money from the officer as birthday-tilak to the leader. Mr. Wahaab politely denied and said that he didn't accept bribes to pay bribes further on. Although very gently executed... his words wounded the perky politician so deeply that he attacked his house with his gang one evening.

The hapless man was electrocuted, kicked and mauled so badly that it ultimately led to his demise. His wife just clung her 11 year old son Abdul to her but could do nothing to her husband's rescue. An honest Govt officer lost his life so cheaply in the hands of a statesman and the birthday of one brought doom to another.

He was arrested later on, remained in jail for some time and was released on bail. He died next year... and carried the cache of his crimes with him. Abdul's widowed mother left the country forever and migrated to his brother in Saudi Arabia with her son where she reared him up. She was a devout lady and had a strong belief, that nobody could escape his sins, and will be rewarded accordingly by Allah. But Abdul had seen the grisly end of his father with his own eyes. He remembered the scene and could not forget it, and came to India as he got the chance.

He went to that UP city and to his ex-house where his father breathed his last. It had now given way to new constructions. Abdul was disheartened to know that Umakant had died long before. His revenge began to languish... as his motive was somehow achieved directly or indirectly. He thought of returning back but in the process of meeting people and making enquiries, he happened to get a family photograph of the villain, in which our Swamiji also stood alongside his father.

Incidentally, he appeared just identical to his father in looks. This photograph aroused Abdul's anger again. He saw the same wicked Umakant in him. Like father... like son! So he surmised and decided to shift his revenge on to the poor Swami Ji. Finally having ascertained his whereabouts, he came to this Noida location of him for the purpose.

He thus finished his story, and as he stopped speaking, a shroud of depressed silence gripped all. He seemed much at ease now and breathed deeply. Swami Ji didn't utter a single word in between and just listened in remorse. He stared at the same photo that Abdul had just handed over to him. His wrinkled and bearded face drooped more and more with guilty conscience. He brooded deep ... for he was the fruit of the same poisonous tree.

At last, he solemnly took out the same dagger from under that pile of blankets, placed the grasp of it carefully in Abdul's palm in the usable position, and then folded the latter's fingers around it with his both hands to plead in the grave tone.

'I am sorry for you man, and am ashamed of myself at the same time. The son has to pay for his father's debts... and I shall be blessed if I could do this. Come on... raise the dagger, and let your purpose be solved.'

Abdul now looked more surprised than being dangerous and threatening. But for a few moments only. He hardened his posture again to utter disdainfully.

'Pandit ji, your regrets can't reduce my sorrows and heal my wounds...' He threw the weapon away into the far corner of the verandah, making a jingling sound and said. 'Let my misfortunes be buried deep inside me now. I would not do you any harm, for you are... unlike your father, a learned servant of God. All I want now is to return back to my country as soon as possible, as I hate India. I shall leave the rest on the almighty. He again looked up at the heavens, beyond the motionless leaves of that Peepal tree, took a deep frustrated sigh and beseeched...Allah!'

He then got up, stepped down the platform, and strode away to the outside. He disappeared within seconds. The patter of his foot steps faded away in the distance. All this happened so unexpectedly, that no one was in a state of speaking a word. We stood there quite nonplussed. Abdul Wahaab... son of late Mr. Ashraf Wahaab was gone. He was out of sight... but could he go out of our minds also?

Some people never go into oblivion, and he was one of them Ramakant Misra alias Swami Ji followed him up to the gate on impulse. Although he knew that there was no point in trying to stop him, and also that there was actually nothing he could do for that man...who had a broken heart. Yet he did cast a searching look out in the street but could not get his sight any more. He then turned dejectedly and dragged his heavy feet towards the sanctum sanctorum.

Terro-Saurs

Our walk back to the car was without any more conversation this time. It was 8:45 already, and we scurried through the evening rush. Both of us were engrossed in our own thoughts. Surprisingly, I was still searching for that stranger in the crowd in vain. We were at the parking within minutes. Anushka took it out from there, and steering to the right, took to the road and drove on. Now, having relaxed for a while, she looked at me and asked to break the silence.

'You are still thinking about that man... isn't it Dad?'

'Yes...' I pushed the seat in the reclining position and yawned. 'But less about him and more about his those cursed words, when he said 'I hate India'!

'But that's quite natural you know. He gained nothing, but lost everything here. And anyone in his place would have done the same.'

'I can understand that. In this case, it was a real tragedy with the hapless man. In fact, our life is a sort of hotchpotch and a series of mixed-up happenings. Some of which are sweet like honey... and some are sour like tamarind. Yet they are the vital fillers, and a single flower makes no garland.' I said like a philosopher and she also added her philosophy to that of mine.

'You are right dad. Our life is like a hilly terrain, so full of ups and downs... and yet enchanting!'

'Smart work! Paying me in my own coin?' I laughed and continued, 'We saw lots of ups and downs of a common life today. There were two remarkable characters before us who displayed the most positive human attitudes in the end. It is difficult to forget the wretched man, but my credit goes to Swami Ji for his persisting modesty. Yet I must salute both.'

'Me too! O rubbish, I totally forgot to ask you about that terrorist remark made by Guruji at the temple. Tell me now, what was all that?' She took me by the wrist.

'That was a shade surprising even to me, as to how he still remembered such an ordinary dialogue that took place between you and me, and which I mentioned to him long time before?' I replied.

'And what was that?' She asked.

'It was when you were a small child, that one day I was watching an old documentary on terrorism over the TV. You were running about in the house purposelessly. Suddenly, you began to pamper me with your endless questions. I hardly answered one, when you asked another...

'Who are these people Dad?'

'Terrorists...'

'Who are the terrorists? Are they beggars?'

'Not beggars...'

'Are they holding guns in their hands?'

'Yes...'

'Do they rob the people with their guns?'

'Yes. Rob and kill the people...'

'Kill why? For not paying money to them?'

'Yes...' I surrendered to put you off as I was in no mood to answer. But you refused to budge and asked again.

'But why the police don't nab them?'

'The police will soon nab them...'

'Do all the bearded people are terrorist?'

'Yes...'I replied inattentively.

You remained silent at that to contemplate for a moment and then offered thoughtfully.

'Do our Swami Ji at Mandir is also a terrorist?'

'No... but why?'

'Because he also supports a big beard...' was your answer.

I was not yet completely finished when Anu began to laugh madly and I added further.

'However, it took me a long time that day to tell you the difference between saadhu and shaitaan.'

'Oh, Dad!'

'By the way, how is Vikramaditya and where is he now?' I changed the subject after those light moments.

'He is always over busy, touring the border areas, regarding his robotic installations and maintenances, etc. He was in Kabul yesterday. I forgot to tell you that he conveyed the New Year wishes to all.'

'Just call him up and let me return the wishes...' I said.

She pushed the car phone on at the panel and fingered the alphabets of his name. Also switched the car on to auto-drive mode and steered it into the left side's auto driver's lane. Having done this, she waited... and I could read her enthusiasm clearly.

'Hi... Anushka!' A wise looking face appeared on the screen.

'Hi... Vikram, where are you?' She chirped.

'In the remote town of Herat, near Iran border

'Doing what?'

'Working still...'

'Working so late! Are you crazy?'

'So late, why? It's still day light here Madam. You should know that there is a time difference of three hours in India from East to West. Moreover, I am doing overtime today to finish the work quickly. And you are driving may be as I can see your seat belt?'

'Yes, going shopping with Dad, who is right here with me...'

'Hello Uncle...'

What's up Vikram?'

The panel phone lens had angled towards me by itself now, sensing my voice.

'It's fine... although the work schedule is so tight. Yesterday was all wasted away in new-year celebrations till late night at Kabul club, and that's why, I decided to coverup today. Yet I must not regret that, as the quality of music, dance and food was just top class, at this premier club of North-Western India.'

'Late night party...and in Afghanistan? Life seems to be quite ultra modern there nowadays?'

'It is no more Afghanistan Uncle. It is Gandhar Pradesh now. Modern time Kabul is not different from our Bangalore and this Herat is a mushrooming town. Our national legal policy of exiling the culprits to the border areas have proved very fruitful. These people have totally changed the landscapes of these places by dint of their hard work. They have turned the barren lands into fertile ones with the mass afforestation. More and more green patches are increasing fast due to the developed agricultural techniques adopted by the government. By the way... have you never been to this place?'

'Not yet...'

'Uncle, you have been to Moon, and have missed your own country? That's not fair...' He rubbed his nose the way that I couldn't help laughing and decided to make a note of my family's 'Moon trip' in my time-book to preserve those very precious moments forever, as soon as I get the time.

'You're right, I am looking to visit the province at my earliest. And specially, the Khyber-Pass, and Bamiyaan... the biggest Buddhist pilgrimage centre in the Northern part. How do those resurrected grand statues of Lord Buddha look to the eyes?'

'Marvelous to behold! They are very popular among the tourists, who come through the national highway that connects it to Amritsar via Kabul, Rawalpindi and Lahore.'

'What sort of culture exactly dominates that part now?'

'It's a mixed one. Every faith and colour is intermingled with each other. South Indians are here, East Indians are here, and Marwaris are here. Moreover, the Government has provided the pieces of land to those exiled outlaws, who have completed the terms of their punishments and are unwilling to go back. Overall, the new generations are building up a modern society. Jeans-Top clad young girls and women can be seen walking the streets or watching the movies at multiplexes anywhere.'

'Well...it was a nice chat with you. When you'll be back?'

'May be tomorrow or the day after, as soon as I finish.'

'We'll dine together when you're in Delhi. Coming by road?'

'By both the means supposedly. I have got my own aircar as I have to go a lot of places now.'

'Good! Which model?'

'Its Maruti's common... Hawk-QTX. It's with hydrogen and bio-fuel, dual option. It's an excellent machine.'

'God bless you! Bye for now... see you soon.'

'Bye Uncle.'

He disappeared from the screen, but left me with my thoughts wandering. I felt proud of my country but Abdul's words echoed in my mind again and again, 'I hate India...I hate India.' I desperately wanted to erase it from my inside, and it became a sort of emotional struggle for me. Just then, Anu switched the car Music Player on. The instrument took a few seconds to read my patriotic mood, and then selected one of my favourites from the collection of the old melodies.

"Jahaan daal-daal par sone ki
Chidia kerti hai basera
Woh Bharat desh hai mera
Woh Bharat Desh hai mera..."

The sweet voice of Mohd Rafi descended down to my soul and I felt exhilarated. I closed my eyes... and listened silently. It was like the small sips of 'Finest Scotch' going down my throat. Anu had marked our destination that was some 15 miles away, on the GPS controlled auto-navigation system. She had to do nothing and was in a talking mood. So as the car stopped by itself at a red signal, she sounded a click with her thumb and finger near my ear and interrupted.

'Where are you Dad? I want to say something...'

'Hmm...'

'I have a senior friend who got married in West Punjab recently. She has moved to swat-valley, with her husband. She keeps sending me the e-mails and tells about the place that is far more beautiful than Kashmir. How about going there by car sometime on a long drive?'

'No vacations till the next six months at least...' I declared, and then enquired 'What's her husband doing there?'

The Music Player had gone silent automatically while we talked together.

'He is posted in a Medical College that was a big Madarsa (Muslim School) previously. It was the stronghold of some Taliban and Qaida sort of people and as she told me, they ruled the region once on gun-point and even banned the women even to show their nails from behind their Burkaas. I wonder, if there were no Govt or law to check them?' She looked at me.

'Well, it was in the hold of religion-struck, mentally wicked terrorists, who produced only two things... opium poppies and hatred. The shoulders of those uncivilized gangsters again carried two burdens at the same time... the deadly guns and their pre-historic brains. They were so heartless, that they killed anyone in a moment with the flick of a finger and ironically, it was all the State Sponsored.' I explained and she jumped up in excitement in the end.

'Wow! It sounds like the land of modern time Robin Hoods. I wish I could go there at once.'

'Robin Hood robbed the rich to give to the poor. But

they tormented the common folks! Banning even the haircuts, music, films, TV, fashion, etc. was the sheer vandalism in the name of Islam. And they declared it, 'The wish of Allah'

'It is only the act of defaming the very image of the Almighty...' She said.

'That's why Allah alias Shiva finally had to show his magical dance Tandava that totally wiped the terrorists out from the area.

'And thus the Terro-Saurs vanished from the continent like the mighty Dino-saurs! She announced dramatically.

'You're right.'

But the question is that as to how they ever came into existence? She asked again.

'The structure of Talibans, etc. was erected by West-Punjab, known as Pakistan formerly. But slowly the former assumed so much power that many individual warlords began to emerge out of them to make their own ethnic groups. They became a constant threat to India. Luckily for us, a changed constitution had taken the reigns from the imperialism at home at the same time. The new government began an all round strike on these insurgents in and around the country. All the terror camps were hence being destroyed with firm resolution and occupied Kashmir was taken back first of all.'

'The action led to a civil war within Pakistan which broke it into many self declared free parts. Now, the state-Taliban coalition committed the decisive blunder. They dared to attack India in frustration and this proved to be a misfire. Our forces romped home through Pakistan, finally taking the complete military and diplomatic control over it.

Later on a referendum was procured under the flag of UNO, regarding its re-union with India and people chose rightly the protection of their parental country. Again... in the similar circumstances a decade later, Afghanistan too preferred to get the protection of India and became its subsidiary state, having the certain constitutional powers to exercise.'

'But over all, this overwhelming success owes to the new genre of our politicians who proved to be 'the Jewels in Rags', and dazzled the world by their sparkle. They adopted an aggressive, yet progressive diplomacy to govern. Home and foreign policy was being made bold and penetrating with the help of the administrative officers...' I explained in detail.

A beeping sound distracted both of us, as GPS indicator was showing the Mahabazar in the vicinity. The gaudy lights of the same were right in front of our eyes. Anu switched the car back to Manual-Drive mode and took the control over. But while doing so, she unknowingly turned it into the wrong lane... all in a jiffy. And within moments, a uniformed Police personnel appeared in front and motioned her to stop.

'Yes officer?' She enquired apologetically as she slid the window glass of her side down.

'Do you have the license to drive Madam?' He enquired.

'Yes, I do...' She opened the cabinet and took it out. Then she placed it on the extended hands of the cop.

He gave it a searching look... and here, I took my wallet out to pay the fine. And before he could speak, I offered myself.

'How much officer?'

'One thousand only...' He took out his small official gadget and entered Anu's thumb print code, taken from her license. He then added a few more details and returned the license to her. He now put his machine in front, for her thumb impression and so did she. A small slip creaked up its slit. He handed it over to her, accepted the bill from me and smiled quite professionally.

'Thanks for your contribution to the State's economy sir! Take care the next time...' He suggested.

With this, he turned and walked away.

Enigma of an E-Mail

3rd January, Friday 2031

The same cryptic e-mail puzzled me even more. It always danced before my eyes, whenever I went through my P-top messages. Although the coming of such mails on systems is not so unusual at all... and mostly they are deleted from the record even unread. I also thought of doing the same at times, but don't know what stopped me. It had such a peculiarity in language that it gave me an aversion on one side and lured me on the other. I was feeling the same both while looking at it again yesternight. There was no sender's name beneath.

Anu had gone to sleep in her room and I was in bed with Tina, who sat beside me with her back reclining on cushion. She busied herself in knitting a head scarf for herself, from a multicoloured cashmilon yarn. She needed it on these wintry mornings and evenings while going to and coming back from her salon. The ball of wool whirled about on the Rezaai sometimes like a whirly-gig, and her fingers did a sort of pole-dancing around the needle. I had watched them curiously earlier, trying my best to understand the swift manoeuver... but it ditched me everytime.

'Damn fucker!' Suddenly I uttered in anxiety and it put a break to her artistic work.

'What is this?' She asked me with surprise.

'This is Bermuda triangle of an e-mail, that's tangling my mind since the day before yesterday.' I nodded desperately.

'Let me see...' She took the handset from me and gave it a searching look for the first time. The message was written in many short lines like this...

Hi

How are you?

I am sending here with

STRONG

AC-2031

HEY

WEAR

A

NAPPY...

'What is this?' Looks quite funny. She said while being extremely confused.

'I don't know but the more I think of it, the more complex it becomes to me... just like your this knitting work.' I replied.

She didn't answer and began to scrutinize every word again.

'Strong AC... wear a nappy? It seems to make a sense that someone is sending you an Air Conditioner of the brand name '2031'. But the name of any such I have not heard before however. It may be some latest one, we can suppose. But now... what this Damn nappy is doing here? Are you a kind of 'Tarzan', who lives all naked?' She looked at me and wondered.

'Just suppose, I am the real Tarzan and you are my jungle-love? I began to laugh and gave a caressing nudge to her head with mine and kissed her.'

'I think it's one of those obscene mails, the type of which a woman may send to a man likely...' She said.

'And after all, mine is just the ripe age to get a flirting invitation from someone... isn't it?' I asked.

'This is nothing but a Spam only, and they keep coming every now and then. Just delete it from your Inbox. Why taxing your brains unnecessarily?' She handed the instrument back to me.

'You are right. How do we waste ourselves away in trifles! Life is so short... and the works are so many to do. Let us relax now and have some fun?' I extended my arms and yawned freely and she glared at me.

'Osss... Mr. I was sensing your ill-intent already. Are you alright?'

'Yes... absolutely.'

'Then what is this fun Tamasha every other day?'

'This is not my fault Ma'am, and the poet in me have just coined out a stanza on the subject. Shall I...'

'Why not...' She permitted and I cleared my throat to say.

Where there is an e-mail
There is a spam
And where there is a female
There is a man!

'Good thinking...' She appreciated in a sarcastic manner

and gave a clapping also. I was encouraged more to add.

'And I have already told you the fact that 'Man and Horse never grow old'... remember?'

'And which one are you from the duo exactly?'

'Both. A gentleman at the day time... and a gentle horse at night! But for my dear mare only.'

'My dear Mr. Jeckyll and Hyde. Now you better take your sleep silently. I have got to do my knitting...' and she turned to pick up her needles.

'Throw this prickly stuff away now. We will knit romance with sex together...' I got the hold of her hands and suggested while still making my advances.

'You have gone out of your wits. You were not this much sticky, even when you were newly married. Are you sure that you are not taking any of those dirty blue-pills these days?' She looked in my eyes suspiciously.

'Nope! sure...' I denied.

'But anyhow this excess is spoiling your health. We should fix it to twice a month maximum...'

'Alright. And it starts from today...' I proceeded to kiss her from the neck.

'Wait, Wait, Wait. You want fun, right? Tell you some jokes?' She tried to put the weak resistance.

'No way Ma'am. I like the fun without laughing only... and this is the one.'

'Still, it is not an easy walkover Jawan. Do have some patience. It will take me some time to turn myself on also, and in the mean time, you will have to take an aptitude test...'

'An aptitude test, before taking up the physical one?

Is this the military recruitment procedure or what? I don't understand why you women always choose such delicate moments to harass the men??'

'Tut, Tut, Tut... poor you. I just can't explain as to how I am enjoying your eagerness...' She giggled heartily.

'Yes, ready? It is a simple puzzle and you will solve it so easily, as I have done myself...' She then became serious and encouraged me.

'Can't we take up this ordeal afterwards?' I asked.

'You are just going to sleep after your act is over... so this is the best time to talk to you.' She replied plainly and picked up a women's magazine from the side table to make me more chagrined.

'And am I going out of contest if I happen to fail?' I enquired like a nursery boy.

'Don't be so disheartened...' She began to laugh again. 'You can always hope to get some grace marks, since I am the incharge' She assured and began to flip through the pages of the magazine and then handed it over to me.

There was a squared space at a page. She pointed to it with her finger and added, I was to put it before you the previous night also but then it slipped my mind. The tip for you is that the hint to the solution is hidden within the riddle.

I widened my eyes at the subject, which read like this...

Mind Twister

Use the same four letters Anagram to fill in the blanks in the sentence. What are the missing words? Find the solution at the back page.

On Sunday, a ______ man goes to an antique shop
near the tram ______ where he happens to see
many colorful ______ and likes much. And buying
a grey one, he ______ to pay for it on the ______
And then hurries home as the evening sun
was going down the tree tops.

I went through these lines with a bit of distaste and repeated them again and again. I applied my mind on every word and pondered deep. While Tina entwined one arm with mine, and tapped my shoulder with her fingers in what may be a moral support. She wriggled closer to me as I took sometime.

'Want some more hints?' She whispered in my ear and then blew a puff of breath inside to irritate me. But surprisingly I got the wits with it.

'I've done it!' I exclaimed the next moment and my eyes began to shine.

'Really?'

'It is----post, stop, pots, opts and spot respectively. And the hint you suggested about, is the last word 'tops' in the anagram.'

Shabaash, (Bravo). She cheered up, and kissed me on the cheek. She then invited me with her outstretched arms, 'Here is your mare and you are welcome. I hope you will remain as gentle a horse till the end, as you are...' She said and pulled me upon her lastly.

She looked well prepared now with desire and we both fumbled with each other in passion. After half an hour, we lay beside each other, breathing deeply... in great satisfaction.

'Feeling good?' She asked after some easy moments.

'Yupp... and you?'

'You have turned me sexy as well, like you are yourself.'

'You know, behind every successful person... there is a cooperative wife.'

'Shall I thank you for the compliments?' She asked.

I didn't reply. Something had dawned upon me all of a sudden and the hairlines of my eyebrows shrank by itself. I sprang up from the bed and threw the Rezaai aside in frenzy. And just like Archimedes had done centuries ago, I cried out madly.

'Eureka eureka!'

'What happened to you?' She was extremely startled.

I jumped down on the floor. Picked up my P-top from the bed and rushed to the study table in the corner. I opened its drawer and searched for a pen and a paper. Then, I worked the same troubling message up on the screen, and copied it down on the paper. Now I fidgeted to unscramble the words to the best of my wits.

I stood near the table stark naked and just worked intently. Tina watched me in sheer panic, while lifting her head up the pillow. My silence had made her worried even more. Finally, she got up to sit upon the bed and began to wear her lingeries quickly.

It took me about Five minutes to finish, and when I did it, my face was glowing as never before. I hammered the table with my fist and cried out excitedly...

'I have got it!'

'Got what?'

I didn't reply again, took the letter pad instead and

returned to my position at the bed. I seated myself comfortably this time underneath the quilt, while she was seething in anger by then.

'Why are you not answering me?' She burst out.

'Relax Tina... I have solved the puzzle of that e-mail at last. It is actually the simple New Year greetings, sent to me by one of my old college friends. We had not been in touch since then, and that's why I couldn't understand it at once. I must thank you for asking me that mind twister, which brought the idea to my mind. What a big fool I had been so far...'

Then, I showed the small letter pad to her that contained both, the scrambled and unscrambled messages in due order. She began to read curiously. The corrected one read like this in the same format...

Hi	Hi
How are you?	How are u
I am sending here with	I am sending here with
STRONG	*Congrats*
AC-2031	2031
HEY	*A*
WEAR	*Happy*
A	*New*
NAPPY...	*Year*

'It now makes some right sense at least.' She lifted her face up after sometime and commented. Some mixed expressions could be noticed in her voice. She compared the both again closely and then scoffed at.

'I just don't understand why the same wishes couldn't have been sent quite plainly? The unnecessary mental exercise... huh! Who is this sender anyway?'

'It's V.D.'

'V.D.? It's some Vidhyadhar or Vidhya Devi?'

'It's Vandana. She was fond of scrambling the words up in the college also...'

'Your classmate?' A woman inside her had begun to surface.

'Hmm...'

'I see... there is some other connection maybe?'

'What connection?'

'The language of the mail indicates a lot.'

'You know such things are so normal when we are young...' I tried to put forward a defence and she became more aggressive.

'You did something with her also?'

'Nope! We just kissed each other...'

'How many times?'

'Two or three times maximum. My god... why you wives are so over cautious with husbands?'

'Was there nothing else?'

'Absolutely not.'

'Swear by me...'

'It's by you... okay?'

She seemed to understand for a while but asked again the next moment.

'Was she beautiful?'

'Yes, she was.'

'More than me?'

I hesitated; and then chose the words wisely to deny.

'No... you are prettier than her.'

'Speaking truth?'

'Yes, it is true!'

Being contented at last, she prepared to sleep. I was not feeling sleepy, so folding my arms over the pillow and beneath my head, I quietly watched the moonlight that was trying to filter into the room through the window. It tempted me to write about my overdue moon voyage. It was full moon in the clear sky and I watched the disc with a steady gaze. I knew the shadows visible on the surface were the places where sunlight was not reaching properly. It was such a wonderful territory to walk on. Had I really gone there last year...I wondered? I then returned to my study table and opened my T-book to write...

Moon Voyage

It was a memorable day for my family when we reported at the Sriharikota base on 14th May last year, six days prior to the schedule date of flying as compulsory. Harsh and Anu were so excited that they wanted to join the station even earlier than directed. The funny craze of the young Blood!

At the base, we had to go through the special pre-flight training programme. It comprised many tough modules of acclimatization, such as weightlessness, space suit and parachute jumping, etc. to deal with the outer space atmospheric conditions. There were some particular exercises to do also. Regular classes and slide shows also followed to teach the same. Our batch consisted of 50 voyagers in all, and a medical certificate of a healthy heart was necessary for each. Anyway, going to moon is not as easy as going to Simla or Kashmir for holidaying, and it is expensive too.

Finally, the dream day came when we boarded the space shuttle one by one. Most of the passengers were going for the first time, so there was high excitement around. The heart beats sprinted when the 'Space Hostess' announced to fasten the seat belts and the takeoff counting began soon after. Four... Three... Two... One... Zero! And the craft shot up, giving us a sudden inertial jerk, that was however minimized by the technically designed seats.

And Wow! It was breathtaking to see the base-station

disappear into the state, the state into country... and country into continent within a few seconds. After all we were traveling at the breakneck velocity of 22 km/sec, Both Anu and Harsh glued to the window, and may be never winked while looking outside.

The ship had six crew members on board, which included Mr. Purushottam Kamath, who was Three-in-One on flight. He was our host, doctor and the guide at the same time. Harsh had made a sort of friendship with him during the training and thus asked him thousands of questions on the entire trip, regarding space technicalities, moon and even about other stars and satellites.

Our first destination was 'Indian Space Station' that twinkled like a star in the distance and drew near every moment. Soon, the craft dropped its fuel tank down into the Bottle-Green Pacific Ocean, while escaping the Earth's gravitational field. Within minutes, it got coupled with the I.S.S. softly like a boggy does with the train. All of us then came out and alighted at the platform, while swimming through the air like birds in the special suits.

Mr. Kamath showed all of us the station around. Along with other things, part of it also hosted the powerful receivers and transmitters, which received electricity, produced on moon and being conducted without wires therefrom. It is further transmitted to the three big power houses in the South, Central East and Northern India respectively, simply by rectifying the received microwave signals with the help of the sophisticated equipments. Today, moon produces more than 50% of the total electricity required in our country and since it has become more essential to us.

Finally, after the 18 hours long flight, the craft landed at the Moon-base of the Indian territory of the planet, with the help of a mammoth parachute. I am not able to express exactly now, that how much ecstatic to me was my first step on the soil of Chandamama. What I remember well is that I took Tina's hand in mine and we both set our feet together on the rocky surface gingerly. And the moment we did it, an electrifying wave ran through our bodies each! It was unparallel joy to see our National Tri-colour standing proudly there like a soldier on the Border Anu and Harsh had already jumped down like kids. All the voyagers, however saluted the National Flag solemnly.

There was a big fibremade, conical shaped structure nearby and we were all led into it. We covered the distance by jumping like balls. However the atmosphere inside was akin to the earth, being created specially by using magnetic waves for generating extra gravitation. The glass pyramid was centrally oxygenated. There were numerous separate cabins made for two, so we were given the cabin numbers and some big capsule type big refreshments also, before everybody was discharged to take rest. Kamath now announced to all...

'Friends. I do welcome and congratulate everybody on this part of the Universe. It's our own familiar moon. Be prepared tomorrow as it will be the first of our three days long lunar- expedition. I will guide you through the ninehour trip, that will cover one third of the satellite's total surface, with stopovers at the land mark places. Till then... it's good night!'

We had a comfortable and profound sleep that night as we were dead tired. Next day after everyone was ready, we were led to a unique hovercraft, that waited for us outside at a small ground near the camp. It was shaped like a flying saucer, and was quite big to accommodate all. Two of the crew did the piloting job, although it flew automatically on the autopilot. It used the processed 'Helium-3' as fuel. Its name was Tarangini, that was written in Hindi on its belly.

Passengers were provided with the special Lunar Suits this time, with inbuilt oxygen supply and a clear walky-talky system to talk to each other. I had never imagined that I will fly in a flying saucer one day and in all, it was the marvelous achievement of the Indian scientists.

Our first stop was the famous Batukeshwar Dutt-Urja Kendra.' (Energy Center), just two kms away. The power house produced electricity by using Helium-3 found all over the moon like sand. The big transmitters transmitted the production nonstop to the powerful receivers on the I.S.S, wirelessly. From where it is sent further away on earth continuously. A staff of four scientists remained here every time who welcomed us and showed around. Although every work is done digitally by the Robots there, yet a total of 13 scientists stayed at the panel round the clock to supervise. They are replaced by the fresh substitutes from India from time to time.

So, for the next three days, we scanned the rugged surface of the moon. We walked the ridges, descended down the awesome ditches, and climbed the mountains also. Trekking is particularly easy there, as even a small jump takes us six times higher than on earth. We saw queer rocks, meteors and craters, etc. and also took the countless photographs of the landscape.

It was a busy itinerary. On the last day, we were taken to the place where first man on Moon had set his foot seven decades earlier. It was situated in the U.S. territory. The astronaut 'Neil Armstrong's footprint was still preserved clearly in the sand. There is no air or climate on the planet and the atmosphere is absolutely stark!

The last point to visit in the end was a high plateau, where a powerful telescope was fitted. We were taken there in late evening. And what we saw there on the top was hair-raising. A big and beautiful blue coloured globe had risen-up in the western horizon. Anu jumped up madly at the sight of it and exclaimed.

'Look Dad... that's our own Earth!'

I didn't answer and kept staring at the wonderful view. Tina was also enthralled. Mr. Kamath who had guided all of us through the tour so far and who also carried out the routine check-up of visitor's health regularly, again came up to explain as a guide.

'Friends, This is the concluding part of our trip and its name is 'Glimpse of Earth...' He said and went on. 'It's quite emotional for us to see our motherland from such a long distance. Incidentally, the Indian part of our globe is illuminated before our eyes today. And if we do concentrate, we can mark out the famous landmarks of our country easily. So enjoy for two hours and behold the most beautiful part of the universe, from where we have come and shall be returning to tomorrow.'

So, ladies were allowed first to view through the telescope, who made a sort of queue for the purpose. Kamath had seated himself on a big boulder to relax with Harsh on his side as always. I also joined them there. Kamath gave me a helping hand and pulled up the boulder easily. A fine milky earth-light filtering through the velvet-black moon sky, made the surrounding quite mysterious and unique. An interesting fellow as he was, Kamath asked me wistfully.

'How I wish I could smoke a cigarette here! Have you one with you?'

I was surprised for a moment... but then began to laugh. We both kept laughing together for sometime. Harsh stared at the earth unblinkingly. He said to me at length.

'Dad, I can see clearly everything even with naked eyes. Look... that hairline above India is the Wall of China, He pointed up, 'And the eyebrow visible little below is our Himalayan Range.'

'And that dot below the Indian coastline is Sri Lanka. Kamath added and they began a long discussion again. I silently watched the massive globe, remembering my childhood, when during moonlit summer nights, I lay flat on my bed at the roof top and often watched the resplendent Moon till I closed my eyes to sleep.

Suddenly, I had an eerie feeling in that extreme wilderness, that startled me up. I clearly felt a soft touch... as if some supreme being were sitting close to me on that boulder. My hair stood on end, yet there was no fear. I became carried away for sometime. My old time spiritual guru Kokul's words began to resound in mind when he had said.

"In many different ways, the existence of a supreme power of the universe can often be perceived!"

I wanted to sit there for the whole night but had to return back to the camp. But before leaving the place, Harsh took all four of us to some distance on the same plateau, and stamped his foot at a spot on the sand and asked us to do the same. We gave our foot prints carefully side by side as advised. Then, Harsh engraved the names of each below the respective print with pointed gravel on the white, sticky and powdery sand and then announced triumphantly.

'These prints will remain here for ever... like Armstrong's.'

'But he was not wise enough like you to write his name below... Hmm?' I commented to make him feel shy. After all, he was one of the Indians who are so fond of carving out their names on the monuments and elsewhere they happen to go.

So our moon trip came to an end the day after, and I brought back the heaps of memories from there. Eight months have gone since, but that short sojourn on the boulder on the last evening at the planet, stands out in my memory afresh. To see the shimmering blue earth rising up and that Magical Touch still thrills me deeply. I simply feel blessed at such times and tell to myself proudly.

"Everyone desires to touch the Moon. But don't limit yourself as the whole universe is within your reach!"

It is well past midnight now and I am feeling sleepy. But I am happy to finish the details of this journey. I shall start my journey yet again, but into my interesting past this time as soon as possible in the coming days.

My Glorious Past

June, 2005

At the time of Entrance Test for Software-Engineering, my test centre was at A.P.I.I.T. College Panipat, and it was the month of June in 2005. I did well and headed home being a happy man after the test. I had no conveyance to go back because my father had dropped me in the morning and now, I had to walk nearly one Km to reach G.T. road, from where I could get an auto to the city. I had walked hardly a furlong, when a car approached from behind and I instantly waved for a lift. It slowed down and came to a stop near me.

'Yes?' The gentleman at the wheel peered out of window.

'Uncle, are you going to the city side?' I enquired.

'I don't know about the place much... however, we are going to Delhi...' He said.

There were two boys on the back seat. And the front one was occupied by another man. So, I could be easily taken.

'Could you drop me on the way sir?' I requested.

'Come...' He obliged without hesitation. I was given small room behind by the boy who sat near me. He appeared unfriendly at first. He had a strong built and his projected chin made him look like a wrestler. I introduced myself as the car moved on.

'Hi, this is Tapan, a localite....'

'I am Himanshu and he is Pavan, my cousin...' He returned not so warmly and the hand shakes were exchanged. His firm grip at my hand although showed his confidence. The other boy wore the specks and he asked me this time.

'Came to take the test at this college?'

'Yes... and you?' I replied.

'We too...'

'Did well?'

'Excellent! It was not so difficult...'

I don't know why his positive reply made me sink like a ship. I can't tell whether the same thing happens with others or not?

'What about this college young man?' The man who drove the car asked me.

'Don't know much uncle. It is affiliated to Staffordshire University UK. and prefers the practical method of education. Just can't tell more for sure.'

Between the same short and formal conversation, Barsat Road came and I got down the car. This was the first time, I had met Himanshu and Pavan.

Thousands of people come across us in life and we do reciprocate the names together, and then we simply forget. But I didn't know at the time, that this couple was going to be the most intimate of my friends, in the college life to begin. And I must describe it from the very first day hereon...

1

My first day at college
August 2005

I parked my bike at the stand and looked around. Some placards attracted me. They were fixed on tree trunks and elsewhere along the passage that led to the college building.

"Freshers are welcome to Mini-Auditorium", It read.

I followed the arrow marks. I was late by fifteen minutes and no other student was in sight. It surprised me and I wondered whether I was the only new admission in the college? The pointers led me to the first floor... and a humming noise of the crowd reached out to me as I came near the auditorium. I hesitated for a moment, and then entered.

It was jam packed. Hundreds of eyes looked at me all at once, and it sent my heart racing. A strange fear like the Ochlophobia crept inside me. Crossing the hall on my way to the back to find a chair for myself, gave me such nervousness that I had never experienced in life before.

There were a few empty seats behind and I took one. After having seated comfortably, I looked around with searching eyes. It was an A/C hall... occupied by a mixed lot of about one hundred and fifty boys and girls, all of whom were the new comers. The entire atmosphere was superior to what I had seen in the schools so far... and now I was also the part of it. I felt proud. 'Ah my first day at college!' It was like a dream come true. I took a deep breath and relaxed.

Just then, I spotted the two boys, I had taken the short car ride with two months earlier. Those were the only familiar faces among the strangers. I forgot the name of the spectacled one but remembered the other's who was Himanshu. He was also looking at me, and wished the recognition as our eyes met. I also returned the same with a smile. They sat at the far corner in the back. He pointed to an empty chair near him and gestured to come and I did so without any hesitation.

We did the handshakes as I took my new seat.

'When did you guys come?' I asked.

'Yesterday only... and got accommodated in the hostel' Himanshu said.

'It's nice to see you again...'

They gave the smiling nods.

'What is going on here?' I asked

'It's a lecture on Motivation...' Pavan replied this time.

A gentleman got up from the front row and ascended up to the dais. He took the mike to speak and everyone in the hall became silent to hear. He began his very short speech.

'Hello Students, This Asian Pacific Institute of Information- Technology welcomes all the new-comers to the college. We are gathered here to get some most valuable motivations from the wellknown name in the field. Please give a big hand to Mr. Anil Keswani.'

And amid the clapping, another man came to the stage from the front row. He held a diary in his hand which he opened and took out an equal sized paper from it. He placed his diary aside at the lectern and came to the middle. He was lean and frail. Mr. Keswani raised his hand up in a gesture to stop the applause and then embarked on his peculiar jugglery without speaking a word.

He threw that piece of paper in the air, aiming to send it farther from him. Picked up from the floor and repeated it with more effort. He did the same many times with the professional agility of a sorcerer... and I watched him like others, being quite nonplussed of his motives.

After some fruitless encores, he stopped trying any more and came to address the audience in explanation.

'Friends, I was trying to throw this piece of paper away to some meters, but it's not working and I am confused. Could any of you help me do that?' He did cast an expectant glance over us but no one moved or spoke a word.

He waited and asked again.

'Excuse Me. Could you please tell me whether it is possible or not?'

'It is not possible sir.' Someone said from ahead.

'Do you all agree with that?'

'Yes sir...' There came a few voices.

'But I will make it possible to you...' He smiled. 'Just let me try the other way...'and with this, he began the technical work of giving it many folds in a specific manner, and produced a paper plane soon. He raised it up to show and prepared to throw it in the air. He let it go the next moment with perfection... and the plane began to travel straight. It flew over and fell behind me in the end of the auditorium, while all eyes chasing it curiously.

'It's a miracle!' Keswani exclaimed and initiated the clapping himself this time to be followed by others and said. 'You see... it was a simple piece of paper that refused to go. But when moulded in proper shape, it went farther than expected. Now you guys are also 'raw' just like this, but if moulded in the right way... you can go beyond the stars!'

The loud cheers came at once, and he continued.

'Remember... you are not born with the written fate, and it's you who hold the reins of your own destiny.'

He waited for a while and then pointed to a boy from the third row.

'You... Gentleman! Have you ever fallen in love with someone? Please tell me in yes or no.'

'No sir...' He answered shyly.

'Not even with your parents?'

'Yes sir! I mean that's a different thing sir...'

'You are right, and please take your seat. I also meant that different love only...' He smiled meaningfully. 'Could anyone tell me, as to how do we know that the person we love, do loves us also?'

A buzzing sound, mixed with the giggles arose from the students and continued till Mr. Keswani began again.

'The vital medium here is our eyes. The very feeling simply overflows from our eyes that are the reflectors of a human being. An experienced company HR can see the level of your knowledgebase + confidence in them easily. Our mind is a bank of unending memory cells. Do fill them with the power of knowledge, the way that its light should begin to overflow from your eyes to get you a worthy place in any company in the future.'

He then turned back without wasting any time and switched the projector on which projected three big A's on the screen boldly. He continued to explain...

AAA

'Each 'A' here stands for Aptitude, Attitude and Altitude respectively. And do keep in mind that it is not Aptitude, but Attitude that will decide your Altitude in life. The great saint Valmiki's life is the finest example of this. He was a man of great Aptitude but his Attitude made him a dreaded dacoit known as Valiya Bheel. He applied his skills in looting and killing people initially but when he changed his Attitude... he climbed to such an Altitude as a sage that he succeeded to script the epic Ramayana.'

He waited again between the sounds of applause and continued after a while.

'Students, Our life is like a sailor's compass that has different degrees and directions. It navigates the sailor to safety through the clueless sea. Its pointer always looks northwards, and makes all the sense of a compass. Likewise, the same pointer is hope in our life. Hope gone... life's compass gone! Do always remember two things in your life.'

'One/Our thoughts are our navigators, so always set the high aims for you. '

'Two/Today will never come again. So don't let it go just easily.'

'And now...' He said again. 'I will ask everybody to close your eyes and think about what you want to become after four years of graduation here. Just be positive in your imagination for a few seconds and see how your ambitions begin to materialize.'

The entire hall did the same as advised quite in a state of hypnotism. Mr. Keswani picked his diary up and took his leave with this while expressing his gratitude before getting down the dais, and going out of the auditorium.

He had finished and was soon gone but nobody moved from his/her seat as if his lecture was still on.

I must admit that the motivation class was so powerful to shake my nerves that day. Yet, it was only a shadow of the hair-raising and live motivation that was given to us by the Red Triangle during my last semester at college.

2

Himanshu found me at college canteen after the classes were over and where I had just stopped to have a hot patty before going home.

'Hello Tapan...'

'Hi!' I smiled.

He sat down in front of me in a sluggish manner and reading his face, I asked.

'Looking a bit off colors today?'

'I want some outing badly to refresh the brains.' He said lazily.

'Why? Only four days at college and you have a sour brain already? Just imagine, four years are a long journey to go.'

'Leave it Yaar. The motivation lecture the first day was so damn dangerous. that right from the moment I solemnly decided to do only three things in life, and it was study, study and study only. I got a few books issued the same day and didn't leave my hostel room after college since then. I couldn't sleep properly at nights and eventually returned the ghosts of those books to their graves in the library today. It is only after that I am feeling a bit normal...' and he took a deep breath in.

The way he completed his sorrowful statement without a break, made me neither laugh nor feel sorry for him anyway.

Strangely, it seemed to me that he was not explaining himself, but me instead. However, I offered with a smile.

'Rome was also not built in a day. So relax... and have some chai. Quite like you, I have also gone mad for the last three days, reading various books on Hacking.'

'Hacking? Want to hack the bank account of somebody?' He looked interested.

'I may also do so, if required. But for the ethical purpose only...

'That's exciting to know. But my condition is serious at present. And as overeating spoils the digestion, my head is similarly spinning with the overdose of 'vitamin knowledge'. Tell me what to do?'

'Then I must prescribe you some entertainment urgently. Better go and watch a movie outside at theatre...' I laughed.

Just then, Pavan also joined us there. He was accompanied by two classmate girls. And while we sat around together after the introductions, he enquired:

'Tapan, you belong to Panipat and we are all new to the place. Could you afford to take us around tomorrow evening?'

'Yes!' Himanshu seconded his proposal as once. Both the girls also attuned in their thin voices to make me weak, and for the sake of the girls, I agreed to take them to city the next day.

I always went to college by motorcycle and it was my favourite red coloured 'CD-Dawn'. So the next day, I returned home after college to get my dad's car that I had already booked in the morning, and rushed back. I found the group outside the college gate waiting for me. They had swelled to six in all. Himanshu, Pavan, Jaiswal, Anjali and the other two girls whom I met the day before were Bindu and Vandana. I adjusted both of them on the front seat while the other four took the back one.

'Where are we going to in Panipat Tapan?' Vandana who was sitting next to me asked as I put the car into gear. The railway crossing gate ahead was closed as usual, so turning left down the road to take the unmetalled underpass to cross over, I replied...

'We are going to the old city. There is not much to see at all here. I will take you to the Durgah of Qalandar Sahib. This is nationally renowned and is the only noted place to see around. We will cover most of the distance on foot through the streets. It will take us roughly three hours to return. One can also shop in the market on the way.'

Vandana almost sat in the middle of both the front seats, and her shoulder brushed with that of mine sometimes. She wore Churidaars and her right leg was coupled with the gear in such a manner, that every time I shifted it, my left hand nudged her thigh softly, just like a golfer's club would do to a ball while near the hole. The game of this car-golf gave me a tingling sensation and I could have driven even up to as long as Kanya Kumari in the same position.

However, the car turned left before Skylark petrol pump, and I stopped it for a while near the tomb of Ibrahim Lodhi. The littered vicinity marred the importance of the historical monument, so without getting down, I told the fellow folks briefly about it.

'Who was Lodhi?' Vandana showed her interest in history.

'He was an Afghan warrior who ruled Delhi...'

'The place is badly neglected...' Jaiswal commented.

'I was taking a walk at Devilal Park last evening. It has a bigger than lifesize statue of the ex-state leader in the centre. It seems to me that the late leader had more historical value than this poor Lodhi for the state?' Pavan ridiculed and gave an indication of being a keen politics critic for the first time.

An argument followed between the group and they busied themselves in answers and cross questions on the topic. Passing through a line of private hospitals, I parked the car near the Bikaner sweet shop where all of us got down.

Vandana again glued to me. May be she had discovered some appeal in me... and I was flying. We two walked ahead of others, talking. While passing under the grand Salarjung gateway, I told her about the famous local battles, eg. Lodhi fought the first battle of Panipat in 1526 with Babar, and lost his life along with 20,000 soldiers on 26th April. This was the birth of Mughal Empire in India... I explained.

Going through the Gher-Araiyan locality at gentle pace, we were at the Quila ground in half an hour. Catching the sight of the green municipal park, everyone decided to have some rest. So all took the round platform around a Neem tree.

'You call it Quila. But there is nothing such visible here?' Vandana asked me while casting a wide look around.

'It's gone long, only the remains can be seen now...' I told.

'It is a manmade mound, in the time of battles may be?'

'I don't know, but looks like a natural formation. The kings and Sultans always chose the places at higher altitudes for fortification purposes...'

While talking, we had come to the north corner of the park from where we could see the houses and green fields below. I pointed north-westwards and told her.

'Look! Our college is there... where we can see the chimneys of oil refinery. That building with some green patches is Darpan Cinema and oúr college is right behind it.'

'Good! This is our first meeting only and you are showing me the cinema already?' She looked in my eyes cutely. Her manner was so prankish that I felt embarrassed at first and couldn't understand whether it was an invitation or what? But I dared to welcome her.

'Thanks for the Idea! Shall we fix it for the coming Sunday?' I offered boldly.

'Your calculation about the college is however pretty good...' She changed the subject in style but her cheeks had become more reddish.

'And memory too! I don't forget people and things, I come across...' I boasted.

'Really?'

'You may try anytime...'

'Ask you about something, you have seen many times so far?' She looked at me deeply.

'Sure...' I wore a cautious smile on my face.

'Then tell me, how many stone bastions are there in counting over the Salarjung Gate?'

The question stunned me and I stood like a simpleton. The draughts of breeze coming from the ravine below seemed to blow the remaining senses away from me. I began to bring the gateway's shape before my eyes and tried to count, but I had no clue. But an answer must there be, so I took a chance at random to reply.

'The bastions are twenty in all...'

She chortled and seemed to enjoy

'Out by dips!'she then said in delight

'What did you say?'

'Stupid Boy! I had just scrambled it up, like you seem to be yourself...' And she began to laugh.

'Holy Shit! How could you scramble that so fast?'I wondered

'It is damn easy for me...'

'And why you called me a stupid?'

'Because the exact number is seventeen. They are flanked by two corner pillars that make them nineteen in a row... understand?'

I just nodded like a puppet, but my lips were sealed. Descending down the mound towards east, I was thinking of herself and her notable ability of observation. I couldn't know when we found ourselves in the courtyard of the Durgah.

The boys and girls spent almost one hour there, ambling around, washing their feet at the pond and rubbing their articles of gold at the black coloured and unique touchstone pillars in the portico.

The excursion ended with a happy note, but none of us realized that a couple of college seniors had noticed us and the coming day was not going to be as happy as that one.

3

'There is a senior with Red Tag at the gate, who is making enquiries about us...' Himanshu informed me during lunch at the mess.

'Enquiring what?' I asked.

'About those, who went to the city yesterday.'

'Don't you worry. Take this Samosa and rejoice...' I handed him over a small piece of snack and crammed the remaining large chunk into my mouth to munch.

'Two senior girls were also asking Anjali the same outside...'

'Come on Yaar, and fuck the twats!' I answered carelessly.

'I am serious Tapan. We are going to be ragged.'

'Going around the places is not an offence, you know?'

'This is not the question of right or wrong. We will have to pay the price of being the juniors.'

Just then Pavan entered with some more news.

I have been ordered to assemble all the city visitors outside the syndicate room in the evening.' He said and loomed over us with his mouth agape.

'Sit down, you stupid camel. Do you never have any good news to tell?' Himanshu growled with anger and pulled him down on to the chair.

'Just cool down... have some cold drink?' I pushed my bottle towards him at the table to ease him up.

'You are carefree because you may be spared being a localite. But why should you worry for us?' He taunted.

'Have some courage He-man, let me think.' I said.

'He-man? And me?'

'Why, your physique and name both give the same indication.'

'This is not the time to make jokes, and get ready for a grind.'

'Don't worry that much... I assured him. I won't let the bastards cross any limits.'

And just before 4:00 pm, while all the accused had lined up at the directed place, Himanshu alias He-Man was quarrelling with Anjali.

'This is your fault only. Why did you tell the names of others to them?' He scolded her.

'I'm not a scapegoat... you understand?' She objected.

'You have little wits in such a big pumpkin that you always carry over you...'

'And you? You have no wits at all in the much bigger pumpkin of yours!' She retorted.

'Shut up!'

'You shut up!'

'Stop it!' I shouted at He-man. 'Let us take the things wisely, and nobody shall blame others. We are going to face the ragging and there must not always be a reason behind that.'

There was a tense break for some moments before Jaiswal reflected.

'I think they are going to call us in one-by-one...'

'And what they may do to us?' Bindu asked timidly.

'Anything from physical abuse to the mental-rape...' Anjali replied.

'One may be asked to do striptease or anything like that...' Pavan feared.

'Do any of you also know how to do mujra (Musical Performance)?' I enquired seriously and He-Man admitted to that.

'Yes, I do... and will prefer it over those horrible push-ups.'

'I am not going to follow their mean orders...' Bindu came to a firm decision.

'What will happen now?' Vandana said to me in a low voice. Her cheeks had lost a bit of pink.

'Don't panic! We are going to obey them, until they are not vulgar in language or indecent in behaviour. After all they are seniors, and this is the part of college life...' I advised.

'And don't forget to wish a 'good afternoon' to all...' Pavan suggested in the end.

A boy appeared at the door of syndicate room from inside. He brandished his finger towards us and dictated.

'Hey you nuts, Come in all together... quick!'

His word 'together' gave me a great relief. So we were not going to be isolated at least. We went in to see five boys and four girls, sitting on chairs in an arc. A fear again crawled inside us as we positioned ourselves cautiously right in front and wished each of them.

We stood just silently after that, and I did cast a cursory look at each. They were glaring at us, as if they were the

Pakistani Intelligence, and we were the Indian spies. Another fresher girl already stood there, a little away with the pulled face. Maybe she was also a similar victim like us. There was a pin-drop silence for some time, and there came the first order from a Bandit-Queen looking senior.

'Give your introductions to the bench...'

There was a round of introductions, and lastly a desperado looking boy whose name was Rahul, subjected me to a long interrogation.

'So you are that localite... huh?'

'Yes sir.'

'Why you took the new college 'chicks' to city on Friday?'

'There were the boys also...' I protested.

'Really? You were four boys with three girls... how did you manage the things at all? He enquired, with keen interest

'Manage what?'

I mean what you all did there together?' He chuckled clumsily.

'We were on a sightseeing trip only.' I remained composed.

'Are you running a traveling agency also?'

'I was simply requested by all to accompany and guide.'

'Free service? And what can you do for us?'

'Take you to the similar city-trip, if you like?' I offered.

He looked disoriented at the unexpected reply and couldn't speak further. And another boss chipped in this time.

'Mr. Local Hero... are you trying to make a sort of gang in the college?'

I remained silent.

'Don't try to be over smart and just behave like a Junior... got it?' He inculcated.

I nodded in submission, and two of them in the middle now began to whisper something in the ears of each other. A wise looking girl began to address us after that.

'You Guys are in professional college now, and need to learn some discipline to start your careers as Freshers. Don't fear, we are not going to subject you to any torture or humiliation here. This is a goodwill interaction only between you and us. And the sole purpose is to mix old with the new, and to make good relations with each other.'

She stopped her speech and a boy now exclaimed dramatically.

'The all you are going to do now is to play a sort of a game in the pairs of a male and a female each. You can select your partners yourselves. This girl Vinny shall be included in your squad to make four separate pairs in all. And you will walk free after this very short game is over.'

We were surprised at the mode of punishment and exchanged the doubtful glances with each other. Are we going to be asked to propose to each other or to perform a dance in couples? To sing a duet or what? I was calculating wildly, and drew closer to Vandana to be her partner in the game.

However, soon we were standing a bit apart in four different pairs and it was in the following formation:

Pavan + Anjali
Jaiswal + Bindu
He-man + Vinny
Vandana + Myself

'Now each girl from every pair shall pick up an envelope from that table, and come back to their respective positions...' there came the next direction and it was followed in the same manner.

Everyone stood absolutely quiet, expecting the next move in suspense. He-Man's pair was summoned first of all. The girl Vinny was directed to open the envelope. She tore it open with care, as others watched curiously. The enclosed content was visible in a moment, and what came out of the wretched envelope was...

A Rakhi!

My eyes widened in shock. The very sight of the thing gave me sheer abhorrence and the heart began to pound in dismay. Me and Vandana both looked at each other and turned the eyes away. Why that uncommon feeling was there... I was utterly confused about? I could not even know when two pairs went outside after finishing the job, and the third of Bindu and Jaiswal was taking the ritual solemnly. She had tied the holy thread at the wrist of the hesitating Jaiswal and the seniors showered the grains of rice over them to bid farewell.

'God Bless You!'

Both also walked away and then they motioned us to come forward. And it was the deadliest call I ever came across in life.

I was shaken from my thoughts, and we both came ahead

like puppets. What should I do next? I was struggling with myself. I was not willing to get a Rakhi from Vandana. But what about her? Is she going to tie it on my wrist like others did so easily? Should I leave the decision on her?

I was thinking fast and then opted to just wait and watch for her move. We now stood in front of each other, and I looked at her deeply. The envelope trembled in her hand, and she didn't tear it open. I got the message within moments and decided to revolt! I took the envelope from her hand and turned to the performers of that funeral-service of the freshers.

'The juniors must take a leaf out of the senior's book. So, please proceed with it first with your batch mates...' I said politely to Rahul who was grimacing at us like others so far, but had become colourless now.

'So, you are going to teach the moral philosophy to us... hum?' He growled and got up from his seat.

'No! Just want you to give me a practical exposure...'

'You certainly need an exposure, but a different one...' said the 'Bandit-Queen' this time and turned her glares at Vandana.

'And you Bitch! Have your parents sent you so far away here to just flirt around with the boys? They were aplenty in your own city there... why?'

Vandana couldn't stand it any more. Her face had flushed with shame. Her legs trembled and before she should fell down, she gave me a parting glance and ran out of the room.

I was now left alone there in front of those adversaries, and something untoward was to follow. Rahul had got up from his seat viciously but to my good luck, the peon entered the room at the same moment to announce.

'Vacate the room at once. The lecturer's meeting is going to take place here sharply...'

Rahul stopped his menacing advances but threatened me.

'You seem to be a hard nut to crack. Would like to see you next time...' and in a quick motion he picked the glass of water from the table and threw the remaining used content on my crotch! It made my trousers quite soaked at the zip, and I was totally taken aback.

'Now you need not explain to any, about what happened with you inside...' His grimace returned, and they all got up to leave. And it was me to remark this time in vengeance.

'Hey Rahul... come out to city some time and I will make you do the real Piss!'

4

The lecturer Mr. Venkat entered the class and switched the computer on. He attached his Pen-Drive to the USB extension near the mouse, and a big 'C' was projected on the screen behind him.

'Hello! Students...' The lecturer introduced. 'Our topic today is 'C'. Do you know what is C all about?'

'Yes sir! This is the third letter of the English alphabets.' Someone replied but the answer was so plain that many students began to laugh in a suppressed manner.

'Excellent! But this is the name of a language too...' Mr. Venkat appreciated and asked again.

'And how do we communicate with others?'

'By expressing ourselves to others...' One of the girls said.

'By talking to each other...' Came another reply.

'Now, how do we talk at all? I mean what do we speak?' He asked.

'Language sir! We talk together by using our own different languages...'

'Exactly! We do communicate in a language that we know, and are sure that the other understands as well. Similarly, 'C' is the kind of language, the computer understands. And to communicate with it, you need to understand it also.'

He continued his lecture Blah... Blah... Blah...

'That's all for today...' He said to finish at last. I could catch a little of whatever he had orated and finally he left the room with his book.

I was packing my bag when I heard some commotion behind. I turned to see a group of seven-eight boys there, exchanging a verbal war with two others in front. I got up to see and recognized Himanshu, who was one of the two and he was shielding the other from the rivals.

I rushed to the spot. Pavan who was accompanied by two others, whom I didn't know, had also come to our side in the mean time.

'What's up here?' I asked He-Man, but Jaiswal who presided the rivals replied in a blunt manner instead.

'This is Mayank, our classmate...' He pointed with eyes, and he was the fellow who made enquiries about us at the mess gate that day wearing a Red Tag of the seniors.

I looked at the lean boy who appeared gentle to me at first.

'So?' I returned to Jaiswal coolly.

'He is the bloody informer! And I am gonna thras(thrash) him...' He was used to misspell the letter "sh".

'And I won't let you do so...' He-Man amused.

'Who are you to stop me?' Jaiswal flared up.

'He is under my protecson(protection), and you can't touch him even with a finger!' He-Man imitated his accent while warning him.

'He will have to answer for his acson(action) at any cost!' Jaiswal still insisted.

'You may ask him in front of all, whatever you want to.'

'Okay, let him stand forth, right here!'

He-Man pushed Mayank forward deliberately and watched Jaiswal who came closer to the boy threateningly.

'You Swine! How dare you...'

'No obscenities...' He-Man warned him half-way with his finger and directed to Mayank, 'Come on, tell them why you did that?'

'I was forced to do so by the seniors...' He said helplessly.

'No! You offered to help them yourself...' Jaiswal shouted.

'He is telling truth, and the matter is over.' He-Man interrupted again.

'How long can you protect him Boss?' Jaiswal smiled vilely.

'I do apologize to all who have suffered...' Mayank pleaded this time to make the former's stance softer. Vandana and Bindu had also come around by now and stood behind silently.

'Let's forget now. We should infact be thankful to Mayank for helping develop some new relations between us. Here are my congrats to all the newlymade brothers and sisters...' I said to finish.

There were all the smiles, but Bindu still had the unpleasant taste, so I hailed her.

'You are still looking upset Bindu?'

'Yes, I am very upset you know. How can the seniors force anyone into some relations? I am not in college here to make brothers around. I have two at home already...' She shook her head carelessly and there were the sniggers in the whole party.

'And what about this poor Jaiswal?' He-Man asked her jovially and looked at him, who turned and strode out of class in anger.

'He is from my home state Jharkhand, so you can suppose we are in the same relation already. But it was all absurd that day...' She jerked her neck.

'I am sorry again Bindu, but I have something that might help you smile...' Mayank said to her this time. He then opened his bag, took a book out of it and extended to her.

She took it and glanced at the cover. She then opened it and turned a few pages, and then began to laugh without effort. The book was the 'cartoons collections' by a famous cartoonist.

'Don't mind...' She said softly to Mayank. I know it was not your fault at all. She then returned the book and went away. Others also moved, and it was here that Pavan introduced the accompanying two boys to me.

'He is my roommate 'Rohit' from Delhi... and he is Sumit, a local village chap as you are.'

And there were the zealous handshakes between us.

5

'What are you doing this evening?' He-Man came to me as I started my bike after the college. Rohit and Pavan also appeared from behind. 'Our second semester had begun now.'

'Nothing much...' I replied.

'Come to hostel and I have got all three parts of Matrix... He-Man said.

'Movie is okay, but there is a big Noooo to the English. A plain Hindi one will do...'

'You are grown up baby. Do start viewing the foreign stuff. It is real bomb you know?' Rohit suggested to me and I gave up.

'I wanted some soft entertainment... but as you feel like' I shrugged.

'I have Nayak in my lappy.' Pavan suggested. 'It's a great movie. I have seen it 22 times already, and could do once again...'

'He is deeply infected by a political bug and that's why always talks about the rotten subject...' Rohit taunted curtly.

'I think the fresh releases like 'Page 3' and Iqbal are exactly your types...' Pavan calculated.

'If you want to see something like pages only, then simply pick up a particular North Indian Hindi newspaper. It's second last page is really sexy stuff yaar, with the pageant of almost bare-breasted beauties!' Rohit said again.

'And a sex bug has infected this man...' Pavan returned desperately.

'Why only me? You can ask our 'Dinosaur'... I mean Dean Sir about that! While in office, you will find him lost in the same Page-Eleven only.'

We began to laugh and Rohit added further.

'But will fold the paper up neatly to see someone approaching...'

'And what about your own experience?' I remarked.

'Me? I am a virgin so far, and shall remain so, till my marriage.' Rohit caught his Adam's apple.

'I know you don't wear the underwear, and I wonder if there is any connection between the both?' Pavan enquired.

'How on earth you came to know about that?' I exclaimed in utter astonishment.

'Don't misunderstand me, and stop guessing wildly...' He tried to explain. 'I discovered it only recently when taking a shortcut at hostel stairs, he jumped down and tore his pants at the crotch to reveal his entire kit outside!'

We all began to laugh madly.

'Shut up...' Rohit grinned and He-Man turned to me to ask.

'So, are you coming Tapan?'

'Yes, but how could an outsider stay in there for so long?'

'Come on... rules are made to be broken. The watchman can't remember nearly two-hundred inmates by face all the time.'

'I shall be there...' I said and moved.

And three hours later...

'Man vs. Machine... this is the movie all about?' I stretched my legs on the chair and yawned after the first part was finished.

'Sounds like a new theme...' He-Man said.

'We are no match for these fucking westerners...' I said.

'But what this Matrix exactly stands for?' Rohit frowned.

'It is a womb or a mould in which a type is cast...' He-Man explained but Rohit was not impressed.

'It's a big bore. I hate the animated or superfluous characters' He said.

'I also abhor the sound of clanking metal...' Pavan also added.

'This is technology and requires something 'here' to understand' He-Man tapped his own head to show.

'The idea of this technology came to the Indians first, when they wrote the same Matrix six decades ago...' Pavan replied calmly.

He-Man eyed him gingerly as if he had some loose screw.

'Really?'

'Yes!'

'Are you alright?' I feel the movie has spun his brains... He-Man looked at the remaining two for confirmation, and Rohit cried out in discovery.

'NOooooooo! He is talking about politics again.'

Pavan didn't react but continued further.

'The movie is a simple story about how men created the brainy machines for their own benefit, and which eventually overcame its own creators... isn't it?'

'Hum...' He-Man grunted.

The same was conceived by Dr. Bhim Rao Ambedkar, and his learned associates, when they scripted the constitution of India. He said.

You want to say that we are the suffering folks similarly, and the politicians are those created machines... I pondered.

'Tell me one thing...' Pavan asked again, without answering me. 'What do we do with the batteries after use?'

'Simply throw them away...' I said.

'So give power to those machines, and you are discarded like that.' He explained.

There was a contemplative silence that was broken by Rohit.

'He is right! Politics here is a game of power, and has developed as a cottage industry...' He reflected at the point.

'Constitution + Matrix = Democracy in India.' He-Man also equated thoughtfully and Rohit looked at him in surprise.

'Hullo! You are not as dullheaded as we had assumed about you earlier...' He remarked.

'And what about you?' He-Man returned.

'He has no brains to prove anything about himself ever since he decided to do the Engineering...' I told and just then the situation changed suddenly there. It was some noise outside. We looked at the door, and in came Rahul from there with three other seniors following behind.

He came straight to me and stationed himself comfortably

right in front. My heart beats began to rise. Staring at me with scorn, he said.

'You local canker! Do you think this hostel is your city theatre here?' With this, he gave such a kick to my chair that it toppled down with me. But, I jumped up in a moment and began to dust my cloth. He-Man got up from his seat and tried to stand in between us.

'Let me talk to him...' Rahul pushed him aside and turned to me again.

'How dare you come in here?' He took a step towards me but He-Man blocked his way by keeping his right hand on his chest and said.

'And this is not the syndicate room of the college and we are the freshers no more! This is my room right here... and the rules are different also.'

'And we have to abide by your rules... is it?' He cocked his eyes.

'If it is the matter of my room... the answer is Yes!'

'Who the hell are you bastard? Let me fix you first...' Rahul gave a blow on his chest and took his collar menacingly. He-Man also gripped his arm to free himself and they got locked together. Both had the same stocky built and appeared at par with each other.

A scuffle took place, and it was ominous. Pavan, Rohit and I had also come to assist now. The loud voices reaching outside attracted a lot of others inside the room.

They both fell on to the bed with a thud, while still trying to overcome each other. We three were also raring to go any time. Any such move could have turned into a fierce fight, but a few of the seniors rushed forward wisely to separate them from each other.

The hostel supervisor accompanied by one of the gatemen also came rushing in, and we were taken to his office down-stairs while other hostlers stood outside waiting for some news.

'Why you entered the hostel?' The supervisor asked me as he took his seat.

I had no answer to that and He-Man said.

'I invited him to my room, sir, to watch a movie together.'

'Did you take the permission for that?'

'No sir.' He-Man replied.

'Then you better keep quiet...' He rebuked and turned to me.

'So you also initiated a fight with the hostelers?' He asked.

'That's not true. We were sitting in the room when Rahul attacked me.'

'For no obvious reason at all?'

'There was the big reason, of course, and it was ragging...' I had decided to open the cards.

'Ragging?' He repeated slowly and fell silent. The very word made him tentative to decide what to do next? He then looked at each of us with penetrating eyes. A few of questions and answers followed between all, and I was fined for just five hundred rupees in the end. Rahul and He-Man were warned to be expelled from the hostel in case of any further disturbance.

6

My college life moved on at a fast pace. Months came to pass one after the other. I still had some confrontations with disgusting Rahul, but it was not anything serious. The worst was to come in the coming months, however.

Vandana and I were still going on good terms. I called her VD now, because she belonged to Vidisha, Madhya Pradesh. And she christened me Tipu in return.

Our class had divided into two groups after the Jaiswal-Mayank conflict. One was 'ours', including six boys mainly, who had become most intimate so far and mostly remained together. Jaiswal had formed a rival group, which included more than a dozen students from Jharkhand, Chattisgarh and Bihar. And we had nicknamed them JCB's.

Bindu and Mayank had become close friends after that, but Jaiswal hated it. He nursed a grudge both against him and our group as well. The trifling arguments, however, took place sometimes between each other, but the situation worsened after that session on communication techniques during our fourth semester in the college. And the main reason was Jaiswal's same inability to pronounce 'Shhh'. An expert lecture was going on in the class that day and the subject was Phonetics.

The lecturer had worked up two words on the screen.

Pillar / Pilla

'How will you pronounce the first one?' She asked and pointed to Sumit, who got up to answer.

'It is Pillar!'

'And the second?'

And before he could answer, a JCB boy Abhinav got up from behind and answered while pointing his finger towards Sumit.

'This is Pilla!' (Cub of a Dog)

And there were the mocking laughters from his entire group. The south Indian lecturer did cast a surprising look around, but could understand nothing as she didn't know Hindi. She continued after a while, however.

'This second one is the correct pronunciation of the first word...' She told and there were a few more similar examples after that. She displayed a set of another words on the screen after some time.

Sure / Shuar

And it was, unfortunately, Jaiswal to be interrogated about the first word in the previous manner this time.

'It is syor...' He said in his own peculiar style.

'Shuar...' She spelled it rightly but he still insisted at the same word.

'Syor...'

'Shuar! Say I am shuar...' She encouraged.

'I am Suar' (Piglet).

And it was our turn now to laugh even more loudly. Not only we but the whole class was rolling in fun to make him highly baffled. The south Indian lecturer was again at a loss to know what was going on. Just then He-Man offered a solution.

'I have a suggestion for him Ma'am...'

'Yes...' She looked at him confusedly.

'He should practice this line again and again...'

'She sells sea shells on sea shore!'

More laughters came at the funny idea.

'And what about "Shom-Shom-Shom-Shamo-Shasha?' Rohit exclaimed to make every one absolutely mad, but making the lecturer utterly bewildered by that time, who exited from the class without a word in frustration!

It was only after this particular class, that the enmity of both the group intensified and stray cases of scuffles also began to take place between the members of the same.

7

Outside the college, we had made our den at a tea-kiosk. It was at the Huda crossing near rally ground. We often spent the wild time there. The name of its owner was Yaksha Prasad, and it sounded a bit peculiar. But he was a jolly man and soon we had become good friends together. And on other times we chatted endlessly while standing in front of the coffee shop in Yamuna-enclave for a change.

It was Rohit's offer to have some coffee that day so we two came there with He-Man and Pavan after the college. While going in to the shop, Rohit's eyes stayed at a cute girl who was coming out of the shop. He turned back to have a last look at her and heaved a cool sigh.

'She is a beauty, buddies.'

'Nothing so special... every girl is a beauty for you.' Pavan said with unconcern and seated himself. But I took the subject as pastime and said to him.

'Come on...' Every one has the right to express oneself.

'Because the beauty lies in the eyes of the beholder.' He-Man corroborated.

'And it has different meanings for different people...' I said again.

'As unlike Rohit, a poet finds it in the nature...' He-Man exemplified.

'And a drunkard in a wine shop...' Pavan said this time.

The coffee was ordered and we proceeded with a few more examples turn by turn. Suddenly, Pavan sniffed at something in the air, and pressed his nose with fingers before asking.

'Now,... what is this Rohit?'

'Me?' He prentended ignorance and tried two-three quick sniffs.

'I don't know... but it's definitely not the fragrance of coffee.' He suggested.

'Let's come outside in the open, and I will tell you about an interesting instance...' Pavan said and got up. We also followed him out where we settled ourselves across the road in front of the shop. It was fresh and cool there, and Pavan started his short tale at once...

'A thief sneaked into a house, and hid himself under the bedstead, waiting for the opportunity. When the house owner and his wife came to sleep there, the wife suddenly began to smell something frantically in the air and said to her husband with surprise.

Darling, I do recognize the smell of your fart very well. My small baby's stuff smells milk only. As far as I am concerned, I have not done this. Then, what the hell this alien fart is doing here? 'And thus the exotic smell led to the discovery of the thief!'

'So? What your silly story has to do with me?' Rohit asked.

'Darling I live in the same room with you and recognize you well, quite like that lady'

'Rohit grinned and brazened out with a suggestion.'

'I have only a small piece of poetry to answer you. Shall I?

Pavan nodded the Yes and he began.

A belch, a sneeze and a fart
Makes a man so smart!

'That's okay! But do start wearing underwear for God's sake! It works as a filter too...' He-Man said and the rest three of us began to shake our guts badly.

'Is that Mayank coming?' Just then I said with surprise, still trying to control myself, and others saw that he was striding towards us from the gate side. He stopped near us soon and tried to ease up. But his tension could be easily noticed. Yet Rohit gave him a welcome torture.

'What happened? Has Bindu raped you again?' He asked.

And all four of us began to laugh again like real nuts at the question. And Mayank looked at us like a crank.

'I have decided to leave the hostel...' He said dejectedly after some time.

'Leaving? And going where?' Pavan questioned and before he could answer He-Man asked.

'Why leaving at once baby?'

'The seniors have made my life miserable there. They are ordering like masters every time. I do feel like a service-boy than being a collegiate.'

'Why didn't you tell us about it before?' He-Man asked.

'It was not all that serious... but they are crossing all the limits now!' He widened his eyes.

'What limits?' Pavan asked.

'Rahul has begun to demand the cell no. of Bindu...'

'Hmm... now you came to the real point!' I said.

'Then simply pass her number to him dude. Why making the mountain of a mole-hill?' Rohit gave his wanton advice.

'Stop your fun all the time Rohit... this is a serious matter.' Pavan scolded him at that and tried to assure Mayank, 'Don't you worry and stop following the bastards like a slave from today. He-Man, Rohit and I are there already to help you any time.'

'But it's decided now... and this is final. I have negotiated a room at the first floor of a building Kansal Bhavan in front of Yamuna Enclave there...' He turned and pointed southwards to add, 'I am going to shift tomorrow morning...'

'So what can we do now... if the decision has been taken?' He-Man asked.

'I want you all to help me packing and stay with me there at that time please...

And the next afternoon, that was a Sunday, we had just loaded almost all his packed belongings onto the hired autorickshaw, when Rahul came to encounter us like a ruffian.

'What's up boys...? What's going on here?' He danced his finger at the auto.

'Mayank is leaving the hostel...' Pavan replied in brief and busied himself to do the necessary adjustments of the luggage.

'People are coming here at will, and going out at will. This is a Hostel or a public house?' He asked in a mocking tone.

Two-three more seniors came there and he got the moral support to start the trouble.

'You are all leaving together?' He asked again.

'One going or all going, you have nothing to do with it.' He-Man retorted this time.

'We definitely have to, and what the shit we are doing here?'

Nobody responded and there was no need either. He then aimed at Mayank.

'Where are you shifting to baby... at the house of this local hero?'

Without replying, Maynak prepared to ride the auto, but Rahul got irritated by this negligence. He came ahead to grip his shirt from behind and pulled him back.

'You bloody wanker! Do you hear what I say?' He roared.

I was really out of control and couldn't contain myself any longer. I clutched at his hand and shook it off from the grip.

The action made him offensive and he suddenly hit me at my jaw. I was stunned by the impact and staggered at my feet. But it was He-Man's turn now. He came ahead quickly and hit him back at the nose. The blood began to drip.

The situation was becoming alarming. Other seniors tried to overpower He-Man, but Pavan and Rohit resisted and a violent fracas took place. More boys began to come out of their rooms and the commotion increased. Soon, we were all exchanging blind blows with the seniors.

Watchman and hostel warden came running, and with the help of other hostelers, they pulled us separate from each other. Mayank had also tried his hands bravely that day. The atmosphere was tense... so we were all shooed from the hostel premises away without delay.

Fortunately, it was our last conflict with Rahul. But he proved to be a cog of the wheel that ultimately took us away somewhere into the mystified world, and we were lost?

Hardly ten minutes later, the auto came to a stop in front of Kansal Bhavan. I had followed it on my bike along with Rohit and Pavan. He-Man and Mayank got down the auto... and I glanced at the twostoried building casually. It had a provision store at the ground floor that had no sign-board on it. It was a mediumsized structure... not very old. It was daubed in dull pale colour inartistically. Its name was carved out in front along with the date in cement plaster that was patchy at places.

I don't know what interested me about it, but I couldn't take my eyes off the facade. There was something peculiar with that building... and I stopped dead at the seat of my bike. I had never come there before, yet I began to recall uselessly. A strange confusion bogged me down.

'Tipusss...' Rohit shouted, 'do some work my son! You are not a guest here...'

I was distracted and found that he was calling from the gallery of the first floor above, and I was alone at the spot. The remaining two-three bundles lay on the ground around. I pulled the stand of the bike open with my foot and made it lean against the same. I picked the bundles up and went upstairs, where all others sat with Mayank in his new room... and relaxed on his luggage.

I also took my seat on a bundle I had carried along. Everyone just sat silent for some time, inspecting the injuries. Someone had bruised his fingers and someone lost the buttons of his shirt. I had got a sore jaw and groped it often.

'You started the entire clash there. What was the need to hit Rahul?' I broke the silence at last and said angrily to He-Man.

'It was a real He-Man's show today...' Pavan said with a lusterless smile.

'He had hit you and I would have broken his nose.' He-Man looked at me and replied my complaint.

'That's what you have done already...' I said, but only to excite the manhood of Rohit.

'I would have broken his teeth also... but thanks to the others who saved him at the right time.' He added impudently.

'The disciplinary action will follow now... and perhaps against all three of you.' I said and He-Man showed his usual carelessness at my warning.

'What the hell the management will do at last? Expel us from the hostel?'

'A rented accommodation is far more convenient...' Pavan suggested and Mayank's face bloomed with an idea.

'You can put up here also.' Two rooms are already vacant at this section of the floor, and we are four in all. We can share it comfortably...

Nobody gave an instant reply and just thought over his offer.

And the expected notice appeared on the board the next afternoon. It read...

'Himanshu, Pavan and Rohit (Roll Numbers...) have been expelled from the hostel. They are instructed to leave within two weeks.'

(Dean)

8

The things began to take strange shapes after that. I didn't see Mayank in the class for two days. I tried his mobile but it was not responding. The next one was an off day, so I went to see him on Wednesday afternoon. Actually, it was not he, but the very place that attracted me and I don't know why.

I stationed my bike near the grocery store that was run by the building owner himself. I just looked up at the house to read once again.

Kansal Bhavan

23 / 03 / 1971

I then took my steps to the stairs.

As I jumped my way up, one man began to come down from the top, and he crossed me half way. I looked at him curiously. He was of mahogany complexion and wore some different type of holy looking dress of orange or light tangerine shade. He offered me a smile as our eyes met, and gently said as he went past me.

'Om Shanti!'

He didn't wait for any return gesture from me and was gone within moments, while I stood there thinking of him.

A sort of peculiar feeling swept through me, that I am unable to explain exactly. It was like... like I had seen him somewhere. But where? I yearned to have more free view of him, so I descended the stairs and peeped outside in search... but he was nowhere to be seen. I turned and began my ascend again, but slowly this time. I was thinking that this building, this man and even these stairs were known to me. Certainly, this was not a case of reincarnation and after a bit of struggle... I came to the vague conclusion that I had come here sometime in my dream.

I found the door of Mayank's room closed, but it opened to inside when I gave it a slight push. He was sitting on a chair... all cuddled up. He raised his head up to look at me, and a shade of recognition flickered on his unshaven face. But he didn't speak a word and sagged in the same posture again. He had a coarse blanket on his knees.

I came near, closely observing him and the room around. His hair were unkempt and he had not taken a bath for days. The room was untidy and some of the packets still lay here and there unopened. That unhealthy development baffled me and I asked with surprise.

'What is wrong Mayank, are you not feeling well?'

'I am dying...' He groaned hoarsely.

'Dying... what nonsense?' I put my hand on his forehead, but there was no fever.

'Unhappy things are happening with me since the day I came here...' He said again.

'What happened to you at all?' I took my seat on the brink of his folding bed nearby.

'There is not a single thing to tell. Misfortunes never come alone Tipu...'

'Will you please tell me what the matter is?' I yelled at him.

'Matter?' He almost began to cry at my stern approach. 'Everything has gone wrong badly during the last couple of days. I am having bad dreams,. couldn't sleep a wink for the last few nights. Bindu has also gone away from me and I am completely undone! My end has come near now...'

'Wait... wait! Let's take the things one by one. Tell me why didn't you sleep at nights?' I forgot to ask him, however, how could have he taken those evil dreams without taking a wink?

'This is an eerie place... like those haunted ones. Strange noises come at nights from nowhere. And above all, there is a tenant next door who looks like a real ghost and I am sure that he is involved in some spectral connections.' He went on to explain in a weak and fretful tone.

'Is your neighbour the dark complexioned one... and looks like a devout?' I asked.

'Yes, yes! Have you met with him?' His dull eyes gave a weird spark.

'Not met... but just saw him in the stairs while coming up right now.'

'I am talking about the same man. He knocked at my door at the dead of night on Sunday... and asked for a matchbox. It was load shedding in the area at that time, and to see him abruptly in that absolute dark was a horrible experience for me. I was so frightened that his apparition haunts me at nights now, and I am sleeping on this chair for the last two days.'

'It is nothing but delusion only. He is a human being like us. What does he do by the way?'

'Don't know much about him. But, some males and females do come to him in early morning to practice meditation and some yoga type things. But I tell you for sure that he is not all that human exactly.'

'And what about Bindu?' I ignored his suggestion and changed the subject.

'Don't talk of her. She has betrayed me. She has poisoned me...' He began to tremble.

'Poisoned?' I jumped up.

'She has fed me with a dangerous 'virus' and it has crept up into my mind cells. It slowly erodes into... like termite does to the wood. Now, I am going to die within three months... ah!'

I was stunned at his nonsensical prattle and couldn't know what to say or do for sometime. I looked at him carefully. He was apparently in a state of hallucination and I was confused.

'How can she do this? And where the hell she got that virus from?' I asked.

'Her brother is a microbiologist at Delhi... she obtained the stuff from him.'

'How do you know that?'

'She told me so herself...'

'And when and how she managed to feed it to you?'

'I got her phone call on the same Sunday evening ...' He went on dreamily and told me about his disastrous experience with her girlfriend. It was an odd but interesting account to hear, and it took place like this...

'Hi Mayank... where are you?' Bindu called him up.

'At my new room and getting bored...'

'Give you a surprise? I am very near to you at the moment.'

'Where?'

'At Yamuna-enclave, and was thinking of you...' She said.

'Then come over here at my room...'

'No, Let's have some chat at the coffee shop here. Are you coming?' came the sweet voice.

And he was there within fifteen minutes.

'When you came back from Delhi?' He asked as he took his seat in front of her.

'Early this evening, and you know I missed you very much this time...' She looked into his eyes amorously and put her hand onto his to make him thrilled.

'I also miss you so much these days and I think this is the right time to meet your dad...' Mayank was carried away.

'Dad! But why?'

'To ask him for your hand...'

'Then go to Delhi and see him if you want to...'

'Really? But when?' He became excited.

'Hmm... I think any Saturday or Sunday morning will suit you properly. Dad goes to the Radha Krishna Temple near our house, between 8 to 9 am everyday and you better meet him inside there...'

'Inside the Temple?' He asked with distaste.

'Yes, because people don't wear the shoes there.'

He couldn't understand for sometime and then suddenly began to laugh clumsily.

'You really have a good sense of humour Bindu...' He looked blank.

'This is not humor mister. What you don't know is that, he is a very short tempered man, but leave it. This marriagewarriage is the most stupid thing one ever does in life. It leads to sheer death of romance.'

'You are talking pretty good philosophy today...'

'Why? This is the universal truth that the men do keep the double standards about women. They generally adore the lovers and abhor the wives! I am not talking about you...' She abruptly softened her stance and pressed his hand again cozily. Adding the killing sweetness in her voice, she said. 'You are different from others Mayank... and that's why I like you so much.'

'You're but trying to look at the things your own way...'

'You know this world is full of shameless people like a westerner who paid his homage to his deceased wife in a unique way. He inscribed an epitaph on her grave in satanic verses. I have read it in a magazine recently and memorized for the purpose of telling you. The lines go like this...' She said and then recited four lines of a limerick.

Here snug in grave
My wife does lie
Now she is at rest
And so am I...

Mayank began to laugh freely at this.

'This is the western culture, but ours is different. We have some fine examples like one Shahjahaan, who created a peerless Taj Mahal in the memory of his beloved Begum Mumtaaz. Why don't you look at the brighter side of the things?' He asked.

'But he had another brighter side, I am looking at...'

'Like?'

'He had many Beghums(Queens) at a time. Are you also fond of many like him?' She asked so innocently.

'Are you in a crazy mood today?' He again let out a wan laugh.

'Oh my God!' She suddenly looked bewildered and snatched her handbag from the table. The next moment she was fumbling inside it wildly.

'What happened?' He asked.

'My key...' She shrieked in panic and then turned the bag upside down on the table. Many articles fell out from it... making a mixed sound. There were lipstick, face powder, comb, hanky, tissue papers, some Rupees and change, etc. and along with all this treasure... there came out a small vial only two inches in size. It was like an injection type and contained some peach-coloured fluid in it. A typical danger sign was pasted on it... two cross bones and a skull in black colour, with Poison written above in red. Its presence was quite unusual in a girl's bag, so he picked it up and enquired.

'What is this?'

'Damn it! This is my brother's official stuff and I carried it with me mistakenly. He told me that this is a dangerous 'virus' and kills anyone within three months if taken orally or being injected intravenous. How an absent minded fool am I...' She nodded and took it from him. She dropped it in her bag in a gesture of self annoyance. It was incidentally or intentionally the last item to go back into her bag.

Just then, the boy served the coffee. It was steaming hot. She picked her mobile up and looked at it with concern. She then handed it over to him, requesting to put it on charging. He got up, went to the charging cabinet in the corner, plugged it in and came back. She was mixing her coffee with spoon.

The aroma of the fine brew could be smelled in the air. He took a sip from his cup and felt the flavour.

'It is too strong...' He complained with a bit of bitterness.

'Sorry... I needed some strong coffee. Shall I add some sugar in yours?' She asked tenderly.

'No, it's okay...' He denied and then both chatted over different topics.

'I returned at my room in about one hour...' Mayank finished the tale of a date with his girlfriend here. It was so good so far, but the awesome part of it was to come now. He stopped speaking for sometime, as if unwilling to tell more.

'What happened after that?' I asked impatiently.

'I had never imagined that she is a real villainess...' He said in a broken voice. He was almost on the verge of crying and began again after a short break.

'I got her call around 9 pm the same day, and it surprised me.'

'Hi honey...' She said, 'How are you?'

'What a surprise... I was not expecting your call now.'

'Don't expect it also ever in future again. I have called to tell you that your days are numbered now. You are going to die within three months...'

'What is this Bindu... are you mentally disturbed today?' I was greatly surprised at her tone.

'Listen... I have poisoned you! Remember that virus in the phial? It creeps up to one's brain soon and starts decaying it slowly. I had mixed it in your coffee...'

'Her words were coming into my ears clearly and I was just shocked by her changed attitude. She was certainly not joking but I could make out nothing at once and my tongue was stuck to my palate...' He rested for a moment before telling about her again.

'I had specially ordered the strong brew to conceal its taste, and sent you away for charging the mobile!' She disclosed her plot further, but I couldn't believe it still.

'You want to kill me... but why? I asked at last and she replied...' Mayank ended abruptly there and I asked this time.

'What she replied?'

'She said...' He began to say but stopped again.

'Come on... Speak up.' I became more curious to know.

'I can't tell you that...' He suddenly resigned to give me sheer disappointment.

'But why?'

'It is no use telling that now. Please leave me alone...' He pleaded.

'Damn it and go to hell!' I shouted in exasperation, 'I am going...' I got up and moved outside. But I turned at the door and came back. I took the hold of his arm and commanded.

'Let's go to the doctor. Get up.'

'No doctor can cure me at this stage. That virus has already gone into my brain. I am just going to die now and let me do so peacefully...' He protested and got his arm released from my grasp rudely.

I was rendered helpless by his non-cooperation. I stood there looking at him for sometime, and then came out of room slowly. I was worried for him. He couldn't be just left alone in that condition. Someone was required to nurse him and stay with him all the time.

I turned my bike towards hostel where I met Himanshu, Pavan and Rohit and explained everything to them in detail.

'What drove Bindu do so?'

'Poisoning Mayank... that's impossible!'

'There must be some secret in it...'

There were many questions like this but I had answer to none. However, Pavan prepared to shift at Mayank's room at once as decided mutually by all. Moreover, ten days had already gone since all three of them had received the notice from the college.

9

I couldn't see any of them for the next two days as I was out of city. But we were in touch by our mobiles, and thus, I came to know that Rohit and Himanshu had also shifted to Kansal Bhavan, after their terms were settled with the owner. They all managed to take care of Mayank as best as they could. He was unwilling to eat and had become weak. The very thought was embedded deep in him that his death was imminent.

I met the three at college late on Friday and the main topic of discussion was Mayank who was absent from college for the five consecutive days and remained indoors.

'He is still silent and not telling anything...' Pavan told me.

'Looks badly desperate over something unknown to us...' Rohit also said with unease.

'Let the bastard die... he has no right to live!' He-Man crooned disdainfully.

'Why are you getting so rude?' I asked.

'It's a case of same fucking timepass with girls... huh!'

'But we can't let him die like this...' I protested but he made me the next target at once.

'You have the special sympathy for him because both of you are sailing in the same boat. Now, you do scratch his back, and he will scratch yours.'

'You also need some medic urgently, and your case is more serious than Mayank's...' I suddenly became aggressive.

'Leave him. You know, he is such an eccentric by birth...' Rohit tried to cool me down.

'We must stop this nonsense and should talk to Bindu clearly about the matter...' Pavan suggested.

The silence was taken as unanimous consent and we cornered her after the last period. But, the interaction with her proved to be very brief and fruitless.

'Bindu... have you really poisoned Mayank?' I asked her pointblank without wasting the time.

'Yes, it is true...' She admitted plainly.

'And what was his sin?'

'He knows well why I did this.'

'But we want to know it from you...'

'I don't want to talk about that fellow any more. Better ask him directly and he will tell you all himself...' She said and walked away without any word. I couldn't even stop her.

But as she disappeared round the corner, Vandana appeared from the other side.

'Why this Bindu is looking so upset?' She asked as she came near.

'She is a bloody sinner. She has plotted to murder Mayank' I said in anger and she made a jarring reaction at that.

'What?'

We made a briefing of the whole case to her and finally prepared her to be a mediator between Bindu and us. She had gone back to hostel, so Vandana also left to have an open discussion with her over the imbroglio. We then made our way to see Mayank.

We found the door of his room bolted from outside, but it was not locked. The stairs of the building opened on the first floor right in the middle of two wings, the left and the right wing respectively. Mayank and friends occupied the right one and the entire left one belonged to that devoted type person who was quite unknown to us so far. We still stood there wondering about our missing pal, when the same fellow came out of his room on the left side and hailed to us.

'Come over here friends... Mayank is with me.'

We rushed there and he let us inside. Mayank sat still there on a green coloured blanket and sipped chai comfortably. Our host directed us to take our seats also. We removed our shoes and sat down on the other blanket with the legs crossed. There was no sign of any sofa or chair in the room.

'My name is Kokul and I am from Sri Lanka...' The man introduced himself while approaching a small table in the corner. Some crockery was neatly placed upon it. He continued in a steady voice, 'I do work with a south Indian company at refinery. I was late for my office today, but as I came out to go, I saw your friend standing in the balcony in front of his room. He was not looking well and nearly fainted due to weakness before my eyes. But luckily, I held him before he should collapse and took him to my room. Mayank is simply undernourished, but has taken some food since, and is feeling better now...'

He gave his long explanation casually and finished. He had the tea ready in a big thermos flask, which he poured out to us in the small bone-china cups after that. We accepted it thankfully and then he seated himself on a cushioned altar in front of us. It seemed to me a 'Gurukul' like situation where he was the guru and we were the pupils. I felt such a deep contentment within me at the time that I had never experienced before. My friends were introducing themselves to him and I was just looking at him, being quite enchanted.

He was a man in his late thirties and had a stately appearance. He wore a safari type suit of holy colour, and on his right wrist, he had a band of off-white beads. And as for the place... it was a prayer or meditation hall, made by connecting two rooms together. It was painted in very light mixture of lemon and apple green shade. The walls were partly pictorial with some sacred emblems on it. The hall was well ventilated with sufficient sunlight, and the atmosphere in there was very soothing to the senses.

'Mayank has told me about the tragedy that has taken place with him...' Kokul said with a friendly smile.

'He has told you all?' Pavan asked eagerly.

'What he has told me is simply that a girl has deceived him...'

'Yes, she has poisoned him...' I said.

'How do you know that?' He asked.

'It is Mayank who told me about that!'

'And he is still stable even after consuming the poison?'

We had no answer to give and began to look at each other like fools.

'But the girl has also admitted to it herself...' Pavan tried to convince him this time.

He gave a meaningful smile in return and said like a thinker.

'Remember... we have no control over the consequences of our actions. What we actually are at the moment is the result of what we have done in the past...'

None of us said a word in reply and he crossed his legs on his one foot high altar. He then concluded in a grave tone.

'Some wounds are too deep to be healed by a medicine. But yoga is the remedy to all the worldly woes. He must practice the meditation regularly and he will be alright very soon...'

There was a silence for a few moments before he said again.

'Excuse me friends... this now is the time of my evening time prayers. I shall be glad if all of you come to attend the yoga session with Mayank in the morning and you will find it helpful. So see you tomorrow...' With this, he raised his hand in a gesture of good bye and we also had to take his leave silently. We got up and bowed our heads. He closed his eyes before we came out from there.

Mayank rushed to his room way ahead of us. As if being freed from the jail and Rohit commented at him.

'This holy man Kokul is quite right about Mayank. The boy is just reaping the crop he has sown himself'

'This rascal has certainly played some vile or dirty game with Bindu...' He-Man calculated.

'And now she is playing a psychological game with him in return...' Pavan said.

'On the whole, this particular man has a photogenic personality...' I also expressed my views and just then my mobile began to sound. It was VD on the other side who told.

'Bindu has gone back to Delhi, before I could meet her...'

'Then let us simply wait for her to return. Anything else?'

'I just called to inform you... bye!'

'Hmm... but listen-listen.'

'Hum?'

'We are going to attend a yoga class here at Mayank's building tomorrow morning...'

'Yoga class? Grown the fitness mania?' She laughed.

'I am just trying, and you are also coming...'

'Me? But how can I...'

'Get ready early and I shall be at your hostel gate by 7:30am. And please don't ask questions now. You will know all tomorrow... bye.' I disconnected.

'This meditation and yoga things are all rubbish. Who the hell has so much time to spare?' He-Man said carelessly as he entered his room with others.

'He is an exorcist for sure. And such fellows are usually very dangerous!' Mayank said rudely. He was not happy with his ex-host for his comments about him.

'Don't you worry. He can do you no further harm as you are already going to die within three months' He-Man made his fun, but I took it seriously.

'Shut up Himanshu... this is the limit of madness'

'That's okay, but I didn't like the yoga fellow that much myself. And these types of soft exercises are suitable to the girls only.' He said.

'And to me also, it is so insulting to just sit around and give a twist to my body limbs in a sexual way...' Rohit said.

'Who is inviting you there? But I am certainly not going to miss this n-w experience...' I affirmed.

'I am als‿ coming with you...' Pavan supported me, 'I am deeply impressed with this spiritual guru. Every word of his was so balanced and true!'

10

'Everyone of us has two supreme powers within ourselves...' Kokul said while seated on his altar, 'First of them is soul, the purest element in the whole universe. This is eternal and this is none other than Aum. And second one is mind, the fastest thing in the universe. It has the wavering nature and is never at rest. It is faster than light and only meditation is capable of putting breaks to it'

'So close your eyes and immerse yourself in the same. Closing the eyes helps to concentrate, and as the concentration increases, the tendency of the mind to waver decreases. It is then more sharply focused. Yoga means the steadiness of mind only. It is like the flame of a candle. If it does not flicker at all... the yoga is achieved.'

With these words, he closed his eyes and so did all others. Everything became so quiet in the hall for sometime, and the meditation continued.

Pavan, VD and I were taking that class on Saturday morning. None of the three others had accompanied us. At the end of the session, when the outsiders were gone, Kokul gestured for us to come and sit down near his altar. VD bowed to him before doing so and I gave her introduction.

'This is Vandana, my classmate and friend.'

'Did you like the session today? It is different from the college classes...' He asked her to allay any hesitation.

'This was a wonderful experience for me, Sir. Could we come again?' She asked curiously.

'You guys can come everyday. The practice will help concentrate in your studies too.'

'But this morning time is not suitable to us please...' Pavan requested and he began to think.

'I shall manage to spare some time during evenings. Where are your other friends today?' Kokul assured at last and asked.

'They are still sleeping...' I replied.

'This is the best thing to do...' He began to laugh.

'Meditation is Detention to some like those...' VD said and he looked amused at her skill.

'All of us are guided by our own conscience. By the way, that's an interesting comparison of words, you have just made.' He exclaimed

'She has some special abilities, Guruji. She can scramble or unscramble any word and can solve the riddles so easily....' I said in her praise.

'Riddles?' He started up at the word.

'Yes...'

'What a coincidence!' He exclaimed and fell silent abruptly. It was an awkward reaction from him so I asked in return.

'What coincidence?'

He didn't reply. He was unwilling to talk after that and was lost in deep thoughts. May be he is a man of quickly changing moods, I surmised and could make out nothing of his behaviour. We waited for some moments but he didn't open his eyes. He was muttering some prayers. We looked at each other as we were getting late for college. We then bade him adieu silently and came out from there.

Back at home, I waited for the next evening to come impatiently. I don't know why he charmed me more and more and my urge to meet him increased every moment. But, an unfortunate thing happened at Kokul's place the next day that rendered us shocked for sometime.

Next evening, Pavan, Vandana and I had taken Mayank with us also. Although he was not willing to come but Pavan insisted and we got pretty late in the procedure. It was the beginning of September and the sun had already gone half down the horizon, when we entered Kokul's hall. There was no sign of him anywhere. We stood there waiting for some time and in the meanwhile, the probing Mayank began his searching adventure around.

There were two adjoining rooms at the right side of the hall and they were for Kokul's personal use. One of them was bolted from outside, and the other that was locked yesterday, had no lock on it at the moment. It indicated that he may be inside. Mayank was exactly near it by that time. Here, Pavan was about to call out 'Guruji' when Mayank motioned him to keep quiet.

He then gave a gentle push to the same door, and we could see a slit emerging as the door leaf opened a bit. Surprisingly, there was dark inside, and a narrow beam of flickering pale light, like that of a lantern fell on his face. He was straining his eyes to see something, and we couldn't stop him to trespass. We just watched him senselessly.

He stared at something inside with intent, and the expression of his countenance began to change rapidly. It soon became contorted in sheer horror. His body shuddered and he closed the door within moments. But, he was careful enough to do it silently. He then dashed to us without noise. We could see the drops of sweat on his forehead as he came near. He stopped suddenly for a while in front of us.

'Have you seen some ghost inside there?' Pavan asked.

'This man is a bloody ghoul, and will kill all of us!' Mayank said with broken breath, 'Now come on fast and run from here if you want to save your life...' With this, he jumped and ran out of the hall. He had created such a sudden alarm that we also began to follow him in panic. But as we came out in balcony, I came to a stop and raised my hand for Pavan and VD to stop also. Mayank had disappeared into his room by now. Both looked at me and I said in annoyance.

'Aren't we behaving like absolute idiots?'

None of them responded to that. I read the confusion in their eyes and said again.

'This Mayank is a coward of first water. He fears even his own shadow these days... '

'Yes, he may be just crying wolf, We must go back and see what is actually going on in there?' Pavan suggested rightly. VD also looked convinced and we turned back in accord.

The hall was deserted like before. We hesitated there and listened. No sound was coming from anywhere. We approached the same door stealthily and there we stood motionless near it for some moments. We then braced ourselves for the next step. Our hearts were racing. My hands trembled in excitement as I placed it on the door to give a slight push. Both of my friends crammed into me to see inside. VD clutched at my shirt with her fingers from behind and stood on her tip-toes to have a view from over my shoulder. Now, the very next moment could bring anything in front of our eyes.

I finally opened the door hardly nine inches apart. The room inside was all dark but a dim candle light originated from a table at the far corner. And near it sat Kokul on a chair solemnly. He held a top-like round thing in his hand that was suspended from a string and he moved it in a circle over what looked like a computer and keyboard. It was a bit hazy inside, and some fragrant smoke permeated in the air outside the partly opened door.

There hung a small canvas screen on the wall in front of him, and some shades appeared and disappeared on it intermittently. It was fixed at such an oblique angle from our position that we could see nothing clearly. However, Kokul glued his eyes to it and murmured something earnestly... like a sorcerer chants the mantras. The atmosphere inside was quite mysterious.

Suddenly something went wrong with our manouvre and it worked as the spoil sport. And it was VD, who was responsible for that. In order to have a clearer view, she tried to gain some extra height from over my shoulder, and pulled me a step backward in the effort. That step of mine landed down on her left toe and she let out a muffled shriek in pain.

'Oooeee...'

It alerted Kokul of our presence there. He turned his face with a jerk and glared at us with his natural red eyes, which bore the ghastly sparkle in that yellow candle light. I became so frightened that I closed the door with a bang. We exchanged the wild glances with each other and then we fled from there.

We came straight to the room and sat down in a bewildered state. Rohit and He-Man were still absent and

Mayank stood in front of the photo frame of Lord Bajrang Bali placed in a niche of the room wall. He was reciting the lines of Hanuman Chalisa in audible voice.

Bhoot pisaach nikat nahin aave
Mahavir jab naam sunave...

We listened silently until he finished, and as he did, I said to Pavan ruefully.

'We should not have run from there like this...'

'So?'

'He has recognized me, and I am feeling ashamed on our thievish action.'

'Are you crazy? Should we have stayed there to take the wrath of his curses on us?' Vandana said.

'Just try to understand. He is not an exorcist or like that' I protested.

'And what was he doing there at all?' She asked.

'He was practising the black magic. I saw that with these eyes...' Mayank poked his superstitious nose in and pointed to his extra opened eyes with both hands.

'You must be thankful to Hanuman Ji for you are still alright!' Pavan replied coolly.

'You have gone mad, and your bad times have come near...' Mayank said to him in a desperate tone.

'Do you want to say anything else?' Pavan asked.

'I just want to warn you that we should leave this place at once' This place is cursed you know...

'You better keep your dirty mouth shut now. Enough is enough' He yelled.

'That's okay. But I can't stay in this haunted house any more. I am going to arrange another room for me'

'When?'

'Right now!'

'My pleasure!' Pavan swayed his arm towards outside and Mayank stamped away to the same direction angrily.

'Let him go to hell...' Pavan shrugged after he was gone and VD resumed the topic after a while to ask me.

'So what you think the man was doing in there at that time?'

'I think he was not practising any black magic, but it was some form of science instead.' Pavan replied in place of me.

'That sounds better...' I was encouraged

'And how?' VD asked again.

'We just saw there that some images were coming on a screen in front of him... isn't it?' He said.

'Yes!' She admitted.

'But you didn't notice another important thing...'

'What?' I asked.

'That those visuals were coming on it without any apparent projection system?'

'This fact startled me. I had not thought about it at all.'

'That's true!' VD exclaimed in astonishment.

'But how is that possible? Was that an LCD?' I asked.

'That's the screw here...' He got up and began to pace up and down the room in deep thoughts. There was a silence of one minute before he opened his mouth to say something, but I also began at the same time.

'I wonder why I am having some unusual experiences these days...' I said.

'You too? I can't believe this' Pavan gasped and pleaded, 'But let me have my say first...'

I gave a silent nod and he continued.

'It may sound absurd and I wanted to disclose it earlier on also that I am viewing some unclear visuals in my dreams for some time. And the things we are confronting these days seem to be quite connected to them'

'What a coincidence!' I got up in excitement. 'That's my own story... a ditto! More than often, I do also have the same perception.'

'Tipu, you are repeating the words of Kokul exactly...' Pavan came near and frowned at me.

'Good Lord! Something is destined to happen to us. But what is that?' I took a deep sigh.

'Coming events do cast their shadows before.' Someone replied and we were stupefied to see Kokul standing at the door. He was a changed man now. He was smiling and his red eyes had retained that usual softness of friendship. It took us sometime to recover and then Pavan answered with a quick wit.

'And yet the future is so unpredictable.'

'Like my unexpected appearance here at this time? I was just going down stairs, when the sound of your voices attracted me. This door was wide open, so couldn't help overhearing you...' He explained.

'Guruji, we are sorry for overseeing you that way. It was not intentional you know...' I tried to explain with a sense of guilt.

'I do trust the intentions of you guys, and that's why I am here again. Let's forget it. I am in a hurry at the moment but

I know that you have a lot of curiosities, and I must disclose all to you. So let's meet the next fortnight as I am going to 'Mcleodganj' to see my own spiritual guru in the meantime...' He said and turned to go. And before any of us could say anything, he had gone away.

11

17th September 2007

Mayank had gone missing. He was not attending the college and didn't even return to his room earlier. He was behaving more and more oddly those days. He had become morose and excessively superstitious. He spent most of his time in prayers. He had also stopped talking to the mates, and had virtually become a lone wolf. He had not got a suitable separate room yet and was still trying desperately for that. And living in the same room with him was becoming difficult for others, as he used to get angry even on the trifles. On the whole, he was both physically and mentally in pieces and I was worried for him.

Bindu had not returned from Delhi till Tuesday. She came the next day and VD managed to talk to her.

'Do you have some dispute with Mayank?' She asked and Bindu became irritated at once.

'Don't spoil my mood Vandana...'

'I know you are hurt and I can understand that.' She said softly, trying to drag her into conversation.

Bindu remained silent.

Please tell me what the matter is?' VD asked.

'I trusted him as a friend but he betrayed me...' She opened her mouth at last.

'What has he done?'

She didn't reply again and kept looking at nowhere blankly.

'You certainly have a lot to say...' VD again started after some moments.

'He's a real bastard!And I don't want to say anything else.'

'Did you really feed him with some virus?'

'Yes I did, and he deserved the treatment.' She lashed out at him. She then sank her face in her knees and cried. VD tried to console her and succeeded in the effort soon.

'You can confide in me Bindu', She said, 'It may be of some help to you...' And she placed her hand on hers.

Bindu felt relieved and it took her sometime before she began to open up slowly. She had nothing to say much, however, and finished soon. But, what she told about Mayank was an act of sheer wickedness and it infuriated VD, too. She was herself very upset in the end. They concluded the meeting by working out a possible solution to the crisis. And Bindu handed over that poison marked tiny vial to her before departing.

College was to end when I gave the information to the friends in detail and then we began our conference in the library. I began the proceedings in the low voice with that vial between my fingers.

'Friends We will know about some wonderful qualities of dear Mr. Mayank today. But for this we will have to go to his Scrapbook in his Orkut profile. And last of all, we also have to do the task of deleting the certain contents.'

'But it is only he who can do it, and he is still absent...' He-Man replied.

'He must be somewhere in or around Yamuna-Enclave and we are going to find him out...' I said.

'You didn't tell us whether she has really given him some lethal dose or not?' Pavan enquired.

'She has done nothing of the sort. It was a hoax only.' I revealed.

'But why?' Rohit asked.

'To teach him a befitting lesson. She knew that Mayank had the foolish superstitions and was prone to become delusive very easily.'

'I told you already that she is just playing a game with him...' He-Man reminded carelessly.

'This poor Mayank is quite helpless as we all know that he is so fond of girls...' Rohit said.

'Actually, a region at the centre of his brain called, Ventral-Tegmental area lights up and starts producing a feelgood chemical Dopamine as soon as he comes in contact with the opposite sex...' VD said.

'And he just gets carried away so easily...' I explained further.

'And it should simply be a girl. No matter she is beautiful or dreadful!' Rohit added in his particular style, and it made all of us laugh loudly.

Librarian gave us a warning glance and we got up from there to come out.

But what tragedy had there taken place with Bindu? She had opened Mayank's Orkut profile randomly, while at home in Delhi last time, and as she did so, it began to give her shock after shocks! It was filled up with a 'blue' album and the featuring girl had the face of none other than Bindu on her shoulders

She also went in details of his scrapbook after that obscene discovery and that led her to the profile of another boy and she found that a lot of vulgar hot scraps were exchanged between them regarding her. She had never expected it from Mayank and she was broken. And then out of fury, she decided to retaliate in a quite different way.

It may be just raunchy or indecent to give the note of all the details and dialogues she had discovered from there, so I am citing only one of them, e.g.

'Who is this girl Bindu?' The other boy enquires.

And here comes the ugliest reply of Mayank...

'She is a good timepass... and very hot at intimate times'

However, we found out Mayank at the temple in Yamuna-Enclave after about one hour search that evening. He wore a long customary Tilak on his forehead. We brought him to his room and gained his confidence. Slowly, we succeeded to finish our required work from his Orkut profile.

The next day, as planned, Bindu confessed to him in front of us that she had deliberately lied to him for the purpose of giving some real shock waves! Mayank was much relieved from her truth. But she didn't forgive him. And quite regardless of her feelings, he began to recoup after that.

He shifted to his new room a couple of days later. Slowly, we had little touch with him. Here, we got involved in some very-interesting adventures with Kokul and his supernatural world. But I owe it to Mayank only. I shall always remember him for he got us in touch of our spiritual guru who gave us the divine light.

May be this was the only good deed of a badman, and that was Mayank.

12

19th September 2007

The disliking for each other between He-Man and Anjali had continued by that time, and it increased before the preparation of another project, Information System. He had refused to include her in his group assignment. And they often pooh-poohed each other openly after that, till the day of the presentation came when their topsy-turvy relations finally took a funny turn.

He-Man had achieved the notoriety of a Rakhi-Boy in the college so far. He had the treasure of not less than four Rakhis from the different girls with him. But other boys including me were unlike him and had the same 'Kuch-Kuch-Hota-Hai' type mental disposition towards girls. I still wonder why on earth, boys do relish this suicidal tendency so commonly? However, it sometimes becomes the root of a big problem as happened in my case.

So, the working groups for the said project had been mutually formed by the students. I represented one along with Rohit and Sumit. He-Man formed another with Pavan only, and Vandana was the part of yet another group separately. The thing we IT-students boasted of at the time was that, we completed a two month assignment in the last three days only. And always succeeded in getting the grading in A's and B's as well.

And it was no wonder anyway. Our simple mathematics worked out in the following proportion.

60 Days x 1 Student = 1 Assignment

3 Days x 20 Students = 1 Assignment

And that's how we are called the engineers.

Against the college rules, we had made it a practice to reciprocate the needed information with other groups as per our suitability. But this is the infamous 'Plagiarism' that was strictly unacceptable by the management.

However, our group started the work accordingly and we arranged to finish it by 3pm on the last day of submission. No files were accepted after 5'o' clock, so I rushed through my remaining job madly. I copied all our documentation in my Pen-Drive, and was just to get up, when Vandana came to me in the computer lab.

'Hi, Tipu!'

'Bye, VD...' I said slowly while still busy.

'What is this?' She looked perplexed.

'Sorry, I'm in a hurry. I still have to go through the printouts, arranging them in the file, and submit. So, really have no time to talk. Have you finished your work?'

I left my chair with this and got up to go. But I couldn't move as she was absolutely motionless. I looked at her face and it was downcast.

'What's the matter? You know this is the last day of submission, and only two hours are remaining...' I searched.

'Yes I know... but our work is not finished yet.'

'Any problem?'

'I want the 'Analysis' part of your assign...' She hesitated.

'What? But it was not your share to do that part in the group...'

'Yes, it was not my work, but you know if any part of the assignment remains incomplete, it affects the overall marking of the whole group.'

'Oh! That's true...' I began to think and then ventured to explain to her sincerely.

'Look VD... the assignments of mine and He-Man's group are almost same with slight changes only. And if another one happens to resemble, then it is going to be a problem for all. Now tell me what to do?'

'But who will do the 'Post-Mortem' on the files? Nobody has this much time...'

'I do agree with you. But suppose some obsessive type idler happens to examine them... then?'

My reasoning silenced her and she couldn't speak for some time, while I watched her helplessly.

'Never mind...' She gave a wane smile in the end and turned to move. But her feet were heavy and she almost trudged away. It perturbed me and I called her back in submission.

'Stop VD...'

She turned and came back slowly. She read me within seconds, as the girls always have the special ability to do, and said in a firm voice.

'I can understand Tipu, I'll manage it.'

'It is always a problem for me whenever you are in a problem. You can take that 'Analysis' component of mine with you. But be careful to put some necessary changes in it.'

And without her response, I sat down again and copied the component on the Desktop.

The Presentation Day

I reached the college ten minutes before 10am and entered canteen to see a few of the students taking their routine breakfast. I came to Rohit's table who fed himself with a bread sandwich in hurry.

'Hi Tipu... Sandwich?' He offered.

'Thanks! Four stuff Paranthas are already crammed inside here...' I caressed my stomach.

'Ah! It's a long time since I ate the Paranthas in the breakfast...' He sighed. No one knows about the pain of the diners at mess!

'Eat faster and I want to give you a patty from my side as encouragement. It is the presentation day today, and you know that you are our group leader.'

'Presentation is no problem, but this patty is very emetic to me. Oooo...' He showed with disgust, how to vomit?

'What's the schedule buddies?' Pavan who led He-Man's group came and enquired while taking his seat in front.

'Don't know... but here comes Sumit also.' I said.

He was rushing by with a cup of coffee. Some snacks filled his mouth and he answered without being asked.

'The list will be on the notice board by noon along with the time table...' He gulped the content down his throat and rushed away.

'But there is one problem here.' Pavan said. 'Mr. Dahiya has been appointed the project supervisor.'

'What? Everyone knows that he is the mental dud! And the documentation of our two particular groups is a ditto copy...' Rohit said.

'Nothing to worry much. There are hundred forty students and thirty five assignments in all. There is absolutely no chance of detection...' I said carelessly.

'It is possible only when it happens to fall in sequence, by sheer bad luck!' Pavan said.

But that particular day was not an auspicious one for us. At noon, the notice board made my heart stop. Rohit also stood near me. I saw that Vandana's group was listed just before our, and both came to be second last and the last in day's schedule. My eyes were still glued to these two numbers, when Rohit commented in a shaking voice.

'Bull Shit! We are in deep waters my son.'

He had actually made quite a new discovery at the board there but I was ignorant of that so far.

'Yes! Our turn is right after Vandana's and both have come in sequence...' I said with great concern, but he suddenly gave me a whack on the neck and I looked at him like a dimwit.

'When will you stop dreaming about the girls every time?' He raged in anger.

'What happened?'

'Happened what? Vandana is the deity, you are the priest and I am here to sound the bell like a fool devotee, Right?'

'But what is wrong with you Rohit?' I barked at him.

'It is Pavan's presentation next to us, and the very first tomorrow... look here.' He tapped at the spot with his finger and added, 'It's deadly sequence here and you are lost in Vandana's dreams.'

I stared at that point and began to faint. I then stumbled to a bench at the short distance and fell on it feebly. Rohit also scurried behind. He looked very worried and caring now.

'Are you alright? Shall I fetch you some water?' He touched my forehead softly with his hand.

'Yes... Noooo!' I answered both his questions at a time, making him even more confused.

'What is this? You want to say yes or no?'

'I am alright, and I don't need water...' I explained.

'Don't you worry! We will make some way out of it...' He tried to console but I groaned again.

'The problem is not ahead, but the real problem is behind'

He could understand nothing. He then lowered his eyes behind at my rump to give an examining look for a moment and then wondered.

'Do you have piles... and at this age?' I can't believe this

'No, no, no... it's VD' I protested.

'Venereal Disease? Are you mad? I never imagined that you are fond of those dirty habits too!'

'Shut up Rohit... our real problem is Vandana' I cleared the matter up.

'But what the hell this Vandana is doing here in our matter?'

'I gave her the Analysis component of our project earlier...'

'What?

'And it was submitted by her without any change' I dropped the second bomb to kill him.

And after some moments, it was he who reclined on the same bench and gasped deeply like a patient, while I attended on him carefully. I felt his forehead in worry and asked.

'Are you alright? Need some water?'

'How can you do this?' He moaned painfully.

'Well... I will go to the water cooler and fetch it in a glass!'

'Go to hell!' He suddenly burst out and almost jumped on me. The sign of violence made me retreat a couple of steps back, and I watched him in fright from the distance.

'Why did you do that?' He was cluttering his teeth and I just stood thinking.

'All three presentations are in a perfect sequence, and we are finished now!' He shook his head to and fro in frustration,

'We have only one chance to take...' I ventured at last and waited. He didn't reply and I continued.

'We must skip the presentation today on some pretex.'

However that was the worst day of my life so far. The supervisor Mr. Dahiya denied accepting any such excuse to avoid our turn and we had to take the presentation at last. When the slides of my Analysis part came to the screen, I began to give the summary of the same. And when it was over, he encircled it with a red pen on the file as feared by me already. He then proffered with a smile.

'It's a case of Plagiarism Mr. Tapan! The previous one resembles it exactly.'

There was nothing for me to answer. I remained silent and came out.

Vandana's group was called yet again and was duly interrogated. One of the members plainly admitted having copied it from mine, as there was no other way to save our skin. Their file was also marked in similar manner after that. So, we finished the day in a tense note.

There was no time to go home that evening so we got assembled at Kansal Bhavan immediately. All five of us sat here and there in a subdued posture and not talking much to each other. Everyone was angry with me and a couple of them wanted to shoot me at once!

'All the assignments are now going to be labeled as plagiarized with the third and last presentation tomorrow...' Sumit said slowly after some time.

'Can't the presentation be avoided in the morning somehow?' I struggled in vain.

'Stop talking nonsense! We don't need your ideas any more...' Rohit was still boiling.

'Dahiya is strict to the schedule, and we are going to draw a big zero for non-appearance...' Pavan said.

'We are trapped.' Sumit said again. 'Now, get ready for the retake next year.'

'No retake will be done. We are going to swap our assign tomorrow morning...' He-Man announced dramatically and a hush fell on all for some moments.

'Swap it! But how?' Rohit asked with extreme surprise.

'We are going to change the whole documentation tonight, and the original file will be replaced by the new one in the Dahiya's cabin tomorrow morning...' He said calmly.

There was pindrop silence for some time. Moments later many questions followed from all sides and he answered each with confidence.

'It is not as easy as you think...' I said.

'But we have no other option left to save all.' He replied.

'The file may be locked in his almirah...' Rohit calculated.

'Our Lalaji, the owner of this building's numerous Godrej type keys will make it...' He assured.

'And what if we are caught red-handed?' Pavan feared.

'Suspension from the college for one week, or the fine of Rs. Five Thousand maximum.'

'He is right...' Sumit supported him, and a hot argument took place between all. Finally, the plan was being agreed unanimously after many ifs and buts.

So, the required tools for the operation were arranged within no time. A hurried dinner was taken outside together. And then,... five laptops and five wouldbe engineers began the hardwork of conspiracy and treachery at 9pm. Necessary data was downloaded from the internet. Parts of work were divided between each other, and a new assignment was eventually ready by 3am in the morning. Having done this, all of us sprawled here and there, being both physically and mentally broken.

The day began with the fast action. He-Man collected dozens of those godrej type keys from Lalaji's store below, and also some red ball pens as planned. Dahiya used the same ink for markings. We were finally at college by 9:30am. No one was visible there except two sweepers who did the cleaning work around. They didn't pay any attention to us, however.

Without wasting the time, Pavan and Sumit sneaked into the building, while the rest three stayed outside to keep watch. Pavan carried the required outfit in his bag, and he was to do the main operation. Sumit was in regular touch with He-Man by his cell, and he gave the running commentary from inside.

'We are in the cabin now...'

'There are dozens files on the table...'

'Fuck! Our file is not in the lot...'

'Almirah is locked...'

'Pavan is trying the keys but none is working...'

'Try again and turn hard...' He-Man insisted impatiently.

'We have tried again, but one key is stuck inside.'

'Pull it out! It shouldn't remain in there...' He shouted and listened to the struggling sounds from the other side desperately.

'Hurry-up! Some faculties are coming in...' He looked worriedly towards the college entrance, and just then he heard the sound of a hollow bang on the cell and with that came Sumit's voice.

'It is done! We are coming out...'

And five minutes later, we all sat around in the playground to decide the next move.

'Our only hope is also dashed!' The comments began to rise from each one.

'All the hardwork of the night is wasted away...'

'I am feeling very sleepy...' Sumit began to yawn, but He-Man stopped him half-way.

'Shut this dirty mouth up' He threatened.

'It is all Tipu's fault you know. Why you guys are sharpening your tongues on me?' Sumit protested and He-Man clutched his neck in one hand at once.

'I will wring you like a towel, you rascal!'

'Stop it! This is the time to use brains and not the hands...' Pavan meddled with.

'But nothing is possible to do now...' Rohit said in disappointment.

'We still have one chance left, and it is to swap the file before presentation in the class...' I suggested.

'But how?' Someone asked.

Right then, Vandana also came around and we included her in the plan. The strategy was worked up fast and she was provided a new SIM, purchased by a group member recently.

At 10:30, He-Man and Pavan followed Dahiya sir into the classroom as planned. Sumit had stayed outside deliberately. Dahiya carried a few files with him including the questioned one and took his seat to proceed.

Sumit, Vandana and I were in regular touch with each other through tele-conference. Sumit was stationed outside the class. Rohit and I hovered around the reception below and VD stayed away in the ground. She called the reception as soon as Sumit told her about Dahiya's entry into the class.

'Hello!' The receptionist squeaked.

'Hello... please get me to Mr. Dahiya.'

'Who is speaking?'

'I am his daughter...'

'Just wait a minute...' She connected Dahiya's cabin

intercom and waited, but there was no response and it was not possible either.

'He is not in his cabin...' Any message?

'Please make him talk to me right now...' It's urgent.

'Well...' She hesitated but then realized that mobile was not allowed even to the lecturers in the institution.

'Okay! Please hold on...' She obliged and sent the peon for him quickly and put the receiver aside.

There outside the classroom, Sumit saw Dahiya sir going out with peon and informed Vandana immediately, who disconnected the phone. Her role was finished. Below stairs, I watched Dahiya come at the reception, and pick the receiver up. My heart beats increased as I saw him turn back after trying unsuccessfully to get a response from other side.

'He is going back to the class. I whispered to Sumit in panic.'

Sumit passed the same message orally to both inside the class and kept guarding the door. He-Man still fumbled through the pages of the file to find out the special markings if any. Luckily, there was only one such on the first page of the file. It was written "GN-09" in a circle with a red pen.

Pavan turned his bag upside down in hurry, and all the pens and keys were scattered on to the floor. He hastily picked up the pens and removed their caps. A rough paper was used to match the colour of ink and the mode of handwriting. He was still experimenting, when Sumit blurted out in frenzy from outside the door.

'Dahiya is round the corner... hurry up!'

Pavan took a pen and marked the new file in the similar style quickly. He-Man had collected the pens from the floor, when he heard Sumit's cautionary voice from outside.

'Good Morning Sir!'

'Ready for presentation?' Dahiya asked.

'Yes Sir'

And in a split, second He-Man snatched the original file from the table and flung it outside the open window that was just nearby and tried to be normal. Pavan having done his job was collecting the remaining keys from the floor, when Dahiya Sir came in to utter in extreme surprise.

'So many keys! What do you do with them all?'

'I... I have lost the key to my almirah sir.' Pavan stuttered. 'I have borrowed all these from friends to try that open...' He explained with his voice trembling and face as white as flour.

Dahiya examined him closely and asked.

'Really?'

'Yes Sir...' And without meeting his eyes, Pavan began to chain his bag up.

'You sound like a Burglar to me...' Dahiya said seriously and then suddenly began to laugh, to give much relief to both. He reoccupied his seat with this.

Fortunately for us, one of the faculties came in to meet Dahiya just then and he also took his seat near him, giving He-Man some time to go down and collect his discarded file. He came out and rushed down stairs madly. I saw him on the way and began to follow without knowing anything. I soon found him in the side garden, standing right below the window of our classroom, and looking around in a perplexed manner.

'What is the matter?' I asked.

'I threw the file down that window...' He pointed up while still panting.

'And where is it now?'

'It is nowhere to be seen...' He said.

The file was gone.

Rohit had also followed me there and all three of us stood simply wondering. There was a green bush nearby, and after a while out came from behind it Anjali with the same file in her hand. He-Man rushed to her at once, and they stood facing each other silently for some moments. Then both began the silliest talk together, quite like two stupids.

'I am going to hand it over to the management...' She said.

'Don't do it. I will be rusticated from the college...'

'And why you expelled me from your last project?'

'Because you had called me a pumpkin-headed that day...'

'That was because you had also called me the same before...'

'Give the file to me...'

'I wouldn't...'

'I am also gonna give you something in return...'

'Really?' And she handed it over to him without further protest. He-Man put his hand in his pocket and produced a Rakhi to display before her eyes. And there were all the smiles on the faces of both and on ours as well.

13

22nd September 2007

'Whatever you saw last fortnight in my room, was not a magic or witchcraft. It was the result of my hardwork that I have been doing for years...' He opened his eyes after the yoga and came to the previous subject after a bit of relaxation. He had returned from his trip only yesterday.

Rohit and Himanshu had also come along with us that day, mainly out of curiosity to know about the occult man in detail. We had begun the evening with regular meditation, and both of them had also taken part in it without any protest.

'And what had you been working on?' I asked.

'I had been working on my own concept of a C.V.P., and I have done it now'

We looked at each other quizzically, being unable to understand the alien term.

'This is the Computerized Visual Planchette system...' He explained at our lingering silence.

'Visual Planchette? Do you summon the ghosts on it?' V.D became over excited.

'Not ghosts... but the spirits of the deceased ones.'

'Do they appear on that special screen in their live form?'

'Yes!'

'This is unbelievable!' She said and we all just sat still, feeling a fearful tingling in our pores.

'But what prompted you to embark on such a grisly work?' Pavan asked after a while.

He began to laugh and then composed himself to clarify.

'It may be gruesome for you, but it is devotion for me.'

'Devotion for the dead people?' He-Man shrank his brow.

'Dead people do become the angels lastly. Don't forget that they had lived a life, like we are doing at present. So going into their life account is very interesting at times. But this is not the only reason of this infatuation of mine...'

'So?'

'A divine personality is responsible for that. Kokul raised his eyes up in reverence and then closed them to contemplate. We did let him take his time to speak further, and to our utter amazement, he disclosed in a calm voice.

'It is Lord Gautam Buddha!'

We all looked at him with our mouths open. We could make out nothing of what he was talking about. No doubt... he was a morbid personality, but was he insane also? Sometimes his character appeared doubtful to us, yet there was something very appealing in him.

'You sound so confusing to me Guruji...' I said at last.

'It's a long story that we may discuss at some time of leisure. But the summary here is that, I am an Electrical engineer from Colombo University Sri Lanka. I am Buddhist by faith. I was deeply interested in 'souls and spirits' from the very beginning. I started to do Planchette with my friends as fun in the college, and my passion increased with the success'

'One day, I thought that if I can have a dialogue with the ordinary souls, then why can't I do the same with some great souls like Buddha's? This thought drove me crazy and I began to try it after that. I succeeded in my effort to some extent and received the desired signals from time to time. But, those messages were not trustworthy, as they had always been broken and unclear. I was not discouraged however and tried harder and harder...' He collected his breadth here and took a sip of water. But, before he could continue, VD asked with surprise.

'But Lord Buddha is dead for 2500 years!'

'A soul never dies. It is immortal, and he may still be around in some form...' He said calmly.

'What happened after that?' Rohit asked.

'It was during an ordinary séance, when an idea came to my mind that if I can talk to the souls, then I can see them as well. I had a burning desire to see my icon live on the screen. So from that day on, I applied myself to work that idea up into some method that could enable me to view the spirit I am interacting with. I devoted my full time for the same quest after the graduation. It took me years and by the grace of Almighty, I succeeded to bring it off at last.'

A light of contentment illuminated his face as he concluded the absorbing detail of his wonderful discovery. But, the fog of doubt that had gathered in our minds earlier... had become more dense now and we wanted to know more. One thing was clear by that time that he was a gifted person and had many talents at the same time.

'And did Lord Buddha appear on your system... what you call that device?' He-Man enquired with a frown.

'It's a C.V.P.'

'Did you see him on your C.V.P. ultimately?' He asked again and Kokul deflated his lungs in a bit of dismay.

'Not yet. But he is so gracious that he won't deprive me of my hope much longer...'

'Which kind of spirits do you come across during your meetings with them?' Rohit asked this time.

'They also possess different qualities of nature, like the human beings. Some are benevolent, others are malevolent too. Some are funny, some are abusive and some of them do have the secretive nature. They don't expose themselves so easily. They may send the cryptic messages before to intrigue you, and can do so for a long time also. I do generally ignore such ones and they discontinue by themselves if not attended properly. But here...' he sealed his lips and began to ponder.

'Here what?' I asked.

'A couple of them are coming to me with nagging regularity for sometime now. I don't know why I am not able to ignore them. I am sure that someway, directly or indirectly, they are coming from none other than Lord Buddha. Please don't make fun of me. I can't be wrong this time. The problem here is that the received signals are in a coded form. This is not like our typical ASCII coding... but is an alphabetical one and I do know absolutely nothing about that. But I hope Miss Vandana can do it for me...'

'Me?' It was her turn to be surprised.

'Why? It was Mr. Tapan who told yesterday that you can solve the riddles easily.'

'That's why you were so startled at the topic that day?' Pavan asked.

'Yes, the information was so relieving to me and I must be thankful to God who has sent her for my help...' He smiled.

'You can relax now. It's like cakewalk for VD...' I affirmed.

He winced unexpectedly at the last two words.

'VD? Who is he?'

'Not he. It is she, and it is this Vandana...' I pointed to her.

'My God!' He opened his mouth wide open and began to stare at her in a bizarre manner and she began to shrink.

'What's wrong Guruji?' I asked.

'I was looking for her for such a long time...' His words were coming deep from his throat, and eyes almost double their normal size.

'But why?' I asked again.

'Wait, wait, V..a..n..d..a..n..a...' He spelled every word of her name separately and still wondered.

'Is she really the same VD?'

'Of course, she is. But, what is so unusual in her nick name?' I asked in desperation.

'Because this name appears in one of those messages very prominently.' He did the explosion very calmly.'

'What?' The voice was stuck in my throat.

'That's quite impossible. I can't believe this...' Vandana whispered in awe.

'But, it is all clear to me now and let me arrange the events properly before all of you to make it understand easily.

There is an anonymous caller who wants to appear on my system. But beforehand, he sends some cryptic signals to be deciphered as a pre-condition for his appearance. It is obvious that the entity has the supernatural powers as it knows all of us even by our names. It began to appear on the system in the shape of a flashing Red coloured Triangle at first, and continued to come and go for many days during the séance...' He said, took a short pause and continued...

'However, I paid no attention to it initially as I told you that this type of peculiar signs and symbols do keep coming on it off and on. I can't forget the evening when it persisted on the screen and refused to go, and it was just a couple of days back.'

'You could not see his image, but did you have some dialogue with him?' Pavan asked.

'Yes, I did. Although it answered only a fewer questions of mine verbally, yet I remember them very well. My fingers were slipping fast on my keyboard to ask. Our conversation was exactly like this.'

'Who are you?'

'It's Red Triangle.'

Sorry?

Red Triangle...

'This sounds like a logo or trademark to me, but what is your real name?'

No answer...

'Are you listening?'

'I want to give you some messages...'

'For whom and why?'

No answer...

'Why don't you come on to the screen here?'

'You will have to identify me for that...'

'How can I do so without seeing you?'

No answer...

'Hello! Are you there?'

'Read the messages...'

'He didn't reply any more questions after that and the keys of my computer began to work up and down by itself speedily. Some confusing words began to emerge on the screen one after the other. There were three different messages in all... like three small poems of very short lines, written neatly. I have copied them down on my notebook accurately...' He began to grope hither and thither and then produced a small notepad from under the cushion of his altar. He then turned a few pages and said while extending it over to me to read.

'I think, there are only two messages in actual, and the third one is meant to serve as a clue for me to get VD's assistance.

I took the notebook and all my friends got squeezed together in a tight circle to gaze at the contents curiously. I ran my eyes over it. There was only one message on one page and it was written in the same format.

(1)

GRRABS

A

DASHING

HAT!

----

(2)

Hi!

HUGH

JARS
SAVE
A
MURDER
----
(3)
HARK!
VD
HAS
THE
DUE
SHAPE!

I turned those small pages off quickly and repeated it again and again. We were so eager to read that one head shunted the other and a sort of human pyramid was formed. The act clouded the words beyond legibility due to darkness and then there began the desperate round of pad snatching in turn. It finally came into the hands of VD and she looked deeply at the last message.

'The sender seems to be quite impressed with your shape or figure, and I think he is absolutely right in his observation...' Rohit commented to her playfully.

His words brought the smiles on every face and she blushed modestly. Kokul also enjoyed the humour and said.

'The word 'shape' here signifies the shape or nature of the two messages and not her. It figures out clearly that only she has the right answers to it.' He explained.

'I shall try my best to solve it Guruji, but it is still so astounding to me as to how come the sender knew my name?'

She wondered.

'As I mentioned earlier, there is nothing unknown to the Supreme Being. We are simply the puppets in the hands of circumstances and destiny...' He smiled but He-Man who was silent so far raised a different suspicion.

'I am looking at the things from the different angle. I think, some restless spirit wants to draw our attention towards a felony. You can see that the second message is clearly hinting at some attempted murder and the first one is the short and clear description of the plotter...'

His assertion made Kokul thoughtful for some moments. It also sounded reasonably true to us as well.

'It may also be possible, but the key is in the hands of VD, now. However, I strongly believe that this is only my Lord Buddha and no one else. It is only Gods who come to test the human beings from time to time...' He preached in his own style in the end.

'Could we also take part in your Séance Guruji?' Rohit ventured to ask the question, almost all of us had in mind already.

'It seems to be destined to us. I have one more thing to tell you here, that it was not merely a chance meeting with you guys. I had some premonition about it many days before.' he revealed in the same posture.

His words thrilled us and I do humbly admit here that I became more devoted to the super power after that evening.

14

24th September 2007

Now, the last four overs remained to be bowled by India and 54 runs were required by Pakistan to lift the first ever 20:20 world cup. They were chasing a meager total of 157 and the scale had tipped in our favor at this juncture. The excitement was at its peak. This was the first time, I viewed a cricket match with so much interest. Our friend circle, together with numerous other collegiate friends glued to the TV screen in the college mess and shouted madly at every ball delivered.

The passage to victory looked smooth until that dreadful over came when the Pakistani batsman Misbah-Ul-Haque pounded the spinner Harbhajan for three towering sixes to change the complexion of the game. A mournful silence became dominant at the scene.

'This damned over of the 'Sardar' has ruined everything!' Someone gasped in sheer exasperation.

'It's no chance for us now. These Pakistani cunts are fierce fighters...' The other said in more desperation after sometime when the other bowler Sreesanth was also ruthlessly hit for another two sixes to dash the remaining hopes. The only good thing was that, he had taken a wicket and only the last pair occupied the crease now. And from there on... everybody began to shout out-out at every ball hysterically.

The different comments came from the congregation every now and then. The batting pair dashed for a run in the mean time and completed successfully.

'They are scuttling like rats for runs, and they are going to make it for sure...' One of the viewers speculated.

'They are the marked runners on the battle-field as well, and this is the only department they do outsmart us in. I can bet that these scum-balls are going to loose this battle also...' came a jealous reply.

And just then the fabulous catch was taken at fine-leg or third-man as the batsman tried to scoop the ball in overexcitement. And the dining room was blown to pieces by the rumbling hue and cry of all the watchers. Chai and snacks began to come in after that and quite thankfully, no mess in-charge came there to check the partying savages.

Niketan.... a 1st year junior, who weighed at least 100 kgs, began to dance in merriment. He carried loaves of fat around his waste, yet he danced with perfect rhythm and others started to follow him soon. His moves, steps and quick reflexes surprised me for sometime and then I was also lured to come to the floor

We had seen the first world cup victory of India in our lives, so we decided to make it memorable. The dancing lad Niketan had given us the idea. So, the next day, our group and some other went to the Dean Sir to seek his permission for organizing a Disco-Jockey (DJ) party in the college to which he granted easily. Few of the boys began to do the collection immediately, and everything was done accordingly. The DJ was ready to go by 3pm at last.

The mishap took place around 5pm, and the jubilation was disrupted unpleasantly. At that time, we were doing the wildest dance we ever did before. Like most of others, we also didn't know even ABC's of this exotic art. And it may be funny to admit that we were doing a sort of somersault instead!

The problem began when amid his frolicking, a junior happened to collide with our classmate and Jaiswal's gang member Abhinav. The impact was so light that it was not noticeable at the first instance. But, as the bad luck would have it, he repeated it mistakenly a couple of times in a careless manner, and had to pay for the blunder.

Abhinav could not bear the outrage and gave two blows on his back one after the other. The sound of this brawl attracted others and we saw the former still baring his teeth at the poor junior who was pleading 'sorry-sorry' again and again. Now, here was just a suitable, case for He-man and he took it in his hands without delay. He came ahead and tapped at the villain's shoulder gently.

'Leave it Abhinav... the boy is apologizing already.' He said but unfortunately, the friendly pat worked as a goad to irritate him even more. He turned and confronted the trespasser with the frowned brows.

'Who are you to interfere between us?'

'Come on man. Everybody is enjoying the moments, and such trifles should be overlooked at such times...'

'I don't need your advice and you better mind your own business...' He returned.

He-Man gave him an unpredictable look for some moments and said coolly.

'Everything that is going wrong is my own business here in the college, you know?'

Both the rival groups had begun to assemble on their respective sides for support by now. The changed moods had clouded the whole atmosphere. Other students had begun to look curiously in some anticipation. The music was going on without action now, and Abhinav became more offensive to give a sharp retort to his opponent.

'But I don't give a fuck to the bosses like you. Get lost...'

A short tempered guy as he was, Himanshu lost his patience at once. He gripped Abhinav's neck instantly by his collar, and gave him a close and deterring growl.

'I do like the quick learners only, and not a 'dildo' like you are...'

A minor scuffle followed as a result. JCB's had outnumbered us by now... headed by Jaiswal. Fortunately, some seniors, along with a couple of lecturers came to intervene, and separated them with each other to avoid a certain group clash. Both the warriors were then warned and reprimanded for their actions.

The paused DJ was reintroduced soon and the awkward situation was over without a further fuss. Although Rohit was still rolling his sleeves up while exchanging the hostile glares with Jaiswal and Co.

The session was over by 6pm and I headed home on my bike. Rohit was sitting behind me and as I overtook a group of boys outside the college gate, an unhealthy taunt came from them.

'Look! There goes a brave Eunuch from Haryana...'

It was unmistakably Abhinav's voice, clearly being aimed at Rohit. I really couldn't understand what happened to him all of a sudden. In a spasmodic action, he jumped down from the running bike and raced away to Abhinav. He seized the latter by his shirt at the shoulder and rained the sharp jabs on his bust in anger, giving him no time to react.

He was, however, dragged away soon by others and brought back to the bike, where he was pulled on to the back seat again. It all happened so fast that I hardly got the time to alight from the vehicle. Someone gave it a forward thrust to go... and I also accelerated without any protest. I drove it on silently there from, but I stopped it on GT Road and turned back to enquire.

'Did you hurt yourself?'

'No...'

'I never saw you losing your temper that way ever before...'

He didn't reply and I laughed lightly in admiration.

'The fist of fury... Huh?'

'These JCB's deserve the more befitting treatment...' He answered gravely this time and I put the bike in the first gear again with my left toe to move ahead in a jolting manner.

But this was only a prologue of a big happening to come in the following months. The matter took another twist the same evening when Rohit's Mobile gave a ring in his bed at Kansal Bhavan.

'Hello...' He took it in a sleepy voice.

'It's Jaiswal here...' The caller told from other side.

'Yes?' He opened his eyes wide open at the mention of name.

'I want to talk to you, and sorry for disturbing at the late hours.'

'That's okay, but I have no ready prescription with me to enable you a sound sleep...' Rohit replied.

'I don't need that...' He laughed away. 'What I want to say is that, we shouldn't quarrel like kids together anymore.

Let's bury the hatchet and make some good relations with each other.'

'Well... that's a good idea! But you are too late my dear. I have already sent my hatchet to the whetstone.'

There was an ominous silence for sometime, as if the conversation had broken midway. But then came the blunt reply from Jaiswal.

'I know that you guys are inciting the juniors against us to fabricate a ragging drama in front of the college management for the purpose of trapping us... Hum?'

'So?' Rohit was surprised at the allegation.

'Remember... if you are going to do anything of the sort, I shall send my hatchet to the whetstone as well, and you will repent that.' Jaiswal retorted.

'That's all you wanted to say?' Rohit asked in rising fury.

'Yes!'

'Now listen carefully. We are not going to do any such act of cowardice first of all, and secondly you must fulfill your desires if any, as early as possible.' Rohit challenged.

'Thanks for the suggestion but...'

'But take my words for granted...' Rohit grumbled in excitement to leave him incomplete. 'Abhinav called me a eunuch today and infact the whole lot of you JCB people is eunuch enough to do anything manly.'

'And what is this JCB all about by the way?'

'This is Jharkhandi, Chattisgarhi and Bihari respectively. And last of all... my damn prick right here!' With this he switched his mobile off and threw it underneath his pillow scornfully.

15

It was Thursday, 27th September, 2007 and I remember this date precisely. That day, VD informed me at college that she had solved the riddles last night. I was not too enthusiastic about it at the time as I had busy schedule in the class. So all five of us got assembled at Kansal Bhavan at five in the evening and as we settled down to relax, she said.

'I have solved them, but there is no encouraging news for Guruji...'

'Why?' I asked.

'It has nothing to do with Lord Buddha!'

'You just convey to him whatever it is, and your duty is over.' Rohit suggested carelessly.

'Correct! Let's go to him now, as I am dying to see his pet ghosts on that screen...' He-Man craned his neck towards others and both Pavan and Rohit also gave a consenting nod.

'What do both the messages want to say by the way?' I enquired.

'Whatever they want to say is something very startling...' She became serious.

Everyone pricked his ears up at this and began to look at her keenly.

'And what is that?' I asked again.

'It is the self introduction of two great National heroes....'

'National heroes? Who are they?'

'*Sardar Bhagat Singh* and *Shivram Rajguru!*'

'What?' Pavan sprang up on his feet.

'Yes!' She nodded coolly.

'What did you say?' Rohit asked in disbelief this time, and repeated the names one by one.

'The same that you have heard...' She answered.

'Now please don't make it so enigmatic VD...' I said wearily.

'I am not joking Tipu...'

'Have you worked them up properly?'

'You know that I don't make mistakes in anagrams...'

She then opened her bag and took her notebook out. She turned a few pages and showed it to us.

(1)	
GRRABS	
A	*"SARDAR BHAGAT SINGH"*
DASHING	
HAT!	

----

(2)	
Hi!	
HUGH	
JARS	*"SHIVRAM RAJGURU"*
SAVE	
A	
MURDER	

'But this is unbelievable! How on earth can these great men come to communicate with us and Guruji?' I wondered.

'Nobody had an answer to that.' Pavan was lost in deep thoughts. Suddenly, he put up a question to all.

'Do you remember that the entity had quoted itself as the Red-Triangle to Guruji?'

'Yes, he told us so...' He-Man replied.

'Then where is the remaining third angle of this triangle?'

'Third angle?' Rohit looked quite confused.

'I mean where is *Sukhdev* missing? He should also be around somewhere...' And he began to walk impatiently. Suddenly, his eyes lit up like torch and he began to shout madly.

'O My God! He is also here. He is also here...'

'But where?' Almost all of us got up in excitement and he turned to Vandana.

'That last message in your name is definitely Sukhdev!' He was becoming crazy. 'That is a dual message in meaning, I am sure...'

Vandana was simply amazed at the revelation and could not speak at once. She then singled out that third one and began to examine carefully. Pavan became more impatient and drew closer to her to command.

'Come on...' unscramble it fast.

All heads stooped over the paper as she started to jot down the different words in a specific way. She hardly took three minutes and finished, and finally looked up at Pavan in resignation.

'Absolutely!' She exclaimed in a subdued voice and extended her notebook to others. She had written it down like the earlier two and in the similar fashion.

(3)
HARK!
VD
HAS *SHAHEED SUKHDEV THAPAR*
THE
DUE
SHAPE!

Pavan's face began to gleam with joy as he read it. He clenched his fist in jubilation and yelled.

'Yesss! I knew that it could be Sukhdev only!'

'It means, all three martyrs are still together here and they want to communicate with us, and this is amazing!' VD gasped.

All felt silent for some time after that and just sat thinking mutely. Each had many questions in mind but there was no answer to any. VD zipped her bag up again and said ruefully.

'I am angry with myself for why couldn't I catch it before? It was so crystal clear though.'

'And I am still very much upset about what is going on at all?' He-Man was getting agitated.

'Get ready man...' Pavan said to him, 'The fabulous trio is coming to meet you and us all'

'But why?' He asked.

'I don't know that...'

'And why only we?' Rohit asked.

'And what they must be wanting from us?' I tried to calculate.

'I have got it!' Rohit made the announcement and all eyes rolled towards him.

'Pavan has always been talking about revolutions, country and leaders, etc. Now, they are coming to take him with them to prepare for yet another revolution...'

'Aha.... this will be the best way to get rid of him.' He-Man also uttered with joy and continued, 'I am already fed up with his political crooning all the time.'

'Shut your mouths up now and move out of here. It is the time to see Guruji...' I dismissed the class and all got up. We were in his meditation hall within two minutes.

He was present at his altar. We took some yoga exercises first and then told him about all the development. He was very anxious to know about the expected results but when VD explained the otherwise, he became thoughtful and didn't speak for sometime. It was an unexpected turn for him.

'Om... Shanti!' He uttered at last and smiled. And thus we also felt relaxed. He went on to say in deep tone.

'Electricity power flows along the wires to do different type of works...' He said, 'It cools down in a refrigerator and warms up in a heat convector. Likewise,... God also can transform into any shape, depending on the nature of the work. My intuition can't be wrong. They are the divine ambassadors, being deputed by the Lordship itself to accomplish some necessary work.'

'Necessary work?' I asked.

'Yes!'

'And use us as the tools for that?' Rohit asked with a shade of fear.

'He began to laugh and said.'

'I just told you that we are the different forms or mediums only. This incident here seems to be a forerunner of some divine action to take place imminently. And to know about that, we must interact with these angels.' With this, he got up and began to move towards his Séance room... waving us to follow and so we did without delay. We were jumping with thrill.

Although we were overjoyed as we approached his spiritual work place behind him, yet an unknown fear lurked inside everybody. VD clutched at my hand in apprehension... as if she were going into a trap, being laid out especially for her.

And then, we entered that secret room for the first time. The room was dimly lit and was decorated religiously. Saffron and white combination existed everywhere. Interior was tasteful with simple furniture and some wood work. Handicraft items were placed here and there selectively, and the floor was covered with jute mattress. He loved greenery and grew a variety of creepers in the tainted goblets in a corner that crept up to a big wooden frame above and got entwined with it. And a couple of ageold lanterns also hung down from the same frame... giving the room an overall mystic look.

He embarked on his work soon, while we watched him silently like school children. He was seated on a chair and we stood around him. There in front of him was his computer on a table and what surprised us most was that there were two keyboards attached to it at the same time. On yet another small table, there was a mini transformer type device nearby. And about ten feet straight away, there hung that screen or canvas on the wall.

He switched some buttons on at the electric panel. He then lighted an incense-stick and a candle. Finally, he switched his computer on and sat still with the eyes closed. That semi-red screen on the wall had also become illuminated now.

It was an ecstatic moment for us and we waited for something to happen any time. Kokul had picked up a top-like instrument that hung from about one foot long string and began to move it in a circle over the black coloured keyboard. Neither he had spoken a word so far, nor did any of us dare to ask him anything.

Five minutes ticked away like this and our heart pounded more and more. Suddenly, to our horror, the keys on the same keyboard began to work automatically, giving a clicking sound. The room had filled up with some special energy and we began to feel quite hypnotized. Kokul opened his eyes at last and looked at the screen in front where some bold letters were emerging out of nowhere. And in the background, a pyramidic shape of a triangle was flashing not so brightly. The letters read...

'Hi... We are here!'

'Who are you?' Kokul asked verbally and the keys began to work again.

'It's Red Triangle!'

'Anyway... me and my friends do welcome you here!'

'Thanks!'

'I am glad to tell you that we have recognized you...'

'Our special thanks to Miss Vandana for that'

'Will you now please define to us, the meaning of this Red Triangle as we are so confused about it?' He asked.

'As you know, we are three in number... that's what makes it a triangle simply.'

'And if the revolution has any colour... it is only red.'

'The martyrdom is written with blood... and the colour is again red! We hope it is clear now.'

The three sentences appeared to be expressed by each of them separately. But, I was a bit frightened to read the last one.

So far, Kokul was talking to them verbally and they were answering in written only. So he requested.

'We want to hear and see you on our screen here please...'

But before we could get this opportunity, something untoward happened and the scene changed at that spot dramatically. There was a sound of a thud beside me, where VD had stood a short while ago. She was absent from there now. I looked down and found that she had collapsed on the ground. It panicked me. I bent down and tried to shake her back to consciousness. Someone gave me a glass of water that I poured in the hollow of my hand and splashed on her face repeatedly. She began to show the signs of recovery. Suddenly; an alien but commanding voice sounded amid that confusion.

'Don't worry... she is alright.'

It surprised everyone and all eyes sprang back to the screen that was blank as before. The waves of some throbbing energy could be felt easily in the atmosphere around. Kokul had the operation still under control.

'Who are you?' He asked and there came the reply in verbal.

'I am Shivram Rajguru.'

The astounding introduction left us stupefied! Rajguru? Was the legend really around us? We began to locate him about blindly. The sound of the voice was so steady and sturdy that it gave us a cool shudder.

Pavan lost his control and even without the permission of Kokul, he implored in the trembling words.

'Please come before us, Sir...'

'Our friend Vandana is little frightened, so take care of her today. We shall be back tomorrow evening at the same time...' He said and finished. There was a deep silence after that. Kokul also wound up. He switched his appliances off and came to VD, who had been seated on a chair by now. She had regained her senses fully.

'What happened to you?' He placed his elderly hand on her head and shook slightly.

'I don't know what went wrong with me when I saw my name on the canvas...' She said feebly.

'Were you scared?'

'Yes, I was!'

'Then you better avoid it from the next time...'

'It's okay! No, no... I mean I am absolutely alright now!' She stuttered desperately to stay in the show.

'Well... It sometimes happens in the beginning.' He smiled.

'I am sorry for spoiling such an important séance...'

'Do not regret and get ready for the morrow. You're fortunate for the great men were addressing you.'

'But was it really the voice of the real Rajguru?' He-Man enquired skeptically.

'I haven't listened to it before, but it certainly was.' Guruji replied.

'How I cherish the moment when he responded me.' Pavan sighed with shining eyes.

'Could we also have a view of him and other two, Guruji?' Rohit asked like a kid this time.

'Why not? But it's possible only when the caller wishes so, as the spirits do have the subtle forms only...'

'Devising such a unique system is not an ordinary feat. Where you got the idea from?' I asked while all of us had taken our seats to relax.

'My necessity made me do so, and an incident helped me by my good luck.' He was ready to explain and did so happily.

'You know I loved Planchette but did it in the orthodox way in the beginning. The method was so timeconsuming and very less communicative, and I always wanted to do something new. Later on, when I came to India and got a job in refinery, I saw there was a particular area inside known as No-mobile zone.

'One day I was strolling about inside the same, just thinking about my spiritual work when my mobile suddenly beeped twice. I had unknowingly carried it with me in the restricted area. I then came out of there and took it out of pocket to see.'

'There were two freshly arrived messages in it. But, to my surprise, they were in ASCII coding, featuring in ones and zeroes only, and there was no sender's name! It could only be a joke being played by the service provider company or someone else but I didn't understand as to how could that be possible?'

'When I decoded them, they turned out to be the names of two persons whom I didn't know. That evening when I was doing the Planchette... the same strangers came to the board uninvited and talked to me. They also admitted having sent those messages earlier in the day. It shook me and also gave me the vague idea for the first time that if I can receive the signals from the spirits directly... then why couldn't I talk to them verbally as well. But it was possible in the specified range of an electromagnetic field only. So, I decided to create the same in a confined space as in this room.'

'Here, my electrical engineering stood me in good stead and I put my heart and soul into the work. And after trying numberless permutations and combinations, I succeeded at last in making a small device that was capable of generating the same electro-magnetic waves around by creating a sort of vacuous atmosphere in a limited area...' He took a restful breath here and began again after a while.

'Having done this, I fitted the sophisticated receivers and adapters in it to catch the wanted signals and connected them to my computer speakers. The result was overwhelming. The voices began to come in during the séance. Thus, I initially devised a C.A.P. (Computerized Audio Planchette) and worked with it for a long time. The present C.V.P. in front of you now is the refined version of the same.'

'In order to catch the possible images of the spirits, I installed those dish type receivers to the original device in addition...' He pointed where in an open closet, numerous small electrical instruments were fitted compactly. There were rings, wires, coils and other tangled things that were beyond our knowledge.

'But how do you manage to bring the pictures on that ordinary canvas?' I asked a feasible question.

'It's is no wonder at all. There is a concealed LCD underneath that...' My curiosity made him laugh, 'It is a special canvas that simply refines the signals of uncertain wavelengths or frequencies, coming on the LCD through my system.'

There was a long query regarding this new experience of ours and he answered with patience.

'And what is the orthodox method of doing the Planchette, Guruji?' VD asked.

'It is usually done with a board on which the alphabets and digits are written all around. There may be some diagrams or drawings and a Yes and a No is also written on it. Four pieces of a cork or wood are used as concentration blocks. It may require many people to operate it at a time. And the methods may differ also.'

'Do you never feel any problem with the ghosts... I mean the spirits?' This was the time for He-Man to ask.

'No! They don't harm physically. But sometimes some of them are the 'poltergeists' also. They like to play pranks like moving the articles... and even knocking them down. They are to be handled most patiently and then they simply go away.'

'And what if they refused to go?' The other asked.

'It never happened with me so far...'

'Could we call any of the dead persons we like on the board?'

'We can try only. But it will come or not, it depends...'

'Do the spirits know about all the worldly things?'

'It depends...'

'Guruji, could they also tell the locations of the hidden

treasures?' Rohit came to his funny point and all of us began to laugh. Kokul didn't reply, however. He got up and began to walk towards the door... smiling, and we also followed him outside.

16

28th September 2007

I can't tell about others, but I tossed in my bed that night. I never waited for a day to come that way in my life before. And never were the hours so longer either. The urge was intense and unbearable... and it is inexplicable in words now. I saw the Great Bhagat Singh & Co. in my dreams during my irregular sleep.

The morning was more tense than night. Was I really going to see them live today? How will they be looking like? How and what shall we talk to them? They were dead for almost eight decades, then how could they appear before anybody like living beings now? Are they still alive in another world? What is their purpose to send a message in the name of VD? The more I thought about it... the more intricate it became.

So, the evening came anyhow and we rushed to Kansal Bhavan after college. The meditation hall didn't charm us that day, and we wanted to go in as soon as possible. Kokul began his work at the time of dusk as usual and we got seated around like the eager spectators. He plugged the wires in and connected the instruments. The canvas lit up at last. He was still busy in preparations, when a voice came from the system.

'How are you Guruji?'

He looked up with a start and replied.

'I am fine...'

We heard it clearly. It was a young male voice, but the style and accent was different from that of yesterday. Kokul had not yet taken up his stringed top to summon any spirit, so it was an out of routine development for him. The canvas was still blank there on the wall. He became baffled and asked.

'Who said that?'

And the answer came from the speakers promptly.

'It is me... Bhagat Singh.'

'Bha...gat Singh? Good Evening Sir...' Kokul became extremely nervous at the very name, although he was a cool customer.

'Jai Hind!' Came the reply.

'Where are you Sir?' Pavan could not help speaking again.

'We are here close to you!'

'Please appear on the screen so that we could see you all...' Kokul pleaded.

We didn't wait longer and there began an incredible show of the configuration process before our eyes. The tiny dots accumulated into some obscure shapes at the canvas, and those shapes then slowly turned into some perceivable forms. Now these forms became clearer and clearer every second. Soon there was the live picture of the three men... or young boys rather, smiling gently and sitting side by side on what appeared to be a round plinth work around a tree.

We stared at them like statues. There could be no mistake in recognizing the legends. They were the same!

Bhagat Singh was in the middle and Rajguru and Sukhdev, to his left and right respectively. The former looked stylish in a hat over the shirt, and the other two appeared more impressive in Kurta-Pyzama and jackets. They supported traditional caps on their heads.

Thus we watched a magic we had never seen in our life before. Their overall appearance was so august that we forgot even to blink. Their glorified eyes met straight with ours and seemed to penetrate deeply. Their faces glowed with a divine light, and each had a 'halo' around him. We were dazzled so much that all of us suddenly left our chairs and stood up in a haphazard manner in utmost respect for them.

'Don't fear us friends...' The man on the right said. His smile increased more.

'Are you Sukhdev sir?' Pavan ventured to ask him.

'Yes... I am!'

'Can you see and hear us from there?'

'Yes... and that's how we are talking to you.'

'But I can't believe this...' Rohit opened his eyes wide like balls.

'How will you then believe Rohit?' Sukhdev asked.

'Well... tell me the color of my shirt?' He thought for a moment and tested frankly.

'It's blue. The color of your pant is khaki. This is what you are dressed in for everyone to see clearly. But shall I also tell you in front of your friends, what you are not wearing at all?' Sukhdev amused and Rohit got deterred at once.

'No, no... it's okay! I do believe it now.' He said hurriedly.

None could help laughing including the trio at his

undue worry. However, it worked to make the situation more adaptable to all. Here, Rohit opened his frank questionnaire before them without any hesitation.

'Sir, I want to know more if you don't mind.'

'Yes?'

'Are you three the same real ones?'

It put Sukhdev in a fix for a moment and he couldn't reply easily. Bhagat Singh came to his assistance and said.

'We can understand that you are living in modern India where three essential C's... currency, commodities and chauvinism are available fake at every step. But, you can trust that we are as real as you are...'

'But you were dead long ago?'

'Yes we were... but only physically and not spiritually.'

'And what brings you here after such a long time?'

'There is always a purpose behind every action. And you know this world is so selfish...' He smiled.

'Similarly, we do also have some motives, as our work is still unaccomplished here...' Rajguru said this time.

'I see... is it some money matter?' Rohit asked scrupulously. But VD got angry with him at once and tried to hush him down for his lewdness.

'What nonsense Rohit? They have nothing to do with worthless money.' She said slowly.

'She is right. It is not the worthless money but a treasure trove instead...' Bhagat replied.

'That's it! He cheered up, 'I knew that the spirits can tell about the locations of hidden treasures exactly. And here you want us to unearth it for you... am I right?'

'Right.' Singh accepted humbly.

'And what will our share be out of that?'

'It depends upon you...' He smiled.

Rohit looked at each of us thoughtfully and then there came a surprising reply.

'Then, I will demand an equal share for my 1.1 billions fellow Indians...'

An absorbing silence followed for some moments, and then, there came the applause from the trio.

'You are cleverer than we had estimated Mr. Rohit...' Singh acknowledged in the end.

'Now, you can disclose the location of that treasure to us...' Rohit said in reply.

'But should we trust you so early?'

'You have come to the right place sir! We are not going to ditch you...'

'We know it, and that's why we have found you guys out among millions other...'

'Forgive me for my kidding sir. But I know that you have certainly brought something unique for the countrymen after those so many years.'

'Well... let us talk about some friendship now and try to know each other more...' Rajguru changed the subject.

'You are right sir. Pavan said quickly to agree with him.'

'Now this is not fair that you people are calling us 'Sir' again and again...' He complained.

'So?'

'You can call us by our names as there is not much difference in our ages.'

'No... you are most respectable to us and it is against our culture also.' Pavan denied.

'Then you may give us an affectionate name as you have given to Gandhi Ji and Nehru Ji. If they are Bapu and Chacha of the nation, are we not the brothers of the same?' Sukhdev asked intimately.

The martyr had touched us on the raw and all of us felt embarrassed at the notion. The subject was a sort of national shame. It was there that He-Man offered his thoughtful suggestion to us.

'Shall we call them Bhaiya?'

'Yes... it gives some sense of family association at least.' Pavan consented, but VD rejected the idea.

'No! We will call them Dada... as the Bengalis do address their elder brothers with affection.'

'It sounds quite suitable to the Big Brothers...' I seconded the proposal and others also accepted it with a cheer.

And there at the screen on the wall, Sukhdev turned to his companion in the middle.

'What do you say Bhagat? We have been given a new name after such a long time...' He said.

'And there couldn't have been a better present on your 'Centenary-Birthday..." Rajguru added.

'Centenary birthday?' I repeated.

'Yes! It is a great day for us. Bhagat was born exactly 100 years before on the same day of 28th September, 1907. And, we had chosen this day specially to meet you all...' Rajguru said.

An applause for him came up from our group this time. Sukhdev and Rajguru also accompanied. Bhagat raised his hand to stop and said.

'I do return the same gesture to our friend VD, as her B-Day also falls on the same day.'

This was a surprise for all. Even I didn't know about it before. However the clapping began for her this time.

Her cheeks turned rosy at the treat.

'Thanks! But I never celebrated my birthday before...' She said modestly.

'We never did either...' Bhagat said, 'I was born 100 years ago, Sukhdev has completed his century already earlier this year and Rajguru will be a centenarian next year. But all these statistics are quite insignificant to us. We are more or less still twenty three years old, as we were on 23rd March 1931, when we went to the gallows. And that proud day is a real and combined birthday for us...'

He stopped for a while before speaking again.

'Me and my friends are more energetic now than before, as more work is yet to be done!' His voice became emotional but he controlled himself quickly to take his leave.

'Well friends... it was nice meeting you and it is time for us to move.' And they got up to go.

'But Dada... we are not even well acquainted with each other yet?' Rohit hailed in agitation.

'Leave it on the next time...' Singh gave a smile.

'Next time when?'

'We have marked out 23rd of every month to meet you...'

'Sure?'

'See you at the same time.' He said and they turned to walk away. They disappeared after going a few steps... and the same blank dots and contrasts returned to the canvas as before.

17

It was the October evening next month in 2007 when after returning home, I took the key from the concealed point as the door was locked and Mom was out. It was quiet inside. I was feeling tired, so I decided to take a nap, and fell on the bed without changing.

I woke up at 8pm after having a good three hours sound sleep. Mom returned soon from a neighbour Aunt's Bhajan-Kirtan (Group singing of Hymns) and carried Prasada in a leaf-cup. And giving a share to me, she triggered the series of questions.

'When did you come back?'

'In the evening...'

'Why didn't you carry your lunch box?'

'I forgot...'

'Ate something or not?'

'Yes, Samosa at canteen.'

'Only Samosa? You must be feeling hungry. What will you eat now? Come to the kitchen at once...' She ordered angrily.

Eat, eat and eat... do these Moms think of nothing else? I wondered. And why don't we ever think the same about them? May be they are made of some special soil. The poor doting Moms.

We had a small Temple inside near the main entrance

of our home, where during Navratras, she was used to light a wick in the small silver lamp in the evenings also. Whenever she returned home from somewhere, it was her custom to peep inside first of all to check whether the Jyoti(Flame) was still on or not. She did the same this time also and her face glowed with satisfaction.

She had also cast a look at the two earthen pots, which lay nearby in a corner. Dad had sown some barley seeds in each, five days earlier, and now the numerous green straws stood straight in both of them. I remember how much tense she had been, when the seeds didn't sprout up for the first three days, although the pots were watered regularly. However, she was eventually eased up on the fourth day to see the positive signs.

Another big concern earlier was a rat that had burrowed a hole in the soil of one pot, may be to find a cool resting place for him. And the food was also available aplenty there. It was necessary to turn him out of his new house to save the paddy straws, and the task was entrusted to me by Mom.

It was anyhow a tedious work to search, chase and then trap the intruder under an upside-down waste paper basket after creating a big turmoil. Encouraged by the success, I trapped two other family members of the rodent, one after the other. I did announce my achievement to Mom every time and then travelled about hundred yards to release them near a police personnel's house in the colony. I heaved a sigh of relief when the entire family disappeared inside one by one, and nobody had noticed me as well.

A door banged shut in the lobby where I stood and it gave me a start from my thoughts. I felt that a storm was brewing outside. Window panes had also begun to creak. I took to bolt all of them one by one and came outside at the terrace.

A strong gusty wind was blowing. The margosa tree standing in our garden, overlooked the terrace. Its small conical leaves fluttered ominously and flew away in all directions. The sky was dotted with stray clouds. I paced there restlessly for some time just thinking. A storm... and may be the following rain on the eve of the Dussehra-Day? Has this happened ever before?

My thoughts then drifted to Dussehra ground, where I had promised to take our group to attend the funeral of the three demon brothers tomorrow evening. Girls were especially over-excited for this adventure. But, will the erected effigies be able to sustain this strong storm today? What if they fell down and get damaged by rain?

I kept thinking and the thoughts changed like scenes on a screen. Mind compared them with the living Ravanas of my motherland, who reigned it. I wondered as to when the blessed day will come that will prove to be their ultimate doomsday? It is better if the effigies fell down by themselves today, before being publicly disgraced tomorrow.

A thread of fluorescent lightening flashed away on the eastern horizon. Something was happening quite uncommonly. I had no idea at the time that these were the heavenly signs of change that was to come imminent and was going to be a milestone in the chronicles of Indian political scenario.

18

And our favourite tea point the next day. Rohit and Pavan sat on one bench, while He-Man and I sat on the other, facing them.

We sipped Chai and waited for Sumit who had gone to bring the girls from the hostel. Vandana, Anjali and Bindu were coming to go to the Dussehra ground.

It was 3pm and a pleasant breeze blew through the leaves of Baalam-Kheera trees gently. However, some traffic was disturbing the peace.

'The place is losing its charm now. How deserted it had been during our 1st and 2nd year...' Himanshu yawned.

'Yes. It is the same frustrating human jungle everywhere...' Rohit said.

'Animals are better than the humans. They are charming, but the latter is alarming! Pavan said aridly.'

The sound of drums and cymbals attracted us. A band of saffron clad devotees was coming towards us. They were chanting the holy slogans and in the middle of them walked a man disguised as Lord Hanuman. He was painted with ochre from head to feet. He wore a peculiar mask that had an attachment of a ten feet high ornate steeple above it. A devotee walking beside carried the Lord's wooden club on the shoulder.

All three friends of mine watched them with extreme

curiosity as the procession came to a halt for a while at the crossway near us. The Image was made to bow its head there and the steeple came down. A guavasized explosive was tied to the crossbar of the steeple and another man set its wick on fire. And with this, the Image straightened his back again.

The wick burned fast and the next moment the bomb exploded with a bang! The rumble gave some vigour to Pavan, who appeared excited to ask me.

'What is this all about Tipu?'

'This is the local Dussehra procession to mark the monkey brigade's victory over the demons.' I explained and as I did so, Kaka got up from his seat and dashed to the image. He fell on his feet in prostration and returned with the Prasada of an orange. Taking the clue from him, Rohit also got up to go.

'I will also get the blessings...' He said and went away. We three also followed and came back with three Bananas. Rohit however, caressed his back, for he had got a heavy slap on it from the Holy character.

'Got the lion's share of the blessings?' Pavan asked him and we both began to laugh. But He-Man was looking moody so our attention was diverted to him.

'Why He-Man? Why are you looking so off your colours??' I nudged him with my elbow.

'May be he is missing Anjali...' Rohit jested.

'Anjali? His fourth sister??' Pavan frowned seriously.

'But why are you so sad? She is also on the way...' Rohit said this time. He and Pavan were bent on pulling his legs together.

Himanshu tossed the Banana peel aside lazily and didn't reply the remarks. But Pavan teased him further.

'Don't you ever think He-Man that you have some sort of a sister-mania?'

I think he needs to consult a sexologist. It's a serious problem somewhere...' Rohit fired another shot and Himanshu eyed him acidly this time.

'And may be the okay sexed ones don't wear the underwear as a symbol.' He asked.

'This is my private matter and you have nothing to do with it...' Rohit looked flat at once!

'Then you better keep this freaking trap of yours shut'

'I had just given a suggestion to you. But it is damn confusing to me as to why you always discover a 'sister' in every girl?' Rohit tried to molest him more.

'And quite in contrast... you always discover just a girl in every sister!' He-Man returned.

'The bloom of the young age and this college life is not going to come back again my dear. So, enjoy the life as much as you can' I said to him fancifully but he was in a different mood that day.

'Sorry, we are here to study and not to go romancing with girls. Our parents are not paying to do all that you know...' He professed.

'But they are not paying to make the sisters either...' I said.

'Making friends is not so bad. A short term infatuation with the opposite sex is good for the mental health also...' Rohit said like a psychologist.

'This is the most enjoyable thing in the world dude! Rohit can tell you in detail if you have some problem. Thirty minutes tuition from him everyday will teach you the necessary tactics so easily...' Pavan suggested to Himanshu and looked at Rohit who accepted the offer at once.

'You see, the concentration, devotion and determination are the three keys to achieve any goal successfully...' He began seriously but his attention was caught by a pack of dogs, that had just passed by. It was the month of October and canine's love season was in full swing. Inspired by the sight, he began again.

'Here are the animals who represent the raw nature and wise men say that the nature is our best teacher.'

'And luckily, we have so many specialists together. One, two, three, four, eight, nine...' Pavan started to count them.

The entire pack walked in passion. Leading in the front, were three or four bitches... and the followers were the devoted dogs. They didn't know at all where they were going to. But their only aim was to just follow, and they did so mindlessly. They walked to some distance, then took a sudden turn and began to come towards us again.

'Just watch their moves closely, and you will learn the basics very today!' Pavan now suggested to Himanshu.

'And my God!' Rohit exclaimed as they came near, 'These bastards will do exactly whatever their female counterparts do. And it will continue ceaselessly, until one wins the bitch over. And this is the finest display of the three key qualities I mentioned earlier.'

By now I was in a fit of uncontrollable laughter. A sudden spasm made my 'chai' coughed out of my mouth and I got up to control the coughing. Himanshu's seriousness was also gone now, and he was tittering too!

'This is the festive season and that's why they are having a rave party.' He also commented at last.

'And this is the wildest of the rave parties, ever enjoyed by the human beings.' I said and all of us began to laugh madly. A couple of passers-by stopped in their tracks to look at us like fools, when Rohit added more.

'And sometimes, this is a kind of a relay race. One gives up and another takes charge. But the race goes on...'.

'There is at least one species on earth, that is not less than fifty years advanced to Americans in respect of showing their love so publicly...' I said.

The pack of canines had now gone out of sight, and our remaining friends had not come yet. It took us some time to compose ourselves, when we regained our seats on the benches and ordered the fresh 'chai'.

'You are Ph.D in dog-science! He-Man appreciated Rohit, 'So tell me, why do the dogs sniff at the arseholes of each other as a welcome gesture?'

'This is a very good question my dear, and fortunately I have an answer ready for it also. But it's a long story to tell...' And he began to relate even without getting our reactions.

Ages ago, the dogs got concerned about their status in the world and their agitation slowly increased. Eventually their leaders organized a rally, like one that takes place in the ground there in front of us so often. He pointed to show for example and continued... so an old and wise veteran presided the rally. Some aged and experienced ones also expressed their views on the subject. One of them said

'Respected president and other dignitaries seated on the dais here. My dear friends, brothers, mothers, children and all other ladies and gentle dogs...'

'We are deemed to be the most damned species in the world by all. The human beings are the ones, we serve most loyally, and yet they do treat us with contempt. They even use our name as a slang to address each other. This is very insulting to us and has now become a prestige issue for our society.'

'Why shouldn't we change the name of our race?' Someone suggested.

'It won't work at all. We need an overall change!' The other speaker rejected the idea and a debate went on. Finally the president concluded in his speech.

'Lord Brahma has created the whole world! We must meet him directly and make a request to turn us into some respectable beings...'

The proposal was applauded unanimously with the barking-cheers from all around. And then a group of some energetic and brilliant minded volunteers was formed to set-off on the long journey.

After the many long days, they reached the abode of Brahma in the Himalayas, who asked them about the purpose of their visit. The group leader explained everything to him and then pleaded to do the needful. After listening to him intently, the Lord was in a fix. He thought for sometime and said with a godlike smile.

'Look my children! I am just the creator and my role comes to an end after that. You are a living being and this department comes under Lord Vishnu, as he is the protector. He may be able to help you...'

All of them went to the second Lord with new hope.

'A new structure can't be erected at a place, without destroying the existing one. Lord Vishnu said, 'And since I am the protector only... so I can't do this. Go to Lord Shiva, who is the destroyer. He may help you in this...'

'Your lordship! We have already traveled so far with great difficulties. Lord Brahma and you are so good in nature, but Lord Shiva has a tendency of getting furious so soon, and we do fear his wrath! Kindly give us your reference letter that could solve our purpose accordingly...' The leader requested.

'Alright! But do keep the epistle safe, as the mount Kailash is far from here...' With this he wrote some lines on a Bhoj-Patra (Birch-leaf) and handed it over to the leader.

They started their pilgrimage again with it. But it was the most arduous track so far in the forests and hilly terrain. Many of the members died of cold and hunger on the way, but they kept their march continued with fortitude. None of the dutiful canines worried for its life as the safety of the special epistle was above all for them.

The members of the pack held it in their mouths turn by turn. But it was very much prone to be spoiled in rough weather. So to protect it from rain and rivers, the leader got a unique idea. He rolled it thinly and wrapped in a banana leaf. Then he inserted it inside the 'Arsehole' of a volunteer carefully. Having done this, the caravan moved on with relax.

But as the bad luck would have it, the biggest tragedy of the canine history occured on the way, and their mission failed miserably. May be while crossing a gushing mountain stream, the courier-dog was swept away by the strong current without any trace. And the poor creature lost his life while doing his duty, but none of others knew about his sacrifice.

They came to the conclusion that the courier-dog had run away deliberately to avoid the hardship of the journey, because after all every dog has its day! The remaining members returned back, searching for him desperately. Slowly the news of this shocking treachery spread all around in the community. Eventually, the entire race took an oath to find the traitor out at any cost.

And thus, the determined creatures are still looking for the mentioned truant even to this day. They do sniff at, and also peep inside the arseholes of each other in hope to discover that missing letter!

Here Rohit finished his whimsical story at last. We had already shaken all our guts badly, and had no more stamina to laugh. Tears flowed from our eyes and faces became cherry red. But thank God! Our awaited friends arrived at the right time to save us from a possible heart-attack.

19

'How was your Dussehra friends?' Sukhdev Da asked.

'It was very special this time. Tipu had taken all of us atop a house, adjoining the 'Devi Mandir' ground and we had a clear view of the demon brother's funeral from there...' He-Man answered.

'So all of you enjoyed to see how thousands of people lynch the three poor villains?' They began to laugh.

'And this is also against Bapu's principal of non-violence.' RG amused.

'That is simply the part of a festival Dada...' I smiled.

'It is true that Ravana was a villain, but he had a bright side too!' VD gave her opinion.

'He was a great scholar, right?' Dev said.

'Yes Dada...' Kokul admitted this time, 'That's why he is worshipped in many parts of India and Sri-Lanka even today. There are his idols and temples too.'

'There is a village in my home district Vidisha in Madhya-Pradesh, named Ravangram. A ten feet long idol of the demon is situated there in a reclining position. The villagers believe that something ominous will occur if someone ever tried to place it in a standing posture...' VD added and Rohit let out an awkward gasp to exclaim.

'It means someone is going to make him stand up soon.'

'What do you mean?' Kokul asked.

'Guruji...' He hesitated, 'As you know, I am having some inexplicable dreams for some time, and I again saw a bizarre one last night!'

'Here is another breaking news!' He-Man said.

'You may continue Rohit...' Kokul encouraged.

'I saw the burning of Ravana and brothers...'

'And what is so unusual about that?'

'It is that the triad had the uniquely changed features.'

'Unique?' Kokul asked.

'Instead of the customary demons, they were the enlarged copies of Gandhiji's three trademark monkeys in place of them. And each of them sported a big badge on his chest, reading... 'I am the voter.'

'That's pretty interesting...' Guruji nodded.

'But it was even more interesting presence at the big ground there. In the form of tens of thousands of devotees around... there were men and women of every age, who had willfully lost their lives for country as freedom fighters and also in the battle fields as soldiers. All of them had a Martyr written badge on, as their distinction marks.'

'I saw our friend Dadas there... and I also saw Aazad, Netaji Bose, Bismil and numerous others, who stood and watched. A brigade of angels, holding the bow and arrows in their hands like warriors, surrounded the effigies and rained their arrows on them furiously. And again... they also wore the different logos this time, reading... "Long Live Revolution."

Rohit finished his fantasy in almost one line and became silent. None of us spoke a word and just looked at the great men in expectation. At last the contemplating Singh said.

'Well... our dreams are usually the mirror of the coming events, and sometimes they do reflect the present also. Here the typical Bapu-monkeys do symbolize the most of our fellow Indian voters, who are in fact so negligent about their own motherland and self-powers that they are virtually the Deaf, Dumb and Blind individuals.

'And what about that 'revolution' force there?' Pavan asked.

'Revolution is not bloodshed always and it had never been our philosophy as well. It simply means Change. This very word is the rule of the existence and the secret of human progress too. The angry archers are shooting the arrows of awareness at such common folks to wake them up.'

'But it is the politicians, who should wake up rather...' VD argued and it brought an ironic smile on Singh's lips.

'How funny! It is like punishing others for the crime you have committed yourself. British... who ruled over us for about 250 years, can't be blamed alone as they were the tradesmen, who came to India just to extend their business. But the responsible were those, who provided the necessary tools to them, to gain power and become powerful. And now those monkey-brand voters are repeating the history once again by nourishing a wrong system of ruling the country by casting the votes. He argued.

'And still showing their proud Fingers-Up after doing that.' RG Dada said.

But showing a finger in that manner has a 'different meaning' too... Kokul Guruji hesitated but couldn't say clearly.

Exactly. It also seems to express, 'Look... I have been fucked! Rohit exclaimed and everyone began to laugh.

'A guru is always a guru...' Dev commented with glee at Kokul.

'By the way, Mr. Kokul has reminded me of my own

Guru, Bhai Parmanand Ji who always gave me some valuable lesson in old days...' Singh began to recall and was lost for some moments.

'It will be good to hear a few words about him after a long time...' RG encouraged him.

'It was a cold January morning of 1927 in Lahore, when I was sitting in front of him at a cement bench on his house's roof...' Singh began to tell.

'We both had come upstairs to enjoy the warm sunlight after having taken the stomach-full breakfast of Paranthas stuffed with grated radish along with potato-peas, butter and Lassi. He had called me following the complaint of my father Sh. Kishan Singh Ji, about my involvement in revolutionary activities...' He laughed lightly and continued.

'I remember I was wearing pyjama-shirt, coat and turban at that time, all made of khadi and felt too cold. It was however an emotional and inspirational meeting with him. I took his advice and blessings in the end and came back, and it was the last time I saw him...' He concluded.

'He was the source of great encouragement to all.' Dev commented.

'Pyjama-shirt? Like Dev and RG Dada are wearing?' I asked with surprise.

'Well... they both look great in the attire, but it is not made for you. You look stylish in this western dress only... and may be that's why you like it most.' VD flattered.

'She is right. This pant-shirt and the dashing Hat makes a striking appearance of yours!' Pavan gave his approval to her.

'And you look like a real Dada in this pointed and robust moustache...' Rohit added in his best way but I admonished him for his choice of words.

'Shut-up Rohit! Why just doing comedy all the time? Dada... you please don't take him seriously. You know that he is such a dimwit already...'

'In fact, you are so handsome, and thousands of girls must have had a crush on you... isn't it?' VD smiled and so did the young Singh. The other two also began to chuckle.

'This particular dress was conceived and given to me by both of them...' He pointed to his right and left. 'And that's why I love it so much. It was the time when after 'Saunders murder, me and RG were to leave Lahore. I was dressed in the same disguise along with Durga Bhabhi (The wife of great revolutionist Bhagvati Charan Bohra), and I also deem it lucky for me, as it made our escape successful... although the success was not possible without RG.'

'RG is really a remarkable actor...' Dev said. 'He had chosen the role of Bhagat's servant during the journey, and also got dressed accordingly.'

'He had shaved his head and carried a tattered bedding under his armpit. He stayed overnight at Bhabhi's house with me before departure and acted like a faithful servant all the time.' Bhagat could not help laughing again.

'And early next morning, on their way to Calcutta, he traveled third class, while his 'sir and madam' traveled first class. Incidentally, Aazad Bhai had also taken the same train in the perfect disguise of a devoted Sadhu, but he got down somewhere on the way...' Dev told.

'However, Rajguru played his part like no one other can do for his friend.' Singh added and Rohit who was listening intently, let out a deep sigh.

'How I wish my friends were also like RG Dada!' He regretted.

'Why... what is wrong with you?' Dev asked.

'I am talking about Himanshu. He leaves no stone unturned to disturb me at night, and I can't sleep properly. He will bang the doors of almirah and washroom shut. And sometimes, would even drag the folding bed around to make a shrill sound. I do already suffer from the disturbed sleep. And he does all that to tease me only...' He finished his woeful experience at last.

'It is Rohit himself who disturbs others instead. We often find the room light on at midnight and see him operating the computer or roaming about in the corridor outside aimlessly like a ghost.' Pavan said in protest.

'And that's why he gets up well past 9am...' He-Man got the encouragement and turned to Rohit.

'Shall we stop our natural wants for the sake of your sleep?' He growled.

Rohit was shying away from him when RG said to us in a very light and relaxed mood.

'This is not an exception. Dev and Singh had also been doing the same with Rajaram Shastri and Bhagwan Das Mahour in the college days...'

They both began to laugh at the taunt.

'Who were these Rajaram and Mahour?' Pavan enquired.

'Rajaram was the librarian at the Dwarka Das library near our college in Lahore, and was a good friend. Dev and Singh often found him out, whenever he went to the Ramakrishna's Dhaba to take lunch and began to share his meals uninvited. He hated Bhagat's eating in his plate... and was forced to order the separate lunch for him every-time. Bhagat was also fond of eating Rasgullas and ordered it shamelessly. And they never paid for the free meals.' RG stated and took a pause.

'Both of them usually took their seats on his left and

right respectively to make him a sandwich between them so that he couldn't move or leave from there.' He told and began to laugh.

'What happened after that?' I asked.

'Happened what? One day Rajaram gave them a deliberate slip and vanished from the spot on pretext of fetching a Paan (Betel-Leaf) for himself and turned up only when both of them were about to be beaten up by the shopkeeper and the staff because they had no money to pay the bill. RG smiled.

'And what about the other Mr. Bhagwan Das Mahour. I asked again between the laughters.

'He was a revolutionist friend of ours and according to Bhagat, he was also a missing link between apes and human beings during its evolution...' Dev told this time, 'Bhagat had nick-named him Orangutan with affection and the latter never took it amiss. He was so beautiful at heart and Bhagat had many interesting altercations with him from time to time'

Post-Script
26th February 2031

I still remember that we had several other interesting discussions with them about their life that day. They told us about their friends and many other things and I can recall many of them up to this moment when I have decided to add a few more lines to this previous page of my diary today. All of us were asking many questions and they were answering one by one. Here is the gross summary of that. And it is not important that who asked a particular question and who answered the same.

'What was your picture in front of a common man?'

'Two examples are enough to answer that... one is Jatin Das who died on 13th September, 1929 in Bostol jail Lahore, while doing the Hunger-Strike with us and many others. We were demanding the status of political prisoners for us and also the facilities like good food, newspaper etc. He died on 63rd day of the strike and his dead body was taken to his home at Calcutta. You know, thousands of people gathered at the stations between Lahore to Calcutta to see him and more than 150 thousand were following his funeral procession at home!'

'The other was Chandra Shekhar who was born free and died free, and that's why he was Aazad. Just imagine, people worshipped the 'Tree' he died underneath and took its leaves home with reverence as keepsake. The spot had become a place of pilgrimage and the British had to cut it down to stop people flooding the scene.'

'What about your personal likings or hobbies?'

'Sukhdev was so fond of eating Maize Corn, Bhagat Singh liked Books and Rajguru liked Shooting.'

'What inspired you to be the violent-revolutionists'?

'All of us were deeply impressed by Mahatma Gandhi in the beginning. But it was a shock to us when he took his Non-cooperation movement back in 1922 after an incident at Chaura-Chauri. It forced us to make a separate way or line of action to attain freedom.'

It was the first time for us to realize that the great men like RT were also like us. They also enjoyed the life, pulled the leg of others and played the pranks like the common young men. The only difference was that we do only dream about our goals, but the great personalities do bring their dreams to reality.

20

It was Sunday so we decided to meet at the T-Point in the afternoon. I took my bike but as I reached near the HUDA ground of Sec 13-17, the barricades and the policemen stopped me to go ahead. One of them swung his arm like a robot to the road going to my right.

'I just have to go at the crossing there...' I pointed in front, but without speaking he repeated the same action, a bit contemptuously. I could see the little bunch of my friends standing at the far corner, who waved to me. They were He-Man, Pavan, Rohit and Sumit. I also waved my arm anticlock wise in response to show that I was coming by the directed de-tour.

As I reached there, I saw that the landscape had remarkably changed there within a couple of days. The coal-tar road had been re-laid and heavy electric cables being detached from the poles to facilitate the landing of the Helicopters.

'Where is the tea kiosk?' I asked in surprise and glanced around. 'It has been removed by the security and the police...' Someone replied.

'But why?'

'CM and a few party leaders are coming to the ground tomorrow...'

'Damn it!'

'Let us take our seats on the grass in this park.' Rohit

suggested and all agreed. It was a small green area, just across the road and was surrounded by merely a two feet high boundary wall. We selected a clean looking corner and squatted down lazily to begin our Panchayat.

'Another rally, huh?' Pavan looked away at the ground where dozens of policemen and officers were having a sort of official stroll. Numerous Goverment vehicles also stood there. Red lights flashed and sirens buzzed.

'The total state police will be here tomorrow, as if another Panipat battle were going to take place at this ground....' He-Man yawned and a debate began.

'VIPs will come and there will be the same deceiving speeches and announcements.' Rohit said.

'And the show will be over after wasting crores of rupees...' Pavan said.

'A deputy commissioner is the in-charge of a district. Why can't he make such announcements on the local cable or in front of the media on behalf of the Govt?' Rohit questioned.

'To save all these lavish spending that could well be used for public welfare?' He-Man added.

'The whole drama is the fucking leader's personal and party propaganda only....' Pavan picked a piece of rubble up from the grass and threw it away in scorn.

A chopper came humming from the Delhi side and began to circle over the city. It then circled the ground for two-three times and hovered over to land in the middle. Many people came out of it when it finally did.

'They are the intelligence men to survey the security arrangements of the VIPs.' Rohit calculated.

'But whom are these leaders afraid of so much?' Sumit asked this time.

'This is you and me. And this is the every citizen of the country...' Pavan replied.

'And what can be their real purpose of coming here and elsewhere?'

'They are actually undertaking a business tour and do only come to lure the people. Opportune declarations as free plots, free electricity, loan exemptions, reservations, subsidies etc for the chosen cast-creed based sections of the society are some examples of their art.'

'Moreover... free sarees, free TVs, wheat or rice to be made available @ throwaway prices of Rupee 1/2 per kg are some other jugglery items of these expert magicians.' He-Man supplemented this time.

'To say... they do pick up their targets very cunningly.' Rohit also gave his expert comments.

'But how such provisions can be made possible in a poor country or state, such as ours?' I wondered.

'It is very simple. Taxes will come and the whole society will suffer the consequences. There will be the increase or addition of a couple of new taxes to more than five dozen different ones already being imposed on the people. These politicians are simply playing the game of roulette with public's hard earned money...' Pavan replied.

'And the economic structure of the country will crumble further more. The middle class will manage to remain middle class any how, but the poor will increase. As they are doing year after years since 1947...' I acknowledged.

'Hey... what you goons are doing here?' A police officer came near the low boundary wall of the park to enquire impolitely.

'Plotting to assassinate the CM...' Pavan replied seriously.

'What?' May be the officer couldn't hear clearly.

'We are just sitting around to chat...' I promptly clarified and smiled.

'Get up and move away...' He brandished his rule and ordered dutifully.

There was no use of doing any argument with the cop, so we silently got up and came out where Sumit's and my bikes were parked. The tea seller Yaksha Prasad also joined us there as we rested on the bike. Sumit heaved a frustrated sigh.

'Police are not to be blamed. They are forced to wag their tales in front of these so called Very Important Persons...' He said.

'And what is our status? Do we deserve no respect as the citizens of the republic??' Rohit asked.

'No! We really don't. We are simply the 'PONI's... or the Persons of No Importance.'

'You mean, we are the mules who carry the loads?' Rohit scowled.

'Yes! A mule is a beast of burden and similarly, we are also bearing the burden of these VIP's existence.' Sumit said.

'Friends, I just don't understand why do they close my business whenever, a leader comes to this ground...' Yaksha said in a distressed voice.

'Because you are also a 'PONI' as we are...' He-Man began to laugh.

'There is something utterly wrong with the whole system somewhere...' I said.

'Hopefully, the arrival of Bhagat Singh & Co. at this

juncture, heralds some changes to happen...' Rohit said fancifully.

'Good Lord! It is still hard to believe when I saw them for the first time...' Pavan said in response.

'What are you talking about? Where is Bhagat Singh??' Sumit asked in surprise and Rohit did the quick correction carefully.

'He came in Pavan's dream last week.'

'Shit! He is so fond of having such baseless dreams. Hey... why don't you think about a girlfriend rather? You ought to be romantic and not patriotic at this sweet age.'

'Pavan didn't reply Sumit's comment.

'I've seen in movies that the soul of the diseased keeps wandering ceaselessly, if its wish remains unfulfilled...' I said.

'Till it achieves its goal anyhow, right?' Rohit added.

'They wanted freedom and the country became free after sixteen years of their death. So their souls should have rested in peace eventually...' He-Man said.

'Did they sacrifice themselves to attain this freedom?' Rohit asked and stressed on the word 'this'

'If this is the freedom, then we were free in British Empire also.' Pavan replied.

'British are gone after transferring the power to the Indians, and that's what everyone wanted?' He-Man said and Yaksha, who was silent for a long time, gave his expert comment.

'It is true that the British departed. But before doing so, they gave something to their successors, which they are using successfully to this date...'

'And what is that?' I asked with curiosity.

'It is in the form of a short poem written by me...' He gave a hint and began to look at us for the permission. We granted the same silently and he started to cite in a particular style...

Congratulations India, Good wishes to all
We hail your freedom, as the British fall
Good luck my friends, now it is your turn
For after the long ages, we have to return
This is your land and, we were only guests
So to bid you Goodbye, we give you a chest
It is a simple box, a small souvenir gift
But lid of the same, you may never lift
Golden is the color, and so is its key
But locked as it is, should it ever be
No cash, no diamonds, as they are too small
Yet it holds something, most precious of all

It was a touching poem, so there were all the praises for him.

'You are a good poet too, Yaksha Kaka... but the poem looks still incomplete. What was there in the box at all?' I asked.

He smiled and explained further.

'Quite like you, all Indian leaders couldn't resist the temptation of opening it, and finally did what they shouldn't have done. There lay a piece of velvet neatly folded inside. And when being unfolded, it read in golden words.'

Here are the useful, teachings of our school
Golden key to power is, just divide and rule!

He finished with a bang and bowed his head in the end.

Nobody spoke for sometime. The verses were the expressions of a common man and we just kept thinking about them.

'They took the boxfuls of precious wealth away to England, and left an empty box behind, with dynamite inside.' He-Man gave his views at last.

'It went to England before the socalled Independence... and is going to Switzerland etc now.' Sumit commented.

'Yes... the post independence rulers have been doing the same. Nothing has changed ever since except the ruling hands.' Pavan added.

The chopper in the ground lifted up in the air with a roar and flew away. Yaksha mixed some lime to his chewing tobacco to relax and busied himself in mixing it together on his palm with his thumb. He gazed at the diminishing speck of the flying machine with contracted eyes and asked a question unexpectedly.

'Friends... why don't you people take their places now?'

'What?' We began to look at each other like fools.

'What do you mean to say?' I asked again.

He tucked the pinch of tobacco behind his lower lip and began to explain.

'I mean to say that the older people are running our country for decades, and almost all of them are near or past their retirement age. They dominate the front pages and news headlines. But to me, it is so frustrating to see the same faces everyday and their same lackluster policies have become discordant to the ears now...' He stopped for a while to spit and then resumed...

'I wondered to see how some of them can't even walk without help. Yet they are too anxious to carry the burden of the nation on their tired shoulders...' Yaksha finished and then questioned.

'And do you know why?'

'Why?' I asked.

'They have become so habitual of the kinghood that they simply don't want to let it go.'

We wanted to listen him more so just remained silent in anticipation. And he asked again.

'Tell me... can the old and the rusted steel make a safe and solid building?'

'No...' Someone said.

'Then how can the same build a strong nation?'

No one still replied and he continued further...

'It requires the fresh and high quality steel. And this steel is found aplenty in our country. Our graduate youths, learned teachers, and millions others are that required stuff exactly'

We were stunned at his notion. He had simply brought forward a new ideology of our political system. That little educated tea seller had the real country in his bosom. Yet the things were not clear enough for us to understand easily. It demanded more explanation.

'But how the hell will it be possible?' Pavan asked in a perplexed manner.

'If I prepare tea with the sour milk... will you still sip it?'

He asked to make us understand.

'No!' Pavan replied at once.

'Then tell me how can we sustain the sour system? We need more awareness to achieve the necessary reforms. Throw the perpetrators away who are separating the communities with each other like the tart does to the milk. Never accept anything that our consciousness denies. Otherwise, it will become an accepted practice or system as at present, and will persist for ages.'

The stunning facts revealed by him, left us pondering deeply. All of us were already impressed by that man from the beginning and liked him as well. He was a different case of a tea seller.

21

It was 23rd November, 2007 and we were in Kokul's room together. Although the coming days were going to be hectic for us and we had no time to spare. Yet the temptation of a rendezvous with 'Dadas' was so big that nothing could stop us. So Kokul was on his customary seat in the evening and we were face to face with the trio. Rajguru Dada began in a very friendly manner. May be he was impressed by Rohit's carefree interaction in the first meeting with them.

'What is the matter Rohit? You are looking a bit upset today.' He asked.

'It's nothing so special to mention here...' Rohit appeared taciturn.

'Your studies are not going on well, I think?' RG asked again.

'It's an important assignment a couple of days later, and I have done nothing yet!'

'What is this assignment all about?'

'Its name is P.M., but you won't understand that...'

'P.M.? Assignment Prime Minister??'

'It's Project-Management. But let's talk something different from studies...' Rohit said wearily, and Rajguru Da did the further chaffing.

'Any allotted work must be taken seriously. Can we help you in that someway?'

'This is Engineering. Dada...' Vandana suggested this time, 'It is not your subject.'

'Why not? We have also done the Engineering. But our was the different type...' He looked at the other two and they began to laugh together.

'All of you are just laughing away and I am very very tense here.' Rohit complained a bit peevishly.

'You are tense because you are dependant on others for the accomplishment of your work. And this tendency makes one stray off the main target. We also committed the same blunder long time before, while doing our assignment of A.S...' Bhagat Da tried to soothe him down this time.

'Assignment and you? And what does this 'A.S.' stand for??' Vandana frowned.

'This was Assassination Scott.'

'Please tell us more about that Dada...' I said and Bhagat Da took some moments before he began the narration.

'It was when Lala Lajpat Rai was opposing the public safety biil that he was beaten to death in the Lathi-Charge ordered by Superintendent Scott. And to avenge his death...'

'Wait a minute Dada...' Pavan interfered to make him stop and then gave quite an unusual suggestion to surprise all, 'We know that you do possess the supernatural powers. Can't you make us experience the same as real please? It will be a great experience for us.'

'Do you mean to say that you want to see it live?' Rajguru Da asked with surprise.

'Yes we want the same...' Almost everyone including me said unanimously.

'But it is not so easy you know...' He sealed his lips and

ruminated. Than they looked at each other and began to confer. Sukhdev Da consented after a while.

'Well, we shall try to take you to the spot in your subtle forms, if you are insisting that much...'

'But your bodies shall remain in the same room in that case...' RG gave the further explanation.

'Hurray...' everyone jumped up at the benign acceptance and the room became noisy. Sukhdev Dada quieted us down with the humorous warning.

'Stop it! And don't shout about like this at the place where you are going now, because that one is the secret mission...'

The other two were also delighted at his suggestion, and the former asked again.

'Now are you ready to go?'

Nobody spoke this time but gave a big nod silently like kids.

'So... here all of you are going to Lahore now! It is 17th Dec, 1928. The day is Monday, and the time is 3:45 in the evening. Its eighty years earlier to this date and the venue is near the famous DAV College in the city...' Singh introduced.

'Right now Jai Gopal, one of our confederates is waiting for a 'Firangi' (Briton) to come out of the nearby Police station. We are also around to do our important assignment. You can view live what is going on further at the spot...'

'But remember some vital instructions before you go. You may experience the partial or total lapse of memory during the course. You may also have the bizarre feelings that can mystify or confuse you...' RG warned.

'And it is the time for all of you to start the meditation for a while under the supervision of Guruji...' Dev said after a short pause, and we straightened our spines at once at his command. We closed our eyes and concentrated as Kokul began to recite the sacred word and we followed a long humming in chorus.

'Aummmm...'

We went into the trance soon after. It was not long when all five of us found ourselves away at the mentioned spot. We had simply travelled back in to the past where the place, incident and the characters were real, but we were the specters of the future! And we had now little memory of our present.

Vandana and I stood at the road side at the time, and she was looking about searchingly. It was a busy road. A lot of cycles, rickshaws and tongas were going to and fro. She turned to me after a bit of survey and then asked with surprise.

'Tipu... Are you also observing the same as I am doing?'

'What?'

'This is a big city, but no car is visible on the road? I think petrol has come to a finish.'

'Well, it may be quite possible...' I admitted thoughtfully.

'I knew it was to happen one day...' She concluded and began to examine me cap-a-pie.

'What are you looking like this?' I asked.

'Are not you looking so funny I think?'

'Funny... why?'

'All the people around are wearing Kurta-Pyjamas, Dhotis and woolens like gentlemen. And you...'

'And me?'

'You are looking like a joker in the printed T-Shirt and jeans.' And she began to laugh.

I bent down and looked at me. I then glanced at the other three friends who had gone ahead to some distance where a man was stooping over his bicycle to find out some fault.

'But He-Man, Pavan and Rohit are also dressed like me and you too?' I disclosed while pointing to her.

'It really looks a bit ridiculous...' She wondered as she also examined herself.

'Yes, it is.' I admitted.

A chilly breeze swept through and we advanced our steps towards the others. They were now standing a few steps away from the cyclist, watching him curiously, and we seemed to recognize the man! Rohit could control himself no longer as habitual, and ventured to help him.

'Why Jai Gopal bhai, how you got your cycle chain off the pulley? And where are you going to??'

Jai Gopal didn't reply and kept fiddling with the chain. He didn't see or hear us, and it was not possible either. He was looking at the nearby police station from the corner of his eyes, as if waiting for someone to come.

Rohit was going to ask him another question when He-Man dragged him back by tugging at his collar and threatened in the hushed voice.

'You fool! Why you keep braying like a donkey every time and everywhere?'

'Don't you know that he is on some secret mission, and is just pretending to repair the cycle?' Pavan also said in hushed voice.

'Ossss....' Rohit crossed his lips with his finger and apologized silently. We moved away from there after that and began to walk towards the D.A.V. College. We saw Rajguru coming towards Jai Gopal from that side at the same time. His eyes were extremely alert. He didn't notice us and went past carelessly. He then ambled away towards the police station, and we reached near Bhagat Singh who also ambushed at some distance.

We were watching that entire manoeuver with our subconscious minds. We kept looking at the three in some anticipation turn by turn. What we knew, was that they were on some mission and something was going to happen soon. But exactly what the same was... we didn't know anything about.

All was so quiet there so far. But, suddenly there began a horrible action. A police officer in uniform came out of the station, and he started a red colored motorcycle standing outside near the verandah. A constable, who stood there came to attention quickly and saluted him. The officer kicked the motorcycle and mounted it as the engine roared. But before he did so, Jai Gopal had already mounted his cycle. It was a signal to Bhagat Singh, who examined the Firangi carefully from over the low boundary wall of the police station. The next moment, he was surprised at the wrong signal and waved frantically to Rajguru to stop him.

'Nossss... He is not Superintendent Scott!'

But Rajguru mistook his gesture for the start of action. He couldn't hear Singh's low calling. He was so enthusiastic to do something that he came into open to confront the officer at once. He lifted the front part of his Kurta up, snatched the pistol from his waist band with a jerk and brandished it on him at the point blank range.

The cop had by now come out of the premises and they were face to face with each other. A renowned sharp shooter as Rajguru was, he fired a single shot without wasting the time. There was a loud sound of explosion, and the bullet made a hole into the poor officer's scalp. He instantly toppled down on to the road along with his motorcycle, and there was the ghastly sight of red blood oozing out.

We watched the mayhem on the road with wide open eyes. Bhagat Singh had rushed to the spot to cover Rajguru. He also emptied his pistol's chamber on the already dead man. Both of them then turned and came running towards us. We all huddled close together in fright and moved quickly away from their path. They ran away towards the college without paying any attention to us. Jai Gopal had also paddled away on his cycle in the opposite direction unnoticed by now.

There was complete silence around for some moments and then the tumult began to rise. Some police men started to come out of the police station. And, Lo! They dashed straight towards us. This development now was even more frightening to us. Assuming that they were coming to catch us, we bolted out and began to run madly after the duo to save our lives! We were quite unable to realize that it was actually needless to do, as no one could see or hear us anyway.

The duo running ahead was suddenly intercepted by a traffic inspector who approached from the other side. I came to know later on that his name was 'Fern'. Rajguru fired his pistol at him also but it missed. And immediately, he struck Fern with such a wrestling trick that he was lying flat on the road in a trice. This interruption had made us stop also and the things were happening very fast there.

Just then, we heard the sound of the heavy foot falls behind. And as we turned, we saw a Sikh constable came charging. He was followed by two-three other sepoys also. He gripped his official rule in a threatening manner and prattled furiously.

'My name is 'Chanan Singh'. And I will not leave you...'

All of us thought that he was aiming at us so we jumped up to see him so near and began to run wildly again. He was clearly in a dangerous mood and was calling out the slang words also. But as we started to run, he perhaps became more furious and shouted out loudly.

'Stop you bastards... or I will kill you!'

And as I heard this call, I ran faster in panic. Bhagat Singh and Rajguru were ahead of me, and my phantom friends behind me. Just then a mustached and robust looking handsome young man appeared from inside the college boundary grill with a pistol in his hand. And at the sight of him, Vandana cried out.

'Who is this man?'

'Don't worry...' He-Man replied from behind, 'He is brother Chandra Shekhar Aazad. And with this we ran past him.'

Don't know why, Rohit had lagged far behind in the mean time and Chanan Singh had reached at his arm's length now. Rohit was trying his best to go away from him. But surprisingly, the constable was not trying to catch him. He seemed to over take him instead, but the determined Rohit won't let him do so.

Aazad had aimed his pistol on Chanan and warned him to stop. But he didn't, and the next moment the former fired the shot. The bullet appeared to go straight into the Rohit's chest, who was unfortunately positioned right in the middle of Chanan and Aazad at that time. Rohit also saw the bullet coming towards him and he fell down in shock immediately and one of us yelled out a heart-rending shriek aloud.

'ROooooHIT...'

And the next moment, we were back from our long trance.

Soon, I opened my eyes to discover that my heart was beating very fast. I naturally searched around for Rohit and found him near me in a shocking state. His face was yellow with fear... and he was still panting. I glanced at others and found everyone perspiring, as if being exhausted from that life-saving sprint.

'So... how was our assignment?' Rajguru Dada laughed away lightly while looking at us turn by turn.

None of us gave any reply although we had come back to normal and Bhagat Da tried to give us some balm.

'We told you already that you can feel the hallucinations during the journey. Are you alright now?'

We nodded in yes and he went on to explain.

'Our was in fact the case of wrong identity. The killed officer was 'Saunders' and the main target Scott was lucky to escape scot-free. He fled to England after that and never came back. Chanan Singh died unnecessarily in the hands of Aazad bhai, who was giving the covering to us as per the plan. He was never happy to kill an Indian but the undue stubbornness and the hatred for the revolutionists, cost the cop his precious life. And depending blindly on Jai Gopal for that 'crucial work' of identification did cost us ours.'

'What happened with Jai Gopal after that?' Pavan asked.

'He was arrested later on and became an approver against

us. But we have since forgiven him because, he simply wanted to live... and we wanted to die for the country.'

'Now, what is the moral of all this exercise Rohit? Sukhdev Da asked to conclude.'

'I have understood Dada...' He woke up from his stupor and said, 'I shall do all my work myself from now on.'

'Good! And I expect the same from others as well.'

'All is well that ends well. Here are our hearty congratulations to Rohit for he is still alive' Rajguru Da quipped to make everyone laugh.

Thus, our meeting ended that evening by giving us a valuable lesson. And I do cherish that lesson even to this day.

22

One evening, I was busy in computer lab with Pavan. We were doing some pending documentation work, when a junior who was almost out of his breath, came hurriedly to inform us that Rohit was involved in some strife near the canteen below. We left the work on the spur of the moment, and ran outside in helter-skelter.

We skipped over many stairs at a time and were at the spot within a minute. The scene there was not encouraging for us and our hearts sank to see Rohit cornered by about a dozen JCBs. He was poorly stuck to the wall. We forced our way through the surrounding crowd to face him.

'What happened?' Pavan asked.

'The reforming process is going on...' Abhinav smiled..

'You must listen to this peace of beauty before you should open your mouth.' Jaiswal came ahead. He opened his laptop and fingered the button to play an audio to us. It was the same argument that had taken place between Rohit and Jaiswal months before.

The audio ended soon and we were speechless to listen that. We just stood thinking what to say or do, when my mobile began to vibrate. It was He-Man's number on the screen.

'Yes?' I enquired.

'There is a gathering of 16-18 JCBs outside the college

and it looks suspicious to me...' He said, like the shorthand dictation, and put the question mark in the end, 'What to do?'

The news disheartened me more and I was in sheer panic. So, it was the planned ambuscade? Certainly, the trouble was brewing for a long time and now this evening is going to be the Rahu-kaal (Inauspicious time) for us for sure... I thought.

Pavan was reading my colourless face. I disconnected the phone by instructing He-Man to stay out there. I didn't want to invite him in, as he had the easily excitable temperament. My mind was working too faster for the first time in life. And then, I decided to take the bull by the horns cleverly.

'Rohit... is it your voice?' I asked him with the stern approach.

He gave a half-nod in response.

'You will have to take your words back...' I commanded.

'It's an old story now, yet I shall do if they want to? Rohit surrendered.

'Why Jaiswal?' I turned to him, 'You know it was just a mistake and he wants to apologize... okay??'

'Well, let's come outside the college and close this chapter...' He began to push Rohit, showing his mal-intention clearly. I put my hand on his to check.

'Wait... let me call Himanshu here first.' And without waiting for the permission, I made my way out of that cluster to be alone. I pushed a few digits on my handset, and as someone responded, I gave the signal 'SOS' in brief and low words. Having done this, I came back to announce.

'He is coming shortly...'

My sole intention was to delay the proceedings till the appropriate time, as we four were no match for those werewolves! But Abhinav and others began to push Rohit again to take him out of the college premises and we had to move with them helplessly.

We kept our pace slow however and after coming out of the main gate, we headed westwards to the village side. The other lurking members had also begun to join them and they swelled every moment. We had not gone very far when He-Man came running to us and everybody came to a stop. He looked excited, but I gestured for him to have patience and asked the rival leader pointblank.

'Now what do you want Jaiswal?'

'That's the real sportsmanship...' He smiled.

'We want Rohit only, and have nothing to do with others...' Abhinav said.

'But why?'

'To teach him a last lesson before he gets his degree from this college...' He replied.

'We are proud that we are Jharkhandi, Chattisgarhi and Biharis respectively. But he must also know today that the JCB is a sort of machine that can move the earth as well.' Jaiswal said this time.

'So... what do you want to do now?' I repeated.

'It's time not for us but for him to do something instead.' He pointed to Rohit.

'And what is that for example?'

'Not much! He will have to do a very simple thing for just two minutes...'

'Like?'

'He has insulted not only us in the college, but the millions of other citizens of our states as well, by calling them the eunuchs. Now he will perform their typical clap dance before all these gentlemen from the same states. And that's all.'

'Wow...' A victorious cheer came from the crowd at that and there were the mocking whistles and comments.

'It will suit him very well...' Someone shouted.

'And he may turn out to be a real one also...' Another suggested and there were the laughters all around.

'What nonsense? What the hell is going on here??' He-Man again got heated up with rage and I had to calm him down. Then pointing to Abhinav, I resisted.

'But this is he, who had started the word-war first of all...'

'And if such an act is going to take place, it will be a duo performance...' Pavan said.

'Don't waste the time. I am going to count up to three before he starts. Otherwise...' Abhinav gave a meaningful smirk.

'Otherwise?' Himanshu challenged.

'All of you are going to be The Dogs on all your fours!' He took his belt out and began to roll in his hand to make a sort of strap threateningly.

'I shall pull your tongue out of this bloody mouth...' He-Man became furious and caught him by the neck. Abhinav gave him a violent push in return and the fight took place at once.

The four of us immediately formed a small ring with our backs touching each other... like the lions of Ashoka pillar.

And then we began to exchange blind blows with whosoever came ahead. But within a minute, it became difficult for us to defend ourselves. They outnumbered us by a good margin and we were soon bruised badly.

My only hope lay on the road that led to the city... and it had disappointed me so far. I was hopefully glancing at it again and again, when my eyes began to shine. Three bikes were rushing towards us, and soon they stopped near with a squeak.

Mounted on them were eleven boys from my locality, led by Birjesh, my colony friend whom I had informed on my mobile earlier. Six of them carried the cricket stumps in their hands.

They immediately jumped down to take part in the fray and brandished the wooden weapons menacingly at Jaiswal & Co. The latter were taken aback by this new turn, and the action came to a stop for the time being. I then gave stunned Jaiswal a whoop.

'Come on buddy... let's have the real business now!'

'Involving the street bullies in our personal dispute is no business anyway...' Came the subdued reply from him.

'Twenty against four is no equation also anyway...' I returned.

'Why the others then? Let's we both come to the ring only, to try our muscles together??' He gave an open challenge to me and I couldn't react at once. His heroic offer was however cheered loudly by his team-mates and he appeared quite dauntless. He then threw an intimidating glance at me and snarled.

'What are you thinking baby? Shall we begin the game??'

I searched him carefully this time. His body structure was heavier than mine. He-Man came near and held me by the arm. We exchanged the silent glances. He looked worried and concerned. Rohit and Pavan also came closer, in that short conference. They were clearly not happy at the suggestion, knowing that I had never done such violence type thing ever before. He-Man protested in low tone.

'Tipu, I shall take this fight and not you. I am going to break the teeth of this dirty swine.'

'Don't worry and have trust on me. Our team's pride is on stake and I won't let you down...' I patted on his arm and assured, 'I shall fulfill your desire for sure.'

I then turned to Jaiswal and glared at him.

'We will fight with each other till one of us falls dead. And remember... nobody will come between us to intervene. The only survivor will be the winner.' I declared in loud voice.

Both the groups then began to retreat to make way for the fatal contest in the middle. Two-three volunteers took the enthusiastic job of clearing the ground of any rubble rapidly. Finally we prepared ourselves for the deadly scuffle in that makeshift arena.

It was a small enclosure in a field near the road. The encouraging shouts began to emerge from both the sides as we drew closer to each other. It was as if we were the fighting bulls rather and not the human beings. We locked our horns together soon after.

Whack!

Whack!

Seven or eight minutes later, both of us lay in the dust half unconscious. Our blood stained cloths had turned to the dirty rags. At the beginning of the fight, I had filled my heart with the feeling of hatred and vengeance for my rival, and thus was able to attack him with all the might. And now I lay poorly still. My left cheek rested on the ground the way that my breath blew the dust away. My mouth was bleeding and blood mixed saliva trickled down cheaply.

Yet my listless eyes were still fixed on Jaiswal, who lay flat and motionless hardly a yard away. I was trying to gather my remaining strength to follow him, in case he gets up again. But his eyes were closed and he panted with exhaustion. I couldn't know when the fight was declared finished undecided by Birjesh. Pavan then approached me. He came near and I badly needed his support. But to my surprise, he extended his hand to Jaiswal.

'Get up Jaiswal... the fight is over.' He said calmly.

At the same time, Rohit and Abhinav came over together to support me. Both of us were anyhow made to stand on our feet. We staggered feebly to maintain the balance as Birjesh delivered the most astonishing words of quite different disposition to our rivals. His voice was deep and not to say, that it was aimed at me also.

'Let's pass the sponge over whatever has happened so far. These petty battles won't earn you a medal. You are not here to do this nonsense. One of you might win this time and the other next time. But both will have to suffer the overall loss!' He sermonized seriously .

'It is our final year and this is the time to work hard. We should concentrate on our careers rather. And only that will be the real victory for us.' Abhinav also said wisely after that.

'And now both of you should beat the dust of enmity

and hatred off your clothes, and come forward to shake the hands of friendship...' Birjesh entreated.

The inspiring address worked wonder at everybody from both the groups. A loud cheer came rolling from all. Some boys really began to dust our clothes, and then both Jaiswal and I were stood to face each other. Our hands were extended to hold each other but we didn't do the handshakes and it was all over after that.

The slanting rays of evening sun had made both of us look ghastly and we seemed to be two odd looking scare-crows in a field.

Both the groups however never vied with each other after that. And Jaiswal gave us a beautiful surprise later on.

23

Coming few days were restful for me. I took the leave from college and nursed my injuries at home. During this time, I read plenty of literature on the National Martyrs. Rohit e-mailed a lot of e-books to all of us and even bought some other from the market. We were so keen to know more and more about them.

Now we usually exchanged the books and other information regarding them with each other and discussed the different contents vehemently whenever we met. Those days, we had become so obsessed with the topic that my friends carried those books to the college also and the classmates asked the numerous questions.

On Sunday, I invited my friends at home to lunch. Vandana came first of all, and when she entered my room, I was surfing internet while munching the crisp pakoras (fritters) leisurely.

'Wow! Eating the delicacies all alone here?' She complained as she took the seat near me and I passed the plate to her.

'Try some... the yam-leaf pakoras are mom's speciality.'

She picked up one and examined the rolled layers carefully.

'This is the fine art indeed...' She exclaimed and placed it back.

'What happened?'

'Just avoiding oily things. Have put on weight these days...'

'Routine exercise will help you loose some...' I suggested.

'Tut! It seems damn boring to me...'

'Fast actions like aerobics won't bore you. If you want to do something interesting, you can do it in some dance form... as Garba. And again, if you want to do something more exciting and sexy... then you must try the pole-dance! And this is so scintillating yaar...' I winked my eye at her.

'Really?' She angled her neck.

'And doing it under my supervision will help you more...' I advised further.

'Shall I call mom to tell her about your 'ideal thoughts'?'

'Do not disturb her. She is preparing lunch for all...'

'Then I am going to help her in the kitchen.'

'Go! Kitchen is also a sort of gym for ladies. And she must also be needing your help.'

'You are not all that bad my boy. You have some good qualities too.' She patted my shoulder in appreciation and I gave a girlish blushing.

'Thanks for the compliments.' I said.

'Do you also help in her daily chores or not?' She asked.

'Why not? I do make dough-balls for her to fry Kachoris on festive days. Sometimes do apply oil to her hair, and also message her feet, whenever she is tired. I do copy a design from 'net' and apply myrtle on her palms on the eve of Karva-Chowth (Ladies festive day) every year. I also help her buy the green-grocery from the nearby market as well. And then carry the load back to home on foot.' I described my feats her in pride.

'Is there still left anything, you didn't tell about?' She asked with irony.

'I think that's all.' I nodded my head in contentment.

'Good job! And you get a lot of blessings in return?'

'Blessings? I get a lot of scolding everytime. She still always blames me to work lousily. You have bought the old dated bread, you drive the bike so rash and carelessly etc... etc. Now I have become habitual, but on my occasional trips to the grocery market with her, I have learned a valuable lesson without doing the M.B.A in marketing... and that's, 'how to haggle over the prices successfully.'

She began to laugh at that. Then she got up and made her way to the kitchen. It was not long when Rohit, He-Man and Pavan arrived. Rohit said in a querulous tone as he came near.

'I have searched everywhere but no books are available particularly on RG and Dev Dada in the market, and it is so disgusting...' He threw some titles on my study table that were mainly on Bhagat Singh.

'Internet is also not providing much information about the two and lot many other martyrs...' I answered desperately.

'But the details of the post-independence leaders is available in wholesale...' Pavan said.

'This is the necessary general knowledge for the school children today...' Rohit blurted out.

'Cool down... cool down! And have a glass of water.' He-Man handed one over to him from the tray that VD had just brought in.

Rohit seated himself and took the small draughts down his throat. And Pavan declared after some cool moments.

'I have made a startling discovery from the books...'

'What?'

'There are some intriguing peculiarities that associate all of us with the trio in some way, and may be that's the reason which have brought them to us.'

'Now please stop creating the suspense...' VD said.

'Tell me what is your date of birth?' Pavan asked her in return.

'Mine?' She looked surprised at the question and then said, 'Well... it is 28th September.'

'And your Himanshu?'

'24th August... but why?'

'And mine is 15th May. And for your kind information, Singh, RG and Dev were born on the same dates respectively.'

A deep silence gripped everybody for some moments. All began to reflect on the mysticism that was surrounding them and then realized that the knowledge gained recently from various books on revolutionists, supported Pavan's explanation.

'That's quite true!' He-Man whispered at last.

'There is another interesting connection with the Sudoku of this date game...' Pavan began to laugh this time.

'And that's the day when the Kansal-Bhavan was being inaugurated...' Rohit jumped up with his own idea.

'Exactly! And that's 23rd March, the day when they kissed the deadly loop...' Pavan said.

'Really! This is how so unusual happening?' I wondered.

'God forbid! This all seem to be a spell of black magic or voodoo to me...' VD said.

'God knows what is fated to happen next? Is this a web to ensnare us someway? Or some form of benevolence on us??' Rohit appeared a bit concerned.

'Don't worry, the facts will come to light soon...' Pavan tried to assure him.

'But there must be something spectacular...' He-Man said.

'Ah! I still feel so excited whenever I think of their grand appearance...' Pavan exclaimed.

'Leave it! We have forgotten the main issue in between the other gossips. Do tell us Tipu, how are you now?' He-Man gave a heavy slap on my thigh and I let out a painful moan.

'Oof!'

'Sorry... sorry! Are you hurt?' He begged.

'My yes or no will make no difference now...' I cried out..

'You are a real hero, and heroes don't feel pain.' He tried to encourage in his own special way, but it made me more annoyed and I glared at him and cursed.

'It should have been you in place of me to know that...'

'That's what I had suggested you at that time!' He said and others began to smile.

'Whenever I think of that fight I feel ashamed of myself for I underestimated 'JCB' states and its people...' Rohit regretted in the end and everybody began to look at him.

'I am responsible for that incident alone...' He said again.

'Combats are the ornaments of brave men. But one thing is true that the undivided Bihar have been a great state indeed...' He-Man professed.

'You are right... VD said, 'It has the illustrated history. Some starry names are associated with it. The renowned emperors of Magadh, Chandragupt Maurya and Ashoka belonged to it. Kautilya, the noted economist also came from there. And the evolution of Jainism also began from the same land...'

'And the numerous revolutionists like Praful Chaki etc and Kunwar Singh, who led the 1857 sepoy mutiny from the region also hailed from Bihar...' Pavan added.

'You must thank me for how all of you have become wiser after the fight...' I said and others began to laugh.

And then there was the delicious lunch at last. Mom was nice enough to attend all of them so motherly.

24

23th December 2007

'Have you recovered from your injuries Tipu?' Dev asked.

'Yes Dada... it's more than three weeks now.'

'No doubt, it was a gutsy fight from you...'

'How do you know that?' Rohit blinked his eyes like a turkey.

'We were there at the moment. But I don't understand why you guys are wasting your talent and energy in such trifles? If you really want to fight, then do it for your fundamental rights. Do it against those people who are sucking the blood of others by ruling over them hereditarily. These social evils are still present in our society exactly as they were in the British times.' Dev said with the unexpected and persisting anger.

'O... Sukhdev, keep the voltage down and don't discharge that much current all at once.' Singh began to laugh at his lengthy monologue.

'He won't change ever.' RG also joined him and enjoyed the situation.

'What's wrong with you?' Dev looked baffled at the mimicry of the two.

'It seemed to me that you are delivering an ardent speech to the fellow members of our former party 'NBS' (Navjavan Bharat Sabha) in your college...' RG said.

'So what? These friends of mine make no difference to me...' He replied, 'And in fact, they look to be the new version of the same NBS, under the similar national circumstances at present. However I am not trying to mould them in our cast. I just wanted to instill some exemplary principles in them...' Dev reasoned.

'We are sorry for that...' Pavan realized and said to him with compunction.

'Do keep your spirits reserved for some bigger goals in life.' Singh tried to finish with the friendly advice.

'You are right Dada. We should set the bigger goals indeed, as you did when you blasted a bomb in assembly. Do you remember that?' Rohit suddenly put a strange question, and an interesting argument to place.

'Certainly we did that in 1929...' Singh smiled.

'Where you got the noble idea from?'

'I was inspired by the book "Anarchism and other essays".'

'And why you did so?'

'To stop the presentation of the public safety bill that day...'

'But why simply doing the blast without hurting anybody?'

'The blast was merely to mark the protest against British government.'

'And why you and other people were against the British Government?' Rohit asked in reply.

'We wanted the freedom and self rule...'

'Then kindly do a similar blast again...' He implored.

'Again?' They looked at each other and began to laugh.

'Yes! But to bring the Public Safety Bill in force this time..'

'And why?'

'Because the public need the safety more than it ever required before. And we demand the self-rule again also!'

'And what do you exactly mean by this self-rule?' Singh asked with frown, similar to that of an examiner.

'It is such a transparent governing system, that should be open to all those who desire to serve their country. It is such a novel democratic system without the existence of the parties and... and I don't know how to explain the exact structure of the same at the moment but...' He suddenly remembered something there and widened his eyes in astonishment.

'Dada... why are you asking the innocent questions? Do you really know nothing about it? That is impossible. I have got it now that you guys are just testing us here. Aren't you?'

'We know that you also want the same as we do. You are here not just to hear and tell the tales only. You definitely have some strong motive behind it...' I also corroborated.

'You are absolutely right!' RG admitted.

'And what that motive may be?'

'The same. To bring the freedom and self-rule to our countrymen...'

'And when and how are you going to do that?' I asked with impatience.

'Let's work it out carefully and it will be executed with your assistance. It is time for you also to do something...' RG said.

'We can't do it alone because it will be a long fight for us from British kingdom of the past to the Leader's kingdom of the present...' Singh said.

'You know Dada... this Leaders is incidentally a scrambled word. The right one is 'Dealers' instead.' VD provided interesting information at that.

And what about the Secularism... the main tool of the ruling class? Guruji asked as if to test her.

She began to think deeply.

Well... it gives a better sense as being Islam's-cure. She replied after some moments.

Absolutely right. Curing or giving the undue attention to muslims is what the secularism all about in India... He-man professed as a thinker

RG began to laugh at her magic.

'Just Very Dangerous!' He then uttered joyfully.

Very Dangerous What?' I enquired.

'This is what VD actually stands for. This Vandana can turn anything upside-down in a moment...'

Everyone gave her an appreciating smile.

'She is right Dada. Our country is reigned by the opportunists and the unworthy people. Our Parliament is the fine example of the same. It is choked with the 25% of the total MPs, who have the criminal records...' Pavan said.

'And the whole House do rejoice to sing in chorus.' I also added my sarcasm this way...

Mind and Body
Heart and Soul
We are Hooligans
Most of All.

The verses brought the laughs on every face this time.

'It's a superb piece of poetry but, merely cursing and criticizing them wouldn't do any good. It's time to open the eyes instead...' Dev Dada said seriously after a while to make everybody thoughtful.

'Remember... the thousands of Martyrs, whom Rohit saw in his dream last month, had not gathered there just purposelessly. Ah... how they struggled and succumbed to their ambitions for freedom! And where is that freedom now? Just imagine why they happily did that and what is the cost of their lost lives? Their souls are still wandering restlessly and they are asking the thousand questions. All the country folks today do stand liable to answer them.' Dev challenged this time.

'So what to do then? Should we stop casting our votes at all??' Pavan enquired in confusion and a series of testing questions ensued between both of them.

'To run away from a problem is not a solution at all. You must cast your votes to bring the worthy ones to power only.'

'And where to bring those worthy candidates from?'

'Why not try other if one is tainted?'

'There is not any... they are all the professional tradesmen like the British were.'

'Then the freshers should come to contest. 70% of the Indian population is below 35, but this country is being run by the rest of only 30%. type... why?' Dev argued.

'No party will allot tickets to them...' Pavan said.

'They can fight as independent contestants as well.'

'It's no use. They do become the part and parcels of the ruling party after winning.'

'All are not the same. Suppose it is you the next time?'

'The blunt question made him silent and thoughtful and he couldn't reply.

'Well... he will also do the same!' Kokul Guruji offered an answer this time.

'That's disgusting! I never expected that from you guys...' Dev gave up at last.

'Dada... Tell me what the shape of water is?' He asked.

'None! It simply takes the form of the container it is put in...'

'And if we put it in a Gutter?'

'It will become contaminated naturally...' Dev replied.

'Then how can we blame the water for that? The politics in modern India is the polluted business to invest and earn. This is the game of money and might. The name of the deadliest narcotic in the country is... Power!' Guruji argued.

'You mean there is no party in the country ideal to rule?' Dev asked desperately.

'Absolutely not!' Pavan said, 'All the parties have the same goal under the different banners. It is only to gain power by hook or crook and stay in there as long as possible...'

'They may however look different but they are actually hand in glove with each other. Luring the masses in the name of cast, creed, language, religion and unfair incentives etc is their secret agenda...' Rohit said.

'A voter is quite helpless, as he has to trust atleast one of them... and is finally made to shed his vote in the name of democracy and to repent his decision thereafter.' VD added this time and RG Dada asked in the end.

'Do you people know the meaning of democracy?'

'It is a Government chosen by the people...' I replied.

'Then who is to blame? You are suffering the results of your own deeds!'

'And why should I suffer for the deeds of others?' I reasoned.

'Who others?'

'You know it is mostly the backward and illiterate voters, who are making the governments in India?'

'So?'

'The elections are nothing more than a festival for them and they just relish it. They are not capable of judging right or wrong about the real nationalism and our constitution allows the parties to tap this rich resource legally...'

'Most of them are usually the blind supporters of a particular party or cast and their only goal is to cast the vote, without knowing its value...' He-Man said.

'Secondly, such class tends to sell the next five year of their future for some paltry temptations, offered by the parties...' VD said also.

'And sometimes they even happily exchange their votes for a bottle of liquor only.' Rohit gave his opinion.

'Then why don't the educated people like you take active part in the polling?' RG asked.

'Well... I can't say about others, but for me it is like being asked to choose the weapon I have to die with. And I am not even given the option to say no.' I said.

'But you can definitely say no here. The Section 49-O of our constitution gives the right to a voter to cast a negative vote. He can reject the contenders in the fray...' RG answered.

'And if the total negative votes do outnumber the

positive ones, the polling could be cancelled and the same candidates couldn't contest again even in the repolling, as the voters have already expressed their views against them...' Dev told this time.

'But how? This section is just safely closed in the books and is never listed in the ballot papers. It is surprising why the election commission has not exposed such a clause to the general public. They are clearly working as the associates of the parties.' I said again.

'Dada... Our country's cancer is this damned party kingdom, and you are asking us to nourish it more?' Pavan reasoned.

'It was a single East India company in ancient time but it is mainly two Pvt. Ltd. concerns now who are ruling over us almost alternately since the British departed...' Rohit said.

'And the same structure exists in every state and it comprises mainly anti-socials, corrupt and powerful as its directors...' VD said.

'We can still remember how some criminal MPs were brought from the jail recently, to help a particular party win the vote of confidence in parliament...' I said.

'So how can you expect us to reinforce such a sick, immoral and unfit political system? Tell me, is it the same India you people wanted to see?' Pavan demanded reasonably.

'I also have a question to ask Dada...' I hesitated.

Rajguru looked at me with approval.

'Although we love your company very much, but I am still confused about your clear and viable motive behind coming to us...'

'We have told you already and let's make it very clear to

you again. We are expecting a successful revolution this time, and it will take place with your help.' He exclaimed.

'Revolution?' All of us began to look at each other with a start. Were we going to fall prey to some conspiracy?

'Yes, it was quite incomplete when we lost our lives trying the same...' Singh said.

'But how will it take place in the present circumstances?' Pavan asked

'I think nothing can happen of the sort in this country now. It's quite hopeless situation...' Rohit said in a dull manner.

'The parties have such a strong base that either you die or accept the system...' Vandana said.

'And what do you think Tipu?' Singh looked at me with disappointment. Otherwise they were quite contented so far.

'I do also feel the same Dada...' I said slowly.

'Slavery has been rooted deep in the blood of Indians since the long long time. And now the family rule or the kinghood has been accepted as the real democracy in India by one and all...' He-Man replied.

'It was not Bapu or Chacha who brought the so called freedom to the country. It was only after the Second World War that England had become too weaker to rule and owing to the international pressure, they were forced to leave the country forever. Indians did nothing neither at that time nor can they do now.' Pavan expressed his terse views plainly.

Our argument made them speechless, but seemingly they were not happy with the proceedings and their moods were showing the signs of deep chagrin over our dismal show of inability.

'This system needs to be changed... as the change is the only constant thing in the world.' Kokul Guruji also expressed his views and took a deep breath.

'But how will this happen? No one can change the voters, and no one can change the politicians also. This business will keep going year after year quite as it is. Only some miracle can do this now...' Pavan looked quite hopeless and broken.

There was again an ominous silence at that.

So you people can do nothing at all? Singh enquired.

Nobody still spoke a word in the nervous moments.

'Shall we assume that we are at the wrong place?' Singh heaved a sigh at length and looked at his companions.

'A single spark can make big fires. Changes always come with the madness, but here is no sign of such ambition in anybody...' RG consented with him.

'Let's start our journey to find the right people for the job once again...' Dev also resigned and before any of us could say anything, the Trio slowly disappeared from the screen without any further discussions, leaving us in total bewilderment.

25

27th January, 2008
Sunday

It is now two months since we met them and their sudden departure was a real shock to us. Still, we hoped to meet them yet again as before. RT didn't appear last month and it made all of us so worried and dejected. Together, we often remembered their last words and discussed about our approach before them in December last month and asked each other, 'Were they really gone for good?' We also kept asking Kokul repeatedly, regarding any message from their side. But, there was not any.

Subsequently, we tried to forget the past events but couldn't. We had become so attached with them sentimentally that I often saw tears in Vandana's eyes at the mention of the trio. The weeks passed by and slowly we tried to busy ourselves in college schedule. But the days were so melancholy and different during that period.

We now, desperately wanted to do something unique like they did but we had no clue about what to do and how to prove ourselves. We desperately wanted our lost esteem back, but how? Fortunately for us, Rohit provided a chance to do so and it proved to be invaluable to us in the coming months.

However, I noticed a distinctive change in my friend's room during those days. Mayank had taken his idol of Hanuman Ji with him earlier and Rohit had adorned the same niche with the pictures of Singh, Dev and RG.

2nd February, 2008
Saturday 10.10 pm

It's a chilly evening today and I am sitting in my bed at the moment, all enveloped in a warm quilt and still thinking about the Red Triangle. The lonely night is shrouded in dense fog and darkness outside. The power supply is off in this locality for the last two days, owing to some major fault in the grid and our house inverter has already gone dead. This is the common occurrence in this northern part of the country during winters.

The fog however, is so beautiful and cool! It makes the life halt for sometime and works as a natural silencer as well. It is so quiet inside here in my room that I can hear the ticking of the wall clock like a gong.

A candle is burning steadily on the stand at the cornice of the bed behind me. And its yellow silky flame is lighting this page of my diary as I am writing these lines. It is making me drowsy too. But I am inclined to mention about an interesting encounter I had with Rohit this evening and it gives me a new hope

After dinner, I had gone to Huda sectors for some work, and was coming back when I decided to drop in at Kansal Bhavan for a while. I parked the bike and went upstairs. No one was in sight in the outer room. The pictures of Singh, Dev and RG adorned the same niche on the wall. I found Rohit operating his PC silently in the inner room. He was alone in the flat.

Quite lightfooted, I came behind him and positioned myself in such a way that he shouldn't see my reflection on the screen. He was surfing a website, and the very name of the same gave me a shock.

'Suicide without Pain? Have you gone mad Rohit??' I shouted in panic.

He jumped up in surprise to find me near so unexpectedly. But became at ease soon.

'Yes, I was trying to find an easy way to die.' He then answered sedately.

'But what is wrong with you all of a sudden?' I asked.

'I am left with no other option now. Our friends 'RT' are already gone and the same stupid Bapu-Monkeys are haunting me at nights these days and I am dreading the sleep.'

'So you have seen yet another weird dream again?' I began to laugh in relax.

'It is still shocking for me to think of the parting with our divine friends. I am fed up with my life now...' Rohit said.

'Let's hope they should come back. But, they have shown the way to us and we must do at least something for our country. They had high hopes on us and we disappointed them.' I said, but he didn't reply and remained silent.

'You are inconsistent with your yoga these days and need some exercise to have a profound sleep and get rid of the bad dreams...' I suggested again.

'I have lost my interest in the meditation these days and now those mocking-primates have drained all the life out of me...' He said desperately.

'Okay, ok! I am in a hurry to go and have only five minutes to listen to your nonsense...' I dragged a chair near him.

'And where are the other two descendants of the same primates?' I asked about He-Man and Pavan.

'They have gone to dine out, but let them go to hell. And suggest me some remedy if you can...' He became vexed.

'Come on buddy... the dreams always keep coming every night, so just open the eyes in the morning and forget the stuff. It is not such a problem at all.'

'That's what I am already trying to... but these hallucinations have blocked the very functioning of my brain.'

'It was blocked to some extent already. You need a pacemaker for your brain urgently.' I began to laugh and added after a while, 'But so sad... it is not being invented so far.'

He didn't reply and silently busied himself to open some window on the PC, and after having finished, he said.

'Look at this...'

It was a short animated clip, titled... 'The Awakening'.

It began with the same Dussehra ground scene as he had mentioned in the earlier meeting with the Red Triangle. The huge idols of the symbolic Ravana bros are tethered firmly in the center of a ground and are surrounded by the angels. The demons are in the form of Deaf, Dumb and Blind monkeys like before, bearing the badges on the chest I am the Voter and they are being riddled with the arrows of the angry crowd of Martyrs.

A caption flashes on the screen after a short pause.

"These three monkeys are the real Ravanas and deserve to be set on fire instead. These are the virtually deaf, dumb and blind Indian individuals who willfully and knowingly voted a wrong system to power for decades and ruined the country."

And the scene changes wonderfully soon after.

The motionless emblems appear to come to life for the first time in history. And surprise... surprise! They begin to breathe like human beings the next moment. Now the first of them removes his hand from the lips and begs to the almighty in earnest prayer. The rest of two also uncover their eyes and ears respectively to beseech one by one after him.

"Asto Ma Sadgamaya..."

O-Lord... Take me to the truth from the falsehood.

"Tamaso Ma Jyotirgamaya..."

Let there be light in my life, And,

"Mrityorma Amritam Gamaya..."

Take me to the immortality from death/

And with this, the wild monkeys do transform into the cultured ones. They are not naked anymore and a formal dress comes to their bodies to attire each. Allthough still tethered, they now get up from their slavish cuddles, and do stand upright in resolution side by side. The one in extreme right, raises his arm up with the clenched fist and demands in authority...

I want freedom!

Again the other in left also yells after him.

We want freddom!

And now the third and last in the middle, throws his arm up to shout out with command, and to be repeated in chorus by all three.

We want self rule.

Long Live Revolution!

A mirracle happens with this. Their fastenings do fall

down by itself to set them free and the small badges of the voters are replaced by the new ones at their shirt pockets, showing... 'The awakened Indians'

The moral upheaval of the nation is over, and the heavenly bodies seem to be quite contented with the change. They are now showering flowers and not the arrows over the 'three' to reward that notable reform. And there comes a mesage written in bold letters to conclude...

"Remember... No revolution can be successful unless the common man becomes awakened."

The wonder clip came to an end, and I got up in excitement.

'This is sensational man!' I exclaimed, 'You have changed the basic meanings of this age old monkey funda so impressively. What on earth made you do that?'

I don't know, but I have simply moulded my imagination into this animation to make everybody understand easily.'

'I have no doubt about one thing now...' I looked at him searchingly.

'What?'

'To make your brain work properly, you require a pace maker... absolutely not. Your mind is already running fast.'

'Thanks! And now to tell you one thing... I was not finding the suicide ideas for myself. You can consult me if you ever decide to commit the same.' Rohit said very seriously.

I didn't reply and got up. I then ruffled his hair with my hands in silent praise, 'Good night!' I smiled and came back from there.

Now, back in my room here, the window panes are at present covered with grey haze, and the same sleepy haze is covering me from within as I am thinking about the same clip. The burning candle at my back is throwing my own blown-up reflection on the wall to my left side.

Five minutes before from now, a surge of nap suddenly swept me and I saw the same short clip of Rohit in my dream. I woke up within minutes however, and than began to think deeply about the dreams.

Why do we see them at all? Do they simply represent our ambitions? Or do they reflect our failures? Do they guide us from the darkness? Or they are just the delusive labyrinths...

Post Script
Dated 7th March 2031.

I had left this page incomplete that night, twenty three years earliers. The sleep had simply gripped me and I was lost in myriad dreams again, with this diary lying open on my bed. The candle burnt itself out and I found the stand all filled up with wax in the morning.

Let me sharpen my memory for a while to recollect as I have to add a few necessary details here today to make the journal reasonably apprehensible. And why? Because I could find absolutely no record of events for the next five six months herein after february 2008.

Well, I can remember that our group did a wise thing the following week. We e-mailed the same clip to all the students in the college, with request to forward the same to the maximum number of people as possible, for the sake of nationalism. Quite wisely, we also included Jaiswal and Co. in our list later on. It was our enterprise to try improve the relations with them, although we were not so positive about getting any response from the boys.

In the meanwhile, our college life went on as usual. We still remembered RT whenever we all got assembled at college canteen and also at our favorite T-point, where we spent more and more time in the company of Yaksha Prasad in the following months. However our meetings with Kokul Guruji also continued and we became more and more curious to know more about the disappeared trio.

The days were although not as cheerful as they were before, yet they were going smooth and there was nothing unpleasant anymore. Then came the month of May, and it was the time of our summer vacations? I Got the unexpected reply from jaiswal during that time it read...

I had received your e-mail and went through the clip again and again. All the thanks for sending me this wonderful message. I found it so damn inspiring that I have forwarded it to all my acquaintances here and elsewhere since then.

It is to inform you that the clip is making its way fast to the students and others here in my city as well. I have also formed a Google-group on 'Gmail' for the purpose and am getting the overwhelming feedback.

Do keep me in reckoning as a friend from now on. Do also keep sending the other informative e-mails on the same Google-group of ours. Kindly accept its membership with your group. See you after the vacations.

With best wishes.

Jaiswal.

This was the surprising message from Jaiswal that I received at home. But it was so cool to read it in the scorching heat of the season. In the meantime, I kept frequenting the T-kiosk alone in the absence of my friends as they had gone home on vacations. Yaksha Prasad always gave me the valuable knowledge and tips as always, and I forwarded the same to the G-Group from time to time. Jaiswal & Co. had become our good friends during those vacations and it was a big achievement for us.

We had also decided to resurrect Navjavaan Bharat Sabha (NBS) in the memory of our beloved trio. Now, the G-Group was identified as NBS, and it had swollen to thousands of members by that time and was still flourishing exponentially.

Surprisingly for us, the awakening got circulated far and wide within a few months, and became extremely popular with the people of every genre. The featuring slogan uttered by the monkeys, was gaining tremendous attention everywhere. People began to realize for the first time that they really needed to open the eyes, and also that why did'nt they think about it before?

I would like to mention with great interest here that the slogan could soon be seen almost everywhere one can imagine. It was being printed on T-shirts and vests, on towels and handkerchives. Even on stickers and as monograms. Also on the back side of the tickets of the private buses, as the members belonged to different trades.

And how this magic had taken place?

One of the members of N.B.S. had begun an S.M.S. war, and slowely the short message clouded the millions of mobiles in the country. It was a plain and touching, maxim...

I want freedom and self rule.

Do you?

I dont know who the person was? But I do take my hat off to that hero!

However a 'single spark can make big fires'... were the last words uttered by RT, and we were happy that we had produced that spark at last. All we required now was the necessary fuel that could be ignited. But who was to guide and motivate us further?

We missed our divine friends so much. We needed them the most at that juncture. But it was heart breaking that they had left us so stranded.

26

My Diary, some day in the end of July 2008

Our college life went on once again after the vacations were over. But, all the usual excitement is gone and it is quite monotonous now. I had an individual project of animation still pending to work on. And now, it was to be presented immediately after the holidays. We were to make an animation clip of about two minutes each along with documentation. I am well adept in MM flash, so Sumit and He-Man relied on me for their projects. And knowing that I usually work at the eleventh hour, they had just waited in faith.

On the first day, I chanced my arms with volleyball for some time. I decided to return home in the afternoon to finish my work and as I came out of the ground, I encountered Vandana near the parking area. She had gone to Vidisha for holidays, so had not seen her since the last two months. She looked gorgeous as ever... but a shade pale in complexion this time. Her eyes sparkled feebly as she saw me.

'Hi Tipu... How are you?'

'Fine! When did you come back?'

'This morning only...'

'Are you alright?' I asked.

'Not feeling so well. I am dead tired from the journey...'

'Then go to hostel and have a sleep till morning... Simple.'

'Can't do that. I am tense about my project. Haven't done anything yet...' She said.

'That's not good, and we have to submit it tomorrow...

'Please help me do that...'

'But I have to go home. Mom is on fast and she must be waiting for me...'

'Is she almost always on fast?' She smiled.

'Not always...' I returned, 'Just once or twice a week. Why don't you also come along? We can finish our works there as well.'

She thought for a while and consented.

'Okay! It's a long time since I listened you play guitar...'

'But the work first.'

'No... the guitar first.'

'Okay...' I began to laugh and gave up.

At home, mom was waiting for me eagerly for lunch. She smiled naively to see VD and flowered her blessings on the girl. We went straight to the dining table as I was feeling hungry. I ate like a glutton, but VD took some salad only. We were in my study soon to start our work.

She was fond of my singing and playing guitar, so without a word I picked the instrument up and unzipped it. I adjusted the strings and did the testing with plectrum for some moments. I started with the chord.... 'Bm', and slowly reached the erescendo. Finally I was singing my favorite number from the eagles. The strings of guitar had now begun to release the melodious music in the room.

On a dark desert highway
Cool wind in my hair
Warm smell of colitas
Rising up through the air
Welcome to the Hotel California

I sang to her in my rhythm and she listened to it most contentedly. The song was not yet over, when Mom entered with chai and snacks in a tray. Knowing that I don't take tea after meals, she had brought only two cups. And handing one over to VD, she took the seat beside her. Both sipped silently while listening to me and as I finished, she began to scold me.

'Have you nothing else to do except wasting time all the day? You are going to fail in engineering.'

'Oooo... Mom!' I began to laugh and she turned to VD to enquire solicitously.

'How does he play Vandana?'

'It is so excellent Aunty...'

Mom's face glowed with pride. But, she again changed her color the next moment.

'He has obtained only 62% in the last semester... and now I am going to give his guitar away to the scrap dealer.'

' NOooo.... mom!' I cried out in protest and VD came to my rescue.

'Don't do that aunty. Music is so wonderful thing in the world. According to scientists, listening or playing just a few minutes of our favourite music everyday, releases nitric oxide in the body. It prevents build-up of blood clots and harmful cholesterol. It is like a tonic for body and brain!' She explained.

'Understood Mom? It is good for you also...' I was encouraged.

'Huh...' She turned her nose up and now focused her attention on VD to praise her dress. She wore a deepnecked Kaliyonwala (Flower-printed) salwar-suit of light maroon shade and the multistoned bangles to make a nice matching. But, I was wondering about the extra ordinary ability of women to change the topics so quickly. And also, about how versatile talkers they are! Finally, she left the room after some time, telling me that she was going to the Mandir. And I heaved a sigh of relief.

'These moms are the eighth wonder of the world...' I said and gave a sudden stroke to the strings.

She didn't reply. Her eyes were although rested on me, but the mind was elsewhere. She appeared quite mesmerized. Some moments passed and then I stroked the guitar again a bit loudly to attract her. It worked this time. She gave a start and the lucidity returned in her eyes.

'You were looking so cute in that absentminded gaze.' I laughed, 'Where were you lost honey?'

'You remember Tipu...' She got up from her chair and came to sit near me at the settee and continued. 'Kokul Guruji had once told that every one of us have an 'aura' around our body. It is called 'halo', and it is invisible to the eyes?'

'Yes...'

'And also that this halo has the different shades in everyone according to one's own Karma. And it exerts its own negative or positive impressions on the other people, who come into close contact with them?'

'Yes...'

'I have felt the same strange vibrations with me.' She

exclaimed. 'Whenever I come here at your house, my heart beats calm down considerably and I find myself at great ease...' She put her hand on her bosom to show.

'Really?'

'Believe me. You can feel it yourself...' and the next moment she took my hand in hers and placed it on her breast to feel. She inhaled a lot of air and closed her eyes in relax.

It was a never before experience for me. An electric current sparked in my body and my own heart raced @ 400 beats / min. I became restless... and it was not long when she felt my fingers groping around, and she removed my hand from the place abruptly. She gave a glare in the end.

'You are not trustworthy... naughty boy!'

'I was just trying to find your heart out...' I grinned sheepishly but she gave me another admonition at once.

'Good boys don't do the pranks... got it? Now tell me how to play guitar?' With this, she snatched the instrument from my lap and tried to hold it in right position.

'It is not a day's game Miss.' I advised but she had begun to fiddle with the delicate strings with her bare fingers so wishfully that I couldn't help smiling.

'Come on... tell me how to play?' She egged me on again.

'My God...' I shook my head in submission. Got up and came behind the settee, from where I stooped over her and adjusted the instrument properly under her armpit. I then took her fingers to place at the strings rightly and finally gave them the motion with her hand in mine. A broken tone began to flow out. But, she was mentally absent from that particular work too. Her grips suddenly slackened off, and she sang quite a different tune in deep voice.

'Tipu, you told me about your choice of the eighth wonder of the world and I also want to tell you about the first seven of mine...'

Her wayward suggestion surprised me, yet I gave her a short encouraging croon.

'Hmm...'

'To me, these wonders are not located outside, but are rooted within us. Don't you think that, to feel, to hear, to laugh or cry, to see, to taste, to touch and to love... these seven are the actual wonders of the world?' With these words, she tipped her head back to rest at the cushion, and raised her eyes up to look into mine above her, earnestly.

I couldn't answer and just stopped dead in the same crouching posture. She was so near to me that I was feeling her fragrance, and it was clouding me quickly. Her breath went straight down my veins like ale, and I began to loose my senses quickly.

Her moist lips fell slightly apart... as if inviting me, and they were only inches away from that of mine. I don't know what happened at that time, but within moments. Our lips were locked together and we were kissing each other with burning heat. I gave a support to her chin with my left hand to keep her face lifted up and kissed her more lustfully. She also entwined her arms around my neck and remained glued to me with desire.

The heat of passion was carrying both of us away... and the time flew merrily. We were heading towards the forbidden path blindly. But all of a sudden, the guitar slid from her lap and fell down on the floor with a dull sound. The humming of the hollow timber plucked us off our embrace, and we got separated from each other. The love express had come to a halt and soon we were trying to compose ourselves from our excited and disheveled conditions.

It was already 6 pm so we stuck to my PC without delay. I dropped her at the hostel gate well before 9 pm. She looked lighthearted now, and before going in... smiled sweetly to me.

'Thanks Tipu... I never imagined getting my work done so soon. Now, I can sleep peacefully tonight.'

'The credit goes to that wonderful kiss only. It was a big step towards our early success.' I said in a secret manner.

'Really?' She sharpened her eyes to kill me.

'It's not me but Guruji who had said. "Most of our worries are like thin fog that disappears by itself by taking a single step.'

'Shut up and good night!' She waved her fingers and walked away cutely.

And the next morning at college...

Himanshu looked formidable. He caught the hold of my collar and brandished his fist right in front of my face and clattered his teeth in retaliation. Sumit also stood nearby to assist him.

'You dirty dick-head... where were you last evening? Your cell was also switched off.' He-Man barked at me.

'It must be sounding out of reach...' I tried a ready excuse. 'I... I was out of station yesterday.'

'But who will make our assignment now?' Sumit asked rudely.

'I will do it... Don't worry.'

'Then move and do it right now...' He-Man dragged me to the computer lab straightway. I was made to sit down at once and mind my business from the world go: I began to Google the internet to download, and did the necessary changes. I worked clumsily and almost finished by 3 pm. During this time, I was kept under strict surveillance by both and was given a cold patty and a glass of water only. I was tired and hungry too.

'Both the clips are ready, now please let me go...' I pleaded at last. But, Sumit still objected to my request.

'How can you go without adding the introduction and documentation to it?' He frowned.

'But you can do it easily yourself...' I tried to explain.

'We can do nothing now. Finish the work soon...' He-Man ordered.

'You can't keep me as hostage anymore...' My anger began to rise and I got up from the seat. I took my pen-drive out of the pocket and tossed it on the table carelessly.

'You can copy that part from it...' I said and without waiting for any reaction, stamped my feet to outside.

I was preparing to go home that evening when both of them met me at the parking.

'Are you coming for the yoga this evening? It is long time we did it last time...' He-Man handed my pen-drive back to me and began very seriously.

'Let's begin from tomorrow. By the way, I have been visiting Guruji in your absence also...' I replied.

'Anyway, where had you gone yester evening Tipu?' He-Man changed the subject suddenly.

'I know that very well... he had gone to Prem-Nagar. Sumit answered before I could speak something.

'Prem Nagar? Where is this situated and how it looks

like?' He-Man wondered mockingly and I became more confused.

'What's this crap?' I asked.

'There is Vandana's assignment in your pen-drive and the time was 8:45 pm. You were doing her work at that time, and you are telling the tales to us here.' Sumit said to me coolly.

I was speechless and had nothing to reply. It was better to run from the spot, so I kicked my bike and sped away without a word. And there came a shouting from behind.

'Have some shame... you rabbit!'

27

7th September 2008

"Control your breathing and meditate on your inner light. Do compare it with a candle flame and don't let it move slightly. Focus your attention on the ultimate silence... as it is the voice of God. It heals the wounds of soul. Silence to mind is what sleep is to body..." Kokul was uttering slowly and deeply and we enjoyed his meditation sessions as always. But Singh, Dev and RG were never out of our minds while doing so.

'Aum Shanti!' He heaved a deep breath and concluded after some time. All of us opened our eyes and came at ease. Rohit asked him after a while.

'Guruji, where our Atma or soul goes to after death?'

He smiled before explaining and replied.

'There are many other worlds in this endless universe. And, where the soul goes immediately after leaving the body... is a complex subject to know about so easily. But, it keeps coming back like the reverberating sound waves... Sometimes on its own and sometimes on being summoned by somebody.'

'Couldn't you summon our lost friends yet again? Isn't there any way to locate the whereabouts of the RT?' Rohit asked with frustration, quite unexpectedly.

'I am afraid, there is none. Until they give some indication about it themselves...' Kokul replied.

'You have just told that the souls keep coming back like the sound waves. We might find them once again if you try...' VD begged wishfully.

'It is more than eight months since they have departed. And seemingly they are not around any longer. Maybe they are not interested to return...' Kokul said.

'But atleast, do try to invoke them this evening for our sake Guruji?' I also entreated abjectly.

'Please Guruji, don't say no...' Everyone began to insist in one voice after me.

He didn't reply for some moments and kept thinking. Then, he silently got up and motioned for us to come behind. And, so we did with the renewed hopes.

We were soon in his séance room after a long time. The same old fragrance could be felt around and I took some deep breaths. The place was very soothing indeed. My heart beats began to rise, as I looked at his CVP and other devices.

He took his seat immediately and commenced his customary process of invocation. He lighted the incense-stick and candle. Switched the PC and other instruments on and sat still with his eyes closed for some time. He had picked up his top-like instrument to move it in a circle over the black coloured keyboard. The semi-red screen on the wall had also become illuminated. And all of us stood there with our hands united in earnest prayers and the closed eyes.

Minutes ticked away. Kokul was muttering something and finally he gave a call.

'Hello... are you around Dada? Please come on to the screen. We are so anxious to see you again.'

We waited but nothing happened. He repeated the request many times without any result. The screen was still blank as before. Finally, Guruji gave up and looked at us in despair.

'I told you already that they won't come. And this is also not the 23rd day of the month...' He said and proceeded to switch his instruments off. Our faces sank with that.

But, suddenly a miracle happened in the room and it was Rohit who noticed it first of all.

'Stop it! They are here, they are back...' He began to shout like a small kid and pointed towards the screen. All eyes turned to the spot and Guruji withdrew his hand from the switches.

I saw a faded form of our familiar Red Triangle, glow and disappear on the blank screen of the CVP and my joy knew no bounds. There were many transitory glows of the Triangle one after the other. Slowly, the form became clearer and darker in shade. And soon it stayed there firmly and within moments it flashed brightly to dazzle our eyes. Suddenly, a voice struck our ears.

'Jai Hind friends...'

It were the Trio on the screen right in front of us again and we couldn't blink. They were smiling as usual and we were staring at them in disbelief. Nobody spoke for sometime and then there were tears of happiness in our eyes. VD and Pavan actually began to cry with emotions.

'Is everything alright?' Dev asked softly with the same warmth of intimacy in his voice.

'We missed you a lot since you departed...' Rohit began at last, 'It's long long months when we saw you last time.'

'We missed you too.' Dev said, 'And that's why we are back. Now, cheer yourself up!'

'We are sorry for we had disappointed you...' He-Man said.

'It's better late than never. We received The Awakening clip of yours, and it has worked to awaken us about you too.' Singh appreciated this time.

'But, we had not e-mailed to you any...' Rohit wondered.

The Trio began to laugh in response.

'It was a good work and your stimulating message is travelling fast across the country...' RG also opened his mouth.

'Where had you been all these months?' I asked.

'We were on our mission Discovery of India, and went to every nook and corner during this time...' Singh said.

'And what you discovered around?' I asked.

'It's a long story to tell, and will take much time. Let's discuss about it later on...' Singh replied.

'But we want to hear a lot from you Dada please...' VD implored with the tears still in her eyes.

'Well... It was a journey that had many suns and shades. We saw many shocking faces of our country during the course. On one side, we saw children dying with hunger and certain people wallowing in wealth on the other. We saw the legislators and officials having the boxes, full of black money and also the common people being crushed under the burden of taxes...' Singh took a pause while explaining and RG continued the travelogue after that.

'We saw the sale purchase of judiciary system and the denied justice to the distressed ones. We saw the ousted Kashmiri residents living the miserable lives in the camps at

Jammu, and we saw the Bangladeshi infiltrators enjoying the Indian citizenship and economy in the north-eastern states by the grace of the leaders...'

'We saw the super-rich Dalits (So called downtrodden) enjoying the luxury of reservations and other facilities, and the super-poor uppercasts + majorityclass being neglected by the governments to do the politics of vote. And, we also went into the hefty Swiss-Bank accounts of the traitors...' Dev finished this time.

'Do you also know about the secret Bank Accounts of them?' Rohit asked with surprise.

'Yes we do...' Singh said.

'Even the account numbers of the same?' Rohit gasped out.

'Yes, Bhagat has prepared a list of all. We all know well that he is so fond of reading and making notes...' Dev said.

'That's the hidden treasure I hinted at, during our very first meeting...' Rohit said in excitement.

'We were never uncertain about your talents Rohit...' Singh said and it brought smiles on every face.

'We were talking about your journey. What is the conclusion you arrived at in the end?' Kokul asked thoughtfully.

'It's only one. We must change the ruling system of the country.' Singh replied.

And then, there was a short but interesting session of GD (Group Discussion) between us.

'Do you guys have any suggestion about the supposed structure of the future legislature?' Dev asked in the end.

'First of all, it should not be based on parties.' Pavan began.

'How can we imagine the politics without the existence of parties?' Dev asked again.

'We don't need politics anymore. What we need is work and progress only.' VD said.

'It can also be a twoparty system like in USA.' Kokul argued.

'This is India Guruji, where the entire political class wants to enjoy the regal chair by hook or crook. It is virtually no opposition here. We have seen the instances of the archrivals having shaken their hands together to share the power when there was no clear majority for any one.' Pavan replied.

'This bi-party system is therefore, not effective here.' VD rejected the idea rightly.

'It should be open to every individual who is eligible for the job....' He-Man gave his opinion.

'And what should be the eligibility criteria?' Singh asked.

'There should be an age limit of 50 years for the area representatives. They must clear the IQ (Intelligence-Quotient) test + some psychometric tests, being organized by the states like the company recruitment procedure, at the same time, districtwise and nationwide. The tenure should be limited to 2-3 years and the willing Ex MLAs and MPs should be provided the Govt jobs as per their abilities.' He-Man took a short pause and continued...

'The top three ranked ones from every district after the tests should be brought before the concerned citizens through the local cable-network in a contest. It will be similar to the talent shows we see on the TV everyday and much more exciting than those absurd looking 'laughing and dancing' programs. Thus, the people could select one of the three to stamp it as a genuine democracy.'

'Right! And these interesting shows on the local cable could also get the easy sponsors to meet the expenses.' I consented.

'And how the people will cast their votes to the favourite candidate, featuring on the local cable?' Rohit asked.

'India is the IT (Information Technology) hub of the world. We can easily implement some method to replace the ageold and expensive voting system?' Singh replied.

'Exactly! We can provide a UIC (Unique Identification Code) to every voter along with a password, enabling him/her to vote through the Toll free number, SMS and through the Internet also. By this online process, we can save billions of rupees spent on polling by both, the country and candidates. And the voting percentage can also be increased marginally.' I replied this time.

'What if the willing candidate is illiterate or has some criminal record, as most of our present leaders do?' VD questioned.

'Do you think that even a small organization would provide even a low grade job as of a clerk to an illiterate or characterless person?' Rohit did the counter-question in return and answered himself after a while, 'obviously not! Then how could a whole nation be jeopardized by allowing such individuals to rule?' Dev answered.

None of us gave any reply or reaction at once and there was not any either. He was absolutely right. There were so many other hot discussions about judiciary, terrorism and national defence etc but RT's answer was very plain and only one.

Cut the roots of the existing poisonous tree and more than 99% of the needed reforms will come by itself with this change...

Everyone looked convinced with the absorbing debate at last and there was a lingering silence for some time.

'Do you have some doubts in mind Himanshu? You are looking so disoriented.' Dev asked him.

And He-Man commenced a quite different subject.

'I have no doubt about what you said, but dada, I am feeling something strange for sometime these days...'

'What?'

'Rohit is not sleeping at nights for a few weeks...' He said.

'That's all what has made you so worried?' RG smiled.

'I am worried because he has the tendency of sleepwalking also.'

'Really?' RG asked.

'Sometimes, he would even open the room door and walk out in the dark corridor...'

'That's no problem at all. You better place a candle stand, with a candle and matchbox near the door...' RG bantered.

'Like you view in the horror movies so often, when the resident ghost moves around in the bungalows at night...' Dev also added to the fun.

'It is not a joke Dada...' Pavan also said gravely, 'I have also seen him working secretly on his PC during certain nights. I saw him typing something at an abnormal speed yesternight also. It was well past midnight and I was disturbed from my sleep. I wanted to ask him about that, but I couldn't get up from the bed and was fast asleep soon again.'

'Why Rohit... what was so special to do at the dead of night?' RG asked him and he appeared obviously upset at the charge.

'I don't know what rubbish he is talking about?'

'Nothing to worry much, for this is a form of stress only. Rohit must devote some more time to yoga and meditation for the peace of mind...' Guruji tried to relieve him with his alltime remedy and the three Dadas wore a mysterious smile on their lips.

'You are smiling Dada... why?' I asked.

'Let me now disclose it to you all, that Rohit has not been doing some useless work at nights. He had been typing the reformed sections of the Constitution and Indian Penal Code, as dictated by us. The work is complete now and it is in the shape of a book...' Singh exclaimed to give us the shocks of surprise.

'But where is that book?' I gasped.

'Well... I know that you are quite good at window hacking, and the particular file is Super Hidden in Rohit's laptop. Now it is your work to help him open that...' He revealed and smiled.

Whatever he was saying was quite unbelievable to us and we stood stunned for sometime. Then, I took Rohit's laptop and followed the specific path to open the Super Hidden files...

Start> Run> Type 'Regedit' and hit enter.

On the left side, there were certain folders and I took the thread as follows.

HKEY_CURRENT_USER\ Software\ Microsoft\ Windows\ CurrentVersion\ Explorer\ Advanced\ SuperHidden

Right click on the key and Select 'Modify'.

Set the registry value to '1'.

Click "OK" and reboot for changes to take effect.

And I finally found the file named Red Triangle in a super hidden folder on the desktop.

The content was in the form of an e-book. It took me some time to remember the right path to reach there. I was doing my work and Dada's were preparing to leave.

'Take it easy. You have a lot of time to do it. Go through the contents carefully. You guys have more than two weeks, before we meet again to discuss about the subject. We'll be back on 23rd of the same month...' Dev said.

They motioned to leave, but we won't let them go so easily this time and we became impatient.

'Are you going Dada?' VD asked.

'Yes, we are...' Rajguru replied.

'But please don't disappear like before...' She begged.

'Hope you will not forget us again...' Pavan also said.

'You are always in our hearts, quite like the one billion other Indians, and it is they who have forgotten us instead.' Dev replied.

His words sealed our lips and then they were gone as ever.

The Secret File
21st September, 2008

During the previous two weeks, we all tried to read the same e-book again and again but it was too complex to understand so easily. The distasteful literature irritated us in the beginning, but slowly, it aroused our interest and we scrutinized it together deeply.

It was composed in two parts. The first one was about

the constitution and the second one being about the IPC (Indian Penal Code). There were the notes of hundreds of sections, clauses and references of the original prints and then followed the meticulous amendments of the same, made by the RT very adroitly. It was notable that all the given reforms were the same, we have been discussing together all these years.

It was a hard and sophisticated work done by the masters and it actually reflected 'India of their dreams'.

Only two days are left for our scheduled spiritual meeting and we are waiting for that keenly. Every single day is trudging along like a long year.

28

23rd September 2008
7.30 pm

They appeared in the séance without delay this evening and after the routine exchange of courtesies between us, Dev's eyes rested on Rohit and he couldn't help asking.

'Why are you looking so serious Rohit?'

'Dada... how you people came to know about the certain sections of the constitution and IPC?' Was the very first and plain question that Rohit put before them.

'That's very simple! Bhagat is so fond of reading and he has gone through it many times. We do so often discuss together about the worthless sections of both' Dev answered.

'You have found out many flaws in the IPC...' Rohit told.

'Well... the Indian Penal Code was drafted by a Briton to protect the ruling Britons from the Indians. It gave them tremendous powers and made us handicapped before them...'

'We were always against it and Brother C. Aazad had openly censured the act, but it is still unchanged since then' Singh asserted.

'But why?' Rohit asked.

'It is only up to you to calculate ...'

'I will tell you why?' Pavan said, 'It was intentionally kept intact by the new rulers for the purpose of keeping us down trodden as before.'

'And still it is democracy by the people?' I asked.

'By the People or buy the people?' He-Man asked.

'Let's stop the criticism any more...' VD changed the subject and turned to Singh to ask, 'Dada, if you are still fond of reading, then you must also have finished the Lenin Book that you had left unfinished on your last day?'

'Yes I have. He had been my favorite character.'

'I wonder how one can behave so naturally, like reading a book in such a grim situation?'

'What situation?'

'I mean...'

She couldn't explain further and Singh did it himself.

'Do you know that Pandit Ram Prasad Bismil was doing his routine exercise just before the hanging? That my Idol Kartar Singh Sarabha had put on 8 kgs after hearing his death sentence? That thousands of those martyrs whom Rohit saw in the ground were just proud of this achievement? And that... this Raj and Dev were waiting for the 'Rope' like an outbound passenger does for the departure anxiously. Do you know why? Because everyone of them had the same purpose in mind, and it was to offer only the fresh flowers to their Motherland... and not the languished ones!' He finished in single breath

'You people had no fear of death at all?' She asked.

'Everyone of us have to get that one day...'

'But how, when one knows that it is just a few hours away?'

'I never experienced such a thing... so I can't answer that.'

'Dada... we want to see your last moments in jail please.' I made quite an unexpected demand all of a sudden.

There was a stunned silence for some moments and then others also began to raise the same voices. And it made the trio extremely surprised.

'You mean that you want to go to the Central Jail to view our assassination?' Bhagat Dada asked.

'Yes!' We all nodded like kids.

He looked at his friends and RG tried to skip the topic.

'We shall try for that sometime, but why do you want to go there at all?'

'You guys were really crazy. We want to see and feel your amazing and unyielding spirits till end...' I said.

'Amazing are those soldiers who march to their deaths happily on the frontiers, to protect their country from the enemies. Only that one is the sacrifice of the highest calibre. We are not even the shadows of such daredevils!' RG said gravely.

'Do you have any such ideal?' I asked.

'There are so many, but I would like to mention about a couple of them. One was Khudiram Bose of Midnapur, who opposed Bengal division in 1905, and was hanged on 11/08/1908 at Muzaffarpur Jail at the teen age of 19 only...'

'And the other one?' I asked again.

'It is Major Shaitan Singh and his resolute army of 122 soldiers.' RG replied.

'Who was Major Shaitan Singh?' Pavan asked.

He didn't reply for some moments, and Dev enquired from us seriously this time.

'Do you know who Michael Jackson' is?'

'Yes, we do...' Almost all replied in unison at once and were ashamed of ourselves the next moment, when he congratulated us.

'I must greet you guys for your good knowledge about the Rockstars but alas! You know nothing of your own National Stars who were like the real Rocks.'

We had no answer to that and Singh Dada began to tell us about him.

'He was the commander of a small company, who fought with the mighty Chinese during 1962 war. And the way they did so, was unparallel and it has become the greatest war ever being fought anywhere in the world.'

'We want to know more about that encounter Dada...' VD requested.

'Well, this heroic tale was written in Ladakh sector, and the writers were few of those who walk the earth with the deathwish in heart' And he began to tell about the same.

'It was the year of 1962 and the war with China was in full swing on almost every front. At that time, one hundred and twenty odd soldiers of Kumaun regiment, forming the three different platoons, were posted to protect the strategic pass near Chushul peak at 18000 feet. The name of this army was Charlie-Company. I remember it was the same November month and may be an early dark morning of 18th, when the Chinese attacked.'

'This company had the ordinary 303 rifles with limited ammunition, and their uniforms were also not capable to tolerate the sub-zero cold. Whereas the intruders were well equipped with automatic machine guns and suitable outfits. Yet our soldiers played such havoc with the enemy that they ran all around like rats. Only the handful of those intrepid men brought doom to more than 1000 Chinese, and one killed ten of them at an average.'

'We saw them stabbing the enemies even with the bayonets fiercely when there were no bullets in the end. Finally, all of them lay dead by the same evening, but held their points firmly till last. Everyone of them still gripped the rifle in his hand when he breathed his last!'

Singh took a short break here, as all of us listened with extreme devotion. He continued again after a while, but he was seemingly lost somewhere this time.'

'The great festival of Diwali was around and being away from their homes, they celebrated both Diwali and Holi at the same time together... with bullets and blood. Imagine... the whole company gave its life away to the nation till the same evening! They knew already that there was no comeback from that snow desert, yet they strode on into the valley of death quite daringly and happily. It is a tale of matchless bravery and endurance. And it was the purest offering of fresh and fragrant flowers at the feet of dear Motherland. All of them died like champions in the end...'

His eyes suddenly got filled up with tears, and we were shaken to see that he had begun to cry silently. Dev tried to say a few finishing words, but he too was down with sentiments and couldn't speak properly.

'They are the ones who are eternal even after the death.' Singh said somehow and there was a lingering silence after that.

'And we are the ones who are dead even while being alive!' Pavan commented at last.

'Our thousand salutes to those all and countless others

like them...' RG said this time, 'How we wish, we were the soldiers of the same Charlie Company... as we always wanted to die like one. Bhagat had even requested the British authority from the Jail, to shoot him like a soldier but...'

He heaved a sigh and fell silent.

'You really saw that particular battle by your own eyes?' He-Man asked.

'Yes!' RG said.

'Live on the spot?'

'Of course... and it was quite unbelievable to see those great warriors in action.'

'Can you go anywhere and anytime you want to?' It was Kokul Guruji who asked this time.

'Yes, we can.' RG replied again.

'And were you still there in Afghanistan when the Taliban were piercing the grand statues of Lord Buddha madly with bullets and cannon balls at Bamiyan?'

'Yes, we were there at the moment.' He admitted.

'What?' Kokul was shocked and his voice became emotional, 'And you still didn't try to stop them?'

Singh now gave him a sympathetic smile before speaking.

'Try to understand Guruji... we can do nothing material on our own. You are a knowledgeable person and can understand that we do exist in the subtle forms only. We have no bodies to do the worldly acts. But we however, can give our powers to some human being or beings, who are worthy and are willing to act on our behalf...'

'And don't worry, the days of such Taliban type outfits are numbered now. It won't be long before those grand statues will be resurrected with the equal grandeur...' Dev assured him.

Kokul realized the fact soon and looked remorseful. Rohit on the other hand had also become so inspired like others, that he couldn't help speaking.

'Dada... we do have the strong will and bodies to act for you. Do tell us as to how can we bring the complete freedom to our country? I am also a young and fresh flower and I also want to die for my Motherland as you people did.' He offered passionately.

'I also want the same... many voluntary voices came up from us instantly, and Singh's eyes began to shine at the dedication in such a way that it was difficult to encounter them.'

'Superb. I can see none other than Batukeshwar Dutt, Jatin Das, Ashfakulla Khan, Veer Savarkar, Mangal Pandey and Durga Bhabhi reincarnate in all six of you!' He exclaimed and began to clap for us. The other two also joined him.

What I remember even to this day was that it was just great feeling for me to be honoured by the great men like that.

'We knew that you guys are different and that's why we are here. Let's celebrate the spirit and call out unanimously once again...' It was now RG who invited and commanded .

'Inquilab...'

'Zindabad!' The reply was quick and spontaneous from us.

'Let's say Vande Mataram...'He jerked his arm up again.

'Vande Mataram!'

'Remember... giving your life is not the only way to do the sacrifice. You can also do so while being still alive. It is 'you six' who are going to finish our unaccomplished work with the help of your so gifted intellect.' Singh revealed in the end.

'But how and when?' Pavan was so excited by the proposal.

'Do have some patience and the time is coming fast now. You will soon be engaged to do the most important task for the country...'

'And what to do with that particular Secret File? VD asked.

'You are not the small kids,yet to learn how to walk? Tell me what was your purpose of floating NBS? And what are you going to do with that??' Singh frowned.

'We are sorry Singh Dada... I have already decided the next step. I will e-mail the amended contents of the Secret File to all the members of the NBS nationwide to know about their reactions....' Pavan did the correction.

'Is that sufficient?' RG asked.

'No, I have found the e-mail ID of President also. It is presidentofindia@rb.nic.in. I am going to e-mail a copy of the same to him along with The Awakening clip with the request to acknowledge soon as he is the highest authority of the nation and he can't ignore it.'

'That is what we expected from you.' Dev appreciated with an encouraging smile.

Pavan's idea surprised us greatly at first and then we felt proud of him. He was a real revolutionist in the making.

'Wait for the reply till we meet you again on the same day after the two months from now...' Singh bade the goodbye and they were gone again.

29

25th September 2008

We dispatched the necessary contents to both 'NBS' and the 'President' yesterday through the e-mail. And today we were mentally refreshed to take up the very interesting presentation of our crucial project that VD had prepared at my home previously.

Earlier in the day, Macromedia Flash lecturer Mr. Adit inserted a CD in the system and announced.

"Students! All of you have done the hardwork to make some superb clips. It was not easy for me to do the proper grading of all, but here are two of them that got the highest marks. Some of you might like to view them. The reason why I have chosen them is that the makers of both have tried something different."

The first work of animation, that came on the screen was worked up by Pavan and was titled.

'Vande Matram.'

Some cartoon characters of small students and their teacher appeared while viewing an old black and white movie 'Jagriti' in a school. And a popular song was going on.

Insaaf ki dagar pe
Bachcho dikhao chalke
Yeh Desh hai tumhara
Neta tum hi ho kal ke...

The movie finally came to an end, and a curious looking small boy who was greatly inspired by the film and song came to his teacher to ask.

'Sir, I also want to be a leader in future...'

'Shabaash! The children like you are the proud of the country.'

'But what should I do for that?' The boy held his chin.

The teacher scratched his bald head to think and replied.

'Well... you have to do nothing much my son. It is a very easy task in fact. Tell me if your parents are doing the politics already?'

'No sir...'

'Is your father a don or some notorious type of criminal?

'No sir...'

'Then your parents must be very wealthy or famous?'

'No sir...'

'That's very disgusting. You have absolutely no chance to lead your country in that case, so forget it.'

The boy could not speak and the teacher said again.

'However, there is only one thing for you to do...'

'What sir?'

'Just study hard and grow up. Then try to find a job for

yourself. Your destiny now is to cast your vote in favour of any of the mentioned class of people and serve them for the rest of your life...'

'Vande Matram!'

The poor boy fell flat on the ground on hearing this and fainted!

The animation earned a loud applause from the class.

And the other one made by Vandana. was titled...

'The other side of a coin'

It contained no knowledge or message like that of Pavan's. It was just a superb piece of scrambled mimicry that cheered the whole class up. It featured the interaction between two cartoons... a boy and a girl each. The latter stood near a photostat sized machine, and told the boy about her innovation and its qualities.

'I have made a device that brings out a hidden woman from inside of every man. All we have to do is to write his full name on the back of his Postcard sized photograph and drop it in the slit here. It will instantly come out of the other slit from there...' She pointed. 'And you will see that it has changed into a woman.'

'Look...' She said and began to insert the cards into the slit one by one. They popped out from the other the next moment. The innocent looking cartoon boy just looked at every converted photograph clapped in glee and let out a prankish giggle. Few of them were as below.

Narendra modi / Mandodari	*(converted)*
Rahul Gandhi / Dulari	*---do---*
Sachin Tendulkar / Tulika	*---do---*
Paresh Raval / Sarla	*---do---*

Ghulam Nabi / Mubina	*---do---*
Shahrukh Khan / Rukhsana	*---do---*
Aamir Khan / Kiran	*---do---*
Nitish Kumar / Sunita	*---do---*
etc.	

There were about three dozen such displays one after the other. It was very funny to see men converting to women... along with the proper attires and make up also! The whole class enjoyed the clips. The thumping followed at every change. It may be peculiar to mention that some of the faces looked more attractive and suitable as females.

30

Two days after, it was a friendly Volleyball competition in college. Our team had just lost to the adjoining Senior School boy's team shamefully and we now relaxed near the college temple, waiting for the next match to commence. I was a bit dejected as I was not able to deliver the services from my position at the centre as usual.

Jaiswal and his group were also with us and we all sprawled here and there leisurely. It was hard to imagine that we had been sworn enemies just a few months before. The boys from both the groups were now on very friendly terms with each other.

Meanwhile, a group of small students also stood solemnly near the boundary wall to watch the games. My thoughts began to drift while looking at them. All my friends and some other boys and girls also sat or stood around. I was silent so Abhinav placed his hand on my shoulder and enquired.

'Are you still thinking of the defeat?'

'It was a bit disheartening to loose to the school boys, but they have really played well...' I said.

'They are the nation's future to come after all...' He began to laugh.

'That's what I am trying to find out in these small kids. They are reminding me of that animation clip of Pavan.

'You are thinking about that? Good Lord... that's why you didn't play well today?' Jaiswal said.

'What do you think about that, I mean about Pavan's work?' I turned to him.

'No doubt... there is absolutely no chance in politics for the millions of youngsters like us.' Jaiswal answered.

'This damn Democracy is in the grip of a few dozen ladies and gents only, since 1947...' One of the JCBs commented.

'Brown Sahibs succeeded the White ones and we got the freedom. What a joke! Ha ha ha...' Another JCB also ridiculed.

'Yeh desh hai tumhaara, neta tum hi ho kal ke... my foot! We are fated to just cast our votes in favor of these kings and queens as long as they live.' Abhinav said.

'No... as long as we live! Their generations are coming up to take their places...' Jaiswal said.

'I wonder how this squeaking wheel is still moving on?' Sumit said and Pavan also shared his views at last.

'It will stop and break down soon. Everything is mortal on this earth'

'Yes. Even "Saas bhi kabhi bahu thi" has also come to an end...' He-Man proffered this time. He then inserted his index finger straight into his ear and began to give it a violent shake and his manner frustrated me.

'Think of your career boys. Time is difficult ahead.' I changed the subject.

'What do you want to say?' Abhinav asked.

'We are not the damned leaders. All we have to do is to find the jobs for us...'

'Hold on...' He-Man took his finger out of the ear and sniffed at the tip of it tastefully to feel more comfortable.

'But why do you worry? Almost all of us have already got

the offer letters' He then said at ease.

'I think you should stop day dreaming now...' I said.

'Are you talking about the US sub-prime crisis and the recession?' Pavan asked.

'Yes. The companies have not only stopped the new recruitments, but are sacking the existing employees instead.'

'Our jobs are not safe any longer and the game is in the hands of merited ones now.' Jaiswal said.

'And what will happen to all others?' Abhinav asked.

'They can apply for the post of security guards of the V.I.P's.' He-Man commented again and began to laugh.

'More difficult time is coming ahead for country's majority class, with the increasing reservations everyday...' Someone said.

'I think 'sex education' should be provided to the non-reserved class to help increase the overall percentage.' Rohit also gave his different suggestion as usual.

'That will be a great option for any collegiate! 99% of them are going to score 99% in the subject.' Sumit consented at once.

'Exactly! Our fellow Indians are the great people already. They do know about the secrets of this art very well even without learning.' I said.

'That's why we are more than a billion today...' Jaiswal said.

'And still increasing rapidly...' Abhinav added.

'And who teaches the animals? They do it more perfectly and confidently than we nuts do.' Pavan extended the argument.

'You are right. Even a small piglet of a few months knows well how to screw?' I said.

'And you can see one of the bloody bastards, trying so in the streets of a slum locality of any town... any time!' Rohit gave a finishing touch to bring the hearty laughters around and behind, the girls chuckled slyly including VD.

31

23rd November 2008

'Guruji, it's getting late and our friends must be waiting for us...' I reminded impatiently after the meditation and then we all headed towards the séance room following Kokul.

He took his seat immediately and commenced his customary process of invocation. Soon there was the familiar Red-Triangle flashing on his CVP and the three Dadas appeared inside.

'Jai Hind friends!' Dev Dada cheered with a smile, and they took the seats. We also returned the same slogan in response. The rendezvous began with a queer silence from us. We were so curious after those two months that we wanted the business from the world go! Singh Dada looked at each of us searchingly and asked.

'Why are you all so silent today? Didn't get any reply so far?'

'We did get the overwhelming response from the co-members of the NBS. They returned the feedback of almost every minute change...' He-Man began.

'But sorry to say there is not a single word from the respected President so far.' Pavan added. He is also getting thousands of 'I want freedom' S.M.S. every day.

'I have also sent the mail to his office repeatedly.' Rohit told.

'' He is not going to respond at all. The best way of denial is to just keep silent... VD opined.

He will have to react sooner or later. The pressure is building up slowly, so let him take his time. We all know that he is such a busy person and we must think positively' Singh gave the assurance.

Nobody moved and just looked expectantly at the Trio.

'So, what to do then?' Singh asked after a while.

'We want to go to jail.' VD said plainly.

'Go to jail?' Dev began to laugh.

'Sorry friends... that's not possible.' RG objected to the proposal and VD shifted in her chair impatiently to complain.

'But you had made a promise Dada... please!'

'Try to understand Vandana. It will require the nerves of steel to behold that gory incident of our hanging.'

'Come what may! But it has great personal values for us...' Rohit said adamantly.

'I think we shouldn't break their hearts and they might also get some needed motivation from that...' Singh tried to reconcile his unwilling partner and RG shrugged helplessly in response as a result.

'What do you say Guruji?' Singh now turned to Kokul.

'You are right Dada, It will work as the wonderful inspiration for the guys, and they need it too! All of them are strong at heart as well. I wish I were also with you, but I shall stay at my duty here till you come back. So good luck to all and happy journey...' Kokul raised his thumb in farewell.

'Hum...' Singh grunted thoughtfully and said to us this time.

'Okay... but don't forget the same instructions again that you may have vague perceptions and fancies like you do experience in a dream. And also that you may undergo the matter related realistic feelings, once you are in a trance. So be careful...'

Singh took a short break here and Dev did the continuation on his part.

'And within moments from now, you will find yourself in Lahore again. Now, just imagine that you have become invisible to others during this time. Nobody could see, feel or hear you, but you can do that all. So do concentrate and get ready to go...' And he began to cast his steady spell.

I felt as if a merry-go-round was taking me higher and higher. I remember very well that my hair had stood on end. All of us were raring to go in such a way that the runners do at the starting post. We loosened our hands to relax and closed our eyes to hear when our spiritual Guru Kokul, exhorted in a calm voice.

'Aum...'

'Aum...' We all chanted solemnly after him and there came the slow and hypnotic voice of Singh.

'You guys are now going to Lahore. It is 23rd March of 1931, and the day is Monday. The time is 6pm in the evening...'

Our senses were slowly swept away and we went into a trance while still hearing his words. The scene changed quickly thereafter. It was a partly cloudy afternoon. And we stood in front of a big jail. The high stone walls of the prison extended to both of our sides.

Many excitedlooking people were gathered outside the main gate. All of them were anxious to know about the fate of the three patriots. A Sikh and aged gentleman who had just come out, was trying to cool them down. He was Sardar Kishan Singh Ji, Bhagat's father.

'I was not allowed to meet him for the last time...' He moaned out in grief and there were the angry slogans of disapproval from the crowd.

'This is injustice...' Someone shouted and so did the many others. Agitation and anger was rising up and passing across them we were right in front of the main entrance soon.

We stopped dead there to see an armed Sikh Sepoy, guarding it alertly. His appearance frightened us and we dared not to come near. The small side gate was opened, and we could see some movement inside. May be some released inmates were preparing to leave.

'Enter.' Pavan pushed me from behind.

'But he won't let us go in...' I pointed to the fearsome Sardar.

'He can't see us fool... we are invisible now.' He scolded and went forward to be very close to the guard. He then stepped inside the gate without any fear and without being noticed by him as well. He then waved us to come also.

Assured now, we also followed one-by-one carefully and rushed immediately inwards. On the way, while crossing the Jailor's office, I saw the wall clock inside telling 6 pm. We were in an open ground shortly, where there were the one storey building blocks all around. We stood there for sometime, just casting a searching look about, and wondering where to find the prisoners in question? The evening had come down and there was a deathly silence in the whole premises.

Right then, a few British and Indian officers came out of the offices behind, and rushed past us so close that one of them brushed me and Rohit together, and we had to move away from their path in alarm. But smiled as we realized immediately after, that we were merely the apparitions now and not the regular human beings to have the worldly worries.

However, being unable to decide what to do next, we began to follow them at random. Turning at many bend-ups and passing through the corridors and pathways behind them, we finally reached an enclosed place which was surrounded by the high walls from all sides. There was a raised platform at one side and the ominous vision right there, sent the very feeling of horror down our spines. That was the gallows!

Three brand-new rope halters hung thereupon in a row and waited thirstily for the preys to come. The ropes were suspended from a strong wooden framework above. And further, three lifesize weighty effigies were made to stand below the each halter, with their necks ensnared inside the loops, and their feet resting on the planks below. Three long black baglike cloth headgears lay neatly on a stool near the wall. And fixed on the ground below near the platform were some mechanical accessories, like levers, handles... etc.

That entire place wore a haunted look and some jail staff was busy in brisk work in that death-workshop. They were preparing for a rehearsal of the hanging. All of them stood in attention at the entry of the officials. The Magistrate and Jail Superintendent climbed the steps to the platform and inspected the proceedings for a while. One of them groped at the rope to feel the strength and the other tried to push the wooden planks at the floor with his shoe and asked the hangman, who stood at their service solemnly quite like a ghost.

'Why Mr... everything alright?'

'Yes sir!'

'Shall we test try the execution?'

'Okay sir...' He said and took his position at the lever dutifully.

The officer now raised his wrist and looked at his watch. He was a squarefaced and cruel looking creature, quite fit to be an executioner himself.

'It is 6:45 pm... ready?' He raised his other hand up and brought down suddenly with a jerk. The hangman pulled at the lever and planks fell down with a thud. The effigies disappeared below in the dungeon in a split second and the performance brought a thirsty smile at the barbaric face of the Firangi.

'Excellent!' He chirped in murderous glee and then peeped down, where the effigies had gone. He now ordered the Indian Jailer who stood silently below the platform.

'Only thirty minutes are now left for the execution officer. So get the things tidied up fast.'

The Jailor silently and sadly embarked on to give the necessary instructions to his staff, and I looked at my friends with some concern.

'But where are they shut in this honeycomb of this prison?'

'It won't be easy for us to find them out... and the time is running out.' VD responded.

'Hurry!' Pavan became excited at the answer, 'Let's go to find them in their cells...' He turned and began to run towards the inner area, and the rest of us following close on his heels.

Quite unknown to the place as we were... we strayed on our way back in the meandering and came to the barracks where hundreds of other prisoners were kept. I found all of them restless and angry. They were talking about the same premature execution of the three. I overheard one of them deploring badly.

"This will be the blackest day in Indian history and it has never happened before. These fair-skinned beasts are going to kill the brave young men this evening only... And one day before the scheduled time"

Another sore voice struck my ears on the bend-up ahead, where an inmate implored to the Jail barber, while holding his hands firmly through the bars.

"You have already brought a pen and a comb to Ehsaan Ali and Virendra respectively, as the token of parting gifts from Bhagat Singh. Kindly bring something to me also from Rajguru and Sukhdev."

"They have donated all their belongings to the friends around already and they have not the much time left for them now..." The barber answered somehow before he should start crying and went quickly away.

I had halted there, to hear for a moment and then started to run again. Pavan was leading and I was trailing behind all. I was not sure where were we going to, and exactly where the condemned cells were situated in that vast prison?

But, I soon found myself in Ward No-14, and right in front of none other than Rajguru's cell. My other friends were not visible to me at the moment. I however, looked inside and suddenly couldn't believe my eyes to see the real personality of the mighty revolutionist, who made the British shudder with fear. I came closer to the bars and fixed my thirsty and wide opened eyes at the icon.

He was sitting on the bed... all ready to go. His face was resplendent with some divine light and he was crooning some folksong in his mother tongue Marathi. I was thrilled and shocked with surprise when he suddenly looked up at me and blew out a whistle from his lips. The next moment, I noticed some movement on my left and turned my face to see two cops, opening the lock of his cell door. Their hands were however, trembling while doing so.

So the whistle was for them and not for me... I realized and slid myself aside. The wretched metal door opened to inside with a creaking sound and I also sneaked into the cubicle behind them. I stood myself cautiously at the foot of his bed for some moments. I ran my hand over it to feel and then took it to my forehead with reverence. I then waited for the next moment silently. My heart was pounding fast. The two cops also just stood silent in front of him... unable to speak. The stalwart prisoner, however, gave them a sharp and searching eye and asked authoritatively.

'Is everything ready over there brothers?'

'Yes sir...' one of them replied while trying to stifle his emotions. Rajguru got up from the bed and prepared to leave. He put on his slippers, trimmed his hair and cloth with the fingers in a keen manner... as if he were going to some party instead. Finally, he came out of his cell, where he let the cops tie his hands behind as per the rules.

Just then Sukhdev also appeared from his cell followed by the cops a little away from there. He stretched his arms up at leisure and yawned carelessly to shake the lethargy away. RG looked at him and greeted with vigour.

'O... Sukhdev! Our train has already come to the station,

and you are not ready yet?'

'I was just dozing off yaar... but thank God! I will sleep on my birth soundly now.' He replied and let the cops tie his hands also in the meantime.

'And where is Bhagat?' He then tried to find him out around.

'I am here friends.' Came the energetic voice from the farther corridor and both saw him walking towards them in a royal manner. Two other cops also followed him. I saw VD and Rohit were coming behind him, and two other, He-Man and Pavan were already standing near Sukhdev.

'Sorry for being late...' Singh regretted as he came near and revealed, I was trying to finish the biography of Lenin. But you know, some things do remain unfinished in life at last. Now, it is time to move friends... lest our train should leave. He then turned and roared like a Lion!

Inquilaab...

Zindabad!

Inquilaab...

Zindabad!

Inquilaab...

Zindabad!

The slogans rolled like thunder along the dark corridors and reached every nook and corner of the Jail at once. The sickly silence around was thus, broken eventually and the responding slogans began to rebound in the hundreds of gloomy barracks. Slowly... a mixed hue and cry began to emerge from all sides. And amid that very unusual welcome... the three carefree men strode on towards the scaffold.

They were singing in passion on the way and thousands

of prisoners around in the barracks were calling Zindabad to their names. The latter were shouting, waving and shaking the barred doors violently in protest. We were also following the condemned 'heroes' closely, circling around them just like the butterflies do hover around the flowers. We were wishfully touching and feeling each of them again and again.

'You know...' VD caught me by the arm and said in a strange and emotional excitement. Her voice was broken and choked 'I was in Singh's cell with Rohit a short while ago, and what we saw inside there is utterly inexplicable for me.... He lay on his bed... reading intently, as we normally do before going to sleep. Just imagine... you are going to die, and you are reading a book. My goodness... what the different stuff this man is made of! He had absolutely no worry of the coming hour. I don't know this is frenzy, madness or what? I really wanted to cry to see him so cool, and if I were at his place, I would have been half-dead already' She expressed in almost single breath, while scurrying behind that funeral procession. Her face had turned red and she was panting, with her eyes half full of tears.

'Yes...' Rohit also corroborated, 'What I saw for the first time in my life was a 'Heart of Steel' working in a human body, and it seemed to me that the molten lead is flowing in his vessels instead of blood!' He shook his head in awe.

'It is that special revolutionary stuff which makes the history turn' Himanshu also exhaled an exasperated air from his mouth, 'These all people are damn crazy like that. I was near Sukhdev with Pavan, when two messengers of Yama came to his door to take him. And quite unconcerned about the coming business... he was having the luxury of a slumber. My God... we were staring at his relaxed face and wondering how that uncommon oddity in the human behavior can be possible on earth? Whether he is an ordinary man or a Super Man?'

The macabre march took a final turn to that official slaughter house while we were talking together. The mixed hullabaloo of the locked-up prisoners had become weaker and distant at that place. And, it was there that a delusion began to grip us. Although, at the beginning of that supernatural session, we had already been warned about the possible occurrence of some abnormal feelings, yet we forgot the advices and reality, and assumed the real characters of the relevant time. The anguish now began to rise in all.

'But why the trio is doing all this? I don't know why the hell they are doing this supreme sacrifice?' I conjectured.

'Just to bring freedom to us and billions of other Indians...' He-Man said.

'And what are we doing for them in return? Look at these senseless Indian cops, who are taking them away to be killed...' Rohit said.

'Such people do like to remain the slaves forever. And the concept of freedom has no substance for them...' Pavan reflected with disgust.

'The poor cops are not to be blamed, as they and others are simply doing their duties. It is these red-faced British monkeys who are playing this vicious game...' VD said.

We had now followed the cavalcade right up to the steps of that deadly platform, where the Jail officials were anxiously waiting for them. The eyes of both, the Magistrate and Superintendent gave a voluptuous spark at the very sight of that triple-prey and Rohit tossed a slang towards the formers.

I wish I could hang both the morons right here...

'What do these fucking bastards think? Will they do anything they like? Will they kill anybody at will?? No! This is carnage... He-Man also blurted out.

And right then, the sarcastic voice of a white man intervened our angry conference. He was directing to the executioner staff, while aiming at the doomed prisoners.

'Take the additional care boys. Don't forget that they are the hardcore revolutionists.'

And there came the even more cutting but cool retort from the undaunted Singh at once.

'Don't you worry Mr. Magistrate. You won't be disappointed in the end. In fact, you people present here are going to be the most fortunate ones today, to witness not only one but three Indian patriots together, going so happily to the gallows. And remember... this is the spectacle you will cherish for the rest of your life.'

The white officer was all mute and flushed before that intimidating and commanding invitation. He couldn't speak another word and cowered away behind others. And with a proud smile on their faces, the trio took their feet up the steps. While climbing, they had formed a perfect Triangle, with Singh a step ahead in the middle, and the other two following a step down to the left and right behind.

They mounted the platform in a royal manner... as a wouldbe king ascends his throne to be crowned. They stood atop there in anticipation, with their bosoms swelled-up. The aggrieved Jailor came ahead to accomplish the final rituals, and asked then in a broken voice.

'Do you have any last wish before death?'

'Yes Jailer Sahib! The complete freedom for our countrymen from the imperialism is our only last wish, and shall remain so in the other world as well. However... we want our hands to be unfastened at the moment, so that we could embrace each other, before we breathe our last.' Singh replied.

The Jailer nodded and they were freed from the fastenings. They thirstily came closer and locked themselves with each other. A few pearls of tears dropped down in the soil from their eyes and the parting emotions began to overflow.

'The only regret is that we couldn't do even a fraction of what we wanted to do...' Dev regretted.

'I am sure, the coming generations will fulfill our dreams' Singh asserted and Rajguru shouted out in affirmation.

Inquilaab...

Zindabad

Long live...

Revolution

Down with...

Imperialism

Soon after, they took their respective positions in front of each noose themselves, and held it firm in their hands in warm reception. Then, they kissed those overhanging jute ropes and closed their eyes in supreme relax.

The time ticked by. The jailer nodded again and their hands were tied behind yet again. The things began to happen faster now. The faces of all three were covered with the black colored headgears, and the loops being garlanded in their necks. The moment of doom had come at last, and it was the time for us to panic.

We had been standing like statues so far... Just watching the tense proceedings go on, and now the final countdown had begun. The jailer had fixed his eyes at the wrist watch and the executioner had fixed his own at the former, while tightening his grip at the lever-handle. He was all ready to go at a flick, and we were looking at both of them by turns, while standing beside him.

The scene was heart-rending for us and we were utterly bewildered. Up there, the revolutionists had once again begun to raise the same slogans from beneath their masks as lively as before. I was becoming numb and desperate. Will they be killed before my eyes? I worried.

Suddenly, a fit of emotions swept me... and I pulled my belt out of my pant loops. I hurriedly gave it a single twine around the lever, right below where the executioner was clutching at. Now, VD and I took the buckleside and Pavan held the other with Rohit. And thus, with perfect mutual understanding, and being guided by our instincts, we prepared to 'jam' the crucial functioning of the apparatus, by tugging at it in the opposite direction.

'Pull!'

I commanded, and we all four tugged at both ends of my leather belt with all the might. He-Man began to do the same with his bare hands. We were now convinced that the lever won't move even slightly. And the executioner will give up after a few futile attempts.

Only a couple of moments remained when Jailer's face began to react quickly. His trembling hand got the momentum and the signal of death came like lightening. The professional hands of the official murderer moved in brutal force, and there was a sharp click of the metal.

He had accomplished his task successfully inspite of our great resistance. In a split second, the trio had disappeared from the platform without a trace. The sound of slogans had also sunk down deep somewhere. And an eerie silence ruled the whole slaughter-house very ominously.

The brisk patter of shoe-soles on the pave stones broke the uneasy calm. I saw with dimmed eyes that the Magistrate was rushing up to the platform. He came to the spot where the rectangular wooden planks had been some time before, and peered down in the dark abyss curiously. His face bloomed in satisfaction and he turned to the staff more sincerely.

'Well done boys! But the work is not over yet. Go down fast and pack the bodies up without delay. We have to get rid of their remains as soon as possible.'

Everything was preplanned and the next round of more diligent work began at once. And there standing still, we were shocked to our nerves. For some time, it was hard to believe and we just stood dead, as if the blood was squeezed out of our veins. Our effort to their rescue was fruitless and it didn't take me time to realize why?

After all, we were merely the onlookers of the bygone past, being specially replayed for us by the Red Triangle. We couldn't have avoided the certainty and what we did was a sudden rush of blood, driven by the natural instinct. However, we had seen a peerless historical event live, and its impact was a bit deeper on all and specially VD, who began with the sobs and soon burst into tears.

Nobody tried to console her, and her lamenting made the wretched place more desolate. I looked up at the sky with tears in eyes. The dim stars twinkled sadly above, but down there, three bright stars were sucked up by a blackhole in front of us.

However, the pale light of a kerosinlit incandescent lamp was trying to fight the increasing dark in vain. It hung from a wall-peg at the platform, and threw the ghostly shadows around. Just then, beyond the high walls, a melancholy dog let out a wailing weep in the street. And the piercing tone of that unpleasant 'elegy' stirred me from my emotions. I turned to VD and said in a steady voice.

'The death of the Martyrs is not to be mourned over. It is the moment of national pride for every Indian. This triple sacrifice will prove to be the last nail in the coffin of the imperialism. They are not dead... but are immortal now!'

'Clap... Clap... Clap.' The sound of applause was coming from the hands of Rohit, He-Man and Pavan. They had come around in a circle... still applauding, and trying to smile with watery eyes and distorted faces. It was the most sentimental tribute to the Martyrs.

We then went up the platform and to near the pits. Those three ropes now suspended loosely in each. We bent down and touched the ground there, and took some soil to apply on our foreheads. It was more than just visiting a pilgrimage for us.

Right then, I noticed some movements down in the basement, and tried to see what was going on there? The gleam of a scimitar like weapon's blade flashed in lamp light, and the sound of some quick blows followed. My eyes widened in horror at the sight. Some men or butchers were busy there in some most gruesome work, and it was just abhorring even to watch!

'My God... they are cutting the bodies into pieces!' I exclaimed in awe and all began a frantic search. Unfortunately, VD got the view and could not sustain the bloody-business even for a second. She let out a distressed shriek that rebounded amid the high stone walls around...

And the next moment, we were back in Guruji's room, sitting on the chairs in front of the trio like before, with VD still crying and the divine bodies smiling. I was so moved by that shocking journey that I was looking around to believe both, the present and the past. Was I really in Central Jail of Lahore? It was as if I were being woken-up from a thrilling dream all of a sudden.

But what a treasure of dream it was! Every minute detail of that odyssey still stands out in my memory afresh to this day.

However, the ashen faces of everybody were coming back to normal, when Dev Dada looked hither and thither among us in search and asked in humorous astonishment.

'And where is VD guys? Have you marooned her somewhere on the way?'

'Why Dada... she is sitting right here with me.' Pavan gave the surprised confirmation.

'But she is not our same Vandana...' He pretended to recognize for a moment and rejected the suggestion.

'Because she is shedding tears like a baby doll.' RG explained with a smile.

The remark made her embarrassed. She wiped her eyes with her small hanky and appeared steadfast at once. And it was time for Singh to smile.

'That's it.' He said, 'It is no use crying over the past. We must cry out for the coming future instead. We shall have some more useful discussions next month, and all of you may have to do a lot of work thereafter. Now, could anyone tell me what message you got in the course of journey today?'

And it was VD who again displayed her special art of grasping at the little things so easily.

'You people had stressed the hope on the coming generations, for the fulfillments of the tasks you had left unaccomplished...' She replied.

'Exactly!' RG said, 'And now this is the time for us to wait for the President's reply till we meet again.'

And thus, that meeting of ours came to an end.

32

'How are you Kaka?' I asked the owner as I came to the tea kiosk. Sumit, He-Man, Pavan and Rohit were busy in some argument a little behind. The shop owner had fixed his 6x6 wooden structure again after the rally, to earn his bread and butter. But this time, he was made to change it's location a little away from the road.

My eyes slid itself at his small cash box whereupon his name was written in white as always.

'Yaksha Prasad'

'It's many days since I saw you guys last time...' He smiled while pouring the chai to the two customers and before I could answer, he asked again.

'And where are the other four Pandavas left today?'

Pandavas? I was entertained by the epic designation.

'Because you are almost always five in number whenever I see you' He answered

'Kaka has given us a combined name today... Pandavas!' I said to He-Man as they came near and all nodded gently while taking their seats on the benches.

'He is Yaksha, and we are the Pandavas. It is such a dramatic situation of Mahabharata to think about...' Pavan said after a while.

'May be the original Yaksha was one who owned a Pond and who refused to give water to Pandavas before getting the answers to his questions?' Sumit asked.

'Yes, and this is the second one here.' The former owned a Pond and he owns a Tea-Shop. Pavan replied.

Each one was making his own merry-quips to add to the gossips when Kaka announced to us.

'You will have to wait a bit for chai...'

'Do we also have to answer your questions for that?' He-Man asked seriously and the rest of us began to laugh.

'Milk is finished, and the milkman is on his way...' He clarified and came out from his seat. He sat down on the bench near us and said again while preparing his tobacco.

'This is not a condition however as you said, and I fear that you may also not be able to answer the complex Yaksha questions to me.'

'Then let us try that...' Pavan replied and looked curious.

'It will be a good option to kill the time at all...' Sumit said.

'Yes Kaka, go ahead...' Others also encouraged. He then pushed the pinch of tobacco behind his lower lip at ease and then began at last.

'Okay! Get ready if you insist, and here is my first question...'

'Tell me what is heavier than earth?'

'It is Jupiter...' Rohit answered at once.

'No, it's a wrong answer.' Yaksha rejected.

'He is not asking the science questions here you apeshit' I scolded Rohit.

'This is the moral science understand?' Sumit tried to teach

'The right answer is Mother. I have viewed the serial Mahabharata many times...' One of the aged customers who stood nearby replied this time, but only to face an embarrassing question from He-Man.

'But whose mother?' He asked with surprise.

'I wonder how on earth you passed your primary school...' I gave him a whack on the back and he grinned in response. However, Kaka looked at the responding customer in disapproval.

'I do admit that this was the right answer 5000 years ago, but the same is not relevant in the so called India Shining.'

Pavan took the clue quickly and replied.

"Throne or the Chair of Power is heavier than earth!.'

'That's right!' Kaka looked at him with hope and proceeded.

'What is faster than the wind?'

Bribery.

'Where is the Sun established?'

'It is established at Delhi.'

'Who moves around it?'

'The Yes-Men move around it.'

'Who helps the Sun to ascend?'

Brainless Voters.

'What is higher than the sky?'

Cast and Creed is higher than the sky.

'How does a man become intelligent?'

Selfishness makes a man intelligent.'

'What is sorrow?'

'Losing a Constituency by close margin is the sorrow.'

'Who keeps his eyes open even during his sleep?'

Corrupt.

'Who does not make an effort even after taking birth?'

Offspring of the politicians.'

'What is knowledge?'

'Right calculation of areawise and castewise vote percentage is the real knowledge.'

'Who is scholar and who is fool?'

'Illiterate leaders are scholars and their highly educated staff is fool.'

'What is the supreme wealth among all the wealth? What is chief gain among all the gains? What is supreme joy among all the joys?'

'An account in Swiss Bank is the supreme wealth. The chair of Ministry is the chief gain and to behold one's own and family statues at the public places is the supreme joy'.

'What are innumerable than the straws?'

'Bundles of black-money.'

'What is wonder?'

'Thousands of crores of people's taxes disappear without trace every year, yet none wants to know about it. This is the greatest wonder!'

Excellent! You are a promising boy... Yaksha Prasad's eyes began to shine at last and he began to applaud Pavan cheerfully. And so did the other two aged customers also. One of them said to Kaka this time.

'I am inspired to ask you an important question if you please...'

'Yes...' Kaka replied.

'I want to know that who gave the country its name Bharat and what is something so significant about him even today?;

'It was King Bharat, the ancestor of Kauravas and Pandavas. He was the first man to sow the seeds of true democracy in this holy soil. He had nine sons, but selected a gifted subject from outside his family, as his successor. And the fellow was Bhumanyu, the son of Bharadwaj.'

Kaka received the round of applauds from all of us this time for his knowledge.

But on the contrary, here exists quite the opposite and ugly democracy today. This is an overall trend of family rule and not only sons and wives but even the servants of the ruling dynasty could be enthroned with the due stamp of democracy... The same customer commented in the end.

'Hummm... everyone present there admitted the fact with the thoughtful crooning and then Kaka got up to receive the milkman who had just arrived and we waited for the chai that was coming finally.

33

25th December, 2008

It's a black 'X-Max' this year as yet another big terrorist attack has taken place in the country. Hotel Taj at Mumbai was under siege this time. The marauders came by sea and took the daring hold of it. The seizure continued for the consecutive three days. More than hundred people lost their lives apart from the invaluable properties that were damaged. It is disgusting.... Damn disgusting! One attacker was caught alive however, but what will happen to him... only God knows.

Already the prime accused of the Parliament attack is still feeding himself on Indian tax-payers in jails for the last ten long years. I wonder if ours is an absolutely lawless country? hello... where are you Mr. President? And what are you doing there in your 5-Star residence? Why don't you order to hang him at once?? After all you have the certain national duties to do.

Come on Mr. President... this is your job to kill such parasites, and you must do it. You have already seen how a passenger plane IC-184 was hijacked about a decade earlier and some hardcore terrorists were released by our proud leaders to pay the ransom.

Do you know that those released gentlemen later on

masterminded to kill thousands of innocent people in and outside the country? Are you waiting for the encore of the same? Knock... knock? Are you there? But there is no answer from anywhere and nor had I with me as I am writing this page. And it was the topic of current discussion with the Red Triangle that took place day before yesterday.

Unfortunately it was our last meeting with them.

The Trio was silent and serious at their appearance in the room and didn't speak a word for some time.

'Is everything alright Dada?' Rohit ventured to ask at last.

'How can you be alright when you are bleeding?' Dev said.

'Recent attack on Mumbai was 'shocking news' for us...' RG explained the reason.

'News? Were you not present there at that time and as usual?' I asked knowingly.

'Yes... we were there!' Singh admitted, 'But we were unable to stop the bloodshed.'

'And it was not our duty as well...' RG said in frustration and anger, and it was the first time that we saw him so upset. But, it gave an encouragement to Pavan who exclaimed to him in sympathy.

'We can understand your anguish. It was your home state after all'

'Stop this nonsense!' RG suddenly became violent at his words and threw a knife-sharp glare to give him a chill in the spine.

'I am Indian above all and every single inch of this holy land is my own home.' He said after some tense moments.

'States are only the different parts of a single body as the human beings do have...' Dev said softly this time.

'They are not to blame Dev. Countrymen are simply learning what they are being taught by their democratic lords...' Singh said to him.

'And according to them, every part or limb is a different body or country within the same country... i.e. India.'

'It is true as far as the southern states are concerned...' Kokul couldn't help commenting at that. 'Just go to Tamilnadu and you will get the feeling that you are roaming about in Sri-Lanka! Absolutely no sign of our national language Hindi anywhere. People can't speak and can't even understand the same in the rural areas...'

'And this is possible in India only that a certain state like Kashmir has its own constitution. And that the rest of the country and its people have absolutely no right to claim there...' VD asserted.

'And yet thousands of crores of people's taxes go there every year as a state grant.' Pavan added in the end.

'The same structure is taking shape in Maharashtra as well.' He-Man said and became excited to ask, 'Does anyone know about where is our central government? Is it sleeping soundly? Has it any role to play at least? No... they are just doing the politics, and the country may go to hell.'

'We can't do the endless wait for the President's reply. It requires a blast to make the deaf hear.' I said.

All turned to me in surprise and I faced RT with resolution.

'Kindly give us the numbers of those secret foreign accounts and we are going to forward it to the President' I asserted.

'And what if there is still no reply?' Dev asked.

'We are going to make it public through thousands of our NBS members and media as well. It will be the biggest blast like that you did in the Assembly in your time.' I replied.

'Exactly! Media is the only channel to achieve our goal. It will then be 'Rulers v/s Public' openly.' VD said.

There was a deep pause in that unique séance. Singh, Dev and RG contemplated my suggestion for some long moments. And there came the cool conclusion from Singh.

Don't expect any magic from us guys, as we are not the magicians. We are the mentors alright, and want to remain the same. It is the best time to prove that you people can also do something.

But how can we know about the questioned account numbers? Rohit asked.

You have got the brains and sufficient ability to do so... RG encouraged.

I think an ethical-hacker must know about his right job... Dev said and everyone began to look at me.

Me? But it is next to impossible...

That's right. Just concentrate on what you just said... 'Im-possible' = 'I m possible'. Dev smiled.

You can do it Tipu and we all know that... He-Man gave an encouraging pat on my back and everyone consented with him.

I fell silent and began to ponder over the Herculean task.

Moments ticked away and it was too late already. We then noticed such a strange thing that we can't forget till we are alive. The trio were looking a bit dejected that evening.

'Why are you looking so downcast Dada?' VD asked.

'Well..., simply because we have fallen in love with all of you, during all these months...' Singh tried to smile.

'And love is a strong bond. It gives us strength, and not the weakness. We needed it most before we met you guys and we are thankful to you for that.' RG said.

'We do also feel the same. VD answered weakly.' May be she was sensing the untoward parting with our beloved friends.

'We are feeling stronger and extremely contented now. The climax of events will reach a happy ending soon.' Dev said.

'All of you are so special to us and we do trust you. We do also appreciate your ideas and motives. We are proud to say that you are few of the real Revolutionists of the present time.' Singh said and our heart beats were rising.

'When are we meeting next?' Rohit asked impatiently.

'We shall celebrate the success together. We shall wait very anxiously to see the happiest day of our life. In the meantime, wish you all the best and all the thanks to Guruji for his vital cooperation all these days. We shall be back as and whenever required...' RG finished abruptly.

And the next moment, they vanished from the room quite like the elusive character of 'Vetaal', who disappears from the shoulder of King Vikram after telling the story.

25th January 2009

It is almost one month since I have been trying to hack the database of Indian account holders in the banks of Switzerland. I burnt the midnight oil day after the day, struggling to unfold the national mystery and I wish to mention about my interesting quest in my diary here today, as I am feeling extremely relaxed now.

Hacking a certain database of a website is quite similar to entering a strongly fortified building. Let's take a rat for example here. Suppose it is determined to go in, so what is it supposed to do? It will naturally go around the building, looking for a small hole, drain, crack or breach in the outer wall, that may have been left open by mistake. And any smallest inlet will solve its purpose.

Similarly, one needs to track down the loopholes in the website. There are various techniques in use to hack a website but most suitable are SQL injection, cross site scripting and network penetration. I used network penetration to prefer over others.

It is a long account how first of all I found the IP address of the website and then did the port scanning through which I analyzed the web server, the application or the operating system used. So, I would like to finish in brief here.

The website sometimes has loopholes to enable the entry into the application, which are immediately healed by the website owners with the help of patches. But sometimes, these patches do create extra loopholes to enter the database and occasionally some loopholes are left unhealed and one needs to find those loopholes to enter the database like the above motioned rat.

However, to find the required loopholes is the most taxing work to do. I used the metaexploit tool to hit and try on thousands of loopholes step by step and then succeeded at last! Ultimately, I found the way through which I could access the database. Now, to hack the password of database, I used bruteforce attack and fortunately found the administrator password. It took me more than a week's continuous sitting to get the needed work done. And finally, after running the SQL query, I copied down all the information about Indian account holders successfully.

I triumphantly shared the discovery with my friends this morning, and they couldn't believe the well known names involved. The real identification and designation of many of the depositors was, however still not clear, so we e-mailed the same to Abhinav for help. We are hoping to get the necessary details soon.

15th February 2009

The state-wise NBS members are quick enough to provide the required information about such names within the last two weeks.

They include the ministers and legislators of many political parties. The government officers and high profile brokers are also in the list. It is a well established syndicate and all of them are part and parcels of each other. It simply reminds me of an ancient and interesting tale of...

"Ali Baba & 40 Thieves"

34

16th March 2009

We had mailed the same blacklist to the President soon after and waited. It was the last week of February when we got the news of the President's address to the nation. We hopefully checked the Inbox and there we found a short acknowledgement of our sensational e-mail. We began to jump with joy to see the positive signs and embraced each other on our initial success.

However, we glued to Kokul Guruji's TV in time for the phenomenal address that evening. The President briefly reflected on and indicated about the possibility of some radical changes in our constitutional system.

He told that the proposal was being worked out in detail to be put before the Parliament on 23rd of March, 2009. It now depended on the House to give its sanction to the amendments. He also demanded the moral cooperation and support from the common folks to get it sanctioned.

The Prime Minister's address also followed the next day and he also stressed the need of major reforms in the IPC as well. To our utter surprise, he also summoned all the politicians, beaurocrats etc to surrender their black assets till the prescribed date to avoid the stern actions.

Both the addresses were taken by media very hotly. They

were duly provided with the copies of the amendments. There followed the endless arguments on the news channels and newspapers on the proposed legislative structure. The move was welcomed by one and all.

In the mean time, the members of our NBS played the important role country wide. The members went to the villages, streets and the remote townships to awaken the citizens and to tell them about the real Independence. A slow thunder storm had thus begun to sweep the country.

Now, one week is left for the historical day to come and all of us are waiting impatiently for the moment.

23rd March 2009

So many things happened together in a single day and it is very difficult for me to condense the whole drama on paper. So, I am giving only the brief account of the same. It was a war-like situation inside and outside the Parliament at New Delhi. There were hundreds of thousands of people around the Parliament, awaiting the heroic sanction.

But our respected Parliamentarians were not the actual heroes to do the same so easily. There was a great uproar and then followed the walkout of the members from the house finally. But, outside the angry crowd were ready to welcome them and they had to return back to the protection of house.

People watched the proceedings live on TV sets country wide. Finally, MP's were forced to give their sanction to all the amendments and thus a new 'sun of hope' arose in the horizon of nation. Subsequently all the black money and secret foreign accounts were surrendered by the defaulters following the Prime Minister's promise of the amnesty to the accused ones.

And the procured wealth if being amassed at one place, could equal the Mt. Everest in height.

The caretaker houses of Parliament and the State Assemblies were to work till the formation of the newly accepted test based and finally the democratically chosen legislators the next year on the same day. It was like the declaration of real self-rule for the country men for the first time in Indian history.

Sometime in June 2009

College was off after the final exams and all my friends took their leave one by one. Kansal Bhavan was also deserted by He-Man, Pavan and Rohit. And, I was left alone in the city. Sometimes I still went there to meet Guruji. We had tried to call 'RT' for the consecutive two months after our last meeting with them in December but they didn't appear thereafter and we desperately stopped trying anymore.

VD's parents came from Vidisha and she left with them suddenly. We couldn't meet each other before her departure, but she rang me up and bade me a hurried bye before leaving. She took a part of my heart away with her. Quite understandably, I didn't try her mobile from my side in the coming days and she also didn't give a call to me.

Days flew away. It was about one month later when I received her mail. It was very balanced and straight forward.

Hi Tipu

How are you? Give you some news? I am getting married next month. Surprised na? Even I couldn't believe it myself, but it is true. I think it will not be easy for me to forget you. But, your love shall remain with me as a symbol of strength... and not the weakness. Do you remember the same words of RG Dada in our last meeting with them? Those were the golden four years I spent with you in the college and outside. You will stay in my memory as a true and affectionate friend forever.

My sincere regards to Mom.

Good Bye

Vandana

Her mail made me forlorn and I couldn't help giving her a congrats call. But, I was disappointed as she was not using her Haryana SIM anymore. I then wisely opened my Phonebook and deleted her name from its memory with heavy heart, and prayed to God for her happy married life. Incidentally, I also got married soon and we had no contact with each other after that.

35

23rd March 2010
11.42 pm

Rohit, He-Man and Pavan have come to Panipat specially to attend the first ever Revolution Day together. They are staying with me, and as I am writing these lines, they are sleeping peacefully in the guest room of my flat. We were very tired after retuning from Delhi, but we went straight to Kokul Guruji's place to see him. It was such an emotional get-together after one year, and we missed Vandana much.

Earlier in the day, Guruji didn't come with us, as he was busy in his packing. He was leaving the city forever to move to Mcleodganj (The mini Tibet in Himachal Pradesh) to spend the rest of his life in spirituality while being near to his own guru.

But apart from that, a piece of surprising news was waiting for us there and that one was madly exciting. He had not disclosed anything about that earlier in the day, when he unexpectedly called me up at Delhi and simply invited all four of us to have a farewell dinner with him.

Revolution day

However, back at Delhi, it was a great show of liberation

at Rajpath. The newly elected Assemblies and Parliament took an oath today in the States and Center all together. The old and stinging crop of politicians had gone, and a new era had begun. It was the real Republic Day in the making.

There was as if a new sky above and the new colors were all around. Thousands of new hopes were gathered there in the form of people... with their eyes glittering with dreams. And there was a new smell in the air. I saw a big flock of white migrating birds high up... flying freely and going northwards. It was an effortless flight of freedom and I kept looking at them until they faded away in the horizon.

It was a sheer passion all the way, and we stood silently near India Gate, watching RT's dream come true at last. This must be the happiest moment for the 'Trio, I thought. But where were they lost all of a sudden? There was above all, an aching feeling in my heart that they had disappeared so mysteriously, without even having a last word with us.

Officially, there was a speech from the ex President, announcing the handover of the reins to the new national concept. He briefly told about the reshaped constitution and also about the reformed Indian Penal Code. And in the end, the newlyelected President who was half the age of his predecessor did also put forth the new promises for the country.

Lastly, it was time for us to make a move. We were still on the outskirts of the Capital, when my mobile began to buzz. I picked it up and glanced at the screen. It read

Guruji.

Three hours later, when we had taken our dinner with him, he disclosed calmly while wiping his hands with the towel.

'And now, I have a surprising piece of news for you...' He Said

'What?' Rohit asked.

'There is an e-message for us from the Red Triangle!'

His words did an explosion and drove everybody crazy. And there was an array of questions and reactions.

'But after such a long time?'

I know that they cant forget us like that.

Really? And when did you received it??

'This evening only. I was in my casual séance when the message began to flash on the CVP...' He got up and headed towards the inner room without answering much. We followed him.

He switched his PC on, and there was the long awaited farewell message from our beloved Trio. There lay safely in his window, were some most intimate lines and we were crying while going through them again and again. The message read

Dear friends,

Sorry for being away for a full long year. You are now on your way back after attending the Revolution day. And, by the time you will reach Kansal Bhavan, we would have perhaps taken a new birth somewhere!

Death after life and life after death again is what the system of nature all about. Rebirth may, however be delayed sometimes, but it is for some specific purposes only. Our mission is accomplished here and it was not possible without your combined help. Being extremely satisfied, we have to depart now, but it was so nice meeting you for all these days. It is also the beginning of your respective careers and our wishes shall remain with you forever. Life is a long journey and there may be some difficulties on the way, but never stray away from your path

Remember... It is not the destinations but the travelers who are lost. And just a right step takes us there so easily. We do pray to God that we should come across you guys again in physical forms in this material world sometime... somewhere. We might not recognize each other at that time but it is greatly satisfying to think of that at the moment. It is goodbye to all of you from us. May God bless you... Jai Hind!

Parade of Liberty

24th March 2031
11.07 pm

Well, I am quite contented after having finished the long journey into my scintillating past now. Yesterday morning, I opened my eyes to witness the rise of yet another day. But, this was unlike the other ordinary ones to just come and go. It had so precious sentimental value for me, for not less than three reasons apiece.

One/The same bunch of Fabulous Five of my college time friends were at Delhi to celebrate the 22nd National Revolution Day together.

Two/The whole country commemorated the centenary year of the Red Triangle's martyrdom (1931-2031) with reverence. It was an event, not just to remember those 'three' only but also to pay homage to thousands others who sacrificed and burned themselves like flairs to lead the path of the nation through the darkness.

And the third and the most phenomenal of all/Our group saw such an inexplicable miracle in the end that the day has gone down in the annals of my memory for as long as I live!

However, my son Harshvardhan was back from Calcutta

on vacation. And he, along with Anushka and Tina, all were so keen to meet the whole of my notorious gang together. Although my family had come across everyone of them separately at occasions except VD, who had also come this time, with her husband from Madhya Pradesh on my request. Her husband had a sprawling Tendu Leaf business there. However, we met her for the first time since 2009.

Kokul Guruji had also come down from Mcleodganj. Rohit, He-Man and Pavan were accompanied by their wives. And it is honorific to me that all three are the successful personalities today. Around noon, we met each other like crazy people, and our this tryst was also as peculiar as we were ourselves. Imagine... we got assembled at no where else but zoo near Pragati Maidan! And it was simply because everyone found it convenient to reach. There is no happiness greater than meeting the old pals and it was a great reunion after twentytwo long years. And, the hours flew away.

Rajpath 7:30pm
23rd March 2031

It was the breathtaking spectacle on the promenade... and a treat to the eyes. Just imagine the entire strip full of people of every age. They were although attired differently, but represented only one culture and one faith as well... and it was Indianness. They held the colorful candles in their hands and almost everyone sported the symbolic caps of Basanti shade (Yellow) including us.

We had stationed ourselves close to the floodlit India Gate and silently watched the patriotic mood of united India. Every heart was as illuminated as the big screens that were fixed at certain places, showing the people dancing and enjoying all around. Everywhere up to the Rashtrapati Bhavan, media were busy hither and thither, taking short interviews of men, women and children and telecasting it live on screens. Thousands of them wore the fancy dresses to look as deities, martyrs and the historic warlords.

Three very big yellow balloons were being hoisted up high... bearing 'Long Live Revolution' in red, with one separate word on each. And to add to the whole madness, the sound of a variety of music instruments sprang up continuously from all over. Absolutely, everything was so morale boosting, but it made me down with emotions. And, soon I realized that not only me, but the whole lot of 'we-6' was feeling the same. That's why He-Man wistfully heaved a cool sigh and said to me.

'It's how so beautiful to watch! This is the genuine liberty of India, we all dreamt of...'

I looked at him. The words were coming deep from his heart and he had the restrained tears in eyes. He didn't look at me in return, however.

'Yes! And, it were our dear Dadas only who made it complete for us. Otherwise, it was merely a token freedom in 1947...' I answered in a damp voice.

'It were those who gave this transformed revolution to the nation...' He-Man said.

'Eventually, they did after death what they couldn't do in their life time' Pavan said.

'But they have left a big vacuum in our lives and nothing can fill it up!' Rohit said.

'It seems to me as if each flame of a candle represents an individual martyred soul here and 'they' are somewhere among them...' Pavan said.

'Papa, it is marvelous to see thousands of candles swaying at a time at one place' My son Harsh wondered and Anushka commented at that.

'Not only thousands... but hundreds of thousands all together. I have not seen such a magnificent view after what I had seen on moon.'

'Lord Buddha must also be looking down at this 'new galaxy' from the heavens above...' Guruji looked up and united his hands in 'Namastey' and closed his eyes for a moment to remember the lordship. And VD who was 'Mrs Jain' now, also atoned dreamily.

'You are right Guruji. It is the whole universe on earth tonight, how I wish the time should come to a stop here and now! I have been looking for this 'Lovey-Duration' for a long time anxiously...'

'What? What is this you just said??' I asked in surprise and as if she came back to her senses.

'Lovey Duration... I mean 'Revolution Day'. I am sorry.'

'You are still as enigmatic as you were in your college days Vandana...' Guruji began to laugh at her plight and her husband came to her rescue.

'She keeps me entertained like this with her great sense of anagrammatic humor. She has really unscrambled my puzzled life since the very day she entered it...' He said while looking at his wife fondly, and it was the right time for Tina to add a humorous reason.

'Maybe, this is the aromatic effect of the Tendu Leaves (Tobacco) that you deal in.'

And there were all the laughters to make Vandana blush! She was almost as young as she was twenty two years before. I remembered the same venue way back on the same 23rd March

2010, which had marked the eradication of imperialism from the country in practical and when the first ever Revolution Day was introduced.

At that historic moment, we were all there together like this... but VD was missing. But yesterday, it was just blissful to be with her and all other friends yet again. I had experienced so many colors of life's rainbow all in a day! There was happiness, there were emotions, there were some unfulfilled wishes... and there were some regrets too! But all these sentiments are the parts of our life, which ultimately goes on...

'My dear fellow country folks...'

'Jai Hind!'

We were suddenly attracted by the voice of country's President appearing on the big screens. He was a young man of about thirty-five and was walking the 'Rajpath' at brisk pace while addressing the nation, and also meeting the people on the way. He was flanked by a dozen odd Parliamentarians on both of his sides. And, it was a bunch of collegiate looking boys and girls even younger to him.

He continued with his address further...

'I do congratulate you on this great day, and welcome the ones who are present here with me to take part in this Annual Parade of liberty'

'This is the National Revolution Day...' He waved and roared enthusiastically and a surging applause followed from the sea of people all along. And after it had subsided, he said again.

'Revolution is a journey and it never comes to an end! It is not only the 22nd year today since we are celebrating it... but the 7666th day, starting from way back 23rd March

2010, and it was the day when India's future was written in golden words!'

There was a short pause to make way for the deafening cheers before he regained his speech.

'The very word revolution has the thousands meanings, and it is progress progress and only progress again and again! Forgetting our failures and moving ahead apace is the real revolution. We are proud that we are all the Revolutionists today... and let's take a vow to make a new revolution every day from now on...'

There were the rumbling shouts of approval from all over. It was a very brief, lively and terribly inspiring address, which swept the masses away. And there came his commanding voice once again.

'Now everybody present here and all over the country, shall come to join me to chant the Magic-Mantra after me...' He waited for a while for the complete silence to come. He then waved his arm up jubilantly with the fist clenched in determination and called out aloud.

'Long Live...'

'Revolution!' There came the thunder of millions of voices and rolled slowly away in distance. We also sang the same in chorus and stood there silently to listen to the echoes travelling all around! Mr. President had finished in the meantime and the panorama of people reappeared on the screens thereafter to continue.

However, when the night was far more advanced, we moved out of there to reach our caravanserai for the night halt. It was already been booked by me a couple of days before. Anu and Harsh were not coming with us. They were to go back home at New Greater Noida.

Quite interestingly, there was my old guitar in my van and it was carried at the behest of all, who were so crazy to see me play and sing once again and the night was going to be wild with music and gossips.

Will it Ever Come True ?

Our convoy of two eight-seater family vans and eleven people in all, was running slow on Bakhtavarpur road, on the northern outskirts of Delhi. We were trying to locate the farm house where all of us were to stay for the night. Rohit was leading me in his van along with He-Man and Pavan. And, I was following with VD and Kokul Guruji, in my own. All of us were in couples except the latter.

It was now long time that we were driving clueless around a short area in the proximity. The GPS of both the vans were showing the destination home, but it was nowhere in sight. I had just pushed the digits of Rohit's palmtop from my dashboard, when he stopped his van at the road side ahead and came out. I also did the same and as I joined him, he said.

'I think there is something wrong with the location...'

'Let's enquire somebody about that...' I suggested and all the co-passengers began to gather around us to know. All were throwing the searching glances on both sides of road in perplexity. The sky was all dark, but the beams of high pole-lights in the center of the road, made the place well illuminated. It was a pleasant late March evening and a gentle breeze was blowing across.

Just then, we saw an open jeep approaching us from behind, with the headlights dimmed. It was not coming very fast. I took a few steps forward and waved it to stop. And so it did with a screech. Seated in the vehicle were three young men of around twenty. One of them occupying the driving seat, had the pinkish complexion, and a pair of small, pointed and juvenile mustachio over the handsome and sharp features. He looked at me with his shining eyes and enquired.

'Yes?'

'Could you tell me where is Aranya Kutir around?' I asked.

'Aranya Kutir?' He turned to his companion at the front seat for the confirmation. That youngster was having a tasty bite at the roasted maize corns. He replied to me while still munching.

'It is so close to you uncle. Just turn right at the bend-up there... and you will find it the first address in the right lane.' He pointed.

'It is in fact the boundary wall of the same, we are standing in front of now. You can see even a small board there...' The third boy sitting at the back seat pointed at a place towards the outline of trees, and all strained their eyes to spot a small board, being camouflaged between the yellow-green autumn foliage, bearing the obscure name. It was however, not so easy to locate, and I heaved a sigh of relief and surprise at the discovery.

'Oh really! And, we were circling around like nomads for the last twenty minutes or so. But how on earth could you locate that patchy board? I asked the backsitter.

It's damn easy for him, as being the national shooter, he has the eye of an eagle! The corn eater replied.

'But I wonder how we lost it at all!' Rohit exclaimed in confusion and his words brought a beguiling smile on the cherry-red lips of the driver boy.

'Uncle, it is not the destinations but the travelers who are lost.' He said.

'*And just a right step takes us there so easily...*' The corn-eater also smiled in a friendly manner. And it was time for the third boy who greeted us in a carefree wave of his hand in the end.

'Have a nice time Uncle... *Jai Hind!*'

And, the jeep sped away with a jerk, without waiting for a response. It disappeared at the same bend-up ahead within moments, leaving us in sheer disbelief! Our hair had stood on end in excitement at the very words all three of them had spoken. And all of us... He-Man, Pavan, Rohit, VD; Kokul Guruji and I looked at each other with the bewitched eyes. The touching lines of the last and parting e-message of the Red Triangle we received twenty one years before, resounded afresh in our ears loudly...

We do pray to God that we should come across you guys again in physical forms in this material world sometime... somewhere. We might not recognize each other at that time but it is greatly satisfying to think of that at the moment.

And we stood there still looking in the same direction with the blank and wishful gazes... being absolutely stunned!

THE INDIAN TRADE AT THE ASIAN FRONTIER

THE INDIAN TRADE AT THE ASIAN FRONTIER

Edited by
S. Jeyaseela Stephen

GYAN PUBLISHING HOUSE
NEW DELHI-110002

The Indian Trade at the Asian Frontier

ISBN: 81-212-0946-3

Published in 2008 in India by
Gyan Publishing House,
5, Ansari Road Darya Ganj
New Delhi-110002
Phones : 23282060, 23261060
Fax : (011) 23285914
E-mail: gyanbooks@vsnl.com
Website : http : // www.gyanbooks.com

Laser Typesetting by: Quick Media, Delhi
Printed at : Singhal Print Media, Delhi

Contents

Preface

The essays comprising this volume have been written specially to examine and trace the Indian Trade at the Asian Frontier.

The initiative was taken by the members of the Governing body of the Institute for Indo-European Studies (IIES) gratefully acknowledge their generous support for this volume. I would like to thank all the contributors and many thanks to Dr. Sheela Karta Ram for her advice during the various stages of the book. They have stressed of late that the collective endeavour is more important than individual contribution in the world of scholarship. An effort has been made to provide a thematic unity of the essays by focusing attention on the trade and commerce both on the east and west coasts of India including the hinterland. There are thirteen essays by scholars from four different countries such as France, Germany, United Kingdom and India especially from the university of Mumbai, Goa, Jadavpur, Berhampur, Calcutta, Patna, North Bengal, Pondicherry and Visva-Bharati. I am thankful to Gyan Publishing House, for undertaking and completing the publication within the time schedule.

Editor

Preface

[illegible]

List of Contributors

Aniruddha Ray is Emeritus Professor of the Department of Islamic History and Culture, University of Calcutta. His publications include (ed.,) "*Surendra Nath Sen: Foreign Biographies of Shivaji*", K.P. Bagchi, Calcutta, 1977; "*Some Aspects of Mughal Administration*", Kalyani Publishers, New Delhi, 1984; (ed. with S.K. Bagchi) "*Technology in Ancient and Medieval India*", Sundeep Prakashan, New Delhi, 1986; "*The Rebel Nawab: Revolt of Vizir Alivardi Khan of Oudh*", K.P. Bagchi, Calcutta, 1990; "*Francois Martin Memoires: Travels to Africa, Asia and India*", Subarnarekha, Calcutta, 1990; (ed. with S. Arasaratnam) "*Masulipatnam and Cambay: A History of Two Port Towns, 1500-1800*", Munshiram Manoharlal, Delhi, 1994; "*Adventures, Landowners and Rebels: Bengal, Cir 1575-1850*", Munshiram Manoharlal, Delhi, 1998; (ed.,) "*Tipu Sultan and His Age*" Asiatic Society, Calcutta, 2002; "*Transformation of Bihar: European Discourse*", Kalyani Foundation, Dharbhanga, 2003; "*The Merchant and the State: The French in India, 1666-1739*", 2 vols, Delhi, 2005.

Karubaki Datta, is Reader and Director of the Centre for Himalyan Studies in North Bengal University, Darjeeling. Her dissertation is on "*Remnants of a Receding Empire: Portuguese Trade with Goa and the East, c.1750-1800*", Unpublished, North Bengal University, West Bengal, India, 1994. She has co-edited (with J.B. Subba) "*Religion and Society in the Himalayas*", Gyan Publishing House, Delhi, 1991.

B. Krishnamurthy is the Coordinator of the Centre for Nehru Studies, Pondicherry University. He is a Reader in the Department of Politics and International Relations. His publications include "*French Inthiya Viduthalai Porattam*", (in Tamil) Navajyothi, Pondicherry, 1990; "*Indo French Relations: Prospects and Perspectives*", Shipra, New Delhi, 2005.

Laxmi Narayan Raut is Professor of History in Berhampur University, Orissa. His publication includes "*Socio-Economic Life in Medieval Orissa, 1568-1751*", Calcutta, 1988.

Leena More is a Diplomat at the Embassy of India, Paris, She is the author of "*The English East India Company and the Native Rulers in Kerala: A Case Study of Attingal and Travancore*", IRISH, Tellicherry, 2003.

Martin Krieger is Assistant Professor of History at the University of Griefswald, Germany. His publications include, *Kaufleute, Serauber, Diplomaten Der Danische Handel auf dem Indischen Ozean*, Koln-Weimar-Wien, 1998; *Patriotsmus-Diskurs und die Konstruktion Kollektiver Identitaten in Hamburg in der ersten Halfte 18. Jahrunderts*, Habil-Schrift, 2001; *Geschite Asiens: Eine Einfuhrung*, Koln-Weimar-Wien, 2003; *Land und Meer: Kultureller Austausch Zwischen Westeuropa unde dem Ostseeraum in der Fruhen Neuzeit*, Koln-Weimar-Wien, 2004.

J.B.P. More is a Researcher of the Ecole des Hautes Etudes en Sciences Socials, Paris. He is the author of "*The Political Evolution of the Muslims in Madras, 1930-1940*", Orient Longman, Chennai,1997; "*Freedom Movement in French India: Mahe Revolt of 1948*", IRISH, Tellicherry, 2001; "*L' Inde Face a Bharati: La Poete Rebele*", IRISH, Tellicherry, 2003; "*Bhagavadam ou Bhagavata Purana: Ouvrage Religieux et Philosophique Indien Traduit par Mariadas Poulle de Pondichery en 1769*", IRISH, Tellicherry, 2004; "*Puducheriyil Bharatiyar*", (in Tamil) IRISH, Tellicherry, 2004.

Nicholas Rhodes, specializes on the Himalayas and North East India. He is the Secretary- General of the Oriental Numismatic Society, Council-Member of the Royal Asiatic Society, London and former President of the North East India History Association. His publications include (co-authored with C. Valdettro & K. Gabrisch) "*The Coinage of Nepal*", 1989; (co-authored with S.K. Bose), "*The Coinage of Cooch Behar*", 1999; "*The Coinage of Tripura*" (2002); "*The Coinage of Assam*" in 2 Vols. (2003 & 2004) and (co-authored with Mrs. Rhodes), "*A Man of the Frontier: The Life and Times of S.W. Laden La, 1876-1936*", (2006).

Philomena Sequeira Antony, is Reader in History and Head of the Department at Chowgule College, Margao, Goa. Her publication includes "*The Goa-Bahia Intra-Colonial Relations, 1675-1825*", Goa, 2004.

Rila Mukherjee, is Professor of History at the University of Hyderabad. Her publication includes "*Strange Riches: Bengal in the Mercantile Map of South Asia*", Foundation Books, New Delhi, 2006.

Ruby Maloni is Professor of History at the University of Mumbai. Her publication includes "*European Merchant Capital and the Indian*

Economy: A Study of Surat Factory Records, 1630-1668", Manohar, Delhi, 1992; "*Surat: Port of the Mughal Emperor*", Himalaya Publisher, Mumbai, 2003; (ed.,) with Mariam Dossal, "*State Intervention and Popular Response, Western India in the 19th Century*", Popular Prakashan, Mumbai, 1999.

Surendra Gopal is Emeritus Professor of History of Patna University. His publications include "*Commerce and Crafts in Gujarat, 16th and 17th Centuries*", New Delhi, 1975; "*Mauj-i-Sultani: A Memoir of the Mughal Prince Zubair-uddin Bahadur Gurgan*" (in Hindi with Syed Ejaz Hussian) Darbhanga, 2003; (ed.,) "*India and Central Asia: Cultural, Economic and Political Links*", MAKIAS, Kolkata, 2001; "*Contribution of Hindu Historians to Urdu Historiography in Bihar in the 19th Century*", Patna, 2004; "*Dialogue and Understanding Central Asia and India: The Soviet and the Post- Soviet Era*", MAKIAS, Kolkata, 2005.

Syed Ejaz Hussain is Reader in History in Visva-Bharati. His publications include "*The Bengal Sultanate: Politics, Economy and Coins, AD 1205-1576*, Manohar, Delhi, 2003; *Mauj-i-Sultani: A Memoir of the Mughal Prince Zubair-ud-din- Bhadhur Gurgan*, (in Hindi) edited with Surendra Gopal, Darbhanga, 2004.

Tilottama Mukherjee is Lecturer in History in Visva-Bharati. She had earlier taught at Gargi College, Miranda House and Lady Shri Ram College in Delhi. Her Ph.D dissertation is on *Markets, Transport and the State in the Bengal Economy, 1750-1800*, Cambridge, 2004.

Introduction

Commerce-inland or overseas of the different regions in the world are distinct because they are mainly related to the geo-physical locations. There are significant factors such as the social formations and the local enterprises which determine their uniqueness. Differential configurations of relationships existing within the state systems do play a key role. Commerce always began within its own immediate locations, moved to some areas and then spread to zones covering the whole of any territory. However, there exists the functional interdependence between the centres of production, distribution and consumption. The recognition of significance of trade in Indian history became a topic of interest some decades ago among the historians because until now the economic history of India has been dominated by the study of agrarian economies.

Alexander the Great opened the floodgates of India-West Asia trade during the Fourth Century B.C. During the Mauryan period trade was regulated by the state and it controlled the weights and measures. The traders had to get a license to trade. Special arrangements were made for the protection of trade routes. India exported indigo, various medicinal substances, cotton and silk to Western countries. In ancient India the profit of trade went to the Kushanas who acted as the intermediary of the Central Asia trade.[1] The silk route gave a suitable opportunity at that time to the Indian merchants to take an active part in trade and commerce. After the Kushanas the trade began to decline during the Second Century AD and got diverted to South East Asia and it helped for the development of spice route and textile trade. Thus long distance commerce of India was extended to the Asian frontier.

In India trade was dominated by itinerant or peddling traders belonged to the *vaishya* caste. It is a fact that the initial impetus for commercial activity came mainly from intervillage mutuality. Interdependence in matters of imports and exports of consumption goods among the villages of different regions contributed much to the growth of short distance trade. The funds for commercial activity among the villagers came chiefly from a village surplus by non-productive members of a village society. It is hard to find single evidence suggesting that the merchants acquired the initial money capital by way of making loan from the state. The traders had their supra-local associations for the production of merchandise as well as mutual commercial support. They functioned in South India within the limits and norms set by the local *nadus and nagarams*.[2] Growth of innumerable urban centres developed around the temples had an immediate effect and the producers and artisans sold their goods to whomsoever they liked.

Many places became major centres of trade in South India in the medieval period. Inscriptions mention the varieties of commodities of trade that were found in the region.[3] A stone record of the Alupa King Vijayadita Maravarma (Ninth century) mentions that the king confirmed the tolls due to a city for its upkeep and maintenance.[4] The inscription of Prathvisagara (Ninth century) mentions the custom duties that were collected both in the land routes and waterways and the King donated half of the customs duty to a town and for this he had to take the permission from the local traders.[5] The record of Devaraya II (AD 1430) mentions an agreement between the trading communities of Murukeri and Chaulikeri, and it contains a clause reserving a particular place for the foreign merchants to store the loads of sugar they bring from beyond the ghats.[6] Thus the interest of the traders bringing their commodities from outside for sale in South India were well protected by agreements entered into by the local traders.

A Hoysala inscription gives interesting details on the existence of traders in various regions in South India.[7] Another stone record mentions the different trade guilds in South India and their relations between them.[8] Two famous trading corporations such as *Manigramattars* (from the end of the Ninth Century to Thirteenth Century) and the *Nanadeși Thisai Ayiratthu Ainnuttruvar* (Eleventh & Twelfth Centuries) emerged and they functioned all over South India. The mercantile activity as a mode of surplus earning began to compete in general with other modes of surplus acquisition. We find merchants as distinct functional group of buyers of wares completely separate from the direct producers. *Chettis* converted their precious metal into standard money coins. *Mudaliars* from any other exogenous occupation or source accumulated money.[9] Thus the commercial capital came directly from the appropriation of surplus either by village renters or by village elites.

The Pallava and Chola rulers tried to encourage the maritime trade of South India by sending a series of ambassadorial missions to the Chinese emperors. In the Thirteenth century the Chinese government tried to restrict the export of gold and silver from China to India. Trade in spices from Southeast Asia was also important at that time. Rice and textiles of South India were imported in huge quantities there. Internal trade in medieval South India developed with markets of various types during the Chola and Vijayanagara period. We can distinguish sharply between three models of exchange, such as reciprocity, (exchange of goods that takes place neither through markets nor through administrative hierarchies) redistribution (movement of goods up to an administrative centre and their resultant downwards to consumers) and market (exchange of goods at prices based on supply and demand).[10] The Vijayanagara state used *Hamsa-mudhra* to ensure the quality of unadulterated goods sold in the markets.

The North Indian commercial scene in the medieval period of the Delhi Sultanates presents a different picture. We find that there developed a number of urban rice centres and grain merchants in towns. But this growth of inland commerce in grains was not autonomous or voluntary. An official *iqta* holder or a village headman of that period did not impose any extra claim on village output. The commerce conducted between the town and the village was indeed forced upon a village which was under a compulsion to pay fifty per cent or more of its crops as royal tax. A band of caravan traders or wealthy grain merchants emerged who came into being only as by product of the royal tax policy.[11] Import of food grains from rural areas was the basic dynamic of commerce and an emphasis was made on the role of coercion in augmenting town supply of grains. We notice that imprisoning the caravan traders' families or their transport animals happened if the traders failed to procure stipulated grain provisions for the capital city of Delhi.

Horses were a major item of import while slaves were exported in large numbers. Alauddin Khilji's market regulations included prices of various types of slaves, which were comparable to those of inferior horses and milch cows. Indigo was in demand overseas. Delhi, the capital of the Sultanates received betel leaves from Dhar, muslin from Devagiri and striped cloth from Bengal and thus the inland trade was handled by the merchants. Further, the absence of a well regulated monetary system caused the merchants or traders to have their minting of the ruling currency, billon - a copper currency mixed with silver alloy and this was permitted only in Delhi and Agra.

The commercial situation gradually began to improve in North India in the period of the Great Mughals. The most important items of inter-regional trade were foodstuffs and textiles. The rural transactions in goods constituted the main dynamic of Mughal commerce. The trading activity as wealth accumulating venture shaped the rural commerce which fed the urban business. Under Akbar to Aurangzeb with the development of commerce in the rural areas there also grew a comprehensively well designed system of revenue assessment and collection, permitting public minting of centrally standard coins in a large number of local mints spread over the various *Subhas* of the Mughal empire.[12] Further, emergence of towns as a dominant buyer's market and the villages mainly as sellers market for agricultural produce and nonagricultural commodities was a noteworthy feature. The movement of goods was made by a network of merchants, *gumastas* (agents) and *dalals* (commission agents). Two types of *hundis* (bills of exchange) such as *Darshni* and *Miti* facilitated inland trade and a class of professionals called *saraffs* had specialized in dealing with *hundis*. The growing overseas demand for the Indian goods and the trade conducted by the Portuguese, Dutch and the English East India Companies supplanted the growth of inland commerce too. A series of interdependent commercial endeavours dealing with intra-local, inter-regional and international transactions grew up as the distinct features of Mughal commerce.

India was well connected with trade routes in Asia especially from Agra to Quandhar through Thatta or Kabul. There was another route from Agra to Lahore, Kandahar to Isfahan. Yet another caravan route had developed from Agra to Lahore, Kandhaar Farrah, Tabas and Isfahan. Places such as Kabul and Khandhar were mainly connected in the trade network to Lahore, Multan, Agra, Delhi, Patna, Kasimbazar and Banaras, on the northern and eastern trade routes. Ahmedabad, Burhanpur and Cambay on the western overland trade route were linked with Delhi and Agra. Most of these trading marts were centres of inter-Asiatic trade and were involved in considerable commercial exchange of important wares to Persia, Egypt and Gulf countries.[13] Thirteen main overland routes connected the major towns and ports in South India including the royal city of Vijayanagara and the details are traced from various sources such as inscriptions, literary texts, Portuguese records and travelogues.[14]

Inter-continental trade in the early modern period known variously as the age of commercial capitalism and the age of European expansion in the East is a well studied one. However, the continental trade within Asia and the significant role of India with detailed studies on particular branches of trade, areas of production, commercial routes or points of distribution have yet to be done. It is hoped that this volume will be a step in the right direction in the Asian context especially because of the growing interest. The works of Andre Gunder Frank[15] Immanuel Wallerstein[16] and Eric R. Wolf[17] have drawn attention to the significance of the pre-modern era for our understanding of the distribution of wealth and power. Their views and basic assumptions are contradictory and also remain controversial. J.C Van Leur was the first to move away from the Europe-centred approach.[18] K.M. Pannikar followed him later and he depicted the course of world history from an Asian/Indian perspective in clear contrast to Western view points.[19] Maritime historians have begun to challenge the conventional view of world economic history that the European merchants overwhelmed their Asian counterparts and the early modern age is described not as an age of conflict or competition but as an age of paternership.[20]

I

While this being the case, in this book the first section deals with ports, maritime trade and shipping. Rila Mukherjee examines the location of the port of Samandar in early medieval Bengal. According to her studying Bengal's independent commercial policy, not only on the Husain Shahi period is important but on an earlier period-the Ilyas Shahi Sultanate from 1342 to 1487, except for a short interregnum between 1410 and 1435. The Ilyas Shahis had brought an immense commercial boom in Bengal. By way of commerce they placed Bengal within an expanding network of Islamic states that radiated from east Africa through southern Europe, Mecca, Central Asia and China through a mixture of religious (charitable works such as the foundation of mosques and *madrassas* at Mecca), diplomatic (mission to Herat), trade (between East Africa and China; at least one giraffe from Africa was sent by the Bengal sultan to China) and tribute (voyages to China) missions. The Ilyas Shahis therefore negotiated a vast physical space: from China to Central Asia and Africa. This was the first Islamic network and it was indeed an era of cosmopolitanism for Bengal. On the one hand the Islamic conquest of Bengal inserted the region into a vast maritime network stretching from Spain, Persia, West Asia and East Africa up until the China coast. On the other hand, Mongol invasions on the northern Chinese border made the Chinese abandon the traditional overland silk route through Herat and Mashd and look southwards through the port of Ch'uan Chou or Zaitun for tribute and trade. This gave a great boost to oceanic trade in the eastern Indian Ocean. Zaitun became the premier mercantile city in the eastern Indian Ocean by the thirteenth century. The conquest of Chattagram was not accidental nor was it the reflection of a haphazard policy on the part of the Ilyas Shahis. From the eleventh century this area, nominally under the rule of the Chandras of Dhaka-Vikrampur, was a heavily commercialized zone. The importance of the Chattagram/Arakan region-this amorphous zone that was fought over by Tripura, the Ilyas Shahis, the Husain Shahis (and later the Mughals) and the Arakanese-should therefore not be underestimated. The commercial dynamism of this area was cut short in the Sixteenth Century due to three circumstances and they are (a) Environmental: (b) Political (c) West Faced Commercial Policy. However early Arab accounts of South Asia have referred to the existence of a mysterious port called Samandar; mysterious because to this date we are not sure as to where exactly it was located, or whether it was situated in Bengal at all. Mohar Ali locates the shadowy Samandar, to be in eastern Bengal, on the Meghna to be precise, as the premier port of Bengal during this period. But apart from the confusion regarding Samandar's location within Bengal, there is also a doubt whether Samandar was situated in Bengal at all, for there are certain problems with Mohar Ali's identification. She concludes that Samandar may well have been Sagor and Sagor's name has also been proposed as an interim port. Both Sagor and Bakla in the Sundarbans area were functioning ports from the twelfth century. But this identification, too, is not conclusive. We see therefore that our search for a port in Bengal in the period between the seventh and thirteenth centuries remains inconclusive. Until we are able to locate a port in the region our researches into Bengal's commercial position in the mercantile map of South Asia will remain uncertain.

Aniruddha Ray next explains the various causes for the rise and fall of the port of Satgaon in medieval Bengal and he tries to make a reconstruction of the morphology of Satgaon. He says that the defeat of the Hindu ruler and the victory of the Sultan in 1298 signalled the beginning of the process of urbanization of Satgaon, The establishment of the mint in early Fourteenth century would suggest the growth of mercantile activities of the area that must have started from an earlier period and one could speculate that the conquest of Zafar Khan Ghazi was to control the port that was bringing precious metal from outside, if not the horses desperately needed by the newly founded State. Before moving on to the discussion on the change of the course of the river Bhagirathi, one may suggest that it is quite possible that Satgaon was functioning from the late Thirteenth Century as an inland port. It is also possible to speculate that the rise of Satgaon as an overseas port occurred after the second half of the Fifteenth century, when the capital was transferred from Pandua to Gaur. It is in this context that one may discuss the change of the course of the river Bhagirathi and one may perhaps put up a chronology for such a change, which has been suggested by Nihar Ranjan Ray. However, he says that the rise of Satgaon is important at least in the middle of the Thirteenth century. Its importance as an urban centre was significantly helped by administrative measures. The inscription of a mosque at Triveni under Malik Barbak Shah of 1455 A.D. shows that the mosque was built by Ulugh Ajmal Khan under Iqrar Khan, Wazir of Arsa Sajla Mankhabad. Nasiruddin Mahmud then was the Sultan. Around 1494 A.D. Satgaon was full of houses of rich people and it has become a big urban centre. If we believe Bipradas, Satgaon has developed into a big town by the end of the Fifteenth century. In his account, one could see the existence of sizeable Hindu and Muslim population in the town and Bipradas has enumerated some of the professions of the Muslims as well. Obviously there was a quick development of the urban area of Satgaon, which was probably due to its closeness to the capital Gaur that was becoming quickly populated.

Satgaon had become the headquarters of the *Sarkar* by the middle of the Sixteenth century. The granting of *farman* by the Emperor Akbar to the Portuguese in 1579 gave the Portuguese the permission to make a settlement at Hughli. It has been hailed as the beginning of the rise of Hughli and the fall of Satgaon. Obviously the Portuguese request for the settlement at Hughli would signify that the port of Satgaon was declining or having difficulties with the flow of water. Caesar Federici had seen thirty big and small ships anchored in the port of Satgaon. This was almost the last mention of the ships in the port of Satgaon in the Sixteenth century. In 1590s Satgaon continued to draw goods from the hinterland and neighbouring areas for its markets, although one is not clear whether the port of Satgaon was still functioning at least in the transportation of goods. That the port was still functioning in transporting goods in the 1620's could be seen from two English letters written from Patna in which they mentioned that the Portuguese had brought goods from Southeast Asia to Satgaon and they are then transporting these goods to Patna. It was only after the Mughal conquest in 1632 of the Hughli port held by the Portuguese, that the Mughals transferred their customhouse from Satgaon to Hughli, which finished the importance of the port of Satgaon.

The two sketches of Bengal by Joao de Barros and Broeke are compared in this connection. There are many differences between the two. Broeke did not mention Betore, but shows that the river was falling into the Bhagirathi channel opposite Calcutta. But the bigger difference was that Broeke had shown Satgaon on the northern bank of the river Saraswati, which in actuality was located on the southern bank. The town of Satgaon began to move towards the east i.e. towards the Hughli river, then must have been a small stream, and it also began to move towards the south making at the same time a semi-circular appearance that we notice in the sketch of Barros. It may be that the after the river has taken the southward turn, its course was not steady, which may explain the inability of the inhabitants to settle there. At the same time, it is possible that by that time the principal bank of the river, the southern bank, has been saturated, the withdrawal of water from the Saraswati was becoming more rapid and there was a tendency of the inhabitants to move towards the Hughli channel rather than going towards the west. We find that there is no detailed record on the port of Satgaon in the writings of the European travellers. This must have led the modern historians to conclude that Satgaon had declined with the rise of the port of Hughli established by the Portuguese in 1579. But that is not the entire story. Perhaps there was another reason for the dislocation of the function of the port of Satgaon. Once again, the modern historians, bent on concluding that that the silting of the Saraswati was the real and only reason for the decline of the port, did not pay much attention to the functional differences of the port and the town of Satgaon. The proximity of the prosperous town of Hughli, although in decline since the middle of the Eighteenth century, helped the town of Satgaon to continue without the port. The town of Satgaon however continued to function till the end of the Eighteenth century.

In the third essay J.B.P. More and Leena More examine the political and commercial role of the Raja of Cannanore in the Sixteenth and Seventeenth centuries. They mention that the port of Cannanore was part of the kingdom of Kolathanadu, whose ruler was known as Kolattiri and it was an insignificant place prior to the Eleventh century. According to them Jurfattan is the name given to Cannanore by Ibn Batuta. The place had several wealthy Muslim merchants and it was emerging as a Muslim–dominated port. The growing importance of this trading centre into a town in northern Kerala is seen from the Fourteenth century onwards and we find the discovery of Chinese ceramics which suggest that the Chinese had trade relations with Cannanore in the Fifteenth century itself. While this is so, when the Portuguese came to Malabar, the king of Cannanore wanted to assert his separate identity and so he had sent presents to both the King and Queen of Portugal. Later in 1502, when the Portuguese founded a factory in Calicut, the ruler of Cannanore wanted somehow to strike an alliance with the Portuguese king in order to counter the might of the Zamorin of Calicut. As a result of the overtures made by the King of Cannanore, the Portuguese sent their representative Pedro Alvares Cabral to visit Cannanore. In the meantime the ambassadors of the rulers of Quilon and also Cochin had also reached Cannanore. These ambassadors along with the ambassador of the King of Cannanore boarded Cabral's ship and sailed to Lisbon to meet Dom Manuel I, the king of

Portugal. Thus the Portuguese had a good understanding with the Raja of Cannanore and the merchants there. Hence the Portuguese could continue their trade in the port for 160 years. The Raja also well reciprocated his friendship with the Portuguese and he exercised his command over the trade in the hinterland of the port.

With the Dutch occupation of Cannanore in 1663 we find that the situation has not much changed because the Raja of Cannanore continued to have control in the hinterland trade. In fact maritime trade in the port of Cannanore began to flourish well because of the Muslim merchants and especially their trade with Maldives at that time under the patronage of the Raja. In the Seventeenth century Zamorin and the other local princes including that of Cannanore wanted the Dutch to chase the Portuguese away from their country, rendered little help to the Dutch during the wars. In fact the new Dutch chief of Cannanore, Van Weerden was blamed and accused of not stipulating a monopoly in spice trade and also in the cardamom and opium trade. In fact the powerful Muslim merchant prince, Ali Raja, dominated the hinterland trade in spices, cardamom and opium even under the Portuguese control of the port of Cannanore. This singularity of Cannanore seems to have paved the way in the beginning of the Eighteenth century for a stronger emergence of the Arakkal house as an independent political entity in the name of the Ali Raja. The latter even quarreled with the Kolattiri of Kolathanadu to demonstrate his independence. Ali Raja was so powerful during the Eighteenth century that he laid claim over the Maldive islands in the Indian Ocean, invaded and even imposed a certain control over the trade which traditionally had its own king. In fact the attempt of the Maldivians to get rid off Cannanore's interference in their affairs during this period, met with failure, for the Maldivian prince himself was taken in 1758 as a prisoner to Cannanore. However, after 1792 with the annexation of Northern Kerala including Cannanore as part of the Madras Presidency of British India had put an end to the sway of the Ali Raja in Cannanore.

Martin Krieger records that in 1616, King Christian IV founded the first *Ostindisk Kompagni*, and four years later the Scandinavians succeeded in acquiring the trading settlement of Tranquebar on the Coromandel Coast of India. The beginnings of this enterprise were promising, but Denmark's participation in the Thirty Years War lead to a decline of the intercontinental trade between Copenhagen and Tranquebar. So there was no traffic existed between 1639 and 1668 between India and Denmark. In 1650, the first Danish East India Company was dissolved. A recovery of the Danish economy from its deep economic crisis led to the foundation of the second *Ostindisk Kompagni* in 1670, which existed until 1729. The author analyzes the role of Danish shipping and trade between Tranquebar on the Coromandel Coast of India and Southeast Asia during the Seventeenth and Eighteenth Centuries. Like other Europeans the Danes also not only carried on their trade between India and Europe, but also joined in the race of intra-regional commodity exchange in the Indian Ocean. A lack of capital and a low number of intercontinental voyages forced them to seek profit within this intra-Asian trade. Their enterprises between India and South East Asia constituted an eminent lifeline to Danish Asia-trade. Especially after the collapse of the intercontinental trade between Copenhagen and Tranquebar entirely after AD.1639, intra-Asian trade between Coromandel and Southeast Asia became the major source of income and the basis of the survival of the very few remaining Danes – next to the gains of Danish piracy in the Bay of Bengal.

The study investigates into the Danish intra-Asiatic voyages between Coromandel and Southeast Asia and looks deep into the Danish motives for launching such trade in the 1620s, structural changes and the reasons for its end in the Eighteenth Century. An examination of the Danish intra-Asiatic trade between South India and Southeast Asia raises three basic questions: 1. To what degree did this trade function as a complement to intercontinental trade? 2. Who profited from this trade? 3. Why were the Danish East India Companies unable to gain legitimacy for their trade-monopoly concerning their own employees? The author concludes that the primary function of the Danish intra-Asiatic trade was to endow the intercontinental voyages to Copenhagen with sufficient commodities for the Europe-bound vessels. And the first intra-Asiatic voyages from Tranquebar to Mergui on the Malayan peninsula certainly responded to such expectations. As a consequence of the increasing discontinuity of intercontinental trade, intra-Asiatic trade under Danish colours increasingly became independent from intercontinental voyages. In this context, we witness the fact that the structures of intercontinental trade shaped the structures of commodity-exchange on the Bay of Bengal: Either its main aim was gaining return-cargoes such as pepper or the Danes merely participated in the traditional intra-Asiatic trade which mainly consisted of bartering South-Indian textiles against Southeast Asian spices and sandalwood without caring for the needs of the East India companies at home. The choice of the various trading emporia frequented by the Danes supports this thesis. While trading via Macassar between 1627 and 1640, the main interest was purchasing cloves for the sale in Masulipatnam. But when the Danes headed for Bantam after 1670, they mainly procured pepper for exporting to Europe. While the initial capital for the Danish intra-Asiatic trade mainly came from the merchants of Copenhagen – be they of Danish or Dutch origin – and the royal Danish family, it was indeed, to some degree, the investors were not benefited by their investments in ships and trading settlements.

Regarding the question of gains from this trade, Martin Kreiger opines that we have to separate the periods of regular intercontinental traffic and those with only irregular sailings or of an entire collapse such as between 1639 and 1668. During the period of interrupted intercontinental traffic it was mainly the merchants at the shores of the Indian Ocean seeking shelter under the Danish flag profited from the Danish enterprise in the Indian Ocean region – mainly by utilizing company-vessels, trading-settlements and Danish neutrality for their own purposes. On the other hand, intra-Asiatic trade was carried out to the Copenhagen shareholders' benefit during periods of regular intercontinental sailings. The trading-policy of the Kingdom of Denmark was, such as in many other countries, characterized by a mercantilistic policy during the Seventeenth and Eighteenth centuries. Even more it is astonishing that the various Danish trading companies never pursued an effective trading monopoly in the Indian Ocean. The explanation for our observation might be found in the fact, that the Danes – as a minor trading-nation in the Indian Ocean – never would have profited by such a monopoly since they depended on private trade and on trade with their European or Asian competitors as a result of their lack of own trading-capacity in the Indian Ocean. This fact resembles the main difference between Danish and Dutch intra-Asiatic trade, because the Dutch successfully maintained a trading-monopoly in the Indian Ocean until 1743.

II

The second section deals with merchants, middlemen and business. Here Laxmi Narayan Raut examines the role of private and official trade in medieval Orissa. He underlines the importance of the local merchants, agents and brokers in the trade besides the role of the European trading companies. They Europeans were in need of the local merchants and brokers to assist them in their overseas trade. The Mughal officials and the Factors of the European companies played a key role in private trade. The internal and the external trade of Orissa received new strides with the advent of the Europeans and with the participation of indigenous merchants but could not continue to flourish for long. Many factors were at work which hindered the prosperity. The European companies had to pay customs and transit duties to the Mughal authorities on all transactions on import and export. Even though the merchants paid the normal duties their commercial activities were not free from difficulties. To a great extent, the conduct of trade depended on the privileges secured through *farmans*, *nishans*, *parwanas* and *dastaks* granted by Mughal emperors, princes, *subahdars* and *diwans* respectively. Since the trade privileges were very often infringed by the Mughal officers at the provincial level, procurement of repeated confirmations of such trade privileges had to be obtained by the

Europeans. Such an administrative requirement for trade operation was considered very irksome for certain reasons. Firstly, the merchants had to offer bribes and presents to the Mughal officials for obtaining trade privileges. Again there was a rush to procure more and more trade privileges by all the European trading companies. Although the main purpose of granting privileges was to facilitate the trade activities, it could not become so. The merchants with the passage of time became subjected to harassment by local officers. Further, it indirectly encouraged official corruption, and adversely affected the trade. The frequent changes in governorship of Orissa and their short tenures which became a common feature during the later part of the Mughal rule in Orissa also hindered the trade. It was customary for a new governor to renew the existing trade privileges. But it often became a difficult affair on the part of the merchants to deal with all the local governors and their subordinate officers. As a result, various exactions of Mughal officials, their interference with the free passage of merchandise, receipt of bribes and forced presents in the form of money, guns, horses, and luxury articles etc., became very common. Under such situation trade could not flourish.

After 1670 the rulers introduced various exactions, imposition of transit duties and so the oppression and harassment of the Mughal governors in Orissa went on increasing. An important administrative change which caused uncertainty in trade and commerce was the transfer of jurisdictions over Balasore from Orissa to Bengal. On important policy matters pertaining to Orissa decision was to be taken in court of Murshidabad in Bengal. The Mughal Viceroy of Bengal exercised control over Orissa through his deputy. These new developments were not considered to be favourable from the commercial point of view. If the merchants were oppressed, the immediate relief was not sought from the local officer at Balasore but from the Viceroy of Bengal. By the time such grievances were examined and set aside a lot of time would entail and a large amount of loss to the trade was carried on. Further, the geographical factor for the decline of trade in the port-towns such as Balasore, Pipli and Hariharpur had to be mentioned because these commercial centres were suffering from accumulation of silt on the mouth of the river. As a result, ports at the mouth of these rivers became unsuitable for ships to come in. Again the Indian traders who belonged mostly to the nobility and state officials of the empire had lost their larger-share in the trade owing to foreign competition. The general impoverishment of the nobility, the political turmoil in the twilight of the Mughal empire and the crisis in the economy resulted in setting a trend of decline in trade.

B. Krishnamurthy in his paper mentions that the French on the Coromandel Coast when began to trade and establish settlements they had some problems such as lack of expertise in the local language, customs and manners, as well as inadequate funds at their disposal to invest in their commerce. These factors forced them to heavily rely on intermediaries, who were naturally the indigenous merchant community of the locality.. In his opinion, the commercial intermediaries had served the French Company at two stages. The *Mudaliar* (*Courtier* or the Chief *dubash*) served as a bridge between the Company and the local merchants and the individual held the highest post for which any Indian was eligible or entitled to under the French organization of trade. In the second stage, the native merchants served as the intermediaries between the Company and the actual producers/ manufacturers. The home authorities were not quite happy about the role of intermediaries in the import and export trade of the French Company in India and they wanted to do away with them in a phased manner. They advised the *Conséil Supérieur* to instruct some young Frenchmen in the local languages, so that the middleman might be replaced in due course. But, the efforts of the *Conséil* and the gratuity offered, failed to encourage the youngsters to take the trouble of learning the native tongues. While the other European trading companies, as corporate bodies never attempted to have joint ventures with the natives, the French Company had really taken a fancy for them. Its poor financial condition and its inability to monopolise intra-Asian trade, must have prompted the French to resort to joint ventures.

In the later period (the early years of the Eighteenth Century) we find also the mention of *marchands de la Compagnie* (Company merchants) with whom contracts for piece-goods were signed year after year. Regarding the mode of procurement of the Indian merchandise, especially textiles, it is noticed that the *dadni* or the system of advances, was widely prevalent. Under this system contracts were prepared with the native merchants - individuals as well as those who have organized a joint-stock Company – to supply a stipulated quantity of certain varieties of textiles, the pattern, quality and price being specified. Besides their commercial enterprises the French Company had also indulged in revenue collection in the territories under their jurisdiction. To ensure a fixed and assured income, they have resorted to the *ijara* system or the tax-farming. Those native merchants who associated with them in their commercial activities, had entered into tax-farming. In 1702, the Company merchants as a corporate body took to farming of the sale of tobacco and betel at the rate of 200 *pagodas* per year for two years. The Courtiers of the French Company at Pondicherry like Guruvappillai, Kanagaraya Mudali and Ananda Ranga Pillai took to tax-farming, personally or through their agents, such as land revenue collection, customs and transit duty collection, tobacco and betel nut farming, arrack farming, salt farming, etc., The intermediary merchant community thus turned out to be quite indispensable to the French Company authorities on the Coromandel Coast.

The chaotic political situation of the Carnatic region in the absence of a strong central power and the competition from other European trading companies, which vied with each other to monopolise the Indian commercial scene, forced the French to understand the futility of seeking the agents and the sources of supply of local merchandise from far-off production and manufacturing centres in the hinterland. Moreover, the French realised that the presence of wealthy merchants in their colonies would enhance their prestige as well as the steady revenue from their territorial possessions. The French conferred on the Courtiers titles and awarded them with medals, by way of recognizing the meritorious services rendered by them to the Company. They provided the native merchant community several avenues of accumulating wealth like participation in the import-export trade, shipping, money lending and exchanging, tax-farming and minting. Being a commercially and economically weak power, the French Company had to cooperate with the locals to get its business going. Only the religious intolerance of the French system proved to be insurmountable hindrance between the company and the merchants. The local merchants served the Company in the disposal of the imported European goods.

Ruby Maloni in her essay records that the Portuguese in the Sixteenth Century had extended preferential treatment to the Jains, to counteract the Arabs. Therefore the Jain merchants were visible and active in the ports occupied by the Portuguese. These Jains had mainly exported cotton textiles, indigo, wheat, rice, agate goods and even leather items to West Asian ports like Ormuz, Mocha, Jiddah, Muscat and Aden from the ports of Porbandar, Jamnagar, Diu and Cambay. Among the Muslim merchant communities of Gujarat, the *Shia Khojas* and *Sunni Memons* were also highly active at that time in the Arabian Sea trade. Taken together, the entire group of the merchants of Gujarat it may be said that they had formed a strong part of the commercial elite of the India -West Asia trade. Further, we know that Gujarat had also been well interlinked and developed trade connections with the east African coast. Gujarati shipping called at Kilwa, Mombasa, Malindi and Pate, as part of their round voyage to the Red Sea brought gold and ivory in exchange for textiles. Thus Indian trade in the western Indian Ocean, flowed along the two established maritime channels, one through the Red Sea, Cairo and Alexandria, and the other through the Persian Gulf and up through Basra and Baghdad.

The emergence of the Ottoman, Safavid and Mughal empires had set a new scene for maritime trade. These three major early modern Muslim dynasties established an effective *pax Islamica* linking the traditional civilizational centres of West Asia and South Asia. Merchants of India, Arabia and Persia operated within a broad commercial and even in a linguistic environment. The Safavids and the Mughals energetically encouraged the pilgrim traffic to the Islamic holy cities in Hijaz. To these factors the development of the trade in Yemeni coffee also occurred. Turkish merchants became the principal purchasers of coffee in Yemen and this pre-eminence was not challenged by the European buyers even at the height of the European coffee trade in the early Eighteenth century. The trade between the Red Sea and Gujarat had also been dominated by the Karimi merchants, the Cairo-based mercantile organization for a long time, but they did not hold a monopoly of the traffic. In fact, easier access to the Red Sea and the Persian Gulf, following the decline of Portuguese power, strengthened the position of the Surat merchants *vis a vis* the *Multanis* and other merchants on the caravan routes between India and Persia. The merchant navy of Surat had been developed and in 1650s we find fifty ships, many of them large and well-built. In 1651, the Mughal administration initiated a building programme for sea-going vessels, and four to six large ships were built for the voyages to Bandar Abbas and Mokha. The importance of Surat at that time was chiefly reflected by the emergence of 'merchant princes', entrepreneurs of a hitherto unknown wealth and status. Virji Vora was a leading merchant and later we find Mulla Abdul Ghafur, the owner of seventeen seagoing ships based at Surat. The small-scale merchants competed actively with the well-established merchants. Many of them were the agents of other merchants, earning a commission on the proceeds of the transactions. However Abdul Ghafur was unable to establish a monopoly in his favoured Red Sea trade because he was unable to cope with the multitude of minor merchants. Gujarati brokers or *Dalals* and moneychangers or *Sarrafs* became very indispensable for the supply of specific commodities and transfer of funds.

Throughout the Seventeenth century, Gujarati trade to the Red Sea and Persian Gulf continued in force, and neither the English nor the Dutch affected the flow adversely. Since the conveyance of spices had abated, this phase may be considered to be the high tide of India's textile trade to West Asia. Significant items of export to this region included foodstuff like rice, sugar, pulses, wheat and oil, for which there was considerable demand. Such food commodities helped to feed port cities like Ormuz and Aden. Trade in Bulk goods fetched relatively less profit. Gujarat also exported raw cotton to the West Asian markets. Specialty items such as *pan* or betel leaf coveted in the Safavid court were also exported. Soon after tobacco began to be cultivated in Mughal India, it also became an important item of export. By the end of the Seventeenth century, Indian carriers not only lost the trade in pepper to a substantial extent, they also lost, albeit to a lesser degree, the carriage of indigo since European ships diverted this trade to Europe. The Indian imports were concentrated on bullion and horses, and specific items such as dyewoods from the Persian Gulf. Further, many types of wines, silks, carpets, rosewater and medicinal gum resin only made the list of imports from West Asia impressive.

The crucial significance of the West Asian market was for the Indian import of bullion. While Mocha was known as the treasure house of the Mughals, the Persian Gulf also yielded a rich bounty of precious metals, and it was on these markets that India depended for the inflow of the much-needed currency. The direct shipment of silver from the Persian Gulf and the Red Sea made the Gujarat economy more monetised. The trade to the Red Sea in particular brought in large consignments of bullion every year in August and September. The Spanish *rial* of eight was the dominating coin of those which were imported, which included European, Turkish and Persian bullion, not to speak of gold and silver in bars. Gujarati merchants moved northwards from Bandar Abbas to Isfahan, the splendid capital of Shah Abbas. There were already settlements of Indian merchants there, who had come by land routes. The fall of the Safavids in 1722 disturbed the internal situation in Persia. Both the demand for Indian commodities in Persia and for Persian commodities in India fell off. In the Red sea, the trend was in the same direction. The Gujarati merchants projected a sophisticated network of mercantile practices, since they came from an urbanized milieu. There had been approximately sixty urban centers in the Mughal *Subah* of Gujarat. As middlemen and moneychangers, the Gujarati merchants utilised their mercantile expertise even when venturing outside their own regional base. Thus the Gujarati merchant class had been one of the mercantile categories who responded actively and sturdily to the incursion of European trading companies in the Indian Ocean.

In the next essay Philomena Sequeira Antony examines the role of Hindu dominance in the Goa-based long-distance trade during the Eighteenth Century. She mentions that many factors and forces such as the steady decline in the trade of pepper and spices, loss of many Indo-Portuguese settlements and territories, challenges posed by the other European rivals in trade in the Seventeenth Century compelled the Portuguese Crown to slacken its policy over the monopoly of commerce in the Indian Ocean. This led to the entry of private merchants into an arena that was Crown monopoly earlier. The three Portuguese ministers, Marquis of Pombal, Martinho de Melo e Castro and Dom Rodrigo de Souza Coutinho, influenced by the liberal movements in Europe, stressed on keeping pace with the economic reforms in the continent. Lisbon opened itself to liberal ideas and ended up throwing the doors of economic opportunities open to its subjects. Native Hindu merchants of Goa were quick to take advantage of the need of Portugal. They joined in the commercial nexus as subordinate partners. Utilising their business acumen, knowledge of local languages and their contacts outside the *Estado da India*, they entered the trajectory of trade at various levels. They played the lead role in the official trade involving sale of tobacco for a century and a half. They also monopolized the contracts for the sale of snuff in Goa from 1675 to 1825. When Bahian leaf tobacco was introduced in Goa by way of direct imports, the Hindu traders took the contracts of this trade between 1775 and 1825. They acted as suppliers of a wide range of goods that formed part of the official, reciprocal trade to Brazil, Lisbon and Africa on the tobacco account. They also joined in the race for the long-distance private trade to the empire, covering Africa and America, besides Portugal. Seven indigenous merchants and their associates had monopolized the sale of American leaf tobacco spanning the forty seven years (1775 – 1822). These native merchants of Goa were active players in the long-distance private trade as well. State participation in seaborne trade was minimal during this period. Lisbon largely depended on and benefited from the collection of duties at various entry and exit points of the *Estado da India*. Remittances of goods by Goan Hindu merchants were regular and they are reflected by ample references in the records preserved in the Historical Archives of Goa.

Commodities such as textiles, pepper, cinnamon, diamonds, incense, tea, porcelain and sealing wax were exported to Lisbon as well as Luanda and ports of Brazil. The trading network of these Hindus such as Bulla Naik, Govinda Naik and Dugu Kamat, had spread across parts of India, Asia, Africa and America for forty years (roughly,1725 onwards). They had their agents in Balaghat, Macau, Mozambique, Bahia, Angola and Portugal. These native merchants did not hesitate to appeal to the authorities in Lisbon for redressal of grievances. Petitions by the above mentioned merchants and others like Custam, Hari, Venkatesh Kamat and Vitogi Kamat – were addressed to his majesty seeking royal protection for their trade. They claimed that their goods dispatched in December 1765 and February 1766, and earlier sent to Bahia and Lisbon in 1763 and 1764, were sequestered in Lisbon, resulting in heavy losses to them. Although Hindus were reduced to a clear minority in Goa by the end of the Seventeenth Century, yet we find that their economic power remained intact and the dependence of the Portuguese on this native Hindu mercantile community had continued. It is learnt that the Portuguese could not have lasted for a long time in Goa without the significant economic role played by the Hindu merchants.

Surendra Gopal in his paper mentions that the Hindu Indian traders in Russia had mostly hailed from the North-Western India and they were popularly known as *Multanis*.

These Hindu Indians traded in the cities of Russia, mostly lying along the Volga river such as Kasan and Saratov went also up to the Russian capital Moscow. They were money lenders who met the credit needs of small farmers, ordinary soldier, lower-rank state functionaries and traders. They also actively participated in the Russo-Persian trade since Indian merchants were present in all the important Persian cities. Once in a while only we find in the Russian records the presence of *Marwari* traders. The author examines the role of one of the Marawri traders namely Marwari Barayev, an Indian in Russia in the Eighteenth Century. He describes the career of this *Marwari* trader, who in a decade and half emerged as the richest and most influential Indian trader in Astrakhan. Marwari Barayev is first mentioned in the year 1721 in the "Register of Petitions and Reports Received in the Chancellory of the Governor of Astrakhan". The year 1726 unmistakably confirmed Marwari Barayev's financial clout and we find that he had purchased from his fellow Indians fifty-two loan deeds worth 3047 *roubles* executed in the past and due for payment in the coming years. Marwari Barayev had successfully built up his business of money lending, financing of imports and sale of imported commodities at whole-sale rates. Some of the borrowers had mortgaged their immovable properties before obtaining the loan. Supply of credit and capital and attaching movable and immovable properties of borrowers had made him very rich. He was lending money even to his compatriots.

Marwari Barayev was invited to Orenburg by the promoters of the new trade centre, I.K. Krillov, V.N. Tatishchev, I.I. Neplyuev and P.I. Richkov. He went there and prepared a document which listed four trade routes leading to Indian capital Delhi from Astrakhan. He favoured the Central Asian line for promoting Russo-Indian trade in future. He supported his contention by referring to the decay of trade in Persia and Astrakhan following the outbreak of anarchy after Nadir Shah had come to power. According to him when peace prevailed in Persia, two hundred Indian traders annually visited Astrakhan. Now the number had come down to eighty. The Bukharan route was the shortest. If security of life and property could be ensured, he was confident, around six hundred Indian traders would come every year. He also prepared a list of Indian goods and Russian goods imported into and exported from Orenburg. The Empress Anna Ivanovna concurred with the proposal of Krillov in her Edict of 11 February 1736. She ordered one thousand *roubles* should be advanced to Marwari Barayev from the Royal Treasury to purchase goods to be sent to India through his agents from Orenburg. Marwari Barayev was to return the money after his agents returned. However he never made the trip to India. He could not send his agents to India. When he arrived in Astrakhan from Orenburg, the local Governor, V.N. Tatishchev, arrested him on flimsy charges and put him in gaol. Tatishchev feared that the rise of Astrakhan as a commercial centre of eastern goods would result in his loss of income and authority. This was the beginning of his misfortunes and probably he never recovered from the slide in his fortunes.

The study throws much light on the range of the trading activities of Indian merchants, the different dimensions of usury they practiced and the hurdles they faced. It shows that these Indians were not lacking in entrepreneurial skill; what hampered them were non-commercial factors. Extending loan on condition that the borrower would go out of Russia and bring specified goods to be purchased by the trader who had given the loan, seems to have been an accepted business practice. Marwari Barayev had the entrepreneurial talent. Starting as a small moneylender who had lent a tiny sum of twelve *roubles*, he, within a decade, became an owner of assets worth between 50,000 and 77,000 *roubles*. Besides cash he also owned immovable properties in and around Astrakhan. He prospered because he kept on exploring new avenues of business. From a moneylender he turned into a supplier of capital to Russian, Indian and foreign merchants. He traded as a wholesale merchant and made a fortune. But he was in position to confront the local bureaucrats, who had turned hostile to him. This was the fate of Hindu merchants in foreign lands extending from the peninsula of Arabia, to Persia, to Iran, to Central Asia, to Russia. Absence of explicit state support prevented them from successfully standing up to local bureaucratic oppression.

III

The third section in this book deals with commodities, commerce and coinage. Syed Ejaz Hussain in his paper mentions that India and Persia (modern Iran) have been distinct but not dissimilar civilizations. Geography has made the two countries close neighbours sharing a common border between Baluchistan (now in Afghanistan) and Iran. When Herat was the capital of Persia under the Timurids India had a common boundary with Persia. Indian rulers from Babur (1526-30) to Aurangzeb (1659-1707) possessed Afghanistan except for Qandhar which Shah Jahan lost to Iran in 1649 and never recovered it. Qandhar served as the common overland corridor between India and Persia. On the sea route Indian ports like Ahmedabad and Cambay (in Gujarat), Calicut (in the Western coast), Bhatkal (in the kingdom of Vijayanagar), and Chittagong (in Bengal) had commercial traffic with Persian Gulf through the ports of Hormuz (captured by the Portuguese in 1515), Lari Bandar and Bandar Abbas (originally known as Gombroon that rose after 1515 and fell in 1760), and finally Abu Shahr.

India and Iran have very intimate cultural relations from early times. The Persian culture particularly after Firdausi's Shahnama (completed cir.1009-10) began to envelope a large area in its domain. Indian sultanates - Delhi as well as provincial kingdoms of Bengal, Gujarat, Malwa, Kashmir, Jaunpur and the five Deccan kingdoms of Qutubshahis (of Golkonda), Adilshahis (of Bijapur), Nizam Shahis (of Ahmadnagar), Imad Shahis (of Berar) and Barid Shahis (of Bidar) had a massive infusion of Persian culture practically at all levels. Cultural relationship was further reinforced by the economic ties. Indian merchants - even Jains and Marwaris - exported textiles, indigo, sugar and spices (including ginger and cardamom), sandal-wood and saffron, even *paan* (betel leaves) to Persia and brought Pearls, gold, silver and other rarities to India. The Persian merchants used to bring silk textiles, carpets and war-horses from their country to India for sale as per the Indian royal needs. Trade exchange between India and Persia got revitalized during the Safavid-Mughal period. One noteworthy manifestation of the two powerful oriental kingdoms was their strong and stable currency system. The Safavid rulers from Shah Ismail I (1502-24) to Shah Husain I (1694-1722) and the Mughal rulers from Babur (1526-30) and more specifically from Akbar (1556-1605) to Aurangzeb (1659-1707) maintained a strong silver currency and in many aspects their monetary pattern was similar. Every city of importance both in Persia and India had its mints. The mints in Persia were farmed out to private persons in auction to the highest bidder. While in India the mints were fully a Government run department. The mints, however, produced huge quantity of coins in both the countries and catered sufficiently to the demand of money by the people in general and the merchant class in particular.

Commerce in Safavid Persia and Mughal India was conducted largely in cash. The money-oriented commerce and tax pattern were the two fundamental factors that facilitated both the countries to produce a high standard coinage in huge quantity. A tri-metallic currency (gold, silver and copper) was maintained in both the oriental kingdoms. However, silver coin was their principal currency. In spite of this, Persia had a chronic shortage of silver throughout the Safavid period. The Indian *banias* who resided in Persia (it is reported that there were ten to twelve thousand in Isfahan alone) used to send back their profits of usury to India in the form of silver and gold made the situation worse. John Chardin notes that these Indians, like true leeches extracted all the gold and silver of Persia and send them to their own country so that in the year 1677 when he departed from Persia, he could not see there any more gold or silver. On the other hand, the Mughal India, though devoid of domestic sources of silver, maintained exceptionally pure and standard silver coins not only during the period of the great Mughals but even after that for several decades. The main reason for this was the enormous currency influx to the empire coming in transit trade. A Dutch factor in 1634 remarked that the total value of textiles, indigo, sugar and gum lac exported annually from Agra, Lahore, Sind, Gujarat and Daulatabad sold in the markets of Iran was 2,130,350 *Muhanunadis* or 24.20 metric tons of silver. The merchants of Surat alone had imported annually 22.7 metric tons of silver as reported by another Dutch factor. According to an estimate, on an average of 25 metric tons of silver was exported to the Mughal empire from the Iranian ports in the second quarter of the Seventeenth century. The author concludes that the Indian mints received silver from the trade through the Red Sea as well as the caravan trade via overland route. The Indian mints therefore, at least till the time of Aurangzeb never experienced any scarcity of silver. However, after the death of Aurangzeb the situation changed and the imperial mints began to face the silver shortage abysmally.

Nicholas Rhodes in his study describes the trade across the Himalayas based on the numismatic evidences. He mentions that the coinages of the Himalayas are of silver or gold, even though there are no silver or gold mines in the area. The precious metal used for the various coinages must have been acquired in the course of trade. A study of these coinages gives interesting insights into the trading patterns at different times. The author attempts to consider the various coinages struck in or near the Himalayas. Copper mines, however, existed in many parts of the Himalayas, and the existence of copper coinage in the region also sheds light on trade patterns. The period covered by this study is mainly the Seventh century until the Eighteenth century, although occasional references to earlier and later coins are also touched upon. The area covered will be from Kashmir in the west, up to Assam in the east. This is a period when documentation regarding trade is scanty, and knowledge of trading links is much less than for it is the Nineteenth century, when the British started to maintain detailed statistics of the wealth they were able to extract from their Empire.

Salt was always in demand, because the lack of other sources of iodine caused goitre, and it had to be obtained, either from India in the south, or from the Tibetan salt lakes to the north. At higher altitudes, crops were scarce and very seasonal, but the Tibetan frontier was close. Many Himalayan people were involved in modest barter trade across the frontier, exchanging grain for salt, wool and other commodities from Tibet and beyond. The trade that is mainly dealt with here in this paper is the large scale trade, involving high value products in bulk, financed and organised by rich professional traders or monasteries – and often involving the local Himalayan people only as porters. As regards the Himalayan States, it was purely transit trade, but the local people and rulers were able to benefit from the existence of this trade, not only by providing labour for carriage, but also by charging taxes and customs duties of various kinds. In particular, they could also insist that bullion was struck into local coinage before being sent on to be used for the purchase of goods, and in that way the controller of the mint could benefit from the hidden tax represented by the seigneurage levied to cover minting costs and profit.

Trade with Western Tibet and Central Asia had previously been mainly routed through Kashmir. Then it was also rerouted through Kangra. The trade with Tibet was brisk, and the extent of the coins certainly proves that the economic activity in the valley was considerable. In addition, there was considerable activity in the artistic field, with stone and bronze images being commissioned for the first time, indicating the existence of relatively large numbers of specialist stone and metal workers. As neither gold nor silver are mined in Nepal, the metal must have been acquired through trans-Himalayan trade. The gold probably came from Tibet, in exchange for goods exported from India. Coins of this type are sometimes found in Bihar, and must have been used to purchase such trade goods, with the Nepalese king cleverly profiting from the seigneurage. Most probably he required that all gold bullion from Tibet had to be taken to his mint to be struck into coin, before it could be exported to India. Silver coins have not yet been found outside Nepal, so the silver may have been another trade item, possibly acquired from India. Trade between India and the Himalayas was not always trans-Himalayan trade with Tibet or Central Asia, but occasionally local produce became an important export. One commodity that was produced in the Himalayas and that was in demand in India was copper. The copper mines existed in many areas from Kashmir to Bhutan, although the cost of extraction meant that the mines were no longer commercially viable. One period when numismatic evidence demonstrates the importance of this trade was during the reign of Akbar. Throughout the reign, two of the most productive mints for copper coins were Dogaon and Bahraich, both situated just south of the Nepalese border to the west of Kathmandu.

The trade with Tibet brought immense wealth to the Valley of Nepal, as testified, not only by the coinage, but also by the construction of temples and the commissioning of works of art by the Newar traders. Tibet agreed that all trade with India, even though conducted by other than Newari merchants, would be channeled through the Kathmandu Valley in preference to the routes to the east (i.e. via Sikkim, Bhutan or Tawang). One mechanism used by the Nepalese at this time was to forbid the export of silver bullion. Any trader importing silver from India or from Tibet, either as bullion or as coin, had to take the silver to the mint, where it was struck into coin. The Nepalese kings made considerable profits from the alloy and from the seigneurage charged by the mint. This mechanism was also used by other Himalayan states, allowing them to profit from transit trade. The Garhwal king probably copied the Nepalese, in insisting that silver bullion could not be exported, so that traders had to bring their silver bullion to his mint. Nicholas Rhodes concludes that bullion, and in particular silver, played an important part in this trade, and striking silver coins was a way in which the Himalayan states could profit from the transit trade, which might otherwise have provided them with little benefit.

Karubaki Datta in her paper mentions that at the time of the arrival of the Portuguese in India, textiles had been more used in the country trade. Piece goods of India were exported to the ports of South East Asia to be exchanged for pepper and spices. Presumably, till the third decade of the Sixteenth Century the Portuguese home demand for cloth had been met through the supply of the Dutch merchants who in return took salt and Indian goods. The confiscation of the Dutch ships and cargoes by King Philip II and closing of the Iberian ports in 1585, 1595 and 1597 brought the traditional practice of the country trade to a standstill. Thereafter the Portuguese began to import directly cloth for their own internal market and the practice continued till the third decade of the Seventeenth Century. One reason for this development was the demand generated by the slave trade in African countries – especially São João de Mina from where they obtained the maximum number of slaves. In this context the author discusses the significance of Portuguese trade in Indian cotton textiles during the late Eighteenth Century.

Trade in cotton textiles was carried on and we find that funds were regularly remitted from Lisbon for purchase of Indian cloths during the middle of the Eighteenth Century. Indian cotton textiles by this time had become suitable for use by the slaves of Brazil and Angola. There is enough documentary proof to show clearly the nature of this lucrative slave trade and textiles. By the middle of the Eighteenth Century there was so much of illegal trade with textiles suitable for the slaves of Africa that it adversely affected the official Portuguese trade. Unfortunately for the Crown, the scope of this was provided by a Royal order itself. Permission was given on 17 November 1761 to vessels returning from India to halt at the port of São Paulo de Assumpção of Angola and even to trade with the articles which were being carried from India. One customs house was set up exclusively for this purpose. The officials of the ship took the advantage to start full fledged trade in textiles particularly in those varieties which were coarse and plain and therefore known as cloths for the blacks. These were used not only in Angola but in Brazil as well. Since the ships did not have the permission to halt at the ports of Brazil an entrepot was set up in Angola itself. This adversely affected the interests of the metropolis which reserved for itself the monopoly of trade with the colonies. Only those pieces that did not sell in Angola were carried to Portugal and there they failed to fetch the desired price. This interrupted the usual trading practices of the country.

Some cotton factories had been by this time set up in Portugal to process the raw cotton imported from Brazil and produce some piece goods for Angola. This parallel and illegal trade blocked that line as well. With a plan to check this practice the King of Portugal issued a new order whereby all the ships then onwards were ordered to transport their stock of piece goods directly to Lisbon. They were no longer allowed to unload their cargo of textiles in any port other than Lisbon, be it for use in the metropolis or elsewhere. Heavy punishment and fine awaited for those who ignored the order. As expected, this curb on cotton trade of the Indian merchants created resentment among them. There is no evidence that the Government in Lisbon paid any heed to these grievances. It only points out the importance of Indian textiles in the economy of Portugal during the first half of the Eighteenth Century. While it is true that the Portuguese trade in Indian cotton textiles did benefit from the Napoleonic wars, the upsurge seems to have begun a few years before the war broke out. According to statistics we find that Angola exported almost 700,000 slaves during the 70 years from 1701 to 1770. Over half of these went to Rio de Janeiro in Brazil. It was in this background that trade in cotton textiles expanded in the last quarter of the Eighteenth Century. There was a series of tax regulations the objective of which was to increase the trade through the port of Goa. The main objective was also to connect Goa with other colonies of Portugal, particularly those in Brazil where we find some tax concessions that were announced for those articles which were re-exported by Portuguese ships to the ports of Brazil and the African coast. On the whole there was special encouragement to export coarse cotton textiles to Brazil that had the highest demand. In slight modification to the previous order, concessions were also announced in 1783 for articles which were produced elsewhere but loaded in Goa. These articles which were to be re-exported from Portugal were to enjoy certain tax concessions while no such concession was given to commodities which were to remain in the country. Even in this category some exceptions were made for certain cotton cloths like *Zuartes, Coromandels, Chellas, Cadeas, Lenhas, Languins* and some more varieties from Gujarat commonly grouped together as cloths for the blacks. These no matter re-exported or not, would have to pay only half the taxes. These textiles were collected from Surat, Balaghat, Daman and Diu in the West coast of India. Lisbon merchants were also conscious of the textiles available in Madras and Bengal. Thus the textiles carried from India were used in Portugal in three different ways such as consumption within the country itself, re-export to the ports of Brazil and the African coast, re-export to other European countries. All the three however were interlinked.

A big portion of the textile varieties used for trade came from Surat. The items of export from this port were many. It included the most common among them *being zuartes, cadeas, chelas and lenhas*. These items were also available in Coromandel but the Portuguese preferred to collect these from Surat because the price there was found to be low. These articles were also in high demand in West Africa. *Dotis* were used for printing and dyeing in Portugal. In other words the tax concessions for cotton textiles were declared not out of a mere goodwill to regenerate the *Estado da India* but out of a definite motive to use the imports from Goa to serve the interests of the metropolis and her colonies of greater importance. This was done either through exports to other European countries or to colonies in the North Atlantic. Thus Goa, whose contribution to the overall economy of Portugal had become negligible by this time but it was again brought in the orbit through her contribution to the regeneration of Portuguese economy in general.

Finally, Tilottama Mukherjee in her essay discusses trade and the regional economy of Bengal and makes a reassessment on the functioning of the Early English East India Company State. She states that the tendency in the existing historiography is to view eighteenth-century Bengal as a fragile economy (whether or not historians state that assumption explicitly) that collapsed with the incursion of the Company. The sources, however, tell a different story, with coexisting and multiple routes and markets existing well during the period of the Company's first intrusion and indeed feeding into its networks of procurement. The Company's checks on the flow of trade or its infrastructure of revenue-collecting institutions along roads and embankments, all exhibit a concern to collect its revenues and to procure commodities in a situation of great fluidity. If at a higher level, it was trying to centralise, for instance by destroying a level of local *zamindari* markets, in the early years of its rule no such wholesale reorganisation of the Bengal's market was even considered. The ambitious nature of the regulations was belied by their haphazard manner of being put into practice, which moreover stuck closely to existing paths of trade as it proceeded along a decentralised network of diverse routes. She in her paper considers the ways in which the Company State tried to intervene, or to control various aspects of the economy and this measures either success or failure. Though much work has been done on the nature of the Company State, its involvement with the economy has often been an emotive and contentious issue, with very contradictory pictures being painted in different writings. To some, the Company was a basically exploitative interloper that destroyed a delicate network of indigenous co-operation that had developed over centuries. For others, the Company was the prime mechanism of modernisation in Bengal, opening the region to a wider range of international and intercultural contacts. Tied into local estates and the revenue collection of landed élite and rulers, as they were, these market formations were difficult to dislodge entirely or to regulate out of existence by collecting duty and taxes at a different source. Evidences suggest that the economy was so decentralised that the Company dispensation could not initially subordinate it in Bengal.

Tilottamma discusses the grain trade, the cotton weaving industry, the silk industry, the volume of trade and the role of the English East India Company state in Bengal. She mentions elaborately the efforts of the Company State to intervene in Bengal's trading and marketing circuits and related aspects of the local supply chain. Existing infrastructural networks always preceded the State; markets, merchants and commodities did not come into existence due to state regulation. The highly market-responsive and cost-competitive structure of production was mainly determined by the sophisticated economic infrastructure. Evidences suggest the notions of widespread decline in late eighteenth-century demanding for a reappraisal. This is not to deny that the economic sphere suffered fractures, but to specify their limited and commodity-specific, rather than structural, nature. The wider 'modification', which authors such as Datta, or 'collapse' as Chaudhury and Sen have depicted, seem to attribute to the Company State more power and influence than it actually exercised in the early years. The Company's depredations, in practice, certainly created some major losers like the Jagath Seths or Omichand or Khwaja Wajid, largely on account of these rich bankers and merchants extensive connection with the political regimes displaced by the new State. From a perspective of hindsight, it may be inappropriate in the context to apportion blame to any particular individual or group for 'complicity' in colonialism.

Though the use of force could sometimes rebound upon its agents, an increased armed presence as manifested in armed guards in factories and the growth of cantonments and military garrisons, betray a more aggressive and territorial motive than merely policing commodity flow. Incidents of dacoities are mentioned in our records, especially in the 1770s and 80s. The economic, ecological and political instability of this time occasioned major disruption in many spheres of life. While during the *Nizamat* period, travellers had noted the relative safety with which they moved, Company records refer to looting and plunder. Guarded boats carrying treasure could fall prey to mass groups of as many as 100-150 people although in 1753 merchants could send bullion from one part of Bengal to another protected only by two or three peons.

The Company's objectives, at least on paper, were to encourage and promote free trade internally and through import and export markets with neighbouring districts and adjoining countries. 'Public markets', according to this rhetoric, were to be kept free and monopolies abolished; as the Company reserved to itself the prerogative of regulation, no duties were to be imposed on goods brought to market except for fixed customs authorised by the State. The crafts and industry of the natives was to be encouraged and assistance and protection granted to all manufacturers willing to return to their former occupation, if it should appear that any such manufacturers have either abandoned their settlement or quitted their Business. The Company espoused a benign language of fostering local activity, promising government protection to the manufactures of particular districts, which appeared jeopardised by international trade. In their interpretation of the Company state, some may have placed too much credence in the official account. The state regime was more exploitative than their stated aims suggest, as in practice, the Company imposed and extended monopolies, far from completely suppressing fiscal barriers, it multiplied transit taxes. The State's inability to oversee the actions of its intermediaries, whose levies remained in place even when jurisdiction had formally passed to the Company regime, meant that much trade fell foul of some version of 'double taxation'.

It is undeniable that there was 'market contact' in the late eighteenth century, in the sense that peasants went to market in order to sell produce to pay the state revenues. It is difficult to believe, however, that commercialisation was not also market-oriented, determined by different parties' parlaying of their interests in their context of a relatively free negotiation process. Farmers, traders and intermediaries did not, then only approach the market because of institutional pressure of revenues. The increase in the number of markets over this period was possibly due to the easing of population pressure following famines and the opening of new cultivable lands. If Company efforts at regulatory enforcement largely failed, it may also be true that the positive effect attributed to the Company policies in the form of increased revenue pressure leading to the intensification of commercialisation might well be an overstatement. The presence of numerous buyers, including the English East India Company, in the Bengal economy created a huge demand, although the attestation of an emergent State providing the crucial link towards market integration may err too much in the direction of a state-centred analysis. Though scholars have painted a very bleak picture of its impact on late eighteenth-century Bengal, the evidence rather suggests a patchwork of change and continuity, with a variety of pre-existing local modes subsisting beneath the level of Company jurisdiction.

There were many viable markets that preceded the intervention of the Company and many effective forms of market facilitation and oversight. The *Nizamat* was not an inept as a broker of trade, nor was the Company State an all-pervasive presence conditioning every form of commerce, at any level, that went on under its jurisdiction. The Bengali elite maintained a vigorous presence along the routes of trade, rather than retiring feebly to cities as some commentators have suggested and the land was not simply stripped to tend to their luxuries. Trade and the resulting wealth propelled local rulers to act as coordinators or facilitators of commerce and sometimes even direct participants. Economic exuberance in early modern Bengal took a variety of forms that resisted ossification or state control in so far as innovation offered a commercial advantage. During the period, Bengal had a functional infrastructure and a working labour market; merchant groups could mobilise in collective defence; accountancy was practised; and highly developed and price-responsive marketing systems and forms of credit and monetisation were in place. Yet, economic historians such as Om Prakash do not hesitate to characterise even the early Company state as being successful in its imposition of unilaterally determined terms and conditions over suppliers, artisans, weavers and peasants. The major changes of this period, by contrast, are not in the structure of trade as it represents a surrogate for the exercise of political power, but in the sizeable upheavals affecting the ecological, demographical and political spheres of eighteenth-century Bengal. If in politics and economics, incremental change produces the most enduring results, in a cruel reversal of this process, Bengal suffered a jarring reversion into famine, and gradually shrinking overseas demand.

It may be said that all the essays in the three sections of the book have been neatly arranged. They reflect the themes and sub-themes on trade and commerce. The ports, their rise and demise, overseas trade, merchants and brokers, commodities and coinage, markets and internal trade have been presented in this volume that refer in one way or another, to the Indian trade at the Asian frontier.

Notes and References

1. Giridhari Prasad Das, India, *West Asia, Trade in Ancient India, 6th Century BC to 3rd Century AD*, New Century Publishers, New Delhi, 2006, See p.vii, & ix.
2. Meera Abraham, *Two Medieval Merchant Guilds of South India*, New Delhi, 1988.
3. *Epigraphia Carnatica*, (henceforth E.C.) New Series, Vol. IX, Belur, No. 171.
4. *Epigraphia Indica*, (henceforth E.I) Vol. IX, pp.22-23.
5. K.V. Ramesh & M.J. Sharma, (eds.,) *Tulunadina Shasanagalu*, Mysore, 1978, pp. 33-34.
6. K.V. Ramesh, *A History of South Kanara*, Dharwar, 1970, p. 261.
7. E.C., Vol. IX, Belur, No. 181.
8. E.C., Vol. IX, Belur, No. 171.
9. S. Jeyaseela Stephen, Medieval Trade of the Tamil Coast and its Hinterland, AD 1280-1500, in *The Indian Historical Review*, Vol. XXV, No. 2, January, 1999, pp. 1-37.
10. Kenneth R. Hall, *Trade and Statecraft in the Age of the Colas*, Delhi, 1980; S. Jeyaseeela Stephen, *The Coromandel Coast and its Hinterland: Economy, Society and Political System, 1500-1600*, Delhi, 1997.
11. Irfan Habib, *The Social Distribution of Landed Property in Pre-British India*, p.295. See also, Agraian economy op.cit., Ch. III, Sec 3., pp. 82-86. See, *The Cambridge Economic History of India*, Delhi, 1984..
12. Irfan Habib, Potentialities of Capitalistic Development in the Economy of Mughal India, *Journal of Economic History*, XXIX (1), March 1969, pp. 32-78.
13. There was a route from Multan to Ashkabad on the northern shores of Caspian which had a large population of Indian traders. See, Stephen Dale, *Indian Merchants and the Eurasian Trade, 1600-1750*, Cambridge, 1994.

14. *S. Jeyaseeela Stephen,* The Coromandel Coast and its Hinterland: Economy, Society and Political System, 1500-1600, Delhi, 1997, p. 97.
15. *Andre Gunder Frank,* World Accumulation, 1492-1789, New York, 1978.
16. *Immanuel Wallerstein,* The Modern World System: Vol. 1, Capitalist Agriculture and the Origin of the European World Economy in the Sixteenth Century; Vol. 2. Mercantilism and the consolidation of the European Word Economy, 1600-1750, New York, 1974, 1980.
17. *Eric R. Wolf,* Europe and the People Without History, Berkeley, 1982.
18. *J.C Van Leur,* Indonesian Trade and Society, The Hague, 1958,
19. *K.M. Pannikar,* Asia and the Western Dominance: A Survey of the Vasco da Gama Epoch of Indian History, 1498-1945, London, 1953.
20. *Sushil Chaudhri & Michel Morineau, Merchants,* Companies and Trade: Europe and Asia in the Early Modern Era, *Cambridge, 1999; See also, Jag*dish Narayan Sarkar, Private Traders in Medieval India, British and Indian, Calcutta, 1991.

SECTION–I

Ports, Maritime Trade and Shipping

1

An Elusive Port in Early Medieval Bengal: The Mystery of Samandar

Rila Mukherjee

Les Khorasan l'appellent Douzakhast..ce qui signifie en arabe un enfer rempli des biens' (The Khorasans call it [Bengal] in Arabic 'a hell full of abundance') Ibn Batuta, *Voyages,* Tome III, (Tr). Defremery, E.C., Sanguinetty, B.R., 1982, Paris. (My translation).

Bengala, a most spacious and fruitful province, but more properly to be called a kingdom, which hath two very large powers in it, Purb and Patan, the one lying in the East, the other on the west side of the river Ganges...the chief cities in it are Ragamahat and Dakaka. It hath many havens and ports belonging unto it, which are places of very great trade. (Edward Terry, *Voyage to East India*, London, T.Wilkes, MDCC LXXVIII : 84-5)

'It (Bengal) is one of the largest and most Potent Kingdomes of Hindostan..blessed with many fine Rivers that issue out into the sea of Gulph of Bengala viz. below Point Palmirs..and the Arackan Shore..some of which are navigable both for great and small ships..This Kingdome is now become the most Famous and Flourishinge' (Thomas Bowrey, *A Geographical Account of the Countries Around the Bay of Bengal 1669-1679*, R.C. Temple (Ed)., Cambridge, Hakluyt Society, MDCCCCV : 131.)

I
Conceptual Formulations
Questioning the Primacy of Bengal in the late Medieval Period

During the seventies and eighties, the idea of 'the primacy of Bengal' in the commercial history of eighteenth century

South Asia was a well-established canon in academic studies. The notion of primacy concerns itself with Bengal's diversity of manufactures, demand for its products overseas, abundant agricultural produce and low prices. These contributed to what has been regarded as Bengal's prodigious riches. Historical studies till date focus on the 'primacy' of Bengal on the mercantile map of South Asia.

Yet generation after generation of researchers have also been struck by the curious fact that despite the so called primacy, Bengal seemed to display no independent commercial momentum of her own in the late medieval period. While the second half of the eighteenth century is definitely a period of overall commercial decline for South Asia, the non-existence of a historically vibrant merchant community in eighteenth century Bengal is particularly glaring. Instead of merchants emerging on their own initiative, controlling the home market and moving on to conquer others (as was attempted by the Gujarat merchants in at least the Malabar from the middle of the fifteenth century) trade in late medieval Bengal operated seemingly in a 'protected domain'. Moreover this 'protected domain' had a marked 'royal' nature. This did not mean that all rulers participated in trade in their official capacity, what it did mean is that rulers granted farms, monopolies and other favours to a clique of a few courtiers. This was hardly a commercial-political nexus except in a very loose sense of the term. In eighteenth century Bengal therefore we frequently stumble across references to merchants such as Umichand and Ramkrishna Babu who had 'powerful friends' in court[1]. But this did not imply a strong mercantile influence on the court; indeed the contrary. Merchants worked as the protégés of courtiers. Traders did not venture out of the state to control networks emanating from other ports along the eastern seaboard.

The absence of a vibrant commercial culture manifested itself by the fact that there was hardly an organised indigenous and vocal mercantile community worth its name as in Surat, the Malabar or the Coromandel in the same period. The energetic Chintaman Shahs and Khemchands of the seventeenth century[2] translated into the politically active but commercially dependent Katmas[3] who acted as suppliers (known as *dadni* merchants) to the English East India Company or the EEIC. By mid-century we find them withdrawing from trade and functioning as Chief Brokers to the EEIC[4]. In other words, instead of the courtier becoming an independent merchant, the merchant became a courtier in eighteenth century Bengal. This reinforces our impression that an autonomous, energetic and sovereign mercantile community was yet to emerge in Bengal.

Let us now see the reasons for this contradictory picture: on the one hand we have glowing references that reinforce our notion of a commercial primacy and on the other hand a picture marked by an absence of commercial dynamism. Which picture is true for Bengal? Was an autonomous, energetic and sovereign mercantile community yet to emerge in Bengal? Or to put this another way, had such a community existed in previous times and was now on the wane in Bengal? The latter formulation demands a probe further back into Bengal's commercial past .

Studies of Bengal's trade focus on three political realms in its history. These are, the Nawabi period of the eighteenth century, the Mughal period in the seventeenth century and the Husain Shahi Sultanate period in the sixteenth century. M.R.Tarafdar romanticised Bengal's trade and wealth in the Husain Shahi period[5], Mughal historians were unanimous in praising Bengal's prosperity in the seventeenth century and European accounts of eighteenth century Bengal were largely responsible for establishing the notion of the 'primacy of Bengal' in modern times. However we should bear in mind that, except for the sixteenth century, Bengal's trade was integrated into a greater transcontinental trade that was part of the Mughal and then the European world economy. Her produce was taken out of the state by Mughal and European merchants and ship-owners to meet the demands of these economies. Bengal had no independent position in these networks that were run first from Agra and executed through Surat, and then from London and executed through Calcutta. What was the situation in the period prior to the Husain Shahis?

Ilyas Shahi Bengal as an Independent Commercial Unit of Analysis

Bengal as a region state, as an independent political unit, therefore forms the first focus of the essay here. And in studying Bengal's independent commercial policy I will focus, not on the Husain Shahi period, but on an earlier period-the Ilyas Shahi Sultanate-that lasted from 1342 to 1487, that is almost a hundred and fifty years, except for a short interregnum between 1410 and 1435.

Atul Chandra Roy claimed in his History of Bengal : Turko-Afghan Period[6]: The Ilyas Shahi dynasty occupies a distinct place in the history of Bengal. This dynasty preserved remarkable political consistency and produced a chain of able rulers who ruled over a vast kingdom like Bengal for such a long time at a stretch with a short interregnum..The greatest political contribution of this dynasty lies in the fact that it not only recovered Bengal's political independence (from Delhi) but also preserved the same against Delhi's repeated aggressions..It was Ilyas Shah who restored Bengal's political and administrative unity under one authority (by introducing) some sort of a central government. The Ilyas Shahi rulers were also great conquerors..Bengal witnessed a large territorial expansion under the rule of the Ilyas Shahis. The Ilyas Shahis were tolerant, enlightened and great builders too. ..(They) were patrons of art and architecture and built numerous mosques and public buildings.

Not only were the Ilyas Shahis all of the above; they also motored an immense commercial boom in Bengal. By way of commerce they placed Bengal within an expanding network of Islamic states that radiated from east Africa through southern Europe, Mecca, Central Asia and China through a mixture of religious (charitable works such as the foundation of mosques and *madrassas* at Mecca), diplomatic (mission to Herat), trade (between East Africa and China; at least one giraffe from Africa was sent by the Bengal sultan to China) and tribute (voyages to China)[7] missions. The Ilyas Shahis therefore negotiated a vast physical space: from China to Central Asia and Africa. This was the first Islamic network and it was indeed an era of cosmopolitanism for Bengal. One author who takes account of the vast physical space of Ilyas Shahi activities (albeit only to the East) is Haraprased Ray whose data on fifteenth century trade, routes and China-Bengal diplomacy has proved invaluable in reconstructing much of the mercantile history of Bengal in the Ilyas Shahi period[8]. Hence one of the main arguments of this essay is that this period, and not the Husain Shahi period, is crucial for understanding the peculiar mercantile history of Bengal and that we should see Bengal as part of the first Islamic-Mongol network from the thirteenth century onward, one that stretched from North Africa into China of which Ibn Khurdadbih, Ibn Khaldun, Ibn Batuta and the Chinese have left us their impressions.

The Ilyas Shahi period in Bengal insinuated itself into two favourable conjunctions for Bengal's commerce. On the one hand the Islamic conquest of Bengal inserted the region into a vast maritime network stretching from Spain, Persia, West Asia and East Africa up until the China coast. On the other hand, Mongol invasions on the northern Chinese border made the Chinese abandon the traditional overland silk route through Herat and Mashd and look southwards through the port of Ch'uan Chou or Zaitun for tribute and trade. This gave a great boost to oceanic trade in the eastern Indian Ocean. Zaitun became the premier mercantile city in the eastern Indian Ocean by the thirteenth century.

Pala-Sena-Chandra-Varman Bengal as a Commercial Unit

The Ilyas Shahis were the first Muslim rulers to give a cohesive political shape to the region we know as Bengal. Prior to them, Bengal was ruled by the Palas and then Senas in the west and the Chandras and then the Varmans to the east. A less political identity existed for the whole region; we shall see that there were two centres for the articulation of political power: Gaur and Dhaka-Vikrampur. While the great port of the Ilyas Shahis was undoubtedly Chattagram, it is the identification of a port in the eastern region, prior to the rise of Chattagram, which is the focus of the essay here.

The eleventh century trade revolution in the Indian Ocean, mentioned by Kulke[9] and refined by Lombard[10] and then by Christie[11] further to encompass the period between the tenth to the thirteenth centuries, placed Bengal at one end of an arc that ran from China and the countries of South East Asia.

But the trade revolution of the tenth to the thirteenth centuries was not confined to oceanic trade. A new land route from the thirteenth century led to an increase in Bengal's commercial map. Other than the Mongol putsch to the south, the introduction of a new silk route by the Mongols, called the Southern Silk Route, impacted favourably on Bengal's commerce at this time. New towns such as Karampatan, famed for the horse trade for both China and Lakhnauti, Mardhan Kot built on the model of towns in Mongol China by Gurhasp Shah on his return from China in Kamrup on the Brahmaputra, and Ku'lam, known for its Chinese style ceramics and famed for its trade in aloes, became important off shoots of the new silk route. These towns on the northern frontier of Bengal, running through Kamrup and Ava into Chinese Turkestan and Tibet, introduced a new pattern of trade into Bengal by the end of the thirteenth century. Through Bengal's fabled waterways Bengal's ports now began to connect with these caravan trading towns. Bengal's ports prospered from this time and the area-stretching through Bengal into south China and encompassing Kamrup, Ava, Arakan and much of Assam-formed an independent and unified economic realm by the fourteenth century. Chinese tea and porcelain was exchanged for Bengal cotton and Kamrup aloes. Trade in the sturdy hill horses from Turkestan and Tibet mediated this process.

The Importance of the East in Bengal's Commercial History

In the fourteenth century, by the time the Ilyas Shahi's ruled at least one portion of Bengal, Chattagram emerged as the premier port of Bengal. Initially under an independent king Fakhruddin, whom Ibn Batuta called the King of Bangala as opposed to the King of Lakhnauti or Ilyas Shah, Chattagram fell into Ilyas Shah hands soon after[12].

The conquest of Chattagram was not accidental nor was it the reflection of a haphazard policy on the part of the Ilyas Shahis. From the eleventh century this area, nominally under the rule of the Chandras of Dhaka-Vikrampur, was a heavily commercialized zone. It stood in stark contrast to land bound Gaur, ruled by the Palas, where, it was said, commerce was shrinking. Indeed economic developments on the easternmost part of Bengal had sculpted this region into a different political entity; what Terry claimed as Purb and Patan in the seventeenth century, and what Ibn Batuta had claimed as Bangalah and Lakhnauti much earlier.

The commercial vitality of the Dhaka-Vikrampur region, which was mostly Buddhist in religion, had already placed this deltaic area (comprising *samatata* (Dhaka-Suvarnagram) and *harikela* (Chattagram) as the traditional political/cultural divisions), into a wider network of a pilgrimage circuit and trade emanating from Pagan and then Arakan to Bengal's east, Bodh Gaya to Bengal's west and Ceylon to Bengal's south[13]. The Chandras claimed lineage descending from the Arakan royal house and issued standard silver coins for trade in the Bay of Bengal in the eleventh century. The Bengal-Arakan association proved durable. In the fifteenth century Narameikhla, the Arakan king, regained his throne with help of the Ilyas Shahi sultan. He soon after started a mint at his capital Mrauk-U, with the help of Bengali mint experts. The result was the distinctive Arakanese coin with Buddhist symbols and the Buddhist name of the ruler in Arakanese script on the one side and with Arabic numerals and the Islamicised name of the ruler on the obverse[14].

The importance of the Chattagram/Arakan region-this amorphous zone that was fought over by Tripura, the Ilyas Shahis, the Husain Shahis (and later the Mughals) and the Arakanese-should therefore not be underestimated. The commercial dynamism of this area was cut short in the sixteenth century due to three circumstances. They are (*a*) Environmental: Between the sixteenth and the eighteenth centuries rivers in Bengal started an eastward shift that resulted in the introduction of six new rivers into the landscape[15]. The east now became an active delta; many ports now moved in the west or silted up in the east. Moreover, the new tributaries connected the eastern rivers to the western branches. Therefore the importance of rivers such as the Karatoya for sailing up to the north east was diminished. The Brahmaputra and the Padma-Meghna waterway were no longer indispensable for going upwards into north and north east Bengal, the hinterland upon which the Dhaka-Vikrampur region relied for its commercial dynamism. (*b*) Political: The withdrawal of China, Bengal's largest foreign trading partner in the east from active trade with Bengal by the end of the fifteenth century, became even more detrimental for the fortunes of the eastern sector of Bengal. (*c*) West Faced Commercial Policy: Finally, perhaps as a response to these changing fortunes there developed a Commercial Policy, from the beginning of the sixteenth century the Husain Shahis started developing the western delta to the detriment of the east. Saptagram in the west became the new port of the Bengal sultanate. In 1506 Ala ud Din Husain Shah connected it by way of a bridge with the new towns of the region-Nabadwip and Tribeni. From this time Vanga-the heartland of Gaur-assummed iconic status in Bengal's history. No such urban initiative was undertaken in the east,

Thus by the time the Husain Shahis appeared on the political map of Bengal, the commercial picture had changed substantially. Efforts were made by these sultans to concentrate on trade with the Gangetic plain and not with the northern Bay of Bengal. If the Ilyas Shahis looked east then the Husain Shahis looked resolutely north, despite their efforts to wrest Chattagram from the control of Tripura in 1516.

In the sixteenth century the world map of commerce changed substantially as well. New empires appeared on the stage-the Ottomans, the Persians and the Mughals. These formed the second Islamic world economy; a somewhat weaker one than the first Islamic world economy that was in place at the time of the Ilyas Shahis, because it had to face the new threat emanating from the Portuguese presence in the Indian Ocean.

II

Why is the Search for Samandar so Important for the Commercial History of Bengal?

We have seen in the preceding section, the commercial dynamism of Bengal in the early medieval period. It is to be expected, therefore, that references be found for ports in deltaic Bengal that carried on such a trade. While there are references to Sripur and Bakla functioning as ports from the twelfth century, and somewhat hazy references to early Arab traders congregating at Chattagram from the tenth century; there is no mention of earlier ports. From the time of decline of Tamralipta in the seventh century and the meteoric rise of Chattagram in the thirteenth century, there is no record of port activity in Bengal. It is therefore difficult for us to document Bengal's position in the Bay trade given that no references exist for a premier port in Bengal. Trade in post Tamralipta Bengal seemed to have concentrated on Chilka which is much further down the coast.

However early Arab accounts of South Asia have referred to the existence of a mysterious port called Samandar; mysterious because to this date we are not sure as to where exactly it was located, or whether it was situated in Bengal at all. Mohar Ali locates the shadowy Samandar, to be in eastern Bengal, on the Meghna to be precise, as the premier port of Bengal during this period.[16]

The Claims of Mohar Ali

Let us now examine Mohar Ali's claims. What are his sources? According to him the ninth century *Al-Masalik wa'l Mamalik* names ports on the eastern route as Nagapattinam (called Bullin by the Arabs), Ganjam (Kanja) in present day Orissa, the unidentified Samundar thirty miles north of Ganjam (somewhere between Bengal and inland Assam?)[17], Nicobar Islands, Kedah, Java and Khmer and this was the preferred route from the eastern sea board to China according to Ibn Khurdadhbih.[18] It is striking that there is no mention of Chattagram (Chittagong), the great eastern port, in this ninth-tenth century account; however by the time of Ibn Batutah's voyages in the fourteenth century Chattagram had emerged as the greatest port on the eastern sea board after the Coromandel ports. It probably dated from the tenth century as discussed earlier. By the fourteenth century it had surpassed all other Bengal ports in the volume of its trade. The flourishing production and foreign trade centred on the Chattagram-Suvarnagram complex was described by Chinese visitors as well as in the Chaitanya Mangala of Jayananda in later centuries.[19]

Yet it is certain that production and trade continued in Bengal; was indeed given a boost by the eastern Indian Ocean 'trade revolution' from the tenth century. Which port then served as port for the Dhaka-Suvarnagram production complex? There are substantial references to Bengal (and Bihar to the north) being part of a flourishing Buddhist network that linked Japan and China, South Asia and Ceylon. Which were the ports for the flourishing Buddhist complexes in eastern Bengal: for Paharpur, Mahastan and the Mainamati-Lalmai complexes? Was Samundar the chief port of Bengal in this interim period? We are told that it was the principal market and port on the Ganges delta, inhabited by wealthy merchants from all over the world, the centre point of trade with Assam and Ceylon and trader in aloes-wood (for which there was a great demand, in West Asia and especially in China) brought down from Assam.[20]

Samandar was definitely in existence for three hundred years between the ninth century (Ibn Khurdadhbih) and the twelfth century (al-Idrisi) as sources tell us. Muhammad Mohar Ali places Samundar at/around Sandwip island.[21] It is likely that Samundar may have been an earlier port in the Suvarnagrama region; in that case however it cannot be thirty miles north of Ganjam. Or was Samandar located in the area around Saptagram? Samandar can then be identified with Gangabandar/Tamralipta as Tarafdar claimed. According to al-Idrisi, as Mohar Ali interprets him, Samundar was near the confluence of the Meghna and the Brahmaputra near the present port town of Chandpur in Bangladesh. Since al-Idrisi wrote in the twelfth century we know that Samundar functioned as a port for at least three hundred years. The earliest reference to Samandar dates from the ninth century (Ibn Khurdadhbih)]. Riverine changes may have silted this port up so much so after this time that the next great port was destined to be Chattagram on the Karnaphuli further east.

Early Accounts of Samandar

But apart from the confusion regarding Samandar's location *within* Bengal, there is also a doubt whether Samandar was situated in Bengal *at all.* For there are certain problems with Mohar Ali's identification. Al-Idrisi wrote[22]:

Samandar is a large town, commercial and rich, where there are good profits to be made. It is a port dependant upon Kanauj, King of this country. It stands upon a river which comes from the country of Kashmir..Aloes wood is brought hither from the country of Karmut fifteen day's distance by a river of which the waters are sweet. The aloes wood which comes from this country is of a superior quality and of a delicious perfume. It grows in the mountains of Karan...to the north at seven day's distance from Samandar, is the city of Kashmir the inner, celebrated throughout India, which is under the rule of Kanauj..This is a fine commercial city which gives its name to the King of the country (Kanauj). It is built upon the banks of a large river which falls into the Musala..the River of Perfumes. It rises in the mountains of Karan..and at length falls into the sea.

Mohar Ali's identification of Samandar as a port in eastern Bengal hinges on three key facts. First, the identification of Karmut/ Karan with Kamrup, the legendary producer of aloes wood; second, with the identification of Musala as the Meghna and third, as being the premier port for receiving and exporting aloes wood in the east. But how do we reconcile this identification with other facets of al-Idrisi's description: that the river (Musala) comes from Kashmir and that 'the city of Kashmir the inner' is at seven day's distance from Samandar?

A Samandar in The West

Indeed there is a confusion about the name Samandar. Samandar could be in peninsular South Asia as well. The

Jamiu-t Tawarikh of Rashi'du-d D'in of the early fourteenth century (1310) mentions Duru Samundar (Dwara Samudra) 'adjoining M'abar Island'.[23] But it could equally be located on the west coast, in Sindh province, in the Multan and Kandahar/ Kabul area which also produced aloes.[24] In such a case the reputedly sweet and perfumed waters of the Musala-which Mohar Ali takes to be the Meghna on account of the trade in perfumed aloes-could apply equally to the Mihran (Indus). The twelfth century account of Ibn Haukal tells us that the waters of the Sandaruz (Sind-rud) whose waters were 'sweet and abundant' joined the Mihran above Basmad.[25] And there was a Samandar on the Mihran. The book of Abu Ishak al Istakhri, composed aound the mid-tenth century, tells us that Samand 'is a small city situated like Multan on the east of the river Mihran' and adds that the distance between Multan and Samand was two parasangs (roughly eleven miles). According to Abu Ishak it was also called Samundur.[26]

There are also Basmand, and Basmat in Sindh as well as Sandur, 'situated on the banks of a river which falls into the Mihran (Indus) above Samand'. There is no mention of aloes but al-Idrisi mentions its wealth and commerce[27]; and this may well be the Samandar taken by Mohar Ali to be in eastern Bengal .

Therefore all indications point to Samandar being situated in Sindh. But the identification of Samandar hinges on its association with aloes. Was this region a producer of aloes wood? Yes. We have already seen that Multan in Sindh province as well as the Kabul/Kandahar region produced aloes in plenty.[28] Moreover this seems to have been the chief source of revenue to the rulers of Multan; and a brisk trade in aloes wood was carried on by pilgrim merchants when they visited the temple at Multan. We do not know what idol the temple housed as it is referred to as the 'idol' of Multan, or occasionally as 'Multan' as well. This is what 10th century Muslim travellers had to say about it:

The idol called Multan is situated in the environs of Mansura (in Sindh) and people come on pilgrimage to it. They bring thither the Indian aloes called al-kamrun from Kamrun the name of the country where it grows. These aloes are of the finest quality. They are given to the ministers of the temple for use as incense..Merchants buy them of the ministers of the temple.[29] And, 'the greatest part of the revenues of the Kingdom of Multan is derived from the rich presents brought to the idol of the pure aloes wood of Kumar..and one *man* of which is worth 200 dinars.[30]

A Samandar in the East

So where was the kingdom of Kumar/Kamrun located? According to Mohar Ali this was Kamrup, but again, there are problems in reaching this conclusion. Abu Zaidu-l Hasan tells us that the kingdom of Kumar 'which produces the aloes known as kumari' was situated 'on that side that faces the country of the Arabs' , that is, the western side of South Asia.[31] But Ibn Khurdadba tells us that Kamrun was 'contiguous to China'[32] which exported 'aloes to Kilkan, Luan and Kanja by the freshwater route in fifteen days.[33] 'Kanja is probably Ganjam (Orissa) so a fifteen day river journey is likely from Bengal down there. Moreover, Ibn Khurdadba wrote that the distance between Samandar and Urashir was twelve pharasangs[34] (12 pharasangs is roughly a distance of 70 miles). If Urashir is Orissa, as seems likely, then Samandar was situated on the west Bengal coast, and not on the Meghna, as Mohar Ali claims. Al Idrisi noted that Samandar was situated thirty miles north of Ganjam[35]. If that is the case then Samandar may well be identified with Gangabandar as Tarafdar claimed.[36] Other than Kumar there was also the Kingdom of Kaman in the east which, al-Masudi tells us, was next to the kingdom of Rahma.[37]

Is Kaman then Kamrup? If so, where is Rahma? Rahma (or ruhmi) was the name given to that part of Bengal that bordered the Arakan region, that is, the easternmost part of the province. Elliot and Dowson tell us that ruhmi or rahma referred to the Dhaka Arakan region.[38] Suleiman tells us that Ruhmi possessed more troops that Gujarat, it was a producer of fine textiles, it traded through cauris and had gold, silver, rhinos and aloes in plenty.[39] So in actual fact, there may have been two regions producing aloes: Kumar in the west and Kaman in the east.

Mohar Ali, we see, depends largely on al-Idrisi's text for his identification of Samandar. But al-Idrisi's text, we just saw, is inconclusive; rather it is only Ibn Khurdadba's text that contains all three key indicators: aloes, Kamrun as next to China, and the existence of a port called Samundar there. All other texts I have referred to-those of Abu Zaidu-l Hasan, al-Masudi, Abu Ishak, Ibn Haukal-mention some, but not all, of the key facts as we have just seen.

Samundar could be a generic name such as Bandel (a Portuguese corruption of Bandar or port) was to prove two centuries later. Or it could also refer to any port on a wide river. Minhaj tells us that Mardhan Kot in Kamrud (Kamrup) was situated on the banks of the Bangamathi or Brahmaputra. 'When it (the Bangamathi) enters the country of Hindustan it receives in the Hindustani language the name of Samundar. In length, breadth and depth, it is three times greater than the Ganges'.[40]

Finally it is indeed unlikely that there was an active Bengal-Multan trade in aloes as early as in the tenth century; it is therefore more probable that the aloes brought to the temple at Multan came from a source nearer to it. We should note also that while six sources spanning three hundred years, Abu Zaidu-l of Siraf, Al Masudi, Abu Ishak (10th century), Ibn Haukal, al Idrisi (12th century) and Zakari'ya al Kazwi'ni (13th century), mention the idol of Multan and its worship in detail, only two tenth century sources-those of Abu Zaidu-l and al Masudi-mention the trade in aloes at the Multan temple.[41] Had the trade in aloes at Multan died out after that time? This seems unlikely, given the tremendous demand for aloes in West Asia. Had an alternative centre been established on the west coast for the aloes trade? This seems more likely. The trade at Multan declined possibly after the Ghaznavid attacks in the region in the eleventh century. The aloes trade probably moved out of the confines of the pilgrimage circuit and entered the commercial realm at that time.

Samandar may well have been Sagor and Sagor's name has also been proposed as an interim port. Both Sagor and Bakla in the Sundarbans area were functioning ports from the twelfth century. But this identification, too, is not conclusive. We see therefore that our search for a port in Bengal in the period between the seventh and thirteenth centuries remains inconclusive. Until we are able to locate a port in the region our researches into Bengal's commercial position in the mercantile map of South Asia will remain uncertain.

Notes and References

1. British Library, London, See the *Kasimbazar Factory Records* (K.F.R.) for the eighteenth century.
2. Sushil Chaudhuri, *Trade and Commercial Organisation 1650-1720,* Firma KLM, Calcutta, 1975.
3. The Katmas are designated as Cotma in the Kasimbazar Factory Records.
4. Kasimbazar Factory Records, in Rila Mukherjee, *Merchants and Companies: Kasimbazar and Jugdia in the Eighteenth Century* (forthcoming).
5. M.R. Tarafdar, *Husain Shahi Bengal 1494-1538 AD : A Socio-Political Study*, Dacca, 1965.
6. Atul Chandra Roy, *History of Bengal, Turko-Afhgan Period*, New Delhi/Ludhiana, Kalyani Publishers, 1986, pp. 245-6.
7. Sally K. Church, *'The Giraffe of Bengal : A Medieval Encounter in Ming China, Medieval History Journal*, Vol.7.1 : , 2004, pp.1-37.
8. Haraprasad Ray, *Trade and Trade Routes between India and China*, Progressive Publishers, Calcutta, 2003. See also his work, *Trade and Diplomacy in India-China Relations-a Study of Bengal During the Fifteenth Century*, New Delhi, Radiant, 1993.
9. Herman Kulke, 'Rivalry and Competition in the Bay of Bengal' in Om Prakash and Denys Lombard (eds.,) *Commerce and Culture in the Bay of Bengal 1500-1800*, ICHR/Manohar, New Delhi, 1999, pp 17-35 : 33.
10. Denys Lombard, *Le Carrefour Javanais : Essai d'histoire Globale, III, L'Heritage des Royaumes Concentriques*, Paris, Editions E.H.E.S.S, 1990.
11. Jan Wisseman Christie, *'Asian Sea Trade Between the Tenth and Thirteenth Centuries and Its Impact on the States of Java and Bali'* in Himanshu Prabha Ray (ed.) *Archaeology of*

Seafaring : The Indian Ocean in the Ancient Period, ICHR Monograph Series, New Delhi, Pragati, 1999, pp 221-270.

12. This was in the 1340s. The victor was probably Shamsuddin Ilyas Shah.
13. Tilman Frasch, 'A Buddhist Network in the Bay of Bengal: Relations Between Bodh Gaya, Burma and Sri Lanka c.300-1300' in Claude Guillot, Denys Lomabard and Roderick Ptak (eds.) *From the Mediterranean to the China Sea: Miscellaneous Notes*, Wiebaden, Harrassowitz Verlag, 1998, pp. 69-92. See also his 'Coastal Peripheries during the Pagan Period' in Jos Gommans./Jacques Leider (eds.), *The Maritime Frontier of Burma*, Amsterdam, 2002. See also Himanshu Prabha Ray, *The Archaeology Of Seafaring in Ancient South Asia*, Cambridge World Archaeology Series, CUP, 2003. See Radha Kumud Mookerji, *Indian Shipping, A History of the Sea Borne Trade and Maritime Activity of the Indians from the Earliest Times*, Allahabad, Kitab Mahal, reprint, 1962.
14. Narameikhla (Min Sowa Mun) agreed to pay one lakh *tanka* annually to the Bengal sultans as tribute for recovering his kingdom in 1430. To this end he modernised his mint with the help of mint experts from Bengal, as the Arakan coins had only a symbolic value and no proper standard prior to this. The new Arakanese coins were unique in that they had the king's Buddhist name in Burmese characters on one side and the Muslim name (in either Arabic or Persian) and Bengali characters on the other. Arakanese coins in the Bengali style continued to be struck for the next two hundred years. In the seventeenth century Manrique, who visited the Arakan court, alluded to this practice. See also Mohammed Ali Chowdhury, *Bengal-Arakan Relations*, Calcutta, Firma KLM, 2004, pp. 34-44. In traditional scholarship the dependence on Bengal and the fashion of striking coins in the Sultanate fashion was explained either as Arakan's acceptance of Bengal's sovereignty, or tribute, or a fashion (see ibid.) but the fact that not only were coins struck in the Bengal style but that in their rate of exchange the commercial policy of Bengal was followed (ibid.: p.41) points to a more pragmatic reason for following this practice. Fifteenth century Arakan, under the newly restored monarch, wished to play a bigger role in the commerce of the Bay, albeit under Bengal's tutelage, at least initially.

15. P.J. Marshall, *Bengal: The British Bridgehead, Eastern India 1740-1828*, NCHI, Cambridge, University Press, 1987. See also Richard Eaton, *Essays on Islam and Indian History*, Oxford University Press, Delhi, 2000, p.262. The great riverine changes of the second half of the sixteenth century meant that new rivers such as the Bhairab, the Matabhanga, the Garai-Madhumati, the Arial Kha now linked western Bengal and the Ganga through the Padma-Meghna which in turn linked up with the Brahmaputra. This meant that east Bengal ceased to be a remote region. Through the Padma-Meghna system Dhaka could now connect up with the Saptagram-Hugli ports. This meant that north-east riverine sailings up the Brahmaputra to connect up with the older northern route to Upper India were no longer necessary. The drying up of the mighty Karatoya at the end of the sixteenth century was symptomatic of the end of the last great age of connectivity of medieval Bengali ports with the great silk route that ran from China to the west. Eastern goods now found an outlet through the western ports of Bengal. Chattagram became isolated; its claim to Porto Grande status of Bengal diminished. Within western Bengal this change meant the dislocation of ports such as Saptagram (which 'dried' up; from the east bank Saptagram now moved to the west bank), introduction of new rivers and the fragmentation of samatata.

16. Muhammad Mohar Ali, *History of the Muslims of Bengal*, Vol. 1A, *Muslim Rule in Bengal 1203-1757*, Riyadh, Imam Muhammad, Ibn Saud Islamic University, 1985. For more on this see section Routes, Ports and Trading Networks in Bengal in Rila Mukherjee, *Strange Riches : Bengal in the Mercantile Map of South Asia*, Foundation Books, New Delhi, 2006.

17. Samundar has been identified with Suvarnagram by Ahmad. See Ahmad, S.Maqbul, *Arabic Classical Accounts of India and China*, Shimla, Indian Institute of Advanced Study Ahmad, 1989, pp. 24-5. However it could equally be Gangabandar in the region of the ancient port of Bengal, Tamralipta. See Tarafdar, M.R., 1978, 'Trade and Society in Early Medieval Bengal' in *The Indian Historical Review*, January, IV, 20.

18. Ahmad, *op.cit.*, 1989, p. 5.

19. P.C. Bagchi, (ed). *'Political Relations Between Bengal and China in the Pathan Period' Visva Bharati Annals,* 1945,

vol 1, Cheena Bhavana. Jayananda, *Chaitanya Mangala*, Calcutta, 1971, pp.10-11; also Vrindaban Das, *Chaitanya Bhagavat*, Nabadwip, 3rd ed., p.161 in Anirudhha Ray, 'Middle Bengali Literature: A Source for the Study of Bengal in the Age of Akbar'in Irfan Habib, (ed). *Akbar and His India*, Delhi, Oxford, 1997.

20. Ahmad, *op.cit.,* 1989, p. 24.
21. Mohar Ali, Muhammad, *History of the Muslims of Bengal, op.cit.,* pp. 30-34.
22. *Nizhatu-l Mushtak* of al-Idrisi in Elliot and Dowson, *The History of India as Told by its Own Historians : The Muhammadan Period,* V.1, Allahabad, Kitab Mahal: 74-93. See pp. 90-91.
23. Ibid, p. 73.
24. Al-Idrisi, *ibid.*, pp. 91-2.
25. Ibn Haukal, *Ashka'lu-l Bila'd or the Kita'bu-l Masa'lik Wa-l Mama'lik*, *ibid.*,p.40.
26. *Kita'bu-l Aka'li'm, ibid*, pp 28, 30.
27. Al-Idrisi, *ibid*, p.83.
28. Al-Idrisi, *ibid,* pp. 91-2.
29. The additions of Abu Zaidu-l Hasan of Siraf in the *Salsilatu-l Tawarikh* of the Merchant Suleiman in Elliot and Dowson, Vol.1, *op.cit*, p.11.
30. Al Masudi, *Muru'ju-l Zahal*, *ibid*, p.23.
31. *Ibid,* p.8.
32. *Kitabu-l Masalik Wa-l Mamalik* by Ibn Khurdadba in Elliot and Dowson, Vol.1, *op.cit.,* p. 14.
33. *Ibid.,* p. 16.
34. *Ibid.*
35. Al Idrisi, *op.cit.,* p. 90.
36. M.R. Tarafdar, *Husain Shahi Bengal 1494-1538 AD: A Socio-Political Study*, Dacca, 1965.
37. Al Masudi, 'the kingdom of Rahma is bounded by an inland state called the Kingdom of Kaman', p. 25.
38. Elliot and Dowson, Vol.1, *op.cit.,* Appendix A, p.361.
39. *Salsilatu-t Tawarikh*, *op.cit.,* p.5.
40. Tabaqat-i-Nasiri, Vol. II, p. 310.
41. Conclusion reached after an examination of these sources are found in Elliot and Dowson, Vol.1.

2

The Rise and Fall of Satgaon : An Overseas Port of Medieval Bengal

Aniruddha Ray

The rise and fall of Satgaon, called *Saptagram* in Bengali, has remained obscure and controversial even to this day. Various legends are connected with the rise of Satgaon, which is considered an agglomeration of seven villages, namely Basudevpur, Bansaberia, Khamarpura, Debanandpur, Shibpur, Krishnapur and Trisbigha[1]. In the Nineteenth century, Trisbigha has been named as *Adi Saptagram* or the core of the city of Satgaon. Since no archaeological work has been done at Satgaon till now excepting two explorations in the early Twentieth century, which we would see later, it is difficult to substantiate this claim. Nearby is Triveni, a junction of three rivers, which has been referred to in the *Puranas* and is considered as one of oldest towns of the Indian sub-continent. Often the two places – Satgaon and Triveni – have been taken as one, although in the Bengali literature of the medieval period, the two places are shown as distinct and separate. We would attempt here not only to explain the rise and decline of Satgaon, but also try to make a reconstruction of the morphology of the city of Satgaon.

II

Very few scholars have attempted to explain the rise of Satgaon as an overseas port and an urban centre of note during the Sultanate period. This is perhaps due to the simple reason that documents of the period earlier than that of the end of the Fifteenth century are not available, excepting some inscriptions. By the end of the Fifteenth century, it seems that the port and the city of Satgaon was in full swing. This is complicated by the fact that a few scholars have identified the reference of the mid-Fourteenth century Moroccan traveller Ibn Battuta of Sudkawan as Satgaon[2]. There is no need to enter the controversy here on the landing point of the Moroccan traveller and the present view seems to be that Ibn Battuta has landed at Chittagong, which has remained always an overseas port often under the disputed control of the rulers of Bengal, Arakan, Tripura and later the Portuguese[3]. If the account of Battuta cannot be taken as a marker, one can point to the other one, which is less controversial. This is the starting of a mint by the Tughluq ruler at Satgaon from where the coins rolled out from the early Fourteenth century till the middle of the Fifteenth century, which is rather strange, as we would explain it later. If Triveni is taken as synonymous with Satgaon, then Triveni must have been an overseas port of Bengal at least till the end of the Fifteenth century when we have local Bengali documents on the flourishing port and the town of Satgaon. But, as we would see, the contemporary Bengali literature has always seen Satgaon as distinct place from that of Triveni, which we would see later. From the remaining archaeological artefacts at Triveni, we find that it was a place of sanctity to the Buddhists, Jains and Hindus, the latter having gained predominance during the early medieval period[4]. But Triveni has never considered as an overseas port in the contemporary literature, although the merchants of Bengal in the Bengali literature had always anchored their big sea-going boats at Triveni. Since 1298 A.D. when the first inscription of the victory of the Muslim commander, Zafar Khan Ghazi has been found at Triveni-Satgaon area, on the bank of the Bhagirathi[5], the establishment of the mosques, *Madrassas* and tombs continued to multiply giving the area a different character. But these architectural evidences do not necessarily establish this place either as an overseas port or as an urban centre.

One may postulate that the victory in 1298 signalled the beginning of the process of urbanization of Satgaon, although it seems that the defeated Hindu ruler or his descendant had been able to get it back for a brief time later since the Muslim rulers had to lead another operation in the area a few years later[6]. Considering the uncertain political situation, the establishment of the mint at Satgaon in 1328 A.D.[7] is rather strange and does not signify any disturbance at least during that time. The establishment of the mint in early Fourteenth century would suggest the growth of mercantile activities of the area that must have started from an earlier period and one could speculate that the conquest of Zafar Khan Ghazi, cited earlier, was to control the port that was bringing precious metal from outside, if not the horses desperately needed by the newly founded State. If accepted, this speculation of the rise of the port town since the middle or late Thirteenth century would have certain ramifications.

First of all, it would suggest that the Rarh area, the proverbially backward area of Bengal during the medieval period if one goes by the contemporary Bengali literature, was important. That the Rarh area, mostly covering Jharkhand of modern days, of the northwest of Satgaon was an important centre of Buddhist pilgrimage and mercantile traffic during the Eleventh and the Twelfth centuries has been attested by late Nineteenth century archaeological work[8]. The problem lies that such traffic faded away, at least from archaeological works, since the Thirteenth century, although the route from Jharkhand to the Bhagirathi bank and to Orissa remained open for long time to come. Perhaps the problem could be resolved by the second ramification – the change of the course of the river Bhagirathi towards the east.

Before moving on to the discussion on the change of the course of the river Bhagirathi, one may suggest that it is quite possible that Satgaon was functioning from the late Thirteenth century as an inland port. There are two reasons for making such speculation. One is that there is no reference to Bengal's overseas trading earlier than that of the late Fifteenth century. The second reason is that four Chinese delegations, landed at Chittagong and not at Satgaon in the first half of the Fifteenth century[9]. If Satgaon were acting as an overseas port, it would have been much easier for the Chinese to land at Satgaon and march to Pandua, the then capital of Bengal. Obviously the four Chinese delegations, coming one after the other, were not aware of the overseas port of Satgaon, which questions the credibility of the thesis that Satgaon was rising as an overseas port at least from the early Thirteenth century. Given this scenario, it is also possible to speculate that the rise of Satgaon as an overseas port occurred after the second half of the Fifteenth century, when the capital was transferred from Pandua to Gaur. It is in this context that one may discuss the change of the course of the river Bhagirathi and one may perhaps put up a chronology for such a change, which has been suggested by Nihar Ranjan Ray in his classic work.

According to him, the earliest course of the Ganges flowed through the Saraswati river on which stood the port of Satgaon. He cited the *Puranas* to show that the Ganges was at one time flowing through the Tamralipta, which was probably located on the seashore. At one time, the Bhagirathi leaving the Damodar river as well as another course that had joined Rupnarayan river and had gone past Tamralipta, had come near the Triveni junction[10]. From the sketch of Joao de Barros of 1550, it could be seen that the river had left the Triveni junction and had gone towards the west. It is on this river, in its westward movement, that the port of Satgaon stood in the middle of the Sixteenth century. The river after flowing towards the west, then turned sharply towards the south and after covering a distance again turned towards the east to join the course, which was coming straight from Triveni to the south towards the sea, at Betore near Howrah. The river, which took towards the west from Triveni, has been generally called the Saraswati river, although in the contemporary Bengali literature, there is only one mention of this river by this name. Consequently this westward course coming out of Triveni, has been taken as the principal course of the Bhagirathi during the heyday of Satgaon at least till the middle of the Sixteenth century.

There are certain problems in this reconstruction, the principal one being that of setting up a time frame. If there was one river going through the Rarh area past Tamralipta, at which point of time did it split into three rivers? Allied with this is the question at which point of time did the principal course, called Bhagirathi or the Ganges nowadays or the Hughli river by the English, leave the westward channel to form the principal section of the river coming down from Triveni? As regards the rise of Satgaon, it may safely be stated that since Tamralipta was deserted after the Eighth century A.D, the separation of the rivers must have begun at such time as to form two separate river courses. As to the second, it may be stated that the one course, which was coming down from Rajmahal to Triveni, began to draw its water from the other two courses, thus denuding Tamralipta of its existence. But then sometime in the late Twelfth or early Thirteenth century, this course was flowing from Triveni towards the west, which gave rise to the port of Satgaon, the only port in western Bengal after the fading away of Tamralipta. Since no work on historical geography or that of archaeology either at Tamralipta or at Satgaon has been done, there is no evidence to substantiate this thesis. Obviously the process took a long time, perhaps more than four centuries if we go by our proposed chronological sequence. But from the end of the Fifteenth century, the contemporary Bengali writer Bipradas Piplai[11] has praised Satgaon both as a port and an urban centre so much that it is quite possible to believe that Satgaon was becoming important for quite some time, if not for the last one hundred years. If we take the victory of Zafar Khan Ghazi of 1298, which was close on the principal course of the Bhagirathi and not far from Triveni, then we would need to put the rise of Satgaon as an important area at least in the middle of the Thirteenth century.

Whether flow of water from Triveni would have led deep inside Rarh is difficult to say. Obviously the sudden southward turn of the course and then its eastward turn, the latter portion still being visible, gives it the character of a loop. But this southward turn deprived Rarh of the benefit of the flow of the principal course for which the area must have suffered that had given Rarh a bad name in the late Sixteenth century Bengali literature[12]. Even the presence of two rivers – one Damodar and the other joining Rupnarayan – does not improve the character of the area significantly. Therefore the presence of this loop and the establishment of the port of Satgaon since the fading away of Tamralipta become important from the point of view of Rarh area about which unfortunately we do not have any documentary evidence. But we should remember that first two overseas ports of Bengal from the early medieval period – Tamralipta and Satgaon- were both located in the Rarh area that must have been flourishing for a considerable period of time. Unfortunately we do not have a historian to explain the gradual impoverishment of Rarh during the medieval period despite the location of the flourishing port of Satgaon in Rarh.

III

The rise of Satgaon as an urban centre was significantly helped by administrative measures. The inscription of a mosque at Triveni under Malik Barbak Shah of 1455 A.D. shows that the mosque was built by Ulugh Ajmal Khan under Iqrar Khan, Wazir of Arsa Sajla Mankhabad. Nasiruddin Mahmud then was the Sultan. There is a controversy whether Arsa meant a *Pargana* or a *Sarkar*.[13] Without going into such controversy, one may suggest from several other contemporary inscriptions that Barbak Shah was then the Governor of Satgaon, which was then located in the *Pargana* of the *Sarkar* of Arsa. The term *Sarkar* seems to be appropriate here since the area under jurisdiction of Arsa included modern 24 *Parganas*, western part of Nadia and southwest part of Murshidabad. Thus it stretched from north of Hughli to the Kapotaksha river. This was obviously the area that served as the hinterland of the port of Satgaon, which has become an important administrative centre controlling the mouth of the Hughli river. Satgaon had become the headquarters of the *Sarkar* by the middle of the Sixteenth century, which could be seen from the contemporary inscriptions as well as from the contemporary Bengali poems, referring to the existence of administrative officials. In the late Sixteenth century, Abul Fazl confirmed it in his description in the *Ain-i Akbari*[14].

Significantly it was in the middle of the Fifteenth century that we notice the first inscription of the Sultan Nasiruddin Mahmud at Gaur dated 1457 A.D. on a bridge over the road from the *Kotwali Darwaza* towards the palace[15], suggesting the transfer of capital from Pandua to Gaur. This transfer of capital from Pandua to Gaur, from further north to south, at a time when the inscription appears at Satgaon, which could not be wished away as mere coincidence, has been generally overlooked by the historians. If one looks at the location of Pandua close to the Himalayan traffic in the north, then the move towards the south, towards the sea, is important. It suggests the strengthening of mercantile activities on the Bhagirathi river, whose principal course was then flowing through the loop and not through the *Adi Ganga* going past Kalighat as it did in later days. This move is not surprising since according to Nihar Ranjan Ray, Satgaon has become a very big town by 1475, which date he considered as the high watermark of the heyday of Satgaon[16]. Possibly Ray has based his conclusion on the basis of the writing of Bibpradas Piplai around 1494 A.D. who showed that Satgaon was full of houses of rich people and it has become a big urban centre[17]. Obviously there was a quick development of the urban area of Satgaon, which was probably due to its closeness to the capital Gaur that was becoming quickly populated[18]. One would therefore tend to put official patronage as one of the causes of the sudden and quick development of Satgaon as an urban centre. This development was a big change since 1298 A.D. in which the geo-political and economic factor played an important part.

By late Fourteenth century scarcity of silver was becoming clear in the Delhi Sultanate. The Arab geographer Wassaf has mentioned that India was hoarding gold and silver. This is seen very clearly in the scarcity of coins. Even Gujarat with its trade with West Asia was issuing debased silver currency[19]. However, Bengal was issuing silver coins though in a small scale. Historians have wondered about the source of the silver supply to Bengal since Yunan and Burma supplies are becoming rare. Obviously the supply of silver to Bengal was coming through the overseas commerce, which has begun to pick up since the early Fourteenth century perhaps with the establishment of the new kingdoms in South-East Asia. It is reasonable to assume that this has prompted the establishment of the mint at Satgaon in 1328 A.D. as noted earlier. Throughout the Fourteenth century Delhi continued to be deprived of silver supply. So far only four pieces of pure silver coins of the Sultan Firuz Shah Tughluq has been found[20]. One may therefore postulate that the real reason of the two invasions of Bengal by Firuz Shah Tughluq was due to appropriate this supply of silver, which has nothing to do with the construction of the new *Hammam* by the Bengal Sultan as stated by the author of *Riaz-ul Salatin*[21]. Obviously the emphasis was on the supply of silver from overseas trade that might explain the shifting of the capital to the bank of the Bhagirathi river with the port closer to the sea – a shift away from overland traffic to overseas traffic. The existence of Triveni as an ancient and important pilgrimage centre may have helped the process. The question of course remains why the overseas traffic did not take the *Adi Ganga* route or the Hughli route at that time or why the port of Satgaon was not settled far lower south nearer the sea. Obviously the Hughli route was not operative at that time because the flow of water was minimal and did not allow any ship to come by that route. There was no Hughli port at that time and Triveni was not a port in the proper sense of the term. Going by the praise of Bipradas Piplai of the late Fifteenth century, it is clear that Satgaon has reached its nadir as an urban centre by the end of the Fifteenth century.

In this meteoric rise of Satgaon as an overseas port as well as a rich urban centre, the port of Chittagong perhaps has a role to play, if indirectly. As cited earlier, during the first half of the Fifteenth century, four Chinese delegations landed at Chittagong and had gone to the capital Pandua. Even with the struggle for the control of the port of Chittagong beginning from the middle of the Fifteenth century, the port continued to be the overseas port of Bengal intermittently occupied by the kings of Tripura, Arakan and Bengal. From the early Sixteenth century, the Portuguese began to arrive at the port of Chittagong, which they occupied for sometime[22]. Even in 1521, the Portuguese embassy led by Antonio de Britto as well as his rival embassy landed at Chittagong and left for Gaur, the then capital, under the aegis of the officials of the King of Bengal, Nusrut Shah[23]. One wonders if the port of Satgaon was functioning as an overseas port at that tune since in the detailed observations of the anonymous Portuguese interpreter, there was no mention of Satgaon. If it was, then there was no explanation why the Portuguese did not go there in the first place then since they could have taken the boat straight to Gaur without losing too much time on the route. One reason could be that the Portuguese coming for the first time in the eastern waters in the coast of Bengal were not aware of the functioning of the port of Satgaon, which they began to use from the middle of the Sixteenth century. Some scholars including Nihar Ranjan Ray, have suggested that at least till the middle of the Sixteenth century the flow of water at the Padma river was more than that of the Ganges, which they could deduce from the sketch of Joao de Barros, whose sketch of Bengal was drawn probably around 1550. Ray seems to be hesitant at such a suggestion and has compared the sketch of Barros with that of Van den Broeke. He finds that the flow of water in both the rivers remains almost equal between 1550 till 1660, when the sketch of Van den Broeke was drawn. Yet Ray considers that the flow of water was more in the Padma while the contemporary Bengali poets called this river as *Bara Ganga* or Greater Ganges[24]. The Portuguese Government has now published the sketch of Barros on a bigger scale, which shows the flow of water was equal in both the rivers[25]. Besides, neither Ray nor others have seen the sketch of Lopo Homem of 1519, which shows equal water flow in both the rivers[26]. Therefore one could safely reject the thesis that the change of the port activities from Chittagong to Satgaon was due to the increased flow of water in the Bhagirathi from the Padma river. Yet there is a problem of water in the Bhagirathi, which has not yet been attended to by the scholars.

We have seen that in the map of Barros of Cir.1550 A.D the westward channel from the Triveni junction had on its south-eastern bank the port and the city of Satgaon. This channel, as stated earlier, turned south and then east to meet at Betore the stream coming straight from Triveni to the sea near Kalighat. The question may be asked that why the port of Satgaon was located in the westward channel on its southern bank and not on the straight stream coming down from Triveni and which later became the main stream and was called the Hughli river by the English. This is all the more serious in view of the fact that contemporary Bengali literature, excepting Bipradas, always referred to this westward channel as the Bhagirathi. The obvious explanation of these two questions seems to be that till the first half of the Sixteenth century, the straight stream or later the Hughli river was not navigable then and the principal navigational channel was the so-called Saraswati, the westward channel. This would explain why the Vaishnavas had their monasteries on the westward channel instead on the Hughli river and that when Chaitanya had come to one of these monasteries, it was said that he was visiting the bank of the Bhagirathi. There is no mention of Saraswati river in the contemporary Vaishnava literature[27].

The problem of the flow of water comes in perhaps from the seventies of the Sixteenth century. One cannot construct the sequence of the gradual withdrawal of the water from the westward channel to the Hughli river or the straight channel, which slowly denuded the port of Satgaon of the necessary flow of water that would allow the ships to come to the port. It is difficult to propose a chronological sequence since no such work has been done either by the geographers or by the archaeologists. Historians had remained content by simply mentioning that the river Saraswati has silted, which led to the fall of Satgaon as a port. The granting of *farman* by the Emperor Akbar to the Portuguese in 1579[28] gave the Portuguese the permission to make a settlement at Hughli. It has been hailed as the beginning of the rise of Hughli and the fall of Satgaon. Obviously the Portuguese request for the settlement at Hughli would signify that the port of Satgaon was declining or having difficulties with the flow of water. But it seems that the problem has started long before, even before the arrival of the Portuguese in the coast of Bengal in 1517 A.D. We have an inscription of the Sultan Alauddin Hussain Shah of Bengal of 1505, which stated that he was building a bridge between Satgaon and Triveni[29]. Since the bridge is not there, it is difficult to visualize the site of the bridge. But it shows that there was a need to connect the two, which signifies that the river Hughli on which Triveni stood was becoming important. This could be taken as the beginning of the withdrawal of the water from the westward channel while the chronology fits in with the assumption of Nihar Ranjan Ray who postulated 1475 as the high-water mark of the port of Satgaon as cited already. Obviously this does not mean the fall of the port of Satgaon.

That the flow of water was being reduced in the Saraswati channel could be seen from the activities of the Portuguese, who used to take their big ships up to Betore and then transfer their goods to the smaller ships and boats to go to Satgaon[30]. It is difficult to say since when they have started this. But the Portuguese could really establish themselves at Satgaon only from the middle of the Sixteenth century, although they have got the permission to settle at Satgaon and Chittagong during 1530s from the last Hussain Shahi Sultan Mahmud Shah III[31]. Yet it seems that some of the other big ships could come up to the port of Satgaon during the early 1560's, when the traveller Caesar Federici had seen thirty big and small ships anchored in the port of Satgaon[32]. This was almost the last mention of the ships in the port of Satgaon in the Sixteenth century. Later travellers like Ralph Fitch[33] or Vincent Le Blanc[34] did mention Satgaon but did not mention any ship lying there. Actually it seems, but one is not certain, that Le Blanc, who visited Satgaon in 1570s just after the conquest of Bengal by Akbar, probably took the boat via Bhagirathi and then passed into the Saraswati to reach Satgaon. He said that the city of Satgaon, where he stayed in the house of an official, was on a river that came out of the Bhagirathi, thus signifying that the flow of water was not totally withdrawn from the Saraswati channel. Yet it is clear that the area was being deserted and Hughli has not come up. This has been attested by Ralph Fitch, who came to Bengal between 1582 and 1594. He found the route from Satgaon to Hughli full of jungle in which wild animals and the dacoits predominate. He had to take a circuitous route to reach Hughli, which then had few shades[35].

Nihar Ranjan Ray has compared the two sketches of Barros and Broeke. But there are differences between the two[36], which he has not referred to. Broeke did not mention Betore, but shows that the river was falling into the Bhagirathi channel opposite Calcutta. But the bigger difference was that Broeke had shown Satgaon on the northern bank of the river Saraswati, which in actuality was located on the southern bank. The existence of the still surviving two monasteries, referred by the contemporary Vaishnava literature, shows the location on the south bank of the river, whose silted channel could still be seen. Obviously by the time Broeke was drawing his sketch in 1660, the function of Betore for the port of Satgaon seems already to be over. To be fair to Broeke, one must admit that in the map of Barros, there is something common to the settlement on the northern bank of Saraswati river opposite Satgaon, which was probably due to the fact that the area within the Satgaon area i.e. the southern bank of the river, has been fully saturated with buildings. This could be seen from the sketch of Barros as well as from the writing of Bipradas cited earlier. One may also recall that all of the seven villages, including Trisbigha, which was the core area of Satgaon, were in the south bank of the river. It is quite possible that by the time Broeke was writing this, a settlement had begun to crop up on the northern bank close to the Hughli river, which gave him that impression, particularly when Satgaon was then practically deserted.

IV

Two historians of repute of early Twentieth century – Crawford and Rakhal Das Bandyopadhayaya, who was one of the prominent archaeologists of India then, explored the site of Satgaon separately. Although they have visited Satgaon within two years of each other's visit, there are significant differences between them. As we would see, there is also a difference between their identification of sites and the description of such by the contemporary French visitor Vincent Le Blanc. But to understand the implication of these differences, it is necessary to construct the morphology of the town of Satgaon first.

Situated on the southern bank of the so-called Saraswati river, the town of Satgaon extended from the end of the westward channel to Triveni junction in the east. The reason of making such a statement is due to the fact that the Vaishnava monasteries as well as the tomb of Jamaluddin were located towards the end of the westward channel, thus signifying early settlement in situ. If it is accepted that this channel, called generally the Saraswati, is taken at some point of time even as late as the first half of the Sixteenth century as the principal channel of the Bhagirathi, then the town building should have started at the western end of the channel. Since the Hughli channel was not navigable then, the southern bank of the Saraswati was filled first starting from the end of the western end mainly to gain the water of the eastward loop, where the Vaishnava monastery of late Fifteenth century as well as the tomb of Jamaluddin were located showing early settlement. The town began to move towards the east i.e. towards the Hughli river, then must have been a small stream, and it also began to move towards the south making at the same time a semi-circular appearance that we notice in the sketch of Joao de Barros. Such appearance is quite common to the towns located on the bank of the rivers. Within the loop, once the land on the bank has been filled up by the port, the residence of high officials with market nearby, the town would start showing the bulge giving such an appearance. It is quite possible that when the move towards the south or the bulge has become quite big so as to preclude the inhabitants in finding water, there was a move to settle on the northern bank shown in the sketch of Van den Broeke almost a century later in 1660. Obviously Satgaon has become heavily populated by the end of the Fifteenth century as stated by Bipradas, the contemporary poet writing in 1494-95[37]. A later poet Krishnaram Das found that rows of houses on the bank of the Bhagirathi had been so much so that the houses touched each other and the people were sitting on the roofs[38]. Leaving the exaggeration of the poets, it is clear that Satgaon has become heavily populated.

Yet a question remains unanswered. Why the town did not move along the bank of the river Saraswati when it has taken the bend towards the south once its southern bank has been saturated. Why it is that it continues to move towards the south in the middle of the loop and not on the south-western bank of the loop. At least from the sketch of Barros it appears that there was no move to hold on to the south-western bank of the loop when the westward channel bends towards the south. There may be several explanations to this phenomenon but since no archaeological work has been done, no definite answer could be offered. It may be that the after the river has taken the southward turn, its course was not steady, which may explain the inability of the inhabitants to settle there. At the same time, it is possible that by the time the principal bank of the river, the southern bank, has been saturated, the withdrawal of water from the Saraswati was becoming more rapid and there was a tendency of the inhabitants to move towards the Hughli channel rather than going towards the west.

The first of the two explorers of the Twentieth century, D. G. Crawford published his findings in 1908[39] although he did not mention when did he visit the place. He stated that the Saraswati "is now a very small stream but has still on each side a belt of lowlands, about a quarter of a mile broad, which occasionally filled in the rains..on the east side of the road and in southeast of lowlands besides the Saraswati, there is a large quadrangular mass of high mound full of broken bricks."[40]. Crawford considered it a river wall where ships used to anchor. Further east, he found several tanks and many ruins including a mosque nearby[41].

Three points emerge from his brief narrative quoted here, which has not been developed by Crawford or by any other later historian. The first is that the Saraswati bed, even nearly three hundred years after the fall of Satgaon if we take 1632 as such a date, which would be explained later, is nearly a mile broad. This would certainly make it the principal channel of the Bhagirathi in its heyday and one could visualize that during the rainy season the span of the river was more than a mile in front of Satgaon. This should put at rest any controversy regarding the principal channel of the Bhagirathi in its earlier run before it began to withdraw its water for the Hughli course.

The second point is on the southern bank of the Saraswati, Crawford found a quadrangular mass of high ground, which he considered as the port of Satgaon. If this were accepted, this would be closer to the Hughli river near the Triveni junction rather than towards the end of the westward channel. This would mean that the city has started to grow from the eastern end rather than from the western end, which would suggest the influence of the town of Triveni as the starting point. Since Triveni never acted as a port, the port of Satgaon was located further up towards the west particularly at a place where the water was deep enough for the ships to anchor. In that case it is quite natural to accept that the earlier settlers like the Vaishnavas settled their monasteries far from the port at the end of the western channel. The third point is that Crawford has found the ruins all along the bank towards the east i.e. towards the Triveni junction and the Hughli river. We would compare this narrative with that of the celebrated archaeologist Rakhal Das Bandyopadhyaya, who published his findings in 1909 close on the heels of that of Crawford, but in a different Journal[42]. Needless to say the narrative of Bandyopadhyaya is far more specific and we may do well in quoting the relevant portion here.

"From the shrine of Raghunath Das passing eastward along the course of the Saraswati one comes to a huge mound of bricks, which according to the local traditions are the ruins of the citadel of Saptagram (Satgaon)....About a quarter of a mile from the tomb of Jamaluddin..there is a stump of a pillar once belonging to a mosque. The surrounding grounds are strewn with pieces of sculptures and brick works. Whole of the area extending from Trisbigha to Triveni is strewn with bricks and large anchors, chains, cables and ropes of immense sizes are found in the bed of this river...in some places in the district of Howrah has been choked up altogether."[43] Bandyopadhayaya further adds that a pot of coins were found in the riverbank between the monastery and the port, which, according to the people of the monastery, had been appropriated by the Khadim of the mosque[44].

One could discern certain difference between the narrative of Crawford and that of Bandyopadhayaya. As seen earlier,

Crawford had marked this mound as the river wall or part of the port, but Bandyopadhayaya called it a citadel basing on local tradition. The latter thus puts the fort quite a distance from the Triveni junction. It may be mentioned that neither the contemporary Bengali literature nor the travellers, excepting Vincent Le Blanc, had mentioned the fort at Satgaon, although according to the 20th century explorer, such a tradition exists among the local people. But there is a difference between the account of Blanc and those of these two explorers. Le Blanc mentioned the fort close to the Triveni-Satgaon junction or in the vicinity of the Hughli river[45], where no such mound could be seen at present. But the location of the fort in the narrative of Blanc is closer to the location given by Crawford. Both these explorers as well as Blanc had referred to this fort as the one built by the Portuguese, who could have built it only during or after the middle of the Sixteenth century. As mentioned earlier, they got the permission from the Sultan Mahmud Shah III to establish themselves at Satgaon and Chittagong in 1537-38, which they could not do immediately in view of the invasions of Sher Shah and Humayun and the consequent political anarchy that followed for quite some time. Actually in view of the invasion of Gaur by Sher Shah in 1536, the Sultan Mahmud Shah took the help of the Portuguese Diego Rebello who had come to Satgaon with his two ships, on condition of allowing them to build the forts at Satgaon and Chittagong as well as to establish trade. But after Sher Shah was gone, the Sultan changed his mind and did not permit the Portuguese to build forts at either of the places. He however allowed them to establish factories along with their customhouses. This they proceeded to do immediately, thus heralding the establishment of the first European factory in Bengal. Incidentally, the visit of Diego Rebello to Satgaon could be construed as the visit of the first European to this place. Obviously this was done through the Saraswati route since there was no mention of Hughli. The Portuguese could get the permission to construct factories and customhouses and not the construction of any fort[46]. Even if one accepts that the Portuguese had constructed a fort, it seems probable that the fort would be located closer to the Triveni junction than in the east for the simple reason that by the time the Portuguese had got the construction going, the riverbank would be extremely crowded with the buildings while the town was gradually moving towards the Hughli river as the withdrawal of the water from the Saraswati was already underway. Besides, if one accepts the narrative of Le Blanc, that he has seen the fort from outside, it could only be located at the east, close to the Hughli river, since Blanc seems to have travelled via the Hughli river and came shopping at Satgaon. Therefore he could not have been far off from his anchorage, as we would presently see while trying to construct the morphology of the town. Actually this would raise the question that from which end the town of Satgaon started. If the construction is taken near the Triveni junction and if the construction of fort has started after the middle of the Sixteenth century, then the town would have started from the western end of the channel of Saraswati. But there are equal arguments to support the theory that the town has started from the Triveni junction end.

Obviously the port and the principal market along with the temples were located on the eastern side near the Hughli river. Blanc stated that he resided in the house of an official[47], which was perhaps located not far from the port and on the south-eastern bank of the Saraswati. It is of course possible that he walked towards the middle of the town by going along the bank of the river. In that case we could construct the development of the town taking the start from the end of the westward channel and then moving towards the east along the bank of the river, the line that was taken by the two explorers of the Twentieth century cited already. That the Frenchman was not far from the market could be seen in the fact that he had bought some live birds from the market while the noise from the temple was floating by[48], suggesting that the principal market was close by the eastern end of the channel of Saraswati.

The earliest reference to the names of people living on the south-eastern edge of the eastern end of the channel of Saraswati at Satgaon was given by Kirshnadas Kaviraj writing around 1617 A.D.[49]. He referred to the *Ijaradar* of Satgaon, Hiranya Das Majumdar and Govardhan Das Majumdar who had taken Satgaon as *Ijara* for yearly payment of twelve lakhs of rupees in early Sixteenth century, but used to collect twenty lakhs of rupees. Such a big amount should not confuse us since in medieval India the income of the port always included the dependent land around. However the income of the port of Satgaon was at the end of the Sixteenth century was around rupees 30,000 per year as given by Abul Fazl[50]. But that was an assessment done during the Afghan period, which was collected by Todar Mal[51]. Therefore the *Ijara* of Rs. twelve lakhs per year should be of the entire *Sarkar* of Satgaon and not that of the port. These two men were quite rich and obviously were residing at the town of Satgaon. It was stated that they were residing on the south-eastern bank of the Saraswati.

According to Haridas Das, the Vaishnava saint Udharan Dutt was born in 1481 in that area and died there in 1541, whose *Samadhi* was still situated there. The building has been repaired several times and it is difficult at present to locate the original building. Quite close by as one moves towards the east was the monastery of Raghunath Goswami[52].Vrindaban Das, writing in 1563 approximately, wrote that Chaitanya used to go to the temple of Udharan Dutt, which was located on the bank of the Bbhagirathi[53]. Obviously the Vaishanvas had visualized Saraswati as the Bhagirathi and the Vaishnavas had preferred to live quite a distance from the port and the residences of the officials. But the merchants who were converted in Vaishnavism used to live quite close to the port, rather than on the western end of the city, far more closer to the bank of the Hughli river. The *Subarna Baniks* used to settle between Magra and Hughli Railway station, a process that was going on during the second half of the Fifteenth century once the capital was shifted to Gaur from Pandua.

Still the location of the port eludes us. If we take the narrative of Bandyopadhyaya, seen above, that the anchors, cables, chains and ropes as well as a pot of coins were found close to the monasteries, then the port should have been located close by. If we take the account of Crawford, then the port is halfway in the channel of the Saraswati. Whatever the location, it is clear that the flow of water in the Saraswati channel is being reduced by the middle of the 16th century and that the flow of water was going through the Hughli river. The traveller Caeser Federici, writing around 1565[54] found that the big Portuguese ships could not come up to Satgaon and transfer their goods at Betore in smaller crafts. Obviously enough water was not there in either of these two streams – the Saraswati and the Hughli. One could perhaps venture to say that the traveller Federici was at Satgaon at the period of transformation when the disaster to the mercantile world of Satgaon has begun to confront them. Even then it is not clear by which route the Portuguese used to carry their goods to Satgaon port. It seems that the port of Satgaon was not close to the Hughli river. In the contemporary Bengali literature starting from Bipradas, we find that their legendary merchant used to anchor at Triveni and go to Satgaon for shopping. Had there been a port nearby, they would have taken the boats to the port of Satgaon so as to reduce the problem of transporting the goods in to the boats[55]. In that case, it seems that the mound quite close to the Hughli river on the south-eastern bank of the Saraswati was the market or *Dingal Hat* according to local tradition. Such a location of the market would be in accordance to the itinerary of Le Blanc as well as those of the Bengali merchants of contemporary Bengali literature since they followed the Hughli route.

If we believe Bipradas, Satgaon has developed into a big town by the end of the Fifteenth century. In his account, one could see the existence of sizeable Hindu and Muslim population in the town and Bipradas has enumerated some of the professions of the Muslims as well. So far as Hindus are concerned, the poet referred to the thirty six castes, which is a traditional enumeration of the division of the Hindu society[56]. That the Muslim population was there could be seen from the description of Blanc. He found meat of animals and living birds quite cheap in the market. After he has bought some chickens, some people approached him and requested him to release the birds[57]. These people may be Jains or Hindus, whose temples were nearby and from where loud music was being heard by Blanc[58]. As mentioned by us earlier, there is no reference of ships at the port of Satgaon after 1565. Yet Le Blanc, coming immediately after the Mughal occupation of Satgaon in 1575, found the city working in full swing with shops full of goods and the crowd was so much in the market that it was difficult for him to find his way. Although Blanc was requested to release the birds, there was no religious and racial animosity in the town. The worship of the idols, be it Hindus, Vaishnavas or Jainas, with loud music was not stopped either by the *Kotwal* or by the *Qazi*, the proverbial villain of the contemporary Bengali literature of the medieval period. It may be mentioned that by the time Blanc has appeared on the streets of Satgaon, the capital has first been removed to Tanda, on the opposite bank of the Ganges further west by the Sultan Sulaiman Karrani probably in 1565. It was briefly brought back to Gaur by the victorious Mughal general Munim Khan, who along with many others died in the pest and the capital was finally transferred to Rajmahal by the Subadar Man Singh in early 1590's. Yet Satgaon continued to draw goods from the hinterland and neighbouring areas for its markets, although one is not clear whether the port of Satgaon was still functioning at least in the transportation of goods. That the port was still functioning in transporting goods in the 1620's could be seen from two English letters written from Patna in which they mentioned that the Portuguese had brought goods from Southeast Asia to Satgaon and they are then transporting these goods to Patna[59]. This would seriously contradict the view held so far by the historians that the rise of Hughli, apart from silting of the Saraswati, had finished Satgaon by the end of the Sixteenth century. It was only after the Mughal conquest in 1632 of the Hughli port held by the Portuguese, that the Mughals transferred their customhouse from Satgaon to Hughli, which finished the port of Satgaon. Therefore what the Portuguese did in the early Seventeenth century, of taking goods first to Satgaon, was merely to pay the custom tax for which they had a separate house there. The town of Satgaon however continued to function till the end of the Eighteenth century.

The sketch of Barros[60] shows the town of Satgaon in several units of buildings, which perhaps suggests that the town was divided into several wards. He has given it an oblong shape, which he has given in case of two other towns of Bengal. In case of Satgaon, the shape becomes similar to half-moon with a bulge in the centre towards the south of the loop. Obviously after the bank of the Saraswati was crowded, the town began to move towards the south but tending to veer towards the east, towards the Hughli river, thus confirming our suggestion that by 1550, there was a tendency of the inhabitants, particularly living at a distance from the Saraswati, to move towards the Hughli river. Obviously this was the period when the withdrawal of water from the Saraswati and filling up of the Hughli course was becoming markedly clear. This is one of the reasons why the Portuguese wanted to have the permission to settle at Hughli in 1579. By that time, the movement of the city towards the south within the loop has been halted as the flow of water in the Hughli river was becoming more and more clear, thus making the Betore connection redundant. As a result the city looked like an inverted pyramid, but strangely enough, not scrambling yet to get closer to the Hughli riverbank. This was because the Hughli bank has not yet developed, a fact that has been underlined by the visitor Ralph Fitch coming after 1583 but before 1594. From Satgaon he could not go to Hughli by the straight route as it was full of jungles with wild beasts and dacoits roaming in profusion. He did not spare many words for Satgaon and one may quote his comment to show that the town and its market were still functioning. "Satgaon is a faire citie for a citie of the Moores, and plentiful of all things"[61]. Significantly Fitch did speak of boats in Bengal a little later but did not mention any ship or a boat in the port of Satgaon. Therefore the Portuguese kept the port of Satgaon as it is and began to use the port of Hughli, which was then under the control of the Portuguese and becoming notorious as a slave market.

Even if we take the account of Bipradas at the end of the Fifteenth century as the period of prosperity of Satgaon, the merchants there did not always have their happy days. With the arrival of the Portuguese in Bengal since 1517 asking for permission to trade in Bengal, there were debates in the court of the Nusrut Shah, Sultan of Bengal, at Gaur in 1521 on the question of the permission to be given to the Portuguese to trade in Bengal, which has been recounted by the anonymous Portuguese interpreter[62]. This debate in the court partly originated due to the ruthless operations of the Arakanese and the Portuguese pirates in the Bay of Bengal and particularly in the mouth of the Bhagirathi. The Portuguese had already captured two ships of the sultan Alauddin Husain Shah of Bengal and seized all the goods found in the ships. Actually from the beginning of the 16th century, there were problems at Satgaon among the mercantile groups. Tome Pires[63], writing from Malacca during the reign of Sultan Alauddin Husain Shah of Bengal (1493-1519), stated that the Sultan used to oppress the merchants and charged very high taxes. This was probably because the Sultan had his own ships with which he was trading in Southeast Asia. But there were internal dissentions within the mercantile groups. Basudev Ghosh, one of the companions of Chaitanya, referred to at least three mercantile groups at Satgaon, namely the *Subanrna Baniks* (those who deal with gold and silver trading), the *Gandha Baniks* (those who deal with perfumery) and the *Kansa Baniks* (those who deal with mixed metal utensils). Later on the *Subarna Baniks* were divided into two branches, perhaps on the question of giving cooperation to the Portuguese. But Basudev Ghosh had referred to the persecution of the officials of the Sultan on the merchants of these groups[64]. The *Subarna Banik* group was called *Karjana Smaj*, which was referred by the late Sixteenth century Bengali poet Mukundaram Chakrabarty. He stated that the *Subarna Baniks* or the members of the *Karjana Samaj* were very wealthy since they trade with gold and silver, but they never go out of Satgaon[65]. But in the writing of Basudev Ghosh in the early Sixteenth century, one could get a confirmation of the picture given by Bipradas. Basudev Ghosh referred to the existence of physicians, barbers, weavers, merchants, traders, shopkeepers etc. at Satgaon[66]. In the narrative of Mukundaram one finds the same trends excepting that there Hindus of Satgaon were not doing overseas trade and they seem to be controlling the internal trade of Satgaon[67]. The contemporary Bengali literature narrates, rather in a stereotyped version, the journey of the Zamindar-merchant who were taking their boats to the coast of Orissa through the Hughly river, but anchoring at Triveni and shopping at Satgaon. Even we take them as overseas merchants, they were not the merchants of Satgaon, but were coming from the interior of the *Rarh* area. It is quite possible that after the coming of the Portuguese in Bengal and their struggle with the Arab and Turkish merchants, the Gujarati Jain merchants compromised with the Portuguese and carried a share of the South-eastern Asian trade from Bengal, obviously from Satgaon, although there is no specific evidence to support this. Yet the existence of large number of Muslims at Satgaon, first enumerated by Bipradas at the end of the Fifteenth century i.e. before the coming of the Portuguese and then later by Basudev Ghoṣh, who particularly referred to the existence of merchants at Satgaon, create a problem in this regard. One could suggest that Basudev was writing around the middle of the Sixteenth century when the Portuguese stranglehold on Bengal's trade had not become dominant.

The division of the town of Satgaon shown by Barros in the unit of buildings would suggest the existence of different wards, quite a common feature in any Indian medieval big town. In 1521, the anonymous Portuguese interpreter had described such wards at Gaur, where different manufacturing activities and sale of particular commodities were taking place[68]. We do not have a similar statement from any contemporary traveller on Satgaon. But Rakhal Das Bandyopadhayaya, in his exploration in the early Twentieth century, had referred to the continuation of some Bengali words like *Malopara, Kagchipara* etc. at Satgaon[69], which suggests that such kind of division of wards on the basis of occupation and manufacture were there at Satgaon. The reference of so many occupational people at Satgaon, both Hindus and Muslims, would strongly suggest such a possibility. It is therefore clear that like other Indian medieval cities, the division was based neither on class nor on creed nor on the basis of the community, but on the basis of occupation of the people of both communities.

In the early Sixteenth century, Tome Pires, writing from Malacca, had referred to Satgaon as a good port on the

Ganges[70], which confirms once again our suggestion that the principal channel of the Bhagirathi was flowing through the Saraswati till then. Pires suggested, without being at Satgaon and obviously getting the reports from other Portuguese travellers, that Satgaon had a population of about 10, 000 souls[71], which is rather small given the area of the town of Satgaon. It may be mentioned that the contemporary capital of Bengal, Gaur, was more than four times bigger than that of Satgaon in the early Sixteenth century. The population of Gaur has been estimated as more than two lakhs of people[72]. The problem of the Portuguese counting in those days is that they often mentioned souls as hearths, which they did in case of Gaur. If we take the estimate of five persons per hearth i.e. family, as done by Irfan Habib and Shireen Moosvi in case of other medieval towns of India, then we come to 50, 000 persons at Satgaon in the early Sixteenth century[73]. In that case the town of Satgaon would be extremely crowded by the end of the Fifteenth century as explained to us by the Bengali contemporary poet Bipradas cited already.

As seen earlier there is no record of the use of the port of Satgaon in the writings of the European travellers. This must have led the modern historians to conclude that Satgaon had declined with the rise of the port of Hughli established by the Portuguese in 1579. But that is not the entire story. We have seen two letters from the English merchants from Patna during the 1620's, who had referred to the Portuguese bringing goods from Southeast Asia to Satgaon and then transfer these to Patna. Although it is not clear which route the Portuguese then had taken to go to Satgaon and thereafter to Patna, it is certain that the port of Satgaon was functioning till then, albeit for smaller crafts. As seen earlier that the reason for the use of Satgaon instead of that of Hughli was that the customhouse was located at Satgaon till then. It was only when the Mughals had driven out the Portuguese from Hughli in 1632 and had transferred the customhouse at Hughli, then the port of Satgaon had ceased to function, since the reason of its existence was gone. It was only from that time onwards that the port of Hughli began to rise, which perhaps coincided with more water coming through the Hughli river and the establishment of peace and order in Bengal by the Mughals, who now controlled the coastal areas.

With the flow of water being reduced in the Saraswati channel, there would obviously be the problem of going to the port of Satgaon by the Saraswati route. The *Atlas* prepared by Irfan Habib as well as that of Beams reconstructed by B.P. Ambasthya[74] showed that the connection between the Saraswati channel and the Hughly river was cut off, a view that was slightly visible in the sketch of Van den Broeke prepared in 1660. Perhaps the connection at Betore still continued for some time more due to the tide rushing the water through the Saraswati channel, which obviously had failed to fill the connection at Triveni by 1660. It is difficult to say since when this process stated, but given the circumstances, one may suggest that the process of the separation of Triveni and Satgaon had started at least from the second half of the Sixteenth century when the desertion of Satgaon began. This would mean that the Hughli river was becoming navigable quite rapidly and it is safe to postulate that the merchants of Satgaon were shifting to Hughli, and not to Calcutta as some historians had suggested. Their link with Satgaon could continue as the legendary merchants of the contemporary Bengali poets had anchored at Triveni and had gone to Satgaon for shopping. This connection was perhaps based on the land route that Ralph Fitch was suggesting long back. The continuation of the shopping centres at Satgaon would suggest that the merchants of Satgaon were either still there or had settled at Hughli nearby to supply the city of Satgaon. Such supplies to Satgaon become all the more important since till the end of the Sixteenth century, as seen earlier, Hughli has not come up as a town. There is therefore a connection between the rise of Hughli port and the continuation of the town of Satgaon even after 1632 at least till the end of the Eighteenth century.

Perhaps there was another reason for the dislocation of the function of the port of Satgaon. Once again, the modern historians, bent on concluding that that the silting of the

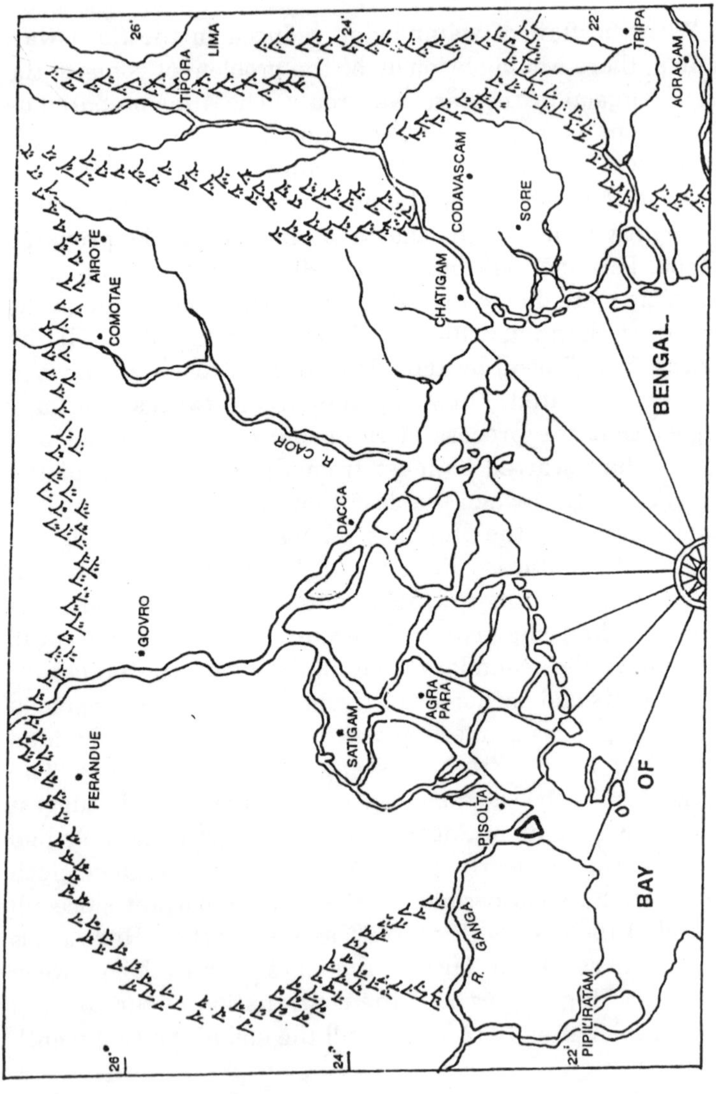

Map 1. Joao de Barros's Map of Bengal, 1615.

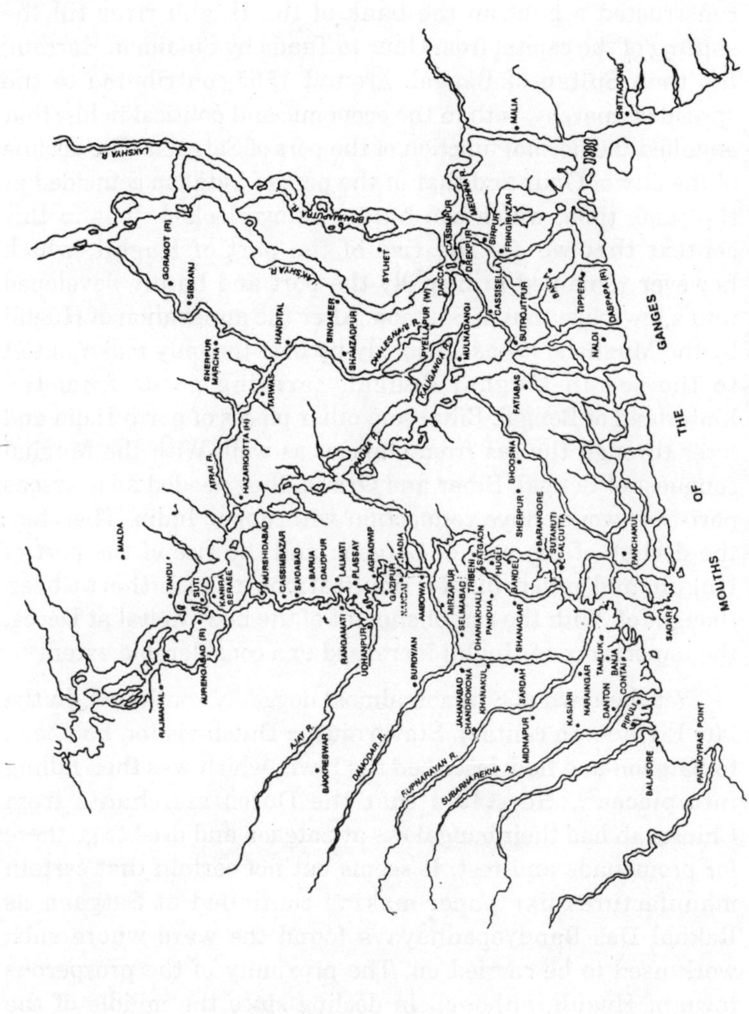

Map 2. Van Den Broucke's Map of Bengal, 1660.

Saraswati was the real and only reason for the decline of the port, did not pay much attention to the functional differences of the port and the town of Satgaon. From the end of the 1530's, the invasion of the Bhagirathi bank including the capital of Bengal, Gaur, twice by Sher Shah, once by Humayun, once by the King of Orissa, who incidentally occupied Satgaon and constructed a ghat on the bank of the Hughli river till the shifting of the capital from Gaur to Tanda by Sulaiman Karrani, the then Sultan of Bengal, around 1565,contributed to the spread of anarchy, both in the economic and political fields, that engulfed the normal function of the port of Satgaon. The decline of the city of Gaur and that of the port of Satgaon coincided at the same time, which can hardly be overlooked. It is in this context that we see the rise of the port of Hughli, which however remained principally the port and hardly developed into a town like that of Satgaon. After the annexation of Hughli by the Mughals, it has obviously become the only major outlet to the sea in Mughal Bengal, carrying goods from the hinterland of Bengal, Bihar and other places of north India and later through the sea from Gujarat as well. With the Mughal conquest of Bengal, Bihar and Orissa, they needed an overseas port that would have connection with upper India. Therefore the decline of the port of Satgaon and the rise of the port of Hughli had much bigger implications than hitherto been thought of. With the establishment of the new capital at Dacca, the importance of Hughli increased to a considerable extent.

Yet the town of Satgaon almost doggedly continued. In the late Eighteenth century, Stavornius, a Dutch visitor, had been to Satgaon and had described the town, which was then falling into pieces[75]. He stated that the Dutch merchants from Chinsurah had their bungalows at Satgaon and used to go there for promenade and rest. It seems but not certain that certain manufactures like paper-making continued at Satgaon as Rakhal Das Bandyopadhayaya found the ward where such work used to be carried on. The proximity of the prosperous town of Hughli, although in decline since the middle of the Eighteenth century, helped the town of Satgaon to continue without the port. The brief but glorious history of the by-gone days of the Bengali merchants who used to get all the wealth by sitting at home was over under the far more ruthless operations of the English merchants in Bengal. The lingering memory of the city of Satgaon blossoms forth in the legends confronting the thin stream that was once the mighty river. In the late Nineteenth century, Jogesh Chandra Basu, on a visit to Trisbigha, had seen the ruined buildings completely neglected by the historians and the archaeologists, still standing isolated splendour[76]. The only satisfaction of the local Municipality remains in naming the core area – Trisbigha- as *Adi Saptagram*, which still awaits its archaeologist.

Notes and References

1. Sudhir Kumar Mitra, *Hughli Zelar Itihas O Banga Samaj* (Bengali), 2 Vols, Calcutta, 1991. II, 1719 post (Reprint).
2. H. A. R. Gibb (tr.), *Ibn Battuta*, New Delhi, 1986. Scholars have expressed different opinions on the landing place of Ibn Battuta. See the earlier work of Harinath De, *Ibn Battuta's Account of Bengal*, Calcutta, 1978. The last one to join the controversy is Dinesh Chandra Ghosh, *Saptagram Uday-Asta* (Bengali), Burdwan, 2004.He suggested that Battuta has landed at Satgaon. There are problems in accepting this thesis.
3. See S. B. Qanungo, *A History of Chittagong*, Chittagong, 1988, Vol. I. 134-136. He has summarized different arguments and came to the conclusion that Battuta had landed at Chittagong.
4. See the article of Rakhal Das Badyopadhyaya entitled "Saptagram or Satgaon" in *The Journal of the Asiatic Society*, 1909, Vol. V, N0, 86, 245-246.
5. See the inscription of 1298 A. D. of Zafar Khan Ghaazi at Triveni (Shamsuddin Ahmed, *Inscriptions of Bengal*, Rasjshahi, 1960, Vol. V, 18-23 for the original Arabic text with English translations and annotations.
6. Mitra, *op. cit.*, II, 722-723.
7. Muhammed Bin Tughluq divided Bengal in several parts in 1328 A. D. and assigned Satgaon to Izzuddin Yahiya. A mint was established at Satgaon and the first coin came out of that mint in 1328 A. D. (see D. C. Ghosh, *op. cit.*, 278).

8. J. D. Beglar, *Report of Tours in South-eastern Provinces in 1874-75 and 1876-77*, Archaeological Survey of India, 1970, Vol. XIII (Reprint).
9. Haraprasad Ray, *Trade and Diplomacy in India-China Relations*, New Delhi, 1993. Mill's identification of the capital with Gaur at that time is obviously incorrect (*Ma Huan* tr. J. V. Gill & ed. By Feng Ch'eng Chun, Cambridge, 1970,159, fn. 3).
10. Nihar Ranjan Ray, *Bangalir Itihas* (Bengali), Calcutta, 1993, 76-79.
11. Sukumar Sen (ed.), *Bipradaser Manasa Vijaya* (Bengali), The Asiatic Society, No date, 124.
12. Mukundaram Chakrabarty, *Chandi Mangal* (Bengali), ed. By Panchanan Mandal, Calcutta, 1992, 196-197.
13. Shamshuddin Ahmed, *op. cit.*, 68-70. Bandyopadhayaya also discussed it (*op. cit.*,248-252). He agrees with Blochman that Arsa was a *sarkar* and not a *pargana* (252).
14. Abul Fazl Allami, *The Ain-i Akbari*, tr. By H. S. Jarret & ed. By Jadunath Sarkar, The Asiatic Society, Calcutta, 1993, Reprint, 3 Vols., II, 137.
15. S. Ahmed for the inscription of Sultan Nasiruddin Mahmud dated 1457 A. D. (*op. cit.*, 49-50).
16. Nihar Ranjan Ray, *op. cit.*, 78.
17. Bipradas, *op. cit.*, 143.
18. Article of Aniruddha Ray entitled "Archaeological Reconnaissance at the City of Gaur: A Preliminary Report" in *Pratna-Samiksha*, Calcutta, 1995, NO. 2-3, 245-263.
19. Article of Simon Digby entitled "The Currency System" in Tapan Raychaudhuri and Irfan Habib (eds.), *The Cambridge Economic History of India*, 1984, Vol. I, 93-101. See also, John S. Deyell, *Living Without Silver*, Oxford University Press, 1990.
20. H. N. Wright, *op. cit.*, 218-19.
21. Gulam Hussain Salim, *Riaz-us Salatin* (Bengali tr.), Dacca, 1974, 77.
22. S. B. Qanungo, *op. cit.*, Vol. I.
23. See G. Bouchon & L. F. Thomaz (eds.), *Voyage,* Paris, 1988, Atlas de Lopo Homem, 1519, N* VI.

24. Nihar Ranjan Ray, *op. cit.*, 74-79
25. A. Cortesao (ed.), *Cartographia e Cartographos Portugais des Seculos XVe-XVIe,* Lisbon, 1935, 2 Vols.; also see, A. Cortesao and A. T. de Motta, *Portugales Monumenta Cartographica*, Lisbon, 1960, 6 Vols.
26. See Bouchon & Thomaz, *op. cit.*
27. See for example, Vrindaban Das, *Chatanya Bhagavat* (Bengali), Nabadwipa, 479 Gaurabda, 1017. These two monasteries are still there, although these have been repaired from time to time.
28. For a full discussion on the Portuguese settlement at Hughli, see J. J. A. Campos, *History of the Portuguese in Bengal,* Patna, 1979 (Reprint), 49-54. Campos has based his account on the basis of the narrative of Manrique and the account of Abul Fazl as given in his *Akbar Nama*. Pedro Taveres was the Portuguese who procured the farman.
29. Shamsuddin Ahmed, *op. cit.*, 173-177.
30. Account of Caeser Frederick in Purchas, *Pilgrimages*, Edinburg, 1911, Vol. V, 410-411.
31. Campos stated that the Portuguese took possession of the customhouses of Chittagong and Satgaon in 1537-1538. But the earliest reference to the Portuguese factory at Satgaon was in 1554-55 (Campos, *op. cit.*,46-47. In any case, the Portuguese factory at Satgaon did not operate before the middle of the Sixteenth century due to the prevailing anarchy on the Bhagirathi belt.
32. Fredericki, *op cit.*, 410-411.
33. For the account of Ralph Fitch, see William Foster (ed.), *Early Travels in India,* Delhi, 1985, 24 (Reprint).
34. Vincent Le Blanc, *Les Voyages Fameux*, Paris, 1648.
35. Fitch, *op. cit.*, 24.
36. He has reproduced copies at the end of his second edition.
37. Bipradas, *op. cit.*, 143.
38. Rakhal Das Bandyopadhayaya quoted the poem in Bengali in his article entitled "Saptagram or Satgaon", *op. cit.,* 264.
39. Article of D. G. Crawford entitled "Satgaon or Triveni" in *Bengal Past & Present*, 1908, Vol. III, 18-26.
40. *Ibid*, 18-19.

41. Ibid.
42. Bandyopadhayaya, *op. cit.*
43. *Ibid, 255.*
44. *Ibid*, 254- 255.
45. Le Blanc, *op. cit.*, 133-134.
46. Campos, *op. cit.*, 37-41.
47. Le Blanc, *op. cit.*, 133.
48. *Ibid.*
49. Description in Mitra, *op. cit.,* II, 721-726. He also mentioned that the late Jogesh Chandra Basu had mentioned that he had seen the ruins of brick buildings in this area (*Ibid*, 730). For the *Ijara* of Saptagram in the Sixteenth century, see Krtishnadas Kaviraj, *Chaitanya Charitamrita* (Bengali), Basumati ed. 1386 B. S. , 9th ed., 185. Obviously the *Ijara* was for the entire Satgaon *sarkar* and not for the revenue of the port of Satgaon only. It may be mentioned that in 1595-96, Abul Fazl put the revenue of the port of Satgaon as Rs. 30, 000 yearly, which was the computation of the Afghan period of at least twentyfive years back.
50. Abul Fazl, *The Ain-i- Akbari, op cit.,* III, 154.
51. *Ibid.*
52. Bipradas, *op. cit.*, 142.
53. Vrindaban Das, *op. cit.*, 1017.
54. Caeser Fredericki, *op. cit.*, 410-411.
55. The merchant of Mukundaram followed it, which seemed to be the traditional line to follow. But Mukundaram did not mention Hughli, although he mentioned Halishahr opposite Hughli.
56. Bipradas, *op. cit.*, 143.
57. Le Blanc, *op. cit.,* 133
58. *Ibid.* Bipradas also stated that the sound of music was coming from the temples.
59. Quoted in L. S. S. O'Malley & M. Chakrabarty, *Bengal District Gazetteer: Hughly*, Calcutta, 1912, Vol. 29, 187-191.
60. In the original sketch kept at the Overseas Archive at Lisbon, it was on a much bigger scale and the separation of units could be seen clearly.

61. Fitch, *op. cit.*, 24-26.
62. Bouchon & Thomaz, *op. cit.*, 328 post.
63. A. Cortesao (ed.), *The Suma Oriental of Thome Pires*, AES, 1990, 93 (Reprint).
64. Article of Manaswita Sanyal entitled "Saptagram, c. 1300-1632" in *Aitihasik* (Bengali Journal), Calcutta, January 1977, N0. 4, 1-26.
65. Mukundaram, *op. cit.*, 324.
66. See supra Note 64.
67. Mukundaram, *op. cit.*, 177, He has given the names of traders and their areas of operations. Haridas Nilambar was from the *Karjana Samaj*.
68. Bouchon & Thomaz, *op. cit.*, 323.
69. Bandyopadhayaya, *op. cit.*, 257-258.
70. Pires, *op. cit.* 91.
71. *Ibid.*
72. Article of Aniruddha Ray entitled "Archaeological Reconnaissance", *op. cit.*, 245-263.
73. For full discussion, see *Ibid.*
74. Irfan Habib, *An Atlas of the Mughal Empire*, Oxford University Press, 1982, Sheet N0 11 A; B.P. Ambasthya, *Beame's Contribution to the Political Geography*, Patna, 1976.
75. Quoted by Crawford, *op. cit.*, 23.
76. Description in Mitra, *op. cit.*, II, 721-726. For the account of Jogesh Chandra Basu on the ruined buildings, see *Ibid*, 738.

3

The Rise and Fall of the Port of Cannanore: Aspects of Trade and Politics in Malabar between the Sixteenth and Seventeenth Centuries

J.B.P. More & Leena More

Various scholars have so far adequately highlighted the role of the Indian and foreign merchants in the port of Cannanore[1] or the relations between the port and its hinterland with special reference to the expansion of Portuguese and Dutch trade.[2] However, except the study of Ruchira Banerjee[3] which deals with conflicts between the English and the Ali Rajas of Cannanore in the Eighteenth century no scholar has dealt in detail the political and commercial role of the Raja of Cannanore in the Sixteenth and Seventeenth centuries. Hence this paper attempts to examine the role of the native ruler with reference to trade and politics.

Keralopatti is largely a mythological and legendary piece of literature which relates the origin and evolution of Kerala. It probably has some germs of historical truth. The kingdom of Cannanore is mentioned in it. It records that the king of Cannanore was the son of a kshatriya woman and to the previous Chera king. It is useful from the historical point of view to note the view of M.G.S.Narayanan who has held in one of his historical works that northern Kerala from Cannanore to Kasargod was definitely incorporated into the Chera kingdom with its capital at Makotai, only around the Tenth century. This seems to suggest that prior to this period northern Kerala was an independent entity. M.G.S.Narayanan has made no reference in his work to Cannanore, either on the basis of the inscriptions or on the indigenous historical manuscripts like the *Musakavamsa kavya* believed to have been composed in the

Eleventh century.[4] This suggests that Cannanore was an insignificant place during this period and even before. Literally speaking, Cannanore which is the anglicized form of the Malayalam *Kannur* means 'beautiful village'. This village was traditionally part of the kingdom of Kolathanadu, whose ruler was known as Kolattiri. It probably evolved into a town from the Fourteenth century onwards. We hardly have any direct reference to Cannanore in the works of the Arab and Persian geographers starting from Sulaiman al-Tajir in the Ninth century, though many of them had referred to the Malabar Coast and the Chinese traders there. The discovery of Chinese ceramics on the Coast, right from Quilon to Cannanore seems to suggest that Chinese had trade relations not only with Quilon but also with Cannanore in the northern Malabar Coast during or before the Fifteenth century itself.[5]

In the beginning of the Fourteenth century, Rashiddudin in his *Ja'mu'ut Towarik* has referred to Quilon (Kulam) and Mangalore (Manjarur). It is quite possible that the town of Faknur situated on the coast between Quilon and Mangalore, mentioned by Rashidudin might refer to Kannur or Cannanore. The great Moroccan traveller Ibn Batuta had referred directly to Manjarur (Mangalore), Calicut and Quilon in the Fourteenth century. Between Manjarur and Calicut, Ibn Batuta had identified Hili, Jurfattan, Dahfattan and Budfattan. He describes Hili (Eli) as an imposing port city where the Chinese ships came for trade. The reference to Jurfattan and its king Kuwayl by Ibn Batuta in his *Rehla* could only point to Cannanore and its ruler. Ibn Batuta adds that the king of Jurfattan possesses many ships which go to Oman, Fars and Yemen and that Dahfattan (probably Dharmapatnam or the modern Darmadam) and Budfattan (probably Valarpatnam or Badagara) belonged to him. But strangely he does not note the presence of Chinese traders in these three ports. Cannanore or Jurfattan seems to be one of the twelve kingdoms of Malabar ruled by Hindu kings according to Ibn Batuta. It is interesting to note that the word 'Jurfattan' is made up of 'Jur' and 'fattan'. 'Jur'.seems to be derived from 'ur' in 'Kannur' and 'fattan' is derived from the Indian 'Patnam' meaning port town. Thus

Jurfattan is the name given to Kannur by Ibn Batuta. The Arab navigator, Ibn Majid also knew about the existence of Kannur or Cannanore in the fifteenth century.[6]

Duarte Barbosa writing about A.D 1510 refers to the tradition of the conversion of Cheraman Perumal to Islam and the division of his kingdom. He refers to Malabar and its three major kings, the Zamorin of Calicut, the king of Quilon and the king of Cannanore, Kolattiri. He tells us that Cannanore was inhabited by Muslim and Hindu merchants who possessed many large and small ships. The great Kerala historian Shaikh Zainuddin who lived in the second half of the Sixteenth century and many others like Joao de Barros, Tomé Pirés, Diogo di Couto and Camoens had referred to this division in the Sixteenth century. Pachu Moothathu in his *Kerala Vishesha Mahatmaya* had also referred to the division of the Malayalam country into eighteen divisions. Tomé Pirés has reported that the ports of Kumbla, Kattakulam, Nileshwaram, Hyeri, Baliapatam (Valarpatnam), Cannanore, Durmapatan (Dharmapatnam) and Madayid belonged to the king of Cannanore ie., Kolathanadu.[7]

The Portuguese under Vasco da Gama were the first west European maritime men to reach the Indian shores in 1498. They actually arrived at Kappad or Kappakadavu about eighteen kilometres north of Calicut. After having met the Zamorin of Calicut, the most important ruler in the Malabar region, Vasco da Gama returned to Lisbon in the subsequent year with presents for the king and Queen of Portugal from the Malabar kings. It appears that Vasco da Gama had contacts with Kolattiri, the king of Cannanore during his stay in Malabar. The king of Cannanore probably in order to assert his separate identity during this period had actually sent presents to both the king and Queen of Portugal.[8] Vasco da Gama was conferred the title of "Dom" by the king of Portugal and also upon his heirs a perpetual right of 200 cruzados, which he might lay out each year, of his own money, in cinnamon, at Cannanore, and send home in any vessel free of freight charges. In 1501 the Portuguese established a factory in Calicut, which was under the control of king Zamorin, who was the most powerful of all the Malabar kings during this period.[9] In fact Quilon which was until then the greatest trading centre was outstripped by Calicut at this time.[10]

It is worthwhile to note that during this period, Cannanore had several wealthy Muslim merchants and was emerging as a Muslim–dominated port. Tomé Pirés further notes that but for the arrival of the Portuguese in Cannanore, all of this kingdom would have become Muslim.[11] All this no doubt attests the growing importance of Cannanore as a trading centre in northern Kerala during this period. Cannanore was a less important port and trading centre than Calicut. The rulers of both Quilon and Cannanore had reasons to worry about the rise in power of the Zamorin of Calicut. In 1502, the very next year after the Portuguese founded a factory in Calicut, the rulers of Cannanore and Quilon wanted somehow to strike an alliance with the Portuguese king in order to counter the might of the Zamorin of Calicut. As a result of the overtures made by the king of Cannanore in particular, the Portuguese sent their representative Pedro Alvares Cabral to visit Cannanore. In the meantime the ambassadors of the rulers of Quilon and also Cochin had reached Cannanore. At Cannanore these ambassadors along with that of the king of Cannanore boarded Cabral's ship and sailed to Lisbon to meet Dom Manuel I, the king of Portugal. The Zamorin of Calicut was extremely worried about this new alliance between Cannanore, Cochin and Quilon. He considered it as a great threat to his sovereignty and authority in the region.[12]

The rulers of Quilon, Cochin and Cannanore seem to have befriended the Portuguese with the sole intention of extricating themselves from the growing influence of the Zamorin of Calicut and his Mappilla allies.[13] The Portuguese succeeded in imposing a monopoly over the spice trade of the entire Malabar Coast partly due to rivalry that existed between the Malabar rulers. But they had to overpower in the process the Muslim merchants who wielded immense power and generally controlled the trade in the area before the advent of the Portuguese. One of the most prominent among them seems to be Mamale Marakkar who was finally caught by the

Portuguese. His hands were first cut off. He was then hanged on the wall of the Portuguese fortress of Cannanore in January 1525. Genevieve Bouchon seems to think that this Mamale Marakkayar was a native of Cannanore. She claims that the Muslims of Cannanore or Kolathanad never bore the title 'Marakkayar' and that Tomé Pirés had mistaken Mamale 'Arakkal' of the Arakkal house, for Mamale Marakkayar. However we know through the studies of K.S. Mathew that there was a Mamale Marakkayar conducting trade in Cochin. S. Jeyaseela Stephen has culled information from the Portuguese archival records on the Marakkayars hailing from the port of Kunimedu on the Coromandel Coast trading with Malabar particularly in rice. He has brought to light the various merchant names and their families such as Pate Marecar and his brother Cunhale Marecar family trading with Cochin besides Mamale Marecar and his brother Cherina Marecar family trading with Cannanore.[14] Mamale Marakkayar had a big godown in Cannanore too. However, the execution of Mamale Marakkayar seems not to have put an end to the influence of the Muslim merchants in the political, administrative and commercial affairs of Cannanore, which became more prominent in the course of time.[15]

Albert Mandelso visiting Malabar during the first half of the Seventeenth century records that sometime back the whole of Malabar was under one king called Sarama Perumal (Cheraman Perumal). He became a Muslim and divided his kingdom into three, Cannanore, Cochin and Chaul, subject to the sovereignty of Calicut. Thus Mandelso had not only made a clear reference to the existence of Cannanore as an entity, but had also stated that Cannanore like Cochin was subject to the king of Calicut. This has great historical significance to the history of these three kingdoms as we are going to see. The Frenchman, Dellon, who visited the Malabar Coast in the latter part of the Seventeenth century, seems to consider the king of Cannanore who was known as Kolattiri as more powerful than Calicut. But another Frenchman, François Pyrad de Laval and the Englishman, Alexander Hamilton, seems to make a more accurate assessment by claiming that the Zamorin of Calicut was the most powerful in the region and was held in respect by all the other rulers including that of Cannanore. By the dawn of the Seventeenth century the Dutch and the English merchants had organized themselves as East India Companies and found their way to India.[16] The Dutch East India Company had actually sent its fleet under Steven Vander Hagen to Calicut. The Zamorin during this period wanted on the one hand to extricate himself from the influence of the Portuguese and on the other to curtail the power of the rulers of Cochin and Cannanore. As a result he entered into a treaty with the Dutch to expel the Portuguese not only from his territories but also from the rest of Malabar. The Dutchman, Jacob Canter Visscher had noted in his letters that the town of Cannanore was actually under the control of a Muslim ruler, subject to the Kolattiri. He was none other than the Ali Rajah of the Arakkal house.[17]

The Dutch Invasion of Malabar and Cannanore

During the Seventeenth century, the Dutch had actually supplanted Portuguese dominance in south-east Asia. They displaced the Portuguese from Malacca and established their headquarters at Batavia, from where they operated in the entire Indian Ocean region. Very soon they established their supremacy in Ceylon and occupied Colombo. Their eyes then turned towards South India, especially the Malabar Coast from Quilon to Cannanore where Portuguese presence was preponderant.

With the intention of evicting the Portuguese from the Malabar and acquiring a monopoly in the spice trade, they raised a mighty army in Colombo under the command of Rykiof Van Goens. A heavily armed fleet consisting of twenty-four warships and other smaller ships set sail for Malabar. The troops were actually split into twenty-seven companies under the overall command of Ryklof Van Goens. Later Admiral Adrien Rothas, Vice Admiral Isbrandt Godskins and Captain Major Pierre Was were in charge of the troops.[18]

On its way to Malabar, the fleet called at Tuticorin which was under the control of the Dutch from 1658, and then passed through Kayalpattinam. Very soon the fleet reached Quilon. The Portuguese who were present at Quilon for the past 150 years seems to have been the first to have opened fire against the Dutch. But the Portuguese were no match to Dutch and very soon they gave themselves up.[19]

The Dutch then blockaded Cranganore situated a few miles to the north of Cochin, with the intention of cutting off arms supplies from that place to Cochin. At that moment the Zamorin of Calicut, the king of Cranganore and other neighboring Malabar princes paid visit to the Dutch fleet and declared to General Ryklof Van Goens their friendliness towards the Dutch nation and their hatred for the Portuguese. They expressed their willingness to guide the Dutch troops and provide them with provisions and fighting men in their attempt to evict the Portuguese. After a prolonged siege which lasted for fifteen days, Cranganore fell to the Dutch. The Zamorin of Calicut, the king of Cranganore and the Malabar princes felicitated Van Goens for the victory.[20]

The next target of the Dutch was Cochin. The Nairs fought valiantly against the Dutch, which prevented the latter from taking over Cochin easily. Besides the Portuguese Governor of Cochin, Ignace de Sermento also acted firmly against the Dutch, along with the king of Porca who was his trusted ally. As a result the Dutch were obliged to retreat. Naturally the Zamorin of Calicut was not very happy with the situation. The Dutch in their turn sought the help of the Zamorin to overcome Cochin. According to a treaty between the Dutch and the Zamorin, 2000 Nair soldiers joined the Dutch forces, along with 300 daily workers. The Zamorin also promised to provide the Dutch company with all the pepper in the region without the payment of any customs duties. He also promised wood, cardamom and other goods likely to be bought by the Dutch without the payment of any duties. On their part the Dutch company would allow the Zamorin to keep Cranganore, Paleport and Vaypin in his hands for sometime and share the Portuguese artillery of the Cochin fort.[21]

Thus with the help of the Zamorin, the Dutch finally vanquished the Portuguese and occupied Cochin on 7 January

1663. With the subjugation of Cochin there was only the king of Cannanore and the Portuguese governor of Cannanore, Antonio Cardoso, who were still resisting Dutch might. Hustaert accompanied by Captain Du Pon and Captain Van Rheede left with the major portion of the Dutch army to overcome Cannanore's resistance. After a few days of intense warfare, Cannanore was captured on 13 February 1663 and the Fort St. Angelo fell into the hands of the Dutch. Although the Portuguese had been well established in Cannanore for the past 161 years, the Portuguese governor Antonio Cardoso was unable to obtain any reinforcement to buttress his sagging fortunes had no choice but to give up the resistance and retreat to Goa. The Portuguese Viceroy in Goa was very unhappy with Antonio Cardoso's feeble defense against the Dutch. According to the Viceroy's orders, Antonio Cardoso was sentenced to death and decapitated.[22]

Plan of Cannanore in the Early 17th century: National Library, Paris

The Dutch in Batavia were very pleased with the conquest of Cochin and Cannanore, which put an end to Portuguese supremacy on the entire Malabar Coast up to Kasargod. It however seems that the Zamorin and the other local princes including that of Cannanore who wanted the Dutch to chase the Portuguese away from their country, rendered little help to the former during the wars. When they did help they did it with the intention of deriving some advantage out of it. With the help of Zamorin when Cochin fell into the hands of the Dutch, Zamorin thought that the Dutch would allow him to be crowned as king of Cochin. But the Dutch politely refused to accede to his demand. The Zamorin then thought of annexing Vaypin to his kingdom. But the Dutch once again opposed. The Dutch had driven the Portuguese out of Malabar Coast from Quilon to Cannanore in order to promote their own interests and certainly not to strengthen the hands of the Zamorin, who could eventually turn against them too. So after driving the Portuguese out, the Dutch sought to conserve and consolidate their conquests on the one hand and also made new arrangements to improve their commercial fortunes in the area.

They seem to have been quite successful in imposing their domination, especially in trade in most of the Malabar areas. But it seems that when the Dutch vanquished the Portuguese in Cannanore their commercial interests were not fully safeguarded. In fact the new Dutch chief of Cannanore, Van Weerden was blamed for such a state of affairs. In the treaty that he made with the king of Cannanore, he was accused of not stipulating a monopoly in spice trade and also in the cardamom and opium trade.[23]

In fact the powerful Muslim merchant prince, Ali Rajah, dominated the hinterland trade in spices, cardamom and opium since many years in Cannanore, even under the Portuguese control of the port of Cannanore. The Dutch had to negotiate with this merchant prince in order to remedy the drawbacks for them arising out of the treaty between the Dutch and the Kolattiri or king of Kolathanadu. The Dutch East India Company had to deliver all its goods to the Muslim merchant in order to procure spices, cardamom and opium. Though the Dutch had conquered the port of Cannanore and entered into a treaty with the Kolattiri, they still could not avoid dealing with this powerful Muslim merchant prince of Cannanore who had a great clout. This seems to be quite strange because the Portuguese who were generally thought to have subjugated and humiliated all the Muslim merchants of the Malabar Coast, had not moved against this particular Muslim merchant prince of Cannanore who not only survived Portuguese domination, but also obtained the upper hand in his dealings with the Dutch. However this was not the case in the southern Malabar region such as Porcad, Eddawa, Calliquilone, Quilon, Karunagapally and Tengapatnam, whose princes not only did not offer any resistance to the Dutch, but also entered into exclusive contracts with them by which all strangers were denied trade in pepper, cinnamon, spice, timber and teak which the Dutch called 'prohibited goods'.[24]

This singularity of Cannanore seems to have paved the way in the beginning of the Eighteenth century for a stronger emergence of the Arakkal house as an independent political entity in the name of the Ali Rajah. The latter even quarreled with the Kolattiri of Kolathanadu to demonstrate his independence. Ali Raja was so powerful during the Eighteenth century that he laid claim to the mainly Muslim Maldive islands in the Indian Ocean, invaded them and even imposed a certain control over the trade in these islands which traditionally had its own king. In fact the attempt of the Maldivians to get rid off Cannanore's interference in their affairs during this period, met with failure, for the Maldivian prince himself was taken in 1758 as a prisoner to Cannanore.[25]

As early as the beginning of the Sixteenth century, the Portuguese factor, Duarte Barbosa had noted that the Maldive islands were inhabited by Malabar Moors and belonged to the King of Cannanore.[26] During this period, the Muslim merchants of Cannanore were using Maldives as a base for trading with West Asia. So it is not altogether surprising to note that the Ali Raja of Cannanore was only asserting his ancestral and traditional rights as the king of Cannanore over the Maldive islands and nothing more. But it still remains in mystery in the history of North Kerala that the year in which the Ali Rajas actually came into existence. However, from the above said it becomes fairly clear that Cannanore was gradually gaining in importance during the Fourteenth century both in trade and politics.

During the second half of the Eighteenth century, the kingdom of Kolathanadu, came under the influence of the Sultans of Mysore. Hyder Ali in the 1760s had captured power in Mysore and invaded northern Kerala. He took possession of the region and also in the process destroyed not only the power of the Kolattiri but also the Zamorin's power. He thus became the master of Malabar between Cannanore and Ponani. The Kolattiri fled to Travancore kingdom in the South. The Raja of Cochin fearing an attack by Hyder Ali offered his allegiance to the Mysore chief. The Ali Rajah of Cannanore threw in his lot with Hyder Ali.[27] The Rajah of Travancore (who had become a power to reckon with in South Kerala with the English help) was the last Malabar power to defy Hyder Ali's might.

In the meantime, the fortunes of the Dutch on the Malabar Coast dwindled drastically. The trade at Cannanore was no more profitable to them. This obliged them to sell the fort of Cannanore to the Ali Rajah in 1771. In the 1780s the Dutch at Nagapattinam on the Coromandel Coast and the Cochin ruler united with Hyder Ali to break up the friendship between the Rajah of Travancore and the English.[28] But the Dutch were no more a power to be reckoned with in the region. With Hyder Ali passing away on 7 December 1782, his son Tipu Sultan succeeded him and continued his confrontation with the English which ended in his defeat in 1792 and the subsequent annexation of Northern Kerala including Cannanore as part of the Madras Presidency of British India. This put an end to the sway of the Ali Rajah in Cannanore and Kolathanadu.

To conclude it may be said that the Portuguese had a good understanding with the Raja of Cannanore and the merchants there. Hence the Portuguese could continue their trade in the port for 160 years. The Raja also well reciprocated his friendship with the Portuguese and he exercised his command over the trade in the hinterland of the port. With the Dutch occupation of Cannanore in 1663 we find that the situation has not much changed because the Raja of Cannanore continued to have control in the hinterland trade. In fact maritime trade in the port of Cannanore began to flourish well because of the Muslim merchants and especially their trade with Maldives at that time under the patronage of the Raja.

Notes and References

1. K.S. Mathew, "Khwaja-Shams-ud-din Giloni: A 16th Century Entreprenur in Portuguese India": in Roderich Ptak & Dietmar Rothermund, (ed.,) *Emporia, Commodities, and Entreprenurs in Asian Maritime Trade, Cir. 1400-1750*, Stutgart, 1997, pp.363-371.
2. Pius Malekandathil, "The Maritime Trade of Cannanore and the Global Commercial Relations in the 16th and 17th Century", in M.O. Koshy, (ed.) *Cannanore in the Maritime History of India*, Kannur University, 2002; See also, Joy Varkey, *Cannanore on the Malabar Coast and the Maritime Trade of India, 1500-1600,* M.Phil Dissertation, Pondicherry University, 1991; Hugo K'S. Jacob, *De Nederlanders in Kerala*, Groningen, 1984.

3. Ruchira Banerjee, "A Wedding Feast or Poltical arena?: Commercial Rivalry between the Alia Rajas and the English Factory in Northern Malabar in the 18th Century" in (eds.,) Rudrangshu Mukherjee & Lakshmi Subramanian, *Politics and Trade in the Indian Ocean World : Essays in Honour of Ashin Das Gupta*, Delhi, 2000, pp. 83-112.
4. Robert Sewell, (ed.), *A Sketch of the Dynasties of Southern India,* Madras, 1883, pp.1,13, 57; P.K Parameswaran Nair, *History of the Malayalam Literature,* New Delhi, 1967, pp.49,113; M.G.S. Narayanan, *Perumals of Kerala: Political and Social Condition of Kerala under the Cera Perumals of Makottai, A.D.800-1124,* Calicut, 1996, pp.91-94; Manuel, Longworth Dames, *The Book of Duarte Barbosa*, Vol. II, London, MCMXXI, p.4 fn; M.J. Koshy, *Encyclopaedia of India – Kerala*, XX, New Delhi, 1994, p. 30.
5. M.R. Raghava Varier, 'Pantalayini Kollam: A Medieval Port Town on the Malabar coast', (in) Kesavan Veluthat, P.P.Sudhakaran (eds.), *Advances in History*, Calicut, 2003, pp.165-168; Haraprasad, Ray, 'Indian Settlements in China – An Exploration of the phenomenon of Indian Diaspora from AD 1015 to 1487', (in), K.S.Mathew (ed.), *Indian Ocean and Cultural Interaction(A.D.1400-1800)*, Pondicherry, 1996; Haraprasad Ray, 'Historical Contacts between Quilon and China', (in), Pius Malekandathil, & T. Jamal Mohammed, (eds.), *The Portuguese, Indian Ocean and European Bridgeheads*, Tellicherry, 2001, pp. 387-402; S. Jeyaseela Stephen (ed.), *Trade and Globalisation, European, Americans and Indians in the Bay of Bengal, 1511-1819*, New Delhi, 2003, pp. 13-18.
6. Mahdi Husain, (tr.), *The Rehla of Ibin Batuta (India, Maldive islands and Ceylon)*, Baroda, 1976, pp.164-197; John Dowson, (ed.), *The History of India as told by its own historians. The Muhammadan Period.*, I, Allahabad, s.d., p.68; G.R. Tibbets, *Arab Navigation in the Indian Ocean before the coming of the Portuguese*, London, 1971, p. 201.
7. M.G.S. Narayanan, *Ibid.,* Calicut, 1996, p.2; Rowlandson, M.J.(tr.), *Tuhfat al Mujahideen*, London 1833, pp.50-56; Robert Sewell, (ed.), *op.cit.,* p.57; Stanley, H.E.J (tr.), *A Description of the Coasts of East Africa and Malabar in the Beginning of the Sixteenth Century by Duarte Barbosa,* New Delhi, 1995, pp.103, 150; Tomé Pirés, *The Suma Oriental, 1512-1515,*Vol.I, London, 1967, pp. 74, 77.

8. Jose Paul, "Vasco da Gama's Discovery of a Maritime Route to India – The Myth and Realities", in K.S. Mathew (ed.) *Maritime Malabar and the Europeans*, Gurgaon, 2003, p. 146.
9. F.C. Danvers, *Report to the Secretary of State for India*, London, 1892, p. 2.
10. Leena More, *English East India Company and the Local Rulers of Kerala: A Case Study of Attingal and Travancore*, Tellicherry, 2003, pp.1-9; G. Bouchon, *'Regent of the Sea' – Cannanore's Response to Portuguese Expansion, 1507-1528*, Delhi, 1988.
11. F.C. Danver, *The Portuguese in India being a history of the rise and decline of their Eastern Empire,* London,1894, ch.3, p.64; Tomé Pirés, *The Suma Oriental,* Liechenstein, 1967, p. 77.
12. Abbé Guyon, *Histoire des Indes Orientales, Anciennes et Modernes*, I, Paris, 1699, pp. 368-369.
13. James Forbes, *Oriental Memoirs*, Vol. I, London,1834, p. 187
14. S. Jeyaseela Stephen, *Portuguese in the Tamil Coast: Historical Explorations in Commerce and Culture, 1507-1749*, Pondicherrry, 1998, pp.129-131 ; See also his another paper on the Marakkayars of Nagore and Kunimedu, «The Role of the Tamil Muslim Mercantile Community of the Marakkayars in the Late Medieval Maritime Trade on the Coromandel Coast : A Study Chiefly Based on Portuguese Sources, AD. 1507-1537 » in *Islamic Culture*, Vol. LXIX, No.4, October 1995, pp. 59-71.
15. J.B. Aquarone, *Joao De Castro, Gouverneur et Vice-Roi des Indes Orientales, 1500-1548*, I, Paris, 1968, pp.211-212 ; Tomé Pirés, *op.cit.,* pp.77-78 ; G.Bouchon, *op.cit.*, 1988, pp.89, 105, 151-175 ; K.S. Mathew, *Portuguese Trade with India in the Sixteenth Century*, Delhi, 1983, pp. 210-211.
16. Leena More, *op.cit.,* pp.20-21; A. de Wicquefort, (tr.), *Voyage Célèbres et remarquables fait de Perse aux Indes Orientales par Mandelso,* Amsterdam, 1727, p.269 ; Dellon, *Nouvelle Relation d'un voyage fait aux Indes Orientales,* Amsterdam, 1688, pp. 82-83 ; Du Val (ed.), *Voyage de François Pyrard de Laval,* 3 parts, Paris, 1679, pp.263-264 ; Alexander Hamilton, *A New Account of the East Indies*, I, Edinburgh, MDCCXXVII.
17. P.C. Alexander, *The Dutch in Malabar*, Annamalai Nagar, 1946, p.4; Visscer, Jacob Canter, *Letters from Malabar,* Madras, 1862, p. 119.

18. J.P.I. Du Bois, *Vies des Gouverneurs Generaux, avec l' abrege de l'Histoire des Etablissements Hollandais aux Indes Orientales*, La Haye, MDCCCXIIL, p. 1.
19. *Ibid.*, pp.193-195.
20. *Ibid.*, pp.196-197.
21. *Ibid.*, 200-203.
22. *Ibid.*, p. 204; Nagam Aiya, *The Travancore State Manual*, Vol. I, Trivandrum, 1906, p. 306.
23. J. P. I. Du Bois, *op.cit.*, p. 204.
24. *Ibid.* p.204; Nagam Aiya, *op.cit.*, p.306; James Forbes, *op.cit.*; Anjengo Factory Records, 1704-1749, Simon Cowse, Anjengo to Court of Directors, June 1704, p.5; Pamela Nightinghale, *Trade and Empire in Western India, 1784-1806,* Cambridge, 1970, p.33; Adriaan Moens, *Memoir written in the year 1781 A.D. Selections from the Madras Government Records, Dutch Record No.2*, Madras, 1908, pp. 45-51.
25. National Library of France, Paris, Mss. Nouvelle Acquisition Francaise, 9359, Memoire ou eclaircissememts raisonnés sur les nouvelles concessions—1755, p. 146 ; Alexander Hamilton, *op.cit.*, pp. 292-93.
26. Manuel Longworth Dames, *The Book of Duarte Barbosa,* Vol. II, New Delhi, 1989, p.104; Bouchon, G., *op.cit.*, pp.118, 161; Pius Malekandathil, 'Merchants, Markets and Commodities: Some Aspects of Portuguese Commerce with Malabar', (in), Pius Malekandathil, & T. Jamal Mohammed, (eds.), *The Portuguese, Indian Ocean and European Bridgeheads*, Tellicherry, 2001, pp. 255-256.
27. Leena More, *op.cit.,* p. 192; Adriaan Moens, *op.cit.*, p. 48.
28. Leena More, *Ibid.*, p. 196; Moens, *Ibid.*, p. 50.

4

Danish Shipping and Trade between Tranquebar on the Coromandel Coast of India and Southeast Asia during the Seventeenth and Eighteenth Centuries

Martin Krieger

The Seventeenth Century was the period of the great North-western European trading companies and their enterprises to the New World, the Arctic region, Africa and the Indian Ocean. A distinct pattern of this trade was its double-function. The Europeans not only carried out trade between foreign continents and Europe itself, but they also joined intra-regional commodity exchange, either between North America and the Caribbean or in the Indian Ocean with its adjoining countries. This pattern gained special importance for the Europeans trading with Asia, and in particular to the minor European trading-companies. A lack of capital and a low number of intercontinental voyages forced them to seek profit within mere intra-Asiatic trade. The Danes were one of these trading nations who joined the traditional trading-networks on the Indian Ocean to compensate an irregular trade between Denmark and Asia. Their enterprises between India and South East Asia constituted an eminent lifeline to Danish Asia-trade.

The Danes who followed the traces of a very ancient trade in the Bay of Bengal had two functions: (*a*) to procure commodities for the Europe-bound ships and (*b*) to gain profits by mere intra-Asiatic trade in the Indian Ocean. They in particular depended on this trade, because much less capital was sent out from Copenhagen than from Amsterdam or London to support the presence of the Dutch and the English.

Especially after the collapse of the intercontinental trade between Copenhagen and Tranquebar entirely after AD.1639, intra-Asiatic trade between Coromandel and Southeast Asia became the major source of income and the basis of the survival of the very few remaining Danes – next to the gains of Danish piracy in the Bay of Bengal.

This paper investigates into the Danish intra-Asiatic voyages between Coromandel and Southeast Asia. It inquires into the Danish motives for launching such trade in the 1620s, structural changes and the reasons for its end in the Eighteenth Century. The records of the Seventeenth Century Danish East India companies are scattered and not very elusive for many decades.[1] We thus also have to study the records produced by the Dutch East India Company (VOC), who always carefully watched the Danish enterprises in the Indonesian archipelago, such as the "*Generale Missiven van Gouverneurs-Generaal en Raden an Heeren XVII*"[2] or the "*Dagh-Register gehouden int Casteel Batavia*".[3]

The kingdom of Denmark constituted a major maritime power of the Baltic Sea and the North Sea during the Early Modern period. It not only creamed off the surpluses of trade by the Sound Toll, but it likewise attempted to assert power over the north German river Elbe connecting the vast Northeast German hinterland to the sea. King Christian IV (1588-1648) ruling Denmark for more than half a century, endeavoured to establish a Danish hegemonic power in the North and to create a major trading nation on the Oceans of the world by joining the European Asia-trade.

The Seventeenth and Eighteenth centuries were a period of the successful northwest-European trading-companies in Asia, which have been described as an "institutional innovation" by Niels Steensgaard due to their ability of raising a high capital and exerting an enormous military power in the Indian Ocean.[4] Next to the successful Dutch and English merchants, the Danes also advanced as a minor, nevertheless a more or less fortunate trading nation in the East. In 1616, King Christian IV founded the first *Ostindisk Kompagni*, and four years later the Scandinavians succeeded in acquiring the trading settlement of Tranquebar on the Coromandel Coast of India. The beginnings of this enterprise were promising, but Denmark's participation in the Thirty Years War led to a decline of the intercontinental trade between Copenhagen and Tranquebar. Between 1639 and 1668 no traffic existed between both the places.[5] In 1650, the first Danish East India Company was finally dissolved. A recovery of the Danish economy from its deep economic crisis lead to the foundation of the second *Ostindisk Kompagni* in 1670, which existed until 1729. During the Seventeenth and Eighteenth centuries, "Danish" trade was not necessarily Danish in a national sense. A large number of entrepreneurs of other nationalities assembled under the protection of the neutral Danish flag in Tranquebar and other minor Danish factories – be they Germans from the Holy Roman Empire, Dutch merchants endeavouring to circumvent the trading monopoly of the VOC or the Portuguese or the French seeking protection especially during wartime.

On the other side, the Danish culture was not at all negligible in the Indian Ocean. As recent studies have shown, a large portion of employees of the Dutch VOC originated from the Danish monarchy, that means not only from Denmark itself, but also from Schleswig-Holstein – the North German provinces of the monarchy – or Norway. Between 1633 and 1640 not less than 20 per cent of the sailors in the services of the VOC were from Denmark-Norway. The number rose up to 35 per cent between 1660 and 1668 to fall again to 20 per cent between 1680 and 1687.[6] In very few cases, sailors had left documents such as the recently published travel account of Jens Mortensen Sveigaard written between 1665 and 1684.[7] At the same time, the Dutch impact on the Danish company-trade was at least of the same importance right from the onset of the Danish enterprise in the Indian Ocean region, such as the Dutch influence on the structures of the various charters of the companies or the influx of Dutch capital.[8]

The Beginnings

Immediately after the Danes had established their settlement in Tranquebar, they were forced to procure pepper as the most important commodity for the Euope-bound ships during the Seventeenth century. Pepper was produced in the western parts of Southeast Asia, mainly in Sumatra, as well as in Malabar, however, not in Coromandel. The records of the VOC reveal, that the Danes first attempted to procure pepper through local merchants in 1621, 1623 and 1624.[9] It very likely reached Tranquebar on the land route via Palghat and Tanjore.[10] Already in 1621, the Danes likewise succeeded in sending their own vessel to Malabar for the same purpose.[11] However, an increasing demand for this commodity resulted in the increase of prices of Malabar pepper and probably in insufficient supplies also.[12] The Danes accordingly resorted to other sources of pepper, mainly from Sumatra. They, however, did not proceed to Sumatra, but to the Malay Peninsula with their large supplies of goods from the entire Archipelago. Danish voyages to Tenasserim are recorded for the years 1621, 1625 and 1627 – compared to the VOC not very many, but from the Danish perspective quite an impressive achievement.

It seems that the Nayak of Tanjore – the supreme ruler of Tranquebar – was willing to support this trade to the Malay Peninsula by issuing letters of recommendation, may be in expectation of the import of elephants by the Danes.[13] Jón Olafsson, Icelandic sailor in Danish company services, reports in his remarkable travel-account:

"[..] the Indian King sent his written greeting on golden paper to the King of Siam, 2400 miles away, with one of the Danish vessels, the 'Copenhagen', which was of 300 lasts, and urgently requested him to provide the vessel as quickly as possible with produce of the country, and that merely at his request, promising him his goodwill and help if needed, in return.

The Siamese King carried out his part well, so that the ship got a full cargo. And the Siamese King offered the King of Denmark such terms and conditions as could best be granted by himself and his subjects, in such matters as permission to settle, and honourable conditions for trading."[14]

It cannot clearly be said, if Olafssons statement corresponded to reality because he was an ordinary sailor and might have come to know all these details only through someone else. However, the story does not seem to be unrealistic if compared to our general historical knowledge. Right from the Sixteenth century, Tenasserim had served as an important port-of-call for Coromandel Hindu traders – being called the "Klings" by the Portuguese. It was an outlet for the trade of Mergui and, at the same time, a transit point for commodity exchange with the Gulf of Thailand and Cambodia. It also served as an emporium for commercial exchange with Sumatra including trade in pepper. Tenasserim itself exported rice to other Southeast Asian ports such as Pasai and later to Aceh on Sumatra.[15] Privileges issued to the European merchants were likewise common for trading on the Malay Peninsula. For example, already in 1518, the Portuguese had been endowed with the right to trade in Ayuthaya, Ligor, Tenasserim and Pattani against delivering European weapons and ammunition to the Ayuthayan king Ramathibodi.[16] The succeeding Toungoo-dynasty of Burma recruited Portuguese mercenaries and likewise imported European weapons to support their territorial expansion on the Southeast Asian mainland. However, evidence of Danish presence during the 1620s is very scarce, and we cannot say if the Danes likewise joined this trade in weapons and military know-how. When Danish intercontinental voyages between Copenhagen and Tranquebar ceased, pepper lost importance and there was no more need for enterprises to Tenasserim, while Macassar on Celebes with its supplies of cloves and sandalwood gained importance for the Danes.

Between Coromandel and Macassar

From the onset of the Seventeenth century, the Dutch endeavoured establishing a trade monopoly in spices in the Indonesian Archipelago. They tried to reach this aim by spoiling clove-plantations as well as by ousting European competitors from the islands by force such as by the infamous "Massacre of Amboina" in 1623. Despite these efforts, the Dutch did not succeed in establishing a trading-monopoly for cloves until the second half of the Seventeenth century, and they never gained control over the pepper production and trade. The town of Macassar on the island Celebes in particular remained an outlet of spice trade out of control of the VOC until the 1660s, however, on a decreasing level since the 1640s. The cloves reached Macassar mainly from the islands of Ternate, Tidore and Amboina. The Portuguese, the English, the Danes as well as the Indian merchants were procuring the spices there before the VOC gained full control of this place in 1667.[17]

The Danes joined trading with Macassar mainly for purchasing cloves and sandalwood. Such commodities were destined for the Indian markets and hardly for exporting to Europe during the period of interrupted traffic to Copenhagen. The first voyage to Macassar was carried out by the "Vandhunden" and the "Jupiter" that reached that place from Masulipatam in 1625. Trading activities were, however, not really promising, and in addition to this, the "Jupiter" ran ashore in Bengal on her way back.[18] Despite this enormous loss, trading with Celebes must have been regarded profitable by the Danish authorities in Tranquebar, who sent the next vessel to Macassar already the following year. Danish ships were also sent there in 1627 and 1628 for procuring cloves. The 1628 voyage was commanded by Roland Crappé, the Danish governor of Tranquebar – a clear proof for the fact that this trade must have been of much importance for the Danes.[19]

Table 1: Danish Voyages between Coromandel and Macassar (1637-1664)

Year	*Ship name*	*Port of origin*
1637	Caritas	Tranquebar
1638	St. Jacob	Masulipatnam
1638	Korsør	Masulipatnam*
1639	St. Jacob	Masulipatnam*
1643	Fortuna	Tranquebar**
1645	Christianshavn	Tranquebar*
1647	St. Peter og St. Paul	Tranquebar*
1649	Christianshavn	Tranquebar
1649	St. Peter og St. Paul	Tranquebar
1664	Fredericus	Tranquebar

* via Bantam
** via Tranquebar and Bantam

Already during the first voyages from Coromandel to Macassar, Danish merchants were regularly left ashore for procuring commodities for the next arrival of a Danish vessel. The purchase of cloves and sandalwood was mainly carried out by the aid of local merchants, however, on some occasions Danish merchants went to the regions of spice production themselves – despite complaints from the Dutch. In 1638, for instance, some Danish merchants having reached Macassar on the "St. Jacob" hired two vessels of Muslim ship-owners and went to Solor and Timor for procuring sandalwood on Portuguese merchants' account. At the same time, the "St. Jacob" left Macassar for a voyage to Larantuka on the island of Solor also for procuring sandalwood.[20] The Danes likewise invested capital in trading enterprises of local merchants between Macassar and other emporia of the Indonesian Archipelago. And they could procure comparatively high amounts of cloves in exchange for the Indian textiles.[21] We may well presume, that the Danes wanted to gain profit by these enterprises for reducing losses arising from the ever dwindling intercontinental trade during this time.

Danish trade to Macassar and other Southeast Asian ports was only partly carried out from Tranquebar, but also from Masulipatnam. The records unveil regular sailings under Danish colours from Masulipatnam at the Godavari-Krishna-delta to Macassar and Bantam, but also to Aceh, Kedah and Japara between 1628 and 1642. Since the onset of the Seventeenth century, Masulipatnam – being connected by land routes to the vast hinterland of the Deccan – had constituted the most important emporium in the Northern Coromandel and an eminent outlet of the empire of Golconda. It exported textiles, indigo, steel and diamonds. The town gained a prominent role especially for trading with Southeast Asia, in particular with Arakan, Tenasserim/Mergui, Aceh, Macassar and Bantam. Trading enterprises were likewise launched towards Bengal, Surat and the Arabian Peninsula. Most European trading companies established factories in Masulipatnam to participate in this lucrative trading network.[22]

Around 1625, the Danes reached Masulipatnam for the first time to establish a small trading-settlement for bartering textiles against Southeast Asian spices. The subsequent Danish enterprises were mainly carried out on account of Indian or the Persian merchants due to lack of own capital. Trading in Masulipatnam must have been very favourable, and already two years later the Danish factory was regarded as being more important to the Danes than Tranquebar itself. This image is supported by the fact that the Danish governor Barend Pessart resided in Masulipatnam instead of Tranquebar itself between around 1636 and 1641. The reason for the increasing importance of this place for the Danes may likewise be found in the collapse of Danish intercontinental trade after 1638. From Masulipatnam, the few remaining Danes in India could better join the traditional intra-Asiatic trade and participate in the extensive local merchants' trading-networks.

It is not always easy to distinguish between the official company-trade of the Danish East-India company and the private enterprises of the Danish employees in this place. We may well presume, that in many instances trading under Danish flag was a mere cover of private enterprises of the Dutch and Danish merchants. However, even obviously successful intra-Asiatic trade between Masulipatnam and Southeast Asia could not keep the Danes away from increasingly becoming indebted by local merchants due to lack of Danish capital from home. Already in 1641, the Danes were forced to abandon their factory in Masulipatnam and had to concentrate their Macassar enterprises from Tranquebar again.

Situation worsened even in Tranquebar during the 1640s when the VOC increasingly hampered independent intra-Asiatic trade via Macassar. The number of voyages from Tranquebar diminished, and in 1642 Antonio van Diemen wrote down about the Danes' situation in Macassar: "De Deense sacken loopen genoegsam desperat".[23] Two years later, he noticed that the remaining Danes were waiting idle without capital in Macassar.[24] The Danes had lost one year in 1646, when they succeeded in selling large quantities of Indian textiles from the vessel "Christianshavn" on Celebes.[25] The last ships for a long time were the "St. Peter og St. Paul" and again the "Christianshavn" reaching Macassar from Tranquebar in 1649. The next vessel reached Macassar only in 1664 – three years before the Dutch succeeded in finally conquering that place and monopolizing trade via Macassar.

The loss of the Macassar spice-market caused a severe economic crisis for the Danish intra-Asiatic trade. To compensate for these losses the Danes commenced a virtual war of piracy in the Bay of Bengal, which was mainly directed against the Muslim trading-vessels. The resumption of intercontinental trade after 1670 led to an end of this piracy, and even more capital from Denmark accumulated within Tranquebar. Instead of reviving the route between Coromandel and Macassar, the connection to Bantam on Java had now emerged as the most important route of Danish intra-Asiatic trade.

Between Tranquebar and Bantam

The sultanate of Bantam was strategically situated between the trading regions of the South China Sea and the Indian Ocean such as Batavia and Malacca. In addition to this, the port town of Bantam was situated close to the most important areas of the production of pepper, spices and sugar. While pepper came from Sumatra, cloves, nutmeg, mace and sandalwood were produced on the Moluccas as well as sugar in North Java. During the Seventeenth century, the sultans of Bantam always endeavoured to establish their own trading fleet as well as attracting foreign merchants, especially after the Dutch appeared to monopolize trade in North Java. Sultan Abdulfatah Agung was especially interested in enhancing commodity exchange with the English, the Danes and the French merchants competing Dutch trade. However, the VOC succeeded in conquering Bantam and ousted the other European trading nations from this place in 1682.[26]

Already during the first half of the Seventeenth century – when trade with Macassar was still flourishing – the Danes tried to procure pepper in Bantam. Even before the first Danish vessel anchored off this town, the Dutch representatives in

Batavia felt highly irritated about these attempts. In 1619, the VOC-merchants were ordered to purchase any pepper in Bantam to precede the expected Danish efforts. The Danes nevertheless succeeded in gaining a foothold in Bantam, however, on an irregular basis. Early Danish voyages from Tranquebar took place in 1622, 1629, 1632, 1638 and 1639. When the vessels "Korsør" and "St. Jacob" reached the town in 1638, they left several merchants back in Bantam for procuring commodities for the next voyage well in advance for the first time. – This policy might be regarded as an attempt to establish a permanent trading settlement there.

Like in Macassar and Masulipatnam, situation worsened after the collapse of intercontinental voyages between Copenhagen and Tranquebar. In addition to this, Danish enterprise was severely hit, when the "St. Jacob" was washed ashore off the Orissan coast on its way back from Macassar and Bantam in 1640, and the entire load of pepper was lost. The officials of the Danish East India Company in Tranquebar finally had no other chance than hiring out ship-space to private merchants instead of carrying out their own enterprises to Southeast Asia themselves due to lack of capital. They offered their vessels not only to local and European merchants, but also to Danish private entrepreneurs, which clearly dodged Company privileges.[27] Hiring out of ship-space enabled the Danes to maintain shipping between Tranquebar and Bantam during the period of interrupted traffic with Copenhagen. During these decades not less than thirteen vessels commuted between both the places based on the data given below in the table.

Trading with Bantam nevertheless did not constitute an appropriate substitute for the lost market in spices of Macassar but it contributed to the survival of the few remaining Danes in the Indian Ocean between the 1640s and 1660s.

It only expanded after the second Danish East India Company had resumed intercontinental voyages to India. In 1669, the merchants of the "Færø" procured pepper in such quantities that they were not able to carry it with in the same vessel back to Tranquebar.[28] Three years later, the "Phoenix"

Table 2: Danish voyages between Coromandel and Bantam (1641-1680)

Year	*Name of the ship*	*Port of origin*
1641	Solen	Masulipatnam
1642	Solen	Masulipatnam
1643	Fortuna	Masulipatnam
1645	Christianshavn (1)	Tranquebar
1647	St. Peter og St. Paul	Tranquebar
1648	Christianshavn (1)	Tranquebar
1653	St. Peter og St. Paul	Tranquebar
1654	Fredericus (1)	Tranquebar
1656	Fredericus (1)	Tranquebar
1660	Fredericus (2)	Tranquebar
1662	Fredericus (2)	Tranquebar
1671	Phønix	Tranquebar
1672	Fortuna	Tranquebar
1673	Phønix	Tranquebar
1674	Haabet	Tranquebar
1675	Pelikan	Tranquebar
1675	Fortuna	Tranquebar
1675	Phønix	Tranquebar
1675	Pelikan	Tranquebar
1678	Fortuna	Tranquebar
1678	Phønix	Tranquebar
1680	Christianshavn (2)	Tranquebar
1680	Fortuna	Tranquebar
1680	Færø	Tranquebar

transported 300 large pieces of Indian cloth to Bantam, and in 1673 the "Oldenburg" reached Bantam directly from Copenhagen, also returning there. This voyage of the "Oldenburg" was the only direct return-trip of a Danish vessel from Copenhagen to Southeast Asia without calling at Tranquebar.[29] A maximum of three Danish ships from Tranquebar anchored off Bantam in 1675 while one of them performed this journey twice.

A certain pattern of Danish trade evolved since the late 1660s, that might be described as a virtual triangular trade on the route Copenhagen-Tranqueber-Bantam-Copenhagen and thus interlinking intercontinental and intra-Asiatic trade. The ships left Copenhagen, mainly supplied with silver and consumer articles to barter them against textiles in Tranquebar, which they brought to Bantam. In Bantam, they procured pepper for the direct return voyage to the mother-country.

Table 3: Danish "Triangular-Voyages" Copenhagen-Tranquebar-Bantam-Copenhagen (1668-1679)

Name of the ship	*Period*
Færø	1668-1670
Phønix	1670-1672
Fortuna	1671-1673
Phønix	1672-1674
Haabet	1673-1675
Phønix	1674-1676
Pelikan	1674-1676*
Phønix	1677-1679

*with one voyage Tranquebar-Bantam-Tranquebar in between (1675)

The "Phønix" made four of these voyages altogether – a quite extraordinary achievement for a Seventeenth-century trading vessel. We may thus discover a significant structural change of commodity exchange between India and Java under the Danish flag: While the Danes carried out mere intra-Asiatic enterprises before 1668, Bantam emerged as an important corner-stone of intercontinental trade. A permanent Danish trading-settlement was established latest in 1673 – an exact date of establishment could not be found indeed. The years before 1682 may thus be regarded as the flourishing period of Danish trade with Bantam, and the loss of the factory proved to have a strong deteriorating effect on trade as well as on the commercial life in Tranquebar itself.

The (most likely) first and only Danish resident in Bantam was Johann Joachim Pauli, who not only had to care for the procurement and sale of goods, but also for the repair of the Danish ships and the communication with the local authorities as well as the Dutch residents in the nearby Batavia. Pauli likewise carried out his own private trade, which clearly shows that the maintenance of company monopolies, East of the Cape of Good Hope proved to be futile. In 1678, for example, Pauli launched a joint venture with the English merchant Robert Parker and the vessel "Bon Avontura" sailing under the flag of Bantam to Manila for selling textiles, pepper and iron.[30] Even if the Philippines had been almost closed for non-Spanish Europeans since 1648, they were regularly approached under the protection of local rulers' flags to gain a share of the influx of silver from the New World.[31] At the same time, Pauli chartered several vessels on account of the local merchants sailing towards West Sumatra, most likely for purchasing pepper.[32] Again, during 1680 and 1681, ships were sent to Eastern Javanese ports of Pekalongan and Cheribon in Pauli's name for the sale of textiles and opium. In 1681 he sent a vessel to Banjarmassin on Borneo.[33] Pauli likewise sought profit from private trade between Southeast Asia and India, and he rented ship-space on English ships travelling to Bengal exporting copper, pepper, tin and silver coins to India.[34] After the Dutch conquest of Bantam, Pauli headed for Dutch Batavia for returning home. He, however, died in Batavia during the New Year's eve of 1683.

The example of Johann Joachim Pauli clearly shows that company merchants were trading in company's name as well as for their own account. For this purpose, they did not utilize Danish ship-space – which easily might have uncovered as an abuse of company monopoly – but employed vessels of local as well as of English merchants. At the same time, they used to rent ships or ship-space on several sailing vessels to minimize the risk of loss of capital.

Between the Straits and Manila (1682-1750)

The end of the Seventeenth century witnessed significant changes with respect to trade between India and Southeast Asia. It is most obvious, that the traditional commodity exchange between Gujarat or Malabar and Southeast Asia on non-European ships almost had come to an end. Even the trade from the Indian East coast seems to have faced a diminution until the 1740s. The decline of trade from Coromandel across the Bay of Bengal especially applied for Masulipatnam for reasons that might be found in the Mughal annexation of Golconda, the loss of Masulipatnam's markets in the hinterland of Golconda as well as in the diminishing influence of the Persian, the Indo-Muslim elites in Southeast Asia, especially in Ayuthya.[35] At the same time, the ever growing town of Madras with it's Fort St. George gained importance as the most important emporium of Coromandel trade of the Hindu merchants with Southeast Asia – especially with Pegu and Syriam, the coasts of Arakan, Tenasserim, Kedah and Malacca on the expense of Masulipatnam, Pulicat and other ports. The Hindu merchants, however, did not only freight their own vessels, but they likewise invested capital in English voyages to Southeast Asia at least until the 1730s. Another major port-of-call was Aceh at the western tip of Sumatra. The sources record regular voyages to this place from Madras, San Thomé, Cuddalore, Porto Novo, Nagore as well as from Tranquebar until the 1740s, when internal political problems in Aceh led to a decline of this commodity exchange.[36] Some of these general patterns outlined here may well be noticed while investigating the Danish intra-Asiatic trade after the Danes' expulsion from Bantam in 1682.

The loss of Bantam was severely felt in Tranquebar, and a period of a moderate prosperity after 1670 came to an end. The sudden end of the highly profitable commodity exchange with Java severely damaged the local economy of the Danes' main settlement. Due to lack of funds, three of the four bastions of *Dansborg* had to be rented out to the Dutch as the Scottish captain Alexander Hamilton notes:

"...the Colony is miserably poor. In Anno 1684 they were so distrest with Poverty, that they paw'd three Bastions of their Fort to the Dutch, for Money to buy Provisions, which then was very scarce and dear in that Country; but next Year they redeemed all again, paying their Debts by an unknown Fund, which still remains a secret."[37]

It remains unclear how the Danes soon managed to redeem their debts to the Dutch in spite of an obviously desperate financial situation and where actually the abovementioned "unknown Fund" came from. New capital possibly poured in, when two Danish vessels from Copenhagen anchored off Tranquebar in 1696 (i.e. one year later than Hamilton would have mentioned in the records). It seems more likely that the Danes resorted to piracy on the Bay of Bengal during those years to raise funds, however, in a doubtful manner. The sources reveal, that Wilke Wygbert, Danish resident at Balasore after 1676, had captured two trading vessels from Surat in 1686.[38] During the same year, one more Armenian vessel was caught by the Danes, the crew being tortured cruelly according to French sources. In September of that year a ship belonging an English private merchant dropped anchor off Tranquebar asking for drinking water and provision. Instead of delivering the requested goods some inhabitants violently entered the vessel, plundering it and sending it off towards Madras.[39]

After ousting of the Danes from Bantam in 1682, they did not entirely abandon their commercial exchange with South East Asia. Instead, they established commodity exchange with ports out of Dutch influence such as the Straits region, the islands of the Riau-Linggam-Archipelago as well as Aceh on the western tip of Sumatra on a small scale. Already two years after the Dutch conquest of Bantam, the Danish East India Company was back in Southeast Asia to conclude a trading contract with the Sultan of Johore.[40] An irregular trade in pepper and textiles between the sultanate and Tranquebar was indeed established by this agreement, but it is difficult to ascertain the exact extent of this exchange. For instance, in October 1690 the "Dansborg" and the "Norske Løve" went to Johore.[41] And even for the years 1705 and 1708 Danish voyages to the sultanate are mentioned in the Dutch sources.[42] Already in 1688 the Danes had also gone to Riau and were permitted to establish a trading settlement there, which could, however, not be realized due to unknown reasons.[43] A journey of a Danish vessel from Madras to Kedah transporting elephants is reported to have been carried out in 1700 – most likely employed by English merchants from Fort St. George.[44]

Even if the Danish enterprises to the Straits were irregular and by no means "very strong" as stated elsewhere, economical situation in Tranquebar slowly improved by the establishment of new trading routes after 1682. This does not only apply for trading to the Archipelago but also along the Indian coasts. Around 1690, the Danes succeeded in founding a factory in Porto Novo (Parangipettai), and they likewise tightened their commercial ties with Madras. On the other hand, the short-term existence of minor factories in Bengal (with the significant Name *Dannemarksnagore*) and in Edavai at the Malabar Coast did not lead to any continuity in these regions. Commercial success led to the erection of some ambitious buildings in Tranquebar during this period, for example a new masonry town fortification in 1696 or the representative Zion Church of the Danish Lutherans in 1701. During these years, Tranquebar had about 6,000, mainly Indian inhabitants.[45]

Scattered trading between Tranquebar or Madras and the Straits must thus have been of mutual benefit for the Danes as well as for the local merchant elites. The Danes succeeded in regaining a foothold in the Archipelago that they have lost in 1682 and could improve the formerly desperate situation in Tranquebar. On the other hand, the merchants and power elites of Johore, Kedah and the surrounding islands were well interested in containing Dutch mercantile power by supporting a competing European trading nation. Even if sources are scarce, we may well presume that such trade raised suspicion among the members of the VOC. While the more powerful English East India Company could maintain at least a minimum of trade with Southeast Asia – for example via their factory in Bencoolen on Sumatra – the weaker Danes might have faced overwhelming Dutch maritime power again. Finally, no more Danish enterprises towards the Straits are mentioned after the 1720s.

The Danes established trade with Aceh instead, which could more or less maintain its independence from the Dutch. Such attempts were more promising and enduring on the long run than trading with the Straits. Aceh had been a major trading port already since the collapse of Srivijaya.[46] Even during the second half of the Seventeenth century as the famous traveller Thomas Bowrey reports:

"Achee is a large City, and populous for these parts of the world, Inhabited by the Natives and many Foreign Merchants as English, Portuguese, Moors, Chuleas and others. …the Port …is never without Ships of English, Danes, Portugals, Moors, Chuleas, Chinesses and others . …all these come in their proper Seasons, with the several sorts of Goods of Surat, the Coast, Bangala, China, and many other places."[47]

The town must have been a virtual hub of Indian Ocean trade and was thus highly attractive for the Danes and Danish shipping services to other European and Asian merchants.

Danish voyages to and from Tranquebar to Aceh are reported already for 1694, 1695 and 1696, that means during the period when the Scandinavians likewise endeavoured gaining access to the Straits itself. A common item to be transported were Indian slaves and Indonesian sugar the other way round for exporting to Europe.[48] By transporting slaves from India to South East Asia, the Danes joint a very ancient trade, that did to only encompass the trade in slaves from the eastern parts of South East Asia and Java but also from India to the Straits region.[49] It nevertheless took about three decades – until the 1730s – when shipping to Aceh gained a higher degree of continuity with at least one annual voyage. The Danish records reveal that it was mainly the company vessel "Christianus Sextus", named after the Danish king, commuting between Aceh and Tranquebar on local private merchants' account, and also regularly carrying slaves, between 1730 und 1745.[50] However, the "Christianus Sextus" proved to be in a desperate condition in 1745, when local Indian merchants denied to entrust their goods to the Danes "due to the vessel's fragility and leakage".[51] Anyhow, commercial exchange between Tranquebar and Aceh soon lost importance for the Danish East India Company when the Danish government abandoned trading in slaves in 1740 due to the influence of the German missionaries and the import of Indonesian sugar to Denmark in favour of Caribbean sugar from the Danish Virgin Islands in 1749.

Only the occupation of the Nicobar Islands in 1755 and the arrival of the German missionaries on the Islands fifteen years later again made Aceh a favourable port-of-call for vessels supplying the Europeans on the Nicobars with provisions. The Nicobars could be reached much easier from Aceh sometimes within a day's journey, while the hazardous voyage between Tranquebar and Nancowry Harbour on the islands proved to last a minimum of ten days. Already before the Scandinavians officially took possession of the Nicobars on January 1st, 1756, the vessels "Kongen af Danmark" and "Ebenezer" called at Aceh where its commanders rented a house in town. Even if they left Aceh already one month later, the renting of a house clearly reveals that the Danes endeavoured permanently settling down here probably by founding a small factory. This assumption is underlined by the fact that the commander of the next ship from Tranquebar, Rasmus Alling, concluded a contract with the ruling Sultan in October 1756, which officially entitled the Danes founding a trading settlement in Aceh.[52] The Danes promised to supply the ruler with cannons and guns instead.[53] The Danes indeed transported weapons to Aceh during the subsequent years, but did not establish a permanent trading settlement and finally could not withstand the increasing British power. The last Danish vessel to call at Aceh left this place in about 1785. Our observations clearly reveal that Danish trading with South East Asia during the eighteenth century was highly irregular. Despite several attempts to commence commercial enterprises, they could never regain the markets which they have lost by the occupation of Bantam by the Dutch.

An outstanding enterprise to Southeast Asia was carried out when the Danes sent an expedition to the Philippines with French assistance in 1745.[54] The Philippines mainly belonged to the economic sphere of the New World, interlinked to the Americas by annual Spanish voyages crossing the Pacific Ocean and transporting silver to the Philippines. Even if the competing European trading nations officially were kept away from the islands after the Peace of Westphalia, this did not mean, that European merchants were completely excluded from the lucrative Philippine markets with their demand of textiles and metals and with their assets of silver. English, Dutch, Portuguese or French merchants simply had to seek for an Indian, Southeast Asian or Armenian ship-owner to transport their trading commodities to the Philippines.

However, the Spaniards did not want to isolate themselves from the Asian markets especially during the European wars that were likewise fought in Asia such as the War auf Austrian Succession during the 1740s or the Seven-Years-War between 1756 and 1763. Accordingly, trade was opened to Danes, the only neutral European nation of the time. On 31 December 1742, the Danes were granted a privilege by the Spaniards that enabled them to carry out trade between the Philippines and other parts of Asia.[55] The French under Dupleix, on coming to know about this privilege, approached the Danes to use the neutral Danish flag for French trading enterprises to the Philippines. Despite a foreseeable abuse of the privilege and Danish neutrality the Danes positively responded to the French approach hoping to receive French assistance when establishing a Danish factory in Bengal. In 1745, the French vessel "Restancier" was renamed and received the well-sounding Danish name "Dansborg". It went to Tranquebar and – after a brief stop at Pondicherry again – safely sailed to Manila and back to Tranquebar again. Its freight mainly consisted of cotton-textiles and tin. In Manila, cowries and silver were procured.

Although the common Franco-Danish enterprise proved to be a single incident, it constituted a bilateral cooperation during the forthcoming years. While the French benefited by the exploitation of Danish neutrality, the Scandinavians found a powerful European partner in Asia to back their ambitions of establishing trade with Bengal. Indeed, the records unveil a substantial French support to the Danes when establishing their trading settlement in Serampore near Calcutta.[56] Only the foundation of the *Asiatisk Kompagni* in 1732 resulted in more continuous traffic under the Danish colours. The Danes now established commodity exchange with China (Canton) and Bengal, where they acquired Serampore. In 1772, the intercontinental trade between Denmark and India was opened to private entrepreneurs, which, until then, was a monopoly of the Asiatic Company. The outbreak of the American War of Independence and even more the Revolutionary Wars eventually lead to an expansion of international private and company trade under the Danish colours, fed mainly by the transfer of Anglo-Indian capital through Danish channels and by clandestine trade between Dutch Batavia and Copenhagen.[57] Many European merchants migrated to Tranquebar from other trading settlements. During this period, the Danes successfully tried to expand the small and almost insignificant territory surrounding Tranquebar.[58] However, economic success in Tranquebar was only of contemporary character.[59]

Conclusion

An examination of the Danish intra-Asiatic trade between South India and Southeast Asia leads us to three basic questions: 1. To what degree did this trade function as a complement to intercontinental trade? 2. Who profited from this trade? 3. Why were the Danish East India Companies unable to gain legitimacy for their trade-monopoly concerning their own employees?

The primary function of the Danish intra-Asiatic trade was to endow the intercontinental voyages to Copenhagen with sufficient commodities for the Europe-bound vessels. And the first intra-Asiatic voyages from Tranquebar to Mergui on the Malayan peninsula certainly responded to such expectations. As a consequence of the increasing discontinuity of intercontinental trade, intra-Asiatic trade under Danish colours increasingly became independent from intercontinental voyages. In this context, we witness the fact that the structures of intercontinental trade shaped the structures of commodity-exchange on the Bay of Bengal: Either its main aim was gaining return-cargoes such as pepper or the Danes merely participated in the traditional intra-Asiatic trade which mainly consisted of bartering South-Indian textiles against Southeast Asian spices and sandalwood without caring for the needs of the East India companies at home. The choice of the various trading emporia frequented by the Danes supports this thesis. While trading via Macassar between 1627 and 1640, the main interest was purchasing cloves for the sale in Masulipatnam. But when the Danes headed for Bantam after 1670, they mainly procured pepper for exporting to Europe.

While the initial capital for the Danish intra-Asiatic trade mainly came from the merchants of Copenhagen – be they of Danish or Dutch origin – and the royal Danish family, it was indeed, to some degree, the investors were not benefited by their investments in ships and trading settlements. Regarding the question of gains from this trade, we again have do separate between periods of regular intercontinental traffic and those with only irregular sailings or of an entire collapse such as between 1639 and 1668. During the period of interrupted intercontinental traffic it was mainly the merchants at the shores of the Indian Ocean seeking shelter under the Danish flag profited from the Danish enterprise in the Indian Ocean region – mainly by utilizing company-vessels, trading-settlements and Danish neutrality for their own purposes. On the other hand, intra-Asiatic trade was carried out to the Copenhagen shareholders' benefit during periods of regular intercontinental sailings.

The trading-policy of the Kingdom of Denmark was, such as in many other countries, characterized by a mercantilistic policy during the Seventeenth and Eighteenth centuries. Even more it is astonishing that the various Danish trading companies never pursued an effective trading monopoly on the Indian Ocean. The explanation for our observation might be found in the fact, that the Danes – as a minor trading-nation in the Indian Ocean – never would have profited by such a monopoly since they depended on private trade and on trade with their European or Asian competitors as a result of their lack of own trading-capacity in the Indian Ocean. This fact resembles the main difference between Danish and Dutch intra-Asiatic trade, because the Dutch successfully maintained a trading-monopoly on the Indian Ocean until 1743.

Notes and References

1. The most important Danish records preserved from seventeenth-century Danish Asia-trade are to be found in *Rigsarkivet*, (henceforth RA) The National Archives at Copenhagen especially *Danske Kancelli*, (henceforth DK), The Danish Office. See for example B244, *Sager ang. det ostindiske Kompagni*; B 245 *Claus Rytters ostindiske Rejse med Skibet "Den forgyldte Sol"*; B 246 *Willum Leyels Arkiv*; B 247, *Tillaeg til Willum Leyels Arkiv*.
2. W.P. Colhaas (ed.), *Generale Missiven van Gouverneurs-Generaal en Raden aan Heeren XVII der Verenigde Oostindische Compagnie*, (henceforth GM) 9 vols., The Hague 1960-1988.
3. J.E. Heeres et al. (eds.), *Dagh-Register gehouden int Casteel Batavia vant passerende daer ter plaetse als over geheel Nederlands-India*, (henceforth DRB) The Hague-Batavia 1887-1931.
4. N. Steensgaard, "The Dutch East India Company as an Institutional Innovation", in M. Aymard (ed.), *Dutch Capitalism and World Capitalism*, Cambridge 1982, pp. 237-257.
5. O. Feldbæk, "No Ship for Tranquebar for Twenty-nine Years : Or The Art of Survival of a Mid-Seventeenth Century European Settlement in India", in: R. Ptak, D. Rothermund (eds.), *Emporia, Commodities and Entrepreneurs in Asian Maritime Trade, C. 1400-1750*, Heidelberg 1991, pp.29-36.
6. Carl Steenstrup, "Scandinavians in Asian Waters in the 17th century. On the Sources for the History of the Participation of Scandinavians in Early Dutch Ventures into Asia", *Acta Orientalia*, Vol. 43, 1982, pp. 69-83. E. Goebel, "Danes in the Service of the Dutch East India Company in the Seventeenth Century", *International Journal of Maritime History*, Vol. 16, No.1, 2004, pp.77-93.

7. E. Goebel, (ed.,) *Jens Mortensen Sveigaards ostindiske rejsebeskrivelse, 1665-1684*, Copenhagen 2005, p.106.
8. R. Willerslew, *Danmarks første Aktieselskab, Historisk Tidsskrift*, Vol. 10,6 (1942-1944), pp. 608-636.
9. H.T. Colenbrander (ed.,) Jan Pietersz. Coen, *Beschieden omtrent zijn Bedrijf in Indie*, 8 Vols., The Hague 1919-1953, Vol. 7, 1, See 3 August 1621, p. 747; Coen, Bescheiden, Vol. 4, See 17 September 1622, p. 563.
10. Regarding trade in pepper between Malabar and Coromandel via land see: S. Subrahmanyam, *The Political Economy of Commerce. Southern India 1500-1650*, Cambridge, 1990, p. 72.
11. H.T. Colenbrander (ed.), Jan Pietersz. Coen, *Beschieden op.cit.*, Vol. 7, 2, See 17 September 1621, p. 563.
12. *Ibid.*, See, 3 August 1621, p. 747.
13. S. Jeyaseela Stephen, *Portuguese in the Tamil Coast: Historical Explorations in Commerce and Culture, 1507-1749*, Navajyothi, Pondicherry, 1998. See the chapter on Trade in Strategic Commodities.
14. D.B. Philpotts (tr.,) *The Life of the Icelander Jón Ólafsson, Traveller to India. Written by Himself and completed about 1661 A.D. with a continuation, by another Hand, up to his Death in 1679*, p. 20.
15. Nicholas Tarling (ed.,) *The Cambridge History of Southeast Asia*, Vol. 2, Cambridge 1999, pp. 9, 127.
16. *Ibid.*, p. 72.
17. Sanjay Subrahmanyam, *The Political Economy of Commerce, op.cit.*, p. 176.
18. DRB, 24 July 1625, p. 181. W. Foster (ed.), *The English Factories in India. A Calendar of Documents in the India Office, British Museum and Public Record Office*, 13 vols, Oxford, 1906-1927 (henceforth EFI), Vol. 3, See 6 February 1626, p. 119.
19. Coen, *Bescheiden op.cit.*, Vol. 7, 2, See 8 June 1628, p.1333.
20. GM, *op.cit.*, Vol. 1, See 22 December 1638, pp.668, 682.
21. Thiele, *Bouwstoffen*, Vol. 2, 2, p. 143; See 3 November 1628.
22. Sinnapah Arasaratnam, "India and the Indian Ocean in the Seventeenth Century", in Ashin Das Gupta, M.N. Pearson (eds.,) *India and the Indian Ocean 1500-1800*, Calcutta 1978, pp. 101 ff.

23. Heeres, *Bouwstoffen*, Vol. 3, p. 46; See 12. December 1642.
24. *"Den Deen sit sonder capitael gants stil"*, *Ibid.,* p. 248; See, 17 December 1645.
25. *Ibid.,* p. 295; See, 21 December 1646.
26. Ashin Das Gupta & M.N. Pearson, *op.cit.,* p. 259.
27. GM, II, p. 91; See, 8 January 1640,
28. DRB, See, 7-8 January 1670, p. 30.
29. DRB, See, 10 January 1672, p. 9; DRB, 30 November 1673, p. 331.
30. DRB, See, 27 July 1678, p. 402.
31. Holden Furber, *Rival Empires of Trade in the Orient*, Minnaepolis, 1976, pp. XII, 4.
32. DRB, See, 21 April 1679, p. 147.
33. DRB, See, 5 December 1680, p. 805. DRB, See, 2-3 April 1681, p. 215. DRB, See, 13 October 1681, p. 609.
34. DRB, 17, See, 17 July 1681, p. 421.
35. Sinnapah Arasaratnam, "The Eastward Trade of India in the Eighteenth Century", in *Politics and Trade in the Indian Ocean World : Essays in Honour of Ashin Das Gupta,* (eds.,) Rudrangshu Mukherjee and Lakshmi Subramaniam, Delhi 1998, p. 210f.
36. S. Arasaratnam, *Eastward Trade of India, op.cit.,* p. 215.
37. William Foster (ed.,) *A New Account of the East Indies by Alexander Hamilton*, Vol. 1, London, 1930, p. 193f.
38. Martin Krieger, *Kaufleute, Seeräuber und Diplomaten*, p. 104.
39. *Ibid.*
40. *En fuld kommen Contracht med Capitn. Herman Bochenhout, paa dets höyeste Danske ostindiske Compag. Vegne*, RA, *Ostind. Komp*. 2188b, See, 1 January 1684.
41. GM, V, See, 26 March 1691, p. 408.
42. GM, VI, See, 30 November 1705, p. 382. GM, VI, See, 15 January 1709, p. 581.
43. GM, V, See, 27 December 1688, p. 224.
44. Records of Fort St. Geroge, (henceforth RFG), Madras, See, 8 September 1701, p. 75.

45. O. Feldbæk, "The Development of an Indo-European Town in Mughal India: Tranquebar in the Seventeenth and Eighteenth Centuries", in: K. Ballhatchet, D. Taylor (eds.), Changing *South Asia: City and Culture*, London, 1984, p. 16.
46. Kenneth McPherson, *The Indian Ocean : A History of People and the Sea*, New Delhi 2001, p.113.
47. Thomas Bowrey, *Geographical Account*, Vol. 1, p. 286, footnote 1. [ist dieses Zitat wirklich von Bowrey selbst? nachprüfen!]
48. ZK, *Dansborg II*; ZK, *Elefanten III*.
49. See for example: Anthony Reid, "Slavery and Bondage in Southeast Asian History", in *Charting the Shape of Early Modern Southeast Asia*, Singapore 2000, pp. 181-216; Jeanette Pinto, *Slavery in Portuguese India, 1510-1842*, Bombay, 1992, p. 36.
50. ZK, *Christianus Sextus*.
51. RA, *As. Komp.,* 1259, See, 10 August 1744.
52. *"Handels accordt imellem Kongen af Danmark, det Dansk asiatiske Compagnie og Cronprintsen af Sumatra eller Achin"*, RA, *As. Komp.*, 2188a, No.38.
53. *Ibid.*
54. Martin Krieger, "Neutrality and Profit: Franco-Danish Relations in 18th-Century India", in K.S. Mathew, (ed.,) *French in India and Indian Nationalism*, 2 Vols, New Delhi, 1999, Vol. I, pp. 155-170.
55. RA, *As. Komp.,* 2188b, 1.
56. RA, *As. Komp.*, 1498, *Protokoller for Kommissionen ang. en ekspedition til, og besvarelse af Kolonier i Bengalen, 1752-1753*. RA, *As. Komp.*, 2019-20, *Rapport Bog over J.C. Soetmanns Expedition till Bengalen ang. en Loges Oprettelse*. RA, *As.Komp.*, *Rapport Bog holden af Hr. Ober Hoved Soetmann og Hr. Ziegenbalg i Bengalen*.
57. O. Feldbæk, "Dutch Batavia Trade via Copenhagen : A Study of Colonial Trade and Neutrality", in *Scandinavian Economic History Review*, Vol. 21, 1973, pp. 43-75.
58. Regarding the motives for extension of territory, See, Martin Krieger, "The Danish Occupation of the Nicobar Islands: The Quest for a "Hinterland" of Tranquebar", in *Pondicherry University Journal of Social Sciences and Humanities*, Vol. 2, pp. 47-62.

59. K. P. Pedersen, "Tranquebars Historie", in *Architectura*, Vol. 9, 1987, p.27. Already during the mid-1780s, Danish trade in Bengal surpassed commodity-exchange in Tranquebar, and in the 1790s, British competition let Tranquebar fall back almost to insignificance. A symbol for the economical decline was the bankruptcy of the wealthy English entrepreneur Daniel Stevenson in Tranquebar by the beginning of the Nineteenth century, whereas the Danish Asiatic Company had abandoned trading-activities in this settlement already in 1796. Denmark's participation in the Napoleonic Wars finally lead to the entire collapse, because the Danish settlements in India were occupied by the British already in 1801-1802 and once more between 1808-1815. After the end of the war, Asia-trade under the Danish flag could not sufficiently recover from its crisis due to the heavy competition from the English East India Company. The Danish Asiatic Company was finally dissolved in 1843, and the Danes sold their possessions in India to the British two years later. At this time, Tranquebar already had changed from a prosperous trading-settlement to the residence of retired Danish officials and finally of their widows. Arabella Due, the last Danish lady residing in Tranquebar, died in 1890. See, Pedersen, *Tranquebars Historie, op.cit.*, pp. 39 & 42.

SECTION–II

Merchants, Middlemen and Business

5

Private and Official Trade with Asia and Europe: Role of the Local Merchants of Orissa in the Medieval Period

Laxmi Narayan Raut

Many Scholars have highlighted the importance of the various European trading companies in Orissa chiefly laying emphasis on their commercial activities and trading settlements. But the role of the local merchants, private trade of the Mughal officials and the Factors of the European companies had not received adequate attention. The reason behind this had been chiefly owing to the paucity of records. Hence this paper attempts to examine the role of the local merchants and private trade in particular besides the commodities involved in the internal and external trade. The growth and decline of such trade and traders in Medieval Orissa has been taken up here for a detailed study.

It is a fact that the European traders during the period 1500 and 1800 had the necessity to engage the services of Indian brokers in their business operations. Some of them were influential merchants on their own account and were exceptionally rich and naturally they played a very important, sometimes dominant, part in the commercial life of Orissa and assisted the foreign companies in commerce.

Local Merchants, Agents and Brokers

The local merchants or native entrepreneurs took active part in trade with different parts of India as well as with foreign countries. They also acted as middle men between the producers and the European merchants. The brokers and local merchants of Orissa belonged to both the Hindu and

Muslim communities. The English factory records as well as the travel accounts mention the names of Khemchand (Chimcham), Chintaman Shah (Chintamund), Suraj Shah, Hira Shah, Kalyan (Calliun), Rai, Rajaram (Roojiram), Ram Narayan (Narain), Gangaram and Gopal as the principal merchants of Balasore. All of them were Hindus.[1] We have also reference to some Muslim merchants of Balasore with whom the English contracted for purchasing goods in 1684.[2] But there is no mention of the names of these Muslim merchants.

These merchants of Orissa had settled down in the port of Balasore carrying on trade with Calcutta. They used to send iron, stone plates, rice and other commodities. Their imports from Calcutta to Balasore consisted of tobacco and other articles.[3] Sometimes before 1684 a *gomastah* of Khemchand purchased huge quantities of *cassas* at Dacca.[4] There is mention of a ship of the merchants of the Gingelly coast being burnt by the Portuguese in the roadsteads of Pulicat in the 1620s.[5] This ship certainly went there on commercial mission. In 1630s Sebastiao Manrique found at Pipli a ship belonging to the local *shiqdar* being sent to Cochin laden with merchandise.[6] Local merchants of Orissa also carried on trade with various parts of Asia. Thomas Bowery in 1670s referred to the merchants of Balasore and Pipli sending their ships for the purpose of trade.[7] In March 1680 Khemchand sent his ship and it brought elephants from Tennaserim to Balasore.[8]

The usual intermediary between the local producers and European companies were the brokers. The European traders had to depend on them for the supply of articles for export as well as for the sale of the European commodities in Orissa. These Europeans competed with one another to have direct access to the original producers through the brokers. The English factors used to give *dadnis* (advances) to the brokers (also known as *dadni* merchants or *dalals)* by taking proper security from them, who were bound to make their contact within the stipulated time and were under the obligation of supplying their goods exclusively to the

English.[9] The merchants were kept under the supervision of a junior English Factor. The English had to remain always alert with regard to their brokers, weavers or artisans who were often seduced by other European factors having trading centres in the hinterland of Orissa. The brokers were obliged to deliver the goods on time i.e. just prior to shipping season or westward monsoon winds. The local merchants in their turn entered into similar agreements with the weavers, manufacturers and artisans, gave them advances on similar conditions, and in turn directed them for supplying their goods to any one save their respective merchants-who gave them *dadnis*. The merchants used to collect the articles of investment at a cheap rate and stocked them in the Company's warehouses. If the merchant failed to deliver the goods on time, or satisfy the Company agents of the quality of the goods delivered and thus robbed the Company of the full return of their investments, the merchant "shale (shall) forfeit and lose his part and share in the investments for ever after provided it were not caused through trouble and stoppage of the goods in the country."[10]

It is sometimes noticed that the English factors entered into direct engagements with the indigenous artisans. Streynsham Master and his Council at Balasore entered into a contract with the local merchants for the year 1679. The latter were to supply Suro *sannoes,* Harapore *sannoes,* Mohunpore-*sannoes, ginghams,* fine and ordinary, *nillaes* to the English factors.[11]

The brokers of Orissa were not only acting as the link between the Orissa producers and artisans and the English East India Company but also sometimes between government officials and local Rajas. In 1673 the Hugli factors directed Hall, the English Factor at Balasore, that Malik Kasirn, the 'governor' (officer-in-charge) of Balasore. must either pay cash for the guns that he would purchase from the Company or Khemchand should buy them for him. The English factors wanted to make this arrangement in order to avoid difficulties in realising the price of guns.[12]

The English in the beginning of their trade operations faced the problem of lack of demands for their goods, lack of ready money and the diminishing purchasing power of the communities in the upper stratum of the society. To scrt out the financial difficulties of the English, the brokers had to arrange selling the overstocked and unsold broad clothes, scarlet and lead. In the commercial operation they took part payment for goods supplied by them in articles imported from Europe. The brokers helped the English in financing them at the payment of three per cent interest on all transaction. Sometimes the English factors paid exorbitant rate of interest as high as fifteen to eighteen per cent per annum to great and powerful brokers like Khemchand and Chintaman Shah. This was however, in the words Streynsham Master, "ordinary rates then paid on outstanding obligations by merchants of the best position and credit".[13]

The local merchants were subjected to the payment of internal customs duties as well as other exactions, to the government officials. When Shaista Khan was the *Subahdar* the merchants of Orissa had to make contributions towards strengthening the naval defence.[14] The merchants belonging to the Hindu community had sometimes to make extra payments. The Hindu merchants of the Gingelly coast besides paying the usual taxes and duties had to pay many extra taxes that the Muslim officer of the place used to charge from them. Although some of the richest Indian merchants lived there, they could not display their wealth for fear of extortion by the Muslim officials as well as for the fact that after their death their properties would belong to the emperor and their descendants could inherit these only by the mercy of the emperor.[15] Sometimes the merchants evaded internal customs duties by eluding the constant vigilance of the officials such as the *faujdar*.[16] They took the risk of procuring raw materials sometimes without paying customary duties to the *nawabs* from the local markets as well as from outside and made them available to the weavers and primary producers. For this attempt at evasion of taxes they had to pay occasionally heavy fines in the shape of occasional financial extortions by the *nawabs* and *faujdars.*[17] The *subahdars* considered the merchants as 'filled sponges' and extorted money from them. Both Saf Shikan Khan (Safi Khan) and Rashid Khan exacted large amount of money from Khemchand.[18] The latter also demanded from other merchants at Balasore money varying from Rs. 10,000 to Rs. 50,000 according to their capacity to pay.[19] Besides being forced to pay large amount of money to the *subahdars,* the merchants were harassed by the local officials in some other ways. When Malik Kasim became governor of Balasore in 1673, Walter Clavell, the Chief of the Bay Factories and his Council feared that he would give trouble to the local merchants at Balasore and force them to wind up their business. Their fear came to be true and in August 1673 Malik Kasim created such conditions as would make the merchants prefer to leave the place.[20] Merchants of Balasore who traded with Calcutta were so much oppressed by a *gomastah* that many of them left the place, and transacted their business at Kuuka (Kanika, in Cuttack district).[21] Some who remained at Balasore were greatly distressed.[22] Thus, the brokers had to reconcile the private financial interest of the Muslim rulers and the trade interest of the English East India Company. It was a period when they had to trade at a highly competitive market, made insecure by the rivalry among the foreign and Indian traders.[23] As early as July 1680 Chintaman was severely reprimanded by the Hughli authorities for 'boggling' about a debt he owed to the Company. In 1681 the Hughli Council refused to give Chintaman Shah any share in the investment because of his private engagements with *nawab* Rasheed Khan (sometime, Governor of Orissa, 1674). However, Khemchand supplied his associate with the proceeds of his own share hoping that the Bay Chief and the Council would pardon him on his representation and continue to employ him as before. In 1685, Chintaman Shah was indebted to the English East India Company. Having little hopes of recovering the whole amount, the Company thought of attacking and seizing his ships at sea by way of part recovery. When a ship owned jointly by Chintaman and Khemchand arrived at the Balasore roadstead, it was seized by Captain John Nicholson on 16th November 1686.[24] It was this conflict among the irreconcilable forces in the economic situation which made their investments insecure and proved their existence precarious.

Some of the brokers of Orissa were wealthy and influential. Khemchand appeared to be very rich. He was the accepted leader or chief and the accredited spokesman and representative of the entire mercantile community of the place. A shrewd and tactful business magnate, he knew his trade well.[25] Even after promising to pay Rs.30,000 to *nawab* Saf Sliikau Khan (Safi Khan) in 1672,[26] Khemchand had resources to indemnify the English and others and this consideration led the English to deliver to Khemchand Rs. 7,500 which was his share in the investment,[27] Khemchand alone in 1673 had in his stock broadcloth worth Rs.30,000.[28] In 1674 he paid Rs.50,000 to Rashid Khan, the *nawab* of Orissa.[29] These details show the wealth of Khemchand. We have also interesting information about the influence of the merchants on the local government and the European factors. In 1654 at the insistence of the merchants Malik Beg the local governor opened the godown of the Dutch at Pipli which was previously sealed by him as the Dutch refused to grant passes to the Indian ships to go to Malaya Peninsula and Achin which were then under the control of the Dutch.[30] The English sometimes solicited the intervention or mediation of the merchants in the hour of need and trouble. The former attempted to procure a *parwana* from the *nawab* Saf Shikan Khan in 1672. Though the *parwana* was procured through the intervention of Boremul (Puran Mai) the governor of Balasore, during the transaction the merchants Khemchand, Haricharau and Suraj Shah accompanied Boremul taking with them some presents for the *nawab's diwan* and other officers and this helped in obtaining the *parwana*.[31] In 1676 there was a dispute between the English and the Dutch over a house and a piece of land at Balasore. The English decided somehow to get *Kanungo's* stamp through the mediation of Khemchand if it be necessary to validate their claim. They also sought the good office of Khemchand and Chintaman Shah in 1685 to settle an affair with the local officials.[32]

The local merchants of Orissa faced numerous difficulties in their trade. They were subjected to unusual custom duties and many other financial extortion from the government officials. The Muslim nobility, on their part, made constant endeavours to exclude their Indian associates and the foreigners from the internal trade and monopoly in particular commodities.[33] There was also heavy competition among the European merchants to reach the primary producers, sometimes evading internal customs duties under the umbrella of the *imperial farman* for duty-free trade. The increasing volume of private trade, the effect of natural calamities like floods and droughts and the political uncertainty owing to wars had added to their difficulties. Gradually the merchants lost their foreign trade. Their condition in some cases became so precarious that as evidenced, they had to give up trading activities and take shelter in religious shrines.

Private Trade of the Mughal Officials and Factors of the European Trading Companies

The prosecution of private trade by the Mughal officials, Factors of the European Companies, interlopers and free merchants was a characteristic feature of commercial life at that time in India. Its volume was great, involving considerable loss to the European trading companies concerned and immense profit to the private traders. But Orissa was an exception to this practice and it is known from the factory records that the prospects of private trade had allured the English Factors to open trade centres in coastal Orissa. *Sauda-i-khas* of the Mughal officials meant monopoly of trade not only in many precious articles but also in the commodities necessary for life on behalf of the governer. Monopoly purchase of the merchandise was made at the centre of production or at the ports of lading and the retail dealers were forced to purchase these goods at increased prices. Private trade was undertaken in by Mughal officers like Shah Shuja, Mir Jumla, Shaista Khan and Azimuddin.[34] Malik Kasi, the Mughal governor at Balasore in 1676 sent iron, coir and other articles of Malik Zindi at Hughli through an English vessel for the purpose of private trade.[35]

Private trade of the servants of the English East India Company was a kind of supplement to their low salaries.[36] But not only the servants of lower category but also officials like Sill (once selected Agent for the Coast of Coromandal), Francis Day (a member of the Council at Masulipatnam), Streynsham Master (Agent at Fort St. George) were engaged in trade on private account. They were not allowed to encroach upon the Company's monopoly and could send to Europe only articles like precious stones. They also sometimes could import certain articles from Europe to India. But inland trade, coastal trade and trade with Asian ports from India were the main concern of these servants.[37] The English East India Company gave legal sanction to protect private trade. In November, 1676 Company's indulgences, allowing their servants and the captains and crews of their vessels to trade in certain goops were 'recommended to be duly observed' by the Agent and his Council in the Bay.[38] While framing the rules for private trade in 1679 the Bay Council also observed that the private trade "being a just privilege of the Company's servants in Bengal" the chief of the Council should assist "all fair private trade".[39]

The following references would show the extent of private trade carried on by the servants of the English East India Company in Orissa. Thomas Colley[40],and Sill[41], English merchants carried on private trade in 1630s in Orissa. The main cause of unwillingness of the Factors to stop trading in the Bay, though it was unprofitable (during the initial stage), was the large amount of private trade carried on board by the *Hopewell* (ship) belonging to Francis Day and Masulipatnam Factors. Francis Day brought some cloves from Masulipatnam to Balasore possibly belonging to his own account for trade. Further, from his personal account he invested a sum of 4003 rials of eight (Spanish dollar) at Gingelly[42] on trade. In January 1676, Hall brought so much merchandise on the sloop, the *Ganges* at Hughli for his private trade that the Company's servants at Balasore had to wait till they could procure boats for unloading these goods and thus the departure of the sloop for the coast was delayed. Moreover, for the quick despatch of goods (60 or 80 *mounds* of long-pepper) to Balasore he hastened the departure of the *Ganges* from Hughli and the Company's goods to be sent from that place were left behind.[43] Streynsham Master did not neglect his personal gain. His letters to Richard Edwards at Balasore (May and June, 1678) revealed that he invested considerable money in long pepper and spelter (zinc).[44] Streynsham Master did brisk business on his private account in 1679 and 1680.[45]

For carrying on their private trade the Company's servants sometimes borrowed money on the security of the Company's funds and also made it obligatory for the Company to repay the same. In 1651 Bridgman and Edward Stephens, the Factors in the Bay (Bengal and Orissa) borrowed money from the 'country people' (local people) in the name of the Company for investing in their private trade. Bridgman made the Company responsible for repaying the same.

For furthering the cause of private trade the servants of the East India Company in Bengal and Orissa secured an order in 1650s with a view to suspend the custom of giving large presents to the local Mughal officers, then prevalent.[46] Mughal emperor Farrukhsiyar's *farman* (1716-1717) exempted from payment of customs duties on the exports and imports of the Company in lieu of payment of an accumulated sum of Rs.3000 per year. On production of a *dastak* or pass from the President of the Calcutta Council, the Company's goods were allowed to pass without inspection at the toll stations. The servants of the Company wrongfully extended this privilege to their private trade. Murshid Quli Khan *subahdar* of Bengal by asking his officer to examine whether the goods were really imported by sea or purchased for exportation by sea prevented the Company's servants from taking privilege of the *dastak* system in the case of their inland private trade but they could easily extend the privilege to their coastal trade. Large scale abuse of *dastak* continued under Shujauddin and Alivardi Khan after the battle of Plassey, the abuse of *dastak* reached such a magnitude that in 1758 the Directors observed in anger that '*dastaks* have been scandalously prostituted'.[47]

To regulate or suppress the excesses of private trade, the authorities of the Company in England framed rules from time to time. It is likely that the Company's servants in Orissa had to abide by these rules. Besides these general rules, we get references to certain measures adopted by the English authorities in Bengal and Orissa for controlling private trade of the Company's servants serving in these places. To prevent smuggling of prohibited goods,[48] Streynsham Master, then Supervisor and Second in the Council at Fort St. George issued an order in 1676 to the effect that goods should be taken neither aboard to sloops nor to the vessels ready for despatch to Europe without a written order from the Chief of Hughli or Balasore or any other person authorised by them.[49] On 28 April 1679 the Bay Council laid down three rules regarding private trade. First, to trade in prohibited goods and to make contracts with the weavers who usually worked for the Company was forbidden. Second, the servants of the East India Company should do all business regarding private trade e.g. receipt, packing and despatch of goods inside the factory and not in a place specially hired for this. Third, investment for private trade should not be made in places where the Company's weavers resided without obtaining prior direction of the Chief of the factory as to the weavers to be employed.[50] But these rules failed to control private trade owing to the luke-warmness of the Company's home authorities and half-heartedness of its servants in India in making these rules effective. Moreover, the tricks of the trade and the corruption of both the English and Indian supervisors and guards helped the private traders to go on with their business.[51]

Official Trade from Orissa With Asia and Europe

Orissa in the medieval period with its agricultural and industrial products carried out inter-provincial and foreign trade. Rice being profusely cultivated, it formed the major export not only to different parts of India but also abroad. Balasore was a centre of rice export to Bengal and different parts of the Mughal Empire. It is to be borne in mind that rice was taken as a share of government from among the people. Khan-i-Dauran says, "as for the Malangi boats for loading rice in, they have not been procured owing to the bad conduct of the *darogha* of the port, get bond from the zamindars of the *mahal* and send rice to the port to be shipped in sailing season."[52]

Balasore was the main collection centre for the export of such commodities from various parts of Orissa.[53] The cotton textiles manufactured in Orissa had a wide market. The principal articles of trade for export from Orissa were saltpetre, turmeric, sugar, cotton yarn, taffetas raw silk, *sannoes,* tincall, *dussuttee* or coarse soil cloth. Saltpetre was most important of them.[54] Gingham and millas were also collected for export. Among other articles exported from Orissa, iron, stone dishes, stone cups, copper pipes, sugar, salt, grains, turmeric, ginger, sandal wood, long pepper and short pepper, brass plates etc. are worthy of note. The principal articles of import to Orissa were lead, quick silver, vermilion, copper, alum, brimstone, broad-cloth, cowries, coral, dried fish, tobacco and various articles of luxury.[55] Elephants, elephant-tusks, arecanuts, cinnamon and conch-shells were also imported.

The Portuguese from Malacca brought to Bengal and Orissa articles like 'brocades, brocateles, cloth, velvets, damaskas, satins, taffetas, tafiosinas, tafissirias escomillas or inusline' of all colours but black colour was considered ill-omened in Bengal. They also brought cloves, nutmegs and mace, and from Borneo the highly prized camphor. From China they brought silks, very valuable pearls and jewels, for labour being cheap in China 'these were made in European style but with greater skill and cheaper. From Maldives they brought sea-shells

(Kaurim] which were current in Orissa as coins and were known as cowries. The bigger kind of shells called chanquos were brought from the Pearlfishery coast in Tamil country. They imported from Solor and Timor both the white and the red varieties of sandal wood.[56]

The trade of the English East India Company in Orissa consisted in the sale of broad cloth, copper, iron, lead and a few other commodities from Europe, and in the purchase of piece-goods, silk, drugs, saltpetre and other articles for the cargoes of their returning ships. The Dutch carried on a considerable trade on their Company's account and in articles like tin, camphor, bengatnin, tuthenaigue, sugar, spices, China-ware and arrack.[57] They exported Orissa cotton textiles, provisions such as rice, butter, oil and opium derived mainly from Bihar in lieu of commodities of the Far Eastern countries like tin, saltpetre and sandal wood.[58]

Orissa had extensive trade and commerce with Bengal, Bihar, Northern India, Gujarat, Surat, Dacca, Kerala and the places in the Eastern Coast viz,, Narasapur,[59] Vizagapatnam, Masulipatnam, Pulicat, Madras and Modapallam.[60] The principal articles of export from Orissa to various places were rice, gram, butter, sugar, textile goods, gingelly seed (sesamum indicum), salt, iron, stone-plates, lead and broadcloth. Orissa also imported mainly articles like tobacco, spices and saltpetre. There are also occasional references to the import of rice and salt into Orissa at the time of scarcity. There was regular supply of Orissa textiles from Balasore to Patna in Bihar. In 1630s Peter Mundy (1628-1634) noted that the cloths of Orissa like *cassaes* / *cassas* or *khosa* (plain good quality muslin) of sixteen, seventeen and eighteen *covads* (cubit) in length and one *covad* in breadth, *ambarees (ambari, amari*— a turban, the canopy of an elephant *howda), chareconnaes* (charkhana, chequered muslin, linen striped with white silk, sixteen *covads* in length and one *covad* in breadth), *hamaones (hammams*— thick stand cloths used for wrappers, linen, eleven *covads* long and one and a qaurter broad) and such varieties of piece goods were available at Patna.[61] Thomas Bowery in 1670s observed that the various cotton manufactures of Balasore like *sannoes, ginghams, orummals (rumals),* cotton yarn and other goods were sent to Patna.[62] Orissa exported salt to Patna. The English factors at Balasore reported (1659) that salt was exported from Balasore to Patna and oxen were used to carry them.[63] From Balasore articles imported by the English like broad-cloth and lead, which could not be disposed away were sent to Patna. Orissa abundantly imported saltpetre from Patna. It was brought to Orissa not for local use but for export to Europe for the military needs. In the mid-seventeenth century the Dutch used to import saltpetre from Patna and its neighbourhood *to Plpli* where they refined it and then exported to Europe. The amount of export was about 2000 tons a year.[64] They further noted that the volume of yearly import ranged between 1000 to 3000 *mounds.*[65]

The close contact between the ports of Balasore and Hugli necessitated constant coastal trade between Orissa and Bengal. Owing to difficulties of navigation in the Hughli river the merchants usually brought down goods from Bengal in small ships and transported at Balasore. The English employed many sloops in carrying goods to Hughli, unloaded from their ships at Balasore.[66] Merchants of Orissa exported salt, stoneware, iron, cloth and rice to Bengal. Balasore stone dishes and cups were greatly priced in the market of Calcutta where duties on these articles were levied.[67] The English factors in Bengal in their letter to Madras (1st September, 1665) made mention of export of salt from Hijli to Hughli.[68] We have references to the export of rice from Orissa to Bengal in the early Eighteenth century. In 1711 owing to a famine in Bengal the English factors stationed there decided to send the *Mary Buoner* to Balasore to bring rice.[69] In the 1750s rice remained as an article of export from Orissa to Bengal. As known from the letter of James Bridgmau (aboard *Lioness* ship) to the Company (15th December, 1650) articles like raw silk, saltpetre, sugar, dry ginger came from Hughli to Balasore. The port of Hughli could also supply bees-wax, long pepper, civet, rice, butter, oil and wheat, all at about half the price of other places.[70] Orissa imported tobacco from Bengal in 1750s.[71]

Masulipatnam received from Orissa products like rice, butter, Gingelly (sesame) seed and sugar. Rice was regularly supplied to Masulipatnam. Of the goods that the seven *junks*72 carried from Gingelly coast to Masulipatnam in February 1629 rice and paddy were important.[73] In March 1634, the *Thomas* (ship purchased from the governor of Balasore) sailed towards Masulipatnam filled rice, sugar and other provisions.[74] In March 1638, the Masulipatnam factors Thomas Clark and Richard Hudson advised John Yard of Balasore to send the freight goods belonging to Mirza Taqi, *dabir* of Golconda.[75] Rice supply to Masulipatnam and the adjacent region was stopped in 1677 due to blockade of the coast by the Dutch.[76] The English Factor at Masulipatam in his letter to Fort St. George (18 November, 1703) expressed their apprehension that rice would become scarce as well as dear there unless it was imported in sufficient quantity from Gingelly coast and Bengal.[77] Sugar was carried in the English ship the *Thomas* from Balasore for Masulipatam in March 1634. A ship was caught in the monsoon at a place 15 or 16 leagues (45 or 48 miles) from Masulipatnam and the sugar was put on a *pinnace* the *Queda* which was also turned over and the entire sugar valued at about 4000 *pagodas* (Rs. 14,000) was lost.[78]

Narasapur, Vizagapatnam, Mọdapallam and Fort St. George (in Madras) also received rice from Orissa. In 1679 Streynsham Master, then Agent of the English at Fort St. George found on the river near the Dutch factory at Narasapur many vessels that were engaged in the rice trade of Gingelly.[79] In 1712 the interference of the Vizagapatnam authorities hampered the import of grain (rice) to that place from Ganjam.[80] The English authorities at Balasore decided on 14 December, 1667 to send rice and other provisions by sloops to Fort St. George.[81] Rice was one of the articles that Job Charnak, then English Factor at Balasore, proposed to despatch in a ship from Balasore to Fort. St. George in 1686.[82]

Alexander Hamilton in 1700s made mention of export of rice from Ganjam to Fort St. George.[83]

We have many references to the considerable rivalry that was going on between the Dutch, the Portuguese and the English for the rice trade between Orissa and Pulicat. Schorer, a Dutch factor at Masulipatnam (1608-1614) made mention of import of rice to Pulicat from Orissa every year.[84] It seems that Dutch settlement to some extent depended on the rice supply from Orissa. In 1616-1617 the Portuguese war vessels started cruising against the Indian boats carrying provisions from Orissa to Pulicat and prevented these from reaching there. As a counter measure the Dutch arranged for a convoy of Pulicat-bound Indian ships.[85] This ship therefore could bring rice safely there.[86] As a result of the rivalry between the English and the Dutch in 1629 and 1633 the former forced the provision boats from Orissa to go to Armagon instead of Pulicat which was their usual destination. The activities of the English were stopped when the Dutch offered protection to the Indian boats carrying such provisions.[87] Schorer informs us about the import of other articles like spices of various kinds and salt to Orissa from Pulicat.[88] It is surprising to note that Orissa which exported salt to Patna and Bengal in 1650s and 1660s, imported it from Pulicat in the early part of the same century.

Birds of Orissa were sold at the markets of Goraghat.[89] Abdul Latif[90] mentioned in 1609 that *maina* birds[91] were brought from Kutch and Orissa to Ghoraghat. Sebastiao Manrique in 1630s found at Pipli a big ship which was loaded with different kinds of merchandise and was bound for Cochin.[92] Francisco Pelsaert writing in the 1620s observed that the merchandise coming from the east country (i.e. Mughal provinces of Allahabad, Bengal and Orissa) passed through Agra, but he is silent about the destinations.[93]

With the coming of the Europeans and the establishment of their factories Orissa's trade and commerce with many countries of Asia and Europe took a new dimension. The European Factors controlled Orissa's external trade. They established contacts with the native merchants and producers of different articles. Amongst the Europeans the English seems to have had a better share in Orissa. References are many in the factory records and European travel accounts. Ceasar Frederick in1560s mentioned that every year in the ports of Orissa about twenty-five or thirty ships big as well as small were laden with rice, various kinds of' bombast cloths,[94] gingelly (sesame) oil, large quantities of butter, lac, long pepper, ginger, mirabolans and large quantities of *herba* cloth.[95] Sebastiao Manrique also informs us that more than one hundred vessels loaded every year with rice, sugar, oil and wax from Orissa.[96] However, both the travellers are silent about the destination as well as size of these vessels. From the ports of Balasore and Pipli as many as twenty-six foreign ships had been recorded in the season 1643-1644.[97] There is again no reference to the size of the ships or to the country where they were exported. From the available records it is known that Orissa had commercial relationship with Persia, Maldives, Junk-Ceylon Malacca, Pegu, Tenassarim, Achin, Sumatra, Batavia and Macao in China. Regarding trade in rice with St. Helena (in Africa) we have only one reference.[98]

Orissa's main articles of export through the European merchant to Persia were cloth, sugar and iron. The English East India Company factors utilised the ocean going ships coming from England during their enforced idleness on voyages to and from Persia carrying articles of Indian merchants in return for freight and investing the proceeds in goods suitable for Persia. In 1642-1643 the English factors of Balasore sold or bartered their glasses, knives, lead, broad-cloth etc. for '*gurras, sannoes, cassas* (textile goods), sugar, iron and *ginghams,* all except the last being intended for Persia.[99] In 1644 Factors at Surat sent to the factor at Balasore one chest of rials with orders to provide for Persia 150 bales of sugar, 10 or 12 bales of *gurras* and the same quantity of coarse *sannoes.*[100]

The Dutch also had traded Orissa goods with Persia. In April, 1653 two Dutch ships from Balasore left for Basra and Gombroon.[101] After founding the Dutch settlement at Batavia (Jakarta) in 1619 they provided the slaves with sufficient textiles besides exchanging Orissa cloth for spices. In order to feed the increased population food grains became indispensable as their local supplies were inadequate.[102] Rice from Orissa was exported to Batavia either via Coromandel or directly. In the 1620s, 1630 and 1650s rice exported from Coromondal to Batavia was procured from Orissa.[103] In 1642 the Dutch authorities at Batavia asked the Dutch factors in Coromondal to procure 600 to 800 *lasts*[104] of rice from Bengal and Orissa. Valentyn in 1720s informs us that besides rice, Orissa (from the port of Pipli) exported sugar, butter, cotton and silk cloths to Batavia.[105] Ralph Fitch who travelled in the Eastern India in 1585-1586 informs that articles like rice, sugar, butter, cloth and long-pepper were exported from Orissa. These ships from Sumatra were coming to the port of Hijli in Orissa and carried articles like rice in large quantities, sugar, butter and cloth of' cotton to Sumatra.[106] In the Seventeenth century Orissa exported rice and muslin cloth to Achin.[107]

Orissa had trade with Maldives. Alexander Hamilton in 1708 observes that Maldives had to depend on Orissa rice as it was not produced there. Further, he informs that Orissa supplied butter and cloth to the Maldives.[108] In the 1780s Abbe Raynal refers to the export of rice, coarse cloths and some silk stuffs from Orissa to the Maldives.[109] Orissa imported cowries and coir from the Maldives. Ibn Batuta (1333-1346) had referred to the import of cowries from the Maldives to Bengal.[110] According to Thomas Bowrey (1666-1679) six or seven ships belonging to the *nawab* of Bengal and the merchants of Balasore, Pipli and Hughli went every year to the Maldives to bring cowries and coir[111] A ship from the Maldives laden with cowries and coir reached Balasore on 8 September 1679.[112] In 1683 two ships came to Balasore from the Maldives bringing cowries.[113] Owing to a *parwana* issued by the king of the Maldives, the Dutch at Balasore enjoyed between 1740 and 1772 exclusive privilege in the trade of cowries brought there by the merchants of the Maldvies.[114] Cowries were passed for money in Orissa seem to indicate that Orissa depended on the Maldives for the supply of cowries. This trade in cowries was highly profitable as a comparison between the prices of cowries in the Maldives and Orissa would show. Cowries were very cheap in the Maldives where 40 or 42 *pans* of cowries (3200 or 3360 numbers) could be bought for six to seven *annas* in 1682.[115] But in Orissa it was sold at a high profit. In 1670s the price of cowries at Balasore varied between 36 *pans* (2880 cowries) to 42 *pans* (3360 cowries) for a rupee.[116] Thus cowries brought from the Maldives could be sold at Balasore at more than hundred per cent profit.[117]

With Malacca and Junk-Ceylon Orissa had established trade by sending articles such as butter, oil and gingelly seed. The Portuguese from Bipilbundar (Pipli) carried butter to Malacca and gingelly seeds in 1620s.[118] Butter and oil used to come to Junk-Ceylon from the coast of Gingelly in the Seventeenth century.[119] In the Seventeenth century rice and muslin remained important items of export from the ports of Pipli and Balasore to Pegu and Tenassarim. Orissa imported from Tenassarim elephants and lead. The Elephants in those days were mainly used in the army as means of conveyance, in religious procession. Persian chroniclers like Shams-i-Siraj Afif, Abul Fazl and others refer to the abundance of elephants in Orissa. It is interesting to note that in spite of the availability of elephants in Orissa, she imported the same from other countries. Thomas Bowery mentions that the ships belonging to the *nawab* of Bengal and the merchants of Balasore, Pipli and Hugli went to Tenassarim every year to bring elephants.[120] In March 1680, Khemchand, a merchant of Orissa brought a good number of elephants for trade at Balasore.

The king of Siam had trade with Balasore and employed some Factors for the commercial purpose. The factors, he sent in 1672 carried on trade in elephants and lead. They had a large stock of lead in the factory at Balasore. This was purchased from Balasore by merchants.[121] In 1679 two great ships of the king of Siam brought elephants to Balasore from Tenassarim.[122] Orissa's articles of export to Macao consisted of rice, butter, gingelly seed and cloth. In 1620s the Portuguese exported the above mentioned articles to Macao from Pipli.[123]

Sri Lanka was dependent on India for rice and so it received large supplies of rice from Orissa. In the 1640s and 1650s the Dutch factors exported rice from their factory at Pipli to Sri Lanka.[124] Thomas Bowrey mentions that ships of considerable burden were plying from the ports of Balasore and Pipli to Sri Lanka on trade mission.[125] Orissa imported elephants from Sri Lanka. Streynsham Master, the Agent of the English at Fort St. George and his associates found on 9 September 1679 two ships that came from Jaffnapatam unloading elephants at Balasore.[126] Bowery also refers to the import of elephants from there to Orissa.[127] The other articles of import include elephant tusks, arecanuts, cinnamon and conchshells.[128]

Orissa's trade with Europe was mainly confined to England. The general practice of shipment was that cotton goods and cotton yarn from Balasore and the neighbouring centres in Orissa, goods procured from Hughli and Patna stored in the godowns were exported according to the East India Company's orders. Various articles were also loaded on the English ships coming annually and anchoring in Balasore. From there these used to sail in November or December for Masulipatnam or Fort St. George and after being finally laden and prepared there set out on the voyage to England about the end of January.[129] The exports from Orissa to various parts of Europe were textile products of different varieties, e.g. *ginghams, sannoes, rutnals, gurrahs, mulmuls, cassas, jiammams, nillaes, salampores, calicoes, peniascoes,* silk *rumals,* cotton *yarn,* sugar, saltpetre lac, turmeric, iron, wax and opium. Cowries which were imported to Orissa from Maldives were also exported from Orissa to Europe. The commodities imported into Orissa from Europe were broadcloth of various colours, scarlet, bullion of gold and silver, rial of eight (Spanish dollar), copper, quicksilver, lead, vermillion, coral, glasses, knives,. brimstone, spelter, ivory, sapan-wood (a kind of wood used in dyeing) and some articles of luxury.[130] All these articles imported were not in demand in Orissa. Hence such articles were transported to Bengal and Patna by the local merchants.

Decline of Trade

The internal and the external trade of Orissa which received new strides with the advent of the Europeans and with the participation of indigenous merchants could not continue to flourish for long. Many factors were at work which hindered the prosperity. The European companies had to pay customs and transit duties to the Mughal authorities on all transactions on import and export. Even though the merchants paid the normal duties their commercial activities were not free from difficulties. To a great extent, the conduct of trade depended on the privileges secured through *farmans, nishans, parwanas* and *dastaks* granted by Mughal emperors, princes, *subahdars* and *diwans* respectively. Since the trade privileges were very often infringed by the Mughal officers at the provincial level, procurement of repeated confirmations of such trade privileges had to be resorted by the Europeans. Such an administrative requirement for trade operation was considered very irksome for certain reasons. Firstly, the merchants had to offer bribes and presents to the Mughal officials for obtaining trade privileges. To cite a few examples Rashid Khan, the Mughal governor of Orissa took Rs.5000 from the Dutch for renewal of their *farman.*[131] For procuring a *parwana,* in respect of their trade privileges the French had to pay Rs. 10,000 to *Nawab* Murshid Quli Khan in 1722.[132] Secondly, a race for procuring more and more trade privileges started amongst the European trading companies. Although the main purpose of granting privileges was to smoothen the trade activities, it could not become so. The merchants with the passage of time became subjected to harassment by local officers. Further it indirectly encouraged official corruption, and adversely affected the trade.

The frequent changes in governorship of Orissa and their short tenures which became a common feature during the later part of the Mughal rule in Orissa which also hindered the trade. It was customary for a new governor to renew the existing trade privileges. But it often became a difficult affair on the part of the merchants to deal with all the local governors and their subordinate officers. As a result, various exactions of Mughal officials, their interference with the free passage of merchandise, receipt of bribes and forced presents in the form of money, guns, horses, and luxury articles etc., became very common. Under such situation trade could not flourish. A careful examination of the European factory records and travel accounts reveal the fact that after 1670 the various exactions, imposition of transit duties, oppression and harassment of the Mughal governors in Orissa went on increasing. For example Safi Khan, the Governor of Orissa earned greatest notoriety in exacting money from the English merchants at Balasore. Similarly, Malik Kasim, the Mughal governor proved very vexatious and exacting to deal with. The English described him as "insolent, proud, abusive rascall", who "used many ways to extort money from the inhabitants and put a stop to almost the whole trade of the town (Balasore)." The English were apprehensive of an end of their trade at Balasore under Kasim's administration.[133] Thomas Bowery, condemned Rashid Khan, the governor of Orissa as a "ravenous wolf". Walter Chavell (the Bay Chief) charged him as "a man of so bad temper that it was difficult to get anything done by him without great trouble and charge in presents".[134] He further complained that "not a worse Nobab *(nawab)* ever come to Orissa than the pressent Ruzzand Chaan (Rashid Khan) who robs the (w)hole country an(d) about Catak (Cuttak)".[135] Rashid Khan took money and broad cloths from the English and also demanded Rs.50.000 from Khemchand, the local merchant.[136] Another governor, Shaista Khan was well known for his economic exploitations.[137] He demanded undue privilege from the merchants, collected money, utilised their ships in carrying out his private trade without any expenses. The above mentioned details show the problems which continued to hinder trade in Orissa.

An important administrative change which caused uncertainty in trade and commerce was the transfer of jurisdictions over Balasore from Orissa to Bengal. On important policy matters pertaining to Orissa decision was to be taken in court of Murshidabad in Bengal. The Mughal Viceroy of Bengal was found to exercise control over Orissa through his deputy. These new developments were not considered to be favourable from the commercial point of view. But now if the merchants were interfered or oppressed, the immediate relief or redress was not to be sought from local officer at Balasore but from the Viceroy of Bengal. By the time such grievances were examined and set aside a lot of time would entail a large amount of loss to the trade they carried on. Of all the European Factors the English alone succeeded in establishing dominance in Orissa's trade and commerce because they had their seat of government at Balasore. But the transfer of the headquarters from Balasore to Hughli as per the decision of the Court of Committees, in the last quarter of the Seventeenth had its adverse influence on the commercial position of Balasore as a port of eminence. Hereafter, the Chief and the Council in the Bay had to stay in Hughli. Though the European ships continued to load and unload at Balasore roadstead, as it was done previously, Hughli was considered "more commodious for receiving orders from all superior officers."[138] Further, with the foundation of Calcutta in 1690, the Hughli port gradually rose into prominence on the Bay. These developments consequently affected the commercial prosperity of the ports of Orissa.

Further, the geographical factor for the decline of trade in the port-towns such as Balasore, Pipli and Hariharpur had to be mentioned because these commercial centres were suffering from accumulation of silt on the mouth of the river. As a result, ports at the mouth of these rivers became unsuitable for ships to come in and this factor is important for the decline. Again Indian traders who belonged mostly to the nobility and state officials of the empire had lost their larger-share in the trade owing to foreign competition. The general impoverishment of the nobility, the political turmoil in the twilight of the Mughal empire and the crisis in the economy resulted in setting a trend of decline in trade. Added to this the English merchants tried in many ways to eliminate both the Indians and other Europeans to establish their monopoly of trade. This brought forth the downfall of indigenous traders in Orissa.

Notes and References

1. Kherachand and Chintaman Shah were the two Gujarati Hindu brokers migrated from Gujarat to Orissa. See, Binod Sankar Das, *Economic History of Orissa,* Calcutta,1978, p. 236.
2. William Foster, *English Factories in India*, London, 1919, (henceforth E.F.I) 1678-1684, New Series, Vol. IV, p. 346.
3. J. Long, *Selections from the unpublished Records of Government, 1748-1767 relating mainly to Social conditions of Bengal,* Calcutta, 1869, Vol. I, p. 250.
4. Journal of Bihar Research Society, (henceforth JBRS), 1954, p. 126.
5. E.F.I., Vol. II, 1622-1623, p. 260.
6. Sebastiao Manrique, *Travels of Fray Sebastiao Manrique*, Oxford, 1927, Vol. I, pp. 440-441.
7. Thomas, Bowery, *A Geographical Account of the Countries Round the Bay of Bengal,* London, 1905, pp. 179-180
8. J.B.R.S., 1954, p. 126; J.N. Sarkar, *Studies in Economic Life in Mughal India,* Delhi, 1975, p. 337.
9. William Bolts, *Considerations on Indian Affairs,* Vol. I, pp. 140-145.
10. Register of papers relating to the English and Dutch East Indies, 1632-1735 in Wilson. C. R., *Early Annals of the English in Bengal,* Calcutta, 1895, Vol. I, pp.381-384 ; *Bengal Past and Present*, Vols. 79-80, Serials 147-148, pp. 34-35.
11. Streynsham Master, *Diaries of Strenyshm Master,1675-1680*, London, 1911, Vol. I, p. 137.
12. E.F.I., 1670-77, New Series, Vol. II, p. 365.
13. Streynsham Master, *op.cit.,* Vol. I, p. 137, *Bengal Past and Present*, Vols. 79-80, Serials 117-148, p. 34 ; Journal of Orissa History, Vol. I, No. 1, Jan. 1980, p. 44.

14. Thomas Bowery, *op.cit.,* pp. 161-163.
15. *Ibid,* pp. 126-127.
16. E.F.I., 1670-77, New Series, Vol. II, p. 365.
17. C.R. Wilson, *op.cit.,* Vol. I, pp. 381-384.
18. Thomas Bowery, *op.cit.,* pp. 152-156 ; E.F.I., 1670-1677, New Series, Vol. II, p. 339.
19. Thomas Bowery, *op.cit.,* p. 155.
20. E F.I., 1670-1677, New Series, Vol. II, p. 331.
21. Kautka (Qjla Katiiki) is situated along the sea coast on both sides of Dharma estuary and extended about 20 miles inland. Its area was 440 square miles. See, Cuttack District Gazetteer, p. 213.
22. J. Long, *op.cit.,* Vol. I, p. 250.
23. William Bolt, *op.cit.,* p. 61 ; E.F.I., 1670-1677, New Series, Vol. II, p. 337.
24. Thomas Bowery, *op.cit.,* pp. 154-155.
25. J.N. Sarkar, *op.cit.,* p. 338.
26. E.F.I., 1670-1677, New Series, Vol. II, p. 339.
27. JBRS, 1954, pp. 123-124.
28. E.F.I., 1670-1677, New Series, Vol. II, p. 358.
29. Ibid, p. 339n. ; Thomas Bowery, *op.cit.,* pp. 152-156.
30. E.F.I., 1651-1654, Vol.IX, pp. 269-270: Francois Valentyn, *Oud en Nieuw Oost Indian*, Amsterdam,1724-1726, Vol. V, Part I, p. 162a ; T.Raychoudhury, *Bengal under Akbar and Jahangir*, Calcutta, 1958, p. 78.
31. E.F.I., 1670-1677, New Series, Vol. II, p. 339.
32. JBRS, 1954, p. 125.
33. W.K. Firminger, (ed.), *Fifth Report from the Select Committee of the HouseofCommons on the Affairs of the East India Company,* July 1812, Vol. II, p. 262.
34. JBRS, 1963, p. 200.
35. Streynsham Master, *op.cit.,* Vol. II, p. 65.

36. The salaries of the second, third and fourth of the Council as fixed by the Company in 1669 were at £ 100, £ 70 and £ 50 respectively. Those of the factors and writers were £ 20 and £ 10 respectively. Love, *Vestiges of old Madras,* 1640-1800, London, Vol. I, p. 452; Wiliam Hedges, *Travels in India*, London, 1793, Vol. II, p. 10.
37. N.K. Sinha, *The Economic History of Bengal*, Calcutta, Vol. I, p. 75; J.B.R.S., 1963, p. 200.
38. Streynsham Master, *op.cit.,* Vol. I, p. 41.
39. E.F.I., 1678-1684, New Series, Vol. IV, p. 198.
40. E.F.I., 1630-1633, Vol. IV, p. XXVII.
41. *Ibid*, pp. 170, 264-265, 268.
42. *Ibid*, pp. 75-76.
43. Streynsham Master, *op.cit.,* Vol. I, pp. 455-456, 477.
44. *Ibid*, p. 74.
45. E.F.I., 1678-1684, New Series, Vol. IV, pp. 220-221, 270-271.
46. E.F.I., 1651-1654, Vol. IX, p. 233.
47. J.S. Mill, *The History of British India,* Vol. II, pp. 21-22; N.K. Sinha, *op.cit.,* Vol. I, pp. 65-68.
48. The prohibited goods for import from India include indigo, calicoes, cinnamon, cloves, cardamom, benjamen, saltpetre, pepper (black or white), nutmegs, maces and cotton yarn ; For export from England, Broad cloth, lead, quick-silver, vermilion, coral and elephants' teeth were included. E.F.I., 1655-1660, Vol. X, pp. 150-151.
49. Streynsham Master, Vol. I, p. 41, Vol. II, p. 89.
50. E.F.I., 1678-1684, New Series, Vol. IV, p. 198.
51. J.B.R.S., 1963, pp. 229-252.
52. J.N. Sarkar, *Studies in Mughal India,* p. 216; Pelsaert in *Jahangir's India* Cambridge, 1925, p.8;

Moreland, W. H., Moreland, *Akbar to Aurangzib,* London, 1923, p.120.Ships used to come during July and September and unloaded themselves. Then being loaded with articles of investment they used to sail in December. See, Proceedings of the Indian History Congress, 16th Session, Waltair, 1953, p. 290.

53. Proceedings of the Indian Historical Records Commission, (henceforth PIHC) Vol. XIV, 1937, p. 92.
54. E.F.I., Vol. VI, 1637-1641, p.335; PIHC, 16th Session, Waltair, 1953, p. 290.
55. PIHC, 16th Session, Waltair, 1953, p. 290; *Bengal Past and Present*, Vols. 79-80, Serials 147-148, 1960, p. 27 ; *Orissa Historical Research Journal*, Vol. VII, Parts 3 and 4, 1958-59, p. 208.
56. J.J. Campos, *History of the Portuguese in Bengal,* London, 1919, p. 115
57. William Bolts, *Considerations on Indian Affairs, particularly respecting the present State of Bengal and its Dependencies,* p. 70.
58. Bindo Sankar Das, *op.cit.,* p. 230.
59. Narasapur is situated (16° 26'N and 81° 42'E) on the Vasista mouth of the Godavari river, 6 miles from the sea. See, Imperial Gazetteer of India, Provincial Series, Madras, I, p. 326.
60. Modapallam is situated (16° 26'N and 81° 42'E) as a suburb of Narasapur.
61. Peter Mundy, *The Travels of Peter Mundy in Europe and Asia,* London, 1914, pp. 154-155; PIHC, 13th Session, Nagpur, 1950, p. 212.
62. Thomas Bowery, *op.cit.,* pp. 231-232.
63. E.F.I., Vol. X, 1655-1660, p. 297.
64. *Ibid.*
65. *Ibid,* Vol. IX, 1651-1654, p. 95.
66. Streynsham Master, *op.cit.* Vol. II, pp. 65-67.

67. *Bengal Past and Present*, Vols. 79-80, Serials, 147-148, 1960, p. 27, J. Long *J. Selections from the unpublished records of Government relating mainly to social conditions of Bengal,* Vol. I, p. 250,
68. E F.I., Vol. XII, 1665-1667, p. 138.
69. C.R. Wilson, *op.cit.,* Vol. II, Part I, pp.15-16.
70. Streynsham Master, *op.cit.,* Vol. II, pp. 67-68.
71. J. Long, *op.cit,* Vol. I, p. 250.
72. Junk is a large ship used by the Chinese and Malay sailors in the Southeast Asian waters.
73. E.F.I., Vol. III, 1624-1629, p. 316.
74. The ship was caught in the monsoon and reached within 15 or 16 leagues (45 or 48 miles) of Masulipatnam where it was unloaded and a part of the goods were transported to Masulipatnam. The remaining goods were loaded in a pinnace hired from the Danes. But the pinnace was turned over due to storm and all the goods were lost. E.F.I., Vol. V, 1634-1636, p. 43.
75. E.F.I., Vol. VI, 1637-1642, pp. 65-66.
76. T. Raychoudhury, *Jan Company in Coromandel,* The Hague, 1962, p. 67.
77. Records of Fort St. George, (hereafter RFSG) *Letters to Fort St. George, 1703*, Madras, 1924, Vol. VIII, p.133.
78. E.F.I., Vol. V, 1634-36, p. 43, *Pagoda* is a gold coin of South India. Its local name was *varaha* or *hun.* Its average value was three and a half of Akbar's rupees. See, Moreland, *India at the Death of Akbar,* pp. 52-53. But T. Raychoudhury, holds that the average value of one *pagoda* was four to four and half rupees. See Raychoudhury, *Jan Company op.cit.,* p. 224. Here conversion from *pagoda* to rupee has been made taking *one pagoda* equivalent to three and a half rupees.
79. Streynsham Master, *op.cit,* Vol. II, p. 169.
80. C.R. Wilson, *op.cit.,* Vol. II, Part I, p. 41,

81. Streynsham Master, *op.cit.,* Vol. II, pp. 70-71.
82. RFSG, *Letter to Fort St. George, 1686-1687*, p. 58.
83. Alexander Hamilton, *A New Account of the East Indies,* London, 1930, Vol. I, p. 203. Schorer's account in W. H. Moreland's *Relations of Golconda,* p. 54.
84. T. Raychoudhury, *op.cit.,* p. 95.
85. E.F.I., Vol. II, 1622-1623, pp. 259-260.
86. T. Raychoudhury, *op.cit.,* pp.105-106.
87. Schorer's account in W. H. Moreland's *Relations of Golconda,* p. 54.
88. Ghoraghat is situated (250° 15'N and 89° 18'E) on the west bank of the Karotaya river.
89. Khwajah Abul Hasan, the brother of Nur Jahan was appointed *divan* of Bengal in 1908 and he had a retainer named Abdul Latif the son of Abdullah Abbasi, a resident of Ahmedabad. Abdul Latif accompanied his master in his journey to Bengal and kept a diary of this journey See, *Bengal Past and Present*, January-June, 1928, p. 145.
90. Coracius Indica and these are a kind of sterling.
91. Sebastiao Manrique, op.cit., Vol. I, pp. 440-441.
92. F. Pelsaert, *op.cit.,* pp. 4n., 6.
93. It means either cotton wool or cotton cloth.
94. Ceaser Frederick in Samuel Purchas, *His Pilgrims*, London, 1910, Part II, pp.171.
95. Sebastiao Maurique, *op.cit.,* Vol. I, pp. 52, 56.
96. W.H. Moreland, *From Akbar to Aurangzeb, op.cit.,* p. 86.
97. In 1676 arrangements were made by the English authorities at Balasore with the captains of the English ships for carrying rice to St. Helena in Africa, See, Streynsham Master, *op.cit.*, Vol. I, pp. 50-51; Vol. II, p. 73).
98. E.F.I., Vol. VII, 1642-1645, pp. 65-66, William Hedges, *op.cit.,* Vol. III, p. CLXXXI.

99. E.F.I., Vol. VII, 1642-1645, pp. 206-207.
100. *Ibid,* Vol. IX, 1651-1654, p. 183.
101. W.H. Moreland, *From Akbar to Aurangzeb, op.cit.,* pp. 76-80.
102. T. Raychoudhury, *op.cit.,* p.167.
103. *Last* is a unit of weight, current in this period in Orissa.
104. F. Valentyn, *op.cit.,* Vol.V, Part I, pp. 178-179.
105. Ralph Fitch, *Travels of Ralph Fitch,* in William Foster, *Early Travels in India,* London, 1910, p. 26.
106. W.H. Moreland, *From Akbar to Aurangazeb, op.cit.,* p. 57.
107. Alexander Hamilton, *op.cit.,* Vol. I, pp. 192-193.
108. A. Raynal, *op.cit.,* Vol. I, p. 419.
109. M. Husain, *The Rehala of Ibn Batuta, op.cit.,* p. 201.
110. Thomas Bowery, *op.cit,* pp. 179-180.
111. Streynsham Master, *op.cit.,* Vol. II, p. 236.
112. William Hedges, *op.cit.,* Vol. I, p. 95.
113. Alexander Hamilton, *op.cit,* Vol. I, pp. 192-193; A. Raynal, *op.cit.,* Vol. I, p. 419.
114. *Proceedings of the Indian Historical Records Commission,* December 1942, pp.86, 88-89, based on two letters of Lawrence D'Costa, the Dutch Agent at Balasore to Issac Fistingh, Governor of the Council at Chinsura dated 23 October, 1787 and 10 October, 1788.
115. Instructions to Mr. Stanley for the Maldives from the Court 20 Sept.1682. Letter Book No. 7, quoted in Thomas Bowery, *op.cit.,* pp. 218n.-219n.
116. John Marshall, *John Marshall in India,* London, 1927, pp. 415, 419; Thomas Bowery, *op.cit.,* pp. 200, 219.
117. Pinak Ranjan Mahapatra, *Some Aspects of Economic Life of Orissa,* Bhubaneshwar, 1984, pp. 175-176.

118. F. Pelsaert, *op.cit.,* p. 8 (for export from Pipli), Cesaer Frederick in Purchas, *His Pilgrimes,* Vol. II, 1711 (For export from Hijli).
119. Thomas Bowery, *op.cit,* p. 247.
120. *Ibid,* pp. 179-180, R.K. Mukherjee, *A History of Indian Shipping and Maritime Activities,* p. 234.
121. Journal of Bihar and Orissa Research Society, Vol. XI, p. 126. PIHC, 1953, p. 293.
122. Streynsham Master, *op.cit.,* Vol. II, p. 256.
123. F. Pelsaert, *op.cit.,* p. 8.
124. T. Raychoudhury, *op.cit.,* p. 168 ; Sir George Birdwood, *Report on the Old Records of the India Office, op.cit.,* p. 190.
125. Thomas Bowery, *op.cit.,* pp. 179-180.
126. Streynsham Master, *op.cit.,* Vol. II, p. 236.
127. Thomas Bowery, *op.cit.,* pp. 179-180.
128. *Ibid*, pp. 180,208.
129. Thomas Bowery, *op.cit*, pp. 179-180 ; J.H. Sarkar, *op.cit.,* p. 320
130. J.N. Sarkar, *op.cit.,* p. 320 ; P.R. Mahapatra, *op.cit.*, p. 247.
131. E.F.I., Vol. II, 1670-1677, New Series, p. XXVIII; Journal of Orissan History, Vol. I, No. 1, 1980, p. 46.
132. Alfred Martineau, *Memoirs de Francois Martin,* Paris, 1910, pp. 19-20.
133. *Bengal Past and Present*, Vols. 79-80, Serials, 147-148, 1960, p. 30.
134. E.F.I., Vol. II, 1670-1677, New Series, p. XXVIII; Journal of Orissan History, Vol. I, No. 1, 1980, p. 46.
135. *Ibid.*
136. E.F.I., Vol. II, 1670-1677, New Series, pp. 338-339.
137. Streynsham Master, *op.cit.,* Vol. II, pp. 80-81.
138. C.R. Wilson, *op.cit,* Vol. I, p. 32 ; J.N. Sarkar, *op.cit.,* p. 341.

6

Indian Commercial Intermediaries and the French East India Company in Coromandel during the Seventeenth and Eighteenth Centuries

B. Krishnamurthy

The French East India Company was established in 1664 to foster direct trade with India on spices and textiles. The first French factory on the Indian soil was opened in Surat in 1668. In due course of time, the French had successfully developed a chain of factories throughout the Western and Eastern Coasts of India. The fact that they could procure cheaper, but at the same time, exquisite varieties of textiles which could be easily disposed off in Europe as well as in the South East Asian markets, prompted the French to venture into the Coromandel Coast.[1] They had settled down at Masulipatnam (1669), Pondicherry (1673-74), Kaveripatnam (1688, but in early 1690s, the French had to abandon it), Yanam (1723) and Karaikal (1738).

Lack of knowledge of local languages and customs as well as inadequate funds at their disposal to invest in their commercial enterprise, forced the French to rely on intermediaries, who were naturally the indigenous merchant community of these localities.[2] These intermediaries have played fascinatingly pluralistic roles: as political intermediaries by providing access to political power and administrative hierarchies in the States where the French were seeking to operate; as middlemen in the world of commerce by bringing the French Company and the actual producers and manufacturers of the local merchandise, which enthused the French to come to India braving all the perils of the sea; and as socio-cultural intermediaries, who were utilized by the

French to assimilate a section of the local population with them on account of socio, religious and cultural ties.[3]

This paper confines itself to the commercial intermediaries, who assisted the French Company in its economic activities. The collaboration between the French Company officials and the locals in private trade too has been kept out of the scope of the present paper.

The commercial intermediaries served the French Company at two stages. The *Mudaliar* (*Courtier* or the Chief *dubash*) served as a bridge between the Company and the local merchants. His was the highest post for which any Indian was eligible or entitled to under the French organization of trade in India. It was expected that by using the *courtier* the costs would be reduced and a greater local knowledge of the market would be brought into play, in favour of the Company. The import - export business of the Company was canalized through the hands of the *courtier*. Whether the Company decided to procure the local merchandise for export or intended to dispose of their European goods, the *courtier* was intimated. He swung into action and sent for the local merchants residing in the French colonies as well as far and wide in the hinterland region.

The most difficult and challenging part of the Courtier's duty was fixing the prices of the merchandise to the utmost satisfaction of both the Company and the merchants. It called for the use all the persuasive power at his disposal to arrive at a reasonable and acceptable price. His failure to satisfy the French Company in this regard would even cost him his post. Thanappa Mudaliar, who happened to be the first native *courtier* of the French East India Company in Pondicherry, was unceremoniously removed and replaced by Nainiappa Pillai as *courtier* in 1708, due to his failure in convincing the local merchants to purchase coral at the price demanded by the French.[4] Ananda Ranga Pillai too alludes to this episode and points out that the dealings of the Company with the merchants as a group rather than as individuals complicated the process of price fixation further.[5] An enterprising Governor like Dupleix tried to impose price of merchandise according to his will either by cajoling the *courtier* and the merchants or by threatening them with utter ruin in case they did not comply with him.

Though all the commercial activities of the Company was canalized through their hands, the *courtier* was not allowed to supply the merchandise to the Company on his own, either directly or indirectly, as this was considered highly detrimental to the interest of the Company.[6] The French authorities even discouraged the private trading activities of the *courtier* in food grains, lest he would use his power and position to enrich himself by unfair means.[7]

The *courtier* stood surety for the advance paid to the merchants and for the proper and timely delivery of the goods. For all the trouble he had to undertake in the service of the Company, the *courtier* was generally given 3/4 per cent of small commission on all purchases, by way of emoluments.[8] However, Ananda Ranga Pillai mentions that the *courtier* by contract received 2000 *pagodas* in return for the service rendered by him to the Company.[9] Any how, the aura and prestige linked with the post attracted the wealthy and capable native hands towards the post and actually, severe and perpetual rivalry between two families, one of Mudaliars and the other of Pillais, could be witnessed to attain this coveted post in Pondicherry.[10]

In the second stage, the native merchants served as the intermediaries between the Company and the actual producers and manufacturers. Lack of funds as well as their inability to approach each and every small producer individually and directly forced the French to resort to this device. The French at Pondicherry, like the English at Madras and the Dutch at Pulicat and elsewhere, provided a considerable part of their Company's investment through a body of merchants organized on a joint-stock basis. François Martin mentions about the formation of such a Company at Pondicherry in the last decades of the Seventeenth century.[11]

Later, during the early years of the eighteenth century the French documents mention about *marchands de la Compagnie* (Company merchants) with whom contracts for piece-goods were signed year after year. Ananda Ranga Pillai even mentions about contracts between the French Company and *la Compagnie des anciens marchands* (the merchants of the Old Company) during 1736-42, thereby implying the existence of a new Company.[12]

The French Company concentrated on individual merchants also for the supply of merchandise, especially textiles. The names of Soukourama (Sungurama Chetti ?), Sungu Seshachala Chetti, Andiappa of Porto Novo, Ananda Ranga Pillai and others appear quite often in the French records as the supplier's of piece-goods to the Company. In 1736, the French Company had ordered for 1471 bales of cloth, the value of which, calculated at the third class rate amounted approximately to 1,20,491 1/2 *pagodas* from Sunguvar Seshachala Chetti and his brother, Lakshmipathi Chetti.[13] In July 1737, the *Conséil Supérieur* signed a contract with Sungurama Chetti for the supply of 1650 bales of piece-goods.[14]

Regarding the mode of procurement of the Indian merchandise, especially textiles, throwing some light on the *dadni* or the system of advances, which was widely prevalent during the Seventeenth and Eighteenth century India is quite obligatory. Under this system contracts were formulated with the native merchants - individuals as well as those who have organized into a joint-stock Company – to supply a stipulated quantity of certain varieties of textiles, the pattern, quality and price being specified.[15] The factors bargained on rates with the merchants and fixed the date of delivery of the supplies at the convenient time for both the parties. Part of the contract amount was paid as advances to the merchants in money as well as in merchandise imported from Europe on finalizing the deal, while the rest was paid only after the delivery of the supplies and their actual inspection and sorting out as acceptable and unacceptable.[16] These merchants, in their turn, approached the actual producers and manufacturers individually, either personally or through their agents, offered them raw materials, victuals as well as little amount as advance and collected their products in due course of time and delivered them to the companies at appropriate time.

While giving contracts for the supply of merchandise, an organization of merchants was always preferred for individual merchants. Generally, the French Company contracted with individuals or indulged in spot purchase, only in case the Company merchants were not in a position to supply required quality and quantity of merchandise through their organization. This was to a greater extent due to avoid bad debts, which created problems between the French Company and the natives. Moreover, it was felt that the advance to be paid to the association of merchants, who among themselves used to pool necessary resources, would be restricted to bare minimum, while in the case of individuals it was next to be impossible.

In case of default in supply or arrears out-standing against the native merchants, they were denied of future contracts. In 1739, Dumas agreed to give a contract for the supply of 2,500 bales of piece-goods to Sungu Seshachala Chetti. Later, when he came to know that Chetti owed the Company 43,000 *pagodas,* Dumas ordered that Seshachala would be given the contract only when the latter paid back the arrears. However, with the complicity of Dumas, Pedro Kanagaraya Mudali, the Courtier, intervened in favour of Seshachala and made good his due to the Company through financial help and by manipulation of accounts and got the contract awarded to him.[17] During the time of Dupleix defaulters and those who tried to cheat the Company by running away into interior after taking some advance from the latter were severely dealt with. Still, the problem of bad debt continued to be a headache for the French factors.[18]

The local merchants served the Company in the disposal of the imported European goods as well. The French records mention Sungurama Chertti, Tiruviti Balu Chetti, Chankarabary (Sankara Pariek ?), a noted merchant and *shroff* of the Nawab of Arcot and several others as the buyers of silver brought by the French Company. Whenever, the Company had some thing to sell, the *courtier* engaged his men to assemble all the native merchants and he served as an intermediary in the fixation of price and in finalising the terms of payment. It seems the local merchants used to join hands and always tried to buy goods from the French at a reduced rate. In 1708, when the Company tried to dispose off their coral at a higher rate, the merchants quoted for some lesser amount and passed on note among them to prevent others buying it as per the French demand.[19] The broad-cloth was sold at auction and cleared off at reduced prices, quite often to avoid its total damage and complete loss.[20] The auction sale of the Company was well-advertised among the native merchants by way of notices in different languages and exhibited in various places like the fort, the cloth market, church and the court house.[21]

The French Company was quite considerate towards the merchants who were their collaborators in their import and export trade. They were over anxious to satisfy them and used to give additional amount over and above the contract price, on true as well as pretension of the merchants of bad times and consequent scarcity, rise in the prices of the material and of labour charges. In a particular occasion in 1731-32, a dispute in the weavers' caste at Pondicherry, forced the merchants to go far a field for cotton stuff and so they demanded for more than contract price. The *Conséil Supérieur* in its anxiety to please them increased its payments by as much as fifteen percent on every item. Moreover, they agreed to pay 450 *pagodas* more towards transport, transit duties and other additional expenses that the merchants had to incur.[22] While disposing the imported items also, the French used to offer lenient payment conditions with handsome discounts to the merchants.

However, the home authorities were not quite happy about the role of intermediaries in the import and export trade of the French Company in India and they wanted to do away with them in a phased manner. They advised the *Conséil Supérieur* to instruct some young Frenchmen in the local languages, so that the middleman might be replaced in due course.[23] But, the efforts of the *Conséil* and the gratuity offered, failed to encourage the youngsters to take the trouble of learning the native tongues. As such, the French Company's efforts to do away with the native intermediaries failed miserably.

Besides their role as suppliers and buyers of merchandise to and from the French Company respectively, the native merchants collaborated with the French in their Indo-European and inter-Asian trade as well. It seems that the native merchants have taken share even in the French Company's Indo-European trade. In 1731, Kanagaraya Mudali and Sungurama Chetti have sent merchandise worth of 401 *pagodas*, 5 *fanams* and 32 *casus* in the Company ship 'Lys' to France. The Company wrote to the *Conséil Supérieur* to give them back the principal with the usual five percent interest per year and settle their accounts. But, in its eagerness to safeguard the interests of the merchants, *Conséil Supérieur* offered them the principal along with 200 *pagodas*, 14 *fanams* and 48 *casus* on the calculation that their merchandise would have fetched at least fifty per cent profit.[24]

While the other companies, as corporate bodies never ventured into joint trips with the natives, the French Company had really taken a fancy for them. Its poor financial condition and its inability to monopolise inter-Asian trade, must have prompted the French to resort to joint ventures. Due to the peculiar circumstances under which the French Company found itself, it had engaged in partnership ventures with prominent Indian merchants living in their colonies as well as in some coastal trading centres like Porto Novo and Cuddalore. From the beginning, the French Company collaborated with the native merchants in the coastal and inter-Asian trade (*Le commerce d'Inde en Inde*) which proved to be mutually beneficial. The home authorities too encouraged the *Conséil Supérieur* of Pondicherry through their letter dated 7 December 1737 to take shared interest in the Commercial enterprises of the natives according to their discretion, bur not exceeding half and not less than one sixth.[25] Accordingly, the *Conséil Supérieur* decided through its deliberation on 14 September 1738, to have a share of at least 1/4th in both large and small business ventures of the privateers and in turn, advised the Local Councils of Mahe and Chandernagore to emulate its example. The French records as well as Ananda Ranga Pillai's Diary are replete with several joint ventures between the French Company and the native merchants. For instance, in July 1738, the French Company had shared interest in a trip to Acheh, organized by the merchants of Porto Novo and also gave them a loan of 15,000 *pagodas* at 16 per cent interest.[26]

The inter-Indies trade was generally conducted in the vessels belonging to the Company. On a particular occasion, when the native merchants were not in a position to set out a business trip for want of a sea-worthy vessel, the French Company came forward to sell its own ship for 6,000 pagodas, with the promise that it would take it back on its return for 4,000 *pagodas*.[27] However, in 1734, as Company's ships were not available, the authorities at Pondicherry decided to send some merchandise belonging to their Company to Manila, in a ship named 'Chankerbary', probably owned by Sankara Parekh (?). It is interesting to note that these goods were dispatched on the name of Pedro, the Courtier, and not on the account of the Company.[28] Again, the brigantine *le Dauphine* belonging to Kanagaraya was often employed by the French in their country trading ventures.

The French emerged as protectors of the Porto Novo shipping, which was quite extensive and pathetically vulnerable to European attacks and harassments. When the merchants of Porto Novo were penalized by the Dutch or the Danes, for not taking pass ports from them or refused of passes due to enmity, the French gave them protection under their flag and pressed into service French sailors and soldiers to protect their business ventures.[29] In the same way, during times of war with their European competitors the French used to send out their vessels under the flag of their native collaborators. The merchant mariners also helped the French Company in transporting the money and merchandise from one counter to the other and also in communicating among different settlements.[30]

However, the French too tried to regulate and restrict the native shipping through the system of passports. The local ship-owners and merchants approached the French for safe-conduct assurances, especially during war times and on the occasion of the menacing presence of their royal navy in the Eastern waters. The passes were generally issued without much fuss, but, especially during the times of war with either the English or the Dutch, the pass-seekers had to bind themselves not to carry any goods belonging to their adversaries.[31] Moreover, the French tried to restrict the nature, and amount of goods carried to particular places in the interests of their own commerce, but not with success to a greater extent.

The French had to import in to India metals like gold, silver, copper and lead to run their business. The prices of these metals too fluctuated like any other merchandise. During the first half of the Eighteenth century, the price of silver per *ser* fluctuated from six *pagodas* to seven *pagodas* and seven *fanams.*[32] Moreover, in converting the silver into local coins, the French Company lost six to seven per cent as conversion charges.[33] At times, local conditions made it very difficult to dispose off their silver profitably.

To avoid all these troubles. and losses, the French began to mint gold *pagodas*, silver *fanams* and copper *casus* from 1699 onwards, without getting due authorisation from the local rulers.[34] All their effort to secure the required permission from the Nawab of Arcot and his masters in Hyderabad and Delhi, failed miserably till mid 1730s. In September 1736, the French had obtained from the Nawab Dost Ali Khan the privilege to mint in Pondicherry the Arcot rupees, the silver coins that enjoyed a wider currency in circulation throughout the Eastern Coast.

In the successful negotiations with the Nawab and his officials, Courtier Kanagaraya played a prominent role.[35] He even maintained constant correspondence with Imam Sahib, a higher official in Arcot, to achieve this goal. The right to mint silver rupees in Pondicherry had not only promoted the image of the French Company but also brought some revenue. It was computed that this privilege would secure annual benefit of 150,000 to 200,000 rupees to the Company.[36] Moreover, the native merchants too got their silver coined in their Pondicherry mint on paying certain charges and this was an additional source of income to the Company.[37]

On Kanagaraya Mudali's representation, Dumas, the then Governor of Pondicherry, decided in favour of conducting the mint there through the merchants, as was the case with Nawab of Arcot's mint in Alambarai. Pedro had also suggested the name of Sungu Seshachala Chetty for the post. Accordingly, the Governor and his Council resolved to appoint Seshachala as the merchant-in-charge of the Pondicherry mint. Tiruvedi Balu Chetti, Gunturi Venkanna Chetti, and Kanagaraya Mudali too involved in the work related to the mint. Three shares were allotted to Seshachala, one each to Balu Chetti, and Venkanna and one-third to Kanagaraya. Moreover, the latter got one half of a rupee for every thousand rupees coined in the Pondicherry mint.[38]

Besides their commercial enterprises the French Company had also indulged in revenue collection in the territories under their jurisdiction. To ensure a fixed and assured income, they have resorted to the *ijara* system or the tax-farming. Those native merchants who have associated with them in their commercial activities, have entered into tax-farming also.[39] In 1702, the Company merchants as a corporate body took to farming of the sale of tobacco and betel at the rate of 200 *pagodas* per year for two years.[40]

The Courtiers of the French Company at Pondicherry like Guruvappillai, Kanagaraya Mudali and Ananda Ranga Pillai took to tax-farming, personally or through their agents, for such farms like the land revenue collection, customs and transit duty collection, tobacco and betel nut farm, arrack farm, salt farm, farm of money changing and of several other heads. For instance, in June 1739, Kanagaraya along with Mouteya (Muthiya ?), the resident of Karaikal, took the lease of five villages around Karaikal for an annual rent of 4600 *pagodas.*[41] It seems that Pedro Mudaliar was also collecting the salt tax at Vanjiyur, in the Karaikal region in the early 1740s.[42] Moreover, the *courtier* had to stand surety for other native bidders for prompt payment.[43] He was also expected to persuade the native renters to pay the Company according to its needs- on scarcity for food-grains to pay the rent in kind or otherwise.[44] The *courtier*'s guarantee for timely and full payment of the amount thus fixed was the most essential part of such a contract between the Company and the locals. Some of the prominent members of the merchant community too indulged in this lucrative enterprise. Quite often these lessees entered into partnership with European officials and settlers or sublet their vast network of farms to the latter.

On 15 September 1738, the *Conséil Supérieur* granted license for the retail sale of arrack, Vichy water, red and white wine to Kariappa, a native merchant, providing that anyone guilty of illicit sale would have his stocks confiscated in addition to a fine of 100 *pagodas*. In Pondicherry and Karikal the exchange of rupees was farmed out to the native bidders and in the former place it fetched about 500 *pagodas* per year around 1706.[45] In 1728, at the request of the local merchants and to attract others from inland, the exchange of rupees was left open for all those who were interested.[46] But, it seems that the farming of exchange of coins was resumed in due course. At Karaikal it was farmed out to one Swaminatha Chetty for three years at 210 *pagodas* per year in 1739.[47]

As the finances of the Company were always in doldrums both at home and in India, the French had to rely many a times on the native financiers and merchants for conducting their business as well as to maintain their commercial presence. In this predicament too, the *courtiers* always came in handy and there were several occasions when they had deposited certain amount with or furnished loans to the Company, which enabled the French to run their show unhindered. For example, André Moutiapa, father of Canagaraya, had deposited a sum of 1,000 Pulicat *pagodas* with the Company on 15 November 1701. This amount remained with the company for about twenty long years and in April 1720, on a claim from Pedro, 550 current *pagodas* were given to him by way of the principal and interest and the account was settled.[48]

When the French were in dire need of funds in August 1739, Kanagaraya offered 10,000 pagodas at eight per cent annual interest.[49] Again, in October of the same year, when the Company expected some additional loan to enable it to strike a deal with the ruler of Tanjavur on the transfer of Karaikal region to the French, Pedro offered 3,000 *pagodas* at the same rate of interest.[50] From this instance, we can infer that Kanagaraya not only helped the French Company to run their business, but also assisted it in ventures that would augment its resources and revenues.

The French had successfully developed a network of factories and trading centres both in the Western and Eastern Coasts of India. Some of their production centres of goods were established in the hinterland. Quite naturally, the French had to face a lot of problems in communicating among themselves and in dispatching money and materials from their head quarters in Pondicherry to other factories situated in different parts of India. Even in solving these problems, Kanagaraya proved himself to be of considerable assistance to the French Company. For instance, in 1736, the authorities of Pondicherry sent some funds to their Masulipatnam counter through his brigantine.

Thus, the intermediary merchant community turned out to be quite indispensable to the French Company authorities in the Coromandel Coast. The chaotic political situation of the Carnatic region in the absence of a strong central power and the competition from other European trading organisations, which vied with each other to monopolise the Indian commercial scene, forced the French to understand the futility of seeking the agents and the sources of supply of local merchandise from far-off production and manufacturing centres in the hinterland. Moreover, they realised that the presence of wealthy merchants in their colonies would enhance their prestige as well as the revenue from their territorial possessions. As such, the French invited the local merchant community from Madras, Porto Novo and other places, to come and settle in their colonies. Again, the French tried to attract the weaver and artisan communities as well to their colonies, so that their dependency on hinterland production centres would be eliminated. To attract both the merchants and artisans, the French offered them land to come and settle down in Pondicherry.[51] Again, the French authorities offered freedom of trade and worship to the settlers to attract men of different faiths to their colonies,

The merchant community, proved to be of great service to the French Company and both found that their collaboration was mutually beneficial. At least, during the times of peace, the merchants felt that the French Company organization was quite conducive to their growth and welfare. This system allowed them to derive income from several portfolios of fiscal management like production, import and export, shipping, money lending and chaining, mint management and tax farming.

There were several men of considerable wealth among the *courtiers* and merchants, who were associated with the economic activities of the French Company.. Some among them like Sungurama have also owned ships and employed them especially in Coastal and inter-Asian trade. As mentioned earlier, Kanagaraya Mudali owned a brigantine *le Dauphin.*[52] Ananda Ranga Pillai's sloop, *Anandapuravi* was sent to Colombo in 1740, and returned in 1742 with his agents Pir Marakkayar and Muttukumara Pillai. Ananda Ranga Pillai mentions about a vessel named, *Chinna Sungurama*, most probably owned by Sungurama and his family members.[53] *Chankarabari*, which was engaged in the Manila trade in the 1730s seems to be owned by Sankara Pariek.

Besides wealth, their association with the French Company had brought new power and status to the intermediary merchant community. The French conferred on the Courtiers titles and awarded them with medals, by way of recognizing the meritorious services rendered by them to the Company, as well as to invest the office of Courtier with a perceived authority in the eyes of the other Indians.[54] One among them, Guruva Pillai was given the Cross of St. Lazar and he was the first Indian to get such a honour. On the occasion of receiving the *parvana*, which allowed the French to mint silver rupees at Pondicherry, Kanagaraya Mudali was honoured in the open council with a medal bearing the figure of the King of France on one side and the Company's coat of arms on the other, along with a gold chain, for the part played by him during the negotiations with the Nawab of Arcot in that connection. The gift of palanquin inlaid with ivory too was made to him.[55] In 1744, even during the time of Kanagaraya Mudali as the *courtier*, Ananda Ranga Pillai was presented with torches by Dupleix in the assembly of leading caste-men and in his honour a salute of seven guns was fired.[56]

By Ranga Pillai's time the office of the *courtier* had acquired considerable pomp and station, in addition to the real power it possessed earlier. Dupleix had delegated some of his powers to him and the latter utilized it in furtherance of the interests of his master and of his own position. He was considered both by the French as well as by the natives as *'le chef des Malabar'* (Chief of the Tamils). He was holding several villages like Thiruvandipuram, Thirumangalam, and Nerkunnam as *jagirs*.[57] Permission to ride on horseback or in a palanquin in the fort area and to move around with all paraphernalia like white flag and umbrella, the right to wear slippers in the Governor's presence and to military honours like gun salute on ceremonial occasions, as at wedding or funeral, were given to him.[58]

Some of these honours were conferred on the Company merchants as well. The occasion of the signing of contract was celebrated with firing of eleven guns and the *courtier*, Chief of the Peons and the merchants were presented with broad-cloth.[59] Twelve merchants of Pondicherry were presented with gold chains in public with usual fanfare in May 1738 by the Company to show its appreciation of their services.[60] Moreover, the French authorities and the native merchants mutually used to offer and take costly presents on ceremonial occasions. However, in conferring these honours and privileges, the French were keen in not hurting the traditional rights of the Right and Left hand caste men. Elements of traditional honours were added with essentially European innovations like gun salute.

To maintain their status and gain popular acclaim the native merchant community engaged in philanthropic activities. Thanappa Mudaliar alias Lazaro de Motta, the first *courtier* of the French Company at Pondicherry, had spent considerable portion of his wealth in building St. Lazaro's church at

Pondicherry. Later, Kanagaraya Mudali had built a church and hosted a lavish dinner for all castes on its blessing day. Some of the wealthy Hindu merchants of Pondicherry donated a huge amount for the renovation and upkeep of the temple at Singirikoil.[61] Ranga Pillai himself had spent considerable portion of his wealth in building and renovating temples and in patronizing art and letters. Thiruvengada Pillai, Seshachala Chetti and other merchants of means provided for *choultries* or rest-houses for the gratuitous accommodation of travelers.

But, everything had not gone well between the French Company and the intermediary merchant community. Though the French were generally generous with the native merchants living in their colonies, they used to restrict them from trading with their European adversaries, especially during war times. They were also prevented from having any commercial relations with the interlopers of different nationalities and with the factors of the Ostend and the Swedish East India Companies.[62]

Though the French authorities offered freedom of trade and worship to the settlers to attract men of different faiths to their colonies, the religious men created a situation in which non-Christian ways of life and worship were impracticable, thereby detracting the Hindu merchants and artisans from coming and settling at Pondicherry.[63] Moreover, the Jesuits insisted on giving the office of the courtier to the native Christians alone. But, the Company authorities found that such a step would be taken only at the cost of its interests. By way of compromise, they created the post of co-*mudaliar* and while Nainiappa Pillai and Thiruvengadam Pillai were *courtiers*, Savari Pillai and Guruva Pillai served as co-*mudaliars*, respectively.[64]

Later, Dupleix tried his best to implore the local merchants to leave Madras and to come and settle under the French flag. Neither his cajoling nor his threat that their properties would be confiscated made them to abandon Madras and to shift their residences to Pondicherry. Thus, the influence that the Jesuits missionaries held with the Company administration nullified all the positive steps taken by the French Governors to attract merchants of means to their colonies and enrich them by their economic enterprises.

As the French were late comers in the Indian commercial scene and also their economic condition was always precarious, (it is generally said, with much truth, about the French Company officials as those who reveled in borrowed money), the part played by the *courtiers* of Pondicherry was especially predominant and fascinatingly dynamic. Again, it may be observed that the service of Pedro Kanagaraya Mudaliar as *courtier,* the highest post, which any Indian could aspire for under the French organisation of trade in India, for more than two decades, is a record of sort, as pointed out by his one-time rival and successor, Ananda Ranga Pillai. *Courtiers* like Kanagaraya and Ananda Ranga accumulated considerable wealth through their multi-faceted financial portfolio management as a merchant, as a ship owner, as a tax farmer, and as an administrator of mint.

Moreover, the French Company provided the native merchant community several avenues of accumulating wealth like participation in the import-export trade, shipping, money lending and changing, tax-farming and minting. Being a commercially and economically weak power, the French Company had to co-operate with the locals to get its business going. The merchants derived at most benefit of this 'enterprise in participation' and they have grown up in wealth, status and ceremonial power. Especially, during the times of peace, the merchant community in general and its native officials in particular, felt that the French Company organisation was conducive to their growth and well-being. On the economic growth and well being of the native merchant community under the patronage of the French Company, one can very well observe the transformation of a merchant-capitalist into a portfolio-capitalist. However, the religious intolerance of the French system proved to be insurmountable hindrance between the company and the merchants for all-out co-operation and that certainly dimmed the scope of any meaningful and mutually beneficial joint ventures of great consequences.

Notes and References

1. François Martin, *Memoires de François Martin*, Alfred Martineau (ed.), Pondicherry, 1931-34, tome II, p. 270.

2. *Bibliothèque Nationale Nouvelles Acquisitions Français* 9227, f.2; Martin's *Memoire*, tome II, p.201. Martin clearly admits: *"Nous étions obliges, pour faire quelque chose, d'engager de gens de la terre avec nous, n'ayant pas de fonds pour agir de nous-mêmes sans assistance".*
3. S. Arasaratnam,"Indian Intermediaries on the Trade and Administration of the French East India Company in the Coromandel 1670-1760" in *Les Relations Historique et Culturelles entre la France et l'Inde XVIIe – XXe Siécles, Association Historique Internationale de l'Ocean Indian, Archives Departmentales de la Réunion, Le Chaudron-97490, Sainte Clotil de France,* 1987, pp. 133-134.
4. *Procès-verbaux des deliberation du Consèil Supérieur de Pondichéry* (hereafter C.S.P.V.) *tome* 1, (1701-1723), *Société de l'Histoire de l' Inde Française*, Pondicherry, 1911-1914, pp. 66-67.
5. *Ananda Ranga Pillai's Diary* (henceforth *Pillai's Diary*) tr. and ed. By J.F. Price and K.Rangachari, New Delhi, 1985, reprint, Vol. 4, pp. 141-142.
6. *Correspondence du Consèil Supérieur de Pondichéry avec le Consèil de Chandernagor* (henceforth *Correspondence avec Chandernagor*), Pondicherry, 1915-18, tome 1, p.65.
7. *Pillai's Diary,* Vol. 4, pp. 247-248.
8. *Correspondence avec Chandernagor, tome* 1, p.110. However, Blancard in his *Manuel du commerce des Indes Orientales et de la China*, Paris, 1806, p.247, maintains that the Courtier got two per cent commission on all purchases, which was known as *'coustumade'*, but not received anything from his master or from other Europeans.
9. *Pillai's Diary,* vol.4, p. 156.
10. Several references in the diary of Ananda Ranga Pillai clearly show this rivalry between these families, one of native Christians and so patronized by the Church and the other of native Hindus, and so could not gain the support of the religious authorities. As mentioned elsewhere, the missionaries intrigued to offer the post only to a native Christian so that their missionary work would gain official support. This factor too added to the heat of rivalry for the post.
11. Martin's *Memoire*, *tome* 2, pp. 444-453, 466,491; *tome* 3, p. 60.

12. C.S.P.V., *tome* 3, p.98; *Pillai's Diary,* Vol. 1, pp. 5, 38, 117, 189.
13. *Pillai's Diary,* Vol. 1, pp. 4-5.
14. C.S.P.V., *tome* 3, p.98.
15. Generally sample-patterns sent out by the Home authorities were given to the merchants to be distributed among the weavers and the printers and painters of cloth, who were expected to follow them while preparing the stuff for the Company. Many a times this expectation was belied than fulfilled.
16. Abbé Morellét, *Mémoire sur la situation de la Compagnie des Indes*, Paris, 1769, pp. 218-219. *Pillai's Diary,* Vol.1, pp. 89-90.
17. Indrani Ray, "The French Company and the Merchants of Bengal 1680-1730" in *Indian Economic and Social History Review,* Vol. 8, no. 1, March 1971, pp. 47-48.
18. C.S.P.V., *tome* 1, pp. 66-68.
19. *Correspondence du Consèil Supérieur de Pondichéry et de la Compagnie 1726-27*, (henceforth *Correspondence avec Compagnie*), *tome* 2, p.14.
20. *Correspondence du Consèil Supérieur de Pondichéry et de la Compagnie 1726-27*, (henceforth *Correspondence avec Compagnie*), *tome* 2, p. 14.
21. *Pillai's Diary,* Vol. 1, p. 89.
22. C.S.P.V., *tome* 2, pp. 263, 328-333, 354; W.H. Dalgleish, *The Company of the Indies in the Days of Dupleix*, Philadelphia, 1933, pp. 91-92.
23. *Bibliothèque Nationale,* Paris, *Departement des Manuscrits Francaise* (henceforth B.N.Mss.Fr.), 8913, f.35v; *Bibliothèque Nationale, departement des Manuscrits Francaise, Nouvelles acquistitions* (Henceforth *B.N.N.A.*) 9352, f.107.
24. C.S.P.V., *tome* 2, pp. 336-337.
25. *Correspondence avec Compagnie, tome* 2, p. 245; *Correspondence avec Chandernagor, tome* 1, p. 186.
26. C.S.P.V. *tome* 3, p. 150.
27. C.S.P.V., *tome* 1, pp. 270-271.
28. C.S.P.V., *tome* 2, p.394.

29. Paul Kaeppelin, *La Compagnie des Indes Orientales et François Martin 1664-1719*, Paris,1908, p. 167; C.S.P.V., *tome* 1, pp. 251-252; Martin's *Memoire, tome* 2, pp. 198, 216-217.
30. C.S.P.V., *tome* 3, pp. 121, 125.
31. *Pillai's Diary,* vol. 4, p. 214.
32. C.S.P.V., *tome* 1 to 3, *passim.*
33. B. Krishnamurthy, The French Trade with India 1664-1754, unpublished Ph.D. thesis, University of Baroda, 1984, pp. 315-316.
34. Kaeppelin, n. 29, p. 540.
35. *Correspondence avec Compagnie*, *tome* 2, pp. 191-192.
36. B.N.N.A. 9354, f. 294v.
37. C.S.P.V., *tome* 3, pp. 80-81.
38. C.S.P.V., *tome* 3, pp. 62-67; Pillai's *Diary*, pp.7-9. Ananda Ranga maintains that Seshachala Chetti was ostensibly proprietor and the man behind the scene was Kanagaraya Mudali, who was even given one share by the former out of his three.
39. B. Krishnamurthy, "The Revenue System of the French Administered Territories in India in the First Half of the Eighteenth Century", in *Revue Historique de Pondichéry*, Vol. 14, 1989-1990, Pondicherry, 1991, pp. 1-18.
40. C.S.P.V., *tome* 1, p. 5.
41. C.S.P.V., *tome* 3, pp. 214-215.
42. *Pillai's Diary*, Vol. 1, p. 240.
43. *Pillai's Diary*, Vol. 1, p.226; Alfred Martineau (ed.), *Lettres et conventions des Governeurs de Pondichéry avec les divers princes Hindous 1666-1793*, Pondicherry, 1914, pp. 78-79.
44. *Pillai's Diary*, Vol. 4, p. 329.
45. C.S.P.V.., *tome* 1, p. 30.
46. C.S.P.V.., tome 2, pp. 190-191.
47. Edmond Gaudart, *Catalogue des manuscripts des Archives du l'Inde Francaise, tome 4, Karikal, 1664-1719,* Paris, 1908, p.6.
48. C.S.P.V., *tome* 1, p. 236.
49. C.S.P.V., *tome* 3, p. 230.
50. C.S.P.V.., *tome* 3, p. 235.

51. C.S.P.V. *tome* 1, pp. 66-67.
52. C.S.P.V., *tome* 3, p. 37.
53. *Pillai's Diary*, Vol. 1, p. 118.
54. Arasaratnam, n. 3, p. 142.
55. *Pillai's Diary,* Vol.1. p. 65.
56. *Pillai's Diary,* Vol.1. p. 245.
57. *Pillai's Diary,* Vol. 6, pp. 381-384.
58. *Pillai's Diary,* Vol. 9, pp. 25, 124, 328.
59. *Pillai' s Diary* , Vol. 1. pp. 4-5.
60. C.S.P.V. *tome* 3, pp. 144-145.
61. *Pillai's Diary,* Vol. 6, pp. 287-289.
62. B.N.N.A. 9357, f.101v.
63. C.S.P.V. *tome* 1, pp. 46-48.
64. Paul Olagnier, Un Grand Colonial Inconnu: Le Gouverneur Benoist Dumas, Société le l'histoire des colonies françaises, Paris, 1936, p. 23; B.N.N.A., 9357, f.14.

7

Straddling the Arabian Sea: Gujarati Trade with West Asia during the 17th & 18th Centuries

Ruby Maloni

By the Seventeenth century, Gujarati merchants had developed a significant presence in the commercial zone of the Arabian Sea. Their trade activities had grown in expanding arcs over the Indian Ocean, from the eastern sector to the western Indian Ocean. Commercial efficacy in the Persian Gulf and the Red Sea owed not a little to the presence of Gujarati merchants. Their role was obvious but not ostentatious and dominant. Operating from their own base centres and commercial nodes in Gujarat, especially the port of Surat, they were able to dominate and even monopolize trade transactions. Eminent 'merchant princes', both Hindu and Muslim, boasted of vertical links with the administration and the ruling elite. There was a close construct of vested economic interests between them and the European trading companies. Out of their own ambit and location, their commercial power and expertise seems to have been exercised in a muted manner. This was perhaps a conscious reaction of the group, as a modus of survival and success.

The Gujarati merchant class integrated itself with apparent ease and some amount of sophistication into the existing milieu of their host regions. The process of assimilation seems to have been seamless. Yet at the same time they remained isolated and contained within their own cultural group, largely impervious to external elements. Much has been said of the resilience of the Gujarati merchants, and their ability of 'bending with the wind'. They were one of the mercantile categories who responded sturdily to the incursion of European trading companies in the Indian Ocean and fitted themselves into the 'comprador' role with the passage of time.

Before the rise of the *Bhatias* and *Lohanas* as competitive business groups, following the emergence of *Pushtimargi Vaishnavism* in the late Sixteenth century, Jains virtually dominated the Gujarati business world, apart from the Muslim mercantile communities. Available evidence suggests that during the Solanki period (942-1304 A.D.), Jains traded with Arab merchants who controlled the western Indian Ocean trade and ports such as Muscat and Aden. In fact, the Portuguese extended preferential treatment to the Jains, to counteract the Arabs, and Jain merchants were visible and active in almost all the ports occupied by the Portuguese. Before the emergence of Surat in the late Sixteenth century, Jains were concentrated at Porbandar, Jamnagar, Diu and Cambay, from where they exported cotton textiles, indigo, wheat, rice, agate goods and even leather items to West Asian ports like Hormuz, Mocha, Jiddah, Muscat and Aden. European travel literature of the Sixteenth and Seventeenth centuries refers to the Jains when the *'Banias'* of Muscat are described. Among other details, it was noted that they were pure vegetarians who took great care in preserving all forms of life, even insects[1]. Among the Muslim merchant communities, the *Shia Khojas* and *Sunni Memons* were highly active in the Arabian Sea trade. Taken together, these above Gujarati merchants formed part of the commercial elite of the Persian Gulf and Red Sea ports [2].

A fact of life, which the student of India's medieval economy has learned to live with, is the relative absence of exact statistics. There is also a paucity of documents, largely limited to the operations of official agencies such the *Estado da India* of the Portuguese, or the Companies of the English, Dutch and French. The history of the foreign trade of the Arabian Sea therefore tends to become a discussion of the structure of commerce and the role of the merchant in it. European and vernacular sources, conjointly used, would illuminate the economic relationships of this broad zone. Until vernacular sources are brought into firm focus, only a rather impressionistic sense of conditions can be created of the Gujarati merchant activities in West Asia.

At the turn of the Fifteenth century, India's mercantile marine on the West coast was largely in the hands of Gujarati Muslim merchants. Indian ships called regularly at the ports of the Red Sea and the Persian Gulf, although the carrying trade in the Arabian Sea was largely in the hands of Arab ship owners. By this time, the loosely jointed structure of overseas trade in the Arabian Sea would seem to have already assumed the form it was to retain for the ensuing three hundred years. Moreover, the important distinction between coastal shipping interests, which were by and large Muslim, and the shore based merchants feeding the shipping lines, among whom Hindus predominated, endured throughout the period. But partly through political changes in the region and partly as a result of European intervention, the deployment of Indian shipping and placement of Indian merchants changed from time to time. Fortunes of particular ports fluctuated sharply and Gujarati maritime trade made adjustments within structures evolved and sanctified by tradition. Initially, European trade fitted itself into the contours of the existing India-West Asia trade. Traditional structures continued, although modified by European commercial enterprise. Major alterations would only come with the establishment of empire.

Gujarat had interlinked and long-standing trade connections with West Asia and the east African coast. It is essential to note the enclave of Gujarati trade which had formed on the east coast of Africa. Gujarati shipping called at Kilwa, Mombasa, Malindi and Pate, as part of their round voyage to the Red Sea, and obtained gold and ivory in exchange for textiles. These Swahili city-states were largely Arab and were the creations of men from Hadramaut though some claimed to be of Persian origins[3]. This east African trade as it was done immediately before the Portuguese came on the scene, only emphasized the cooperation between Indians and Arabs in the western Indian Ocean, a peaceful sharing of profit, which was soon to be overshadowed by other means of doing business.

In the western Indian Ocean, Indian trade flowed along the two established maritime channels, one through the Red Sea, Cairo and Alexandria, and the other through the Persian Gulf and up through Basra and Baghdad. The Osmanli Turks raced the Portuguese towards the Indian Ocean and Salim I overran Syria and Egypt in 1516-17. Aden at the mouth of the Red Sea was secured by 1538, leading to the Red Sea being known as a 'Muslim lake'. Sulaiman the Magnificent, who followed Salim I, consolidated Ottoman conquests in the lower reaches of the Tigris and the Euphrates with Basra at the head of the Persian Gulf falling to him in 1546. The occupation of this city was disputed by the Safavids of Persia who consolidated what became the national territory of Iran, beginning early in the Sixteenth century under Shah Ismail. Somewhat later, the Mughal empire in India absorbed Gujarat in 1573.

It was the almost simultaneous emergence of the Ottoman, Safavid and Mughal empires in the western Indian Ocean which set a new scene for maritime trade. The three major early modern Muslim dynasties established an effective *pax Islamica* linking the traditional civilizational centres of West Asia and South Asia. From the Sixteenth century most rulers of these dynasties consistently implemented standardized political-economic policies that were designed to stimulate both internal and external trade. Indian, Arab and Persian merchants operated within a broadly similar commercial and even linguistic environment. They enjoyed almost unrestricted freedom to carry on their trade within the general framework of Islamic contractual law[4]. Non-Muslim merchants of Gujarat also were familiar with Persian and Arabic languages and usage. What S.D.Goitein has said about mercantile life in the Mediterranean region from the mid-Tenth to the mid-Thirteenth century is also applicable to the conduct of commerce in the western Indian Ocean in the early modern era. According to Goitein, "during the High Middle Ages men, goods, money and books used to travel far and almost without restrictions throughout the Mediterranean area. In many respects the area resembled a free-trade community"[5].

Under the new Mughal-Safavid dispensation, commercial structures now performed with relatively higher efficiency. The Safavids established a better-regulated hinterland for the Gulf ports, and transport in Persia during the Seventeenth century would seem to have been more efficient than in the neighbouring countries. The Safavids and the Mughals energetically encouraged the pilgrim traffic to the Islamic holy cities in Hijaz. The peace of the period, which the occasional Turko-Indian and Indo-Persian conflicts failed to disturb in a major way, promoted a new prosperity for the annual market at Mecca. To these factors may be added the development of the trade in Yemeni coffee which occurred in the Sixteenth century. Turkish merchants were the principal purchasers of coffee in Yemen and this pre-eminence was not challenged by the European buyers even at the height of the European coffee trade in the early Eighteenth century. Merchants from Persia were second only to the merchants of the Ottoman empire in the coffee market, whereas Indian merchants bought much less. However, the rush for Yemeni coffee was utilized by the Indians to good effect to push their textile trade. By the end of the Sixteenth century, the Red Sea had emerged as India's main market overseas.

As early as the mid-Eleventh century, trade of the Red Sea had gained predominance over that of the Persian Gulf, since the latter was unhinged by Seljuq-Turkish interference and Arabian Seaborne commerce had to be re-routed. The north of the Red Sea littoral was controlled by the Mamluk Sultans of Egypt and Syria (1260-1517), while in Yemen in the south the Banu Tahir dynasty supplanted the Rasulids in the mid-Fifteenth century. In between, the Sharif of Mecca and the Sharifian family ruled in Hijaz, and usually conceded suzerainty to the Mamluks. At this time, and afterwards, Gujarati merchants brought their wares to two rather different markets in the Red Sea. One was the market of the *Haj*. This was a conveyor belt by means of which Indian commodities transshipped in India found their way to the European market. The other was the regional market, which included the towns of Hijaz and Yemen, ports like Suakin, Massowa and Zeila on the African coast of the Red Sea, and the towns of the Hadramaut coast like Shihr, Kish and Zofar.

The carrying trade between the Red Sea and Gujarat had been for a long time dominated by the Cairo-based mercantile organization, the Karimi merchants. But they did not hold a monopoly of the traffic. R.B.Serjeant has shown from the evidence of contemporary Arabic chronicles written in Hadramaut that Indian vessels called regularly at south Arabian ports and Gujarati *Banias* had settled already in this area by the Fifteenth century[6]. Even before the arrival of the Portuguese, the *Karim* were under serious pressure from the Mamluk Sultans[7]. A reason for Gujarati shipping to veer towards the western Indian Ocean was the Portuguese determination to oust these merchants. The emphasis on the Red Sea trade was also a result of the diversion of Gujarati shipping from Malacca, caused by Portuguese occupation of the port in 1511. Gujarati shipping which was finding the Malacca voyages as well as the Persian Gulf ports a problem due to the Portuguese presence, found the vacuum created for them in the Red Sea too tempting. Gujarati Muslim ship-owners, vitally interested in preserving the freedom of high sea navigation and retaining hold on the carrying trade of the middle Indian Ocean, were from the outset bitterly opposed to Portuguese penetration. It was they who organized the defence of Malacca against the Portuguese, and once Malacca fell, abandoned that port in favour of Achin and Bantam. Hindu merchants, on the other hand, who were less affected by considerations of freight trade, were less hostile and co-operated with the Portuguese at Malacca. The carriage of spices in the Indian Ocean was now shared by the Hindu Gujarati merchants and the Portuguese. Charles Boxer is of the opinion that more pepper was being carried by Gujarati ships from Achin to the Red Sea at the beginning of the Seventeenth century than was being taken by the Portuguese round the Cape to Lisbon [8].

The Seventeenth century saw the continuation of earlier trends. The international market of the Haj continued to be the principal draw. However, the Zaidi Imams of Sana ended Turkish rule in Yemen in the 1620s and the Imam's port of

Mokha replaced Aden which had languished under Turkish mal-administration. The rise of theYarubis of Oman was a new element in the commerce of the Arabian Sea. Muscat fell to the Yarubis in 1650 and in the next fifteen years the Yarubi navy swept the Portuguese out of all their east African strongholds except Mozambique. Surat, which had constructed and provided maintenance for many Yarubi ships, regretted its own liberality every year when the Muscat ships put in for trade, refit and riot at the Mughal port. Gujarati ships were often the targets of Yarubi attack on the high seas.

Along the Persian Gulf coast, the island emporium of Ormuz had become the centre of a miniature maritime empire, commanding the allegiance of the important *entrepot* of Muscat on the other side of the Gulf and stretching as far as Basra at the head of it. Gujarati vessels called at Ormuz and Muscat, and Gujarati merchants settled in Persian ports and towns, much as they did at Red Sea ports. The Safavids expelled the Portuguese from Ormuz in 1622 with the help of the English, and trade veered to the port of Gombroon, re-named Bandar Abbas after the name of Shah. In fact, easier access to the Red Sea and the Persian Gulf, following the decline of Portuguese power, strengthened the position of the Surat merchants *vis a vis* the *Multanis* and other merchants on the caravan routes between India and Persia.

A significant detail illustrating the growth in active trade between Surat and the Persian Gulf is the fact that Gujarati merchants before the middle of the Seventeenth century freighted, to a large extent, their goods on board English East India Company ships. This was not the result of the Company's pressure on the indigenous merchants. On the contrary, the Company factors were apprehensive of the competition from the merchants who freighted on its ships. But the Company's refusal to freight Indian goods tended to provoke vociferous protests from the merchants and authorities at Surat. Therefore, after the fall of Ormuz, English and Dutch ships made it a practice to carry Gujarati owned commodities from Surat to Bandar Abbas.

The use of the Company ships may be seen as a short-term solution to a bottleneck caused by the expansion in the overseas trade of the Surat merchants. This interpretation appears to be confirmed by the rapid growth of the domestic tonnage available in Surat in the Seventeenth century. Already during the 1640s, freight rates decreased due to the growing number of Gujarati ships available. In about 1650, the merchant navy of Surat contained fifty ships, many of them large and well-built. In 1651, the Mughal administration initiated a building programme for sea-going ships, and four to six large ships were built for the voyages to Bandar Abbas and Mokha. In the following year, the Mughals had six more ships put into commission. In spite of short-term fluctuations, the growth continued during the second half of the Seventeenth century when seventy to a hundred ships were operating from Surat. In 1701, the number of seagoing ships in Surat was at least 112.[9]

The importance of Surat is reflected also by the emergence of 'merchant princes', entrepreneurs of a hitherto unknown wealth and status. In the Surat Factory Records, from 1630 onwards, Virji Vora is frequently mentioned as a leading merchant[10]. He maintained his own agents in West Asian ports, with arrangements for the remittance of large sums of money by *Hundi* or bills of exchange. Virji Vora retired from business in about 1670, and was succeeded by a number of merchant tycoons, among whom appeared in 1701 Mulla Abdul Ghafur, the owner of seventeen seagoing ships based at Surat [11].

Gujarati merchants in the West Asia trade operated in a keenly competitive world. Small-scale merchants competed actively with well-established merchants. The former conjured up the classic figure of the Indian Ocean traveller made immortal by Jacob van Leur. Many of them were the agents of other merchants, earning a commission on the proceeds of the transactions. Among the small merchants, there were also men who owned what they sold, or traded on respondentia. Though their business was limited, both in investment and profit, their presence in the Arabian Sea trade was continuous. In fact, the power of the great was circumscribed by the ubiquity of the small. A major reason why Abdul Ghafur was unable to establish a monopoly in his favoured Red Sea trade was that he was unable to cope with the multitude of minor merchants. This was in spite of the fact that he did manage to drive many of them into bankruptcy. Despite rational calculations and commercial intelligence, even the most affluent merchants had to depend on the caprices of a fluctuating market. Niels Steensgaard has seen in this the true peddling nature of Indian Ocean trade. For instance, the expectation of a good *Haj* would make for frantic purchases in the months of September to January, while news of political unrest in the Persian Gulf would at once create a depression in the overseas markets. The West Asian trade of the English and Dutch Companies was not feasible without reliance on intermediaries. Gujarati brokers or *Dalals* and moneychangers or *Sarrafs* were indispensable for the supply of specific commodities and transfer of funds.

It is obvious that Indian maritime trade was rearranged in the Seventeenth century by the emergence of the English and Dutch trading companies. This rearrangement, however, confirmed the tendency to emphasise West Asia at the expense of South-East Asia. By the middle of the century, Dutch monopoly of the spice trade was real and effective. The Gujaratis gave up the South-Eastern voyages fairly early, not many going to Sumatra after 1618[12]. The near-complete abandonment of Indonesian voyages left the Gujaratis with only the Red Sea and Gulf markets. This was the real reason why the English met with such fierce opposition when they attempted to cut into the trade between Mokha and Surat in the 1620s. Moreover, the trade to the Red Sea came to be more and more in Indian textiles, as spices were no longer readily obtainable. As the English factors at Surat put it, "The merchants of this place are alsoe undone by our trade to the Southwards which hath taken the meate out of their mouthes and overthrowne their trade that way"[13]. Throughout the Seventeenth century, Gujarati trade to the Red Sea and Persian Gulf continued in force, and neither the English nor the Dutch affected the flow adversely. Since the conveyance of spices had abated, this phase may be considered to be the high tide of India's textile trade to West Asia.

There are a multiplicity of references to the sale of Indian textiles in this region. Textiles of the coarser variety were exported to the Red Sea ports, as this was in demand for common consumption. For instance, the Dutch *Verenigde Oostindische Compagnie*, relying on the costlier cloths of Coromandel, could not compete with the Gujaratis at Mocha since Gujarat specialized in the production and export of the cheaper varieties. During both the Seventeenth and Eighteenth centuries, the Red Sea region evinced a preference for cheaper goods, which were not confined to textiles but extended to the entire range of commodities. This does not imply that the more expensive and luxury goods were not in demand among the aristocracy in that sector. Travellers who wrote enthusiastically of the trade in such luxury items were by no means fanciful; but the fact is that the mass of the trade was in ordinary textiles, which nobody would really write home about.

Significant items of export to this region were also foodstuff like rice, sugar, pulses, wheat and oil, for which there was considerable demand. Such food commodities helped to feed port cities like Ormuz and Aden. Bulk trading in such goods fetched relatively less profit. Gujarat also exported raw cotton to the West Asian markets. Specialty items such as *pan* or betel leaf coveted in the Safavid court were also exported. Soon after tobacco began to be cultivated in Mughal India, it became an important item of export [14]. By the end of the Seventeenth century, Indian carriers not only lost the trade in pepper to a substantial extent, they also lost, albeit to a lesser degree, the carriage of indigo since European ships diverted this trade to Europe.

Indian imports were concentrated on bullion and horses, and specific items such as dyewoods from the Persian Gulf. Wines, silks, carpets, rosewater and medicinal gum resin only made the list of imports from West Asia impressive. The crucial significance of the West Asian market was for the Indian import of bullion. While Mocha was known as 'the treasure house of the Mughal', the Persian Gulf also yielded a rich bounty of precious metals, and it was on these markets that India depended for the inflow of the much-needed currency. The direct shipment of silver from the Persian Gulf and the Red Sea made the Gujarat economy more monetised. The trade to the Red Sea in particular brought in large consignments of bullion every year in August and September. The Spanish *rial* of eight was the dominating coin of those which were imported, which included European, Turkish and Persian bullion, not to speak of gold and silver in bars[15]. As Joseph Brennig points out, conscious profiteering from price differentials between Europe and India, however much it might explain English East India Company shipments of specie, had considerably less relevance for the shipment of silver by Gujarati merchants from West Asian markets. In general, these were closely tied to Indian markets and therefore were unlikely to have sharply differing bimettalic ratios. At the beginning of the Eighteenth century also, this movement of silver remained deeply imbedded in the traditional structures of West Asian trade[16].

The Gujarati mercantile diaspora in Persia reflected an asymetrical economic relationship in which the Indian merchants marketed agricultural products, textile manufactures and their own financial expertise. By and large they also enjoyed a competitive advantage in both goods and services. The balance was clearly in favour of Indian trade. A microcosm of this trade relationship can be seen in the way that the English East India Company factors in Surat sold Indian goods in Persia to generate specie for their intra-Asian and Indian trade. Typical of their cargoes that their ships brought from Persia in the Seventeenth century were the 1,000 *tumans*, three horses and some unspecified "freight goods" that arrived at Surat aboard the *Francis* in April 1637[17].

It is well documented that the Mughal-Safavid phase realized an integrated regional market, and the commercial ties between them were quite unprecedented. The relatively high level of stability and prosperity of both states contributed to an increase of commerce between them. The Gujarati merchant diaspora in Persia was substantial. In fact, such a wide dispersal in one region outside India perhaps was not to be seen elsewhere in the Seventeenth century[18]. In 1630, there were approximately ten thousand Indians residing in Bandar

Abbas[19]. The continuity of Indo-Persian trade was also significant, which in value, volume and variety far exceeded India's trade with any other sector in the Arabian Sea region. This commerce was transacted by sea and land routes. Even in the Seventeenth century, overland trade from India had a significant impact on Persian markets, as illustrated by the report that when a thousand camels carrying cloth and indigo reached Isfahan in 1665, local prices fell by fifteen per cent[20]. Both land and sea routes were interchangeable. When the narrow Gulf sea lanes were unusually dangerous, overland trade might increase as much as 300 per cent a year, as Steel and Crowther reported to have occurred for this reason in 1616[21]. The Qandahar crisis would inevitably diminish sea trade. Shah Jahan, for example, in 1640 forbade ships to leave Surat for Bandar Abbas[22].The interchangeability of routes was obvious in the mid-Seventeenth century, when Persian officials told the English factors that if commercial disputes prompted the latter to interdict sea-borne commerce, sufficient supplies would be easily made available through the land routes. On occasions, the opposite was true; when Mughal-Safavid warfare at Qandahar stopped caravan traffic, merchants quickly adjusted to the situation and shipped their goods by sea.

Commercial operations and to some extent, the lifestyle of Gujarati merchants in Persia were noticed and narrated by travellers such as Ralph Fitch, Thomas Herbert, John Fryer, Charles Lockyer, Niccolao Manucci, Manuel Godinho and Jean Chardin. In 1583 Fitch found many Gujarati merchants, Hindu and Jain Banias, in Ormuz. After the emergence of Bandar Abbas, there was a sizeable flow of merchants from Surat, as it was almost at the same time that this port also came into prominence, its volume and value of trade enhanced by the English and Dutch presence. Gujarati traders of Surat operated in close association with the English and Dutch commercial network, enabled as they were to take full advantage of the new business opportunities offered to them in Persia, since the Safavid rulers had forged close commercial links with the Europeans. The English East India Company was permitted to bring in goods customs free, and were also authorized to receive half of the customs duties levied at Bandar Abbas annually. The English had established factories at Bandar Abbas as well as at Basra and took with them their Indian agents, who were usually Gujarati *Banias* and *Parsis*. Their traditional expertise in contacting local traders for sale and purchase of commodities was essential for the English merchants. In times of need, the Gujarati merchants rendered financial assistance to the East India Company servants and discounted bills issued on them to India. They also provided banking services by facilitating remittances. Besides acting on behalf of the Europeans, these merchants also traded on their own and fanned out from Bandar Abbas to other parts of Persia, adding to the number of Indian merchants who had already arrived by the land route.

Thomas Herbert, a young member of the English diplomatic mission that arrived in Bandar Abbas in 1627, describes its flourishing cosmopolitan population and testifies to the substantial presence of Gujarati Banias at this port. The Safavid administration treated them, both big and small merchants, with consideration and permitted public observance of their socio-religious customs. This was probably part of economic expediency, with the aim of developing the trade of the newly established port. Gujarati merchants were allowed to build a Hindu temple, which is described by Herbert as being under the shade of a large banyan tree, and having a shrine with three idols .He also noticed that these merchant communities were vegetarians, and in general did not drink and dine with Europeans, although working closely with them in commercial affairs[23].

The situation had not changed much four decades later. John Fryer arrived from Surat to Bandar Abbas in 1676, and was quick to notice the familiar presence of Gujarati Baniyas. He attested to their affluence, especially of the *Dalals* or brokers of the English and Dutch Companies. He referred to Tockersey or Thackersey, the agent of the English East India Company, who had constructed baths at Kuh-I-Ginso, two miles from Bandar Abbas. Fryer attended religious festivities and a "great concourse" after *Navratri* or the festival of nine nights, and visited two temples. He observed that the Gujarati merchants exercised sufficient influence over the governor to pay him an amount of 350 *tumans* in order to prevent the slaughter of cows[24]. Charles Lockyer, who visited Bandar Abbas in the first decade of the Eighteenth century, corroborated the fact that an annual amount was paid to the governor to avoid cow slaughter[25].

Toward the end of the Seventeenth century, Gujarati merchants were so well entrenched in Bandar Abbas that they could bring considerable pressure on the local administrative authorities. After a dispute with the governor, they left Bandar Abbas *en masse* and shifted a hundred miles west to Kung Bandar, where the governor's writ did not run. As Fryer takes care to mention, they did not return even when importuned by the governor, desisted from transacting any business in Bandar Abbas, and returned only when the governor's tenure was over[26].

Gujarati merchants moved northwards from Bandar Abbas to Isfahan, the splendid capital of Shah Abbas. There were already settlements of Indian merchants there, who had come by land routes. Herbert noted the close ties between these merchants and the East India Company. The entourage in which Herbert was travelling was welcomed two miles off Isfahan by a huge crowd which included "*Banias* in large numbers"[27]. Niccolao Manucci in the 1650s, Manuel Godinho in the 1660s and Jean Chardin in the 1670s wrote of the presence of Indian merchants in the littoral areas of Persia. Godinho found *Banias* from Cambay settled as residents at Bandar Abbas as well as at Kung Bandar[28]. Manucci reported that Lar was "..inhabited by many Hindus, who brought there the goods, brought from Isfahan and other places, and then exported them to many countries, principally from the ports of Congo and Bandar Abbas"[29].The commodities in which Gujarati merchants transacted were not only for Persian markets, but also for other Asian as well as Mediterranean markets. Especially for the latter, they had close dealings with the Armenian merchants who were based in the Persian Gulf ports[30]. A larger section of Gujarati merchants specialized in doing business exclusively in Indian articles, mainly textiles and indigo.

The fall of the Safavids in 1722 disturbed the internal situation in Persia. Both the demand for Indian commodities in Persia and for Persian commodities in India fell off. In the Red sea, the trend was in the same direction. After 1700 the demand for textiles was declining. The reasons for this decline are somewhat obscure, but they may be connected with the contemporary boom in coffee[31]. From 1714 political conditions in Yemen were almost as unstable as in India and Persia.

This period also saw the downfall of the great commercial marine of Gujarat. The debacle of Gujarati shipping may be partly ascribed to the simultaneous political chaos in India, Persia and Yemen. At Surat, the merchant fleet, consisting of 112 vessels in 1701, shrank to 20 vessels in 1750. This decline in Gujarati commerce had begun much earlier than the breakdown in the law and order situation. The increased volume of Gujarat's exports had gradually glutted the markets in West Asia, and their trade operations became low key. At Mocha, Gujarati merchants were fleeced to meet the costs of the Yemeni civil war.

The decline of Surat did not happen all of a sudden. In spite of heavy losses, Gujarati merchants continued with remarkable tenacity, to trade to the 'gulphs'. But they had to face competition from a new variety of merchants, the country traders, who operated primarily under English protection. Based in ports dominated by the East India Company, these country traders enjoyed not only the political protection offered by this affiliation, but often had access to information and privileges only available to Company servants and their 'friends'.

The eighteenth century trade of Gujarati merchants underwent crucial transformations in other ways. The European Companies reoriented production away from traditional destinations into conduits of their own design. Surat changed from a textile and indigo exporting port into a Company entrepot geared towards China exports[32]. European and Gujarati merchants complemented each other often, to maximize their profits.

It was the practice of Gujarati freighters to split their risks even by distributing their freight among the available shipping. Direct investment in shipping was not popular among Gujarati merchants. Ownership was almost always individual. Shared proprietorship was known, but was a rare phenomenon. Except for some affluent merchant families of Surat, such as the *Mulla* and *Parakh* families, Gujarati merchants did not own more than one or two ships. In view of the fact that Gujarati merchants from coastal areas were regularly crossing and re-crossing the Arabian Sea, the carriage of Indian passengers and their goods became a very lucrative part of the business activities of the English East India Company. Charles Lockyer, wrote from Bandar Abbas in the first decade of the Eighteenth century," Freighting (of passengers)...is a main branch of the Company's profit; for they rarely dispatch a ship hence for Surat, but she is deep loaded ..full of passengers, and has vast quantities of pearl and treasure on board; some has to the value of two or three hundred thousand pounds, so that I look upon English ships from Persia to Surat in the latter end of October and November, to be the richest vessels on that side of the world. The Dutch have a great deal of freight, but they sent so many ships together, that they are seldom above half full" [33].

The Gujarati merchants projected a sophisticated network of mercantile practices, since they came from an urbanized milieu. In the *Mirat-I-Ahmadi* there are references to a large number of towns and cities in Gujarat[34]. It is possible to identify over sixty urban centers in the Mughal *Subah* of Gujarat. Merchants were used to a money economy already existing in Gujarat[35]. As middlemen and moneychangers, they utilised their mercantile expertise even when venturing outside their own regional base. Faced with aggressive European mercantile capitalism, they were quick to seize the moment. This may be looked on either as a process of survival or of dynamic change. George Roques, in his fruitless search for an honest Bania from Ahmadabad to Sironj, called them "multifaced"[36], but this diplomatic demeanour enabled them to survive in a transitional and challenging situation, not only in the Seventeenth century, but continue later. As constituting an influential mercantile group throughout the Arabian Sea littoral, they retained their religious, cultural as well as commercial identity. This may explain the felicity with which they were later able to exploit the opportunities and challenges offered by modern capitalism.

Notes and References

1. M.N. Pearson, *Merchants and Rulers in Gujarat : The Response to the Portuguese in the Sixteenth Century*, Berkeley and New Delhi, 1976. Surendra Gopal, *Commerce and Crafts in Gujarat,16th and 17th Centuries,* New Delhi, 1975.
2. Makrand Mehta, 'Gujarati Business Communities in East African Diaspora', in *Economic and Political Weekly*, vol. xxxvi, May 19, 2001.
3. Ashin Dasgupta, 'Indian Merchants and Trade in the Indian Ocean', in Tapan Raychaudhari and Irfan Habib, eds.,*The Cambridge Economic History of India*, Vol.1, 1982, p. 412.
4. Emile Tyan, *Histoire de l'organisation judiciare en pays d'Islam*, Leiden, 1960.
5. S.D.Goitein, *A Mediterranean Society*, Berkeley, University of California Press, 1967-88, p. 66.
6. R.B.Serjeant, *The Portuguese off the South Arabian Coast*, Oxford, 1963, pp. 32-35.
7. W.J.Fischel, 'The Spice Trade of Mamluk Egypt', in *Journal of the Economic and Social History of the Orient*, Leiden, I, 1958, pp. 157-84.
8. Charles Boxer, 'A Note on Portuguese Reactions to the Revival of the Red Sea Spice Trade and the Rise of Atjeh,1540-1600', in *Journal of South East Asian History*, December 1969, pp. 415 -28.
9. H.W.van Santen, *De Verenigde Oost-Indische Compagnie in Gujarat en Hindustan,1620-1660,* Leiden, 1982, pp. 67,78.

   A.Dasgupta, *Indian Merchants and the Decline of Surat c.1700-1750*, Wiesbaden, 1979, p. 286.
10. Ruby Maloni, *European Merchant Capital and the Indian Economy, Surat Factory Records,1630-1668*, New Delhi, 1992.
11. A.Dasgupta, *Op.Cit.*,Ch. II and *passim*.

12. Surendra Gopal, *Commerce and Crafts in Gujarat, 16th and 17th Centuries*, New Delhi, 1975, pp. 59-61.
13. W.Foster, ed.,*The English Factories in India, 1618-21*, Oxford, 1906-27, p. xiii.
14. R.W.Ferrier, 'Trade from the mid-14th Century to the end of the Safavid Period', in *The Cambridge History of Iran*, Vol. VI, p. 475.
15. A.Dasgupta, *Op Cit,* p. 45.
16. J.Brennig, 'Silver in seventeenth century Surat: Monetary circulation and the price revolution in Mughal India', in J.F. Richards, ed., *Precious Metals in the Later Medieval and Early Modern Worlds,* Carolina Academic Press, 1983, pp. 477-493.
17. W.Foster, *The English Factories in India, 1637-1641*, p. 242.
18. Surendra Gopal, 'Indian Traders in Persia in the Seventeenth Century', in *Journal of Historical Studies*, No. 2, December 1996, Patna, pp. 14-35.
19. Ruby Maloni, *Op.Cit.,* p. 28.
20. W.Foster, *The English Factories in India, 1655-1660*, p.128.
21. Richard Steel and John Crowther, 'Journey of Richard Steel and John Crowther from Ajmeer in India to Isfahan in Persia in the Years 1615 and 1616', in Robert Kerr, ed., *A General Collection of Voyages and Travels*, Edinburgh, 1824, IX, pp. 206-219.
22. W.Foster, (ed.) *The English Factories in India, 1637-1641*, Oxford, 1907-27, p. 242.
23. Thomas Herbert, *Travels in Persia, 1627-29*, London, 1928, p. 49.
24. John Fryer, *A New Account of East India and Persia Being Nine Years Travels 1672-81*, Vol. II, London, 1912, p. 167.
25. Charles Lockyer, *An Account of the Trade in India*, London, 1711, pp.238.
26. Fryer, *Op Cit,* p. 326.
27. Herbert, *Op. Cit,* p.121.
28. John Correia-Afonso, *Intrepid Itinerant : Manuel Godinho and his Journey from India to Portugal in 1663*, pp. 91,111.
29. Niccolao Manucci, *Storia do Mogor*, vol. I, reprint, Delhi, 1990, p. 55.

30. Ruquia Kazim Hussain, 'Indian Trade and Indian Merchants in Persia in the middle of the Seventeenth Century', in *Proceedings of the Indian History Congress*, 53rd Session, Warangal, pp. 286-87.
31. N.Steensgaard,' The Indian Ocean Netwcrk and the Emerging World Economy c.1500-1750', in Satish Chandra, ed., *The Indian Ocean: Explorations in History, Commerce and Politics*, New Delhi, 1987, p. 147.
32. Dilbagh Singh and Ashok Rajshirke, 'The Merchant Communities in Surat: Trade, Trade Practices and Institutions in the late Eighteenth Century', in Indu Banga, ed., *Ports and their Hinterlands in India*, New Delhi, 1992, pp. 181-198.
33. Charles Lockyer, *Op Cit*, p. 251.
34. Ali Muhammad Khan, *Mirat-I-Ahmadi*, tr. M.F. Lokhandwala, Baroda, 1965.
35. Ruby Maloni, *Surat: Port of the Mughal Empire*, Mumbai, 2003, pp. 20-35.
36. Indrani Ray,' Of Trade and Traders in Seventeenth Century India: An Unpublished French Memoir by George Rocques', *Occasional Paper No. 26*, Centre for Studies in Social Sciences, Kolkata, 1979.

8

Hindu Dominance in the Goa-based Long-Distance Trade during the Eighteenth Century

Philomena Sequeira Antony

This paper extends very much to the earlier works of some scholars in the sea-borne trade of Goa in the Seventeenth century.[1] It is an oft-repeated credo that after 1600, the *Estado da India* could claim no glory either in terms of its size, or in terms of its profitability to the metropolis. In his unpretentious assessment of Portuguese impact on the east, K.M. Panikkar avers that the *Estado da India* was but a "few square miles of territory at Goa" and that there was nothing scintillating about that first empire.[2] No doubt, Goa, with a miniscule area of 3,701 square kilometers was the capital of the *Estado da India* till 1961. Portugal had lost the *crème de la crème* of her eastern possessions by the Seventeenth century. Thereafter, the perimeters of the *Estado* itself did not extend beyond Goa, Daman and Diu. Portugal, it is believed, was compelled to turn to the Atlantic colony, the milch cow, and neglect the East.

Studies have now shown that the 'Atlantic turning' of Portugal was far from being detrimental to the *Estado da India*. Nor did it imply the isolation of the truncated first empire. On the contrary, colonial Goa had ample opportunities to gain from interface with other colonies. Both official and private trade provided the substratum for sustained commerce during a period when the *Estado* comprising a "few square miles of territory" was believed to have been neglected.

Strength of the Crown Weakens

Steady decline in the spice trade, loss of territories, challenges of European rivals and other factors and forces compelled the Crown to slacken its monopoly over commerce.

This led to entry of private merchants into an arena that was Crown monopoly earlier. Private trade assumed many forms. It began with the freedom to carry specified liberty goods, leading to sale of such articles at ports of call. In 1673 freedom of trade was conceded in textiles, spices and slaves to all Portuguese. The Age of Reason witnessed further liberalization of trade, with focus on individual enterprise and free trade. The three Portuguese ministers, Marquis of Pombal, Martinho de Melo e Castro and Dom Rodrigo de Souza Coutinho, influenced by the liberal movements in Europe, stressed on keeping pace with the economic reforms in the continent. Lisbon opened itself to liberal ideas and ended up throwing the doors of economic opportunities open to its subjects.

The Subaltern Response

Native Hindu merchants of Goa were quick to take advantage of the need of Portugal. They joined in the commercial nexus as subordinate partners. Utilising their business acumen, knowledge of local languages and their contacts outside the *Estado*, they entered the trajectory of trade at various levels: they played the lead role in the official trade involving sale of tobacco for a century and a half: they monopolized the contracts for the sale of snuff in Goa from 1675 to 1825. When Bahian leaf tobacco was introduced in Goa by way of direct imports, they took the contracts of this trade between 1775 and 1825. They acted as suppliers of a wide range of goods that formed part of the official, reciprocal trade to Brazil, Lisbon and Africa on the tobacco account. They also joined in the race for the long-distance private trade to the empire, covering Africa and America, besides Portugal. Their trading nexus with other parts of India was an inevitable factor as Goa depended on the rest of India for commodities meant for export. They were also suppliers of a wide range of articles needed for repairs and provisioning of ships, at the shipyard in Goa.

Role in the Tobacco Trade

Tobacco introduced in India by the Portuguese around the early sixteenth century rapidly turned into a thriving trade.

Local merchants were awarded contracts to collect tax (*Renda*) from tobacco cultivators[3]. Locally grown tobacco leaves were used by consumers during this period. Portugal capitalized on the addiction to tobacco in the *Estado da India* and launched the Tobacco Monopoly in 1675. Lisbon-made snuff was imported from 1675 onwards. Indigenous merchants entered the field as local partners in that trade. The right to sell snuff was farmed out to the merchant contractors annually. After 1700, annual contracts were substituted by triennial contracts as a matter of convenience. Goan Hindu merchants almost monopolized this trade. Christians were conspicuously non-existent in the list of contractors after 1700, though their contribution to consumption was notable, as Convents and Religious houses regularly received their quota of snuff supply.

Table–1 : Hindu Contractors of Snuff in Goa, 1675-1824.

Vantu Naik	Ganaba Sinai Nerlicar
Baxa Babu	Ramaji Sinai
Apaji Naik	Babuso Gauns
Santu Naik	Ramaji Naik
Malpa Chatim	Narayan Sinai
Anta Naik	Seguna Sinai Nerlicar
Gopal Kamat	Vithoji Dalvi
Raghu Naik	Krishna Naik
Pandurang Naik	Tandu Naik
Vithoji Sinai	Venkatesh Kamat
Babea Keni	Pundalik Sinai Kenkre
Govinda Naik	Seguna Sinai Nerlicar
Surya Naik	Santopa Sinai
Ganesh Kamat	Zogu Kamat
Biku Kamat	Kushta Kamat
Narayan Kamat	Fondu Kamat
Narba Kamat	Gopala Naik
Ramchandra Naik	Daquea Naik
Ramaji Naik	Venkatesh Sinai Kenkre

Source: Philomena Sequeira Antony, *The Goa-Bahia Intra-Colonial Relations, 1675-1825*, p. 235.

Native merchants found ingenious methods of undercutting the official trade and its profitability. They supplied locally manufactured snuff at a cheaper rate to the Portuguese territories. In 1768 it was reported from Goa that the snuff factory set up by Poquea Sinai Dumo and his brother Gopala Sinai in Bicholim, had spread the tentacles of the locally made snuff to Ilhas, Ponda, Marcela and other areas. Officials feared that sale of their stocks piled up in the warehouse would be jeopardized by this novel method of contraband. As a remedial measure, the government ordered search operations at check posts and those found with even small quantities of such tobacco were declared liable for imprisonment and exile to Solor and Timor.[4] Such punitive measures were not effective deterrents to men who found means and ways of evading the law. Allegations of corrupt practices were made in 1770 against a number of Hindu merchants who supplied articles like textiles, gold thread, paper, caps and other items.[5] Vitigi Sinai Nerlicar and his son Panduranga Sinai Nerlicar, Custam Pai of Cumbarjua, Santu Parab, Balu Custam, Fondu Chatim, Santu Naik and Siva Chatim, all of St. Luzia, were some of the listed merchants.

Malpractices of merchants had wider ramifications: snuff was mixed with wet leaves and sold at higher than the stipulated rates in Bicholim and Ponda.[6] These tactics amounted to transgression of law concerning price and weight; they also meant exploitation and victimization of their own brethren. Extortion used by the contractors forced many families of Assolna, Velim and Ambolim, flee to Sunda and other neigbouring kingdoms.[7] Clearly, native were motivated solely by higher profits.

New Avenues for Profits

Enthused by the addiction of Goans to snuff, Lisbon resorted to yet another strategy: this time it was the introduction of Bahian leaf tobacco into Goa. Successful at the lucrative snuff trade, Goan merchants plunged themselves into this trade as well. Triennial contracts were awarded to the highest bidder. Seven indigenous merchants and their associates monopolized the sale of American leaf tobacco spanning the forty seven years (1775 – 1822) when this trade prevailed.

Merchants had to pay the contract price and purchase a stipulated quantum of tobacco from the Tobacco Administration at a fixed rate. Though the purchase and sale prices fixed by the authorities were revised periodically, at any given point, the sale price was almost three to four times higher than the former. Contractors found adequate elbow room to earn handsome profits after deducting all their expenses. They vied with each other by offering higher contract price with each passing triennial as shown in the Figure below.

The network of sale was wide enough to create a hierarchy of sub-contractors and agents who handled the lower rungs of the trade structure. Profits percolated to them, though in a smaller measure. These men made inroads into far-flung rural areas, leaving no stone unturned to provide the taste of the "superior American leaf tobacco" to all the colonials. Thanks to the perseverance of these agents, those serving in temples, in the military, at isolated forts, as well as civilians- men, women and children, irrespective of age and economic status ,were roped into the addiction net. This trade, considered a vital branch of the commerce of the *Estado da India*, was turned into a profitable business by the labours of the native contractors and their work force. The vested interest of the native merchants, the subordinate partners in the imperialist game plan, is evident.

Contract Price Offered by Native Merchants for American Leaf Tobacco: 1776-1825

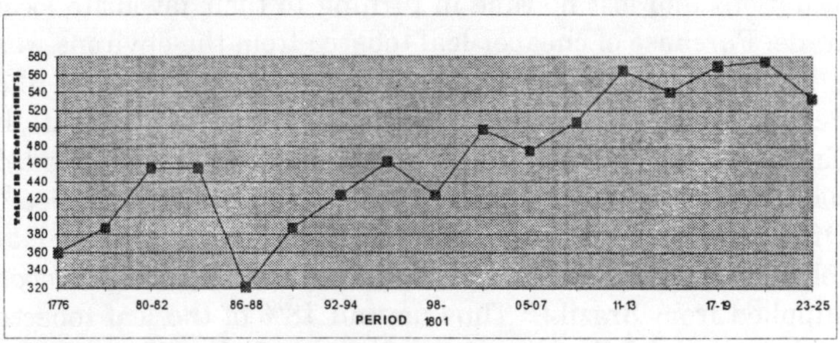

Source : P. Sequeira Antony, *Op.cit.*, p.288.

High profitability was clearly the secret behind the contracts being limited to a meagre number of seven merchants, who secured the contracts repeatedly by offering higher prices. Official figures record the profits of Vitogi Sinai Nerlicar as 20,092=2-23 *xerafins* during the first year, in 1774.Govind Sinai Molio of Cumbarjua earned 91, 519 *xerafins* during 1777-1779, which works out to be 30,000 *xerafins* a year.[8] Though computation of profits at each triennial is almost impossible, there is no doubt that it was a lucrative business to contractors.

Local merchants were not overly charitable to the state. Motivated by self interest, nay selfish interests, they ensured the upward movement of their profit graph at all cost. When terms of the contract demanded that they purchase and sell a stipulated quantum of bales, they retaliated by refusing to buy tobacco of inferior quality. This attitude was not exceptional; it was the trend .Contractor Ramachandra Naik refused such tobacco in 1790, claiming that old leaves were mixed with fresh ones in the bales. Govinda Sinai rejected 86 bales in 1810 and 1811.When authorities were forced to re-examine the rejected bales in the presence of the contractor, several bales were rejected by the panel of officials and government nominees. Govinda Sinai felt vindicated.

Rejection of Brazilian leaf tobacco by native contractors continued unabated. In 1812, 82 bales were rejected; in 1813, 120 bales and in 1814, 24 bales were not collected. The 1816 consignment contained six stones. The bales were of such poor quality that the entire consignment was sent back to Rio. Contractors in Goa sought refuge in such incontrovertible situations and lost no time in turning to their favourite local trade. Purchase of cheaper leaf tobacco from the environs was a far more lucrative business to them. Intermediaries like Seguna Sinai, Ganaba Sinai Nerlicar, Anant Pai, Venkatesh Kamat, Narayan Kamat Raghunath Kamat and others provided tobacco from Balaghat, Ponnani and the South, for sale in Goa.[9] Official records indicate that about 53,875 *arrobas* of leaf tobacco was procured in India as against about 2,90,000 *arrobas* supplied from Brazil.[10] Thus around 18% of the leaf tobacco consumed in the *Estado* was purchased in India. Whatever the reasons for those local purchases, ultimately the contractors were the beneficiaries. Supply and sale of local tobacco provided ample room for manipulation of quality and price.

It is evident that Portugal was totally helpless in the given situation. Being dependent on the American growers of tobacco for supplies on the one hand and on the Goan merchants for sale of tobacco at the other, there was little that Lisbon could do to control the trade. In Brazil, the tobacco suppliers and inspectors were colluders. In Goa, the native merchants worked for their vested interests. They earned their profits by all means: realizing the profitability of the local tobacco trade, they turned to their favorite Indian tobacco and thwarted all official attempts to impose the American tobacco on them. As Goa imported a number of commodities from the neighboring territories, bundles of tobacco were concealed in packages and brought to Ponda and distributed clandestinely. Consumers, particularly in the new conquests chose to buy the cheaper local tobacco procured from the neighboring territories.[11] This spiked the official profits and benefited the local merchants immensely. The iron hand of authorities proved to be a paper tiger with regard to the practice of the trade. Was the manipulative role of native merchants not perceived before the trade was launched?

Officials in Goa were always wary about the trading practices of the native merchants: the century-old snuff trade had clearly revealed their manipulative tactics. State authorities linked up the craftiness and ploys of the Hindu contractors with the poor returns from tobacco trade and promptly reported to Lisbon. It was alleged that merchants were underwriting the actual sales in order to make room for contraband tobacco; and that they indulged in malpractices with regard to quality and weight of tobacco supplied to consumers. Hence, authorities projected higher sale targets and consequently, higher returns from the new leaf tobacco trade. Stringent rules were laid down to keep the trade under control. Contrary to expectations, the practice of trade proved the weakness of Lisbon and the strength of the local merchants.

The upper hand of the indigenous merchants was invidious to the imperialists. Officials in Goa kept fanning the fire by regular reports about the unscrupulous ways of the local merchants: that they dipped inferior local tobacco in a decoction of pepper water in order to artificially flavour it; that Vithogi Sinai Nerlicar, contractor for the first consignment brought to Goa in 1773, exposed the tobacco to cattle urine with a view to bring disrepute to that tobacco and so on.[12] Going by the official version, native merchants were utterly unreliable in handling the new trade. Yet, Hindu merchants, the *béte noire* of Lisbon, monopolised the trade throughout the fifty years of its existence! It was a win-win position to Goan merchants.

Official documentation clearly shows how the leaf tobacco trade proved the steady decline of Portugal's hold over this trade, considered vital to the treasury. Despite clear and repeated warning, Lisbon found itself incapable of providing panacea for the ills that were destroying the very vitals of her valuable tobacco trade. Considering the great importance Portugal attached to the new trade, describing the *Renda do Tabaco* as the "*O Patrimonio de Estado*",[13] and an "important branch of commerce" that needed to be carefully nurtured, the trade was entirely dominated by Hindus, who in her own reckoning , were serving their own interests.

On the other hand, resistance to the new scheme considered profitable to the state, was a natural reaction of the subalterns who were the butt of imperial onslaught on cultural and religious fronts. Hindu merchants could sabotage, if they desired, the trade that could save the *Estado* from the dire financial state it was in, as Portugal depended upon them for its success. The history of this trade clearly reveals that both in Brazil and Goa, the subaltern merchant class turned the trade into an onerous experience to the imperialists. Portugal's vulnerability was exposed by these forces at both the supply and sale point, as official reports clearly reflect. Goan contractors did not permit Lisbon to reap all the golden expectations of this "*novo ramo do comercio colonial*". Outbreak of two successive and almost simultaneous revolts against Portugal in both Goa and Brazil, in the 1780s and early 1820s, might have had their roots in this addiction-based venture. Further research on this issue could throw up factual data on this hypothesis.

Lisbon did not fail to express repugnance to the monopoly of Hindu merchants and take cognizance of their craftiness. Officials in Goa were goaded on to entrust the task to reliable Christian merchants.[14] In 1779, there were 139, 853 Christians above the age of ten, in contrast to 19,220 Hindus. However, local Christians and Portuguese did not figure among successful bidders of contracts. Local Christians were engaged in lesser, contractual jobs like disembarking the bales, depositing them in the warehouse, weighing the stocks and maintenance of records. Wages paid to them varied from a paltry sum of 3 *tangas* and 20 *réis* to 1 *xerafim* a day.[15] Lisbon could do little beyond express disappointment at their own men and the native Christians not being part of this profitable venture.

Role in the Reciprocal, Official Trade

Portugal invested the returns from the snuff and leaf tobacco trade in exports back home. Pepper, textiles, saltpeter, diamonds, cowries and a variety of sundry articles like pearls, tea, musk and porcelain formed part of this reciprocal tobacco-linked trade. The participation of the Hindu merchants as intermediary suppliers of these commodities was inevitable. Upea Kamat, Soirea Parab, Govind Sinai, Soirea Lawande, Vitogy Sinai Nerlicar and others were some of the participants in this trade. Rigid official stipulations of quantity, quality, price and time of procurement of merchandise were often flouted by the merchants. Lisbon found them formidable to deal with, but ended up making adjustments in her strategy. For instance, around 1748, local merchants cited difficulties in complying with orders to procure 100 *khandis* of pepper, just when Lisbon wanted larger supplies. Finally, Lisbon was compelled to reduce the pepper requisition to 50 *khandis* per merchant and shift the focus to diamonds and textiles. Similarly, high-priced procurements by local merchants resulted in losses to the metropolis in the 1740s. In contrast, Portuguese traders were able to supply the goods at a cheaper rate.[16] In the case of textiles too, local merchants gained an upper hand by either supplying goods at a higher price than requisitioned, or procured the goods late. Portugal paid the price: in 1759 textiles shipped on snuff account were sold in Lisbon at 30% loss.[17]

Procurement of supplies involved an intricate system of inter-port commercial networking. Textiles and saltpetre were procured from Bengal by exchanging cotton, sandalwood, rice, coir, cowries and snuff, collected from Surat, Malabar, Mangalore and Bargare. Cotton was purchased in Surat by exchanging ivory that came from Mozambique on snuff account. Local merchants were active participants in all such transactions.

Around 1752 the Bengal Trading Company was planned by merchants in Goa to facilitate procurement of saltpeter and textiles from there.[18] Though Lisbon did not accept the plan, about thirty prominent native merchants, all Hindus, invested their money ranging from 500 *xerafins* to 30,000 *xerafins* as shown in Appendix 2.[19] In April 1760, a ship of this company sailed from Goa to Bengal for trade.[20]

Ship Repairs and Supply of Victuals

The breaking of colonial commercial shackles in the eighteenth century, comparable with the shattering of "a biological *ancien régime*"[21]energized the long-distance trade between Goa, Portugal and the Second Empire. A large number of ships, mainly private vessels, were licensed to trade with the ports of Asia. Twenty Portuguese merchant ships and twenty-one English merchant vessels had anchored at Goa in 1785.[22] Nearly fifty ships linked up Goa and Brazil between 1807-1822, - an average of over three ships a year. As each ship put in at the dockyard in Goa for repairing, wintering or other facilities, it was the indigenous men who provided the required services. At the end of the eighteenth century, there were about three hundred workers on regular pay roll at the dockyard, serving as carpenters, caulkers, blacksmiths, masons, tin workers, painters and tailors. Supply of wood, masts, sails, barrels, sacks, ropes, tar, nails, dyes and other material was supplied by the local merchants .Names of the Kamats, Naiks, Parabs, Mhamai Kamats, Pai and Co. find repetition.[23] They also figure as suppliers of provisions to these vessels. This business provided them with ample opportunities to expand their economic links in other directions.[24]

Private Trade

Native merchants of Goa were active players in the long-distance private trade as well. State participation in seaborne trade was minimal during the period under consideration. Lisbon largely depended on and benefited from the collection of duties at various entry and exit points of the *Estado*. Remittances of goods by Goan Hindu merchants were regular and are reflected by ample references in the Records at the Historical Archives of Goa. Textiles, pepper, cinnamon, diamonds, incense, tea, porcelain, sealing wax and other articles were exported to Lisbon as well as Luanda, ports of Brazil and elsewhere.

Their trading network was spread across parts of India and the empire. For instance, Bulla Naik, Govinda Naik and Dugu Kamat, well known in the trading circles of Goa for over forty years (roughly, 1725 onwards) were involved in extended trade to various parts of Asia, Africa and America. They had agents in ports of Balaghat, the South, North, Macau, Mozambique, Bahia, Angola and Portugal. João Rodrigues, José Rodrigues de Almeida, Frutuozo Vicente Viana Luis Coelho Ferreira, Luis da Silva Pinto and others were their trading partners in Bahia. In Luanda, Angola, Francisco Afonso dos Santos, Thomas da Silva Bautista, João Alberto da Silveira, Francisco Bruno de Lemos, Antonio Morreira Lisboa, José Vieira, Lt. Gen. Mathias da Costa, Thomas da Silva Coutinho and others traded with them. In Lisbon, Caetano Francisco, João André Carabiasos, Anselmo José da Cruz, José Francisco da Cruz e Alagoa, brothers, Tealdo and Croza (?), Ignacio Pedro Quintela, Francisco Antonio Ferreira da Cunha, Felix Maria Reco and Co., widow Calvet, Francisco Manoel Calvet, Bandeira Baugalupe Canoly, Domingo Dias, Jose Alvares Bandeira, Francisca da Cunha, Manoel de Pinho, José Domingos, Bartholomeu Jorge, Francisco Antonio Teixeira da Cunha and Co., and João

Bautista Picardo were partners in trade.[25] Goods were paid for in gold coins. Payment for goods sent to Bahia and Luanda was remitted to specified merchants in Lisbon.

Though quantification of the total value of goods exported remains a problem, a glimpse of the trade can be obtained from manuscripts pertaining to specific years. The *N.S .da Conceição e S. Vicente Ferreira*, captained by Domingos de Faria e Cruz, shipped goods worth 55, 211=1=00 *xerafins* on the account of the above mentioned merchants. In 1765, the *N.S. das Brotas* took textile consignments worth 8,534=0=22 *xerafins* to Bahia. The total value of textiles remitted by these merchants was 10, 476=0=22 *xerafins*. In 1766, the *St. Antonio e Justiça* carried textiles worth 37,512=4=49½ *xerafins*, of which, fabrics worth 23,371=2=42½ *xerafins* were meant for Luanda and 14, 141=2=07 *xerafins* worth textiles were sent to Lisbon, besides spices. The total value of their exports from September 1755 to March 1766 was 3,07,19,967; the duties paid were 185, 998=3=05 *xerafins*, while the *lagimas* were 28, 946=3=45 *xerafins*.[26] It can be surmised that individual trade of Goan merchants was by no means negligible or insignificant. It grew progressively during the peak years from 1792-1806.

Local merchants did not hesitate to appeal to authorities in Lisbon for redressal of grievances. Petitions by the above mentioned merchants and by Custam, Hari, Venkatesh Kamat and Vitogi Kamat – were addressed to his majesty seeking royal protection for their trade. They claimed that their goods dispatched in December 1765 and February 1766, and earlier sent to Bahia and Lisbon in 1763 and 1764, by the vessels, *N.S. da Conceição e S. Vicente Ferreira* and *N.S. da Caridade e S. Francisco de Paula* were sequestered in Lisbon, resulting in heavy losses to them. Portuguese official, José Joaquim de Sequeira Megalhães e Lançöes testified in 1768 that the said petitioners had made valuable contribution by risking large amounts of money which generally exceeded 500,000 *xerafins*, facing risk on land and at sea, maintaining agents at various ports and towns, which benefited the public by way of movement of goods that extended to various parts of the empire; their service to the *Fazenda* included the duties paid on imports and exports .Their distinguished fidelity and allegiance to the Crown in times of need - shown by gifts and donations was all lauded by the said officer.[27]

Hindu merchants had no hesitation to enter into negotiations with Clerics. Fr. Nicolau de Francisco and Fr. João de Sta. Catarina, of the Madre de Deos Convent were found indulging in scandalous commercial dealings and flouting payment of duties around 1770.Quensua Kamat had executed many deals with these priests which included purchase of some ivory.[28] Custam Pai, Anta Naik , Narayan Kamat, Biquia Kamat and Quensua Kamat – all of Cumbarjua testified that they had supplied the said clergy with textiles and other goods.[29]

Conclusions

Hindus were reduced to a clear minority in Goa by the end of the seventeenth century.[30] Yet, their economic power remained intact and the dependence of the Portuguese on this community continued. Native merchant class was resolute in monopolising important branches of trade, and left no room for other competitors. They served as state revenue farmers, as merchant contractors for snuff (1675-1825) and leaf tobacco (1775-1825), they supplied goods for the official tobacco-linked reciprocal trade and were actively engaged in long-distance private trade, having business partnerships with merchants in Luanda, Bahia and Lisbon. They provided brokerage and served as insurers; they were also contractors and suppliers of provisions at the Goa shipyard. The cultural intolerance notwithstanding, they played the role of subordinate partnership with the empire in commercial matters. Merchants received immediate economic rewards and extended linkages in commercial ventures.

M. N. Pearson's observation about the economic role of the Hindus in the Seventeenth century is true of the following century as well. "Portugal could not have lasted for a long time in India without the co-operation of the non-Christians, especially the Hindus", he remarks.[31] This dependence compelled them, in the larger interest of their trade, to amend their strategy in order to accommodate the local merchants' stance, even when it seemed whimsical and onerous. Merchants used their bargaining power to maximize profits while supplying goods for the official trade.

The merchants had their priorities set: their profits were above all else. In the context of the tobacco trade, profits drove them into partnership with the imperialists. They sold tobacco irrespective of quality, and extorted payments that forced villagers from Salcete to flee. As intermediaries in the reciprocal trade, they indirectly assisted the drain of the *cabedal do tabaco* to Portugal. At the same time, they caused enough heartburning to state authorities by resorting to sale of local tobacco and flouting regulations under every possible pretext.

The merchants gained from the Lusitanian move in the direction of liberalization of trade. Reduction of export duties effected after 1783 benefited this class immensely. They seized the tide of steady progress in the long-distance trade during 1792-1806. Private trade continued to engage the Hindu merchants' attention till well after the 1820s. Though some of these merchants had agency houses and were simultaneously managing a variety of business, it appears that they did not own ocean going vessels. Dominance of the Hindu merchant class in the long-distance trade reflects a commercial symbiosis. In spite of the resentment of the imperialists in this regard, the subtle bond of self-interest between the merchants and rulers cannot be ruled out.

Appendix 1

Goods Dispatched to Lisbon by Native Merchants (Bulla, Govinda and Dugu Kamat) 1755-1768.

1755	N.S.da Conceição	Textiles	9 quartas, I bundle
1756	S.Francisco Xavier	Textiles	16 bundles, 1 bale
1757	St . Antonio e Justiça	Textiles	8 quartas
1758	S.José	Textiles & Pepper	18 bundles textiles, 21 bales pepper
1758	Conceição	Cinnamon	50 bales-wild cinnamon
1759	S.Antonio e Justiça	Textiles	8 bundles
1760	S.José	Textiles	35 bundles/ boxes
1760	Conceição	Textiles,	Cinnamon, incense, indigo, lac tea. 127 boxes/ bales
1761	N.S.da Caridadee	S. Francisco da Paula	Textiles 9 bundles
1762	S. Antonio e Justiça	Textiles & Diamonds	21 bundles; 1 *bizalho*
1763	N.S.da Caridade e S. Francisco da Paula		Textiles & Cinnamon 14 bales; 5 boxes
1764	N.S.da Caridade e S. Vicente Ferreira		Textiles & Cinnamon 7 bales; 6 boxes
1765	N.S.da Caridade e S. Francisco da Paula		Textiles 10 bales
1765	N.S.das Brotas	Textiles & sealing wax	25 bales; 1 box
1766	S.Antonio e Justiça	Textiles	21 bales
1767	S.Jose e N.S.da Conceição	Textiles	21 bales
1768	N.S.da Lapa e Trinidade Bom Jesus da	Textiles	15 bales
1768	N.S.da Lapa	Textiles	1 quarto

Source: HAG:MR, 145-B, fls.491-523.

Appendix 2.
Amount invested by Goan Hindu Partners in the Bengal Co.

Merchants	*Residents of*	*Amount (xerafins)*
Rama Parab	N.A.	500
Rama Custam Sinai	N.A.	500
Babulea Parab	N.A..	500
Dessai Vencu Naik	N.A.	30,000
Paquea Sinai Dumo	Cumbarjua	5,000
Bula Naik & Dugu Kamat	N.A.	10,000
Upea Kamat	Betim	10,000
Rama Kamat	Panelim	20,000
Krishna Sinai Cabady	Verem	3,000
Custam Naik Corondo	Cumbarjua	14,000
Anta Sinai	Cumbarjua	4,000
Narsu Naik	Cumbarjua	4,000
Massanea Sinai Molio	Cumbarjua	3,000
Vitoba Sinai Bisalo	Cumbarjua	1,000
Anta Kamat & Surya Kamat	Panjim	2,000
Vitigy Kamat	Panjim	6,000
Suba Kamat Mhamai	Panjim	1,000
Chimenea Parab	N.A	1,000
Rogu Shetty	Naroa	1,000
Vittogi Sinai Coraleiro	St. Luzia	500
Custam Naik Burye	Porpanjim	500
Bapea Naik Burye	Porpanjim	500
Vitogi Sinai Nerlicar	Verem	2,000
Soirea Parab Lawande	Ribandar	1,000
Vencu Keni	Cumbarjua	500
Rama Chandra Sinai	Cumbarjua	500
Narayan Kamat Dolio	Cumbarjua	250
Rama Sinai Rangonkar	S. Estevao	1,000
Vencu Pai Calapurcar	Cumbarjua	1,000
Rogu Sinai	Ribandar	1,000

Source: HAG: *MR*, 144-A, fls.108v-109; 148-A, fls.116-117v.

Notes and References

1. T.R. de Souza, "Glimpses of Hindu Dominance of Goan Economy in the 17th Century", *Indica*, No. 1, vol. 12, March 1975, pp. 27-36. T.R. de Souza 's other articles useful for the role of Goan merchants are, "Mhamai House Records", *The Indian Archives*, XXXI, no. 1, Jan-June, 1982, pp. 25-45 and "Xendi Tax: A Phase in the History of Luso-Hindu Relations in Goa, (1704-1841)", in P.M. Joshi, ed., *Studies in Foreign Relations*, Hyderabad, 1975, pp. 463-471.
2. K.M. Panikkar, *Malabar and the Portuguese*, p.206.
3. Afzal Ahmad, *Indo-Portuguese Trade in Seventeenth Century, 1660-1663*, p. 123.
4. HAG: *MR*, 142-B, fls.454-454v; 458, 464, 465.
5. HAG: *MR*, 149-B, fls.332-334, 335-337v, 338-352v.
6. *Ibid.*, fls.452, 453.
7. HAG: *MR*, 190-B, fls.456-457v.
8. HAG: *MR*, 151, fl.181; 164-G, fl.1744.
9. HAG: *MR*, 195-E, fls.957-957v; *Fazenda*, list 1, nos.1708, fl.1; 1722, fl.5; 1723, fls.1-6;1750, fls.1-5.
10. P. Sequeira Antony, *Op .cit.*, Appendix 7.2, pp.400-404; HAG: *MR*, 202-D, fl. 384.
11. HAG: *MR*,192-B, fls.615-616; 200-B, fl. 216. Duties levied on such imports at Hindu-dominated Ponda, Zambaulim and Canacona netted 37,705 *xerafins* in 1813.
12. Celsa Pinto, "At the Dusk of the Second Empire: Goa-Brazil Commercial Relations, 1770-1825", *Purabhilekh-Puratatva*, vol.viii, no.1, pp.45-47.
13. HAG: *MR*, 191-A, fls.61-61v, 66-67v .
14. In 1779, there were 139, 853 Christians above the age of ten, in contrast to 19,220 Hindus in the old conquests. P. Sequeira Antony, *Op. cit.*, Appendix 7.1, p.399.
15. *Ibid.*, p.287.
16. HAG: *OR*, 1506, fls.1-2, 16; *Fazenda*, list1, no. 1766, fls.100v-102v,108-111v.
17. HAG: *OR*, 1506, fl. 103.
18. HAG: *Fazenda*, list 1, no. 1767, fl. 74v.
19. HAG: *MR*, 144-A, fls.94v-95,108v-109; 148-A, fls.116-117v.

20. HAG: *MR*, 148-A, fl. 120v. For commercial ventures of Portuguese settlers in the eastern coast of India in the 17th century, *vide*, George Winius, "The Shadow Empire" of Goa in the Bay of Bengal" *Itinerario*, vol.1, vii, 1983, 2, pp. 83-101.
21. Quoted in K.N. Chaudhari, *Trade and Civilization in the Indian Ocean. An Economic History from the Rise of Islam to 1750*, p. 221.
22. HAG: *MR*, 195-C, fls. 1335-1335v .
23. HAG: *MR*, 195-E, fls.751-757, 775-775v.
24. T. R. de Souza, "Mhamai House Records", *The Indian Archives*, xxxi, no. 1, Jan-June, 1982, p. 33.
25. HAG: *MR*, 145-B, fls. 491-523v.
26. *Ibid.*
27. HAG: *MR*, 145-B, fls. 467,468-470v; 491-523v; 530-531v.
28. HAG: *MR*, 147-A, fls. 297-298.
29. *Ibid,* fls. 369-383.
30. T.R. de Souza, "Glimpses of Hindu Dominance..", *Op.cit.*, p.30.
31. M. N. Pearson "Indigenous Dominance in a Colonial Economy: The Goa Rendas, 1600-1670", *Mare Luso-Indicum*, vol. II, Geneve, 1973, p. 72.

9

Marwari Barayev : An Indian Trader in Russia in the Eighteenth Century

Surendra Gopal

By 1630s Indian traders had reached Russia; they made Astrakhan (the port at the mouth of the Volga river where it falls into the Caspian Sea) their base of operations.[1] Hindu Indian traders in Russia mostly hailed from the North-western India and were popularly known as *Multanis*. Once in a while contemporary Russian records mention the presence of *Marwari* traders among them.[2] These Hindu Indians lived in a special stone house containing their shops, store-houses and the place of worship. They trade in the cities of Russia, mostly lying along the Volga river, such as Kasan, Saratov, etc. and also went up to the Russian capital Moscow. They were also money lenders who met the credit needs of small farmers, ordinary soldier, lower- rank state functionaries and traders.[3] They also actively participated in the Russo-Persian trade since Indian merchants were present in all the important Persian cities. According to one estimate Indians numbered more than 10,000 in the capital city (Isfahan) Ispahan alone. This paper seeks to describe the career of a *Marwari* trader, who in a decade and half emerged as the richest and most influential Indian trader in Astrakhan. This description will also throw light on the range of the trading activities of Indian merchants, the different dimensions of usury they practiced and the hurdles they faced. It will show that these Indians were not lacking in entrepreneurial skill; what hampered them were non-commercial factors.

Marwari Barayev is first mentioned in the year 1721 in the "Register of Petitions and Reports Received in the Chancellory of the Governor of Astrakhan." The relevant extract indicates that the Indian trader Marwari Barayev had requested that action should be taken against Aleksei Puchkov who had borrowed a sum of twelve *roubles*. He had failed to repay both the principal and the interest even though the stipulated time limit had passed.[4]

Unfortunately the correct name of Marwari Barayev has been nowhere mentioned in other documents. They also fail to indicate when he first arrived in Russia. However subsequent documents reveal the fascinating story of his immense wealth and also his ruination. Another document relating to Marwari Barayev exists in "Register of Astrakhan relating to the money lending operations of Indian traders to the residents of Astrakhan and the surrounding villages." It is a loan deed registered in 1724 in which a gardener Ignatiyev Lukoyanov borrowed on 5 January 215 *roubles* from Marwari Barayev and undertook to repay the sum by 5 April 1724. This is a clear evidence that in the intervening three years he had prospered and was now able to loan more than 200 *roubles* whereas earlier he had lent 12 roubles.[5]

Next year, in 1725, we find Marwari Barayev adding a new dimension to his activity. Kalmyk Sanzhata, through a registered deed hired from him a Tatar Azhimamet Ishyeyev as a domestic servant till 3 May 1727.[6] We have no idea of the profit reaped by Marwari Barayev from this transaction. The locals hired domestic servants from other Indian merchants in Astrakhan as well. A document dated 22 October 1725 shows that an Armenian trader of Astrakhan, borrowed 1550 *roubles* from Marwari Barayev on the following terms. He pledged his stock of textiles, manufactured in Persian towns, with him and promised to repay the sum by 16 May 1726.[7] Marwari Barayev's graph of prosperity was rising as he was now in a position to lend thousands instead of hundreds of *roubles*. We have no idea the rate of interest that he charged. The year 1726 unmistakably confirmed Marwari Barayev's financial clout. He purchased from his fellow Indians fifty-two loan deeds worth 3047 *roubles* executed in the past and due for payment in the coming years.[8]

A loan advanced by Marwari Barayev in 1726 reflects a new aspect of his business. On 3 June 1726, a Tatar Bamamet Zhancheldyev , resident of Astrakhan, borrowed 440 *roubles*. He was to go to Gilan (situated in Persia on the southern coast of the Caspian Sea) and purchase certain specified commodities. On his return Marwari Barayev would purchase all the commodities on the prevailing prices.[9] Extending loan on condition that the borrower would go out of Russia and bring specified goods to be purchased by the trader who had given the loan, seems to have been an accepted business practice. Marwari Barayev on 5 June lent 265 *roubles* to a Persian Armenian who was asked to proceed to Bukhara and to bring goods mentioned in the agreement and deliver it to Him.[10] We have no idea about the nature of goods to be brought and what profit the Agent would gain. Financing of imports into Russia from Persian and Central Asia was an important aspect of the activities of affluent Indian merchants in Astrakhan and Marwari Barayev was pursuing this activity as a part of expanding business operations. Money lending business continued along with financing of imports. On 31 December 1726 a Greek Christopher Matveyev borrowed from Marwari Barayev 537 *roubles*. He was to repay it by 7 May 1727.[11] We do not know the rate of interest the Greek was required to pay.

Marwari Barayev had successfully built up his business of money lending, financing of imports and sale of imported commodities at whole-sale rates. Some of the borrowers had mortgaged their immovable properties before obtaining the loan. When they could repay, Marwari Barayev filed a suit to be allowed to take possession of the mortgaged property according to the terms of the loan. In 1727, he applied to Ivan Alekseivich fon Mengden, the Governor of Astrakhan to permit him to occupy the property of a Tatar Sukhan Toktagov who had defaulted on the payment of a loan of 57 *roubles*. The Governor accepted Marwari Barayev's plea and passed an order in his favour.[12]

The take over of the mortgaged immovable property was an additional means of enriching oneself is also clear from another petition submitted by Marwari Barayev in 1729 to the Governor. He prayed for permission to attach the property of Yunus Ibraimov, consisting of a garden along with all the structures standing on it because he had failed to repay the borrowed amount of seventeen *roubles* within the stipulated time. The Governor upheld his request.[13] On 22 June 1727 Marwari Barayev lent 360 *roubles* to a Tatar of Astrakhan. The condition was that he would go to Gilan (in Persia) and buy certain specified commodities. He was at liberty to sell them there as instructed by him or to hand over the goods to him in Astrakhan. In this case the sureties were Tatar's wife Fatma Yunusaabyzova and his daughter Ertugan Ashirbyzova.[14]

In 1729, Marwari Barayev advanced to Andal Nandaev, an Agrizhanets (children born out of the wedlock of an Indian father and a Tatar or Kalmyk mother) 999 *roubles* on the condition that he would go to Makarevskii Fair held at the city of Nizhniigorod and purchase and bring goods mentioned in the terms of the agreement and hand them over to him.[15] Employing Agents to bring goods from Russian cities and commercial centers in Persia and Central Asia was integral part of the business practices of Marwari Barayev. We have no document naming the buyers of these goods sold by Marwari Barayev. We learn of the rate of interest charged from a document of the year 1726. This document concerns a loan of 120 *roubles* advanced by Marwari Barayev. The interest to be charged is ½ *kopeck* per *rouble* per month i.e. 50 *kopecks* or ½ *rouble* per 100 *roubles* per month or six per cent annually.[16] Throughout 1720s Marwari Barayev was prospering. This is clear from the contents of a petition he submitted to the Governor in 1730. In this he wrote that he had purchased from an Indian trader of Astrakhan Balai Alimchand loan deeds, issued by him in previous years. The borrowers had been asked by the Government to repay the amount to him. However, some of the borrowers had fled. Marwari Barayev prayed for permission of the government to take possession of houses and other properties of the defaulters.[17] We have no idea what relief Marwari Barayev was able to get.

Supply of credit and capital and attaching movable and immovable properties of borrowers had made him very rich. He was lending money even to his compatriots. Gulabra Otomchand took a loan of 250 *roubles* from him on 6 June 1731. He was to return the amount by 6 July 1733. He mortgaged his garden (160m x 79m) with all the structures and workshops standing on its premises and also the 'vegetable and fruit bearing trees.'[18] After a gap of five years Marwari Barayev is again mentioned in a document of 1735. His name crops up in connection with the proposal to establish a new city, Orenburg as the base for conducting Russo-Central Asian and Russo-Indian trade. The Russian desire was necessitated by the political situation developing in Persia after the rise of Nadir Shah. The series of wars the new ruler launched dislocated the normal commercial life in Iran and Indian traders residing in Persia started emigrating across the Caspian Sea to Russia to escape the anarchy. Trade via Iran was unsafe and the Russian authorities had to think of alternative routes. Their choice fell on Orenburg in the steppes east of the Ural mountains.[19] Those officers entrusted with the task decided to consul and seek the advice of Marwari Barayev, the richest and the most famous Indian trader in Russia, about the viability of the project with respect to India.[20] He was invited to Orenburg by the promoters of the new trade centre, I.K.Krillov, V.N. Tatishchev, I.I.Neplyuev and P.I.Richkov.

Marwari Barayev went to Orenburg and prepared a document which listed four trade routes leading to Indian capital Delhi from Astrakhan.[21] He favoured the Central Asian line for promoting Russo-Indian trade in future.[22] He supported his contention by referring to the decay of trade in Persia and Astrakhan following the outbreak of anarchy after Nadir Shah had come to power. According to him when peace prevailed in Persia, two hundred Indian traders annually visited Astrakhan. Now the number had come down to eighty. The Bukharan route was the shortest. If security of life and property could be ensured, he was confident, around six hundred Indian traders would come every year. He also prepared a list of Indian goods and Russian goods imported into and exported from Orenburg.[23]

Krillov was pleased to find emphatic support from the most well known Indian trader of the times in Russia. In his report to Empress Anna Ivanovna on 20 April 1735, Krillov expressed his agreement with Marwari Barayev. He also added that Marwaari Barayev was keen to keen to promote Russo-Indian trade from Orenburg by personally participating in it in the initial stages. He would send agents with goods from Orenburg via Bukhara and Kabul so that more and more Indian traders would be motivated to follow his example and travel to Orenburg.[24] In 1736 Krillov recommended that Marwari Barayev be advanced a sum of one thousand *roubles* from the Royal Treasury to purchase goods to be sent to India. He asserted other Indians would follow his example. He was favouring Marwari Barayev because he could write in Russian and could translate Indian languages texts of his countrymen into Russian. Of course, Marwari Barayev declared he could collect from his compatriots in Astrakhan a sum between one thousand and fifty thousand *roubles*. But in his opinion advancing a sum from the Royal Treasury was a better option. He concluded 'new attempts and enterprises' do involve a loss.[25]

Empress Anna Ivanovna concurred with the proposal of Krillov in her Edict of 11 February 1736. She ordered one thousand *roubles* should be advanced to Marwari Barayev from the Royal Treasury to purchase goods to be sent to India through his Agents from Orenburg. Marwari Barayev was to return the money after his agents returned. His property in Astrakhan was to be placed in the charge of Senate till expedition came back.[26] Marwari Barayev never made the trip to India. He could not send his Agents to India. When he arrived in Astrakhan from Orenburg, the local Governor, V.N. Tatishchev, arrested him on flimsy charges and put him in gaol.[27] Tatishchev feared that the rise of Astrakhan as a commercial centre of eastern goods would spell the doom of Astrakhan and result in his loss of income and authority. This was the beginning of his misfortunes and probably he never recovered from the slide in his fortunes. We do not know how long he was kept in the prison.

According to a document of 1738 he still owned a shop in the Indian quarters and paid eleven *roubles* as rent for eleven months to the Astrakhan authorities.[28] Why only for eleven months? The same document shows that other Indian paid twelve *roubles* as rent for a whole year. Something was definitely amiss. His petition submitted in October 1739 gives us a glimpse into the misfortunes that had befallen on him. He said even though he had been released from prison, a watch was still kept on him. His assets worth 50,000 *roubles* seized by the authorities in Astrakhan had not been returned to him.[29] He was paying the penalty for undertaking the journey to Orenburg. He had been economically ruined; he now lacked the means for his personal sustenance.[30] We have no idea if Marwari Barayev was able to secure justice or not. We learn of his fate from an order sent by the Senate to the Chief Magistrate of Astrakhan in the case of a deceased Indian merchant Sukhanand. It casually refers to the fact that Marwari Barayev had failed to get back his assets worth 77,000 *roubles*. It also mentions the fact that he had accepted Christianity and was now known Petr Fedorov.[31]

This brings down the curtain on the history of Marwari Barayev. Before we end, we might take note of two things. Conversion to Christianity was not new for Indian merchants. In 1726 an Indian had become Christian and assumed the name Feodor Feodorov.[32] In 1729, another Indian convert to Christian religion had been given the name of Petr Ivanov.[33] We have no idea what motivated them to change their religion. Probably they changed their religion to escape harassment from the local bureaucracy to which foreigners and especially those professing a different religion were subjected to. The foreign merchant could not avert the oppression of the local bureaucracy, if it had made up its mind to harass him. Marwari Barayev should have known this. In 1729 he had received a taste of bureaucratic indifference and oppression. He had instituted a case against a soldier Andrei Kosoi (Kosov), who had broken into his shop and stolen cash, broad cloth and other goods worth 1,000 *roubles*. The thief was caught and some of the stolen goods were recovered from him. The thief was also punished but Marwari Barayev was not able to recover his lost property.[34]

To conclude we my say that the career of Marwari Barayev shows the entrepreneurial talent that he possessed. Starting as a small moneylender who had lent a tiny sum of twelve *roubles*, he, within a decade, became an owner of assets worth between 50,000 and 77,000 *roubles*. Besides cash he also owned immovable properties in and around Astrakhan. He prospered because he kept on exploring new avenues of business. From a moneylender he turned into a supplier of capital to Russian, Indian and foreign merchants. He traded as a wholesale merchant and made a fortune. But he was in position to confront the local bureaucrats, who had turned hostile to him. This was the fate of all Hindu merchants in foreign lands extending from the peninsula of Arabia, to Persia, to Iran, to Central Asia, to Russia. Absence of explicit state support prevented them from successfully standing up to local bureaucratic oppression. They rose and fell like a meteor.

Notes and References

1. Surendra Gopal, "Indian Traders in Russia in the XVII Century", *Proceedings of the Indian History Congress*, Mysore, 1969, pp. 460-68.
2. R.V. Ovchinnikov and M.A.Sidorov (compilers) and K.A.Antonova and N.M.Goldberg (eds), *Russko-Indiiskiye Otnosheniya v XVIII v.*, Moskva, 1965, doc.no.48, f.15 (back), p.75. (hereafter cited as *R-I.O. v XVIIIv.*) The document mentions the Marwari Rajaramov, who had lent 600 *roubles* to an Armenian trader Melkun Bagiyev in 1723.
3. Surendra Gopal, "Indian Traders in Russia in the XVIII Century", *The Indian Economic and Social History Review* , Vol. V, No.2, June 1968, pp.141-48: Idem, "Indian Traders in Persia in the Seventeenth Century," *Journal of Historical Studies,* No. 2, 1996, pp. 14-36.
4. *R-I.O.v XVII v.*, doc no. 35, f.103, pp. 56-57.
5. *Ibid.*, doc. no. 40, f.3, p. 61.
6. *Ibid.*, doc. no.41, f. 189, p. 64.
7. *Ibid.*, doc. no.42, f.92 (back), p. 67.
8. *Ibid.*, doc. no. 44,.f.69,75, p. 69.
9. *Ibid.*, f.130 (back), p. 70.

10. *Ibid.*, f.142, p. 70.
11. *Ibid.*, f.288 no.1226, p. 70.
12. *Ibid.*, doc.no.48, f.52, pp. 77-78.
13. *Ibid.*, doc.no.53, f.9, pp. 97-98.
14. *Ibid.*, f.82, p.84.
15. *Ibid.*, doc. no.49, 94 (back), p. 83
16. *Ibid.*, doc. no.52, f.105 (back), pp. 96-97
17. *Ibid.*, doc. no.57, pp. 113-14.
18. *Ibid.*, doc. no. 58, f.150 (back), p. 115.
19. N.A. Khalfin and P.M. Shastitko (eds), *Rossiya I Indiya*, Moskva, 1986, p.77. The founders of Orenburg, I.K.Krillov,
20. R-I.O. v XVII v., doc. no.69, f.9 (back), pp. 128-33.
21. *Ibid.*, pp. 128-29.
22. *Rossiya I Indiya,* p.78.
23. *R-I.O. v XVIII v.,* pp. 129-33.
24. *Ibid.,* doc. no.72, p. 135.
25. *Ibid.,* doc. no.74, f. 498, pp. 139-40.
26. *Ibid.*, doc. no. 75, p. 141.
27. *Indiya I Rossiya,* p. 78.
28. *R-I.O. v XVIII v.*, doc. no.110, p. 157.
29. *Ibid.,* doc. no. 81, pp. 160-61.
30. *Ibid.,* p. 161.
31. *Ibid.,* doc. no.163, p. 327.
32. *Ibid.,* doc. no. 48, f .102 (back), p. 80.
33. *Ibid.*, doc. no. 53, f. 102 (back), p. 98.
34. *Ibid.,* doc. no. 53, f. 142, pp. 100-102.

SECTION–III

Commodities, Commerce and Coinage

10

Mints, Monetary Pattern, Money-Supply and Trade: An Analysis of Safavid-Mughal Coins

Syed Ejaz Hussain

India and Persia (modern Iran) have been distinct but not dissimilar civilizations. Geography has made the two countries close neighbours sharing a common border between Baluchistan (now in Afghanistan) and Iran. When Herat was the capital of Persia under the Timurids India had a common boundary with Persia. Indian rulers from Babur (1526-30) to Aurangzeb (1659-1707) possessed Afghanistan except for Qandhar which Shah Jahan lost to Iran in 1649 and never recovered it. Qandhar served as the common overland corridor between India and Persia. On the sea route Indian ports like Ahmadabad and Cambay (in Gujarat), Calicut (in the Western coast), Bhatkal (in the kingdom of Vijayanagar), and Chittagong (in Bengal) had commercial traffic between the Indian Ocean and the Persian Gulf through the Persian ports of Hormuz (captured by the Portuguese in 1515), Lari Bandar and Bandar Abbas (originally known as Gombroon that rose after 1515 and fell in 1760), and finally Abu Shahr.

India and Iran have very intimate cultural relations from early times. The Persian culture particularly after Firdausi's Shahnama (completed cir.1009-10) began to envelope a large area in its domain. Indian sultanates - Delhi as well as provincial kingdoms of Bengal, Gujarat, Malwa, Kashmir, Jaunpur and the five Deccan kingdoms of Qutubshahis (of Golkonda), Adilshahis (of Bijapur), Nizam Shahis (of Ahmadnagar), Imad Shahis (of Berar) and Barid Shahis (of Bidar) had 'a massive infusion of Persian culture practically at all levels'.[1] Persian functioned as an official language throughout India right from the establishment of the Sultanate rule in Delhi (1192) to the year 1835 when Persian was replaced by English as a lingua franca. As a result scores of books on a variety of subjects like History, Geography, Philosophy, Medicine, Agriculture, Science, Theology, Military Science, Lexicons, Hunting, Cookery and other popular subjects were authored by many scholars. Several Indian poets such as Amir Khusro (1253-1325), Abul Faiz Faizi (1547-95) and Mirza Abdul Qadir Bedil and in modern times Ghalib and Iqbal composed their poetry in Persian. Persian styles in architecture, painting and other fine arts, as also in dress, food, manner and etiquette were adopted in public and private life in India.

Cultural relationship was further reinforced by the economic ties. Indian merchants - even Jains and Marwaris - exported textile, indigo, sugar and spices like ginger, cardamom, sandal-wood and saffron, even paan (betel leaves) to Persia and brought Pearls, gold, silver and other rarities to India. While the Persian merchants used to bring silk textiles, carpets and war-horses from their country to India for sale in accordance with the Indian royal needs. Trade exchange between India and Persia, originated from pre-historic periods, was revitalized during the Safavid-Mughal period.[2]

One noteworthy manifestation of the two powerful oriental kingdoms was their strong and stable currency system. The Safavid rulers from Shah Ismail I (1502-24) to Shah Husain I (1694-1722) and the Mughal rulers from Babur (1526-30) and more specifically from Akbar (1556-1605) to Aurangzeb (1659-1707) maintained a strong silver currency respectively. In many aspects their monetary pattern was similar. Every city of importance both in Persia and India had its mints. The mints in Persia were farmed out to private persons in auction to the highest bidder. While in India the mints were fully a Government run department. The mints, however, produced huge quantity of coins in both the countries and catered sufficiently to the demand of money by the people in general and the merchant class in particular.

The present paper makes a comprehensive study of the pattern of currency under the Safavids in Persia and the Mughals particularly the great Mughals in India. Distinctions and similarities in currency system, types of coins, number of mints, supply of money to merchants and business class, and some other related questions have been attempted to address here. The monetization of the Persian and the Indian economies has also been discussed to understand the increasing role of money in the society, urban and rural, in both the countries.

I

Commerce in Safavid Persia and Mughal India was conducted largely in cash and revenue as well as Government taxes were also collected in cash. The money-oriented commerce and tax pattern were the two fundamental reasons that both the countries produced a high standard coinage in huge quantity. A tri-metallic currency (gold, silver and copper) was maintained in both the oriental kingdoms. However, silver coin was their principal currency.[3]

The institution of pure silver currency in Persia was started by the Ilkhanid ruler, Ghazan Khan (694-703/ AD.1295-1304) who struck the silver *dinar* called *dinar-i-rayij. The dinar-rayij* was equal to six *dirhams* (1 *dirham* = 2.15 gm) and weighed 3 *misqals* (1 *misqal* = 4.3 gm) or 12.9 gm. This silver *dinar* with some modifications continued for several centuries. The weight of 12.9 gm was reduced to 8.4 gm during the reign of Abu Said (717-36/ AD.1317-35). Timur in 792/ AD1390 rechristened the *dinar-i-rayij* and called it *tanga-i-nuqra* or silver *tang. Tangu* that has originated from the Indian term *tanka* or *tank* meant for silver, was adopted earlier by Mahmud of Ghazni. Timor's *tanga-i-nuqra* was half in weight i.e., 5.38 gm of the silver *tanga* of 10.76 gm then prevalent at Delhi in India. When Shah Rukh became the ruler of Persia the silver *tanga* began to be called *Shahrukhi* and its weight was reduced to 4.72 gm that was the weight of one *miscall* at that time. When the Safavid dynasty was established in Persia in 1502, the Shahrukhi-type coin with minor departure was in circulation.[4]

On the eve of the establishment of the Mughal rule at Delhi in 1526 there was no silver coin officially in circulation in north India as the Lodis (Bahlol, Sikandar and Ibrahim) struck only billon and copper coins. Though in provincial Sultanates like Bengal, Malwa and Gujarat silver *tanka* was the main currency. Silver *tanka* called *dirham* was first started by Mahmud of Ghazni from Lahore and later on it was adopted by Iltutmish in Delhi and subsequently it continued as the chief silver currency during time of the Balbans, the Khaljis and the Tughluqs. These were thick flan round pieces with an average weight of 9-11 gms and inscription on both sides preferably *Kalima* or *Khalifa's* name on one side and the ruler's name with mint-name and date on the other side. This silver *tanka* was later on stabilized by Sher Shah Suri whose major coinage was silver *rupiya,* or rupee of one *tola* or 11.6 gm weight and 22 mm breadth and 2mm thickness bearing *Kalima / Khalifa* on obverse and ruler's name with mint and date on reverse in Arabic as well as *devanagri* following the peculiar Indian fabric and calligraphy. Babur (1526-30) and Humayun (1530-40 and 1556), however, struck an exceptionally broad (25 mm) and thin flan (1 mm)-weighing one *misqal* or 4.6 gm approximately *Shahrukhis* coins which were current in central Asia and Persia. This was also a *Kalima / Khalifa* type coin.[5]

II

When Akbar (1556-1605) came to power he initially issued *Shahrukhis* but he soon reverted to the Suri pattern of coins. Since a strong, stable and standard currency along with marvellous architecture (forts, tombs and palaces) and a strong cavalry-based army were the symbols of the State's power and supremacy during the medieval period; there prevailed a sense of competition and craze for possessing these symbols of power among the contemporary rival empires particularly the Asiatic ruling classes of the Ottomans in Central Asia, the Safavids in Persia and the Mughals in India. It was perhaps this coalescence desire that Akbar reorganized the operation of mints in 985/ AD.1577-8 and senior officers were appointed to the officially recognized mints (of Lahore, Ahmadabad, Jaunpur, Patna and Bengal), and a standard pure silver rupee with 11.6 gm in weight (bearing only 4% alloy), 25-28 mm in breadth and 2 mm in thickness carrying *Kalima-Khalifa* pattern began to be struck. Later on coins with different kinds (circular, square, *mihrabi)* and varieties (portrait, couplet, or pictorial motifs bearing a halk or Akbar riding on a horse with a halk) were also struck. *Kalima-Khalifa* was later on replaced by the *Ilahi* creed *(Alluh-o-Akbar Jalla Jalalalui)* in AD 1585. Jahangir, Shah Jahan and Aurangzeb also struck coins in huge quantity and broadly followed Akbars' metrology. Jahangir dropped the Ilahi creed and reinducted *Kalima-Khalifa* pattern. He also struck beautiful portrait and zoidical coins (with 12 zodiacal marks) apart from couplet types. Aurangzeb who considered himself to be a puritan dropped the *Kalima* motif and began a formula - *sanh julus mainanat manus zcirb* -struck at (mint's name) in the year (the regnal year) of the accession associated with prosperity. This formula continued throughout the Mughal empire till the end of the dynastic rule. Besides silver rupee, small denominational silver coins of 1/2 rupee, 1/4 rupee, 1/8 rupee and even 1/16 rupee were also struck particularly from the dawn of the Seventeenth century.[6]

The Safavids in Persia, being the foremost rival of India's Mughals, did not lag behind in maintaining a stable currency particularly a silver one. Shah Ismail I (1502-24), the first Safavid ruler surpassed his Indian contemporaries-Sikandar Lodi (1488-1517) and Ibrahim Lodi (1517-26) who struck billon and copper pieces only. Ismail soon after coming to power introduced a radical change in the pattern of the Persian currency. First of all he dispensed with the earlier lighter coins and started silver *tanka* in three denominations with weights of four, two and one *misqal* (288 grain/18.7 gm, 144 grain/9.3 gm and 72 grains or 4.7 gm). The nomenclature of the silver coin was also changed. Now it came to be known as *Shahi*. The standard silver denomination thus became the silver *Shahi* of 9.3 gm bearing 25-30 mm diameter. 18.7 gm coin was therefore double *Shahi* or *Do-Shahi* while 4.7 gm was *half-Shahi* or *nim-Shahi*. The silver currency of Ismail surpassed the Indian currency which was only copper based. Silver source to the Delhi Sultanate dwindled during this period. But the metrology of the Persian silver currency progressively declined and at the end of his rule *Do-Shahi* was reduced to 120 grain/7.8 gm and *Shahi* contained 60 grains/3.9 gm while *nim-Shahi* had 30 grains or 1.95 gm. Ismail's son and successor, Shah Tahmasp I (1524-76) who ruled for a long period of over half a century and saw the rule of the Mughal's (Babur, Humayun and Akbar) and the Suris in India, produced interesting and extensive coinage in silver. The weight however, further decreased and it ultimately came down to 72 gr/4.6 gm, 36 gr/2.3 gm and 14.4 gr/0.934 gm. After Tahmasp I and the brief rule of Shah Ismail II (1576-77) Muhammad Khudabanda ascended the throne in 1578 and ruled for about eight years till 1586. He followed the last metrology of his predecessor but the designation *of Do-Shahi* was changed and it came to be known as *Muliammadi.* Shah Abbas I (1587-1629) the son of Muhammad Khudabanda reigned for a long period of about forty-two years. He was the contemporary of Akbar and Jahangir. He tried to stabilize the Persian currency and weight of the silver coins was increased. Two *misqcil* i.e., 9.3 gm that was equivalent to 200 *dinars* again reappeared. During his reign the following silver coins were minted: *Abbasi* (2 *misqal*/9.3 gm = 200 *dinars), Muhammadi* (1 *miscal* 1/4.6 gm = 100 *dinars), Shahi* (1/2 *misqal*/2.30 gm = 50 *dinars)* and *Bisti* (1/5 *misqal*/0.92 gm = 20 *dinars).* Later on the weight of the *Abbasi* was reduced to 7.8 gm. The successors of Shah Abbas I i.e., Safi I (1629-42), Abbas II (1642-66), Safi II or Sulaiman II (1669-94) and Shah Husain I (1694-1722) followed more or less the metrology and denominations of Shah Abbas I. However, some heavier silver pieces known as *Panj Abbasi* and *Panj Shahi* worth 500 dinars were also struck. In India the Mughal rulers like Jahangir and Shah Jahan also occasionally issued heavier silver coins. But these were not their regular currency.[7]

Apart from these, there was an unique silver bent bar coinage called *Lari* struck from Lar, the Southern Coastal Iranian province. Weighing 4.5 or 5 gm the *larins* were popular among merchants due to its uniqueness and purity in silver. *Larins* were copied in India by the rulers of Deccan also.[8]

Since the Safavid rulers professed their faith in Shii Islam the names of the Shii twelve Imams along with Kalima appeared on obverse on all their silver and gold coins in different styles and ornamental designs while the ruler's names with his title was inscribed on the reverse. However, the small flan coins with thick engraving of Safi I and his successors did not carry the Shii creed.

III

Decentralization of mints and issue of coins simultaneously from different places is a significant feature of the Safavid-Mughal monetary systems. During the entire period of the Sultanate rule in North India Delhi was the only active mint which produced coins regularly in sufficient quantity. Badayun, Deogir, Daulatabad and Tilang were the other four mints which struck silver coins. During Tughluq period Satgaon, Sunargaon, Lakhnauti and Tirhut also struck silver coins but for a brief spell of time only. Almost the same situation prevailed in pre-Safavid Persia. Not many mints existed there before the foundation of the Safavid dynasty.

In India, Bengal Sultanate was the first provincial kingdom wherein the mints were widely distributed. This practice was followed by Sher Shah Suri who struck coins from a large number of areas. In fact, the operation of simultaneously a number of mints depended on the quantity of supply of silver and demand of the coined money by the merchant class. Sher Shah who rose to power from a rural background of Sahsaram (in Rohtas district of Bihar) where he managed *jagir* of his father, perhaps realized the need to monetize the rural economy to maintain a nice between rural and urban economy in order to augment the revenue resources of the state. That was why he not only widely opened the mints in areas of politico-economic activities struck coins of small denominations too. Akbar, the Mughal ruler, soon grasped the Suri pattern of mint distribution and coinage, and followed it with certain modifications to further improve and stabilize the monetary structure. Babur and Humayun struck coins from Delhi and Agra. Though some coins from Patna struck by the former and Bangala mints issued by the latter have also come up. Their governance was limited and unstable that was why there was crisis of precious metal and hence minimum number of mints and number of coins.[9]

When Akbar assumed power in 1556 initially Agra and Delhi mints produced coins. Soon coins were issued from Jaunpur and later Lahore followed by Patna, Bangala and Ahmedabad mints. The monetary administration was reorganized by Akbar in 985/ AD.1577-8 and officially approved provincial mints viz. Fathpur, Lahore, Ahmedabad, Jaunpur, Patna and Bengal began to strike strike coins. However, this list of officially approved mints falsifies the number of mints known from surviving coins found in different coin-hoards. The Uttar Pradesh coin hoards wherein the largest number of coins are known in dina represent as many as 57 mints which produced silver coins during the time of Akbar. All these mints were not in operation simultaneously; but produced coins at one or the other time during his rule. The most active mints of his time are Agra, Ahmedabad, Akbarnagar, Allahabad, Delhi, Fathpur, Gwalior, Jaunpur, Kabul, Lahore, Patna, Surat, Thatta, Ujjain, Urdu and Urdu Zafar Qarin. During the time of Jahangir the number of mints was reduced to 35. The reason for this is said that Jahangir soon after his accession to power ordered to raise the weight of silver and gold coins by 20 per cent. Hence the silver coin now weighed 212 grains/14gm in place of 176 or 177 gr. /11 gm. But this did not satisfy the ruler and he again passed the order in 1609-10 to increase the weight by 5 per cent. Now the silver rupee became a heavier coin of 222 grains/ 16.25gm approximately, which caused inconvenience to the merchants and *sarrafs* in calculation. Realizing the demand of the coin the emperor rectified himself and ordered to revert to the old standard of 176-177 s/ 11gm in 1611. But the number of mints did not increase and almost the same number of mints produced coins during the reign of Shah Jahan. Aurangzeb, the last of the great Mughals, remained on the throne for quite a long period of five decades (1659-1707) and wielded a comparatively larger area under his sway, had as many as 84 mints producing silver coins. But after Aurangzeb the Mughal empire began to decline in all directions and this had an impact on the silver flow to the Mughal controlled mints, as a result not only the volume of currency declined but the number of mints shrank.[10]

The Mughal mints particularly the mints which produced silver coins from the time of Akbar to Aurangzeb may be divided into three categories: Regular, irregular and temporary mints. Regular mints were those which produced coins regularly during the reign of each ruler and covered almost all the years. These mints were: Agra, Ahmedabad, Ahmadnagar, Ajmer, Akbarnagar (Rajmahal), Allahabad, Burhanpur, Delhi/Shahjahanabad, Kabul, Kashmir/Srinagar, Lahore, Patna, Peshawar, Surat, Thatta and Ujjain. Out of these 16 regular mints Allahabad, Agra, Delhi/Shahjahanabad and Ajmer were located in the North India; Kashmir/ Srinagar in the extreme north while Thatta, Lahore, Peshawar and Kabul were situated in the north-west; Patna and Akbarnagar in the north-east and Ahmedabad, Surat and Ahmadnagar fell in the western India. Ujjain and Burhanpur mints were located in Central India. These mints had regular flow of silver bullion through trade due to their geographical location or commercial importance. Agra was a commercial nucleus and served as a link between Gujarat and upper India markets and production centres in Punjab, Kashmir, Multan even up to Awadh and Banaras, famous for Biana indigo, silk, carpet weaving and cotton goods. The foreign traveller Pelsaert has called it "the junction of all roads from distant countries".[11] Besides, it was the capital of India for a long time. Delhi/Shahjahanabad was the hub of all political and commercial activities and well linked to manufacturing centres in different directions. Ajmer was famous for production of multi-colour dyeing, cotton and wool fabrics as well as saltpetre and fine cotton cloth. Allahabad was important for riverine local trade, boatbuilding, production of coloured dishes, melon and grapes. Kashmir/ Srinagar produced shawls from local wool as well as goat hair of Tibet. Other woolen stuffs and wooden furniture were also produced there. In the north-west direction Kabul was situated on the main routes of the caravan trade. Merchants who came from Iran and Turan supplied perhaps the larger part of the bullion they brought to the mint of Kabul. Situated on the river Ravi and possessing the port Lahore Bandar, Lahore was well connected with the main overland (Grand Trunk Road) and maritime trade routes leading to Persia, Arabia and Central Asia. Lahore produced silk stuffs, fine calico, shawls, satin embroidery, carpets, sugar, fruits like grapes, melon, watermelon, mango, fig, mulberry etc. Peshawar was strategically important and it fell on the main caravan route running to Kabul. Thatta (conquered by Akbar in 1593), a river port, not only facilitated trade with Bandar Abbas and the port of Basra but other Arabian Sea and Indian ocean ports as well. Thatta offered a variety of locally produced items like fine calicos, silk, ivory, sugar, leather and hides. In western India, Ahmedabad (incorporated by Akbar in 1573) was the capital of Gujarat province. It was famous for the production of cotton and silk goods. Indigo, was also produced in nearby area. It was well connected with overland and maritime trade routes. Existing coins of this mint suggest the relative abundance of silver carried to there by trade. Surat (Mughal mint started in 1610) was the chief port of Gujarat and foreign merchants brought bullion in huge quantity there. It was the, chief emporium of trade as it was well connected with the commercial centres of the Middle East and Persia along the maritime trade routes and the production centres in western India during the Mughal period. Ahmadnagar was famous for fine cloth in its vicinity. In central India Ujjain and Burhanpur were distinguished mints. Ujjain was famous for opium, tobacco and sugar production while Burhanpur produced cotton, opium and foodstuffs. Horses were brought there in large number for sale for the Mughal army. Burhanpur (captured by Akbar in 1600) was the headquarters of all the Mughal operations in the South. In eastern India, Akbarnagar and Patna were the main centres of trade. Akbarnagar served as the main gate of commercial transaction between Bengal and Bihar. Patna was well linked along overland and riverine trade routes. Saltpetre, indigo, calico, sugar and turmeric were the main items of trade produced in its vicinity. In 1630 Manrique noted that in Patna alone "over six hundred brokers and middlemen engaged in commerce".[12] In this way, the towns and cities where regular mints were located were major centres of trade on account of their direct connection with riverine and overland trade route, and they produced some important cash crops or other articles of trade.[13]

So far as the Mughal irregular mints were concerned. They were 32 out of which the highest number i.e. 12 mints viz., Bairat, Bareli, Gorakhpur,_Fathpur, Gwalior, Etawa, Jaunpur, Lakhnau, Muhammadabad, Narnol and Saharanpur were located in North India. Multan, Qandhar and Sirhind were the mints which produced coins from time to time in the northwestern borders. Five mints viz., Islamabad (Chittagong), Jahangirnagar (Dhaka), Katak (Orissa), Karimabad and Murshidabad (in present West Bengal) flourished as mint towns in the east. Khambayat (a port town near Surat) and Khujistabuniyad (Aurangabad in Maharashtra) struck coins from time to time in the west India. In South India and the Deccan peninsula places such as Mylapore, Golkunda and Berar, (as many as 8 mints) produced coins in sporadic manner. Apart from these there were 56 silver mints such as Alwar, Anhilwara, Anwala, Balapur, Bandhu, Bangla, Chittor, Chunar, Daulatabad, Dewal-Bandar, Dogaon, Gadraula, Gobindpur, Hisar Foriza, Islam-Bandar, Islam-nagar, Jalnapur, Jaleswar, Kalpi, Khairpur, Kanchi, Kankuli, Karpa, Kaimnagar, Kurnool, Lahori-Bandar, Machlipatnam, Mahmud-Bandar, Mailapur, Mathura, Muradabad, Nagore, Nasirabad, Nusratgarh, Pattan, Patnadeo, Poona, Poonamallee, Purbandhar, Purenda, Ranthambor, Rohtas, Saimur, Sambhal, Sangunner, Satgaon, Sholapur, Shergarh, Sikakal, Sikandara, Sitpur, Toragul, Udiapur and Urdu dar rah-I Dakkan which produced coins only temporarily.

IV

The Safavids in Persia had almost the same pattern of operation and distribution of mints. Shah Ismail I struck silver coins from as many as 52 mints but during the time of his successor, Shah Tahmasp I there operated only 38 mints. This number further fell to 18 during the reign of Muhammad Khudabanda. However, when Shah Abbas I came to power the number of mints producing silver coins rose to 31, But. After him the number of mints again shrank as Safi I had 18 while Shah Abbas II and Shah Safi II had 19 and 14 mints respectively. The last Safavid ruler Shah Hussain I struck silver coins from 14 mints only. A close look at Borgomale's Catalogue of Iranian coins reveal that like the Mughals, the Safavid mints were also of three categories: Regular, irregular and temporary. Regular mints were those which produced coins almost each year during the time of all the rulers from Shah Ismail I to Shah Husain I. Out of the10 regular mints (Ardabil, Ganja, Iravan, Isfahan, Nakhchivan, Rasht, Tabriz, Urdu and Yazd) six, i.e., Aradabil, Ganja, Iravan, Nakhchivan, Rasht and Tabriz, were located in the north-west region while Qazvin was in the north and Yazd was in the south-east. The mint of Isfahan was situated in Central Persia. Such type of regular mints were located in the areas which served as arteries of trade. Besides, the towns in which these mints were situated produced some basic articles of commerce. Ardabil, an important mint town in northern Persia and known as 'the cradle of the Safavids', had a suitable climate for rearing of sheep and thus produced sheep's wool and skins of which woolen hats, caps and other items were produced and sold.[14] An old trade route which ran via Ardabil, linked the town with Tabriz, another significant town of Persia. Ganja, another prolific mint was situated in the town of the same name in northwest Persia in the territory of Azerbaijan. It was one of the best silk producing region. Ganja was in fact a frontier district between Russia and Persia and hence it was of great politico-strategic importance. The city was attacked and sacked in 1803 by the Russian leader Pavel D. Tsitsianov who rechristened it as Elizavet pol that is its modern name. Iravan was also a frontier district on the north-west sharing border with the Ottoman Empire. Armenian and Turkoman merchants were active in cross-country trade in silk, carpets, shawl and precious stones which they purchased from Iravan on regular basis.[15] "Isfahan, also known as *nisf-i-Jahan* (or half of the world) and located in central Persia, rose to prominence from 1591 when Shah Abbas I moved his capital from Qazvin to Isfahan which functioned as the hub of all administrative, commercial and cultural activities for about two centuries until the capital was shifted to Tehran. Well connected with trade routes and with products like opium and cotton textiles, Isfahan continued as a mint town for a long period even after decline of the Safavid empire because How of precious metal to the city never dried up.[16] Another flourishing city during the Sixteenth and Seventeenth centuries was Nakhchivan which was situated in the north-west along the river Ras which fell into (the Caspian Sea. Nakhchivan was a significant frontier district which was attacked by the Ottomans and Russians when the Safavids became weak. Nakhchivan was also a centre of trade and was visited by the Armerian and other merchants.[17] Qazvin, geographically close to Azerbaijan, was not only an important trading and manufacturing centre "with shops of all manner of trades" particularly silk, dye-stuffs and fruits but well connected with major routes to Russia and had a regular traffic in foreign trade. During the time of Shah Abbas the city of Qazvin was "three times as big as the exchange in London".[18] It was made the capital of Persia by Shah Tahmasp I in 1555. However, after a period of four decades i.e., in 1597 the capital was moved to Isfahan by Shah Abbas I.[19] In spite of this Qazvin functioned as a significant frontier town in north-west Persia and produced coins regularly even after the decline of the Safavids. Rasht was traditionally a thriving centre for fine wool, carpet and silk production.[20] It was a major commercial city. It was directly connected along major overland and maritime trade routes as it was situated near the Caspian Sea; south-east of Aradabil and north of Qazvin in the province of Gilan.[21] Rasht played a great role in pre-oil medieval economy of Persia. Another city which had a regular mint producing coin in great number was Tabriz and it was one of the chief cities of the province of Azerbaijan in the north-west. It was an important station on one of the world's great trade routes from the Far East and Central Asia, and as the hub of a network of highroads leading to Mesopotamia and the Mediterranean ports, to Anatolia and Constantinople, and north through the Caucasus to the Ukraine, the Crimea and eastern Europe.[22] Due to this Tabriz was often under attacks of the Ottomans and Russians who tried to capture it time and again. It functioned as the capital under the Mougals, notably under Timur, the Qara Qoyunlu, the Aq Qoyunlu and finally during the Safavids until 1555 when Shah Tahmasp I shifted the capital to Qazvin. Carpet, silk and dyes were manufactured here for export. Dry fruits were also produced in large scale and exported by Armenian, Russian and Indian merchants to different foreign countries.[23] Yazd was located south-east of Isfahan, the Safavid capital. It was a major centre for fine silk textile production particularly brocades with gold floral designs and ubiquitos buta i.e., pear or palm leaf design. Such silk textiles were purchased by the Europeans. Besides fine wool and carpets were also produced and exported to other countries. Ceramics with highly developed designs on porcelain were also an important item of trade. Yazd continued as a nourishing commercial centre even after the Safavid dynasty waned.[24] All the nine regular mints located in nine chief cities (Ardabil, Ganja, Iravan, Isfahan, Nakhchivan, Qazvin, Rasht, Tabriz and Yazd) were thriving centres of trade both internal as well as external. That had been the reason why these mints had a regular inflow of silver bullion which was converted into coins there. Besides, these mint towns were of great strategical and political importance too.

On the other hand, the irregular mints which were eleven in number struck coins from Astrabad, Hamadan, Herat, Howayza, Kashan, Mashhad, Qum, Qandhar, Samakhi, Shiraz and Shirvan. Two mints (Kashan and Qum) were located in the north; Astrabad and Mashhad were the two mints in the north-east while Samakhi and Shirvan were the two mints situated in the north-west. In the south there operated one mint that was Shiraz while in the south-west there was only Howayza. Herat and Qandhar produced coins in eastern Persia and Hamadan mint operated in the west. These mints produced coins in considerable number but with several gaps in year.[25]

The List of mints given against the name of each Safavid ruler in Borgomate Catalogue of Persian coins establish that 47 total mints produced coins temporarily at one or other time from the period of Shah Ismail I to Shah Husain I. In north Persia coins were temporarily struck from as many as nine places like Amul, Barfurush, Damaghan, Damavand, Mazandaran, Nisa, Sari, Simnan and Tehran while seven temporary mints were located in the northwest which include Foman, Lahijan, Lashta Nesha, Savah, Sultaniya, Urduabad and Zanjan. In the north-east Persia at least eight temporary mints existed and they were Abivard, Isfarain, Marv, Nishapur, Sabzvar, Sarakhs, Tiflis and Turbat (or Turbat-i-Haideriya). Abarquh and Lar mints struck coins in the south while Dauraq or Duraq in the south-west. Silver coins were temporarily issued from eight places in the west and they were Baghdab, Bahbahan, Bitlis, Dizful, Dorud, Kirmanshah, Shustar and Van. In the east Kirman operated as a temporary mint.[26]

The number of active or regular and irregular mints spread over the empire in both the Safavid Persia and Mughal India demonstrate the degree of monetization and the scale of money-supply in both the countries.

Types of Mints	*Safavid Persia*	*Mughal India (In number)*
Regular	10	16
Irregular	11	32
Temporary	47	56

The category and operation of mints in both the countries as shown below discerns the fact that Mughal India which run greater number of mints received greater quantity of silver bullion, while lesser quantity of precious metal reached Persia. It is well known that in absence of internal sources, silver in both the countries was imported through trade. The rulers in both countries regarded a stable silver currency as a symbol of prosperity. Silk, carpets and horses were the premier exports of Persia to Europe and Asia particularly India. Sales of these items generated most of foreign exchange to the country. Whenever the relations with the Ottomans strained the silk trade was halted and movement of precious metal to Persia was slowed down and restricted. This caused shortage of bullion to Persian mints. The production and export of silk spurred a new height on account of Shah Abbas's firm decisions in 1603 first, of assumption of a state monopoly of silk and to export the silk directly to Europe via the Indian Ocean. But Shah Abbas's successors abolished the policy of state monopoly of silk and the Indian Ocean route did not develop as a result" of which the shortage of bullion was again caused.[27] This shortage of money was the reason that Shah Tahmasp "never agreed to barter his silk for European cloths and preferred to sell it to any merchant who paid him in money".[28] The other important item that earned precious metal to the Safavids was the supply of Persian horses. Persian horses were in great demand in India and elsewhere and the control of this commerce was in the hands of the Afghan, Persian and Turkish merchants.[29]

In spite of this, Persia had a chronic shortage of silver throughout the Safavid period. The Indian *banias* (or broker-dealers) who resided in Persia (it is reported that there were 10 to 12 thousand in Isfahan alone) and used to send back their profits of usury to India in the form of silver and gold made the situation worse. John Chardin notes: "These Indians, like true leeches extract all the gold and silver of the country and send them to their own country so that in the year 1677 when I departed from Persia, one could not see there any more gold or silver. These usurers had made it disappear entirely".[30] On the other hand, the Mughal India, though devoid of domestic sources of silver, maintained exceptionally pure and standard silver coins not only during the period of the great Mughals but even after that for several decades. The main reason for this was the enormous currency influx to the empire coming in transit trade. A Dutch factor in 1634 remarked that the "total value of textile, indigo, sugar and gum lac exported annually from Agra, Lahore, Sind, Gujarat and Daulatabad sold in the markets of Iran was 2,130,350 *Muhanunadis* or 24.20 metric tons of silver".[31] And the merchants Surat alone imported annually 22.7 metric tons of silver as reported by another Dutch factor".[32] According to an estimate "on an average, about 25 metric tons of silver was exported to the Mughal empire from the Iranian ports in the second quarter of the Seventeenth century".[33] To conclude it may be said that the Indian mints received silver from the trade through the Red Sea as well as the caravan trade via overland route also. Hence the Indian mints at least till the time of Aurangzeb never experienced any scarcity of silver. However, after the death of Aurangzeb the situation changed and the imperial mints began to face the silver shortage abysmally.

Notes and References

1. Irfan Habib, (ed.,) *A Shared Heritage, The growth of Civilizations in India and Iran,* Tulika Books, New Delhi, 2002, pp. xxvi-xxvii.
2. Surendra Gopal, *"Trade Contacts between India and Iran (in the Fifteenth Century)"*, unpublished paper presented in the Seminar on Indo-Iran Relations, Iran Society, Mumbai, 7-9 March 2000, pp.1-18, Idem, *"Indian Traders in Persia in the Seventeenth Century"*, Journal of Historical Studies, Patna University, Patna, No.2, December 1996, pp. 14-36; Idem, *"Indians in Iran in the 18th Century"*, Journal of Indian Ocean Studies, Vol. 4, No.2, March 1997, pp. 160-170.
3. H.L. Rabino di Borgomale, *Coins, Medals and Seals of Shahs of Iran, 1500-1941,* Fitzwilliam Museum, Cambridge, 1945, pp.26-45; H. Nelson Wright, *Catalogue of the Coins in the Indian Museum*, Calcutta, Vol. III, Indological Book House, Varanasi, 1972, pp. 9-190.
4. Peter Jackson and Laurence Lockhart (eds.,) *The Cambridge History of Iran,* Vol. 6, *The Timurid and SafavidPeriods,* CUP, Cambridge, 1986, pp. 556-565.
5. Parmeshwari Lal Gupta, *Coins,* NBT, New Delhi, 1969, pp.111-112.
6. Parmeshwari Lal Gupta, *op. cit.,* pp.113-127; Marie H. Martin, *"The Reforms of the Sixteenth Century and Akbar's Administration: Metrological and Monetary Considerations",*

The Imperial Monetary System of Mughal India (ed.,) John F. Richards, OUP, Paperback, New Delhi, 2000; pp.68-99.

7. Borgomale, *op. cit.,* pp. 27-44.
8. Najaf Haider, *"Global Networks of Exchange, the India Trade and the Mercantile Economy of Safavid Iran",* A Shared Heritage ...., *op. cit.,* pp. 201-2.
9. Parmeshwari Lai Gupta, *op. cit.,* pp.111-12; Syed Ejaz Hussain, "Reflections on Silver Currency output of the Patna Mint", *Readings in Indian History: Syed Hasan Askari Centenary Volume,* (ed.,) Bijoy Kumar Thakur), K.P. Jayaswal Research Institute, Patna, 2001, pp. 334-335.
10. Jaroslav Strand, *Monetary History of Mughal India as Reflected in Silver Coin Hoards,* Harman Publishing House, New Delhi, 2001, pp. 185-187.
11. F. Pelsaret, *The Remonstrainte,* tr., W.H. Moreland and P. Geyl under the title of *"Jahangir's India",* Delhi, 1972, p. 6; B.S. Mallik, Money, Banking and Trade in Mughal India, Rawat Publications, Jaipur, 1991, p. 58.
12. F. Sebastien Manrique, *Travels of Frey Sebastien Manrique (l629-43),* Vol.II, (ed.,) Col. C. Eckford Luad, Oxford, 1927, p.140; B.S.Mallick, *op.cit.,* p. 59.
13. B.S. Mallick, *op.cit.,* pp. 51-70; Irfan Habib, Political and Economic Maps with Detailed Notes, Bibliography and Index, OUP, Delhi, Rep., 1986, pp.1-68; Stewart Gordon, "Burhanpur: Entrepot and Hinterland, 1650-1750", in Sanjay Subrahmanyam, (ed.,) *Merchants, Markets and the State in Early Modern India,* OUP, Delhi, 1990, pp. 48-65.
14. W.B. Fisher, *The Cambridge History of Iran,* Vol.1, The Land of Iran, CUP, Cambridge, 1968, p. 50.
15. CHI, Vol. VII, pp. 946-7.
16. CHI, Vol.1, pp. 104-10; CHI, Vol.VII, pp.445-58; Moustafa Khan Fateh, The Economic Position of Persia, P.S. King & Son, Ltd., London, 1926, pp. 16-29.
17. CHI, Vol. VII, map I, pp. 298, 325.
18. Roger Savory, *Iran Under the Safavids,* CUP, Cambridge, 1980, p. 189.
19. *Ibid.,* pp. 63, 155.
20. *Ibid.,* pp. 95, 141; CHI, Vol.1, p. 549; CHI, Vol. VII, pp. 575, 946-8, 9556.

21. CHI, Vol. I, pp. 50, 552, 554-5.
22. Roger Savory, *op.cit.*, p. 1.
23. CHI, Vol. I, pp. 14-15; CHI, Vol. VII, pp. 14-15, 956-57.
24. CHI, Vol. VII, pp. 544, 931, 946; John Chardin, *Travels in Persia*, London, 1927, pp. 267-8; Roger Savory, *op.cit.*, p. 147.
25. Borgomale, *op. cit.*, pp. 26-46.
26. *Ibid.*
27. Halil Inaleik, "The Ottoman Economic Mind and Aspects of the Ottoman Economy", *Studies in the Economic History of the Middle East*, (ed.,) M.A. Cook, London, 1970, pp. 213-14.
28. Arthur Edwards, "Notes concerning this fourth voyage into Persia, begun in the ninth of July 1568, etc.", *Early Voyages and Travels to Russia and Persia by Anthony Jenkinson and other Englishmen*, (eds.,) E.D. Morgan and C.H. Coote, Hakluyt Society, 1886, Vol. II, p. 411; Najaf Haider, *loc. cit.*, p. 197.
29. Stephen Fredric Dale, *Indian Merchants and Eurasian Trade, 1606-1750,* CUP, Cambridge, 1994, pp. 25-26.
30. John Chardin, *Voyages du Chevalier Chardin en Perse, et Autres Lieux de l'Orient,* (ed.,) L. Langles, Vol. VI, 1811, p. 164; Also quoted by Najaf Haider, "Precious Metal Flows and Currency Circulation in the Mughal Empire", *Journal of the Social and Economic History of the Orient,* (hereafter JESHO), Vol.39, No.3, 1996, p. 307.
31. Najaf Haider, JESHO, loc. Cit., pp. 306-7.
32. *Ibid.*
33. *Ibid.*, p. 307.

11

Trade Across the Himalayas: The Numismatic Evidence

Nicholas Rhodes

It is an interesting fact that many of the coinages of northern India in general, and of the Himalayas in particular, are of silver or gold, even though there are no silver or gold mines in the area. The precious metal used for the various coinages must have been acquired in the course of trade, and hence a study of the coinages gives interesting insights into the trading patterns at different times. The objective of this paper is to consider the various coinages struck in or near the Himalayas, and to consider the light shed by these coinages on trans-Himalayan trade. Copper mines, however, exist in many parts of the Himalayas, and the existence of copper coinage in the region also sheds light on trade patterns.

The period covered by this study is mainly the Seventh century until the Eighteenth century, although occasional references to earlier and later coins may be made, and the area covered will be from Kashmir in the west, up to Assam in the east. This is a period when documentation regarding trade is scanty, and knowledge of trading links is much less than for it is the Nineteenth century, when the British started to maintain detailed statistics of the wealth they were able to extract from their Empire.

When reading this paper it should be appreciated that life in the mountains tends to be tough. Not all the requirements of life can be grown or obtained locally. Salt was always in demand, because the lack of other sources of iodine caused goitre, and it had to be obtained, either from India in the south, or from the Tibetan salt lakes to the north. At higher altitudes, crops were scarce and very seasonal, but the Tibetan frontier was close. Many Himalayan people were involved in modest barter trade across the frontier, exchanging grain and other commodities for salt, wool and other commodities from Tibet and beyond, but this is not the type of trade that tended to involve cash, and not the type of trade that I will be referring to in this study. The trade that I will be considering is the large scale trade, involving high value products in bulk, financed and organised by rich professional traders or monasteries – and often involving the local Himalayan people only as porters. As regards the Himalayan States, it was purely transit trade, but the local people and rulers were able to benefit from the existence of this trade, not only by providing labour for carriage, by charging taxes and customs duties of various kinds. In particular, they could also insist that bullion was struck into local coinage before being sent on to be used for the purchase of goods, and in that way the controller of the mint could benefit from the hidden tax represented by the seigneurage levied to cover minting costs and "profit".

Kashmir (6th Century – 1220 AD)

The first coinages struck in the mountains of northern India were in Kashmir, and many coins have been found in and around the Kashmir valley, dating from the period of the Indo-Scythians, at the very beginning of the Christian era. It is clear from the numismatic evidence, as well as from many other sources, that Kashmir was on a major trade route between India and the central Asian garrison cities of Kashgar and Yarkand. While many of these coins were struck in copper, and only had local circulation, others were struck in silver or base gold, and had a wide circulation in Northern India, so it seems likely that some of the coins were used to purchase goods from the plains.

Another early coinage in the Himalayan area was the silver and copper coins of Kuninda[1], which are sometimes found in the hills of Garhwal. Again, the existence of these coins demonstrates that, for a short period in the early years of the first millennium, this region was growing rich, most probably as a result of trade crossing the Himalayan ranges. Copper coins of Yaudheyas and perhaps also of the Panchalas[2] are also known from the same region, again indicating considerable economic activity in and around the Garhwal hills in the years before the rise of the Guptas.

Moving now to the period after the fall of the Imperial Guptas, when the great Huna king Toramana invaded India through Kashmir in the sixth century, a large coinage in copper or base gold was issued in Kashmir, until the early years of the thirteenth century. The coins are not beautiful, but they were consistent in size, and they do demonstrate economic activity and a well organised economy. Trade must have been brisk, but only on one or two occasions were precious metal coinages struck. During the reign of Sura Varman (933-34)3 a rare gold coin was struck. Then some silver coins were struck by Queen Didda (979-1005 AD)[4], and finally under Harsha (1089-1101 AD), a few very rare silver and gold coins appeared, small in fabric.[5] These precious metal coins were clearly experimental in nature, and their issue was never followed up. On each occasion, the coins struck were very different from those of their predecessors, whereas the copper coinage continued on a very large scale from at least the ninth century AD, with consistent type and weight for several centuries, and was clearly widely accepted as currency, and most probably was struck using locally mined copper. This copper coinage certainly demonstrates that economic activity was at a high level throughout this period, but the copper coinage completely stops after Raja Deva (1214-36 AD), and as the coins of this king are rather scarce, the coinage probably stopped early in the reign, before the year 1220 AD.

Kangra (1220-1350 AD)

Interestingly, just at this time, another large copper coinage commenced in Kangra, and continued for over a century. It is interesting to consider why the Kashmir coinage should have stopped at this time, just as the Kangra coinage commenced. Most probably, trade with western Tibet and central Asia, that had previous been routed through Kashmir, was rerouted through Kangra. It has been suggested that the trade that may have dominated the Kangra bazaar was horses. The Ghorids, who ruled Northern India at this time, relied on horses for their military power, and their supply from Afghanistan would have been cut off in the early thirteenth century, leading them to seek alternative supplies. The establishment of the Palampur horse fair in 1867 AD shows that in later period horses were traded through Kangra, and it seems likely that this horse trade also thrived during the Thirteenth century.[6]

Nepal (575-700 & 1100-25 AD)

Another major trade route across the Himalayas passed through Nepal. The origins of the commencement of this trade route are not well documented, but most probably it was at a high level from the late sixth century AD, when the first copper coins were struck in Nepal.[7] From about 575 AD, until about 700 AD, a large number of copper coins were struck in the Kathmandu Valley, initially during the period when Amshuvarman was ruler of Nepal, initially as Samanta under the Licchavi King, but later as undisputed ruler.[8] At this period, there is some other evidence that trade with Tibet was brisk, and the extent of the coins certainly proves that the economic activity in the valley was considerable. In addition, there was considerable activity in the artistic field, with stone and bronze images being commissioned for the first time, indicating the existence of relatively large numbers of specialist stone and metal workers. This situation could only have been financed by thriving trading activity. It has been suggested the design of the seventh century Lichhavi coins, with the image, often of an animal, surrounded by a border of large dots, may have been derived from the roundels found on Chinese silks of this period, pointing to a silk route passing through Nepal. The silk would have been made in China and exported across Tibet and Nepal, to the Empire of Harsha Vardhana in northern India. The appearance on one particular coin of a winged horse, Pegasus in Greek iconography, also provides evidence of western influence at this period, as this type of image is never found in India.[9] A few coins with the legend *Mananka* have been found in the Kali Gandaki valley, demonstrating the existence of a trade route up this valley at this period.[10]

Some Kushan copper coins have been found in the Valley, and it has been suggested that this proves that monetary activity, and hence trade, commenced much earlier. However, the discovery of a large hoard[11] to the west of Kathmandu, containing many worn Kushan copper coins, as well as coins with the legend *Mananka*, datable to the years around 600 AD, demonstrate that the Kushan coins may not have been imported to Nepal before the sixth century, several centuries after they were first struck. The Nepalese coins certainly must have used these old Kushan coins as the model for their coinage, as they copy the fabric and weight standard.

After the mid Seventh century, the coins reduce in size and weight, but they continue to be struck in large numbers until around 680 AD. Very few coins from the reign of Sivadeva II (680-700) have been found in the Valley, but a large hoard from this period was discovered from Panch Khal, about fifty kilometres east of Kathmandu, along the Kodari road.[12] This may indicate that a trade route also followed the route of the present motorway road during the Seventh century, and indeed the centre of economic power may have shifted eastwards, because of political problems in the valley itself. In any case, after about 700 AD, coinage completely ceases, as do most stone sculptures inscriptions and other large scale religious artistic commissions. Most probably trade with Tibet had reduced considerably.

From then until about 1100 AD, no coins were struck in the Nepal Valley, but around that year, some small gold and silver coins were struck in considerable numbers. As neither gold nor silver are mined in Nepal, the metal must have been acquired through trans-Himalayan trade.[13] The gold probably came from Tibet, in exchange for goods exported from India. Coins of this type are sometimes found in Bihar, and must have been used to purchase such trade goods, with the Nepalese king cleverly profiting from the seigneurage. Most probably he required that all gold bullion from Tibet had to be taken to his mint to be struck into coin, before it could be exported to India.[14] Silver coins have not yet been found outside Nepal, so the silver may have been another trade item, possibly acquired from India. This economic flowering of Nepal was short lived, and after about 1125 AD, hardly any coins were struck in the country until the sixteenth century. Although trade probably continued at a modest level, the volume was considerably reduced from the levels it had reached in earlier years.

Assam (830-900 AD)

Proceeding further east, a copper coinage was struck in Assam during the time of the Salastambha dynasty, from about 830 to 900 AD. These coins are unusual, in that their weights vary from about 2g, to nearly 20g, which their diameter remains constant. The design is also very simple, consisting only of a single Brahmi letter on one side, the other side being blank.

The coinage certainly signifies some economic and trading activity at this time, which is attested by some other anecdotal information. The common currency of Northern India in general, and Assam in particular, at that time was the cowries. However, there was considerable demand for cowries from south western China, because of the rise of the Nan Xiao kingdom in Yunnan, and also because of the reduction in the supply of cowries from the Chinese coast.[15] It is possible that the copper coins struck in Assam at this time were intended to supplement the circulation of cowries, to ensure no local disruption of trade. The cowries could then be exported to south western China in exchange for silver, silk, or some other valuable commodities. After 900 AD the striking of copper coins ceased, perhaps hinting at a reduction in the volume of trade.

Kashmir (1400 – 1560 AD)

About a century after copper coins ceased to be struck by the Hindu kings in Kashmir, a Muslim kingdom was established in the valley. The first Sultan of Kashmir, Shah Mirza, was established on the throne in 1346/7. Initially the Muslim sultans struck very few coins[16], but from about 1440 AD coins were struck in considerable numbers, particularly in silver and copper. The silver coins, interestingly, were struck on a weight standard of about 6.3g, and on a square flan, quite different from the coins otherwise struck in India at this time. The silver must have been imported, most probably from the north, and are never found outside the valley. The copper coins, were struck to the same weight standard as the coins struck by the Hindu kings prior to 1220 AD, which continued to circulate in considerable numbers.[17] Few gold coins known must have been only used as ceremonial issues, and are so rare that no economic conclusions should be drawn from their existence. This coinage continued unchanged until the advent of the Moghuls in about 1586 AD, although it may be significant that no copper coins were struck between about 1540 and 1560 AD.

The impression, as observed through the coins, is of a reasonably prosperous state, which must have been acquiring silver as a result of trade, but the wealth must have been centred in a few hands, as the silver was not dispersed widely[18], and is rarely found in the plains of India. The fact that a different weight standard was chosen clearly shows that the silver coin was not intended to be used elsewhere in India.

Along the Himalayas there is no evidence of significant trade any where at this period, but the situation was to change in the mid sixteenth century, by which time considerable volumes of silver were arriving in the subcontinent, brought by the Europeans, after the discovery of the great silver deposits in central and South America. The silver was in great demand in India, and was used to purchase the spices that were so loved in Europe.

Dolakha (1545)

The first silver coins to appear in the Eastern Himalayas were, surprisingly, struck by the king of Dolakha, in the Tamba Kosi Valley, about fifty miles to the east of Kathmandu. The coins are undated, but were struck in the name of Jaya Indra Simha, who is known to have ruled in the years 1545-47 AD from two inscriptions in his name.[19] The Kosi Valley provided an easy route to Tibet, and the only raison d'être for the coinage must have been trade between India and Tibet, fuelled by silver, which was, by this time, in demand on the plateau. The fact that only about six specimens of these coins survive today, all in the name of the one king, show that it was not a long-lasting coinage, but all the surviving coins are struck with different dies, so the number originally struck must have been quite large. The significance of this coinage in the history of the development of trans-Himalayan trade in the Sixteenth century is considerable, as no other record of the existence of this route survives, and even the existence of this kingdom is not widely known, as it was conquered by the king of Kathmandu later in the Sixteenth century, and largely eliminated from recorded history.

Export of Copper from Western Nepal (1560-1604 AD)

Trade between India and the Himalayas was not always trans-Himalayan trade with Tibet or Central Asia, but occasionally local produce became an important export. One commodity that was produced in the Himalayas and that was in demand in India was copper. Copper mines exist in many areas from Kashmir to Bhutan, although the cost of extraction means that the mines are no longer commercially viable. One period when numismatic evidence demonstrates the importance of this trade was during the reign of Akbar. Throughout the reign, two of the most productive mints for copper coins were Dogaon and Bahraich[20], both situated just south of the Nepalese border to the west of Kathmandu. The only possible reason for locating the mints in that area was the source of the copper ore, which must have been the mines in the area around Baglung and Beni in Nepal, which would have been sent to India via Palpa. Both these mints of Akbar closed when Jahangir ascended the throne in 1605 AD, but the copper continued to be exported from Nepal, and is mentioned in the British records in the Nineteenth century.

Cooch Behar (1555 – 1600 AD)

Soon after Dolakha began issuing coins, the Hindu kingdom of Cooch Behar, a hundred miles to the east, started issuing their own coins. This kingdom controlled the approaches to another route to Tibet, through Paro in Bhutan, and then to Phari. This route would have been convenient for the major Tibetan monastic centres of Lhasa, Shigatse and Gyantse, and was probably able to divert the main trade which had previously passed through Dolakha.

The large numbers of coins struck between 1555 AD and the early years of the Seventeenth century testify to the volume of this trade. Ralph Fitch, an English merchant adventurer, recorded this trade when he visited Bengal in 1583 AD. He noted that musk, wool, agate, silk and pepper were purchased in Cooch Behar, all of which products would have originated in Tibet.[21] Since Fitch does not mention the items exported, it may be assumed that some of these imports were purchased using silver, which was in great demand in Tibet.

After about 1603 AD, trade along this route may have reduced in volume because of conflict between Lakshmi Narayan, the ruler of Cooch Behar, and the Mughals, and the volume of coins struck during the reign of Bir Narayan (1627-33 AD) was quite small. The route was still well known in Bengal, as it was chosen by Cacella and Cabral when they travelled from Bengal to Tibet in 1626 AD. At times in subsequent years the coinage increased in volume, perhaps indicating a growth in the volume of trade, whereas at other times the coinage virtually ceased. For example, no coins were struck between about 1680 and 1695 AD, indicating a break in large scale trade. However, during the 1650's and 1660's, and then in the 1760's and 1770's, the number of coins struck was considerable.

Nepal (1600 – 1750)

In the years around 1600 AD, the valley of Nepal was to emerge as the major player in trans-Himalayan trade, and the coinage demonstrates this dominance very clearly. Although a few silver coins were struck by Mahendra Malla of Kathmandu about 1560 AD[22], it was not until after 1600 AD, and particularly after 1640 AD, that silver coins in Nepal were struck on a large scale.

The trade with Tibet brought immense wealth to the Valley of Nepal, as testified, not only by the coinage, but also by the construction of temples and the commissioning of works of art by the Newar traders.[23] The Nepalese protected their trade, not only by locating trading houses in Lhasa, but also by the exercise of military force. In the early 1640's, Bhima Malla, a brother of Pratap Malla, the king of Kathmandu, led a successful military campaign into Tibet, and forced the Tibetans to sign a treaty under the terms of which:

(*a*) It was agreed that Nepal would mint coins for Tibet; Tibet would use these coins internally and would either provide the silver required for their minting or would pay for Nepali coins with gold.

(*b*) Tibet agreed that all trade with India, even though conducted by other than Newari merchants, would be channeled through the Kathmandu Valley in preference to the routes to the east (i.e. via Sikkim, Bhutan or Tawang)

This treaty shows how the trans-Himalayan trade in the Seventeenth century was worth going to war over, and the Nepalese became the masters of that trade. For the next century, the Malla kingdoms of Nepal sent large quantities of coin to Tibet, not only in exchange for the valuable goods exported from Tibet, but also in exchange for silver bullion. Kathmandu and Bhatgaon, the kingdoms which controlled the routes to Tibet, were particularly active in the coin trade. The coins became seriously debased after about 1720 AD, and as they exchanged coin for bullion on a weight for weight basis, the profits were considerable. The kingdom of Patan controlled the route to India, so that kingdom also profited considerably from the transit trade.

One mechanism used by the Nepalese at this time was to forbid the export of silver bullion. Any trader importing silver from India or from Tibet, either as bullion or as coin, had to take the silver to the mint, where it was struck into coin. The Nepalese kings made considerable profits from the alloy and from the seigneurage charged by the mint. This mechanism was also used by other Himalayan states, allowing them to profit from transit trade.

Tibet in the Seventeenth and early Eighteenth Centuries

Immediately prior to the Seventeenth century, Tibet was not a united country. Several different Buddhist monasteries competed for political power. The situation stabilised only after the Mongol ruler, Gusri Khan, established his hegemony over the country, and established the head of the Gelugpa sect, the great fifth Dalai Lama, as both religious and secular ruler of the whole country. One rival, the Shabdung Ngawang Namgyal, the head of the Drugpa Kagyu sect, moved south into Bhutan, and established an independent Buddhist theocracy there. Similarly the Namgyal dynasty, who patronised the Nyimapa sect, established the Buddhist kingdom of Sikkim. The peace and stability that was thus established in Tibet allowed trade to flourish, and it was the large scale trade that was organised via the great monasteries of Tibet which was routed through Nepal. Small scale trade always existed across the mountains, but this was conducted through barter. It was the monastic trade which was to generate significant wealth for the state through which the trade between Tibet and India was routed.

The economy of Tibet was somewhat upset when a Chinese army arrived in Tibet in 1720 AD, to exert their authority over the country, and to wrest control from the Dzungar Mongols. The Chinese army brought with them large quantities of silver bullion, and the Jesuit missionary, Fr. Desideri, described the situation vividly:

> "Shortly after the Chinese entered Tibet for the second time (Autumn 1720) the whole vast kingdom was flooded with silver, which so diminished in value that reiterated edicts were necessary to force the people to accept it as payment. I must explain that the Chinese had no coinage, but simply large or small pieces of silver. Exposed to some risk, to expense, and to the long journey, the Tibetans sent this silver from Lhasa to Nepal to change into the money of the three petty kings who ruled that Kingdom. They charged nothing, but gave an equal weight for the silver and gained many millions, especially the King of Kathmandu."[24]

The coins provided were only 50-66% fine[25], so in spite of the expenses and risk incurred in transporting the coins to Tibet, the Nepalese did indeed profit very considerably from this trade, and the wealth of the valley is there for all to see.

The Ahom Kingdom of Assam

Until the Seventeenth century, the Ahom Kingdom in upper Assam, was extremely isolationist, and had little contact with the outside world. However, in the early Seventeenth century they came into contact with the expanding Moghul Empire, and were forced to demonstrate their considerable military ingenuity, and mastery over their territory. By the middle of the Seventeenth century, the Ahoms were becoming aware of the world around them, and Jayadhvaja Simha (1648-63 AD) began to strike a fine silver coinage. Apart from normal coins with legend in Assamese script, he issued one remarkable rupee with a large Chinese character on each side, Zang Bao, meaning "Tibet Coin". It is likely that this coin was intended for trade with Tibet, but any ambitions the Ahoms may have had to expand trade with their northern neighbour would have come to naught because of the monopoly exercised by the Nepalese. Only one example of this Tibetan trade coin has survived, so it cannot have been issued in large numbers, but it provides remarkable of an attempt at this time to promote trans-Himalayan trade across the far eastern Himalayas.

From then until the early Nineteenth century, the Ahom kingdom of Assam struck a series of fine silver coins, but the source of the silver has not yet been identified. Some silver may have been acquired as a result of trans-Himalayan trade with Burma and Yunnan. In the Nineteenth century, Assam has a significant balance of payments deficit with Bengal, as they imported significant quantities of salt, in exchange for silver.

Tibet Tries to Limit the Profit made by Nepal

The Tibetan government was somewhat resentful of the domination of their economy by the Nepalese traders, and in 1751 AD, when the Dalai Lama came of age, he wrote to the three Malla kings and demanded that they put an end to their practice of sending debased coins to Tibet. This request was taken seriously, and, in 1753 AD, Jaya Prakash Malla of Kathmandu struck many beautiful fine silver coins, as well as a few rare gold coins. Most probably a trade agreement had been reached whereby Tibet sent gold to Nepal, in exchange for silver coins struck using silver imported from India. The fact that Chinese influence in Lhasa was waning at this period may have meant that the supply of silver bullion in Tibet had reduced. It is also noteworthy that most of the gold coins of Jaya Prakash Malla were found in India, and were carried to Europe by collectors as early as the Eighteenth century.[26]

The Rise of the House of Gorkha (1744-69)

During the Seventeenth and early Eighteenth centuries, a small kingdom to the west of the Nepal Valley, with its capital at *Gorkha*, began to rise to prominence. Gradually this *Gorkha* kingdom allied itself with other small states in this part of western Nepal, and by 1744 AD it had wrested control of the western trade route between Kathmandu and Tibet. Over the next ten years, this little kingdom, under the able leadership of Prithvi Narayan Shah, sought to establish a blockade around the rich valley of Nepal, effectively holding it to ransom. In 1749 AD, Prithvi Narayan struck his first coins, following the same debased pattern as the coins of the Malla Kingdom of Bhatgaon, and he probably tried to get his share of the lucrative coin trade with Tibet, from which the Malla Kingdoms had profited so much, but in this he was not successful. In 1754 AD, however, Prithvi Narayan Shah managed to complete his blockade of the Valley of Nepal, and no trade with Tibet could pass through the Valley.

Prithvi Narayan wasted no time in striking his own fine silver coins in 1754 AD, and he opened up negotiations with the Tibetans to supply the coins to Tibet. Some correspondence has survived from 1757 AD, whereby Prithvi Narayan's agents at Kuti agreed to purchase between twelve and fifteen thousand *tolas* of gold, in exchange for silver coins at the rate of Rs.18 per *tola* of gold. Presumably by "rupees" in this context, the silver coin of 5.6g is meant, normally referred to as a "*mohar*". This would have yielded a handsome profit when the gold was sent to India, where the rate was about 14 *tolas* of silver for one *tola* of gold. Prithvi Narayan struck significant numbers of coins in 1754 and 1756 AD, but thereafter issues were very limited, so this trade of gold in exchange for silver coin may not have lasted very long. Most probably the Tibetans were angry that Prithvi Narayan would not accept the old debased coins as being equal in value to his new fine silver coins. The blockade of the Valley by the *Gorkhas* lasted until the final conquest of the Malla kings in 1769 AD, after which Prithvi Narayan tried to reopen the trading links with Tibet. By this time, however, the main trade had been rerouted by other routes, to the east and west of Nepal.

Garhwal (1693-1815 AD)

One Himalayan state to issue coins in the Eighteenth century was Garhwal, located to the west of present day Nepal. The first king to strike coins was Fath Shah (1665-1716 AD), who struck a few rupees and quarter rupees of Mughal style, but in his own name dated 1750 VS (=1693 AD).[27] He also struck a remarkable octagonal rupee dated 1757 VS (=1800 AD), also in his own name.[28] Both these coins must have been struck for political reasons, to demonstrate independence from the Moghul emperor, although the silver may have been obtained as a result of some trans-Himalayan trade. Fath Shah apparently gained favour with Aurangzeb by handing over one of the latter's brothers, who had sought refuge in the hills. Aurangzeb must have objected to Fath Shah issuing silver coins in his own name, and from early in the Eighteenth century, Fath Shah began issuing copies of Moghul quarter rupee coins with the mint name of Shahjahanabad (Delhi). Initially these coins had the name of Aurangzeb, but most have the name of Furrukshiyar, who ascended the throne in Delhi in 1714 AD. These coins weighed 3 *mashas*, and hence became known as *timashas*, and continued to be struck for several decades, becoming increasingly crude, and barely recognisable as copies of Moghul coins. One of Fath Shah's successors, Pradip Shah (1717-72 AD) struck a few silver and copper coins in his own name, but for the first four decades of his reign he struck mostly the crude copies of the Mughal *timashas*.

The main driving force behind these coins must have been the trade in wool from Tibet, which was much in demand for the fine shawls made in Kashmir and elsewhere. Garhwal controlled the easiest trade route from Western Tibet, where the finest wool producing sheep were reared, to Delhi and

Kashmir. The Garhwal king probably copied the Nepalese, in insisting that silver bullion could not be exported, so that traders had to bring their silver bullion to his mint.

Until about 1759 AD, the coinage of Garhwal was modest in volume, but in that year, the first year of the Emperor Shah Alam, the production increased significantly. This must have been because of the blockade of the Kathmandu Valley by Prithvi Narayan of *Gorkha*. Prior to that, much of the wool was exported from Tibet via Nepal, as a result of the treaty of signed in the 1640's AD. With the closure of the Nepal route, the Kashmiri traders would have sought out alternative routes, and Garhwal was an obvious beneficiary of the increased trade. In 1757 AD, Najib Khan Rohilla had established his authority in Dehra Dun, and probably also benefited from this trade, as is evidenced by the quantity of silver rupees struck in his mint of Najibabad, located just to the south of the hills on the route to Garhwal and Tibet.[29] Indeed, the coinage was mainly organised by the bankers of Najibabad who brought silver up to the hills, sometimes in the form of Spanish coin, and had it struck into *timashas* before paying for local transport and purchasing Tibetan imports.[30]

Pradip Shah of Garhwal died in 1772 AD, and the coinage seems to have stopped, temporarily, with no coins known from the fourteenth year of Shah Alam (=1772 AD), but the silver coinage started again in fifteenth year and continued until about 1780 AD, still in the name of the Moghul emperor, rather than in the name of the king of Garhwal, Lallat Shah. In that year the silver coinage stopped until 1803 AD after the *Gorkha* conquest and it can be assumed that the wool trade was rerouted after 1780 AD.

After the Nepalese conquered Garhwal, the mint reopened in about 1803 AD and continued until 1813 AD. This time the coins had the name of the Nepalese king, Girvan Yuddha, and also of the Moghul Emperor, either Shah 'Alam or Akbar Shah. Presumably the wool trade was routed through Garhwal at this time, and the Nepalese were able to benefit from the seigneurage and alloy in the coin.[31]

Ladakh (1772, 1781-1802, and 1816-41 AD)

By the 1770's AD, the silver *timashas* of Garhwal were widely accepted as currency in Western Tibet, so when the wool trade was routed to Kashmir through Ladakh, it was natural that the Tibetans expected to be paid in that sort of coin. The earliest silver coins struck in Ladakh are copies of the early *timashas* of Garhwal, with the name of the Mughal emperor Furrukshiyar. The earliest pieces have dates 1185 & 1186 AH (1771-73 AD), which fit precisely into the period when there was a gap in the coinage in Garhwal. Presumably, in the year 1772 AD, the wool was routed through Ladakh, and paid for with coins minted in Ladakh. The trade was then routed back through Garhwal from 1773 to 1780 AD, and then again through Ladakh between about 1781 and 1802 AD, when large numbers of silver *timashas*, or *ja'u* as they were called by the Tibetans locally.

Once again, trade through Garhwal must have been disrupted during the war between the British and the Nepalese about 1814-15 AD, and again the wool trade would have been rerouted through Ladakh. Judging from the large number of silver coins of Ladakh, many of which come from Western Tibet, this trade was never again routed through Garhwal. Until about 1840 AD, the wool was paid for using Ladakhi coins, but after then the British Indian rupee became the currency of choice.

Bhutan and Cooch Behar (1760-1780 AD)

After the bulk trade between Tibet and India was stopped by the blockade exercised by Prithvi Narayan, some of the Tibetan trade was routed through passes further east and in particular through Bhutan and Cooch Behar. During the reign of Devendra Narayan (1763-65 AD), in particular, the output of the mint of Cooch Behar increased significantly, and coins of this reign are frequently found in Bhutan. After Prithvi Narayan finally conquered the Malla kingdoms of the Nepal Valley in 1769 AD, he was able to lift the blockade, and he started to encourage transit trade with Tibet, but Nepal was never able to re-impose the monopoly over this trade exercised in the years around 1700 AD. The mint in Cooch Behar continued to strike coins in large numbers, fuelled by the trade with Tibet, until the British closed the mint in 1780 AD. After that date the trade continued, but not on such a large scale, and not in a way that benefited the Cooch Behar state much. The British were increasing their presence and influence in the area, and ensured that the profits from the trade accrued more to the East India Company, than to local states.

The Rise of the British (from 1767 AD)

The trade with Tibet after 1760 AD, was passing mainly through Garhwal and Bhutan, naturally attracted the attention of the British, and in particular of Warren Hastings, the Governor General. The British realised the profits that could be made from this trade, although they probably overestimated the potential. The whole subject of the development of this trade has been ably analysed by Alastair Lamb[32], so I will not cover it here. Suffice it to say that as the British gradually gained control over India, they gradually closed mints in strategic locations, such as Cooch Behar and Garhwal, and by the late 1830's AD they had fully introduced their new standard rupee, which quickly became universally accepted in Tibet.

After about 1870's AD, the route through Sikkim and the Chumbi valley had been opened up, and a considerable quantity of silver rupees was reaching Lhasa. The Tibetans used these rupees to increase the output of debased silver coins from their mint in Lhasa, but the rupees were also very useful for onwards trade with China. An important trade was to develop in the last two decades of the Nineteenth century, whereby musk and wool was exported to India in exchange for rupees, and the rupees were then exchanged with Chinese in Tachienlu for brick tea, which was very popular in Tibet. The British Indian rupees were then melted into sycee in China, but they were also the main currency circulating in eastern Tibet during the late nineteenth century and the early Twentieth century. The British did get concerned about so much silver being sent to Tibet, and took steps to ensure that the trade became more balanced, but the demand for the rupees in the Tibetan markets was so great that the Chinese began to strike their own copies of the Queen Victoria rupee in their mint in Szechuan province.

Finally in this study of Himalayan coinages we find that how coins can shed interesting light on Trans-Himalayan trade. In many cases, they point out the trade routes that were used for bulk trade at different times. Bullion, and in particular silver, played an important part in this trade, and striking silver coins was a way in which the Himalayan states could profit from the transit trade, which might otherwise have provided them with little benefit.

Notes and References

1. S.C. Kala, 'Further Light on the Territory of the Kunindas', in *Journal of the Numismatic Society of India* (*hereafter JNSI*,) Vol. VIII, pp.36-37, describing a hoard of about one thousand silver coins discovered in the year 1880 in the village of Sumari, just above Srinagar, the old capital of the Rajas of Garhwal.
2. A small hoard of copper coins in the name of Bhanumitra was apparently found recently in Garhwal, in the name of Bhanumitra, but of a type slightly different from the known coins of this ruler, and in two sizes. My thanks to Mr. Prashant Kulkarni for informing me of these coins.
3. Singapore Coin Auction, Spink-Taisei, *The Skanda Collection*, 20.2.1991, Lot.164, identified as Kashmir by Dr Devendra Handa, although this attribution has been questioned by other scholars.
4. Robert Tye & Monica, *Jitals*, Isle of South Uist, 1995, p.36 (coin 21e2)
5. Sir Alexander Cunningham, *Coins of Medieval India*, London, 1894, Pl.V Nos. 21-23. These coins are now in the British Museum.
6. Robert Tye, *op.cit.* pp.62-64.
7. Nicholas Rhodes, K. Gabrisch, & C. Valdettaro, *The Coinage of Nepal*, London 1989.
8. Some of Amshuvarman's coins give him the title *Maharajadhirajasya*.
9. One copper coin from Sogdiana, dating from about the year 600AD has a similar image of Pegasus.

10. H.G Huttel, & I. Paap, 'On the Chronology and Periodization of Khyinga Settlement Mound', *Beitrage Zur Allgemeinen und Vergleichenen Archaologie*, Band 18, 1998, and private correspondence from Dr Huttel, noting that several such coins were found at Khyinga, one from Jharkot and another from Garab-dzong near Jomosom. All the coins are now kept in the Department of Archaeology, Kathmandu.
11. Nicholas Rhodes, 'A Hoard of Kushan Coins from Nepal', *Oriental Numismatic Series* (henceforth *ONS Newsletter*), No.155, Winter, 1998.
12. Nicholas Rhodes, 'A Late Lichhavi Hoard from Nepal', *ONS Newsletter* No.155, Winter, 1998, pp. 22-23.
13. Nicholas Rhodes, et al., pp. 52-53.
14. It is worth noting that the famous Tibetan ascetic records that his father travelled in the winter 'to do business in the south in Nepal; in the summer he went among the herdsmen of the north'. 'In this way he became very wealthy'. C.f. *The Life of Milarepa* by Lobsang P. Lhalumgpa, New York 1977, p. 14.
15. C.f. Nicholas Rhodes, & S.K. Bose, *The Coinage of Assam*, Vol. I, Pre-Ahom Period, Kolkata & Guwahati, 2003, pp. 27-45.
16. Apart from a few rare copper coins in 808-13 AH (1408-13 AD). For an account of the coins of the Sultan of Kashmir, cf. Nicholas Rhodes, 'The Coins of the Sultans of Kashmir', *Numismatic Digest*, Vol.17, 1993, pp. 55-146.
17. Many coin hoards from the Kashmir valley include both Hindu and Muslim copper coins.
18. Some account of the routes between Kashmir, Tibet and Central Asia is given by H.G. Raverty, 'Tibbat three hundred and sixty five years ago', *Journal of the Asiatic Society of Bengal (hereafter JASB)* Vol. LXIV, Part I, pp. 82-122.
19. Nicholas Rhodes, Gabrisch & Valdettaro, *op.cit.,* pp. 65-66.
20. Cf. *The Standard Guide to South Asian Coins and Paper Money,* Krause Publications, Wisconsin, 1982.
21. A. Deb, 'Cooch Behar and Bhutan in the Context of Tibetan Trade', *Kailas*, Vol. I, No.1, 1973, pp.80-88, and Nicholas Rhodes, & S.K. Bose, *The Coinage of Cooch Behar*, Dhubri, 1999.
22. The coins of this ruler are very well recorded in the local Chronicles, and hence by historians. Also, the later coins of

Nepal became known as "Mahendramalli Tankas", because it was Mahendra Malla who started to strike silver coins. However, actual examples of the coins of this ruler are very rarely seen and must have been struck in very small numbers. It is possible that their fame as exaggerated for political reasons after the defeat of Dolakha, so that the credit for the introduction of coinage in the region might be claimed by Kathmandu, rather than Dolakha.

23. L. Stiller, 'Cash Resources of the Malla Kings', *Nepalese Cultural Heritage in a Nutshell*, Kathmandu 1979, pp. 77-80.

24. I. Desideri, *An Account of Thibet*, London, 1937, p. 167.

25. RGV, pp. 225-31.

26. Several specimens are in the British Museum collection and other collections in Europe, such as the Museums in Berlin and Rotterdam. One piece was published in Italy in 1791 AD, by Paulinus of St. Bartholomew (*Systema Brahmanicum*).

27. Nicholas Rhodes, 'Some New Silver Coins of Fath Shah of Garhwal', *ONS Information Sheet* No.161, Autumn 1999, Supp. p. 21.

28. Jan Lingen, 'Commemorative Rupee of Fateh Shah of Garhwal', *Numismatic Digest*, Vol. VII, Pts. 1 & 2, 1983, pp. 87-91.

29. The Najibabad mint opened around 1763 AD, and was very active from 1176 AH to 1216 AH (1762 to 1802 AD).

30. F.V. Raper, 'Narrative of a Journey for the purpose of discovering the sources of the Ganges', *Asiatick Researches*, Vol.11, p. 497.

31. The coinage of Garhwal is described in Nicholas Rhodes, 'The Silver Coinages of Garhwal and Ladakh, 1686-1871', *Numismatic Chronicle*, Vol.141, London, 1981, pp. 120-135. Also, for the coins struck under Nepalese rule, see Nicholas Rhodes, Gabrisch & Valdettaro, *op.cit.* pp. 194-200.

32. A. Lamb, *Britain and Chinese Central Asia, The Road to Lhasa 1767-1905*, London, 1960.

12

Portuguese Trade in Indian Cotton Textiles during the Late Eighteenth Century

Karubaki Datta

The Portuguese reached the waters of the Indian Ocean region for trade in pepper and other spices. But from the very early period we know that cotton textiles had constituted an important item of trade with Rome and Greece. However at the time of the arrival of the Portuguese in India, textiles had been more used in the country trade – rather than in trade with Europe. Piece goods of India were exported to the ports of South East Asia to be exchanged for pepper and other spices. A very negligible volume ever seems to have been exported to Portugal. In a discussion of the commodity structure of Portuguese trade in the Sixteenth Century, K.S. Mathew has pointed out that cotton piece goods at this period were mostly collected from Cambay. He points out that the Portuguese also exported diverse sorts of silk and it was brought from China to the Malabar Coast initially and then exported to Lisbon. Thus in 1518 about 2,369 kgs of Chinese silk were exported from the Malabar Coast to Portugal.[1]

Presumably, till the third decade of the Sixteenth Century the Portuguese home demand for cloth was supplied by the Dutch merchants. They in return took back salt and Indian goods to their country. The confiscation of the Dutch cargoes and their ships by King Philip II and closing of the Iberian ports in 1585, 1595 and 1597 brought the traditional practice of this country trade to a standstill. Thereafter the Portuguese began to import directly for their own internal market. The practice continued till the third decade of the Seventeenth Century. One reason for this development was the demand generated by the slave trade in African countries – especially São João de Mina from where they obtained the maximum number of slaves in this period. Due to frequent wars in this period the need for slaves by the Portuguese had increased. They were employed as sailors on the ships and also as soldiers and artillerymen. Slaves were obtained in exchange for Indian textiles.

This demand began to decline in the later period during the fourth decade of the Seventeenth Century onwards. Afzal Ahmad who has described in details the trade of this period points out various reasons for this.[2] Among these were the financial condition of the Portuguese *Estado da India*, corruption among the officials, diversion of private capital in commodities other than textiles which saved a lot of duties, the famine of Gujarat that made collection difficult, the blockade of Goa during 1637-1641 and the Luso-Dutch wars of 1644-1658. All these factors proved to be disastrous for the trade. On the other hand, wars and rivalries in India also raised the price of the textiles.

Afzal Ahmad's conclusion that Portuguese trade in Indian textiles declined after a short spell of expansion is contrary to the general trend in European trade that had set in during the Seventeenth and Eighteenth Centuries. That Indian textiles enjoyed a growing importance in the home bound cargo of the European Companies has been discussed at length by Holden Furber.[3] He points out that this demand in Europe, especially in the Northern Europe was of slower growth due to the extensive use of wool and linen but even there, it accelerated after 1650. From trading in the Coromandel and Gujarat piece goods to the Indonesian archipelago the European Companies found it an easy step to extend their import to Europe itself. It seems that at the beginning, the English had a clear lead over the Dutch and it was only in the second half of the Seventeenth Century that the latter stepped up their European cotton trade. All the European trading companies began to export Indian cotton textiles to Europe and it has been discussed at length by many scholars.

By the third quarter of the Seventeenth Century the popularity of Indian textiles had become sufficiently established as to extend their use to the luxury end of the market. In 1664 the total quantities imported by the English company stood well over 750,000 pieces and their value accounted for 73% of the entire trade of the Company. In two decades the first figure had jumped to more than 1.5 million pieces and the relative share of textiles in total value had increased to 83%. The number of Indian cotton goods sold in Amsterdam by the Dutch Company during the quinquennium 1684 – 89 came to 1.12 million pieces. The 1680s was the great period of expansion for Indian cotton and to some extent the imports of these years were exceptional. The fact that the rate of expansion failed to maintain its momentum in the Eighteenth Century may be attributed to the saturation of market and partly to the imposition of heavy protectionist duties in many European countries, which culminated in some cases in a total prohibition of certain categories of textiles.[4]

The general trend being such, it is unlikely that Indian cloths should lose importance in the economy of Portugal; particularly when plantations were expanding, mines were being discovered and slaves were being employed in increasing numbers. That some trade in cotton was carried on is indicated by the fact that funds were regularly remitted from Lisbon for purchase of Indian cloths in the middle of the Eighteenth Century. By this time Indian cotton textiles suitable for use by slaves of Brazil and Angola had developed into a channel of lucrative trade. There is enough document proof that clearly shows the nature of this trade.[5]

According to an evidence, by the middle of the Eighteenth Century there was so much of illegal trade with textiles suitable for the slaves of Africa that it adversely affected the official Portuguese trade. Unfortunately for the Crown, the scope of this was provided by a Royal order itself. Permission was given on 17 November 1761 to vessels returning from India to halt at the port of Sao Paulo de Assumpcao of Angola and even to trade with the articles which were being carried from India. One customs house was set up exclusively for this purpose. The officials of the ship took the advantage to start full fledged trade in textiles particularly in those varieties which were coarse and plain and therefore known as cloths for the blacks. These were used not only in Angola but in Brazil as well. Since the ships did not have the permission to halt at the ports of Brazil an entrepot was set up in Angola itself. This adversely affected the interests of the metropolis which reserved for itself the monopoly of trade with the colonies. Only those pieces that did not sell in Angola were now carried on to Portugal and there they failed to fetch the desired price. This interrupted the usual trading practices of the country. By this time some cotton factories had been set up in Portugal to process the raw cotton imported from Brazil and produce some piece goods for Angola. This parallel and illegal trade blocked that line as well. With a plan to check this practice the King issued a new order whereby then onwards all the ships were ordered to transport their stock of piece goods directly to Lisbon. They were no longer allowed to unload their cargo of textiles in any port other than Lisbon, be it for use in the metropolis or elsewhere. Heavy punishment and fine awaited those who ignored the order. As expected, this curb on cotton trade of the Indian merchants created resentment among them. They complained to the Secretary of State in Lisbon, explaining how this round-about way of carrying the articles which were in demand in Angola and Brazil had to be taken to Portugal first and then sent to Angola once again. Apart from harassment them this implied repeated payment of customs duties.[6] There is no evidence that the Government in Lisbon paid any heed to these grievances. It only points out the importance of Indian cloths in the economy of Portugal during the first half of the Eighteenth Century.

The trade of Indian cottons further expanded in the last quarter of the Eighteenth Century. If the increasing volume of documents about the trade in cotton textiles of India be taken as an indicator, then this was maintained for the rest of the century.[7] This was a result of some international developments and has to be related to Portugal's economic compulsions at home. Both M.N. Pearson[8] and Celsa Pinto[9] have identified the outbreak of Napoleonic wars and political alignments in Europe as the possible causes of this. In this period of war, Portugal remained a neutral power .The English could do little to stop them and the Portuguese made profits by exporting these goods to Europe while the other traders were stopped by British blockade.

The documents however, give an impression which is slightly different from this. While it is true that the Portuguese trade in Indian cotton textiles did benefit from the Napoleonic wars, the upsurge seems to have begun a few years before the war broke out. A short description of the Portuguese colonies in general will help understand the context. This was a period when in spite of being the seat of Portugal's Indian possessions, Goa was not economically profitable for the metropolis. The number of ships plying between Portugal and Goa had considerably decreased. Goa did not have any product of its own. Orders had to be sent to Bombay, Mahem, Tellicherry and Cochin even for an item as insignificant as a dress. They were driven out from South East Asia, Sri Lanka and Malabar by the Dutch, the ivory trade with East Africa was partially lost to the Omanis and the Northern provinces of Bassein and Salcette had to be surrendered to the Marathas. By this late Eighteenth Century the Portuguese in India were left with little hold over the Indian Ocean ports to collect the cargo that could be transported to Europe.

Trading connection with Portugal therefore became practically limited to a handful of ships plying between Goa and Lisbon. As per one estimate, there was a total of 38 ships that went to India during a period of eleven years from 1738 to 1748. Yearwise the consecutive numbers were four, six, five, two, one, two, one, two, three and six. According to C.R. Boxer the number of ships fell even more from 1751 onwards.[10] The arrival and departure of ships had also become irregular. Sometimes they arrived late from Europe and sometimes they failed to depart in time due to Goa's failure to collect the cargo. In 1778, for example, the Governor complained that for the last three years, the ships were arriving only in December or January and that of 1778 had not arrived till the middle of December.[11] Among the items of export were pepper, saltpetre, coral in small quantity and finally some Indian cotton textiles.

In contrast, the yields from Brazil – known as the second Portuguese Empire, were many and much valuable. In 1738, the Portuguese ambassador to Paris Dom Luis da Cunha commented "in order to preserve Portugal the King needs the wealth of Brazil more than that of Portugal itself."[12] This wealth came from gold and diamond mines, and the extensive sugar, cotton and tobacco plantations. The yield from the gold mines had taken a downward turn in the second half of the Eighteenth Century. In contrast to the 25,000 kg yield from the gold mines in 1720 the yield had been reduced to 14,000 kg by 1760. It became even more insignificant in the following years.

Plantation remained more profitable than with sugar production remaining very high in the late Eighteenth Century. Cotton was another important product. As a result of technological innovations in textile production methods, demand for raw cotton increased in the British markets. Between 1785 and 1789 British manufacturers purchased 13 million pound of Brazilian cotton the amount going up to 68 million pound per year in the 1790s. In addition there were tobacco, rice, some precious stones, cocoa, coffee, hide and some horses to be exported to the metropolis.[13]

The significance of these articles lay not only in their mere quantity and variety but in the fact that a large portion of it constituted Portugal's export outside where these were exchanged for manufactured goods. Gold from Brazil went to places of foreign trade as official means of balancing the trade deficit. Even when the gold production started falling, it was compensated to some extent by raising the production of other plantation products.

Among the Portuguese colonies in Africa Angola was the most important supplier of slaves. In contrast to Guinea and Cape Verde where the golden period of slave trade had passed off in the Fifteenth and the Sixteenth centuries, Angola retained its predominance well into the Nineteenth Century. The important ports were Congo and Luango in the North and Luanda and Benguela in the south. According to one statistics Angola exported almost 700,000 slaves during the 70 years from 1701 to 1770. Over half of these went to Rio de Janeiro in Brazil.

It was in this background that trade in cotton textiles expanded in the last quarter of the Eighteenth Century. There was a series of tax regulations the objective of which was to increase the trade through the port of Goa. This began with the order of 1779 whereby concessions were granted to those articles which were taken from Portuguese ports by ships owned by the Portuguese themselves and then re-exported to other European countries. This was followed by some more such orders of 1783, 1789, etc.[14] The objective was not only to encourage trade from the port of Goa but also from Malabar. Categorical provisions for the articles exported from Malabar indicate a realization regarding the limited scope of trade from Goa. That the main objective was to connect Goa with other colonies of Portugal, particularly those of Brazil is indicated by the fact that some tax concessions were announced for those articles which were re-exported by Portuguese ships to the ports of Brazil and the African coast. On the whole there was special encouragement to export to Brazil. Among the articles that had the highest demand in that country was coarse cotton cloth. Hence this points to a need of this item in that country. In slight modification of the previous order, concessions were announced in 1783 for articles which were produced elsewhere but loaded in Goa. Articles which were to be re-exported from Portugal were to enjoy certain tax concessions while no such concession was given to commodities which were to remain in the country. Even in this category some exceptions were made for certain cotton cloths like *Zuartes, Coromandels, Chellas, Cadeas, Lenhas, Languins* and some more varieties from Gujarat commonly grouped together as cloths for the blacks. These no matter re-exported or not, would have to pay only half the taxes. Those meant for export would have to pay the *consulado de sahida* in addition to this. This implied an incentive to the import of coarse cotton cloths - mainly used by the slaves.

Some more tax exemptions were declared for piece goods exported to the ports of Brazil and the coast of Africa by ships belonging to the Portuguese or otherwise. Those dispatched to the ports of Brazil would be free from paying all the taxes that existed in the ports of that country.The impact was initially encouraging even though there is no authentic account regarding the actual number of ships that became involved in this trade. According to some accounts 24 ships in addition to the regular official ones had left Lisbon for Asia during the decade of 1770 - 1779. There is another set of documents with two reports stating that the number of ships during this period were 36 and 39 visiting Asia.[15] The trade seems to have increased even more in the next decade. The number of ships was higher even though it is difficult to ascertain their destination and ports of halt. This is because the ships had their destinations variously described as Goa, Macao, coast of India, Asia, Madras and Coromandel while destination of some were not described at all.

The total number of ships from the ports of Asia during 1783- 89 was 75 as a whole.[16] On the whole this was a period of increased interest and activity for the Portuguese in this part of the world. Apart from individuals some companies formed by Marques de Pombal for trade with Brazil and even tobacco contractors from Bahia began to take part in this trade. Some non-Portuguese businessmen also sent their ships under fake Portuguese identity.[17] Due to some unexplained reasons the mention of ships in business in Asia becomes infrequent after this. This does not necessarily mean a shrinking volume of trade with India. Celsa Pinto points out that this trade continued well during the first quarter of the Nineteenth Century. The trade received a jolt when the French attacked Portugal in 1807 but picked up rapidly after the immediate effects of French attack had worn out. Disaster struck in another form- the onslaught of cheap Manchester textiles spurred on in part by the opening of Portuguese and Brazilian ports in 1808. During the peak year of 1816, this trade had accounted for 10% of the Portugal trade with Asia. By 1828 this was drastically reduced and henceforth virtually non existent.[18]

These textiles were collected from Surat, Balaghat, Daman and Diu in the west coast of India. Lisbon merchants were also conscious of the textiles available in Madras and Bengal. Private Lisbon shipping even proceeded directly to the east coast for textiles without touching the ports on the west coast.[19]

Malabar continued to dominate the scene. As per one order issued in November 1800 it was explicitly stated that the regulations had failed to equalize the trade from Malabar with that from other ports of the coast of India. The former still dominated the trade from the coast of India. Consequently, some more changes were introduced in tax structure but they did not directly relate to textiles for Brazil.

In fact, by this time Portugal had begun to feel the problem of absorbing the imports items which could no more be re-exported began to pile up in the India House in Lisbon. Around 20 ships were either engaged in this trade or about to leave Lisbon for Asia but it was already felt that goods from Asian ports were already enough for next three to four years, while goods from Bengal and Malabar were enough for six to seven years and two years respectively.[20]

The Portuguese crown's interest in boosting this textile trade from India was not born out of a mere goodwill to regenerate the *Estado da India* but out of a definite motive to use the imports thereof to serve the interests of the metropolis and her colonies of greater economic importance. This could be achieved either through exports to other European countries or to colonies in the North Atlantic. The emphasis on export to Brazil proves the point. But these textiles were also used for some additional purposes. The textiles carried from India were used in Portugal in three different ways such as consumption within the country itself, re-export to the ports of Brazil and the African coast, re-export to other European countries. All the three however were interlinked.

The period was the aftermath of the rule of Marques de Pombal who had tried to regenerate the Portuguese economy through his definite industrial and trade policies. In industrial field Pombal's ideas had rested on two elements such as (a) obtaining raw materials within Portugal itself and the colonies and (b) maintaining and developing small manufacturing units whose output could be integrated into the working of bigger concerns which undertook the finishing process. He set up the *Junta de Comercio* in 1755 to promote industry by recruiting foreign master craftsmen, creating workshops, factories and production units. Factories producing cotton, linen, wool and silk goods, hats, leather goods, hardware, glassware, tapestries, clocks, watches, metal buckles, ivory combs and many luxury items were set up in 1765-66 mainly through private initiative. These manufacturers maintained close ties with the Brazilian trading companies which supplied them with the raw materials for dyeing and weaving. The finished products were subsequently supplied to Brazil. Encouragement to the import of plain white cloth seems to be related to this ten per cent concession policy. This would ensure a supply of raw materials to the units for dyeing and printing. After being processed these could be either re-exported or used within the country itself.[21] A big portion of the varieties used for this purpose came from Surat. The items of export from Surat were many. It included the most common among them *being zuartes, cadeas, chelas and lenhas*. These items were also available in Coromandel but the Portuguese preferred to collect these from Surat because the price there was found to be lower. These articles were also in high demand in West Africa. *Dotis* were used for printing and dyeing in Portugal.[22]

Cotton cloths from India were also used for re-export. A concession of ten per cent was announced on the customs duties paid on such articles in 1789. No alteration was made in this even though some changes were introduced in case of articles meant for home use and re export to Brazil. This emphasis on re-export came from Portugal's economic compulsions at home. In the first half of the Eighteenth Century Portugal's main economic problem at home was the adverse balance of foreign trade where imports exceeded exports by a huge margin. The deficit was compensated with by the gold of Brazil. However, from the 1760s the shrinking purchasing power of the people of Brazil due to declining production of gold and crisis in sugar and diamond mining resulted in a fall in Portugal's trade with England- her largest trading partner. English exports declined drastically from an annual average of £ 12,00,000 in 1750-60 to £ 6,00,000 in 1766-75. In a bid to reverse this trend and to increase the total volume of exports some basic economic reforms were undertaken by Pombal. The crux of his economic policy was to maximize the profits from the colonies which could then be channelised for the benefits of Portugal.[23]

The first of his legislative measures, born out of this objective related to the production prices and transportation of the products of Brazil.[24] The export of African slaves to the plantations and mines was also facilitated. According to the available data between 1757 and 1777, a total of 23,365 slaves were exported to Para and Maranhao from the West African ports, particularly from Cacheu and Bissau in Portuguese Guinea which had hitherto been of minor importance in Africa's slave trade. Angola, as mentioned above was another major source of slaves. The transportation of these slaves was carried on to a large extent by the monopoly trading companies formed on the model of those set up in England, Holland and Spain. Large scale transportation of slaves, it was hoped, would contribute to agricultural development and revive the production and export of sugar, leather, tobacco and cocoa. There was also the Company for whaling and extraction of oil and whalebones. Colonial trade was also reorganised with shipping controlled, capital concentrated and monopolies reinforced.[25] These efforts, initiated by Pombal began to pay off and the objective with which he had launched this was realized when the trend of deficit in Portugal's international trade was actually reversed in 1780.These new economic policies also benefited from two international events. The American War of Independence and the French Revolution and Napoleonic wars after 1789. These provided opportunities to Portugal in the international markets for her colonial products of sugar, cotton, tobacco and indigo. Between 1776 and 1795 Portugal's export to England increased by 90% while imports from England increased by 13% only. Similar changes were observed in trade with other countries. Portugal's European trade produced a surplus in 10 out of 12 years during 1796 - 1807 for a net gain of 88 million *cruzados*. Gold flowed back to Portugal- some of it even reshipped to Brazil. There was an overall betterment in the external trade relations of Portugal.[26] From 1796 onwards there was a constant favourable balance of trade for Portugal with some exceptions once or twice. The trend continued till 1809.

Pombal himself was removed from power in 1777 but the basic principles of his economic policies which had started showing positive results were continued. The policies adopted towards the imports from India also reflected a continuation of those economic measures. Emphasis continued to be put on stimulating agricultural productivity and the export of rice, cotton sugar and cocoa from Brazil. The encouragement to export of Asian commodities has to be placed in this context of Portugal's economic problem and prospects at home. It is true that the Asian trade was not the most important way out for increase of European export but its importance lay in the context of Portugal's economic stake at Brazil. Hence, in order to keep this portion of trade active and growing in consistence with the positive trend in Portugal's international trade, a scope was created, through fiscal concessions for the export of those articles from Asia, even though the economic value of these articles was not very high.

In other words the tax concessions for cotton textiles were declared not out of a mere goodwill to regenerate the *Estado da India* but out of a definite motive to use the imports from Goa to serve the interests of the metropolis and her colonies of greater importance. This was done either through exports to other European countries or to colonies in the North Atlantic. Thus Goa, whose contribution to the overall economy of Portugal had become negligible by this time was once again brought in that orbit through her contribution to the regeneration of Portuguese economy in general. The Portuguese *Estado da India* acted, at least for a few years as a pillar on which rested the second Portuguese Empire with its elaborate network of plantation and slave economy.

Notes and References

1. K.S. Mathew, *Portuguese Trade with India in the Sixteenth Century*, Manohar, New Delhi, 1983, p.133.
2. Afzal Ahmad, *Indo Portuguese Trade in Seventeenth Century* (1600-1663), Gyan Publishing House, Delhi, 1991, pp. 90-105.
3. Holden Furber, *Rival Empires of Trade in the Orient 1600-1800,* Oxford University Press, Oxford,1976, pp 239 -243.

4. K.N. Chaudhuri, "European Trade with India" in *Cambridge Economic History of India*, Vol. I, Cambridge University Press, Cambridge, pp. 401-402.
5. Arquivo Historico Ultramarino, Lisbon, (henceforth, A.H.U) *Mss. India*, Maco 32, dated 19 June1772. Some documents in the AHU bear the original serial number put by the scribe himself. Some documents do not bear any uniform serial number. Many are undated and unsigned. There are documents which are merely drafts, reports and observations submitted by various individuals.
6. *Ibid.,* Maco 126, dated 24 April 1778.
7. For a detailed account of the Portuguese trade of this period see, Karubaki Datta, *Remnants of a Receding Empire : Portuguese Trade with Goa and the East, c.1750-1800,* Unpublished thesis, North Bengal University, West Bengal, India,1994, see the Chapter, Goa : Its Lisbon Connection.
8. M.N. Pearson "Goa Based Seaborne Trade (17th-18th Centuries)" in T.R. de Souza (ed.) *Goa Through the Ages : An Economic History*, Vol. II, New Delhi, 1989, p.171.
9. Celsa Pinto, *Trade and Finance in Portuguese India*, Concept Publishing Company, New Delhi, 1994, p.186.
10. C.R.Boxer, "The Principal Ports of Call in the Carreira da India (16th – 18th Centuries)" in *From Lisbon to Goa, 1500 - 1750, Studies in Portuguese Maritime Enterprise*, London, 1984.
11. A.H.U, *Mss. India*, Maco 143.
12. *Ibid*, Maco 126, Document 82, dated 30 December 1778.
13. Some relevant books for the general description of Brazilian economy are : C.R. Boxer, The *Golden Age of Brazil 1695-1750, Growing Pains of a Colonial Society,* University of California Press, Berkeley,1969; see also his other works, *Portuguese Seaborne Empire*, Pelican, Harmondshire,1969. James Lang, *Portuguese Brazil: the King's Plantation,* Academic Press, New York, 1979, K.N. Maxwell, *Conflicts and Conspiracies: Brazil and Portugal 1750-1800*, Cambridge University Press, Cambridge, 1973; *Cambridge History of Latin America,* vol. I, (ed) Leslie Bethell, Cambridge University Press, Cambridge, 1984.
14. Historical Archives of Goa, (henceforth HAG) Mss. Codice 8089, fls, 1, 22-23, Codice 628, fl. 136 -146. For all the regulations and orders see my thesis.

15. A.H.U, Maco 81, Document entitled – 1779: *Baldeacao a favor das navios que fazem o comercio da Asia*. In one set of undated and unsigned documents there are two rough copies of the same report with slight variations.
16. A.H.U, Maco 161, Document entitled 1791, India, *Correspondencia official enviada pelo Nau Nossa senhora de Conceicao*, No. 1, 31 March 1791.
17. A.H.U, Mss. India, Maco 158, Document 46, dated 15 March 1793.
18. Celsa Pinto, *op.cit.*, pp. 184 -193.
19. *Ibid.*
20. A.H.U, Mss. India, Maco 171, dated 4 December 1801; Maco 48, dated 11 November 1801.
21. For details of Pombal's policies see, C.R.Boxer, *Portuguese Seaborne Empire, op.cit.*, pp. 180-206 and *Cambridge History of Latin America, op cit.*, Vol. 1, pp. 487-497.
22. Karubaki Datta, *op cit.*, p. 140.
23. C.R.Boxer, *Portuguese Seaborne Empire, op. cit.*, p. 186, *Cambridge History of Latin America, op cit.*, pp. 488-491.
24. *Cambridge History of Latin America, op cit.*, Vol. 1, pp.488-489.
25. *Ibid.*, pp. 490-91.
26. E.B. Schumpetre, *English Overseas Trade Statistics (1697-1808)*, Oxford, 1960, pp. 17-18.

13

Commodities, Trade and the Economy of Bengal: A Reassessment of the Early English East India Company State

Tilottama Mukherjee

The tendency in the existing historiography is to view eighteenth-century Bengal as a fragile economy (whether or not historians state that assumption explicitly) that collapsed with the incursion of the Company. The sources, however, tell a different story, with coexisting and multiple routes and markets existing well past the period of the Company's first intrusion and indeed feeding into its networks of procurement. The Company's checks on the flow of trade or its infrastructure of revenue-collecting institutions along roads and embankments, all exhibit a concern to collect its revenues and to procure commodities in a situation of great fluidity. If at a higher level, it was trying to centralise, for instance by destroying a level of local *zamindari* markets, in the early years of its rule no such wholesale reorganisation of the Bengal's market was even considered. The ambitious nature of the regulations was belied by their haphazard manner of being put into practice, which moreover stuck closely to existing paths of trade as it proceeded along a decentralised network of diverse routes.

This paper considers the ways in which the Company State tried to intervene, or to control various aspects of the economy and these measures' success or failure. Though much work has been done on the nature of the Company State, its involvement with the economy has often been an emotive and contentious issue, with very contradictory pictures being painted in different writings. To some, the Company was a basically exploitative interloper that destroyed a delicate network of indigenous co-operation that had developed over centuries.[1] For other, the Company was the prime mechanism of modernisation in Bengal, opening the region to a wider range of international and intercultural contacts.[2] The issue is far from closed and as the finest practitioners have rarely been accorded the last word, something may perhaps still be said on the late eighteenth-century stages of the interaction between the Company and Bengal. This period was simultaneously one of violence, compromise and creativity; accommodation in the economic sphere went hand in hand with a cultural borrowing carried out, whatever other scholars' diagnoses of decline, in a buccaneering spirit of commercial entrepreneurism. All the time, though, the Company State was waiting in the wings, ready to manipulate Bengal's markets in favour of an exploitative interest.

The indigenous trading systems have been the subject of much research over past twenty years.[3] Tied into local estates and the revenue collection of landed élite and rulers, as they were, these market formations were difficult to dislodge entirely or to regulate out of existence by collecting duty and taxes at a different source. The evidence here suggests that the economy was so decentralised that the Company dispensation could not initially subordinate it in Bengal.[4]

The Company State and Trade

The role of the indigenous state itself was neither insignificant nor all encompassing. The English East India Company appears, in comparison, as a more intrusive and different kind of institutionalised state system. The Company's own documents, setting out the terms by which lines of supply and labour would proceed through a chain of intermediary centres to market, confirm the impression of a very hands-on, interventionist body, prepared to distort local methods and priorities to fit preconceived templates. Of course, Company trade networks were limited both in geographical extent and in results achieved. By and large, early eighteenth-century rulers were more permissive or un-prescriptive in allowing the market to run its course. Documents suggesting the Mughal State extracted exploitative revenue from its peasants have been reinterpreted in such a way as suggests the state was never that organised, with outlying regions like Bengal never fully amalgamated into its mode of governance, so that, before the eighteenth century, a posting in Bengal would not have been highly coveted by the *mansabdar*s.[5] Archival records suggest that the Company State understood its interest as modifying existing systems of trade and revenue; it concentrated its efforts at reform in this period towards land revenues, where it insisted on a strict regime of collection from tenants irrespective of circumstances. In the following pages, we explore the interaction of the Company government with the filigree-fine networks of markets and trade in some very important commodities such as grain and textiles.

Trade and Regulations: The Limitations of Central Control

The *Nizamat* and the Company were undoubtedly both interested in trade and commerce. Therefore, they tried to impose certain rules and regulations on the way trade was conducted in various commodities. The differences between the two were nevertheless substantial in terms of the range of the economic policies they pursued. Overall, the Company's varied and ambitious policies appear to have mixed results. The regional economy in some areas weathered the pressures, while in other parts there are evidences of decline, suggesting rather a patchwork rather than clear-cut economic disintegration.

As a result of the grants conferred on the Company in the early years of the eighteenth century, the English Company was exempt from customs in all parts of the Mughal Empire, except for the port of Surat.[6] It annually paid a fixed amount into the imperial treasury at the port of Hughli. It was permitted to buy and sell at its liberty. The Mughal officials annually received the established tribute and were commanded to desist from intervening or interrupting them. 'If any where the least article of their effects shall be made away with', the *rahadar*s and *zamindar*s were to use 'diligence' in their recovery and 'should deliver over the thieves to condign punishment'. The goods were to be returned to the proper owner. Furthermore, wherever they set up factory and bought and sold goods and merchandise, they were to extend their assistance in all matters of contract and with all 'justice'. Farmers were to be made to repay their agents, whatever demands they might have on any merchant, weaver, or anyone else. Neither could anyone harass their agents; nor the boats hired by them nor were their own properties to be stopped for tolls.[7]

After Plassey, conditions were still fluid, for the Company officials noted in 1766 that a local *darogha* stopped several boats in a *ghat* near Burdwan. He declined to obey the *Nawab*'s *parwanas*, orders, under the 'pretence' that they were fictitious and mistreated the *harkaras*, or messengers, sent by the *Nawab*. He extorted money from them before permitting the passage of the goods.[8] Certainly, this was not the first instance of *parwanas* being ignored or flouted. Abuse of *dastaks*[9] was a point of contention between the *Nizamat* and the Company. As the date of the incident indicates, the Company's writ was not being complied with even after 1765. The *Nizamat* had ordained that for the inland trade the English were to pay the same duties as other merchants and take the *dastak* of the 'country government'.

According to the resolutions passed by the Company, the officials were to be particularly observant of the applications made to the President for *dastaks*. The latter was to request the *Nawab* to maintain a strict vigil at the *chaukis* and examine the boats and seize all those that were to be found with English colours without the authorised pass. The Company justified itself by stating that it was an 'imposition' often practised by 'Portegues, Armenians and the Country People' to defraud the government of their customs and 'through the indolence or knavery of the chowkies had succeeded very frequently'. This had been the cause, in a great measure, of the complaints and the Company, according to the reports of their officials, was blamed by the indigenous state.[10]

Historians such as Marshall[11] have noted that the Company government applied contradictory policies, with strict control over some commercial commodities like saltpetre and opium, which had a ready external market and no control over others. By the 1770's, however, the state was trying to engineer some broad changes.[12] The Company tried to prohibit private trade by its officials from 1771 onwards.[13] After 1772, salt was added to the list of restricted commodities.[14] The *dastak*s were abolished and for the encouragement and 'greater freedom of trade', all *chauki*s including *zamindari* ones (except for nine) were to be dismantled. As we shall see in the subsequent pages, even in so-called strictly controlled commodities, the Company's writ hardly went unchallenged.

There were several ways in which the Company's attempted regulations could fail as various letters and reports filed by its functionaries themselves noted over the course of the late eighteenth century:

1. There were only a handful of officials and orders passed in Calcutta, could not be implemented in areas even a few hundred kilometres away. The collection of additional taxes such as *mangun* (cess for superior's life-cycle ceremony) was abolished throughout the region. However, instances of orders being ignored are also recorded. For example, in Krishnanagar, officials stated that boats laden with goods were stopped for the collection of a duty of four and half Rupees on each boat. As a consequence, according to the report, the merchants suffered a great loss and hindrance to business.[15] Krishnanagar was not a remote frontier, but around 100 kilometres from Calcutta. If orders could not be enforced in a neighbouring area, it would have been even more difficult in distant estates and districts.

2. It was virtually impossible to keep an eye on all the custom-houses. As contemporaries noted, the *ghat*s and *chauki*s, where the duties were collected, were so numerous and most so 'inconsiderable', the officers or farmers so frequently changed, that it was scarcely ever possible to collect the papers of more than one or two years. The accounts of the un-farmed *chauki*s, deposited at the head *katchari* of each *pargana*, which were more likely to be preserved, were only in the abstract. Where the *chauki*s either belonged to 'Talook (*taluk*s) or to farms of perpetuity', which were not brought under the annual valuation, the accounts remained in private hands, or were destroyed.[16]

3. If all duties were abolished, they could result in the dismantling of the regular wholesale markets, or *ganj*s. As the Company official Robert Kyd stated, it could not be expected that these markets would be established or supported without the 'visible prospect of benefit'.[17] The numbers of markets were huge by any standards and in some districts (for which data exists) there was an exponential rise in their number over the course of the late eighteenth century.

4. *Ganj* holders were permitted rent of the ground occupied by the retailer. As Company employees noted this could lead to the continuation of the *sair* duties under the rubric of rent.[18] These speculations by individual Company officials do not seem to be unreasonable and instances of such cases were not rare. Reports do indicate that *zamindar*s, in some instances, converted a local fee on the shed or stand of shops, into a land tax and some impositions were renewed under the name of *ganj* duty, which was prohibited earlier under *rahdari*, or road-tax.[19]

In 1772, the state took the first step of prohibiting the collection at the *chauki*s. The abolition of the *zamindari chauki*s, too, appeared to be fraught with contradictions and unclear orders as a 1772 letter to the collector of Dinajpur states, from the tenour of your letter of the 19th instant we are apprehensive you still mistaken the meaning of the regulation which suppresses the zemindary chokies…there never was intention of abolishing the land chokies; that the Regulation only affects Duties on Goods passing by Water, that all duties on Goods carried by land must be levied as formerly but to prevent abuses we now inform you that we thought fit for remove all such chokies as are established on the Banks of Rivers merely for collecting Land Chokies. The duties collected under the name of that Bazar Julcar and Guzzergaut are to be continued without any alteration.[20]

Other officers also made similar observations that they were unaware of new regulations issued by the state abolishing certain taxes 'after being years in office', or the changes that had occurred in them.[21] Unclear orders further made the implementation of such rules almost impossible. Though it was difficult for the Company to implement its statutes, evidence suggests that where it did succeed in abolishing taxes, it adversely affected some farmers and other sections that were previously beneficiaries of the system.[22]

In 1773, 'the Regulations for the future establishments and regulation of Duties of the Country Government',[23] laid down that, all duties levied on grain 'in its transportation from the country' were to be abolished; duties or trade in agricultural produce were henceforth to be collected 'only at the capital towns whither it is brought for consumption' and the management of such levies was to be under five customs houses to be stationed at Calcutta, Hughli, Murshidabad, Dhaka and Patna; 'all road duties (*rahdari*) whether by land or water exacted antecedent' to the regulations of 1773 were to be made null and void; 'all the inferior types of chokies' over all types of trade routes were to be dismantled in a phased manner and the right of the local merchant to be 'at liberty to carry his merchandise wherever he thinks proper for sale' was to be ensured. The duty was fixed at the uniform rate of 2.5 per cent on all commodities, except for salt, tobacco and betel nut, on which certain imposts were levied.[24]

According to Datta, the Company's attitude was that *chaukis* were inimical to fair trade and these tended to push up prices. Hence, the regulations of 1773 were introduced and this had an immediate impact.[25] The Company State, further in 1774, stated that to put the collections of the *ganj* duties on a 'fair and equitable footing' and to 'relieve the merchants from all plea of grievance' no tariffs were to be levied at the *ganjs* except on goods that were actually sold there.[26] The regulations were being modified keeping in mind the ground realities and the reports and complaints of merchants and *raiyats* that were coming from the districts.[27]

Sairs consisted of tolls on shops, on the weighing of merchandise, or on the verifying of scales and weights, on imports and exports, on purchases and sales, on transport by land or by water and on ferries and halting places. Most were levied at markets and the tolls assumed the form of duties and customs at the principal marts.[28] The Company reckoned that these were not inconsequential and therefore perhaps its inclination to intervene in the collection of local taxes. There were significant changes in the structures of local markets and in the relationship between the state and the markets according to some authors. A critical factor in this was the Company's decision to dissociate landed proprietors from collection of local taxes on trade in their respective territories. This supposedly eased the movement of goods under the Company[29] and hence, had a positive effect on the infrastructure.

The evidence suggests that policies were not carried out across the board. The records also seem to indicate that even when the policies were implemented, they did not have the desired positive effects of reducing the burden on merchants. For instance, representations from different *beopari*es who imported grain from Dinajpur and Akbarnagar to Bhagwangola and Murshidabad expressed their inability to continue their 'trade with advantage to themselves', due to the high percentage (5 per cent) of 'imposition', which 'doubly' exceeded the rates that they paid at many *chauki*s and under the head of *mangun*.[30] Far from easing transit, the new directives appear to have further complicated the situation if these petitions are taken into account.

The Calcutta Committee of Revenue noted that some *chauki*s still continued.[31] In a 1775 reference,[32] it was observed that some inland *chauki*s had been recently established. There were in fact thirty-two *chauki*s adjoining 'Rajegunge', an important market in Dinajpur.[33] In another petition, horse traders complained that several landed proprietors exacted duties from them on their way from the west through Ramgar and Pacheat.[34] The system was not perfect as can be gauged by innumerable examples.[35] Conflicts arose over *ganj*s and other markets between neighbouring *zamindari*s or *taluqdar*s and others. Certainly, the Company or other landed proprietors could not enforce their will and arbitrarily appropriate rights without being challenged.

Cornwallis abolished all restrictions on inland transit in 1788, except for a customhouse in Manjee (on the borders of Bihar) for collecting duty on articles coming from Banares, Awadh and other parts.[36] The Company re-established these in 1801 and imposed tariffs at the rate of 3.5 per cent. Regulation IX of 1810 fixed a consolidated duty.[37] According to Charles Trevelyan, the indigenous system levied tolls, in each *pargana* rather than duties. They were negligible amounts and 'simple', fixed on 'well understood quantities' as an ox or camel load. Goods paid in proportion to the distance they traversed, paying by instalments as they proceeded. Though there are inconsistencies in the report about the 'native system', the descriptions do indicate an easily understandable method of levying customs, unlike the later more complicated Company regulations.

The state introduced more modifications in the existing structure of taxation and duties in 1793. The landed proprietors were prohibited from collecting any *sair* and in return were offered compensation.[38] The Company was attempting to break what it perceived as the existing bottlenecks in local marketing systems but not for general freedom of trade, but for its own benefit.

Though the state offered compensation to owners of *ganj*s, many such claims were rejected. What is surprising, however, is that the Company was not inundated with complaints or claims as Chatterjee also notes for Bihar.[39] It is very probable that the landed proprietors realised that the state could not carry out its orders to abolish *sair*. The merchants, who continued to be taxed, did not lodge any protest[40] as they did against the police tax. The police tax, levied in 1793, eventually had to be withdrawn in 1797 due to widespread opposition.[41]

The new regulations were seemingly cutting into the *zamindari* powers. The landed proprietors, however, continued to exercise their power over *hat*s and *ganj*s, and this was not only in a few localised instances. The contention that the Company State's main aim was to take control of the markets of Bengal, what Sen terms as 'conquest of marketplaces' or 'settlement of marketplaces',[42] is difficult to reconcile with the evidence. Local sources of patronage could not be displaced, nor could thorough overhauling of all kinds of duties, privileges and so on as strictly regulate the functioning. The regulations of markets were the concern of the Company's customs administration, in contrast to the actual holders of market rights as under the previous regime. However, the capacity to realise these controls were very limited.

The large number of markets and the clear increase in their number in some districts would negate the notion of close state intervention in late eighteenth-century Bengal, or even large-scale decline. If *chauki*s were dismantled, at least in some parts of the *zamindari*s the exponential rise in the number of markets might be explained by the latter's attempt to recoup resources by direct investment in these markets on a larger scale, as the *Nazim*s themselves were doing. The foundation of new markets continued unabated, especially in the second half of the eighteenth century.[43] The sources also suggest that the *ganj*s were numerous, located well within the *zamindari* estates, or on the 'confines' of the adjoining ones, so as 'not to counteract the general benefit, but if possible increase it, by rendering it the interest of rival holders to reduce the duties as low as possible'.[44] The Company's attempted regulatory management systems appear to have met with partial success and evoked a mixed response.

We have so far discussed only the general regulations, in the next section we turn our attention towards the essential staple commodities of the region and examine how the Company fared in these important sectors of the economy.

The Grain Trade

How did the Company try to regulate the lines of supplies? Its attempted regulations regarding the grain trade and other staple items met with particularly varied results. A chain of indigenous merchants and their intermediaries firmly held the reins of internal markets and the procurement process. The Company had to rely on either prominent merchants or *paikar*s and other intermediate groups as the situation demanded.

Regulations came into force in times of scarcity. A 1774 reference speaks of delayed rains that pushed up price of grain and hence *beoparis* bought and sent it to deficit areas. The Company officials noted that the merchants could not be prevented from purchasing grain, unless there was a prospect of great scarcity or general distress and such a step could not be taken to 'deprive the Merchants or Ryots of the liberty of buying and selling at will'.[45] Similarly in 1781, the Company noted, The vendor of grain (was) to be suffered to carry their grain to such markets as they prefer without hindrance or molestation.[46]

The amount of rice remaining in the districts could not be ascertained particularly 'at this season of the year' (October), as it was no sooner collected, than transported from one *ganj* to another and by being constantly in motion rendered any 'amount impossible to be obtained'.[47] On the other hand, Bogle, for instance, writing in 1770, referred to abuses practised by Company servants who accepted 'presents' or fixed the price of rice in the provinces under their control.[48] Perhaps the Company officials at times tried to control the lines of supplies.[49]

The Company State often resorted to embargoes on exports of grain, which were later forbidden.[50] The free transport of grain was allowed in certain places that were most affected.[51] The Board of Trade clearly noted, however, that there was no established rate for selling grain, the dealers had 'authority to sell at pleasure'.[52] *Raiyats* and landholders hoarded when prices were high, after paying off rents, to ensure continuation of 'exorbitant profits'.[53] The situation was serious enough for the state to issue warnings against hoarding, or not bringing grain to the market and non-compliance could end in seizure of the grain.[54]

The Company's government drew up plans for the establishment of public granaries. The State proposed to buy grain for ready money and deposited it in *golas* (public granaries), constructed of mats and bamboo. If there was a succession of favourable agricultural cycles, stocks were to be maintained by disposing of part of the stored grain during the season when prices were high. Fresh stocks bought at the height of the harvest when the prices were low replaced this. In this way the grain was to be kept without damage and according to the functionaries of the state, the profit from the sale would be adequate for meeting the expenses of collection.[55]

Though a district might have plenty of grain at hand, when the Company tried to buy it for its granaries, the requisite amount was not available. The Company officials noted, as many as 47 *gola*s of grain (containing 200,000 *harrie*s of paddy) besides sufficient amounts with *raiyat*s for their general consumption, might have been present in a particular location, but despite *parwana*s for forming *gola*s and efforts to enforce the orders, not more than 8000 *harrie*s could be procured on the public account.[56] While individual merchants stored rice in numerous granaries,[57] the attempts to buy grain for the Company's *gola*s resulted in a drain on the state's resources, with considerable loss due to mismanagement, high maintenance costs, damage by natural elements and pests, high purchase price and low sale prices. The latter was due to merchants' collective endeavour to control the rates and withdrawing from the auctions.[58] Granaries were finally closed down in 1801. There are numerous instances of seasons of extraordinary plenty in the district of Dhaka. The lowest price of grain appeared to have been 8 maunds or 640 pounds for the rupee.[59] The years 1772, 1795, 1796 and 1797 were also seasons of great abundance.[60] The amount of grain available in Purnea district in 1794 alone was as high as 305000 maunds.[61] A contemporary source in 1791 gives the figure of 43.8 million maunds as the annual turnover of rice.[62] At least during these years, the state's procurement of grain should not have created problems, yet it could not take advantage of the situation.

The Company State also undertook to enforce orders by means of posting guards. The tendency to use force was certainly a significant intervention. Extra-economic measures were apparently necessary for the Company to ensure the continuation of its trade. The state found it necessary to constitute a 'superintendent of Bazars' for the regulation of the *bazar*, as well as for care of public cattle and grain by 1796.[63] Of course, indigenous regimes also had similar officials to look after the *bazar*. Grain could be supplied from 'Bowangunge', Sibganj, 'Sompgunge' and Jamalganj etc.[64] Bhagwan Gola, near Murshidabad, one of the biggest markets, was supplied with grain, oil and *ghee*. The place was well protected and the command of the garrison under a very experienced officer.[65] Thus important central places were well guarded. The complexity of the system of intermediaries and large fluctuations in the production of grain meant that the grain trade was least amenable to control.

Among other staple items, the Company established a monopoly over salt, opium and saltpetre. Between 1781 and 1835 the salt industry grew more rapidly than in the preceding years. However, it declined very sharply after 1835.[66] Throughout the period Indian traders continued to participate in salt trade. The *Nawab*s collected duty on salt manufacture and granted a monopoly of its sale throughout Bengal to Khwaja Wajid.[67] According to another report, before the Company's accession, the trade in salt was 'entirely confined to native merchants'.[68] Notwithstanding the exorbitant duties, demand for salt was great and the profits arising from it so considerable, that despite the initial disruptions, trade continued unabated.[69] Famine caused in 1769-1771 had major disruptions[70] with 'a very considerable portion of the inhabitants' of the salt provinces being affected. The industry was quick to bounce back after 'plenty was restored'. In 1771, the Company once again resumed the trade in salt. The Company continued the salt works with *malangi*s in their employ. Apparently, even if a monopoly existed, other merchants could participate in the trade, possibly as contractors. The Company's profits from this very important branch of trade did not cease. The actual management was not in their hands, but farmed out to *zamindar*s, or contractors. These contractors delivered fixed quantities at the stated seasons. They made 'their returns upon the spot' (where it was manufactured) to the different agents of the Company.[71] In 1780 Hastings brought the whole process of salt manufacture and taxation under direct government control. The salt-producing areas were put under a comptroller and divided into agencies.[72] As a 1793 letter to the Board of Trade noted, the distant provinces were supplied due to the 'activity and intelligence' of the merchants and traders and the increased demand for salt was due to the new markets in the interiors.[73]

Even while Khwaja Wajid enjoyed the salt monopoly or later the Company cornered the trade, indigenous traders continued to participate in salt trade. Similarly, there was no perceptible decline in the production of essential commodities such as sugar. Sugar was an old industry, although in the second half of the century the external market was waning. Markets in Arabia and other places were no longer viable due to competition from sugar coming from China and Batavia.[74] However, the internal market was large and appeared to have sustained this sector.[75]

The State and the Cotton Weaving Industry

> ...[in Bengal] the two most important occupations for mankind, are so happily blended together, that the same hand which at one season governs the plough, at another guides the shuttle, in executing those exquisite textures, which are every where admired, but can no where be equalled. Endeavours in Europe, to connect agriculture and manufactures together, in the same persons and families, have been found in defect, as they always will; and that desirable connection is absolutely peculiar to Bengal..[76]

The weaving industry was a major component of the economy. It is here that the historians have postulated that the Company's policies had their greatest detrimental impact. Economic historians have spilled much ink on the issue of the collapse of the textile industry.[77] Many scholars, such as J.C. Sinha, saw the decline of the cotton industry of Bengal because of the monopolistic control of the Company and the oppression of the *gumashtas*.[78] According to Bhattacharya,[79] the introduction of the agency and contract system in the 1770s and

1780s marginalised the intermediaries in industries such as textiles. Sushil Chaudhury contended that 'ruthless oppression and exploitation' marked the second half of the century. He states that the Company's monopoly enabled it to control what the weavers and artisans produced and how much at a given price, reducing them to the status of 'virtual slavery'.[80] However, in the main chapters of his monograph, *From Prosperity to Decline*, he considers the late eighteenth century only fleetingly.

Paradoxically, those who have studied the cotton textile industry in proper detail have projected a different image of the sector and have seen the later collapse resulting from different reasons. Mitra held the falling overseas demand as being responsible for the decline[81] while Chaudhuri analysed it as a 'low level equilibrium trap', with surplus labour and low wages, which increased output, but not productivity.[82] Hossain, too, focuses on the internal weaknesses that made it vulnerable to emerging forces and pressures and the way in whi[illegible]e Company's policies further aggravated the situation.[83] Al[illegible]n she sees the changes starting early, from the 1750s, the [illegible]72 and 1793 regulations further modified the production process, leading to weavers' indebtedness to the Company. The intermediaries also gained more advantage. According to Hossain, the increasing emphasis on the revenue by the late eighteenth century had led to a shift from manufacture to agriculture, as the returns from the former were not adequate.

However, one can only accept these propositions with reservation. What all these writers tend to ignore, is the sizeable internal market and the presence of indigenous merchants, as well as other buyers - Europeans, Armenians and merchants from other parts of the subcontinent - and the continued prosperity of the internal market. Though there is evidence about increasing pressure on the weavers, there is also contrary data, which suggests a degree of manoeuvrability on their part. The decentralised production process and enterprising people involved in the industry made it difficult for the Company to impose all its directives. The nature of the material does not allow us to delineate sharply the changes occurring in the weaving industry. Though, decline seems to be more of a nineteenth century phenomenon and it appears to have stemmed from several factors, which came into play after 1815. The first part of this section will consider the evidence, which tends to question the existing paradigms. The records also indicate the adverse effects of the Company's impositions, but as we shall see in the second part, the evidence shows local areas of decline, interspersed with areas of considerable economic vitality, rather than a uniform collapse.

Though the external market was considerable, the internal consumption for cotton textiles was immense and involvement of local merchants substantial. Contemporaries estimated the annual value at six million sterling.[84] The Resident at the Dhaka factory reported in 1789 that the province (of Dhaka) produced six times the amount of cloth required by the Company, but 'not of qualities which it can answer for the Company to purchase', or which if they wanted to buy, would not be within their power from the clash of large native capitals, the proprietors of which have certainly more accurate knowledge of what may be termed the mysteries of the business than any Europeans are possessed of.[85] Dhaka district alone had about 40,000 weavers, but the Company controlled or employed only few of them.[86]

Weavers produced cotton piece goods at many different *arangs* scattered throughout the region.[87] Officials noted in their reports to the Company, that there were no manufacturing towns in Bengal as in Europe (though it might not be true for Europe either) and the weavers were dispersed throughout the region, four-five houses in a village. All the European companies trading in Bengal had their establishments in the major cities such as Dhaka. Such establishments, in the contemporary jargon, were known as 'factories'. Every factory had under it a chain of *arangs* or depots at every principal mart and *bazar* of the country. The principal factories at the central place controlled all these. The names of some of these *arangs* under the jurisdiction of Dhaka, for instance, are available in the records - Chandpur, Ratanganj, Masumnagar, Chittagong,

Sylhet, 'Azmaree' and 'Chilmaree'.[88] The main manufacturing centres were in Murshidabad, Kasimbazar, Radnagar *et al.* *Arangs* had a wide hinterland. For example the one at Sonamukhi, extended over the districts of Burdwan, Bishnupur, Birbhum and a part of Rajshahi and had several inferior dependant factories.[89] The *arangs* were central to the Company's procurement system. However, these could not strictly control every aspect of weaving. As a result, of the dispersed nature of the weavers and the *arangs*, officials reported that the Company's orders to 'attend' to the cloths while they were still in the looms were not practicable.[90] Clearly there was no vertical or highly centralised chain of command, which could oversee every aspect of the industry.

It was only in a few central places, such as Dhaka, where Europeans had set up their factories that they could deal directly with *dalals* or *paikars*. In other places, they either had to make contracts with Indian merchants to deliver goods, or employed salaried agents, called *gumashtas*, to make purchases for them.[91] The Calcutta Council tried to encourage weavers to settle in the Company's territory in Calcutta for manufacturing different cloth.[92] Not withstanding its temporary success, the new methods of processing investment did not produce satisfactory results. It vested the *gumashtas*, the agents of the Company with 'powers, which they frequently abused'.[93] The Company's ignorance of local conditions in the early years also meant it issued impractical orders.[94]

The local people involved in the textile industry frustrated any attempts by the Company to impose disadvantageous terms. Apparently, cotton and thread sellers combined with the weavers to thwart the Company's attempts to reduce prices. As an instance of 1766 illustrates, the local brokers would sometimes prevent weavers to bring good quality cotton to the market and they tried to raise the price.[95]

Company officials noted that 'as there is general freedom of trade' the *dalals* and *paikars* brought to the Company whatever assortments they could obtain for ready money purchases at the *hats* or markets. Most weavers, according to one report, refused to take advances as they used to before

1777. It was more advantageous for them to make cloth with the 'little money' they had and bring to the market. They sold it to the Company's *paikar*s or others - 'chiefly the latter' for the higher price they obtained for cloth and other buyers were not 'so scrupulous' in the quality of cloth that they chose. Sometimes *paikar*s used the Company's advances to buy cloth and re-sold them to individual merchants, instead of advancing it to weavers for the Company's assortments.[96] The advances to the weavers were made through 'dusuoreas' settled in the *arang*s. These were brokers and known to weavers and were paid a commission of two per cent for making advances and for inspecting cloths.[97] Presumably, it was easier for the weavers to negotiate and settle terms with a familiar person, rather than a stranger.

In 1787, the Company issued a regulation for the register for weavers.[98] Nonetheless, it appears not to have brought all the weavers under the Company's power, 'for the latter were confidently asserting in their petitions, the markets are open and [the weavers] will sell their cloths where they please - let the Company go to the Markets or establish their Cooties [*kothi*s] here and if to chuse [choose] they will bring their cloths to the Cootie for sale and if they do not they will carry them elsewhere...'.[99]

The early eighteenth-century records amply manifest that the Company could not force the merchants to settle for any price arbitrarily.[100] Even in the later years, the weavers exercised some freedom. Officials noted weavers' unwillingness to work for the Company. They observed that the proposals for 'freedom of commerce and a power to the weavers of quitting the Company's service' were proving harmful for the Company's interest. It would have rendered 'all engagements and estimates on those engagements' uncertain and incomplete, as it did away with all controlling and superintending power over the weavers. It also prevented improvements in quality, which was 'already so much on the decline'.[101]

The economic position of weavers varied across the region. In Malda for instance, they were also farmers. They were 'better protected' from *zamindar*s than any other section of society. The lowest also had their 'hire as manufacturers', perhaps referring to their independence to work for whomever they chose and their condition was better.[102] The high price of cotton and the inability of the Company's functionaries to procure threads were attributed to the decline in the number of spinners as a result of the famine in 1771. The Resident of the Dhaka factory also noted that besides these factors, the more 'forcible reason' was the very high demand for lower kind of *tanjeb*s (white muslin cloth of fine quality), presumably referring to a high demand in the internal market. The market price in the city was nearly double the Company's price. Hence, weavers preferred working for private persons than for the Company in a situation where 'the dearness of the necessaries of life renders it most necessary for him to employ himself to the best advantage'.[103] Even after 1760, the Company was not the sole player on the scene. Buyers included other European companies, private and Indian merchants as well as Armenians, who were exporting cloth from Bengal.[104]

Does the evidence suggest a flourishing textile industry? Contradictory data exists, which point towards different scenarios. The Company tried various ways to control the industry through its system of giving advances, arbitrary valuations and sometimes use of force. Weavers also had to bear the brunt of severe famines and the imposition of intermediaries. In the following few pages, we will examine the different ways in which the weavers were being put under increasing pressure, and whether the industry could persist and survive despite these policies.

The strategies deployed to exploit the weavers were many. The weavers of Santipur in a petition in 1773 stated that the local cloths were woven out of cotton produced in the province. *Beoparie*s brought cotton and retailed it in very small quantities to the *catanie*s or women employed in spinning. The weaver bought the yarn from them directly or from the *paikar*s who collected it in the different villages. The factory made advances in cash to enable the weaver to carry on his business. They complained that they were first obliged to accept money against their will and afterwards forced to part with the goods at an arbitrary valuation, far below the market price. Hence, they received nothing for their labour, as the yarn cost them as much or even more than what they got by selling the manufactured cloth. Having spent all their former savings, they ran up debt to the factory.[105]

The profits they got on *dhotis* and other cloths that their women and children made and sold in the market enabled them to tide over difficult times. Two or three men worked to make a piece of cloth (or one person could take about twenty-five days to make a piece of middling *mulmul*). Even for weaving households in the employ of the Company, the internal market was crucial. This involvement of the whole family had important repercussions on the economy, with greater dependence on the market for everyday necessities. Households in the South Asian variant of the 'industrious revolution'[106] appeared to have put in 269 working days. Twenty-nine days in addition were spent in weaving related activities.[107]

The price of yarn had been gradually rising and the famine had greatly reduced the number of spinners. The price was as much as 25 per cent dearer in 1773. Yet, the value of the cloths remained the same. Although the prices had increased, the *gumashtas* while inspecting the cloths undervalued them by categorising them as of inferior quality ('lower classes').[108] More than price fixing, it was these indirect ways of lowering the prices that affected the weavers more as it appears from the evidence.

The weavers complained that the Company did not pay for their labour at the rate of Rs. 3 for middling *mulmul*. They had to pay the price of the thread in sicca rupees when purchased from the *catanee*s or spinners and in sanout (devalued) rupees when bought from the *paikar*s. They further complained that the various intermediaries took two *anna*s from them as *kharch* or charges. The *dalal*s did not mention this in their account; they took it as a due under the term of *bahar dalali*. The weavers also complained that the intermediaries frequently tied them to a stake and flogged them. The factory *gumashta*s on their part justified it on the account of the weavers delivering cloths of different and inferior classes.[109] The problems enumerated were many. Nevertheless, it appears that the deleterious effects did not lead to a decline in the number of looms, for in 1783, 7000 looms 'for the most valuable assortment' of cotton piece goods were present in Santipur.[110]

If some *arang*s were prospering, some others were not. In Tilbadi *arang* for instance the number of households decreased from 900 to 500 between 1774 and 1788.[111] Compared to quality and fineness, the price increase was less. The famine caused a decline in Dhaka in the mid 1770s, which 'swept away a great part of the spinners' and those who 'should succeed them' were engaged in cultivation of land.[112] Santipur *arang* had also suffered due to 'decay of the Company's investment'. There are instances of prices of *cowrie*s in Dhaka declining due to the weavers' inability to buy because of the 'smallness' of the cloth investment.[113] The Company officials also noted that they had to bear the competition ('rivalship') of other 'foreign settlements' and the great mart of Calcutta. The prices of cloths increased[114] - which were inconvenient for the Company, but of course not for the weavers. Weavers of the 'poorest class' probably carried their goods for sale to the markets, instead of negotiating with the Company intermediaries.[115] Problems arose also because the amount of piece goods demanded was beyond the procurement capacity of some factories. The contractors could be very harsh and ruined many weavers.

The intermediaries played an important role in the negotiations. The *gumashta* of Kaliganj represented that *paikar*s and *dalal*s of that area were privately obtaining cloths from weavers. The latter were able to work only because of the intermediaries' advance. Meanwhile, the commitments to the Company remained unfulfilled. The regulations of 1775 'respecting the freedom of trade' (in effect the Company's trade) expressly addressed such issues. The provisions against arbitrary imprisonment - 'after establishing the absolute right and liberty of weavers and others to sell and trade at their pleasure', declared that it was not meant (in enacting a general freedom of trade) to release them from any engagement that they might have had voluntarily contracted. If the Company caught any weaver in its service selling cloths to private merchants, - while he had not fulfilled his obligations according to agreements - it could punish them.[116]

The stated policy, however, was that the Company shunned the system of coercion. A manufacturer could refuse to enter into an agreement, unless it was at an acceptable price.[117] Other reports stated that weavers were averse to making cloth of unusual lengths, for if the Company did not accept them; it was not easy to dispose to private merchants. This required a 'degree of force' to oblige them to accept an advance.[118]

The Company bought considerably cheaper as compared to other dealers, at 'so great a disparity as to exceed belief, but on the supposition of mere compulsion, which is not the present system'. According to other Company officials, the advantage the Company enjoyed was due to the permanent employment and protection it provided to the weavers. Secondly, the ignorance of other European dealers with the impositions of the indigenous agents they employed gave the Company a competitive edge. Thirdly, it had access to a ready European market. Other functionaries attributed the comparative advantage to the 'superior terms' in which the Company procured goods.[119] The demand for Bengal goods in Europe was also increasing.[120]

Much of the evidence above appears in the forms of complaints of the Company's officials, where the inability to get the required quantity of textiles is sought to be explained by advancing various reasons for the 'decline'. It does not, however, mean that the industry was actually on a downward slide. The number of piece goods, for instance, sold in the external markets, continued to grow through the century. The following figure illustrates the quantities of piece goods imported from the subcontinent and sold at the Company's sales, in the years 1771 to 1792.

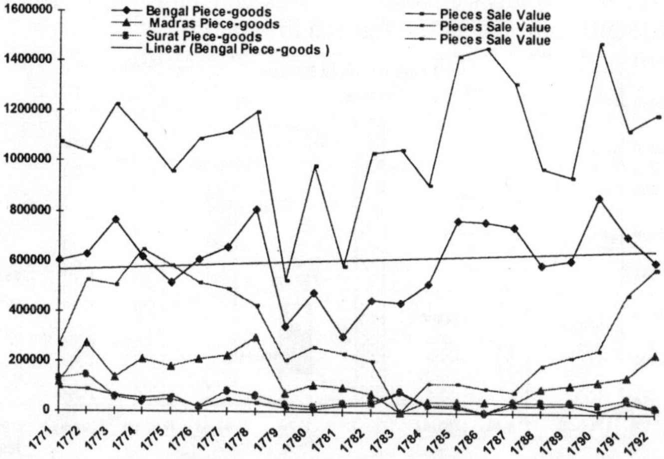

Figure 1 - Company's Cotton Piece Goods Sold in London, 1771-1792.

Source: William Milburn, *Oriental Commerce: A Geographical Description of the Principal Places in the East Indies, China and Japan, with their Produce, Manufacture, and Trade; including the Coasting or Country Trade from Port to Port; also the Rise and Progress of the trade,* Vol. II, London, 1813, p. 234.

Since 1793, according to Milburn, Great Britain was almost constantly on war and at the same time British manufactures were making rapid strides, leading to the decline in the trade in piece goods.

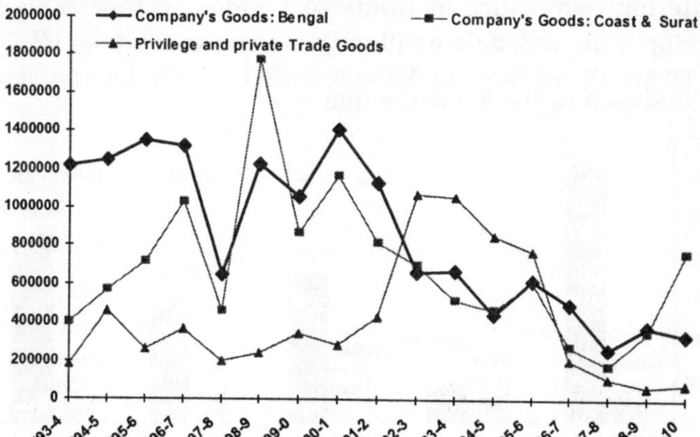

Figure 2 - Cotton Piece Goods sold in London, 1793-1810.

Source: Milburn, *Oriental Commerce*, Vol. II, p. 235.

The Company's investment was considerable in the late eighteenth century as the figures illustrate:

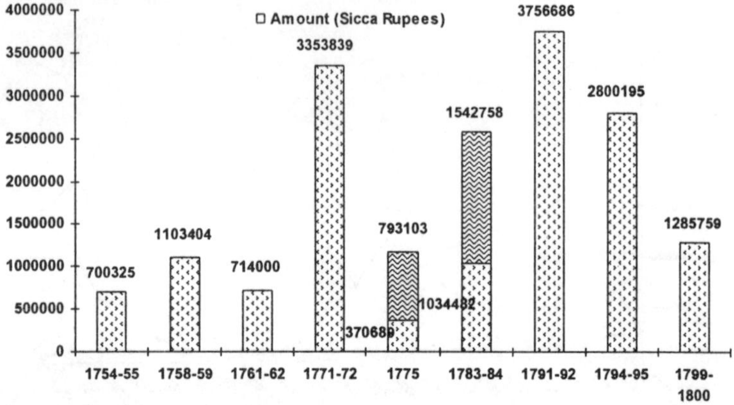

Figure 3 - English East India Company's Investment in Cotton, 1754-1800.

Source: Based on Hameeda Hossain, *The Company Weavers of Bengal. The East India Company and the Organization of Textile Production in Bengal 1750-1813*, Delhi, 1988, p. 98 (figures for seven *arangs*); WBSA, BOT-Comm, Vol. 3 (I), 2 May 1775, p. 204; WBSA, BOT-Comm, Vol. 39, 2 Oct. 1783, pp. 61-62 (the number of *arangs* are greater and hence the column has been divided into two sections for 1775, 1783-84).

If the Company's share was showing a downward trend in the last decade of the eighteenth century, private investment seems to have increased. Tomlinson, for instance, sees it as a vehicle for remittance of funds to London, rather than an indicator of increased demand in the overseas markets.[121]

Private investment in some selected *arangs* for the years 1801 is shown in the following figure:

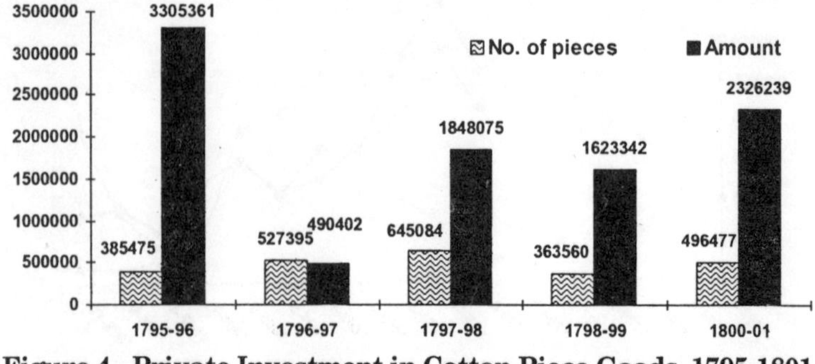

Figure 4 - Private Investment in Cotton Piece Goods, 1795-1801.

Source: Based on Hameeda Hossain, *The Company Weavers of Bengal*, p. 100.

It appears from the above evidence that the cotton textile industry weathered the changing demand patterns as well as the Company's policies in the late eighteenth century. However, the pressures on the weavers were intense, especially in the aftermath of the famines. Despite the impositions of intermediaries - the *dalal*s and *paikar*s and the Company's run of the market as a major buyer, the industry seems to have survived. The actual steep downward slide appears more of a nineteenth-century phenomenon.

The Silk Industry

Silk was an important component of the economy along with cotton. In this section, we will briefly examine how it fared in the late eighteenth century. Here also the internal market was significant and the Company was not the sole buyer. Other European companies as well as traders from other parts of the subcontinent continued to be major players. The industry was decentralised and it embraced new methods of reeling and continued to cater to both the external markets and meet the demand in the subcontinent.

There were two kinds of Bengal raw silk; one reeled according to the old method, commonly called country-wound and the other reeled according to the new or Italian method.[122] Also, by the 1780s, the contract system to the agency houses was in operation, with investment from the Residents and the *paikar*s playing an important role in the procurement process.[123] Mukhopadhyay considers this phase crucial. According to him, one can discern significant changes in the character of the state with the latter becoming an active agent in the production of commodities and 'engineered administered prices'.[124] He sees the Company coercing producers to sell below the cost of production.[125] Nevertheless, some evidence points in a different direction. An 'examination' of a *gumashta* in 1789 seems to show that 'weavers exercised their freedom and set the price:..the chassars refusing to sell them (Buxypore cocoons) under that price (15 & 16 Rs. per maund of 64 Sa wt.)...'[126]

It can be argued that such cases are an exception, but given the competitive nature of the market, it is plausible that weavers continued to have some amount of negotiating power.

The Company was the biggest buyer, but it was neither the only player in the field and nor was Europe or the external market, the sole consumer, a fact which Mukhopadhyay's essay notes in the latter part. He considers the twin mode of usury and under-pricing as significant and the Regulation 31 of 1793 to be of vital importance.[127] The Company did not buy up all the silk.[128] The evidence does not bear with the assertion that silk was almost entirely dependent on the European market, as some authors have suggested.[129] As the Radnogore Resident observed, merchants could buy raw silk from the area in the *bazar*s of Calcutta. Armenians, Calcutta merchants, merchants from Benaras,[130] Gujarat[131] came annually to buy a considerable amount of silk. A number had 'arisen to be considerable farmers and people of wealth'.[132] Merchants exported filature silk to Mirzapore, from where it moved on to Maratha territories and to central and western India.[133] The regular demand is for 'the manufactures..[of] good silk and they seem to be less solicitous about prices, than a steady, constant and uniform supply'.[134] The wars with the other European and country powers affected the investments temporarily.

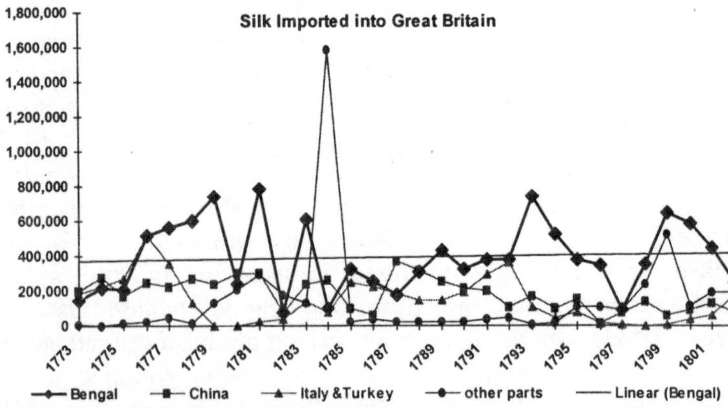

Figure 5 - Raw Silk Imported into Great Britain from Bengal and Other Parts of the World, 1773-1802.

Source: W. Milburn, *Oriental Commerce*, Vol. II, p. 256; Carey Lib. 080, Pam. 19, No. 5, 'Reports of the Committee of Warehouses of the East-India Company, Relative to Extending the Trade in Bengal Raw Silk', London, MDCCXCV, pp. 6, 11.

However, the quality of silk was on the decline. High price and difficulties of obtaining good quality thread caused weavers to mix coarse assortments with the finer ones.[135] There were wide fluctuations, which would have had an adverse effect on the volume of trade.

The following graph gives the quantities of raw silk imported into Great Britain from Bengal, China, Italy, Turkey and other places in the thirty years, from 1773 to 1802.

The overall trend of silk imports from Bengal, however, shows a slight increase. Coercion alone could not have sustained the buoyant demand. Neither there was steady decline in the Company's investments for silk nor did the famine strike a fatal blow. The evidence in the records does not bear out the stark black and white picture of economic prosperity in the first half of the century and complete economic dislocation in the second half. The textile industry appears to have had a rather uneven development, with areas of decline, as well as spots of continued resilience through the eighteenth century.

The Volume of Trade in Bengal

The survival of the cotton and silk exports needs to be considered against the background of the internal and external trade as a whole. The overall figures for internal trade are difficult to obtain. The external trade, however, is more fully documented and the data available shows increasing exports even for much of the late eighteenth century. The amounts of merchandise being exported and treasure coming into the province was considerable. The bullion question has been a much debated issue[136] because it relates to sources of liquidity and hence growth of economic conditions. Much analysis has centred on inflow of precious metal. Quite apart from the silver in circulation, historians often neglect to take into account the stabilising effect of local and little currencies such as *cowries* and copper coins. Without specie and exchanges in local currencies, the massive export of commodities could not have been sustained. Evidence exists suggesting that the Bengal economy retained considerable financial liquidity. *Cowries* constituted almost 40 per cent[137] of the total money in circulation. As Perlin observes, the Company in Bengal solved the problems of mint costs, 'production bottlenecks and competitive access to limited means of payment by continuing to import non-mintable media'.[138] It is probable that the internal economy could sustain itself even in periods of acute silver crisis due to the multiplicity of local forms of currency still in circulation. The term *cowri* or *kaudi* had become synonymous with money itself[139] and these were frequently referred to in literary writings such as the *Mangalkavyas*. It is possible to speculate that shortages of silver affected the revenue mechanism more than local transactions, which were low denomination *cowri* based. There were periodic fluctuations. Indication of the importance and facilitating effects of these local currencies was furnished by the Resident of Golagore.[140] Another official cites the 'inconvenience occasioned' to the investment from the scarcity of *cowri*es in the *hats*.[141] Thus, even local currencies were extremely significant for the Company's transactions.

Merchandise and treasure imported into Bengal from London, excluding the English East India Company's imports between 1802 and 1806, was immense. It follows that such a huge quantity of merchandise being brought, in return, injected money into the local society. As the evidence for internal consumption shows, increasing amounts of English and European goods were making their way into the households of the well-off sections of society in even rural areas, which clearly had the purchasing power and preference for these commodities. Milburn's figures only take account of official statistics, but as Bowen notes that undeclared privileged clandestine trade accounted for an immense amount both in volume and in value, much before the Company's monopoly was abolished.[142] The exports from Bengal to London during the same period were considerable. These goods were bought through a chain of intermediaries with the Company exercising differing levels of control over these functionaries, in a market where there are other competing companies, indigenous merchants, and its own employees working towards their private interests. Extra-economic leverage through its armed and other state functions could give a crucial edge, but the figures here would clearly indicate it could not cut off its rivals and it follows that Bengal's producers, middlemen, transport workers, big and small traders benefited from this considerable trading network, linking it to the world economy on a more equal footing, than what would happen in the nineteenth century.

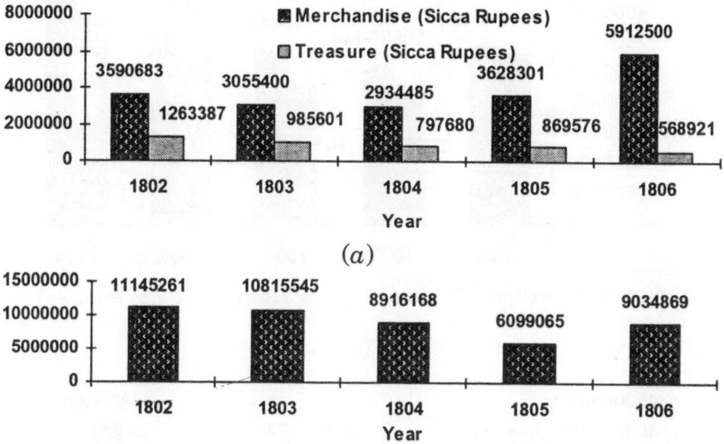

(*b*)

Figure 6 - Merchandise and Treasure: a) Imported into Bengal b) Exported from Bengal.

Source: Milburn, *Oriental Commerce*, Vol. II, p. 112.

The figures for exports from Calcutta, in private and 'foreign' trade were very high as well.

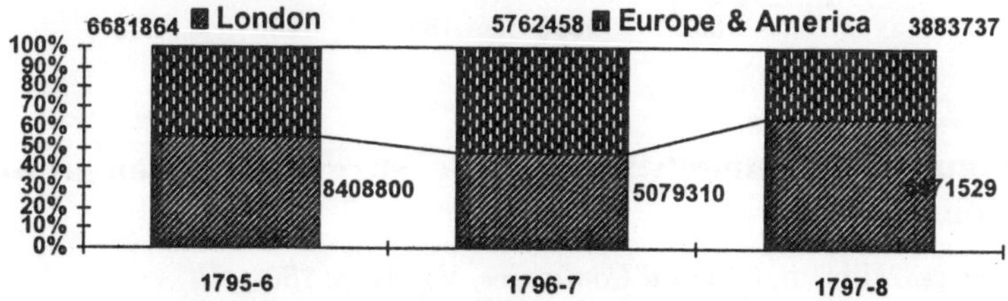

Figure 7: Exports from Bengal, 1795-1798.

Source: Carey Lib. 080, Pam. 19, No. 19, 'Papers respecting the Trade between India and Europe. Printed by order of the Court of Directors for the Information of the Proprietors', April 1802, p. 38.

The merchandise and treasure imported into Bengal from all parts of the world, in the years 1802 to 1806; and exported from Bengal to all parts of the world during the same period is given in the following figure:

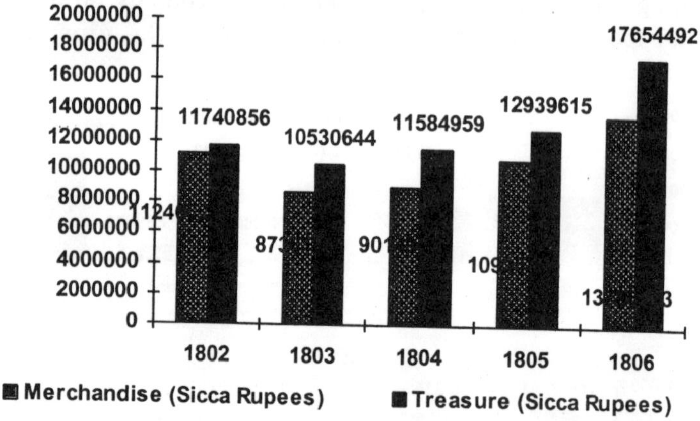

(*a*)

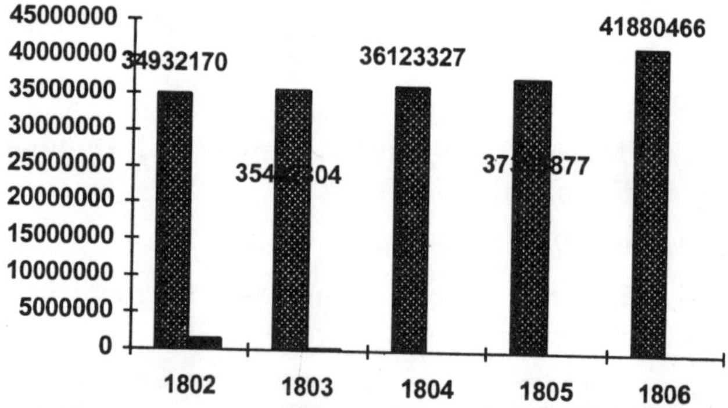

(*b*)

Figure 8 - Commodities and Treasure: a) into Bengal b) from Bengal.

Source: Milburn, *Oriental Commerce,* Vol. II, p. 150.

The Company acquired the right to convert bullion into *siccas* and gold coins.[143] It initiated various regulations regarding mints and other currency reforms. It might be thought that increasingly stringent management of treasuries also resulted in controlling and impeding the flow of metals as it happened during the 1830s. However, it is doubtful whether this was true for late eighteenth-century Bengal, as Chatterjee and others have shown. The attempted amendments did not succeed at this point in significantly diminishing the power of shroffs (*sarraf*s) and bankers.[144] How important the role of these groups was can be clearly seen if we consider the wide range of currencies in circulation and the different species of rupees required at the various *arang*s.

Table I - Variety of Money in Eighteenth-Century Bengal.

Arang	*Rupees*
Barnagore	Arcot
Burron	Sicca
Calcutta	Arcot
Chandernagore	Sicca
Chittagong	Arcot
Cuttorah	Sicca
Dhaka	Arcot
Gollagore	Sicca
Harial	Arcot
Kasimbazar	Sicca
Khirpai & Haripal	Sicca
Lakshmipur	Arcot
Malda	Sonnaut
Midnapur	Arcot or Siccas
Patna	Sonnaut
Rangpur	French Arcot
Santipur	Sicca
Sonamukhi	Sonnaut

Source: WBSA, BOT-Comm, Vol. 3(II), 12 May 1775, pp. 258-259.

Kuroda[145] has argued that the diversity of current currencies can be related to the hierarchy of markets. Mitra, on the other hand, saw this as an indicator of market backwardness. Perhaps, it can as well be seen as an indicator of the flexibility of local trade. Increasing involvement of peasants in rural markets, the independence of local monies made them autonomous from the interventions of the state.[146] Currencies were neither alternative to one another, nor were they equivalent.[147] As trade became more profitable, the monetary circuits increased. Our evidence suggests integrated and at the same time dispersed marketing systems. If the above explanation holds, the eighteenth-century economy was still highly decentralised without this feature proving detrimental to its efficiency.

Concluding Remarks

This essay examined the efforts of the Company State to intervene in Bengal's trading and marketing circuits and related aspects of the local supply chain. Existing infrastructural networks always preceded the State; markets, merchants and commodities did not come into existence due to state regulation. The highly market-responsive and cost-competitive structure of production was mainly determined by the sophisticated economic infrastructure.[148]

The evidence suggests that the notions of widespread decline in late eighteenth-century demand reappraisal. This is not to deny that the economic sphere suffered fractures, but to specify their limited and commodity-specific, rather than structural, nature. The wider 'modification', which authors such as Datta, or 'collapse' as Chaudhury and Sen have depicted, seem to attribute to the Company State more power and influence than it actually exercised in the early years. The Company's depredations, in practice, certainly created some major losers like the Jagath Seths[149] or Omichand or Khwaja Wajid, largely on account of these rich bankers' and merchants' extensive connection with the political regimes displaced by the new State. From a perspective of hindsight, it may be inappropriate in the context to apportion blame to any particular individual or group for 'complicity' in colonialism.

Though the use of force could sometimes rebound upon its agents, an increased armed presence as manifested in armed guards in factories and the growth of cantonments and military garrisons, betray a more aggressive and territorial motive than merely policing commodity flow. It is difficult to know if Bengal's society at this time was becoming more violent as happened in China over a similar time period.[150] Incidents of dacoities are mentioned in our records, especially in the 1770s and 80s. The economic, ecological and political instability of this time occasioned major disruption in many spheres of life.[151] While during the *Nizamat* period, travellers had noted the relative safety with which they moved, Company records refer to looting and plunder. Guarded boats carrying treasure could fall prey to mass groups of as many as 100-150 people[152] although in 1753 merchants could send bullion from one part of Bengal to another protected only by two or three peons.[153]

The Company's objectives, at least on paper, were to encourage and promote free trade internally and through import and export markets with neighbouring districts and adjoining countries. 'Public markets', according to this rhetoric, were to be kept free and monopolies abolished; as the Company reserved to itself the prerogative of regulation, no duties were to be imposed on goods brought to market except for fixed customs authorised by the State. The 'industry of the natives' was to be encouraged and assistance and protection granted to 'all manufacturers willing to return to their former occupation, if it should appear that any such manufacturers have either abandoned their settlement or quitted their Business'.[154] The Company espoused a benign language of fostering local activity, promising government protection to the manufactures or 'arts' of particular districts, which appeared jeopardised by international trade. In their interpretation of the Company state, some may have placed too much credence in the official account.[155] The state regime was more exploitative than their stated aims suggest, as in practice, the Company imposed and extended monopolies,[156] far from completely suppressing fiscal barriers, it multiplied transit taxes.[157] The State's inability to oversee the actions of its intermediaries, whose levies remained in place even when jurisdiction had formally passed to the Company regime, meant that much trade fell foul of some version of 'double taxation'.

It is undeniable that there was 'market contact' in the late eighteenth century, in the sense that peasants went to market in order to sell produce to pay the state revenues. It is difficult to believe, however, that commercialisation was not also market-oriented,[158] determined by different parties' parlaying of their interests in their context of a relatively free negotiation process. Farmers, traders and intermediaries did not, then only approach the market because of institutional pressure of revenues. The increase in the number of markets over this period was possibly due to the easing of population pressure following famines and the opening of new cultivable lands. If Company efforts at regulatory enforcement largely failed, it may also be true that the positive effect attributed to the Company policies in the form of increased revenue pressure leading to the intensification of commercialisation might well be an overstatement. The presence of numerous buyers, including the English East India Company, in the Bengal economy created a huge demand, although the attestation of an emergent State providing the crucial link towards market integration may err too much in the direction of a state-centred analysis.[159] Though scholars have painted a very bleak picture of its impact on late eighteenth-century Bengal, the evidence rather suggests a patchwork of change and continuity, with a variety of pre-existing local modes subsisting beneath the level of Company jurisdiction.

There were many viable markets that preceded the intervention of the Company and many effective forms of market facilitation and oversight. The *Nizamat* was not an inept as a broker of trade, nor was the Company State an all-pervasive presence conditioning every form of commerce, at any level, that went on under its jurisdiction. The Bengali elite maintained a vigorous presence along the routes of trade, rather than retiring feebly to cities as some commentators have suggested[160] and the land was not simply stripped to tend to their luxuries. Trade and the resulting wealth propelled local rulers to act as co-ordinators or facilitators of commerce and sometimes even direct participants. Economic exuberance in early modern Bengal took a variety of forms that resisted ossification or state control insofar as innovation offered a commercial advantage. During the period, Bengal had a functional infrastructure and a working labour market; merchant groups could mobilise in collective defence; accountancy was practised; and highly developed and price-responsive marketing systems and forms of credit and monetisation were in place.[161] Yet, economic historians such as Om Prakash do not hesitate to characterise even the early Company state as being successful in its imposition of unilaterally determined terms and conditions over suppliers, artisans, weavers and peasants.[162] The major changes of this period, by contrast, are not in the structure of trade as it represents a surrogate for the exercise of political power, but in the sizeable upheavals affecting the ecological, demographical and political spheres of eighteenth-century Bengal. If in politics and economics, incremental change produces the most enduring results, in a cruel reversal of this process, Bengal suffered a jarring reversion into famine, want and gradually shrinking overseas demand. Erstwhile robust sectors were rendered marginal with the coming of the railways in the nineteenth century and an increasingly intrusive state structure at just the time that the vitality of its markets promised it a prosperous one.

Acknowledgements

I am grateful to Professor C.A. Bayly, under whose guidance part of the research for this paper was undertaken. Thanks are also due to Dr Raziuddin Aquil for his careful reading and suggestions. The usual disclaimers apply.

Abbreviations used:

BOR-Grain	Board of Revenue-Grain
BOR-Sayer	Board of Revenue-Sayer
BOT-Comm	Board of Trade-Commercial
BOT-Salt	Board of Trade-Salt

BPC	Bengal Public Consultations
BPP	*Bengal Past and Present*
BRC	Bengal Revenue Consultations
Carey Lib.	Serampore Carey Research Library
CCR	Calcutta Committee of Revenue
CCRM	*Proceedings of the Controlling Council of Revenue at Murshidabad*
DFR	Dacca Factory Records
FWIHC	Fort William India House Correspondence
Home Misc.	Home Miscellaneous
Home Public	Home Department Public Branch, Proceedings.
IESHR	*The Indian Economic and Social History Review*
Mf	Micro-film
Mss Eur	European Manuscripts
NAI	National Archives of India
O.C	Original Consultations
OIOC	Oriental and India Office Collections, British Library
PCRD	Provincial Council of Revenue Dinajpur
WBSA	West Bengal State Archives

Notes and References

1. From early Nationalist writings to more recent works repeatedly portray the transition as a period of economic doom. For instance, see Sushil Chaudhury's *From Prosperity to Decline, Eighteenth-Century Bengal*, Delhi, 1995.

2. The Western impact having its benign influence upon social reforms and education has been the theme of some works on nineteenth-century Bengal. David Kopf, *British Orientalism and the Bengal Renaissance; the Dynamics of Indian Modernization, 1773-1835*, Berkeley, 1969.

3. Notably C.A. Bayly, *Rulers, Townsmen and Bazaars: North Indian Society in the Age of British Expansion, 1770- 1870*, Indian ed., Delhi, 2000 (1st publ.1983); Rajat Datta, *Society, Economy and the Market. Commercialization in Rural Bengal c. 1760-1800*, Delhi, 2000.
4. Contrast with Sushil Chaudhury, *From Prosperity to Decline*. Sudipta Sen, *Empire of Free Trade: The East India Company and the Making of the Colonial Market Place*, Philadelphia, 1998.
5. Muzaffar Alam and Sanjay Subrahmanyam, eds., *The Mughal State, 1526-1750*, Delhi, 1998, Introduction.
6. For trade in western part of India, see Ashin Das Gupta, *Indian Merchants and the Decline of Surat: c. 1700-1750*, Weisbaden, 1979. Lakshmi Subramanian, *Indigenous Capital and Imperial Expansion: Bombay, Surat and the West Coast*, Delhi, 1996.
7. NAI, *Home Public*, Vol. 20, 22 Feb. 1763, pp. 236-238. Order from the *Nawab* to the Rangamati *faujdar* for instance, specified that the trade of English *gumashta*s was not to be obstructed on any account, nothing besides the usual customs was to be demanded and no duties were to be levied from those who had the Company's *dastak* (trade permit). NAI, *Home Public*, Vol. 20, 1 Feb. 1763, p. 128. Hence, it was agreed with the *Nazim* that the usual customs were to be paid to the 'country government' upon all goods purchased for the 'inland trade' that was for 'reselling in the country'. Such goods were to be sent from place to place with the *Nawab*'s *dastak* (received from the officer to whom customs had to be paid). After the goods were dispatched, goods were not to pay any 'dustorey', duty or customs to *ghat*s, *chauki*s or others on the road. The goods purchased to be sent to Calcutta went with a *dastak*, and no duties or customs of any sort were to be paid. NAI, *Home Public*, Vol. 20, 1 Feb. 1763, p. 127.
8. NAI, *Home Public*, Vol. 30, 18 Dec. 1766, pp. 1136-1137.
9. Also see Sukumar Bhattacharya, *The East India Company and the Economy of Bengal from 1704 to 1740*, 2nd ed. Calcutta, 1969, pp. 17-68.
10. NAI, *Home Public*, Vol. 20, 1 Feb. 1763, p. 129. *CCRM*, Vol. VII (A), 2 Sept. 1771, p. 9.
11. P.J. Marshall, *East Indian Fortunes: The British in Bengal in the Eighteenth Century*, Oxford, 1976, pp. 138-139.

12. *CCRM*, Vol. IX, 4 Jan. 1772, pp. 6-7.
13. P.J. Marshall, *East Indian Fortunes*, p. 243.
14. W. Bolts, *Consideration of Indian Affairs, particularly respecting the present state of Bengal and its dependencies. To which is prefixed a map of those countries*, 3 Vols., London, 1772-75, pp. 73-74. He observed that '..every manoeuvre of those who govern the English East India concerns and particularly in Asia, seems to have been calculated with a view to facilitate the monopolizing of the whole interior trade of Bengal. To effect this, inconceivable oppressions and hardships have been practiced towards the poor manufacturers and workmen of the country, who are in fact, monopolized as so many slaves'. *Ibid.*, pp. 182-186.
15. *CCRM*, Vol. VII, 14 Nov. 1771, p. 159.
16. *CCRM*, Vol. VIII, 30 Dec. 1771, pp. 100-101.
17. OIOC, Mss. Eur. F 95 (Kyd), ff. 169-170.
18. *Ibid.*
19. WBSA, BOR-Sayer, Vol. 1, 28 May 1790, pp. 153-154.
20. *Proceedings of the Committee of Circuit at Krishnagar and Kasimbazar*, (29 August 1772), Vol. II-III, Calcutta, 1926, p. 182.
21. OIOC, Mss. Eur. F 95 (Kyd), ff. 169-170.
22. *CCRM*, Vol. XI, 28 May 1772, pp. 101-102. A letter from the assistant superintending the 'Pachotra' stated, 'as from the account settlement you will perceive that the agreement with the Farmers has been realized to a very inconsiderable Balance, but it is with the greatest difficulty I have kept up the payment of their Kists, owing to the Abolition of the Gully Mangun, the general decrease in the circulation of Merchandize and the almost universal exemption of duties, from goods passing with a dustic - for all these causes, the farmers were importunate to obtain deductions and to the same causes, is to be imputed the great decay in this branch of the revenue, which I understand used formerly to yield a collection of three lack of rupees'. Ibid. 'Where the Gawts appertaining to this farm used to receive a considerable duty from all Boats passing, they now find themselves excluded by almost all Boats being accompanied by a Dustuck. And as the whole of the Revenue of this Farm arises from the Duties on Boats. The Rents must now of course be

considerably lessened. In consequence of your orders for totally abolishing the Duty Gully Mangun. The farmers... expect to have the Deductions therein specifyed. The Receipts for two or three years at those gauts have been in proportion to this Demand and I imagine.... It should be allowed'. *CCRM*, Vol. VII, 24 Oct. 1771, p. 95.

23. OIOC, BRC, P/49/38, 23 March 1773, OIOC, *Home Misc.*, Vol. 217, pp. 44-49. Also see R. Datta, *'Rural Bengal'*, pp. 36-37.

24. Charles Trevelyan, *Report upon the Inland Customs and Town Duties of the Bengal Presidency* (1834), ed., T. Banerjee, rp. Calcutta, 1976, p. 91.

25. Rajat Datta, *Society, Economy and the Market*, pp. 203-204. A letter to the Board of Customs states, '..as the administration has from a regard to the ease of the merchant and consequently with a view to the encouragement of trade consented to relinquish so great a part of its revenues as the rhadarry duties..'. OIOC, BRC, P/49/44, 1 March 1774, p. 551.

26. OIOC, BRC, P/49/44, 1 March 1774, pp. 551-552.

27. *Ibid.*, pp. 548-551.

28. H.T. Colebrooke, *Remarks on the Husbandry and Internal Commerce of Bengal*, rp. Calcutta, 1884 (first publ.1795), p. 47.

29. R. Datta, 'Peasant Production and Agrarian Commercialism in a Rice Growing Economy: Some Notes on a Comparative Perspective and the Case of Bengal in the Eighteenth Century', in Peter Robb, ed., *Meaning of Agriculture-Essays in South Asian History and Economics*, Delhi, 1996, p. 122.

30. OIOC, BRC, P/49/46, 12 July 1774, pp. 1916-1917.

31. WBSA, CCR, 31 Dec. 1773, p. 103.

32. NAI, PCRD (mf), 30 June 1775, p. 255.

33. Curley places it in the third rung of the hierarchy of markets, this being in the central court of a powerful *zamindar*. The first rung consisted of *khas* markets of Murshidabad and large *khas* markets like Nawabganj formed the next level. David Curley, *'Rulers and Merchants in the Late Eighteenth-Century Bengal'*, Ph.D., University of Chicago, 1980, p. 45.

34. WBSA, *Calcutta Committee of Revenue*, Vol. 14, 20 May 1782, pp. 2161-2164. Ibid., Vol. 15, 6 June 1782, pp. 2528-2529.

35. *CCRM*, Vol. VII, 2 Sept. 1771, p. 12. The *ganj*s of 'Bougdany' and 'Hirgang' were abolished and the officers from those stations withdrawn. The duties being thereby discontinued, necessary deduction had to be made from the revenue of the *pargana*. It was noted, however, that the intention of abolishing all duties hitherto levied at the different *chauki*s seemed to imply sanction for the levying of the customary duties at these *ganj*s. Salt and beetle nut had been exempted from duties ever since 'rowanahs' had been given to the merchants upon the payment of Rs.30 per 100 maunds at the Government's customhouses. But as to tobacco and grain, a small duty had always been levied upon them at different *chauki*s, as upon other articles of merchandise. These were levied under different categories of taxes such as 'Koot Chulluntah', 'Mongon', either upon the weight of the goods, or upon each boat without regard to their tonnage. But, some merchants, especially those who supplied the city of Murshidabad with necessary items, enjoyed particular exemptions by 'long established custom'. Regulation 20th stated that all 'Zemindary Chokies' were to be abolished and none kept but such as immediately dependent on the Government under the 'Punchetra, Bucksh bundar and Shahbunder' subject to such regulations as should be established from time to time. *CCRM*, Vol. XI, May 20 1772, p. 67. Whether *chauki*s were finally abolished or not, contestations did not cease over markets - The *beoparie*s of Aminaganj in the *pargana* of Kasimnagar carry goods there to buy and sell. 'At this time the people of Mongulpore in the Chucla of Rajemehal have oppressively broke down the Flag of the Gunge and without Reason raise(d) a Dispute. They bring sepoys and using violence toward(s) the Beoparies, have stopped all the imports of the Gunge'. *CCRM*, Vol. X, 23 April 1772, pp. 233-234.

36. Charles Trevelyan, *Report upon the Inland Customs and Town Duties of the Bengal Presidency* (1834), p. 91.

37. *Ibid.*, p. 93.

38. Rajat Datta, *Society, Economy and the Market*, p. 205.

39. Kumkum Chatterjee, *Merchants, Politics and Society in Early Modern India, Bihar: 1733-1820*, Leiden, 1996, p. 135.

40. See WBSA, BOR-Sayer, Vol. 5, 11 Jan. 1792. WBSA, Revenue Department-Sayer, 3 May 1793, O.C. No. 2. The *ganj*s were

very often situated on the highways and some peons had to be stationed to prevent 'oppression' from occasional travellers. Otherwise, the *ganj*s would have been deserted. The *beoparies*, as a result, agreed to pay 'something of their own accord under the description of mangunee and ground rent through the medium of the weighmen'. From these collections, *godowns* were built and repairs carried out, - both for keeping salt and for *beoparies* to stay. Further, the charge of bringing water from the Soan, the expenses arising from 'attending' to marching sepoy battalions and transporting them across the Ganges, were defrayed out of this money. WBSA, BOR-Sayer, Vol. 8, 19 April 1793, pp. 408-409.

41. Kumkum Chatterjee, *Merchants, Politics and Society*, pp. 138-140. Basudeb Chattopadhyay, 'Police Tax and Traders' Protest in Bengal 1793-1798', in B. Chattopadhyay, H. Vasudevan, Rajat Kanta Ray, eds., *Dissent and Consensus: Protest in Pre-Industrial Societies*, Calcutta, 1989, pp. 1-35.

42. Sudipta Sen, '*Conquest of Marketplaces: Exchange, Authority and Conflict in Early Colonial North India*', Ph.D., University of Chicago, 1994, pp. 10-11. Kumkum Chatterjee, *Merchants, Politics and Society*, p. 138. Hugh Urban, 'The Marketplace and the Temple: Economic Metaphors and Religious Meanings in the Folk Songs of Colonial Bengal', *Journal of Asian Studies*, Vol. 60, No. 4, 2001, p. 1088.

43. See OIOC, BRC, P/49/47, 21 June 1774 for examples of some *ganj*s set up by the Raja of Burdwan and his family as *debottar* and *mahateran* in the period between 1754 and 1770.

44. OIOC, Mss. Eur. F 95 (Kyd), fol. 169.

45. NAI, PCRD (mf), 8 Aug. 1774, p. 331.

46. WBSA, *Committee of Revenue*, Vol. 7, 12 Sept. 1781, p. 213.

47. NAI, PCRD (mf), 23 Oct. 1775, p. 381.

48. Kate Teltscher, 'The Containment and Re-Deployment of English India Colonial Correspondence: The Letters of George Bogle from Bengal, Bhutan and Tibet, 1770 - 81'.

49. The representation made by the *Naib Diwan* stated, '..[this being] the time of harvest, the price of rice instead of falling rises daily in the markets in and about the city, he therefore requests that orders may be sent to the different supravisors, to enforce an entire freedom of purchase and sale of this

article in the [dis]tricts, to take every measure in their power to prevent monopolies and to remove every obstacle to the transportation of grain from place to place'. *CCRM*, Vol. II, 6 Dec. 1770, p. 20.

50. OIOC, *Bengal Revenue Separate Dept*, L/E/3/158, Vol. 1, Revenue letter dated 15 Nov. 1791, p. 18.
51. NAI, *Home Public*, Vol. 38, 29 Jan. 1772, pp. 208-210. David Curley, 'Fair grain markets and Mughal famine policy in late eighteenth century Bengal', *The Calcutta Historical Journal*, Vol. 2, No. 1, 1977, pp. 13, 21-22. Activities like the grain embargoes were forbidden in 1788.
52. WBSA, BOT-Comm, Vol. 45, 15 Oct. 1784, p. 122.
53. WBSA, *Committee of Revenue*, Vol. 46, 7 Oct. 1784, pp. 182-183.
54. WBSA, *Committee of Revenue*, Vol. 47, Pt. I, 8 Nov. 1784, pp. 97-98.
55. See WBSA, Board of Revenue-Grain-Copies of Governor General in Council Revenue-Grain, letter dated 17 Oct. 1794, pp. 8-9, etc. OIOC, *Bengal Revenue Separate Dept,* L/E/3/158, Vol. 1, Revenue letter dated 29 Dec. 1794.
56. OIOC, *Board's Collection*, F/4/70, Extract of Judicial Cons., 18 April 1799.
57. WBSA, BOT-Comm, Vol. 40, 11 Nov. 1783, p. 99. 'Poostul' *zamindari*, for instance, had as much as 207700 maunds in store.
58. Sayako Miki, 'The English East India Company and Indigenous Trading Systems: The Grain Trade in Early Colonial Bengal', in S. Sugiyama and Linda Grove, eds., *Commercial Networks in Modern Asia*, Richmond (Surrey), 2001, pp. 225-228.
59. This was the rate in 1689 when *Nawab* Shaista Khan, to commemorate such an unusual event, built up the western gate of the city with the injunction that it would remain closed until rice became equally cheap. It remained shut until 1739, when the return of bumper harvests enabled Jaswant Roy, the deputy of Sarfaraz Khan, to reopen it.
60. James Taylor, *A Sketch of the Topography and Statistics of Dacca*, Calcutta, 1840, p. 295.
61. WBSA, BOR-Grain, Vol. 1, 31 Oct.-12 June 1795, p. 34.

62. OIOC, *Home Misc.*, Vol. 434, 28 Feb. 1791, p. 647.

63. Letter to Court, 9 Jan. 1796, A.C Banerjee, ed., *FWIHC*, Vol. XX, Delhi, 1969, p. 589.

64. J.Z. Holwell, *Interesting Historical Events Relative to the Provinces of Bengal and the Empire of Indostan*, Part I, London, 1766, p. 193.

65. *Ibid.*, pp. 194-195.

66. Indrajit Ray, "Imperial policy and the decline of the Bengal salt industry under colonial rule: An episode in the 'de-industrialisation' process", *IESHR*, Vol. 38, No. 2, 2001, pp. 181-205, esp. p. 188.

67. P. J. Marshall, *East Indian Fortunes*, p. 109.

68. The Company had completely 'precluded their servants and all Europeans living under the Company's protection' from trading in that and other 'commodities of Inland Consumption'. OIOC, Bengal Law Council, P/166/84, 5 Jan. 1781. Merchants made advances to the salt workers, the *malangis* employed at the *khallaris* (salt pans). The latter delivered a certain quantity of salt of their respective farms to the merchants at the 'proper' season. If it was a bad season, the merchants were obliged to renew their engagements and repair salt works and 'they made good the deficiencies'. The merchants after making the advances looked for 'bargain contracts and engagements' with other merchants for the sale of their expected returns. These merchants exported salt to different parts of the country after paying a duty to the government (6 per cent for Hindus, 4 per cent for Muslims. Differential duties seem to have been a norm. P. J. Marshall notes that the *Nawab*'s government levied duties on goods passing certain customs posts at 2½ on their current price for Muslims, 5 per cent for Hindus and 3½ for Armenians. Idem., *East Indian Fortunes*, p. 108.

69. The Select Committee resolved that the whole trade was to be carried by a society that was founded on 21 August 1765. In 1767 the Society of inland trade was abolished and trade was 'laid open'. The final dissolution of the society however came later in September 1768. Duties were fixed at 30 per cent and sepoys enforced order. OIOC, BRC, P/49/52, 7 April 1775, p. 45.

70. OIOC, BRC, P/49/52, 7 April 1775, p. 45. The Salt districts did see a decrease in its population during the famine years,

but 'not in so considerable a degree', owing to the 'situation of the country which being low retained what rainfall and enabled people to water and preserve their crops'. The price of grain as a result was moderate and people found means of supporting themselves. The situation was similar in 24 Parganas and Dhaka. Ibid., p. 50.

71. OIOC, *Bengal Law Council*, P/166/84, 5 Jan. 1781. OIOC, BRC, P/49/52, 7 April 1775, pp. 44-49.

72. The *malangis* delivered the salt to the agents at an agreed price. The agents then sold the salt to wholesalers at a price decided by the government. The Company introduced the sale of salt by public auction in 1788 to increase its revenue by raising the price.

73. WBSA, BOT-Salt, Vol. 7, Pt.II, 27 May 1793, pp. 590-592.

74. WBSA, BOT-Comm, Vol. 99, 7 Aug. 1792, p. 325.

75. The sugar industry was apparently not showing a decline, with more or less stable output for jaggery and sugar. The liquid jaggery component of the market was however showing clear increase as the figures for Calcutta indicate. Carey Lib. 080, Pam. 19, No. 3, 'A Report from the Committee of Warehouses of the United East-India Company, Relative to the Culture of Sugar', London, MDCCXCII, appendix 7.

76. Carey Lib. 080, Pam. 19, No. 1, 'To the Honourable the Directors of the Company of Merchant Trading to the East -Indies the following Essay Concerning Bengal' (1770), pp. 26-27.

77. Bhaskar Mukhopadhyay, 'Forced Commercialisation in Early Colonial Bengal: A Model and Beyond', *Calcutta Historical Journal*, Nos. 1-2, 1990-91, pp. 28-82. Hamida Hossain, *The Company Weavers of Bengal*, Delhi, 1988. K.N. Chaudhuri, 'The Structure of Indian Textile Industry in the Seventeenth and Eighteenth Centuries', *IESHR*, Vol. 11, No. 2-3, 1974, pp. 127-182. O. Feldbaeck, 'Cloth Production and Trade in Late Eighteenth Century Bengal: A Report from the Danish Factory in Serampore', *BPP*, Vol. 86, Pt.II, No. 162, 1967, pp. 124-141.

78. J. C. Sinha, *Economic Annals of Bengal*, London, 1927, pp. 86-87.

79. S. Bhattacharya, 'Regional Economy', in Dharma Kumar and Meghnad Desai, eds., *Cambridge Economic History of India*, Vol. II, pp. 270-295.

80. Sushil Chaudhury, *From Prosperity to Decline*, pp. 334-335.
81. D.B. Mitra, *The Cotton Weavers of Bengal*, Calcutta, 1978.
82. K.N. Chaudhuri, *Trading World of Asia and the English East India Company 1600-1780*, Cambridge, 1978, pp. 277-298 etc.
83. Hameeda Hossain, *The Company Weavers of Bengal. The East India Company and the Organization of Textile Production in Bengal 1750-1813*, Delhi, 1988, pp. xv-xvi.
84. H.T. Colebrooke, *Remarks on the Husbandry*, p. 57, Also Carey Lib. 080, Pam. 9, No. 117, 'Wealth of Nations', London, 1837, p. 25.
85. WBSA, BOT-Comm, Vol. 83, Pt. II, 24 Dec. 1789, pp. 400-402.
86. D.B. Mitra, *The Cotton Weavers of Bengal*, pp. 107-108. The Resident of Haripal and Khirpai observed that about 15000-20000 weavers were working in the two *arang*s in 1775. WBSA, BOT-Comm, Vol. 4, 25 Aug. 1775, p. 327.
87. H.T. Colebrooke, *Remarks on the Husbandry*, p. 33.
88. NAI, DFR (mf), 2 Feb. 1736, pp. 27-28.
89. WBSA, BOT- Comm, Vol. 28, 4 Sept. 1781, pp. 386-388.
90. OIOC, Mss. Eur. F 218/11 (Verelst), fol. 14.
91. Letter to Court, 18 Jan. 1754, in K.K. Datta, ed., *FWIHC*, Vol. I, Delhi, 1958, p. 763.
92. *Ibid.*, pp. 762-763.
93. A Verelst, *A View of the Rise, Progress and Present State of the English Govt. in Bengal*, London, 1772, p. 85.
94. For instance, the council sent 'Dooreas to be worked in cusseda' and the Company functionaries at Dhaka wrote, 'Being peremptory in their orders for our getting them done notwithstanding what we wrote in ours of the 4th instant and they although informing us that the cloth they send us is of high prices and that therefore we must take care to be done accordingly by frequently calling on the workmen and taking care that the thread is fine they work with and when they think it practicable to have them done without spoiling the cloth and that if they can have it done in the factory on a small advance for the working they think will be of interest of the Company to agree in that manner. The Broker being called in informed of these orders...told us that he believed it impracticable to comply therewith that there still remained out in the workman's hands near 740 pieces of fine cloth to

be worked in Cusseda work almost all of which is spoiled and when it shall be finished will be very little that the persons that used to undertake that kind of work are almost all of them ruined and not fit to be trusted again, but he said it was possible to get a few pieces done very well but not any quantity, but as for the work being done in the factory it was impossible most of the cloth being worked by women in 'zunnanaes' who on no account would be prevailed with to come to our factory'. NAI, DFR (mf), 28 Feb. 1736, pp. 35 (b)-36.

95. OIOC, Mss. Eur. F 218/11 (Verelst), fol. 15(b). Grueber from 'Buddaul' *arang* further complained that the brokers employed by the Company also supplied the Dutch and the private merchants, at higher rates of profit and their orders were completed earlier and with 'prime quality' goods. Ibid., fol. 16.

96. WBSA, BOT-Comm, Vol. II., Pt. I, 1 April 1777, pp. 61-63.

97. WBSA, BOT-Comm, Vol. 65, 6 March 1788, pp. 211-213.

98. WBSA, BOT-Comm, Vol. 83, Pt. I, 8 Dec. 1789, p. 117.

99. WBSA, BOT-Comm, Vol. 60, 4 Sept. 1787, pp. 6-7.

100. Letter to Court, 10 Jan. 1747/48 in K.K. Datta, ed., *FWIHC*, Vol. I, p. 231; letter to Court, 4 Feb. 1750/51, in K.K Datta, ed., *FWIHC*, Vol. I, p. 468; letter to Court, 20 Aug. 1751, K.K. Datta, ed., *FWIHC*, Vol. I, p. 572; NAI, BPC (mf), 16 April 1722, p. 72 etc.

101. WBSA, BOT-Comm, Vol. 60, 4 Sept. 1787, p. 9.

102. WBSA, BOT-Comm, Vol. 61, 19 Oct. 1787, pp. 350-351.

103. WBSA, BOT-Comm, Vol. 69, 25 July 1788, pp. 468-469.

104. WBSA, BOT-Comm, Vol. 56, 17 May 1787, p. 259.

105. NAI, *Home Public*, Vol. 40, 12 April 1773, pp. 310-313.

106. Jan de Vries, 'The Industrial Revolution and the Industrious Revolution', *The Journal of Economic History,* Vol. 54, No. 2, 1994, pp. 249-270.

107. WBSA, BOT-Comm, Vol. 71, 2 Sept. 1788, p. 29. See chapter 4 for the details. Also see Hans-Joachim Voth, 'Seasonality of Conceptions as a Source for Historical Time-Budget Analysis: Tracing the Disappearance of Holy Days in Early Modern England', *Historical Methods*, Vol. 27, No. 3, 1994, pp. 127-132.

108. NAI, *Home Public*, Vol. 40, 12 April 1773, pp. 310-313.

109. The Company made advances only for the fine *mulmul*s in the early years, and the weaver did not manufacture without 'a certainty of their being taken off his hands'. The middling kinds always commanded a ready sale. The weavers requested the Company not to force them to take money against their will, and the textiles were to cost 40 per cent more. NAI, *Home Public*, Vol. 40, 12 April 1773, pp. 310-313.

110. WBSA, BOT-Comm, Vol. 39, 31 Oct. 1783, p. 359.

111. WBSA, BOT-Comm, Vol. 83, Pt. II, 31 Dec. 1789, p. 583.

112. WBSA, BOT-Comm, Vol. 5, 24 Oct. 1775, p. 116.

113. WBSA, Committee of Revenue, Vol. 14, 30 May 1781, pp. 2343-2344.

114. WBSA, BOT-Comm, Vol. 83, Pt. II, 31 Dec. 1789, pp. 623-624.

115. WBSA, BOT-Comm, Vol. 40, 20 Nov. 1783, p. 297.

116. NAI, *Home Public*, Vol. 52, 28 Feb. 1782, pp. 598-608. The Company official commented that the perfect freedom, which manufactures in Europe enjoyed in 'the disposal of labours', as they (in Europe) worked upon 'some stock of their own' and their being 'fully protected in the possession and use of it to such a degree of freedom, which the manufacturers of India could not at that moment possess'. Whosoever wanted to put them to work, had to advance them money to 'procure materials' and it could often happen that 'the violent hand of delegated power' might deprive them if not of their stock, yet of the means of completing what they undertook to perform'. *Ibid.* Barwell's minute noted that the chief manufacture of Dhaka, that is making of cotton textiles, was much 'decayed' due to the *dalal*s and *paikar*s acting in league, who 'engross' the whole purchases made both for private merchants as well as the Company. The famine, the inability of the State to protect the interest of the weavers and others involved in the process were further impediments. 'The manufacturers required for the publick service have no particular indulgencies are not made the immediate servants of the Company are not engaged to give the produce of their labour at stated rates as formerly are not emancipated from the state of dependence in which they stand to the landholders have not a precise and determinate value fixt to the lands they chuse to cultivate are not freed from the

influence of brokers, a pernicious race of men who feed on the fruits of their industry and whose particular interest it is to take advantage of the necessities of the merchant'. OIOC, BRC, P/49/52, 7 April 1775. The Chief of Dacca factory observed that *dalal*s being men of wealth of the city 'are able to make good any outstanding balances, the great influence they still have over the weavers added to their knowledge and experience of business'. The main drawbacks in employing them 'are the impediments the delolls can throw in the way of owing to their long connections with the pycars and weavers, the ascendancy they have over them on account of the large balances due from them and some risk of their falling off in the quality of the goods provided for the Company from their dealings with private merchants'. WBSA, BOT-Comm, Vol. 3, Pt. 1, 28 April 1775, pp. 169-170.

117. WBSA, BOT-Comm, Vol. 40, 20 Nov. 1783, p. 624.
118. WBSA, BOT-Comm, Vol. 57, 8 June 1787, p. 48.
119. WBSA, BOT-Comm, Vol. 83, Pt. I, 1 Dec. 1789, p. 22.
120. WBSA, BOT-Comm, Vol. 83, Pt. II, 31 Dec. 1789, pp. 583-587.
121. B.R. Tomlinson, 'Bengal textiles, British Industrialisation and the Company Raj: Muslins, Mules and Remittances, 1770-1820', *KIAPS: Bulletin of Asian-Pacific Studies*, XII, 2000, pp. 197-214. P.J. Marshall, *Bengal: The British Bridgehead, Eastern India, 1740-1828*, Cambridge, 1987, p. 105.
122. WBSA, BOT-Comm, Vol. 18, 26 March 1779, pp. 544-546. William Milburn, *Oriental Commerce: A Geographical Description of the Principal Places in the East Indies, China and Japan, with their Produce, Manufacture, and Trade; including the Coasting or Country Trade from Port to Port; also the Rise and Progress of the trade*, Vol. II, London, 1813, Vol. II, p. 243.
123. See WBSA, BOT-Comm, Vol. 57, 8 June 1787, p. 48; Various dates.
124. Bhaskar Mukhopadhyay, *op.cit.*, pp. 42-43.
125. *Ibid.*, p. 59.
126. WBSA, BOT-Comm, Vol. 77, 13 March 1789, p. 324.
127. Bhaskar Mukhopadhyay, *op.cit.*, p. 70.
128. WBSA, BOT-Comm, Vol. 31, 11 June 1782, p. 644. Although French commerce 'was put a stop to' in 1778, the Dutch and Danish commerce had increased. The Dutch trade ceased in

the 80s. However, the French in particular 'since the return of peace' had 'set on foot a violent competition' at several cloth *arangs*. See WBSA, BOT-Comm, Vol. 60, 12 Sept. 1787, p. 126.

129. Rajat Datta, *Society, Economy and the Market*, p. 302.
130. WBSA, BOT-Comm, Vol. 56, 17 May 1787, pp. 259-260.
131. WBSA, BOT-Comm, Vol. 77, 13 March 1789, p. 310. They carried on a 'great deal of business in exchange' between Bombay, Surat and Bengal. Ibid., p. 316. From Kasimbazar, they exported silk to Surat, Nagpore, Mirzapore and to Benares. The exports to these places were always 'governed by the state of the markets'. Ibid., p. 317.
132. WBSA, BOT-Comm, Vol. 56, 17 May 1787, pp. 259-260.
133. H.T. Colebrooke, *Remarks on the Husbandry*, p. 64. Sushil Chaudhury notes that Mirzapore, Lahore, Multân, Aurangabad, Agra, Benares and Delhi were the major destinations in 1775-77. Idem., *From Prosperity to Decline*, p. 256. Also C.A. Bayly, *Rulers, Townsmen and Bazaars*, pp. 150-151.
134. William Milburn, *Oriental Commerce*, Vol. II, p. 244.
135. WBSA, BOT-Comm, Vol. 77, 13 March 1789, p. 320.
136. See Rajat Datta, 'Commercialisation, Tribute, and the Transition from Late Mughal to Early Colonial in India', *The Medieval History Journal*, Vol. 6, No. 2, 2003, pp. 257-291, esp. 265-267. He argues that the Company's imports of treasure were immense even in this period. Also see Om Prakash, *European Commercial Enterprise in Pre-colonial India*, Cambridge, 1998, p. 196.
137. Akinobu Kuroda, 'Seasonal Fluctuation, Multi-Layered Market and Monetary Diversity: How to Make or Not to Make a Single Domestic Currency', Paper Presented to the XIII International Economic History Congress, Buenos Aires, 26 July, 2002, Session 22 Comparative Analyses of Economic Performance Across Eurasia in Age of Early Industrialization, http://www.eh.net/XIIICongress/cd/papers/?D=A, p.4. Frank Perlin notes that 'in Bengal where prices of foodstuffs and labour were unusually low until the late eighteenth century, cauris prevailed as the main subsidiary to silver'. *Idem.*, 'Changes in Production and Circulation of Money in Seventeenth and Eighteenth Century India: An Essay on Monetization Before Colonial Occupation', in Sanjay

Subrahmanyam, ed., *Money and the Market in India 1100-1700*, Delhi, 1994, p. 287. For details of the multiple currency systems, see Sukumar Bhattacharya, *The East India Company and the Economy of Bengal*, ch. 4; and N.K. Sinha, *The Economic History of Bengal, from Plassey to the Permanent Settlement*, Calcutta, 1956, Vol.1, ch. 8.

138. Frank Perlin, 'Changes in Production and Circulation of Money in Seventeenth and Eighteenth Century India: An Essay on Monetization Before Colonial Occupation', in Sanjay Subrahmanyam, ed., *Money and the Market in India 1100-1700*, Delhi, 1994, pp. 290-291.

139. Sanjay Subrahmanyam, ed., *Money and the Market in India*, p. 43. Also see, *ibid.*, p. 39.

140. WBSA, BOT-Comm, Vol. 109, 24 March 1794, p. 327.

141. WBSA, BOT-Comm, Vol. 103, 11 March 1793, pp. 63-65.

142. H. Bowen, 'Monopoly and privilege: reassessing Britain's export trade to Asia c. 1700-1830', Paper presented in Commonwealth and Overseas History Seminar and Modern British Economic History Seminar, Cambridge, 23 October 2003. Also see *idem*, 'Sinews of trade and empire: the supply of commodity exports to the East India Company during the late eighteenth century', *Economic History Review*, Vol. 55, No. 3, 2002, pp. 466-486.

143. NAI, *Home Public*, Vol. 8, 4 Aug. 1757.

144. Kumkum Chatterjee, *Merchants, Politics and Society*, pp.194-204. Shubhra Chakrabarti, 'Intransigent Shroffs and the English East India Company's Currency reforms in Bengal, 1757-1800', *IESHR*, Vol. 34, No. 1, 1997, pp. 69-94.

145. Akinobu Kuroda, op.cit., p.8.

146. *Ibid.*, pp. 8-9.

147. *Ibid.*, p.11.

148. Om Prakash, 'Trade and Politics in 18th Century Bengal', in L. Blusse and F. Gaastra, eds., *On the 18th Century as a category of Asian History. Van Leur in Retrospect*, Ashgate, 1998, p. 242.

149. Alexandre Legoux de Flaix, *Essai Historique, Geographique et Politique Sur l'Indoustan, avec le Tableau de son Commerce, ce dernier pris dans une annee moyenne, depuis 1702 jusqu'en 1770, e´poque de la suppression du privilège de l'ancienne Compagnie des Indes Orientales*, Paris, 1807, Tome I, p. 211.

He wrote that the premiere commercial firms in places as far as Canton, Constantinople, Shiraz and Basra accepted the draft of the house of the Seths; its business extended from China to Turkey.

150. W.K. Firminger, ed., *Bengal District Records-Rangpur*, Calcutta, 1914, p. V. Thomas M. Buoye, *Manslaughter, Markets and Moral Economy: Violent Disputes over Property Rights in Eighteenth-century China*, Cambridge, 2000.

151. OIOC, BRC, P/49/38, 29 Jan. 1773, pp. 697-700.

152. WBSA, BOT-Comm, Vol.17, 24 Feb. 1778, pp. 466-468. WBSA, Judicial Criminal, Vol. 23, 30 July 1795, pp. 23-25.

153. NAI, *Home Public*, Vol. 1, 10 June 1753, p. 169.

154. NAI, PCRD (mf), 28 March 1775, pp. 107-108.

155. See for instance, Sudipta Sen, *Empire of Free Trade*.

156. S. Bose, *Peasant Labour and Colonial Capital: Rural Bengal Since 1770,* Cambridge, 1993, p. 38.

157. Claude Markovits, J. Pouchepadass and Sanjay Subrahmanyam, eds., *Society and Circulation: Mobile People and Itinerant Cultures in South Asia, 1750-1950*, Delhi, 2003, Introduction, esp. p. 9.

158. As Jan de Vries states for Asia. See idem., 'The Industrious Revolutions in the East and West', Session 25 Labour-Intensive Industrialisation in Global History: Asian Experiences and Comparative Perspectives. Paper Presented to the XIII International Economic History Congress, Buenos Aires, 26 July 2002, http://www.eh.net/XIIICongress/cd/papers/?D=A, last accessed April 2003, pp. 7, 9.

159. Rajat Datta, *Society, Economy and the Market*. He observes that it is the English 'Company's intrusion' which 'led to that crucial bit of state intervention necessary for the final crystallization of an integrated market for agricultural production in Bengal'. Ibid., p. 205.

160. N.K.Sinha, *The Economic History of Bengal, from Plassey to the Permanent Settlement*, 3 Vols., Calcutta, 1956, 1962, and 1970.

161. Om Prakash, 'Trade and Politics in Eighteenth-century Bengal', in Seema Alavi, ed., *The Eighteenth Century in India, Debates in Indian History and Society*, Delhi, 2002, pp. 142-143.

162. *Ibid.,* pp. 151-153.

INDEX